THE COFFIN DANCER

"Wake up, Scarpetta fans—Lincoln Rhyme is here to blast you out of your stupor."

—Entertainment Weekly

"This is as good as it gets. There is no thriller writer today like Jeffery Deaver. . . . The Lincoln Rhyme series is simply outstanding."

—San Jose Mercury News

"Deaver revs up the already supercharged tension by cramming all of the action in *The Coffin Dancer* into forty-eight hours."

—USA Today

"Nearly impossible to put down. . . . Draws the reader in on the first page."

—The Denver Post

"Intense and heart-stopping . . . leaves readers gasping at the stunning climax."

—Booklist

"Revelations and reversals punctuate this thriller like a string of firecrackers. . . . Superb plotting and brisk, no-nonsense prose."

—Publishers Weekly

"Quick to the punch, *The Coffin Dancer* is diabolically packed with the good stuff: cover-ups, mystery, action."

—Library Journal

THE
Empty
Chair

Jeffery Deaver

POCKET **STAR** BOOKS

New York   London   Toronto   Sydney   Singapore

This book is a work of fiction. Names, characters, places, and incidents either are products of the author's imagination or are used fictitiously. Any resemblance to actual events or locales or persons living or dead is entirely coincidental.

A Pocket Star Book published by
POCKET BOOKS, a division of Simon & Schuster, Inc.
1230 Avenue of the Americas, New York, NY 10020

Copyright © 2000 by Jeffery Deaver
Excerpt from *Speaking in Tongues* copyright © 2000 by Jeffery Deaver

Originally published in hardcover in 2000 by Simon & Schuster, Inc.

ISBN: 0-671-02601-1

First Pocket Books printing April 2001

10 9 8 7 6 5 4 3 2 1

POCKET STAR BOOKS and colophon are registered trademarks of Simon & Schuster, Inc.

Printed in the U.S.A.

For Deborah Schneider . . .
no better agent, no better friend

From the brain, and the brain alone, arise our pleasures, joys, laughter and jests, as well as our sorrow, pain, grief, and tears. . . . The brain is also the seat of madness and delirium, of the fears and terrors which assail by night or by day. . . .

—*Hippocrates*

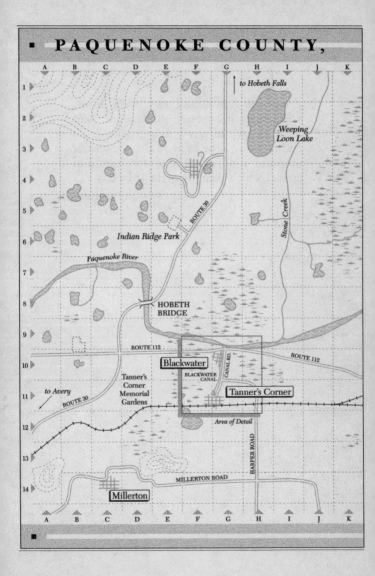

PAQUENOKE COUNTY,

A B C D E F G H I J K

1
to Hobeth Falls →

2
Weeping
Loon Lake

3

4
ROUTE 39

5

6
Indian Ridge Park

7
Paquenoke River

Stone Creek

8
HOBETH
BRIDGE

9

10
ROUTE 112
ROUTE 112

Blackwater
BLACKWATER
CANAL
CANAL RD.

11
Tanner's
Corner
Memorial
Gardens
Tanner's Corner

to Avery
ROUTE 30

12
Area of Detail

13

14
MILLERTON ROAD
Millerton
HARPER ROAD

A B C D E F G H I J K

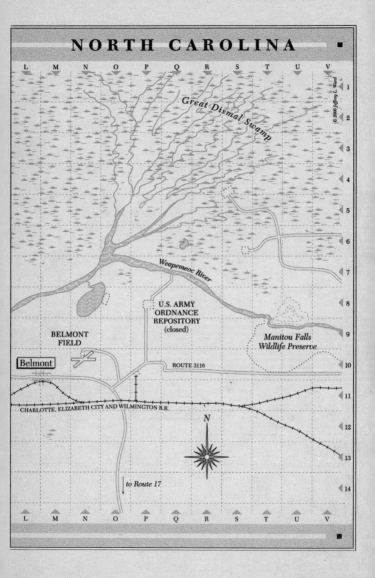

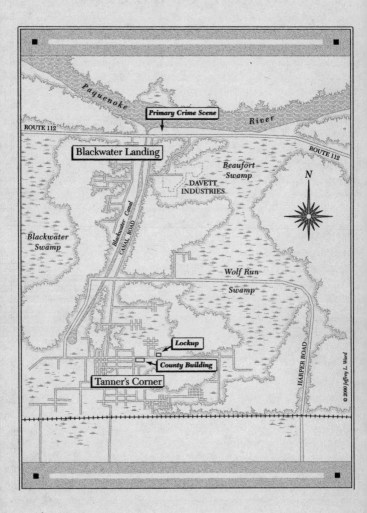

I

North of the Paquo

She came here to lay flowers at the place where the boy died and the girl was kidnapped.

She came here because she was a heavy girl and had a pocked face and not many friends.

She came because she was expected to.

She came because she wanted to.

Ungainly and sweating, twenty-six-year-old Lydia Johansson walked along the dirt shoulder of Route 112, where she'd parked her Honda Accord, then stepped carefully down the hill to the muddy bank where Blackwater Canal met the opaque Paquenoke River.

She came here because she thought it was the right thing to do.

She came even though she was afraid.

It wasn't long after dawn but this August had been the hottest in years in North Carolina and Lydia was already sweating through her nurse's whites by the time she started toward the clearing on the riverbank, surrounded by willows and tupelo gum and broad-leafed bay trees.

She easily found the place she was looking for; the yellow police tape was very evident through the haze.

Early morning sounds. Loons, an animal foraging in the thick brush nearby, hot wind through sedge and swamp grass.

Lord, I'm scared, she thought. Flashing back vividly on the most gruesome scenes from the Stephen King and Dean Koontz novels she read late at night with her companion, a pint of Ben & Jerry's.

More noises in the brush. She hesitated, looked around. Then continued on.

"Hey," a man's voice said. Very near.

Lydia gasped and spun around. Nearly dropped the flowers. "Jesse, you scared me."

"Sorry." Jesse Corn stood on the other side of a weeping willow, near the clearing that was roped off. Lydia noticed that their eyes were fixed on the same thing: a glistening white outline on the ground where the boy's body'd been found. Surrounding the line indicating Billy's head was a dark stain that, as a nurse, she recognized immediately as old blood.

"So that's where it happened," she whispered.

"It is, yep." Jesse wiped his forehead and rearranged the floppy hook of blond hair. His uniform—the beige outfit of the Paquenoke County Sheriff's Department—was wrinkled and dusty. Dark stains of sweat blossomed under his arms. He was thirty and boyishly cute. "How long you been here?" she asked.

"I don't know. Since five maybe."

"I saw another car," she said. "Up the road. Is that Jim?"

"Nope. Ed Schaeffer. He's on the other side of the river." Jesse nodded at the flowers. "Those're pretty."

After a moment Lydia looked down at the daisies in her hand. "Two forty-nine. At Food Lion. Got 'em last night. I knew nothing'd be open this early. Well, Dell's is but they don't sell flowers." She wondered why she was rambling. She looked around again. "No idea where Mary Beth is?"

Jesse shook his head. "Not hide nor hair."

"Him neither, I guess that means."

"Him neither." Jesse looked at his watch. Then out over the dark water, dense reeds and concealing grass, the rotting pier.

Lydia didn't like it that a county deputy, sporting a large pistol, seemed as nervous as she was. Jesse started up the grassy hill to the highway. He paused, glanced at the flowers. "Only two ninety-nine?"

"Forty-nine. Food Lion."

"That's a bargain," the young cop said, squinting toward a thick sea of grass. He turned back to the hill. "I'll be up by the patrol car."

Lydia Johansson walked closer to the crime scene. She pictured Jesus, she pictured angels and she prayed for a few minutes. She prayed for the soul of Billy Stail, which had been released from his bloody body on this very spot just yesterday morning. She prayed that the sorrow visiting Tanner's Corner would soon be over.

She prayed for herself too.

More noise in the brush. Snapping, rustling.

The day was lighter now but the sun didn't do much to brighten up Blackwater Landing. The river was deep here and fringed with messy black willows and thick trunks of cedar and cypress—some living, some not, and all choked with moss and viny kudzu. To the northeast, not far, was the Great Dismal Swamp, and Lydia Johansson, like every Girl Scout past and present in Paquenoke County, knew all the legends about that place: the Lady of the Lake, the Headless Trainman. . . . But it wasn't those apparitions that bothered her; Blackwater Landing had its own ghost—the boy who'd kidnapped Mary Beth McConnell.

Lydia opened her purse and lit a cigarette with shaking hands. Felt a bit calmer. She strolled along the shore.

Stopped beside a stand of tall grass and cattails, which bent in the scorching breeze.

On top of the hill she heard a car engine start. Jesse wasn't leaving, was he? Lydia looked toward it, alarmed. But she saw the car hadn't moved. Just getting the air-conditioning going, she supposed. When she looked back toward the water she noticed the sedge and cattails and wild rice plants were still bending, waving, rustling.

As if someone was there, moving closer to the yellow tape, staying low to the ground.

But no, no, of course that wasn't the case. It's just the wind, she told herself. And she reverently set the flowers in the crook of a gnarly black willow not far from the eerie outline of the sprawled body, spattered with blood dark as the river water. She began praying once more.

■

Across the Paquenoke River from the crime scene, Deputy Ed Schaeffer leaned against an oak tree and ignored the early morning mosquitoes fluttering near his arms in his short-sleeved uniform shirt. He shrank down to a crouch and scanned the floor of the woods again for signs of the boy.

He had to steady himself against a branch; he was dizzy from exhaustion. Like most of the deputies in the county sheriff's department he'd been awake for nearly twenty-four hours, searching for Mary Beth McConnell and the boy who'd kidnapped her. But while, one by one, the others had gone home to shower and eat and get a few hours' sleep Ed had stayed with the search. He was the oldest deputy on the force and the biggest (fifty-one years old and two hundred sixty-four pounds of mostly unuseful weight) but fatigue, hunger and stiff joints weren't going to stop him from continuing to look for the girl.

The deputy examined the ground again.

He pushed the transmit button of his radio. "Jesse, it's me. You there?"

"Go ahead."

He whispered, "I got footprints here. They're fresh. An hour old, tops."

"Him, you think?"

"Who else'd it be? This time of morning, this side of the Paquo?"

"You were right, looks like," Jesse Corn said. "I didn't believe it at first but you hit this one on the head."

It had been Ed's theory that the boy would come back here. Not because of the cliché—about returning to the scene of the crime—but because Blackwater Landing had always been his stalking ground and whatever kind of trouble he'd gotten himself into over the years he always came back here.

Ed looked around, fear now replacing exhaustion and discomfort as he gazed at the infinite tangle of leaves and branches surrounding him. Jesus, the deputy thought, the boy's here someplace. He said into his radio, "The tracks look to be moving toward you but I can't tell for sure. He was walking mostly on leaves. You keep an eye out. I'm going to see where he was coming from."

Knees creaking, Ed rose to his feet and, as quietly as a big man could, followed the boy's footsteps back in the direction they'd come—farther into the woods, away from the river.

He followed the boy's trail about a hundred feet and saw it led to an old hunting blind—a gray shack big enough for three or four hunters. The gun slots were dark and the place seemed to be deserted. Okay, he thought. Okay. . . . He's probably not in there. But still . . .

Breathing hard, Ed Schaeffer did something he hadn't done in nearly a year and a half: unholstered his weapon. He gripped the revolver in a sweaty hand and started forward, eyes flipping back and forth dizzily between the blind and the ground, deciding where best to step to keep his approach silent.

Did the boy have a gun? he wondered, realizing that he was as exposed as a soldier landing on a bald beachhead. He imagined a rifle barrel appearing fast in one of the slots, aiming down on him. Ed felt an ill flush of panic and he sprinted, in a crouch, the last ten feet to the side of the shack. He pressed against the weathered wood as he caught his breath and listened carefully. He heard nothing inside but the faint buzzing of insects.

Okay, he told himself. Take a look. Fast.

Before his courage broke, Ed rose and looked through a gun slot.

No one.

Then he squinted at the floor. His face broke into a smile at what he saw. "Jesse," he called into his radio excitedly.

"Go ahead."

"I'm at a blind maybe a quarter mile north of the river. I think the kid spent the night here. There's some empty food wrappers and water bottles. A roll of duct tape too. And guess what? I see a map."

"A map?"

"Yeah. Looks to be of the area. Might show us where he's got Mary Beth. What do you think about that?"

But Ed Schaeffer never found out his fellow deputy's reaction to this good piece of police work; the woman's screaming filled the woods and Jesse Corn's radio went silent.

■

Lydia Johansson stumbled backward and screamed again as the boy leapt from the tall sedge and grabbed her arms with his pinching fingers.

"Oh, Jesus Lord, please don't hurt me!" she begged.

"Shut up," he raged in a whisper, looking around, jerk-

ing movements, malice in his eyes. He was tall and
skinny, like most sixteen-year-olds in small Carolina
towns, and very strong. His skin was red and welty—
from a run-in with poison oak, it looked like—and he
had a sloppy crew cut that looked like he'd done it himself.

"I just brought flowers . . . that's all! I didn't—"

"Shhhh," he muttered.

But his long, dirty nails dug into her skin painfully and
Lydia gave another scream. Angrily he clamped a hand
over her mouth. She felt him press against her body,
smelled his sour, unwashed odor.

She twisted her head away. "You're hurting me!" she
said in a wail.

"Just shut up!" His voice snapped like ice-coated
branches tapping and flecks of spit dotted her face. He
shook her furiously as if she were a disobedient dog. One
of his sneakers slipped off in the struggle but he paid no
attention to the loss and pressed his hand over her mouth
again until she stopped fighting.

From the top of the hill Jesse Corn called, "Lydia?
Where are you?"

"Shhhhh," the boy warned again, eyes wide and crazy.
"You scream and you'll get hurt bad. You understand?
Do you understand?" He reached into his pocket and
showed her a knife.

She nodded.

He pulled her toward the river.

Oh, not there. Please, no, she thought to her guardian
angel. Don't let him take me there.

North of the Paquo . . .

Lydia glanced back and saw Jesse Corn standing by the
roadside 100 yards away, hand shading his eyes from the
low sun, surveying the landscape. "Lydia?" he called.

The boy pulled her faster. "Jesus Christ, come on!"

"Hey!" Jesse cried, seeing them at last. He started
down the hill.

But they were already at the riverbank, where the boy'd hidden a small skiff under some reeds and grass. He shoved Lydia into the boat and pushed off, rowing hard to the far side of the river. He beached the boat and yanked her out. Then dragged her into the woods.

"Where're we going?" she whispered.

"To see Mary Beth. You're going to be with her."

"Why?" Lydia whispered, sobbing now. "Why *me*?"

But he said nothing more, just clicked his nails together absently and pulled her after him.

■

"Ed," came Jesse Corn's urgent transmission. "Oh, it's a mess. He's got Lydia. I lost him."

"He's *what*?" Gasping from exertion, Ed Schaeffer stopped. He'd started jogging toward the river when he'd heard the scream.

"Lydia Johansson. He's got her too."

"Shit," muttered the heavy deputy, who cursed about as frequently as he drew his sidearm. "Why'd he do that?"

"He's crazy," Jesse said. "That's why. He's over the river and'll be headed your way."

"Okay." Ed thought for a moment. "He'll probably be coming back here to get the stuff in the blind. I'll hide inside, get him when he comes in. He have a gun?"

"I couldn't see."

Ed sighed. "Okay, well. . . . Get over here as soon as you can. Call Jim too."

"Already did."

Ed released the red transmit button and looked through the brush toward the river. There was no sign of the boy and his new victim. Panting, Ed ran back to the blind and found the door. He kicked it open. It swung inward with a crash and Ed stepped inside fast, crouching in front of the gun slot.

He was so high on fear and excitement, concentrating so hard on what he was going to do when the boy got here, that he didn't at first pay any attention to the two or three little black-and-yellow dots that zipped in front of his face. Or to the tickle that began at his neck and worked down his spine.

But then the tickling became detonations of fiery pain on his shoulders then along his arms and under them. "Oh, God," he cried, gasping, leaping up and staring in shock at the dozens of hornets—vicious yellow jackets—clustering on his skin. He brushed at them in a panic and the gesture infuriated the insects even more. They stung his wrist, his palm, his fingertips. He screamed. The pain was worse than any he'd felt—worse than the broken leg, worse than the time he'd picked up the cast-iron skillet not knowing Jean had left the burner on.

Then the inside of the blind grew dim as the cloud of hornets streamed out of the huge gray nest in the corner—which had been crushed by the swinging door when he kicked it in. Easily hundreds of the creatures were attacking him. They zipped into his hair, seated themselves on his arms, in his ears, crawled into his shirt and up his pant legs, as if they knew that stinging on cloth was futile and sought his skin. He raced for the door, ripping his shirt off, and saw with horror masses of the glossy crescents clinging to his huge belly and chest. He gave up trying to brush them off and simply ran mindlessly into the woods.

"Jesse, Jesse, Jesse!" he cried but realized his voice was a whisper; the stinging on his neck had closed up his throat.

Run! he told himself. Run for the river.

And he did. Speeding faster than he'd ever run in his life, crashing through the forest. His legs pumping furiously. Go. . . . Keep going, he ordered himself. Don't stop. Outrun the little bastards. Think about your wife, think about the twins. Go, go, go. . . . There were fewer wasps now though he could still see thirty or forty of the black dots clinging to his skin, the obscene hindquarters bending forward to sting him again.

I'll be at the river in three minutes. I'll leap into the water. They'll drown. I'll be all right. . . . Run! Escape from the pain . . . the pain . . . How can something so small cause so much pain? Oh, it hurts. . . .

He ran like a racehorse, ran like a deer, speeding through underbrush that was just a hazy blur in his tear-filled eyes.

He'd—

But wait, wait. What was wrong? Ed Schaeffer looked down and realized that he wasn't running at all. He wasn't even standing up. He was lying on the ground only thirty feet from the blind, his legs not sprinting but thrashing uncontrollably.

His hand groped for his Handi-talkie and even though his thumb was swollen double from the venom he managed to push the transmit button. But then the convulsions that began in his legs moved into his torso and neck and arms and he dropped the radio. For a moment he heard Jesse Corn's voice in the speaker, and when that stopped he heard the pulsing drone of the wasps, which became a tiny thread of sound and finally silence.

. . . chapter two

Only God could cure him. And God wasn't so inclined.

Not that it mattered, for Lincoln Rhyme was a man of science rather than theology and so he'd traveled not to Lourdes or Turin or to some Baptist tent outfitted with a manic faith healer but here, to this hospital in North Carolina, in hopes of becoming if not a whole man at least less of a partial one.

Rhyme now steered his motorized Storm Arrow wheelchair, red as a Corvette, off the ramp of the van in which he, his aide and Amelia Sachs had just driven five hundred miles—from Manhattan. His perfect lips around the controller straw, he turned the chair expertly and accelerated up the sidewalk toward the front door of the Neurologic Research Institute at the Medical Center of the University of North Carolina in Avery.

Thom retracted the ramp of the glossy black Chrysler Grand Rollx, a wheelchair-accessible van.

"Put it in a handicapped space," Rhyme called. He gave a chuckle.

Amelia Sachs lifted an eyebrow to Thom, who said, "Good mood. Take advantage. It won't last."

"I heard that," Rhyme shouted.

The aide drove off and Sachs caught up with Rhyme. She was on her cell phone, on hold with a local car rental company. Thom would be spending much of the next week in Rhyme's hospital room and Sachs wanted the freedom to keep her own hours, maybe do some exploring in the region. Besides, she was a sports-car person, not a van person, and on principle shunned vehicles whose top speed was two digits.

Sachs had been on hold for five minutes and finally she hung up in frustration. "I wouldn't mind waiting but the Muzak is terrible. I'll try later." She looked at her watch. "Only ten-thirty. But this heat is too much. I mean, way too much." Manhattan is not necessarily the most temperate of locales in August but it's much farther north than the Tar Heel State, and when they'd left the city yesterday, southbound via the Holland Tunnel, the temperature was in the low seventies and the air was dry as salt.

Rhyme wasn't paying any attention to the heat. His mind was solely on his mission here. Ahead of them the automated door swung open obediently (this would be, he assumed, the Tiffany's of handicapped-accessible facilities) and they moved into the cool corridor. While Sachs asked directions Rhyme looked around the main floor. He noticed a half-dozen unoccupied wheelchairs clustered together, dusty. He wondered what had become of the occupants. Maybe the treatment here had been so successful that they'd discarded the chairs and graduated to walkers and crutches. Maybe some had grown worse and were confined to beds or motorized chairs.

Maybe some had died.

"This way," Sachs said, nodding up the hall. Thom joined them at the elevator (double-wide door, handrails, buttons three feet off the floor) and a few minutes later they found the suite they sought. Rhyme wheeled up to

the door, noticed the hands-free intercom. He said a bois-
terous "Open, sesame" and the door swung wide.

"We get that a lot," drawled the pert secretary when
they'd entered. "You must be Mr. Rhyme. I'll tell the
doctor you're here."

■

Dr. Cheryl Weaver was a trim, stylish woman in her mid-
forties. Rhyme noticed immediately that her eyes were
quick and her hands, as befitted a surgeon, seemed
strong. Her nails were polish-free and short. She rose
from her desk, smiled and shook Sachs's and Thom's
hands, nodded to her patient. "Lincoln."

"Doctor." Rhyme's eyes took in the titles of the many
books on her shelves. Then the myriad certificates and
diplomas—all from good schools and renowned institu-
tions, though her credentials were no surprise to him.
Months of research had convinced Rhyme that the University Medical Center in Avery was one of the best hospitals in the world. Its oncology and immunology depart-
ments were among the busiest in the country and Dr.
Weaver's neuro institute set the standard for spinal cord
injury research and treatment.

"It's good to meet you at last," the doctor said. Under
her hand was a three-inch-thick manila folder. Rhyme's
own, the criminalist assumed. (Wondering what the
keeper of the file had entered under the prognosis heading: "Encouraging"? "Poor"? "Hopeless"?) "Lincoln,
you and I've had some conversations on the phone. But I
want to go through the preliminaries again. For both our
sakes."

Rhyme nodded curtly. He was prepared to tolerate
some formality though he had little patience for ass-cov-
ering. Which is what this was starting to sound like.

"You've read the literature about the Institute. And
you know we're starting some trials of a new spinal cord

regeneration and reconstruction technique. But I have to stress again that this is *experimental*."

"I understand that."

"Most of the quads I've treated know more neurology than a general practitioner. And I'll bet you're no exception."

"Know something about science," Rhyme said dismissively. "Know something about medicine." And he offered her an example of his trademark shrug, a gesture Dr. Weaver seemed to notice and file away.

She continued, "Well, forgive me if I repeat what you already know but it's important for you to understand what this technique can do and what it can't do."

"Please," Rhyme said. "Go on."

"Our approach at the Institute here is an all-out assault on the site of the injury. We use traditional decompression surgery to reconstruct the bony structure of the vertebrae themselves and to protect the site where your injury occurred. Then we graft two things into the site of the injury: One is some of the patient's own peripheral nervous system tissue. And the other substance we graft is some embryonic central nervous system cells, which—"

"Ah, the shark," Rhyme said.

"That's right. Blue shark, yes."

"Lincoln was telling us that," Sachs said. "Why shark?"

"Immunologic reasons, compatibility with humans. Also," the doctor added, laughing, "it's a damn big fish so we can get a lot of embryo material from one."

"Why embryo?" Sachs asked.

"It's the *adult* central nervous system that doesn't naturally regenerate," Rhyme grumbled, impatient with the interruption. "Obviously, a baby's nervous system has to grow."

"Exactly. Then, in addition to the decompression surgery and micrografting, we do one more thing—which is what we're so excited about: We've developed some new drugs that we think might have a significant effect on improving regeneration."

Sachs asked, "Are there risks?"

Rhyme glanced at her, hoping to catch her eye. *He* knew the risks. *He'd* made his decision. He didn't want her interrogating his doctor. But Sachs's attention was wholly on Dr. Weaver. Rhyme recognized her expression; it was how she examined a crime scene photo.

"Of course there are risks. The drugs themselves aren't particularly dangerous. But any C4 quad is going to have lung impairment. You're off a ventilator but with the anesthetic there's a chance of respiratory failure. Then the stress of the procedure could lead to autonomic dysreflexia and resulting severe blood pressure elevation—I'm sure you're familiar with that—which in turn could lead to a stroke or a cerebral event. There's also a risk of surgical trauma to the site of your initial injury—you don't have any cysts now and no shunts but the operation and resulting fluid buildup could increase that pressure and cause additional damage."

"Meaning he could get worse," Sachs said.

Dr. Weaver nodded and looked down at the file, apparently to refresh her memory, though she didn't open the folder. She looked up. "You have movement of one lumbrical—the ring finger of your left hand—and good shoulder and neck muscle control. You could lose some or all of that. And lose your ability to breathe spontaneously."

Sachs remained perfectly still. "I see," she said finally, the words coming out as a taut sigh.

The doctor's eyes were locked on Rhyme's. "And you have to weigh these risks in light of what you hope to gain—you aren't going to be able to walk again, if that's what you were hoping for. Procedures of this sort have had some limited success with spinal cord injuries at the lumbar and thoracic level—much lower and much less severe than your injury. It's had only marginal success with cervical injuries and none at all with a C4-level trauma."

"I'm a gambling man," he said quickly. Sachs gave him a troubled glance. Because she'd know that Lincoln Rhyme wasn't a gambling man at all. He was a scientist who lived his life according to quantifiable, documented principles. He added simply, "I want the surgery."

Dr. Weaver nodded and seemed neither pleased nor displeased about his decision. "You'll need to have several tests that should take several hours. The procedure's scheduled for the day after tomorrow. I have about a thousand forms and questionnaires for you. I'll be right back with the paperwork."

Sachs rose and followed the doctor out of the room. Rhyme heard her asking, "Doctor, I have a . . ." The door clicked shut.

"Conspiracy," Rhyme muttered to Thom. "Mutiny in the ranks."

"She's worried about you."

"Worried? That woman drives a hundred fifty miles an hour and plays gunslinger in the South Bronx. I'm getting baby fish cells injected into me."

"You know what I'm saying."

Rhyme tossed his head impatiently. His eyes strayed to a corner of Dr. Weaver's office, where a spinal cord—presumably real—rested on a metal stand. It seemed far too fragile to support the complicated human life that had once hung upon it.

The door opened. Sachs stepped into the office. Someone entered behind her but it wasn't Dr. Weaver. The man was tall, trim except for a slight paunch, and wearing a county sheriff's tan uniform. Unsmiling, Sachs said, "You've got a visitor."

Seeing Rhyme, the man took off his Smokey the Bear hat and nodded. His eyes darted not to Rhyme's body, as did most people's upon meeting him, but went immediately to the spine on the stand behind the doctor's desk.

Back to the criminalist. "Mr. Rhyme. I'm Jim Bell. Roland Bell's cousin? He told me you were going to be in town and I drove over from Tanner's Corner."

Roland was on the NYPD and had worked with Rhyme on several cases. He was currently a partner of Lon Sellitto, a detective Rhyme had known for years. Roland had given Rhyme the names of some of his relatives to call when he was down in North Carolina for the operation in case he wanted some visitors. Jim Bell was one of them, Rhyme recalled. Looking past the sheriff toward the doorway through which his angel of mercy, Dr. Weaver, had yet to return, the criminalist said absently, "Nice to meet you."

Bell gave a grim smile. He said, "Matter of fact, sir, I don't know you're going to be feeling that way for too long."

. . . chapter three

There was a resemblance, Rhyme could see, as he concentrated more acutely on the visitor.

The same lean physique, long hands and thinning hair, the same easygoing nature as his cousin Roland in New York. This Bell looked tanner and more rugged. Probably fished and hunted a lot. A Stetson would have suited him better than the trooper hat. Bell took a seat in a chair next to Thom.

"We have ourselves a problem, Mr. Rhyme."

"Call me Lincoln. Please."

"Go on," Sachs said to Bell. "Tell him what you told me."

Rhyme glanced coolly at Sachs. She'd met this man three minutes ago and already they were in cahoots together.

"I'm sheriff of Paquenoke County. That's about twenty miles east of here. We have this situation and I was thinking 'bout what my cousin told me—he can't speak highly enough of you, sir. . . ."

Rhyme nodded impatiently for him to continue.

Thinking: Where the hell's my doctor? How many forms does she have to dig up? Is *she* in on the conspiracy too?

"Anyway, this situation . . . I thought I'd come over and ask if you could spare us a little time."

Rhyme laughed, a sound without a stitch of humor in it. "I'm about to have surgery."

"Oh, I understand that. I wouldn't interfere with it for the world. I'm just thinking of a few hours. . . . We don't need much help, I'm hoping. See, Cousin Rol told me about some of the things you've done in investigations up north. We have basic crime lab stuff but most of the forensics work 'round here goes through Elizabeth City—the nearest state police HQ—or Raleigh. Takes weeks to get answers. And we don't have weeks. We got hours. At best."

"For what?"

"To find a couple girls got kidnapped."

"Kidnapping's federal," Rhyme pointed out. "Call the FBI."

"I can't recall the last time we even had a federal agent in the county, other than ATF on moonshine warrants. By the time the FBI gets down here and sets up, those girls'll be goners."

"Tell us about what happened," Sachs said. She was wearing her interested face, Rhyme noted cynically—and with displeasure.

Bell said, "Yesterday one of our local high school boys was murdered and a college girl was kidnapped. Then this morning the perp came back and kidnapped another girl." Rhyme noticed the man's face darken. "He set a trap and one of my deputies got hurt bad. He's here at the medical center now, in a coma."

Rhyme saw that Sachs had stopped digging a fingernail into her hair, scratching her scalp, and was paying rapt attention to Bell. Well, perhaps they weren't co-conspirators but Rhyme knew why she was so interested in a case they didn't have the time to participate in. And he didn't like the reason one bit. "Amelia," he began, casting a cool glance at the clock on Dr. Weaver's wall.

"Why not, Rhyme? What can it hurt?" She pulled her long red hair off her shoulders, where it rested like a still waterfall.

Bell glanced at the spinal cord in the corner once more. "We're a small office, sir. We did what we could—all of my deputies and some other folk too were out all night but, fact is, we just couldn't find him or Mary Beth. Ed— the deputy that's in the coma—we think he got a look at a map that shows where the boy might've gone. But the doctors don't know when, or if, he's going to wake up." He looked back into Rhyme's eyes imploringly. "We'd sure be appreciative if you could take a look at the evidence we found and give us any thoughts on where the boy might be headed. We're outa our depth here. I'm standing in need of some serious help."

But Rhyme didn't understand. A criminalist's job is to analyze evidence to help investigators identify a suspect and then to testify at his trial. "You know who the perp is, you know where he lives. Your D.A.'ll have an airtight case." Even if they'd screwed up the crime scene search— the way small-town law enforcers have vast potential to do—there'd be plenty of evidence left for a felony conviction.

"No, no—it's not the trial we're worried about, Mr. Rhyme. It's *finding* them 'fore he kills those girls. Or at least Lydia. We think Mary Beth may already be dead. See, when this happened I thumbed through a state police manual on felony investigations. It was saying that in a sexual abduction case you usually have twenty-four hours to find the victim; after that they become dehumanized in the kidnapper's eyes and he doesn't think anything about killing them."

Sachs asked, "You called him a boy, the perp. How old is he?"

"Sixteen."

"Juvenile."

"Technically," Bell said. "But his history's worse than most of our adult troublemakers."

"You've checked with his family?" she asked, as if it were a foregone conclusion that she and Rhyme were on the case.

"Parents're dead. He's got foster parents. We looked through his room at their place. Didn't find any secret trapdoors or diaries or anything."

One never does, thought Lincoln Rhyme, wishing devoutly this man would hightail it back to his unpronounceable county and take his problems with him.

"I think we should, Rhyme," Sachs said.

"Sachs, the surgery . . ."

She said, "Two victims in two days? He could be a progressive." Progressive felons are like addicts. To satisfy their increasing psychological hunger for violence, the frequency and severity of their acts escalate.

Bell nodded. "You got that right. And there's stuff I didn't mention. There've been three other deaths in Paquenoke County over the past couple of years and a questionable suicide just a few days ago. We think the boy might've been involved in all of them. We just didn't find enough evidence to hold him."

But then *I* wasn't working the cases, now, was I? Rhyme thought before reflecting that pride was probably the sin that would do him in.

He reluctantly felt his mental gears turning, intrigued by the puzzles that the case presented. What had kept Lincoln Rhyme sane since his accident—what had stopped him from finding some Jack Kevorkian to help with assisted suicide—were mental challenges like this.

"Your surgery's not till day after tomorrow, Rhyme," Sachs pushed. "And all you have are those tests before then."

Ah, your ulterior motives are showing, Sachs . . .

But she'd made a good point. He was looking at a lot

of downtime before the operation itself. And it would be pre-surgery downtime—which meant *without* eighteen-year-old scotch. What was a quad going to do in a small North Carolina town anyway? Lincoln Rhyme's greatest enemy wasn't the spasms, phantom pain or dysreflexia that plague spinal cord patients; it was boredom.

"I'll give you one day," Rhyme finally said. "As long as it doesn't delay the operation. I've been on a waiting list for fourteen months to have this procedure."

"Deal, sir," Bell said. His weary face brightened.

But Thom shook his head. "Listen, Lincoln, we're not here to work. We're here for your procedure and then we're leaving. I don't have half the equipment I need to take care of you if you're working."

"We're in a *hospital*, Thom. I wouldn't be surprised to find *most* of what you need here. We'll talk to Dr. Weaver. I'm sure she'll be happy to help us out."

The aide, resplendent in white shirt, pressed tan slacks and tie, said, "For the record, I don't think it's a good idea."

But like hunters everywhere—mobile or not—once Lincoln Rhyme had made the decision to pursue his prey nothing else mattered. He now ignored Thom and began to interrogate Jim Bell. "How long has he been on the run?"

"Just a couple hours," Bell said. "What I'll do is have a deputy bring over the evidence we found and maybe a map of the area. I was thinking . . ."

But Bell's voice faded as Rhyme shook his head and frowned. Sachs suppressed a smile; she'd know what was coming.

"No," Rhyme said firmly. "We'll come to you. You'll have to set us up someplace in—what's the county seat again?"

"Uhm, Tanner's Corner."

"Set us up someplace we can work. I'll need a forensics assistant. . . . You have a lab in your office?"

"Us?" asked the bewildered sheriff. "Not hardly."

"Okay, we'll get you a list of equipment we'll need. You can borrow it from the state police." Rhyme looked at the clock. "We can be there in a half hour. Right, Thom?"

"Lincoln . . ."

"*Right?*"

"A half hour," the resigned aide muttered.

Now who was in a bad mood?

"Get the forms from Dr. Weaver. Bring them with us. You can fill them out while Sachs and I're working."

"Okay, okay."

Sachs was writing a list of the basic forensics lab equipment. She held it up for Rhyme to read. He nodded then said, "Add a density gradient unit. Otherwise, it looks good."

She wrote this item on the list and handed it to Bell. He read it, nodding his head uncertainly. "I'll work this out, sure. But I really don't want you to go to too much trouble—"

"Jim, hope I can speak freely."

"Sure."

The criminalist said in a low voice, "Just looking over a little evidence isn't going to do any good. If this is going to work, Amelia and I are going to be in charge of the pursuit. One hundred percent in charge. Now, you tell me up front—is that going to be a problem for anybody?"

"I'll make sure it isn't," Bell said.

"Good. Now you better get going on that equipment. We need to *move.*"

And Sheriff Bell stood for a moment, nodding, hat in one hand, Sachs's list in the other, before he headed for the door. Rhyme believed that Cousin Roland, a man of many Southernisms, had an expression that fit the look on the sheriff's face. Rhyme wasn't exactly sure how the phrase went but it had something to do with catching a bear by the tail.

"Oh, one thing?" Sachs asked, stopping Bell as he passed through the doorway. He paused and turned. "The perp? What's his name?"

"Garrett Hanlon. But in Tanner's Corner they call him the Insect Boy."

■

Paquenoke is a small county in northeastern North Carolina. Tanner's Corner, roughly in the center of the county, is the biggest town and is surrounded by smaller unincorporated clusters of residential or commercial pockets, such as Blackwater Landing, which huddles against the Paquenoke River—called the Paquo by most locals—a few miles to the north of the county seat.

South of the river is where most of the county's residential and shopping areas are located. The land there is dotted with gentle marshes, forests, fields and ponds. Nearly all of the residents live in this half. North of the Paquo, on the other hand, the land is treacherous. The Great Dismal Swamp has encroached and swallowed up trailer parks and houses and the few mills and factories on that side of the river. Snaky bogs have replaced the ponds and fields, and the forests, largely old-growth, are impenetrable unless you're lucky enough to find a path. No one lives on that side of the river except 'shiners and drug cookers and a few crazy swamp people. Even hunters tend to avoid the area after that incident two years ago when wild boars came after Tal Harper and even shooting half of them didn't stop the rest from devouring him before help arrived.

Like most people in the county Lydia Johansson rarely went north of the Paquo, and never very far from civilization when she did. She now realized, with an overwhelming sense of despair, that by crossing the river she'd stepped over some boundary into a place from which she might never return—a boundary that was not merely geographic but was spiritual too.

She was terrified being dragged along behind this creature, of course—terrified at the way he looked over her body, terrified of his touch, terrified that she'd die from heat- or sunstroke or snakebite—but what scared her the most was realizing what she'd left behind on the south side of the river: her fragile, comfortable life, small though it was: her few friends and fellow nurses on the hospital ward, the doctors she flirted futilely with, the pizza parties, the *Seinfeld* reruns, her horror books, ice cream, her sister's children. She even looked back longingly at the troubled parts of her life—the struggle with her weight, the fight to quit smoking, the nights alone, the long absence of phone calls from the man she occasionally saw (she called him her "boyfriend," though she knew that was merely wishful thinking) . . . even these now seemed fiercely poignant simply because of their familiarity.

But there wasn't a sliver of comfort where she was now.

She remembered the terrible sight at the hunter's blind—deputy Ed Schaeffer lying unconscious on the ground, arms and face swollen grotesquely from the wasp stings. Garrett had muttered, "He shouldn't've hurt 'em. Yellow jackets only attack when their nest's in danger. It was *his* fault." He'd walked inside slowly, the insects ignoring him, to collect some things. He'd taped her hands in front of her and then led her into the woods through which they'd been traveling now for several miles.

The boy moved in an awkward way, jerking her in one direction, then another. He talked to himself. He scratched at the red blotches on his face. Once, he stopped at a pool of water and stared at it. He waited until some bug or spider danced away over the surface then pressed his face into the water, soaking the troubled skin. He looked down at his feet then took off his remaining shoe and flung it away. They pushed on through the hot morning.

She glanced at the map sticking out of his pocket. "Where're we going?" she asked.

"Shut up. Okay?"

Ten minutes later he made her take her shoes off and they forded a shallow, polluted stream. When they'd crossed he eased her into a sitting position. Garrett sat in front of her and, as he watched her legs and cleavage, he slowly dried her feet with a wad of Kleenex he had pulled from his pocket. She felt the same repulsion at his touch that had flooded through her the first time she had to take a tissue sample from a corpse in the morgue at the hospital. He put her white shoes back on, laced them tight, holding her calf for longer than he needed to. Then he consulted the map and led her back into the woods.

Clicking his nails, scratching his cheek . . .

Little by little the marshes grew more tangled and the water darker and deeper. She supposed they were headed toward the Great Dismal Swamp though she couldn't imagine why. Just when it seemed they could go no farther because of the choked bogs, Garrett steered them into a large pine forest, which, to Lydia's relief, was far cooler than the exposed swampland.

He found another path. He led her along it until they came to a steep hill. A series of rocks led to the top.

"I can't climb that," she said, struggling to sound defiant. "Not with my hands taped. I'll slip."

"Bullshit," he muttered angrily, as if she were an idiot. "You got those nurse shoes on. They'll hold you fine. Look at me. I'm, like, barefoot and I can climb it. Lookit my feet, look!" He held up the bottoms. They were callused and yellow. "Now get your ass up there. Only, when you get to the top don't go any farther. You hear me? Hey, you listening?" Another hiss; a fleck of spittle touched her cheek and seemed to burn her skin like battery acid.

God, I hate you, she thought.

Lydia started to climb. She paused halfway, looked

back. Garrett was watching her closely, snapping his fingernails. Staring at her legs, encased in white stockings, his tongue teasing his front teeth. Then looking up higher, under her skirt.

Lydia continued to climb. Heard his hissing breath as he started up behind her.

At the top of the hill was a clearing and from it a single path led into a thick grove of pine trees. She started along the path, into the shade.

"Hey!" Garrett shouted. "Didn't you hear me? I told you not to move!"

"I'm not trying to get away!" she cried. "It's hot. I'm trying to get out of the sun."

He pointed to the ground, twenty feet away. There was a thick blanket of pine boughs in the middle of the path. "You could've fallen in," his voice rasped. "You could've ruined it."

Lydia looked closely. The pine needles covered a wide pit.

"What's under there?"

"It's a deadfall trap."

"What's inside?"

"You know—a surprise for anybody coming after us." He said this proudly, smirking, as if he'd been very clever to think of it.

"But *anybody* could fall in there!"

"Shit," he muttered. "This is north of the Paquo. Only ones who'd come this way'd be the people after us. And they deserve whatever happens to them. Let's get going." Hissing again. He took her by the wrist and led her around the pit.

"You don't have to hold me so hard!" she protested.

Garrett glanced at her then relaxed his grip somewhat—though his gentler touch proved to be a lot more troubling; he took to stroking her wrist with his middle finger, which reminded her of a fat blood tick looking for a spot to burrow into her skin.

. . . chapter four

The Rollx van passed a cemetery, Tanner's Corner Memorial Gardens. A funeral was in progress and Rhyme, Sachs and Thom glanced at the somber procession.

"Look at the casket," Sachs said.

It was small, a child's. The mourners, all adults, were few. Twenty or so people. Rhyme wondered why attendance was so sparse. His eyes rose above the ceremony and examined the graveyard's rolling hills and, beyond, the miles of hazy forest and marshland that vanished in the blue distance. He said, "That's not a bad cemetery. Wouldn't mind being buried in a place like that."

Sachs, who'd been gazing at the funeral with a troubled expression, shifted cool eyes toward him—apparently because with surgery on the agenda she didn't like any talk about mortality.

Then Thom eased the van around a sharp curve and, following Jim Bell's Paquenoke County Sheriff's Department cruiser, accelerated down a straightaway; the cemetery disappeared behind them.

As Bell had promised, Tanner's Corner was twenty miles from the medical center at Avery. The WELCOME TO sign assured visitors that the town was the home of 3,018 souls, which may have been true but only a tiny percentage of them were evident along Main Street on this hot August morning. The dusty place seemed to be a ghost town. One elderly couple sat on a bench, looking out over the empty street. Rhyme spotted two men who must've been the resident drunks—sickly looking and skinny. One sat on the curb, his scabby head in his hands, probably working off a hangover. The other sat against a tree, staring at the glossy van with sunken eyes that even from the distance seemed jaundiced. A scrawny woman lazily washed the drugstore window. Rhyme saw no one else.

"Peaceful," Thom observed.

"That's one way to put it," said Sachs, who obviously shared Rhyme's sense of unease at the emptiness.

Main Street was a tired stretch of old buildings and two small strip malls. Rhyme noticed one supermarket, two drugstores, two bars, one diner, a women's clothing boutique, an insurance company and a combination video shop/candy store/nail salon. The A-OK Car Dealership was sandwiched between a bank and a marine supplies operation. Everybody sold bait. One billboard was for McDonald's, seven miles away along Route 17. Another showed a sun-bleached painting of the *Monitor* and *Merrimack* Civil War ships. "Visit the Ironclad Museum." You had to drive twenty-two miles to see that attraction.

As Rhyme took in all these details of small-town life he realized with dismay how out of his depth as a criminalist he was here. He could successfully analyze evidence in New York because he'd lived there for so many years—had pulled the city apart, walked its streets, studied its history and flora and fauna. But here, in Tanner's Corner and environs, he knew nothing of the soil, the air, the water, nothing of the habits of the residents, the cars they liked, the houses they lived in, the industries that employed them, the lusts that drove them.

Rhyme recalled working for a senior detective at the NYPD when he was a new recruit. The man had lectured his underlings, "Somebody tell me: what's the expression 'Fish out of water' mean?"

Young officer Rhyme had said, "It means: out of one's element. Confused."

"Yeah, well, what happens when fish're out of water?" the grizzled old cop had snapped at Rhyme. "They don't get *confused*. They get fucking *dead*. The greatest single threat to an investigator is unfamiliarity with his environment. Remember that."

Thom parked the van and went through the ritual of lowering the wheelchair. Rhyme blew into the sip-and-puff controller of the Storm Arrow and rolled toward the County Building's steep ramp, undoubtedly added to the building grudgingly after the Americans with Disabilities Act went into effect.

Three men—in work clothes and with folding knife scabbards on their belts—pushed out of the side door of the sheriff's office beside the ramp. They walked toward a burgundy Chevy Suburban.

The skinniest of the three poked the biggest one, a huge man with a braided ponytail and a beard, and nodded toward Rhyme. Then their eyes—almost in unison—perused Sachs's body. The big one took in Thom's trim hair, slight build, impeccable clothes and golden earring. Expressionless, he whispered something to the third of the trio, a man who looked like a conservative Southern businessman. He shrugged. They lost interest in the visitors and climbed into the Chevy.

Fish out of water . . .

Bell, walking beside Rhyme's chair, noticed his gaze.

"That's Rich Culbeau, the big one. And his buddies. Sean O'Sarian—the skinny feller—and Harris Tomel.

Culbeau's not half as much trouble as he looks. He likes playing redneck but he's usually no bother."

O'Sarian glanced back at them from the passenger seat—though whether he was glancing at Thom or Sachs or himself, Rhyme didn't know.

The sheriff jogged ahead to the building. He had to fiddle with the door at the top of the handicapped ramp; it had been painted shut.

"Not many crips here," Thom observed. Then he asked Rhyme, "How're you feeling?"

"I'm fine."

"You don't look fine. You look pale. I'm taking your blood pressure the minute we get inside."

They entered the building. It was dated circa 1950, Rhyme estimated. Painted institutional green, the halls were decorated with finger paintings from a grade-school class, photographs of Tanner's Corner throughout its history and a half-dozen employment notices for county workers.

"Will this be okay?" Bell asked, swinging open a door. "We use it for evidence storage but we're clearing that stuff out and moving it down to the basement."

A dozen boxes lined the walls. One officer struggled to cart a large Toshiba TV out of the room. Another carried two boxes of juice jars filled with a clear liquid. Rhyme glanced at them. Bell laughed. He said, "That there just about summarizes your typical Tanner's Corner criminal: stealing home electronics and making moonshine."

"That's moonshine?" Sachs asked.

"The real thing. Aged all of thirty days."

"Ocean Spray brand?" Rhyme asked wryly, looking at the jars.

" 'Shiners' favorite container—because of the wide neck. You a drinking man?"

"Scotch only."

"Stick to that." Bell nodded at the bottles the officer carried out the door. "The feds and the Carolina tax department worry about their revenue. *We* worry about losing citizens. That batch there isn't too bad. But a lot of 'shine's laced with formaldehyde or paint thinner or fertilizer. We lose a couple people a year to bad batches."

"Why's it called moonshine?" Thom asked.

Bell answered, " 'Cause they used to make it at night in the open under the light of the full moon—so they didn't need lanterns and, you know, wouldn't attract revenuers."

"Ah," said the young man, whose taste, Rhyme knew, ran to St. Emilions, Pomerols and white Burgundies.

Rhyme examined the room. "We'll need more power." Nodding at the single wall outlet.

"We can run some wires," Bell said. "I'll get somebody on it."

He sent a deputy off on this errand then explained that he'd called the state police lab at Elizabeth City and put in an emergency request for the forensic equipment Rhyme wanted. The items would be here within the hour. Rhyme sensed that this was lightning fast for Paquenoke County and he felt once more the urgency of the case.

In a sexual abduction case you usually have twenty-four hours to find the victim; after that they become dehumanized in the kidnapper's eyes and he doesn't think anything about killing them.

The deputy returned with two thick electrical cables that had multiple grounded outlets on the ends. He taped them to the floor.

"Those'll do fine," Rhyme said. Then he asked, "How many people do we have to work the case?"

"I've got three senior deputies and eight line deputies. We've got a communications staff of two and clerical of five. We usually have to share them with Planning and Zoning and DPW—that's been a sore spot for us—but 'causa the kidnapping and you coming here and all we'll have every one of 'em we need. The county supervisor'll support that. I talked to him already."

Rhyme gazed up at the wall. Frowning.

"What is it?"

"He needs a chalkboard," Thom said.

"I was thinking of a *map* of the area. But, yes, I want a blackboard too. A big one."

"Done deal," Bell said. Rhyme and Sachs exchanged smiles. This was one of Cousin Roland Bell's favorite expressions.

"Then if I could see your senior people in here? For a briefing."

"And air-conditioning," Thom said. "It needs to be cooler in here."

"We'll see what we can do," Bell said casually, a man who probably didn't understand the North's obsession with moderate temperatures.

The aide said firmly, "It's not good for him to be in heat like this."

"Don't *worry* about it," Rhyme said.

Thom lifted an eyebrow at Bell and said easily, "We have to cool the room. Or else I'm going to take him back to the hotel."

"Thom," Rhyme warned.

"I'm afraid we don't have any choice," the aide said.

Bell said, "Not a problem. I'll take care of it." He walked to the doorway and called, "Steve, come on in here a minute."

A young crew-cut man in a deputy's uniform walked inside. "This's my brother-in-law, Steve Farr." He was the tallest of the deputies they'd seen so far—easily six-seven—and had round ears that stuck out comically. He seemed only mildly uneasy at the initial sight of Rhyme and his wide lips soon slipped into an easy smile that suggested both confidence and competence. Bell gave him the job of finding an air conditioner for the lab.

"I'll get right on it, Jim." He tugged at his earlobe, turned on his heel like a soldier and vanished into the hall.

A woman stuck her head in the door. "Jim, it's Sue McConnell on three. She's really beside herself."

"Okay. I'll talk to her. Tell her I'll be right there." Bell explained to Rhyme, "Mary Beth's mother. Poor woman. . . . Lost her husband to cancer just a year ago and now this happens. I tell you," he added, shaking his head, "- I've got a couple of kids myself and I can image what she's—"

"Jim, I wonder if we could find that map," Rhyme interrupted. "And get the blackboard set up."

Bell blinked uncertainly at this abrupt tone in the criminalist's voice. "Sure thing, Lincoln. And, hey, if we get too Southern down here, move a little slow for you Yankees, you'll speed us up now, won't you?"

"Oh, you bet I will, Jim."

∎

One out of three.

One of Jim Bell's three senior deputies seemed glad to meet Rhyme and Sachs. Well, to see Sachs, at least. The other two gave formal nods and obviously wished this odd pair had never left the Big Apple.

The agreeable one was a bleary-eyed thirtyish deputy named Jesse Corn. He'd been at the crime scene earlier that morning and, with painful guilt, admitted that Garrett had gotten away with the other victim, Lydia, right in front of him. By the time Jesse had gotten over the river Ed Schaeffer was near death from the wasp attack.

One deputy offering the cool reception was Mason Germain, a short man in his early forties. Dark eyes, graying features, posture a little too perfect for a human being. His hair was slicked back and showed off ruler-straight teeth marks from the comb. He wore excessive aftershave, a cheap, musky smell. He greeted Rhyme and Sachs with a stiff, canny nod and Rhyme imagined that he was actually glad the criminalist was disabled so he wouldn't have to shake his hand. Sachs, being a woman, was entitled to only a condescending "Miss."

Lucy Kerr was the third senior deputy and she wasn't any happier to see the visitors than Mason was. She was a tall woman—just a bit shorter than willowy Sachs. Trim and athletic-looking with a long, pretty face. Mason's uniform was wrinkled and smudged but Lucy's was perfectly ironed. Her blond hair was done up in a taut French braid. You could easily picture her as a model for L.L. Bean or Lands' End—in boots, denim and a down vest.

Rhyme knew that their cold shoulders would be an automatic reaction to interloping cops (especially a crip and a woman—and Northerners, no less). But he had no interest in winning them over. The kidnapper would be harder to find with every passing minute. And he had a date with a surgeon he absolutely was not going to miss.

A solidly built man—the only black deputy Rhyme had seen—wheeled in a large chalkboard and unfolded a map of Paquenoke County.

"Tape it up there, Trey." Bell pointed to the wall. Rhyme scanned the map. It was a good one, very detailed.

Rhyme said, "Now. Tell me exactly what happened. Start with the first victim."

"Mary Beth McConnell," Bell said. "She's twenty-three. A grad student over at the campus at Avery."

"Go on. What happened yesterday?"

Mason said, "Well, it was pretty early. Mary Beth was—"

"Could you be more specific?" Rhyme asked. "About the time?"

"Well, we don't know for certain," Mason responded coolly. "Weren't any stopped clocks like on the *Titanic,* you know."

"Had to've been before eight," Jesse Corn offered.

"Billy—the boy was killed—was out jogging and the crime scene is a half hour away from home. He was making up some credits in summer school and had to be back by eight-thirty to shower and get to class."

Good, Rhyme thought, nodding. "Go on."

Mason continued. "Mary Beth had some class project, digging up old Indian artifacts at Blackwater Landing."

"What's that, a town?" Sachs asked.

"No, just an unincorporated area on the river. 'Bout three dozen houses, a factory. No stores or anything. Mostly woods and swamp."

Rhyme noticed numbers and letters along the margins of the map. "Where?" he asked. "Show me."

Mason touched Location G-10. "Way we see it, Garrett comes by and grabs Mary Beth. He's going to rape her but Billy Stail's out jogging and sees them from the road and tries to stop it. But Garrett grabs a shovel and kills Billy. Beats his head in. Then he takes Mary Beth and disappears." Mason's jaw was tight. "Billy was a good kid. Really good. Went to church regular. Last season he intercepted a pass in the last two minutes of a tied game with Albemarle High and ran it back—"

"I'm sure he was a fine boy," Rhyme said impatiently. "Garrett and Mary Beth, they're on foot?"

"That's right," Lucy answered. "Garrett wouldn't drive. Doesn't even have a license. Think it was because of his folks' dying in a car crash."

"What physical evidence did you find?"

"Oh, we got the murder weapon," Mason said proudly. "The shovel. Were real buttoned up about handling it too. Wore gloves. And we did the chain of custody thing, like's in the books."

Rhyme waited for more. Finally he asked, "What else did you find?"

"Well, some footprints." Mason looked at Jesse, who said, "Oh, right. I took pictures of 'em."

"That's *all*?" Sachs asked.

Lucy nodded, tight-lipped at the Northerner's implicit criticism.

Rhyme: "Didn't you search the scene?"

Jesse said, "Sure we did. Just, there wasn't anything else."

Wasn't anything else? At a scene where a perp kills one victim and abducts another there'd be enough evidence to make a *movie* of who did what to whom and probably what each member of the cast had been doing for the last twenty-four hours. It seemed they were up against two perpetrators: the Insect Boy and law enforcement incompetence. Rhyme caught Sachs's eye and saw she was thinking the same.

"Who conducted the search?" Rhyme asked.

"I did," Mason said. "I got there first. I was nearby when the call came in."

"And when was *that*?"

"Nine-thirty. A truck driver saw Billy's body from the highway and called nine-one-one."

And the boy was killed before eight. Rhyme wasn't pleased. An hour and a half—at least—was a long time for a crime scene to be unprotected. A lot of evidence could get stolen, a lot could get added. The boy could have raped and killed the girl and hidden the body then returned to remove some pieces of evidence and plant others to lead investigators off. "You searched it by yourself?" Rhyme asked Mason.

"First time through. Then we got three, four deputies out there. They went over the area real good."

And found only the murder weapon? Lord almighty . . . Not to mention the damage done by four cops unfamiliar with crime scene search techniques.

"Can I ask," Sachs said, "how you know Garrett was the perp?"

"I *saw* him," Jesse Corn said. "When he took Lydia this morning."

"That doesn't mean he killed Billy and kidnapped the other girl."

"Oh," Bell said. "The fingerprints—we got them off the shovel."

Rhyme nodded and said to the sheriff, "And his prints were on file because of those prior arrests?"

"Right."

Rhyme said, "Now tell me about *this* morning."

Jesse took over. "It was early. Just after sunup. Ed Schaeffer and I were there keeping an eye on the crime scene in case Garrett came back. Ed was north of the river, I was south. Lydia comes 'round to lay some flowers. I left her alone and went back to the car. Which I guess I shouldn't've done. Next thing I know she's screaming and I see the two of them disappear over the Paquo. They were gone 'fore I could find a boat or anything to get across. Ed wouldn't answer his radio. I was worried about him and when I got over there I found him stung half to death. Garrett'd set a trap."

Bell said, "We think Ed knows where he's got Mary Beth. He got a look at a map that was in that blind Garrett'd been hiding in. But he got stung and passed out before he could tell us what the map showed and Garrett must've took it with him after he kidnapped Lydia. We couldn't find it."

"What's the deputy's condition?" Sachs asked.

"Went into shock because of the stinging. Nobody knows if he's going to make it or not. Or if he'll remember anything if he does come to."

So we rely on the evidence, Rhyme thought. Which was, after all, his preference; far better than witnesses any day. "Any clues from this morning's scene?"

"Found this." Jesse opened an attaché case and took out a running shoe in a plastic bag. "Garrett lost it when he was grabbing Lydia. Nothing else."

A shovel at yesterday's scene, a shoe at today's. . . . Nothing more. Rhyme glanced hopelessly at the lone shoe.

"Just set it over there." Nodding toward a table. "Tell me about these other deaths Garrett was a suspect in."

Bell said, "All in and around Blackwater Landing. Two of the victims drowned in the canal. Evidence looked like they'd fallen and hit their heads. But the medical examiner said they could've been hit intentionally and pushed in. Garrett'd been seen around their houses not long before they died. Then last year somebody was stung to death. Wasps. Just like with Ed. We know Garrett did it."

Bell started to continue but Mason interrupted. He said in a low voice, "Girl in her early twenties—like Mary Beth. Real nice, good Christian. She was taking a nap on her back porch. Garrett tossed a hornets' nest inside. Got herself stung a hundred thirty-seven times. Had a heart attack."

Lucy Kerr said, "I ran the call. It was a real bad sight, what happened to her. She died slow. Real painful."

"Oh, and that funeral we passed on the way here?" Bell asked. "That was Todd Wilkes. He was eight. Killed himself."

"Oh, no," Sachs muttered. "Why?"

"Well, he'd been pretty sick," Jesse Corn explained. "He was at the hospital more than at home. Was real tore up about it. But there was more—Garrett was seen shouting at Todd a few weeks ago, really giving him hell. We were thinking that Garrett kept harassing and scaring him until he snapped."

"Motive?" Sachs asked.

"He's a psycho, that's his motive," Mason spat out. "People make fun of him and he's out to get them. Simple as that."

"Schizophrenic?"

Lucy said, "Not according to his counselors at school. Antisocial personality's what they call it. He's got a high IQ. He got mostly A's on his report cards—before he started skipping school a couple of years ago."

"You have a picture of him?" Sachs asked.

The sheriff opened a file. "Here's the booking shot for the hornets' nest assault."

The picture showed a thin, crew-cut boy with prominent, connected brows and sunken eyes. There was a rash on his cheek.

"Here's another." Bell unfolded a newspaper clipping. It showed a family of four at a picnic table. The caption read, "The Hanlons at the Tanner's Corner Annual Picnic, a week before a tragic auto accident on Route 112 took the lives of Stuart, 39, and Sandra, 37, and their daughter, Kaye, 10. Also pictured is Garrett, 11, who was not in the car at the time of the accident."

"Can I see the report of the scene yesterday?" Rhyme asked.

Bell opened a folder. Thom took it. Rhyme had no page-turning frame so he relied on his aide to flip the pages.

"Can't you hold it steadier?"

Thom sighed.

But the criminalist was irritated. The crime scene had been very sloppily worked. There were Polaroid photos revealing a number of footprints but no rulers had been laid in the shot to indicate size. Also, none of the prints had numbered cards to indicate that they'd been made by different individuals.

Sachs noticed this too and shook her head, commenting on it.

Lucy, sounding defensive, said, "You always do that? Put cards down?"

"Of course," Sachs said. "It's standard procedure."

Rhyme continued to examine the report. In it was only a cursory description of the location and pose of the boy's body. Rhyme could see that the outlining had been done in spray paint, which is notorious for ruining trace and contaminating crime scenes.

No dirt had been sampled for trace at the site of the body or where there'd been an obvious scuffle between Billy and Mary Beth and Garrett. And Rhyme could see cigarette butts on the ground—which might provide many clues—but none had been collected.

"Next."

Thom flipped the page.

The friction ridge—fingerprint—report was marginally better. The shovel had four full and seventeen partials, all positively identified as Garrett's and Billy's. Most of them were latents but a few were evident—easily visible without chemicals or alternative light source imaging—in a smear of mud on the handle. Still, Mason had been careless when he'd worked the scene—his latex glove prints on the shovel covered up many of the killer's. Rhyme would have fired a tech for such careless handling of evidence but since there were so many other good prints it wouldn't make any difference in this case.

The equipment would be arriving soon. Rhyme said to Bell, "I'm going to need that forensics tech to help me with the analysis and the equipment. I'd prefer a cop but the important thing is that they know science. And know the area here. A native."

Mason's thumb danced a circle over the ribbed hammer of his revolver. "We can dig somebody up but I thought you were the expert. I mean, isn't that why we're using you?"

"One of the reasons you're using me is because *I* know when I need help." He looked at Bell. "Anybody come to mind?"

It was Lucy Kerr who answered. "My sister's boy—Benny—he's studying science at UNC. Grad school."

"Smart?"

"Phi Beta. He's just . . . well, a little quiet."

"I don't want him for his conversation."

"I'll call him."

"Good," Rhyme said. Then: "Now, I want Amelia to search the crime scenes: the boy's room and Blackwater."

Mason said, "But"—he waved his hand at the report—"we already did that. Fine-tooth comb."

"I'd like her to search them again," Rhyme said

shortly. Then looked at Jesse. "You know the area. Could you go with her?"

"Sure. Be happy to."

Sachs gave him a wry look. But Rhyme knew the value of a flirt; Sachs would need cooperation—and a lot of it. Rhyme didn't think Lucy or Mason would be half as helpful as the already-infatuated Jesse Corn.

Rhyme said, "I want Amelia to have a sidearm."

"Jesse's our ordnance expert," Bell said. "He can rustle you up a nice Smith and Wesson."

"You bet I can."

"Let me have some cuffs too," Sachs said.

"Sure thing."

Bell noticed Mason, looking unhappy, staring at the map.

"What is it?" the sheriff asked.

"You really want my opinion?" the short man asked.

"I asked, didn't I?"

"You do what you think is best, Jim," Mason said in a taut voice, "but I don't think we have time for any more searches. There's a lot of territory out there. We've got to get after that boy and get after him fast."

But it was Lincoln Rhyme who responded. Eyes on the map, at Location G-10, Blackwater Landing, the last place anyone had seen Lydia Johansson alive, he said, "We don't have enough time to move fast."

. . . chapter five

"We wanted him," the man whispered cautiously, as if speaking too loudly would conjure a witch. He looked uneasily around the dusty front yard in which sat a wheelless pickup on concrete blocks. "We called family services and asked about Garrett specifically. 'Cause we'd heard about him and felt sorry. But, fact is, he was trouble from the start. Not like any of the other kids we had. We did our best but, I'll tell you, I'm thinking he doesn't see it that way. And we're scared. Scared bad."

He stood on the weather-beaten front porch of his house north of Tanner's Corner, speaking to Amelia Sachs and Jesse Corn. Amelia was here, at Garrett's foster parents' house, solely to search his room but, despite the urgency, she was letting Hal Babbage ramble on in hopes that she might learn a bit more about Garrett Hanlon; Amelia Sachs didn't quite share Rhyme's view that evidence was the sole key to tracking down perps.

But the only thing this conversation was revealing was that his foster parents were indeed, as Hal had said, terrified that Garrett would return to hurt them or the other children. His wife, who stood beside him on the porch, was a fat woman with curly rust-colored hair. She wore a stained country-western radio station giveaway T-shirt. MY BOOTS TAP TO WKRT. Like her husband's, Margaret Babbage's eyes often scanned the yard and surrounding forest, looking for Garrett's return, Sachs assumed.

"It's not like we ever did anything to him," the man continued. "I never whipped him—the state won't let you do that anymore—but I'd be firm with him, make him toe the line. Like, we eat on a schedule. I insist on that. Only Garrett wouldn't show up on time. I lock the food up when it's not mealtime so he went hungry a lot. And sometimes I'd take him to father and son's Saturday Bible study and he *hated* that. He just sat there and didn't say a word. Embarrassed me, I'll tell you. And I'd nag him to clean that pigsty of a room." He hesitated, caught between anger and fear. "Those're just things you gotta make children do. But I *know* he hates me for 'em."

The wife offered her own testimony: "We were mannerable to him. But he's not going to remember that. He's gonna remember the times we were strict." Her voice quivered. "And he's thinking of revenge."

"I'll tell you, we'll protect ourselves," Garrett's foster father warned, speaking now to Jesse Corn. He nodded to a pile of nails and a rusty hammer sitting on the porch. "We're nailing the windows shut but if he tries to break in . . . we'll protect ourselves. The children know what to do. They know where the shotgun is. I've taught 'em how to use it."

He encouraged them to shoot Garrett? Sachs was shocked. She'd seen several other kids in the house, peering through the screens. They seemed to be no older than ten.

"Hal," Jesse Corn said sternly, preempting Sachs, "don't go taking anything into your own hands. You see Garrett, call us. And don't let the little ones touch any firearms. Come on, you know better'n that."

"We have drills," Hal said defensively. "Every Thursday night after supper. They know how to handle a gun." He squinted as he saw something in the yard. Tensing for a moment.

"I'd like to see his room," Sachs said.

He shrugged. "Help yourself. But you're on your own. I'm not going in there. You show 'em, Mags." He picked up the hammer and a handful of nails. Sachs noticed the butt of a pistol protruding from his waistband. He started to pound nails into a window frame.

"Jesse," Sachs said, "go around to the back and check in his window, see if there're any traps rigged."

"You won't be able to see," the mother explained. "He's got them painted black."

Painted?

Sachs continued. "Then just cover the approach to the window. I don't want any surprises. Keep an eye out for shooting vantages and don't present a clean target."

"Sure. Shooting vantages. I'll go do that." And he nodded in an exaggerated way that told her that he'd had virtually no tactical experience. He disappeared into the side yard.

The wife said to Sachs, "His room's this way."

Sachs followed Garrett's foster mother down a dim corridor filled with laundry and shoes and stacks of magazines. *Family Circle, Christian Life, Guns & Ammo, Field and Stream, Reader's Digest.*

Her neck crawled as she passed each doorway, eyes flicking left and right, and her lengthy fingers stroked the oak checkerboard of the pistol grip. The door to the boy's room was closed.

Garrett tossed a hornets' nest inside. Got herself stung 137 times . . .

"You're really scared he'll come back?"

After a pause the woman said, "Garrett's a troubled boy. People don't understand him and I got more feeling for him than Hal does. I don't know if he'll come back but if he does it'll be trouble. Garrett don't mind hurting people. Once at school some boys kept breaking into his locker and leaving notes and dirty underwear and things. Nothing terrible, just pranks. But Garrett made this cage that popped open if you didn't open the locker just right. Put a spider inside. Next time they broke in the spider bit one of the boys in the face. Nearly blinded him. . . . Yeah, I'm scared he'll come back."

They paused outside a bedroom door. On the wood was a handmade sign. DANGER. DO NOT ENTER. A badly done pen-and-ink drawing of a mean-looking wasp was taped to the door below it.

There was no air-conditioning and Sachs found her palms sweating. She wiped them on her jeans.

Sachs turned on the Motorola radio and pulled on the headset she'd borrowed from the Sheriff's Department Central Communications Office. She spent a moment finding the frequency Steve Farr had given her. The reception was lousy.

"Rhyme?"

"I'm here, Sachs. I've been waiting. Where've you been?"

She didn't want to tell him that she'd spent a few minutes trying to learn more about the psychology of Garrett Hanlon. She said only, "Took us some time to get here."

"Well, what've we got?" the criminalist asked.

"I'm about to go in."

She motioned Margaret back into the living room then kicked the door in and leapt back into the corridor, pressed flat against the wall. No sound from the dimly lit room.

Got herself stung 137 times . . .

Okay. Pistol up. Go, go, go! She pushed inside.

"Jesus." Sachs dropped into a low-profile combat stance. Several earnest pounds of pressure on the trigger, she held the gun steady as a mountain at the figure just inside.

"Sachs?" Rhyme called. "What is it?"

"Minute," she whispered, flicking the overhead light on. The gun sight rested on a poster of the creepy monster in the movie *Alien*.

With her left hand she swung the closet door open. Empty.

"It's secured, Rhyme. Have to say, though, I don't really care for the way he decorates."

It was then that the stench hit her. Unwashed clothing, bodily scents. And something else. . . .

"Phew," she muttered.

"Sachs? What is it?" Rhyme's voice was impatient.

"Place stinks."

"Good. You know my rule."

"Always *smell* the crime scene first. Wish I hadn't."

"I meant to clean it up." Mrs. Babbage had padded up behind Sachs. "I shoulda, before you got here. But I was too afraid to go in. Besides, skunk's hard to get out unless you wash in tomato juice. Which Hal thinks is a waste of money."

That was it. Crowning the smell of dirty clothes was the burnt-rubber scent of skunk musk. Hands clasped desperately, looking like she was about to cry, Garrett's foster mother whispered, "He'll be mad you broke the door."

Sachs said to her, "I'll need a little time alone here." She ushered the woman out and closed the door.

"Time's wasting, Sachs," Rhyme snapped.

"I'm on it," she responded. Looking around. Repulsed by the gray, stained sheets, the piles of dirty clothes, the dishes glued together with old food, the Cell-o bags filled with the dust of potato and corn chips. The whole place made her edgy. She found her fingers in her scalp, compulsively scratching. Stopped, then scratched some more. She wondered why she was so angry. Maybe because the slovenliness suggested that his foster parents didn't really give a damn about the boy and that this neglect had contributed to his becoming a killer and a kidnapper.

Sachs scanned the room fast and noticed that there were dozens of smudges and finger- and footprints on the windowsill. It seemed he used the window more than the front door and she wondered if they locked the children down at night.

She turned to the wall opposite the bed and squinted. Felt a chill slide through her. "We've got ourselves a collector here, Rhyme."

She looked over the dozen large jars—terrariums filled with colonies of insects clustered together, surrounding pools of water in the bottom of each one. Labels in sloppy handwriting identified the species: *Water Boatman . . . Diving Bell Spider.* A chipped magnifying glass sat on a nearby table, beside an old office chair that looked as if Garrett had retrieved it from a trash heap.

"I know why they call him the Insect Boy," Sachs said, then told Rhyme about the jars. She shivered with revulsion as a horde of moist, tiny bugs moved en masse along the glass of one jar.

"Ah, that's good for us."

"Why?"

"Because it's a rare hobby. If tennis or collecting coins turned him on, we'd have a harder time pinning him to specific locations. Now, get going on the scene." He was speaking softly in a voice that was almost cheerful. She knew he'd be imagining himself walking the grid—as he referred to the process of searching a crime scene—using her as his eyes and legs. As head of Investigation and Resources—the NYPD's forensics and crime scene unit— Lincoln Rhyme had often worked homicide crime scenes himself, usually logging more hours on the job than even junior officers. She knew that walking the grid was what he missed most about his life before the accident.

"What's the crime scene kit like?" Rhyme asked. Jesse Corn had dug one up from the Sheriff's Department equipment room for her to use.

Sachs opened the dusty metal attaché case. It didn't

contain a tenth of the equipment of her kit in New York but at least there were the basics: tweezers, a flashlight, probes, latex gloves and evidence bags. "Crime scene lite," she said.

"We're fish out of water on this one, Sachs."

"I'm with you there, Rhyme." She pulled on the gloves as she looked over the room. Garrett's bedroom was what's known as a secondary crime scene—not the place where the actual crime occurred but the location where it was planned, for instance, or to which the perps fled and hid out after a crime. Rhyme had long ago taught her that these were often more valuable than the primary scenes because perps tended to be more careless in places like this, shedding gloves and clothes and leaving behind weapons and other evidence.

She now started her search, walking a grid pattern—covering the floor in close parallel strips, the way you'd mow a lawn, foot by foot, then turning perpendicular and walking over the same territory again.

"Talk to me, Sachs, talk to me."

"It's a spooky place, Rhyme."

"Spooky?" he groused. "What the hell is 'spooky'?"

Lincoln Rhyme didn't like soft observations. He liked hard—specific—adjectives: cold, muddy, blue, green, sharp. Rhyme even complained when she commented that something was "large" or "small." ("Tell me inches or millimeters, Sachs, or don't tell me at all." Amelia Sachs searched crime scenes armed with a Glock 10, latex gloves and a Stanley contractor's tape measure.)

She thought: Well, I *feel* damn spooked. Doesn't that count for anything?

"He's got these posters up. From the *Alien* movies. And *Starship Troopers*—these big bugs attacking people. He's drawn some himself too. They're violent. The place is filthy. Junk food, a lot of books, clothes, the bugs in the jars. Not much else."

"The clothes are dirty?"

"Yep. Got a good one—a pair of pants, really stained. He's worn them a lot; they must have a ton of trace in them. And they all have cuffs. Lucky for us—most kids his age'd wear only blue jeans." She dropped them in a plastic evidence bag.

"Shirts?"

"T-shirts only," she said. "Nothing with pockets." Criminalists love cuffs and pockets; they trap all sorts of helpful clues. "I've got a couple of notebooks here, Rhyme. But Jim Bell and the other deputies must've looked through them."

"Don't make *any* assumptions about our colleagues' crime scene work," Rhyme said wryly.

"Got it."

She began flipping through the pages. "There're no diaries. No maps. Nothing about kidnapping. . . . There're just drawings of insects . . . pictures of the ones he's got here in the terrariums."

"Any of girls, young women? Sado-sexual?"

"No."

"Bring them along. How about the books?"

"Maybe a hundred or so. Schoolbooks, books about animals, insects . . . Hold on—got something here—a Tanner's Corner High School yearbook. It's six years old."

Rhyme asked a question to someone in the room. He came back on the line. "Jim says Lydia's twenty-six. She'd've been out of high school eight years. But check the McConnell girl's page."

Sachs thumbed through the *M*'s.

"Yep. Mary Beth's picture's been cut out with a sharp blade of some kind. He sure fits the classic stalker profile."

"We're not interested in profiles. We're interested in evidence. The other books—the ones on his shelf—which ones does he read the most?"

"How do I—"

"Dirt on the pages," he snapped impatiently. "Start on the ones nearest his bed. Bring back four or five of them."

She picked the four with the most well-thumbed pages. *The Entomologist's Handbook, The Field Guide to Insects of North Carolina, Water Insects of North America, The Miniature World.*

"I've got them, Rhyme. There're a lot of marked passages. Asterisks by some of them."

"Good. Bring them back. But there's *got* to be something more specific in the room."

"I can't find a thing."

"Keep looking, Sachs. He's a sixteen-year-old. You know the juvenile cases we've worked. Teenagers' rooms are the centers of their universe. Start thinking like a sixteen-year-old. Where would you hide things?"

She looked under the mattress, in and under the drawers of the desk, in the closet, beneath the grimy pillows. Then she shone the flashlight between the wall and the bed. She said, "Got something here, Rhyme. . . ."

"What?"

She found a mass of wadded-up Kleenex, a bottle of Vaseline Intensive Care lotion. She examined one of the Kleenexes. It was stained with what appeared to be dried semen.

"Dozens of tissues under the bed. He's been a busy boy with his right hand."

"He's sixteen," Rhyme said. "It'd be unusual if he *wasn't*. Bag one. We might need some DNA."

Sachs found more under the bed: a cheap picture frame on which he'd painted crude drawings of insects—ants and hornets and beetles. Inside was mounted the cut-out yearbook photo of Mary Beth McConnell. There was also an album of a dozen other snapshots of Mary Beth. They were candids. Most of them were of the young woman on what seemed to be a college campus or walking down the street of a small town. Two were of her in her bikini at a lake. In both of these she was bending down and the picture focused on the girl's cleavage. She told Rhyme what she'd found.

"His fantasy girl," Rhyme muttered. "Keep going."

"I think we should bag this and get on to the primary scene."

"In a minute or two, Sachs. Remember—this was *your* idea, being Good Samaritans, not mine."

A shudder of anger at this. "What do you want?" she asked heatedly. "You want me to dust for prints? Vacuum for hairs?"

"Of course not. We're not after trial-quality evidence for the D.A.; you know that. All we need is something that'll give us an idea where he might've taken the girls. He's not going to bring them back home. He's got a place he's made just for them. And he's been there earlier—to get it ready. He may be young and quirky but he still smells of an organized offender. Even if the girls're dead I'll bet he's picked out nice, cozy graves for them."

Despite all the time they'd worked together Sachs still had trouble with Rhyme's callousness. She knew it was part of being a criminalist—the distancing one must do from the horror of crime—but it was hard for her. Perhaps because she recognized that she had the same capacity for this coldness within herself, that numbing detachment that the best crime scene searchers must turn on like a light switch, a detachment that Sachs sometimes feared would deaden her heart irreparably.

Nice, cozy graves . . .

Lincoln Rhyme, whose voice was never more seductive than when he was imagining a crime scene, said to her, "Go on, Sachs, get into him. *Become* Garrett Hanlon. What are you thinking? What's your life like? What do you do minute by minute by minute in that little room? What are your most secret thoughts?"

The best criminalists, Rhyme had told her, were like talented novelists, who imagined themselves as their characters—and could disappear into someone else's world.

Eyes scanning the room once more. I'm sixteen. I'm a troubled boy, I'm an orphan, kids at school pick on me, I'm sixteen, I'm sixteen, I'm—

A thought formed. She snagged it before it swam off.

"Rhyme, you know what's weird?"

"Talk to me, Sachs," he said softly, encouraging.

"He's a teenager, right? Well, I remember Tommy Briscoe—I dated him when *I* was sixteen. You know what he had all over his walls in his room?"

"In my day and age it was that damn Farrah Fawcett poster."

"That's it exactly. Garrett doesn't have a single pinup, a single *Playboy* or *Penthouse* poster. No Magic cards, no Pokémon, no toys. No Alanis or Celine. No rock-musician posters. . . . And—hey, get this: no VCR, TV, stereo, radio. No Nintendo. My God, he's sixteen and he doesn't even have a computer." Her goddaughter was twelve and the girl's room was virtually an electronics showroom.

"Maybe it's a money thing—the foster parents."

"Hell, Rhyme, if I were his age and wanted to listen to music I'd *build* a radio. Nothing stops teenagers. But those aren't the things that excite him."

"Excellent, Sachs."

Maybe, she reflected, but what did it mean? Recording observations is only half of the job of a forensic scientist; the other half, the far more important half, is drawing helpful conclusions from those observations.

"Sachs—"

"Shhhh."

She struggled to put aside the person she really was: the cop from Brooklyn, the lover of taut General Motors vehicles, former fashion model for the Chantelle agency on Madison Avenue, champion pistol shot, the woman who wore her straight red hair long and her fingernails short lest the habit of digging into her scalp and skin mar her otherwise perfect flesh with yet more stigmata of the tension that drove her.

Trying to turn that person into smoke and emerge as a troubled, scary sixteen-year-old boy. Someone who needed, or wanted, to take women by force. Who needed, or wanted, to kill.

What do I feel?

"I don't care about normal pleasures, music, TV, computers. I don't care about normal sex," she said, half to herself. "I don't care about normal relationships. People are like insects—things to be caged. In fact, *all* I care about are insects. They're my only source of comfort. My only amusement." She said this as she paced in front of the jars. Then she looked down at the floor at her feet. "The tracks of the chair!"

"What?"

"Garrett's chair . . . it's on rollers. It's facing the insect jars. All he does is roll back and forth and stare at them and draw them. Hell, he probably talks to them too. His whole life is these bugs." But the tracks in the wood stopped before they got to the jar on the end of the row—the largest of them and one set slightly apart from the others. It contained yellow jackets. The tiny yellow-and-black crescents zipped about angrily as if they were aware of her intrusion.

She walked to the jar, looked down at it carefully. She said to Rhyme, "There's a jar full of wasps. I think it's his safe."

"Why?"

"It's nowhere near the other jars. He never looks at it—I can tell by the tracks of the chair. And all the other jars have water in them—they're aquatic bugs. This's the only one with flying insects. It's a great idea, Rhyme—who'd reach inside something like that? And there's about a foot of shredded paper on the bottom. I'd think he's buried something in there."

"Look inside and see."

She opened the door and asked Mrs. Babbage for a pair of leather gloves. When she brought them she found Sachs looking into the wasp jar.

"You're not going to touch that, are you?" she asked in a desperate whisper.

"Yes."

"Oh, Garrett'll have a fit. He yells at anyone who ever touches his wasp jar."

"Mrs. Babbage, Garrett's a fleeing felon. Him yelling at anybody isn't really a concern here."

"But if he sneaks back and sees you bothered it . . . I mean . . . It could push him over the edge." Again, tears threatened.

"We'll find him before he comes back," Sachs said in a reassuring tone. "Don't worry."

Sachs put on the gloves, and she wrapped a pillowcase around her bare arm. Slowly she eased the mesh lid off and reached inside. Two wasps landed on the glove but flew off a moment later. The rest just ignored the intrusion. She was careful not to disturb the nest.

Stung 137 times . . .

She dug only a few inches before she found the plastic bag.

"Gotcha." She pulled it out. One wasp escaped and disappeared into the house before she got the mesh lid back on.

Pulling off the leather gloves and putting on the latex. She opened the bag and spilled the contents out on the bed. A spool of thin fishing line. Some money—about a hundred dollars in cash and four Eisenhower silver dollars. Another picture frame; this one held the photo from the newspaper of Garrett and his family, a week before the car accident that killed his parents and sister. On a short chain was an old, battered key—like a car key, though there was no logo on the head; only a short serial number. She told Rhyme about this.

"Good, Sachs. Excellent. I don't know what it means yet but it's a start. Now get over to the primary scene. Blackwater Landing."

Sachs paused and looked around the room. The wasp that had escaped had returned and was trying to get back into the jar. She wondered what kind of message it was sending to its fellow insects.

■

"I can't keep up," Lydia told Garrett. "I can't go this fast," she gasped. Sweat streaming down her face. Her uniform was drenched.

"Quiet," he scolded angrily. "I need to listen. Can't do it with you bitching all the time."

Listen for what? she wondered.

He consulted the map again and led her along another path. They were still deep in the pine woods but, even though they were out of the sun, she was dizzy and recognized the early symptoms of heatstroke.

He glanced at her, eyes on her breasts again.

The fingernails snapping.

The immense heat.

"Please," she whispered, crying. "I can't do this! Please!"

"Quiet! I'm not going to tell you again."

A cloud of gnats swarmed around her face. She inhaled one or two and spit in disgust to clear her mouth. God, how she hated it here—in the woods. Lydia Johansson hated to be out of doors. Most people loved the woods and swimming pools and backyards. But her happiness was a fragile contentment that occurred mostly inside: her job, chatting with her other single girlfriends over margaritas at T.G.I. Friday's, horror books and TV, trips to the outlet malls for a shopping spree, those occasional nights with her boyfriend.

Indoor joys, all of them.

Outside reminded her of the cookouts her married friends gave, reminded her of families sitting around pools while their children played with inflatable toys, of picnics, of trim women in Speedos and thongs.

Outside reminded Lydia of a life she wanted but didn't have, of her loneliness.

He led her down another path, out of the forest. Suddenly the trees vanished and a huge pit opened in front of them. It was an old quarry. Blue-green water filled the bottom. She remembered years ago kids used to swim here, before the swamp started to reclaim the land north of the Paquo and the area got more dangerous.

"Let's go," Garrett said, nodding toward it.

"No. I don't want to. It's scary."

"Don't give a shit what you want," he snapped. "Come on!"

He gripped her taped hands and led her down a steep path to a rocky ledge. Garrett stripped off his shirt and bent down, splashed water on his blotched skin. He scratched and picked at the welts, examined his fingernails. Disgusting. He looked up at Lydia. "You want to do this? It feels good. You can take your dress off, you want. Go for a swim."

Horrified at the thought of being naked in front of him she shook her head adamantly. Then sat down near the edge and splashed water on her face and arms.

"Just don't drink it. I've got this."

He pulled a dusty burlap bag out from behind a rock, where he must've stashed it recently. He pulled out a bottle of water and some packets of cheese crackers with peanut butter. He ate a package of crackers and drank half of a bottle of water. He offered the rest to her.

She shook her head, repulsed.

"Fuck, I don't have AIDS or anything if that's what you're thinking. You gotta drink something."

Ignoring the bottle, Lydia lowered her mouth to the water in the quarry and drank deep. It was salty and metallic. Disgusting. She choked, nearly vomited.

"Jesus, I told you," Garrett snapped. He offered her the water again. "There's all kinds of crap in there. Quit being so fucking stupid." He tossed her the bottle. She caught it clumsily with her taped hands and drank it down.

Drinking the water immediately refreshed her. She relaxed some and asked, "Where's Mary Beth? What've you done with her?"

"She's in this place by the ocean. An old banker house."

Lydia knew what he meant. "Banker" to a Carolinian meant somebody who lived on the Outer Banks, the barrier islands off the coast in the Atlantic. So that's where Mary Beth was. And she understood now why they'd been traveling east—toward swampland with no houses and very few other places to hide. He probably had a boat stashed to take them through the swamp to the Intracoastal Waterway then to Elizabeth City and through Albemarle Sound to the Banks.

He continued. "I like it there. It's really neat. You like the ocean?" He asked her in a funny way—conversationally—and he seemed almost normal. For a moment her fear lessened. But then he froze again and listened to something, holding a finger to his lips to silence her, frowning angrily, as his dark side returned. Finally he shook his head as he decided that whatever he'd heard wasn't a threat. He rubbed the back of his hand over his face, scratching another welt. "Let's go." He nodded back up the steep path to the rim of the quarry. "It's not far."

"The Outer Banks'll take us a day to get to. More."

"Oh, hell, we're not gonna get there today." He laughed coldly as if she'd made another idiotic comment. "We'll hide near here and let the assholes searching for us get past. We'll spend the night." He was looking away from her when he said this.

"Spend the night?" she whispered hopelessly.

But Garrett said nothing more. He started prodding her up the steep incline to the lip of the quarry and the pine woods beyond.

chapter six

What's the attraction of the sites of death?

As she'd walked the grid at dozens of crime scenes Amelia Sachs had often asked this question and she asked it again now as she stood on the shoulder of Route 112 in Blackwater Landing, overlooking the Paquenoke River.

This was the place where young Billy Stail had died bloody, where two young women had been kidnapped, where a hardworking deputy's life had been changed forever—perhaps ended—by a hundred wasps. And even in the relentless sun the mood of Blackwater Landing was somber and edgy.

She surveyed the place carefully. Here, at the crime scene, a steep hill, strewn with trash, led from the shoulder of Route 112 down to the muddy riverbank. Where the ground leveled off, there were willows and cypress and clusters of tall grass. An old, rotting pier extended about thirty feet into the river then dipped below the surface of the water.

There were no homes in this immediate area though Sachs had noticed a number of large, new colonials not far from the river. The houses were obviously expensive but Sachs noticed that even this residential portion of Blackwater Landing, like the county seat itself, seemed ghostly and forlorn. It took her a moment to realize why—there were no children playing in the yards even though it was summer vacation. No inflatable pools, no bikes, no strollers. This reminded her of the funeral they'd passed a few hours ago—and the child's casket— and she forced her thoughts away from that sad memory and back to her task.

Examining the scene. Yellow tape encircled two areas. The one nearest the water included a willow in front of which were several bouquets of flowers—where Garrett had kidnapped Lydia. The other was a dusty clearing surrounded by a grove of trees where, yesterday, the boy had killed Billy Stail and taken Mary Beth. In the middle of this scene were a number of shallow holes in the ground where she'd been digging for arrowheads and relics. Twenty feet from the center of the scene was the spray-painted outline representing where Billy's body had lain.

Spray paint? she thought, chagrined. These deputies obviously weren't used to homicide investigations.

A Sheriff's Department car pulled onto the shoulder and Lucy Kerr climbed out. Just what I need—more cooks. The deputy nodded coolly to Sachs. "Find anything helpful at the house?"

"A few things." Sachs didn't explain further and nodded at the hillside.

In her headset she heard Rhyme's voice. "Is the scene trampled as bad as in the photos?"

"Like a herd of cattle walked through it. Must be two dozen footprints."

"Shit," the criminalist muttered.

Lucy had heard Sachs's comment but said nothing, just kept looking out over the dark junction where the canal met the river.

Sachs asked, "That's the boat he got away in?" Looking toward a skiff beached on the muddy riverbank.

"Over there, yeah," Jesse Corn said. "It's not his. He stole it from some folks up the river. You want to search it?"

"Later. Now, which way *wouldn't* he have come to get here? Yesterday, I mean. When he killed Billy."

"Wouldn't?" Jesse pointed to the east. "There's nothing that way. Swamp and reeds. Can't even land a boat. So either he came along Route 112 and down the embankment here. Or, 'cause of the boat, I guess he might've rowed over."

She opened the crime scene suitcase. Said to Jesse, "I want a known of the dirt around here."

"Known?"

"Exemplars—samples, you know."

"Just of the dirt here."

"Right."

"Sure," he said. Then asked, "Why?"

"Because if we can find soil that *doesn't* match what's found here naturally it might be from the place Garrett's got those girls."

"It could also," Lucy said, "be from Lydia's garden or Mary Beth's backyard or shoes of some kids fishing here a couple of days ago."

"It could," Sachs said patiently. "But we need to do it anyway." She handed Jesse a plastic bag. He strode off, pleased to help. Sachs started down the hill. She paused, opened the crime scene case again. No rubber bands. She noticed that Lucy Kerr had some bands binding the end of her French braid. "Borrow those?" she asked. "The elastic bands?"

After a brief pause the deputy pulled them off. Sachs stretched them around her shoes. Explained. "So I'll know which footprints're mine."

As if it makes a difference in this mess, she thought.

She stepped into the crime scene.

"Sachs, what do you have?" Rhyme asked. The reception was even worse than earlier.

"I can't see the scenario very clearly," she said, studying the ground. "Way too many footprints. Must've been eight, ten different people walking through here in the last twenty-four hours. But I have an idea what happened—Mary Beth was kneeling. A man's shoes approach from the west—from the direction of the canal. Garrett's. I remember the tread of the shoe Jesse found. I can see where Mary Beth stands and steps back. A second man's shoes approach from the south. Billy. He came down the embankment. He's moving fast—mostly on his toes. So he's sprinting. Garrett goes toward him. They scuffle. Billy backs up to a willow tree. Garrett comes toward him. More scuffling." Sachs studied the white outline of Billy's body. "The first time Garrett hits Billy with the shovel he gets him in the head. He falls. That didn't kill him. But then he hit him in the neck when he was down. That finished him off."

Jesse gave a surprised laugh, staring at the same outline as if he were looking at something completely different from what she saw. "How'd you know that?"

Absently she said, "The blood pattern. There're a few small drops here." She pointed to the ground. "Consistent with blood falling about six feet—that's from Billy's head. But that big spray pattern—which'd have to be from a severed carotid or jugular—starts when he was on the ground. . . . Okay, Rhyme, I'm going to start the search."

Walking the grid. Foot by foot. Eyes on the dirt and grass, eyes on the knotty bark of the oaks and willows, eyes up to the overhanging branches ("A crime scene is *three* dimensional, Sachs," Rhyme often reminded).

"Those cigarette butts still there?" Rhyme asked.

"Got 'em." She turned to Lucy. "Those cigarette butts," she said, nodding at the ground. "Why weren't they picked up?"

"Oh," Jesse answered for her, "those're just Nathan's."

"Who?"

"Nathan Groomer. One of our deputies. He's been trying to quit but just can't quite manage to."

Sachs sighed but managed to refrain from telling them that any cop who smoked at a crime scene ought to be suspended. She covered the ground carefully but the search was futile. Any visible fibers, scraps of paper or other physical evidence had been removed or blown away. She walked to the scene of this morning's kidnapping, stepped under the tape and started on the grid around the willow. Back and forth, fighting the dizziness from the heat. "Rhyme, there isn't much here . . . but . . . wait. I've got something." She'd seen a flash of white, close to the water. She walked down and carefully picked up a wadded-up Kleenex. Her knees cried out—from the arthritis that had plagued her for years. Rather be running down a perp than doing deep knee bends, she thought. "Kleenex. Looks similar to the ones at his house, Rhyme. Only this one's got blood on it. Quite a bit."

Lucy asked, "You think Garrett dropped it?"

Sachs examined it. "I don't know. All I can say is that it didn't spend the night here. Moisture content's too low. Morning dew would have half disintegrated it."

"Excellent, Sachs. Where'd you learn that? I don't recall ever mentioning it."

"Yes, you did," she said absently. "Your textbook. Chapter twelve. Paper."

Sachs walked down to the water, searched the small boat. She found nothing inside. Then she asked, "Jesse, can you row me over?"

He was, of course, more than happy to. And she wondered how long it would be before he fired off the first invitation for a cup of coffee. Uninvited, Lucy climbed in the skiff too and they pushed off. The threesome rowed silently over the river, which was surprisingly choppy in the current.

On the far shore Sachs found footprints in the mud: Lydia's shoes—the fine tread of nurse sneakers. And Garrett's prints—one barefoot, one in a running shoe with the tread that was already familiar to her. She followed them into the woods. They led to the hunting blind where Ed Schaeffer had been stung by the wasps. Sachs stopped, dismayed.

What the hell had happened here?

"God, Rhyme, it looks like the scene was swept."

Criminals often use brooms or even leaf blowers to destroy or confuse the evidence at crime scenes.

But Jesse Corn said, "Oh, that was from the chopper."

"Helicopter?" Sachs asked, dumbfounded.

"Well, yeah. Medevac—to get Ed Schaeffer out."

"But the downdraft from the rotors ruined the site," Sachs said. "Standard procedure is to move an injured victim away from the scene before you set the chopper down."

"Standard procedure?" Lucy Kerr asked abrasively. "Sorry, but we were a little worried about Ed. Trying to save his life, you know."

Sachs didn't respond. She eased into the shed slowly so she wouldn't disturb the dozens of wasps that were hovering around a shattered nest. But whatever maps or other clues Deputy Schaeffer had seen inside were gone now and the wind from the helicopter had mixed up the topsoil so much that it was pointless to even take a sample of the dirt.

"Let's get back to the lab," Sachs said to Lucy and Jesse.

They were returning to the shore when there was a crashing sound behind her and a huge man lumbered toward them from the tangle of brush surrounding a cluster of black willows.

Jesse Corn drew his weapon but before he cleared leather Sachs had the borrowed Smittie out of the holster, cocked to double-action, and the blade sight aimed at the intruder's chest. He froze, lifted his hands outward, blinking in surprise.

He was bearded, tall and heavy, wore his hair in a braid. Jeans, gray T-shirt, denim vest. Boots. Something familiar about him.

Where had she seen him before?

It took Jesse's mentioning his name for her to remember. "Rich."

One of the trio they'd seen outside the County Building earlier. Rich Culbeau—she remembered the unusual name. Sachs recalled too how he and his friends had glanced at her body with a tacit leer and at Thom with an air of contempt; she kept the pistol pointed at him a moment longer than she would have otherwise. Slowly she aimed the weapon at the ground, uncocked it and replaced it in the holster.

"Sorry," Culbeau said. "Didn't mean to spook nobody. Hey, Jesse."

"This's a crime scene," Sachs said.

In her earphone she heard Rhyme's voice: "Who's there?"

She turned away, whispering into the stalk mike, "One of those characters out of *Deliverance* we saw this morning."

"We're working here, Rich," Lucy said. "Can't have you in our way."

"I don't intend to *be* in your way," he said, switching his gaze into the woods. "But I got a right to try for that thousand like everybody else. You can't stop me from looking."

"What thousand?"

"Hell," Sachs spat out into the microphone, "there's a reward, Rhyme."

"Oh, no. Last thing we need."

Of the major factors contaminating crime scenes and hampering investigations, reward and souvenir seekers are among the worst.

Culbeau explained, "Mary Beth's mom's offering it. That woman's got some money and I'll bet by nightfall, the girl's still not back, she'll be offering two thousand. Maybe more." He then looked at Sachs. "I'm not gonna cause any trouble, miss. You're not from here and you lookit me and think I must be just bad pay—I heard you talking 'bout *Deliverance* in that fancy radio gear of yours. I liked the book better'n the movie, by the way. You ever read it? Well, don't matter. Just don't go puttin' too much stock in appearances. Jesse, tell her who rescued that girl gone missing in the Great Dismal last year. Who ever-body *knew* was gone to snakes and skeeters and the whole county tore up about it."

Jesse said, "Rich and Harris Tomel found her. Three days lost in the swamp. She'd've died, it wasn't for them."

"Was me mostly," Culbeau muttered. "Harris don't like gettin' his boots dirty."

"That was good of you," Sachs said stiffly. "I just want to make sure you don't hurt our chances of finding those women."

"That's not gonna happen. There's no reason for you to get all ashy on me." Culbeau turned and lumbered away.

"Ashy?" Sachs asked.

"Means angry, you know."

She told Rhyme and told him about the encounter.

He dismissed it. "We don't have time to worry about the locals, Sachs. We've got to get on the trail. And fast. Get back here with what you've found."

As they sat in the boat on the way back over the canal Sachs asked, "How much trouble's he gonna be?"

"Culbeau?" Lucy responded. "He's lazy mostly. Smokes dope and drinks too much but he's never done worse than broke some jaws in public. We think he's got a still someplace and, even for a thousand bucks, I can't imagine him getting too far from it."

"What do he and his two cronies do?"

Jesse asked, "Oh, you saw them too? Well, Sean—that's the skinny one—and Rich don't have what you'd call real jobs. Scavenge and do day labor some. Harris Tomel's been to college—a couple years anyway. He's always trying to buy a business or put some deal together. Nothing ever pays out that I heard of. But all three of those boys have money and that means they're running 'shine."

"Moonshine? You don't bust 'em?"

After a moment Jesse said, "Sometimes, down here, you go lookin' for trouble. Sometimes you don't."

Which was a bit of law enforcement philosophy that, Sachs knew, was hardly limited to the South.

They landed again on the south shore of the river, beside the crime scenes, and Sachs climbed out before Jesse could offer his hand, which he did anyway.

Suddenly a huge, dark shape came into view. A black motorized barge, forty feet long, eased down the canal, then passed them and headed into the river. She read on the side: DAVETT INDUSTRIES.

Sachs asked, "What's that?"

Lucy answered, "A company outside of town. They move shipments up the Intracoastal through the Dismal Swamp Canal and into Norfolk. Asphalt, tar paper, stuff like that."

Rhyme had heard this through the radio and said, "Let's ask if there was a shipment around the time of the killing. Get the name of the crew."

Sachs mentioned this to Lucy but she said, "I already did that. One of the first things Jim and I did." Her answer was clipped. "It was a negative. If you're inter-

ested we also canvassed everybody in town normally
makes the commute along Canal Road and Route 112
here. Wasn't any help."

"That was a good idea," Sachs said.

"Just standard procedure," Lucy said coolly and strode
back to her car like a homely girl in high school who'd
finally managed to fling a searing put-down at the head
cheerleader.

chapter seven

"I'm not letting him do anything until you get an air conditioner in here."

"Thom, we don't have time for this," Rhyme spat out. Then told the workmen where to unload the instruments that had arrived from the state police.

Bell said, "Steve's out trying to dig one up. Isn't quite as easy as I thought."

"I don't need one."

Thom explained patiently, "I'm worried about dysreflexia."

"I don't remember hearing that temperature was bad for blood pressure, Thom," Rhyme said. "Did you read that somewhere? *I* didn't read it. Maybe you could show me where you read it."

"I don't need your sarcasm, Lincoln."

"Oh, I'm sarcastic, am I?"

The aide patiently said to Bell, "Heat causes tissue swelling. Swelling causes increased pressure and irritation. And *that* can lead to dysreflexia. Which can kill him. We need an air conditioner. Simple as that."

Thom was the only one of Rhyme's caregiving aides who'd survived more than a few months in the service of the criminalist. The others had either quit or been peremptorily fired.

"Plug that in," Rhyme ordered a deputy who was wheeling a battered gas chromatograph into the corner.

"No." Thom crossed his arms and stood in front of the extension cord. The deputy saw the look on the aide's face and paused uneasily, not prepared for a confrontation with the persistent young man. "When we get the air conditioner up and running . . . *then* we'll plug it in."

"Jesus Christ." Rhyme grimaced. One of the most frustrating aspects of being a quad is the inability to bleed off anger. After his accident Rhyme quickly came to realize how a simple act like walking or clenching our fists—not to mention flinging a heavy object or two (a favorite pastime of Rhyme's ex-wife, Blaine)—dissipates fury. "If I get *angry* I could start spasming or get contractures," Rhyme pointed out testily.

"Neither of which will kill you—the way dysreflexia will." Thom said this with a tactical cheerfulness that infuriated Rhyme all the more.

Bell gingerly said, "Gimme five minutes." He disappeared and the troopers continued to wheel in the equipment. The chromatograph went unelectrified for the moment.

Lincoln Rhyme surveyed the machinery. Wondered what it would be like to actually close his fingers *around* an object again. With his left ring finger he could touch and had a faint sense of pressure. But actually gripping something, feeling its texture, weight, temperature . . . those were unimaginable.

Terry Dobyns, the NYPD therapist, the man who'd been sitting at Rhyme's bedside when he'd awakened after the accident at a crime scene left him a quadriplegic, had explained to the criminalist all the clichéd stages of grief. Rhyme had been assured that he'd experience—and survive—all of them. But what the doctor hadn't told him was that certain stages sneak back. That you carried them around with you like sleeping viruses and that they might erupt at any time.

Over the past several years he'd reexperienced despair and denial.

Now, he was consumed with fury. Why, here were two kidnapped young women and a killer on the run. How badly he wanted to speed to the crime scene, walk the grid, pluck elusive evidence from the ground, gaze at it through the luxurious lenses of a compound microscope, punch the buttons of the computers and the other instruments, pace as he drew his conclusions.

He wanted to get to work without worrying that the fucking heat would kill him. He thought again about Dr. Weaver's magic hands, about the operation.

"You're quiet," Thom said cautiously. "What're you plotting?"

"I'm not plotting anything. Would you please plug in the gas chromatograph and turn it on? It needs time to warm up."

Thom hesitated then walked to the machine and got it running. He arranged the rest of the equipment on a fiberboard table.

Steve Farr walked into the office, lugging a huge Carrier air conditioner. The deputy was apparently as strong as he was tall and the only clue to the effort was the red hue to his prominent ears.

He gasped, "Stole it from Planning and Zoning. We don't much like them."

Bell helped Farr mount the unit in the window and a moment later cold air was chugging into the room.

A figure appeared in the doorway—in fact, he *filled* the doorway. A man in his twenties. Massive shoulders, a prominent forehead. Six-five, close to three hundred pounds. For a difficult moment Rhyme thought this might be a relative of Garrett's and that the man had come to threaten them. But in a high, bashful voice he said, "I'm Ben?"

The three men stared at him as he glanced uneasily at Rhyme's wheelchair and legs.

Bell said, "Can I help you?"

"Well, I'm looking for Mr. Bell."

"I'm Sheriff Bell."

Eyes still surveying Rhyme's legs awkwardly. He glanced away quickly then cleared his throat and swallowed. "Oh, well, now. I'm Lucy Kerr's nephew?" He seemed to ask questions more than make statements.

"Ah, my forensics assistant!" Rhyme said. "Excellent! Just in time."

Another glance at the legs, the wheelchair. "Aunt Lucy didn't say . . ."

What was coming next? Rhyme wondered.

". . . didn't say anything about forensics," he mumbled. "I'm just a student, post-grad at UNC in Avery. Uhm, what do you mean, sir, 'just in time'?" The question was directed to Rhyme but Ben was looking at the sheriff.

"I mean: Get over to that table. I've got samples coming in any minute and you have to help me analyze them."

"Samples . . . Okay. What kind of fish would that be?" he asked Bell.

"Fish?" Rhyme responded. "Fish?"

"What it is, sir," the big man said softly, still looking at Bell, "I'd be happy to help but I have to tell you, I have pretty limited experience."

"We're not talking about fish. We're talking *crime scene* samples! What'd you think?"

"Crime scene? Well, I didn't know," Ben told the sheriff.

"You can talk to *me*," Rhyme corrected sternly.

A rosy blush blossomed on the man's face and his eyes snapped to attention. His head seemed to shiver as he forced himself to look at Rhyme. "I was just . . . I mean, he's the sheriff."

Bell said, "But Lincoln here's running the show. He's a forensics scientist from New York. He's helping us out."

"Sure." Eyes on the wheelchair, eyes on Rhyme's legs, eyes on the sip-and-puff controller. Back to the safety of the floor.

Rhyme decided he hated this man, who was acting as if the criminalist were the oddest kind of circus freak.

And part of him hated Amelia Sachs too—for engineering this whole diversion and taking him away from his shark cells and Dr. Weaver's hands.

"Well, sir—"

" 'Lincoln' is fine."

"The thing is I specialize in marine sociozoology."

"Which is?" Rhyme asked impatiently.

"Basically, the behavior of marine animal life."

Oh, great, Rhyme thought. Not only do I get a crip-phobe for an assistant but I get one who's a fish shrink. "Well, it doesn't matter. You're a scientist. Principles are principles. Protocols are protocols. You've used a gas chromatograph?"

"Yessir."

"And compound and comparison microscopes?"

An affirmative nod though not as assertive as Rhyme would have liked. "But . . ." Looking at Bell for a moment then returning obediently to Rhyme's face. ". . . Aunt Lucy just asked me to stop by. I didn't know she meant I was supposed to help you on a case. . . . I'm not really sure . . . I mean, I have classes—"

"Ben, you *have* to help us," Rhyme said curtly.

The sheriff explained, "Garrett Hanlon."

Ben let the name settle in his massive head somewhere. "Oh, that kid in Blackwater Landing."

The sheriff explained about the kidnappings and Ed Schaeffer's wasp attack.

"Gosh, I'm sorry about Ed," Ben said. "I met him once at Aunt Lucy's house and—"

"So we need you," Rhyme said, trying to steer the conversation back on track.

"We don't have a clue where he's gone with Lydia," the sheriff continued. "And we hardly have any time left to save those women. And, well, as you can see—Mr. Rhyme, he needs somebody to help him."

"Well . . ." A glance toward, but not at, Rhyme. "It's just I have this test coming up. I'm in school and all. Like I said."

Rhyme said patiently, "We don't really have any options here, Ben. Garrett's got three hours on us and he could kill either of his victims at any time—if he hasn't already."

The zoologist looked around the dusty room for a reprieve and found none. "Guess I can stick around for a little while, sir."

"Thank you," Rhyme said. He inhaled into the controller and swung around to the table on which the instruments rested. He stopped and surveyed them. He looked over at Ben. "Now, if you could just change my catheter we'll get to work."

The big man looked stricken. Whispered, "You want me to . . ."

"It's a joke," Thom said.

But Ben didn't smile. He just nodded uneasily and with the grace of a bison walked over to the chromatograph and began studying the control panel.

■

Sachs jogged into the impromptu lab in the County Building, Jesse Corn keeping up the speedy pace beside her.

Moving more leisurely, Lucy Kerr joined them a moment later. She said hello to her nephew Ben and introduced the huge man to Sachs and Jesse. Sachs held up one cluster of bags. "This is the evidence from Garrett's room," she said, then held up more bags. "This is from Blackwater Landing—the primary scene."

Rhyme looked at the bags but did so with some discouragement. Not only was there very little physical evidence but Rhyme was troubled again by what had occurred to him earlier: he had to analyze the clues without any firsthand knowledge of the surrounding area.

Fish out of water . . .

He had a thought.

"Ben, how long've you lived here?" the criminalist asked.

"All my life, sir."

"Good. What's this general area of the state called?"

He cleared his throat. "I guess the Northern Coastal Plain."

"You have any friends who're geologists who specialize in the area? Cartographers? Naturalists?"

"No. They're all marine biologists."

"Rhyme," Sachs said, "when we were at Blackwater Landing I saw that barge, remember? It was shipping asphalt or tar paper from a factory near here."

"Henry Davett's company," Lucy said.

Sachs asked, "Would they have a geologist on staff?"

"I don't know about that," Bell said, "but Davett, he's an engineer and's lived here for years. Probably knows the land as good as anybody."

"Give him a call, will you?"

"You bet." Bell disappeared. He returned a moment later. "I got Davett. There's no geologist on staff but he said he might be able to help. He'll be over in a half hour." Then the sheriff asked, "So, Lincoln, how do you want to handle the pursuit?"

"I'll be here, with you and Ben. We're going to go through the evidence. I want a small search party over at Blackwater Landing now—to where Jesse saw Garrett and Lydia disappear. I'll guide the team as best I can, depending on what the evidence shows."

"Who do you want on the team?"

"Sachs in charge," Rhyme said. "Lucy with her."

Bell nodded and Rhyme noticed that Lucy gave no reaction to these orders about the chain of command.

"I'd like to volunteer," Jesse Corn said quickly.

Bell looked at Rhyme, who nodded. Then he said, "Probably one other."

"Four people? That's *all*?" Bell asked, frowning. "Hell, I could get dozens of volunteers."

"No, less is better in a case like this."

"Who's the fourth?" Lucy asked. "Mason Germain?"

Rhyme looked at the doorway, could see nobody outside. He lowered his voice. "What's Mason's story? He's got some history. I don't like cops with histories. I like blank slates."

Bell shrugged. "The man's had a tough life. He grew up north of the Paquo—the wrong side of the tracks. Father tried to make a go of it at a couple businesses and then started running 'shine and when he got collared by revenuers he killed himself. Mason himself worked his way up from dust. There's an expression 'round here—too poor to paint, too proud to whitewash. That's Mason. He's always complaining about being held back, not getting what he wants. He's an ambitious man in a town that hasn't got any use for ambition."

Rhyme observed, "And he's gunning for Garrett."

"You got that right."

"Why?"

"Mason just about begged to be lead investigator on that case we were telling you about—the girl got stung to death in Blackwater. Meg Blanchard. Truth be told, I think the victim had, you know, some connection with Mason. Maybe they were going out. Maybe there was something else—I don't know. But he wanted to nail Garrett bad. But he just couldn't make the case against him. When it came time for the old sheriff to retire, the Board of Supervisors held that against him. I got the job and he didn't—even though he's older'n me and'd been on the force longer."

Rhyme shook his head. "We don't need hotheads in an operation like this. Pick somebody else."

"Ned Spoto?" Lucy suggested.

Bell shrugged. "He's a good man. Sure. Can shoot good but he also won't unless he for sure has to."

Rhyme said, "Just make sure Mason's nowhere near the search."

"He won't like it."

"That's not a consideration," Rhyme said. "Find something else for him to do. Something that sounds important."

"I'll do the best I can," Bell said uncertainly.

Steve Farr leaned into the doorway. "Just called the hospital," he announced. "Ed's still in critical condition."

"Has he said anything? About the map he saw?"

"Not a word. Still unconscious."

Rhyme turned to Sachs. "Okay . . . Get going. Hold up where the trail stops in Blackwater Landing and wait to hear from me."

Lucy was looking uncertainly at the bags of evidence. "You really think this's the way to find those girls?"

"I *know* it is," Rhyme answered shortly.

She said skeptically, "Seems a little too much like magic to me."

Rhyme laughed. "Oh, that's *exactly* what it is. Sleight of hand, pulling rabbits out of hats. But remember that illusion is based on . . . on *what*, Ben?"

The big man cleared his throat, blushed and shook his head. "Uhm, don't quite know what you mean, sir."

"Illusion's based on *science*. That's what." A glance at Sachs. "I'll call you as soon as I find something."

The two women and Jesse Corn left the evidence room.

And so, the precious evidence arrayed before him, the

familiar equipment warmed up, internal politics disposed of, Lincoln Rhyme eased his head back against the wheelchair headrest and stared at the bags Sachs had delivered to him—willing, or coercing, or perhaps just allowing his mind to roam where his legs could not walk, to touch what his hands could not feel.

chapter eight

The deputies were talking.

Mason Germain, arms crossed, leaning against the hallway wall beside the door that led to the Sheriff's Department deputy cubicles, could just hear their voices.

"How come we're just sitting here not doing anything?"

"No, no, no. . . . Didn't you hear? Jim's sent out a search party."

"Yeah? No, I didn't hear that."

Goddamn, thought Mason. Who hadn't heard it either.

"Lucy, Ned and Jesse. And that lady cop from Washington."

"Naw, it's New York. You see that hair of hers?"

"I don't care 'bout that hair of hers. I care 'bout finding Mary Beth and Lydia."

"I do too. I'm just saying . . ."

Mason's gut tightened further. They only sent four people out after the Insect Boy? Was Bell crazy?

He stormed up the corridor, on his way to the sheriff's office, and nearly collided with Bell himself as he walked out of the storeroom—where that weird guy, the one in the wheelchair, was set up. Bell glanced at the senior deputy with a surprised blink.

"Hey, Mason . . . I was looking for you."

Not looking too hard, though, don't seem.

"I want you to get over to Rich Culbeau's place."

"Culbeau? What for?"

"Sue McConnell's offering some reward or 'nother for Mary Beth and he wants it. We don't need him to mess up the search. I want you to keep an eye on him. If he's not there just wait at his place till he shows up again."

Mason didn't even bother to respond to this bizarre request. "You sent Lucy out after Garrett. And didn't tell me."

Bell looked the deputy up and down. "She and a couple others're going over to Blackwater Landing, see if they can pick up his trail."

"You musta known I wanted to be in the search party."

"I can't send everybody. Culbeau's already been over to Blackwater Landing once today. I can't have him screwing up the search."

"Come on, Jim. Don't bullshit me."

Bell sighed. "All right. The truth? Being as you got a hard-on for that boy, Mason, I decided not to send you. I don't want any mistakes made. There're lives at stake. We've got to get him and get him fast."

"Which is my intent, Jim. As you ought to know. I been after this kid for three years. I can't believe you'd just cut me out and hand the case over to that freak in there—"

"Hey, enough of that."

"Come on. I know Blackwater ten times better'n Lucy. I used to live there. Remember?"

Bell lowered his voice. "You want him *too* bad, Mason. It could affect your judgment."

"Did *you* think of that? Or was it *him*?" Nodding to the room where Mason now heard the eerie whine of the wheelchair. It set him on edge like a dentist's drill. Bell asking that freak to help them out could cause all kinds of problems that Mason didn't even want to think about.

"Come on, facts is facts. The whole world knows how you feel about Garrett."

"And the whole world happens to agree with *me*."

"Well, the way I told you's the way it is. You're gonna have to live with it."

The deputy laughed bitterly. "So now I'm baby-sitting a redneck 'shiner."

Bell looked past Mason, motioned to another deputy. "Hey, Frank . . ."

The tall, round officer ambled over to the two men.

"Frank, you go with Mason here. Over to Rich Culbeau's."

"Gonna serve a warrant? What's he done now?"

"Naw, no papers. Mason'll fill you in. If Culbeau's not at his place just wait for him. And make sure him and his buddies don't go anywhere near the search party. You got that, Mason?"

The deputy didn't answer. He just turned and walked away from his boss, who called, "This's better for everybody."

Don't think so, Mason thought.

"Mason . . ."

But the man said nothing and strode into the deputies' room. Frank followed a moment later. Mason didn't acknowledge the cluster of uniformed men, talking about the Insect Boy and about pretty Mary Beth and about Billy Stail's incredible 92-yard runback. He walked to his office and dug a key out of his pocket. He unlocked his desk and took out an extra Speedloader, clipped in six .357 shells. He slipped the Speedloader into its leather case and hooked it to his belt. He stepped to the doorway of his office. His voice cut through the conversation in the room as he gestured toward Nathan Groomer—a strawberry-blond deputy of about thirty-five. "Groomer,

I'm going to have a talk with Culbeau. You're coming with me."

"Well," Frank began slowly, holding the hat he'd fetched from his cubicle. "I thought Jim wanted *me* to go."

"I want Nathan," Mason said.

"Rich Culbeau?" Nathan asked. "Him and me're oil and water. I brought him in three times for DUI and hurt him some the last time. I'd take Frank."

"Yeah," agreed Frank. "Culbeau's cousin works with my wife's dad. He thinks I'm kin. He'll listen to me."

Mason looked coldly at Nathan. "I want you."

Frank tried again. "But Jim said—"

"And I want you *now.*"

"Come on, Mason," Nathan said in a brittle voice. "There's no call to break your manners with me."

Mason was looking at an elaborate decoy—a mallard duck—on Nathan's desk, his most recent carving. That man has some talent, he thought. Then said to the deputy, "You ready?"

Nathan sighed, stood up.

Frank asked, "But whatta I tell Jim?"

Without responding, Mason walked out of the office, Nathan in tow, and headed toward Mason's squad car. They climbed in. Mason felt the heat bristle around him and he got the engine going and the AC blasting full up.

After they'd belted up, as the slogan on the side of the cruiser instructed all responsible citizens to do, Mason said, "Now, listen up. I—"

"Aw, come on, Mason, don't get that way. I was only telling you what made sense. I mean, last year Frank and Culbeau—"

"Just shut up and listen."

"Okay. I'll listen. Don't think you need to be talking that way. . . . Okay. I'm listening. What's Culbeau done now?"

But Mason didn't answer. He asked, "Where's your Ruger?"

"My deer rifle? The M77?"

"Right."

"In my truck. At home."

"You got the Hitech 'scope mounted?"

"Course I do."

"We're gonna go get it."

They pulled out of the parking lot and as soon as they were on Main Street Mason hit the switch for the gumball machine—the revolving red and blue light on top of the car. Kept the siren off. He sped out of town.

Nathan tucked some Red Indian inside his cheek, which he couldn't do with Jim around but Mason didn't mind. "The Ruger. . . . So. That's why you wanted me. Not Frank."

"That's right."

Nathan Groomer was the best rifle shot in the department, one of the best in Paquenoke County. Mason'd seen him bring down a ten-point buck at eight hundred yards.

"So. After I get the rifle we going to Culbeau's house?"

"No."

"Where we going?"

"We're going hunting."

■

"Nice houses here," Amelia Sachs observed.

She and Lucy Kerr were driving north along Canal Road, back to Blackwater Landing from downtown. Jesse Corn and Ned Spoto, a stocky deputy in his late thirties, were behind them in a second squad car.

Lucy glanced at the real estate overlooking the canal—the elegant new colonials Sachs had seen earlier—and said nothing.

Again Sachs was struck by the forlorn quality of the houses and yards, the absence of kids. Just like the streets of Tanner's Corner.

Children, she reflected again.

Then told herself: Let's not get into *that*.

Lucy turned right on Route 112 then off onto the shoulder—where they'd been just a half hour earlier, the ridge overlooking the crime scenes. Jesse Corn's squad car pulled in behind. The four of them walked down the embankment to the riverside and climbed into the skiff. Jesse took up the rowing position again, muttered, "Brother, north of the Paquo." He said this with an ominous tone that Sachs at first took to be a joke but then noticed that neither he nor the others were smiling. On the far side of the river they climbed out and followed Garrett's and Lydia's footsteps to the hunting blind where Ed Schaeffer had been stung then about fifty feet past it into the woods, where the tracks vanished.

At Sachs's direction they fanned out, moving in increasingly large circles, looking for any signs of the direction Garrett had gone. They found nothing and returned to the place where the footprints disappeared.

Lucy said to Jesse, "You know that path? The one those druggies scooted down after Frank Sturgis found 'em over last year?"

He nodded. He said to Sachs, "It's about fifty yards north. That way." He pointed. "Garrett'd know about it probably and it's the best way to get through the woods and swamp here."

"Let's check it out," Ned said.

Sachs wondered how to best handle the impending conflict and decided there was only one way: head-on. Being overly delicate wouldn't work, not with three of them versus her alone (Jesse Corn being, she believed, only *amorously* in her camp). "We should stay here until we hear from Rhyme."

Jesse kept a faint smile on his face, tasting a morsel of divided loyalty.

Lucy shook her head. "Garrett *had* to've taken that path."

"We don't know that for sure," Sachs said.

"It *does* get a little thick 'round here," Jesse offered.

Ned said, "All that plume grass and tuckahoe and mountain holly. Lot of creeper too. You don't take that path, there's no *way* to get through here and make any time."

"We'll have to wait," Sachs said, thinking of a passage from Lincoln Rhyme's textbook on criminalistics, *Physical Evidence:*

> *More investigations involving a suspect at large are ruined by giving in to the impulse to move quickly and engage in hot pursuit when, in fact, in most cases, a slow examination of the evidence will point a clear path to the suspect's door and permit a safer and more efficient arrest.*

Lucy Kerr said, "It's just that somebody from the city doesn't really understand the woods. You head off that path it'd slow your time by half. He had to've stuck to it."

"He could've doubled back to the riverbank," Sachs pointed out. "Maybe he had another boat hidden up- or downstream."

"That's true," Jesse said, earning a dark glance from Lucy.

A long moment of silence, the four people standing immobile while gnats strafed them and they sweated in the merciless heat.

Finally Sachs said simply, "We'll wait."

Sealing the decision, she sat on what was surely the most uncomfortable rock in the entire woods and, with feigned interest, studied a woodpecker drilling fiercely into a tall oak in front of them.

. . . chapter nine

"Primary scene first," Rhyme called to Ben. "Blackwater."

He nodded at the cluster of evidence on the fiberboard table. "Let's do Garrett's running shoe first. The one he dropped when he snatched Lydia."

Ben picked it up, unzipped the plastic bag, started to reach inside.

"Gloves!" Rhyme ordered. "Always wear latex gloves when handling evidence."

"Because of fingerprints?" the zoologist asked, hurriedly pulling them on.

"That's one reason. The other's contamination. We don't want to confuse places *you've* been with places the perp has been."

"Sure. Right." Ben nodded his massive crew-cut head aggressively, as if he were fearful of forgetting this rule. He shook the shoe, peered into it. "Looks like there's gravel or something inside."

"Hell, I didn't have Amelia ask for sterile examining boards." Rhyme looked around the room. "See that magazine there? *People*?"

Ben picked it up. Shook his head. "It's three weeks old."

"I don't *care* how current the stories about Leonardo DiCaprio's love life are," Rhyme muttered. "Pull out the subscription inserts inside. . . . Don't you hate those things? But they're good for us—they come off the printing press nice and sterile, so they make good mini–examining boards."

Ben did as instructed and poured the dirt and stones onto the card.

"Put a sample in the microscope and let me take a look at it." Rhyme wheeled close to the table but the ocular piece was a few inches too high for him. "Damn."

Ben assessed the problem. "Maybe I could hold it for you to look in."

Rhyme gave a faint laugh. "It weighs close to thirty pounds. No, we'll have to find a—"

But the zoologist picked up the instrument and, with his massive arms, held the 'scope very steady. Rhyme couldn't, of course, turn the focusing knobs but he saw enough to give him an idea of what the evidence was. "Limestone chips and dust. Would that've come from Blackwater Landing?"

"Uhm," Ben said slowly, "doubt it. Mostly just mud and stuff."

"Run a sample of it through the chromatograph. I want to see what else is in there."

Ben mounted the sample inside and pressed the test button.

Chromatography is a criminalist's dream tool. Developed just after the turn of the century by a Russian botanist though not much used until the 1930s, the device analyzes compounds such as foods, drugs, blood and trace elements and isolates the pure elements in them. There are a half-dozen variations on the process but the most common type used in forensic science is the gas chromatograph, which burns a sample of evidence. The resulting vapors are then separated to indicate the component substances that make up the sample. In a forensic science lab the chromatograph is usually connected to a mass spectrometer, which can identify many of the substances specifically.

The gas chromatograph will only work with materials that can be vaporized—burned—at relatively low temperatures. The limestone wouldn't ignite, of course. But Rhyme wasn't interested in the rock; he was interested in what trace materials had adhered to the dirt and gravel. This would narrow down more specifically the places Garrett had been.

"It'll take a little while," Rhyme said. "While we're waiting let's look at the dirt in the *treads* of Garrett's shoe. I tell you, Ben, I *love* treads. Shoes, and tires too. They're like sponges. Remember that."

"Yessir. I will, sir."

"Dig some out and let's see if it comes from someplace different from Blackwater Landing."

Ben scraped the dirt onto another subscription card, which he held in front of Rhyme, who examined it carefully. As a forensic scientist, he knew the importance of dirt. It sticks to clothes, it leaves trails like Hansel's and Gretel's bread crumbs to and from a perp's house and it links criminal and crime scene as if they were shackled together. There are approximately 1,100 different shades of soil and if a sample from a crime scene is the identical color to the dirt in the perp's backyard the odds are good that the perp was there. Similarity in the *composition* of the soils can bolster the connection too. Locard, the great French criminalist, developed a forensics principle named after him, which holds that in every crime there is always some transfer between the perpetrator and the victim or the crime scene. Rhyme had found that, second to blood in the case of an invasive homicide or assault, dirt is the substance most often transferred.

However, the problem with dirt as evidence is that it's

too prevalent. In order for it to have any meaning forensically a bit of dirt whose source *might* be the criminal must be different from the dirt found naturally at the crime scene.

The first step in dirt analysis is to check known soil from the scene—an exemplar—against the sample the criminalist believes came from the perp.

Rhyme explained this to Ben and the big man picked up one bag of dirt, which Sachs had marked *Exemplar soil—Blackwater Landing,* along with the date and time of collection. There was also a notation in a hand that was not Sachs's. *Collected by Deputy J. Corn.* Rhyme pictured the young deputy eagerly scurrying off to do her bidding. Ben poured some of this dirt onto a third subscription card. He set it beside the dirt he'd dug out of Garrett's treads. "How do we compare them?" the young man asked, looking over the instruments.

"Your eyes."

"But—"

"Just look at them. See if the color of the unknown sample is different from the color of the known."

"How do I do that?"

Rhyme forced himself to answer calmly. "You just *look* at them."

Ben stared at one pile, then the other.

Back again. Once more.

And then once again.

Come on, come on . . . it isn't *that* tricky. Rhyme struggled to be patient. One of the hardest things in the world for him.

"What do you see?" Rhyme asked. "Is the dirt from the two scenes different?"

"Well, I can't exactly tell, sir. I think one's lighter."

" 'Scope them in the comparison."

Ben mounted the samples in a comparison microscope and looked through the eyepieces. "I'm not sure. Hard to say. I guess . . . maybe there *is* some difference."

"Let me see."

Once again the massive muscles held the large microscope steady and Rhyme peered into the eyepieces. "Definitely different from the known," Rhyme said. "Lighter colored. And it has more crystal in it. More granite and clay and different types of vegetation. So it's not from Blackwater Landing. . . . If we're lucky it came from his hidey-hole."

A faint smile crossed Ben's lips, the first Rhyme had seen.

"What?"

"Oh, well, that's what we call the cave a moray eel takes for his home . . ." The young man's smile vanished as Rhyme's stare told him that this was not the time or place for anecdotes.

The criminalist said, "When you get the results of the limestone on the chromatograph run the dirt from the treads."

"Yessir."

A moment later the screen of the computer attached to the chromatograph/spectrometer flickered and lines shaped like mountains and valleys appeared. Then a window popped up and the criminalist maneuvered closer in his wheelchair. He bumped a table and the Storm Arrow jerked to the left, jostling Rhyme. "Shit."

Ben's eyes went wide with alarm. "Are you all right, sir?"

"Yes, yes, yes," Rhyme muttered. "What's that fucking table doing there? We don't need it."

"I'll get it out of the way," Ben blurted, grabbing the heavy table with one hand as if it were made of balsa wood and stashing it in the corner. "Sorry, I should've thought of that."

Rhyme ignored the zoologist's uncomfortable contrition and scanned the screen. "Large amounts of nitrates, phosphates and ammonia."

This was very troubling but Rhyme said nothing just

yet; he wanted to see what substances were in the dirt that Ben had dug out of the treads. And shortly these results too were on the screen.

Rhyme sighed. "More nitrates, more ammonia—a lot of it. High concentrations again. Also, more phosphates. Detergent too. And something else. . . . What the hell is that?"

"Where?" Ben asked, leaning toward the screen.

"At the bottom. The database's identified it as camphene. You ever hear of that?"

"No, sir."

"Well, Garrett walked through some of it, whatever it is." He looked at the evidence bag. "Now, what else do we have? That white tissue Sachs found. . . ."

Ben picked up the bag, held it close to Rhyme. There was a lot of blood on the tissue. He glanced at the other tissue sample—the Kleenex that Sachs had found in Garrett's room. "They the same?"

"Look the same," Ben said. "Both white, both the same size."

Rhyme said, "Give them to Jim Bell. Tell him I want a DNA analysis. The drive-through variety."

"The, uhm . . . what's that, sir?"

"The down-and-dirty DNA, the polymerase chain reaction. We don't have time for the RFLP—that's the one-in-six-billion version. I just want to know if it's Billy Stail's blood or somebody else's. Have somebody scrounge up samples from Billy Stail's body and from Mary Beth and Lydia."

"Samples? Of what?"

Rhyme forced himself once more to remain patient. "Of genetic material. Any tissue from Billy's body. For the women, getting some hair would be the easiest—as long as the bulb's attached. Have a deputy pick up a brush or comb from Mary Beth's and Lydia's bathrooms and get it over to the same lab that's running the test on the Kleenex."

The man took the bag and left the room. He returned a moment later. "They'll have it in an hour or two, sir. They're going to send it to the med center in Avery, not to the state police. Deputy Bell, I mean, *Sheriff* Bell, thought that would be easier."

"An hour?" Rhyme muttered, grimacing. "Way too long."

He couldn't help wondering if this delay might be just long enough to keep them from finding the Insect Boy before he killed Lydia or Mary Beth.

Ben stood with his bulky arms at his sides. "Uhm, I could call them back. I told 'em how important it was but . . . Do you want me to?"

"That's okay, Ben. We'll keep going here. Thom, time for our charts."

The aide wrote on the blackboard as Rhyme dictated to him.

FOUND AT PRIMARY CRIME SCENE—
BLACKWATER LANDING

Kleenex with Blood
Limestone Dust
Nitrates
Phosphate
Ammonia
Detergent
Camphene

Rhyme gazed at it. More questions than answers. . . .
Fish out of water . . .

His eye fell on the pile of dirt that Ben had dug out of the boy's shoe. Then something occurred to him. "Jim!" he shouted, his voice booming and startling both Thom and Ben. "Jim! Where the hell is he? Jim!!"

"What?" The sheriff came running into the room, alarmed. "Something wrong?"

"How many people work in the building here?"

"I don't know. 'Bout twenty."

"And they live all over the county?"

"More'n that. Some travel from Pasquotank, Albemarle and Chowan."

"I want 'em all down here now."

"What?"

"Everybody in the building. I want soil samples from their shoes. . . . Wait: And the floor mats in their cars."

"Soil . . ."

"Soil! Dirt! Mud! You know. I want it now!"

Bell retreated. Rhyme said to Ben, "That rack? Over there?"

The zoologist lumbered toward the table on which was a long rack holding a number of test tubes.

"It's a density gradient tester. It profiles the specific gravity of materials like dirt."

He nodded. "I've heard of it. Never used one."

"It's easy. Those bottles there—" Rhyme was looking toward two dark glass bottles. One labeled tetra, the other ethanol. "You're going to mix those the way I tell you and fill up the tubes close to the top."

"Okay. What's that going to do?"

"Start mixing. I'll tell you when we're through."

Ben mixed the chemicals according to Rhyme's instructions and then filled twenty of the tubes with alternating bands of different colored liquids—the ethanol and the tetrabromoethane.

"Pour a little of the soil sample from Garrett's shoe into the tube on the left. The soil'll separate and that'll give us a profile. We'll get samples from employees here who live in different areas of the county. If any of them match Garrett's that means the dirt he picked up could be from nearby."

Bell arrived with the first of the employees and Rhyme explained what he was going to do. The sheriff grinned in admiration. "That's an idea and a half, Lincoln. Cousin

Roland knew what he was doing when he sang your praises."

But the half hour spent on this exercise was futile. None of the samples submitted from the people in the building matched the dirt in the treads of Garrett's shoe. Rhyme scowled as the last sample of dirt from the employees settled into the tube.

"Damn."

"Was a good try though," Bell said.

A waste of precious time.

"Should I pitch out the samples?" Ben asked.

"No. Never throw out your exemplars without recording them," he said firmly. Then remembered not to be too abrasive in his instructions; the big man was here only by the grace of family ties. "Thom, help us out. Sachs asked for a Polaroid camera from the state. It's got to be here someplace. Find it and take close-ups of all the tubes. Mark down the name of each employee on the back of the pictures."

The aide found the camera and went to work.

"Now let's analyze what Sachs found at Garrett's foster parents' house. The pants in that bag—see if there's anything in the cuffs."

Ben carefully opened the plastic bag and examined the trousers. "Yessir, some pine needles."

"Good. Did they fall off the branches or are they cut?"

"Cut, looks like."

"Excellent. That means he *did* something to them. He cut them on purpose. And that purpose *may* have to do with the crime. We don't know what that is yet but I'd guess it's camouflage."

"I smell skunk," Ben said, sniffing the clothes.

Rhyme said, "That's what Amelia said. Doesn't do us any good, though. Not yet anyway."

"Why not?" the zoologist asked.

"Because there's no way to link a wild animal to a specific location. A *stationary* skunk would be helpful; a mobile one isn't. Let's look at the trace on the clothes. Cut a couple pieces of the pants and run them through the chromatograph."

While they waited for the results Rhyme examined the rest of the evidence from the boy's room. "Let me see that notebook, Thom." The aide flipped through the pages for Rhyme. They contained only bad drawings of insects. He shook his head. Nothing helpful there.

"Those other books?" Rhyme nodded toward the four hardbound books Sachs had found in his room. One— *The Miniature World*—had been read so often it was falling apart. Rhyme noticed passages were circled or underlined or marked with asterisks. But none of the passages gave any clue as to where the boy might have spent time. They seemed to be trivia about insects. He told Thom to put them aside.

Rhyme then looked over what Garrett had hidden in the wasp jar: money, pictures of Mary Beth and of the boy's family. The old key. The fishing line.

The cash was just a crumpled mass of fives and tens and silver dollars. There were, Rhyme noted, no helpful jottings in the margins of the bills (where many criminals write messages or plans—a fast way to get rid of incriminating instructions to co-conspirators is to buy something and send the note off into the black hole of circulation). Rhyme had Ben run the PoliLight—an alternative light source—over the money and found that both the paper and the silver dollars contained easily a hundred different partial fingerprints, too many to provide any helpful clues. There was no price sticker on the picture frame or fishing line and thus no way to trace them to stores Garrett might've frequented.

"Three-pound-test fishing line," Rhyme commented, looking at the spool. "That's light, isn't it, Ben?"

"Hardly catch a bluegill with that, sir."

The results of the trace on the boy's slacks flickered

onto the computer screen. Rhyme read aloud: "Kerosene, more ammonia, more nitrates and that camphene again. Another chart, Thom, if you'd be so kind."

He dictated.

FOUND AT SECONDARY CRIME SCENE— GARRETT'S ROOM

Skunk Musk
Cut Pine Needles
Drawings of Insects
Pictures of Mary Beth and Family
Insect Books
Fishing Line
Money
Unknown Key
Kerosene
Ammonia
Nitrates
Camphene

Rhyme stared at the charts. Finally he said, "Thom, make a call. Mel Cooper."

The aide picked up the phone, dialed from memory.

Cooper, who worked with NYPD forensics, weighed in at probably half Ben's weight. He looked like a timid actuary and he was one of the top forensic lab men in the country.

"Can you speaker me, Thom?"

A button was pushed and a moment later the soft tenor of Cooper's voice said, "Hello, Lincoln. Something tells me you're not in the hospital."

"How'd you figure that one out, Mel?"

"Didn't take much deductive reasoning. Caller ID says Paquenoke County Government Building. Delaying your operation?"

"No. Just helping out on a case here. Listen, Mel, I

don't have much time and I need some information about a substance called camphene. Ever hear of it?"

"No. But hold on. I'll go into the database."

Rhyme heard frantic clicking. Cooper was also the fastest keyboarder Rhyme had ever met.

"Okay, here we go . . . Interesting . . ."

"I don't need *interesting*, Mel. I need facts."

"It's a terpene—carbon and hydrogen. Derived from plants. It used to be an ingredient in pesticides but it was banned in the early eighties. Its main use was in the late 1800s. It was used for fuel in lamps. It was state of the art at the time—replaced whale oil. Common as natural gas back then. You're trying to track down an unsub?"

"He's not an unknown subject, Mel. He's *extremely* known. We just can't find him. Old lamps? So trace camphene probably means that he's been hiding out someplace built in the nineteenth century."

"Likely. But there's another possibility. Says here that camphene's only present use is in fragrances."

"What sort?"

"Perfumes, aftershave and cosmetics mostly."

Rhyme considered this. "What percentage of a finished fragrance product is camphene?" he asked.

"Trace only. Parts per thousand."

Rhyme had always told his forensic teams never to be afraid to make bold deductions in analyzing the evidence. Still, he was painfully aware of the short time the two women might have to live and he felt they had only enough resources now to pursue one of these potential leads.

"We'll have to play the odds on this one," he announced. "We'll assume the camphene's from old lanterns, not fragrances, and act accordingly. Now, listen, Mel, I'm also going to be sending you a photocopy of a key. I need you to trace it."

"Easy. From a car?"

"I don't know."

"House?"

"Don't know."

"Recent?"

"No clue."

Cooper said dubiously, "May be less easy than I thought. But get it to me and I'll do what I can."

When they disconnected, Rhyme ordered Ben to photocopy both sides of the key and fax it to Cooper. Then he tried Sachs on the radio. It wasn't working. He called her on her cell phone.

" 'Lo?"

"Sachs, it's me."

"What's wrong with the radio?" she asked.

"There's no reception."

"Which way should we go, Rhyme? We're across the river but we lost the trail. And, frankly"— her voice fell to a whisper—"the natives're restless. Lucy wants to boil me for dinner."

"I've got the basic analysis done but I don't know what to do with all the data—I'm waiting for that man from the factory in Blackwater Landing. Henry Davett. He should be here any minute. But listen, Sachs, there's something else I have to tell you. I found significant trace of ammonia and nitrates on Garrett's clothes and in the shoe he lost."

"A bomb?" she asked, her hollow voice revealing her dismay.

"Looks that way. And that fishing line you found's too light to do any serious fishing. I think he's using it for trip wires to set off the device. Go slow. Look for traps. If you see something that looks like a clue just remember that it might be rigged."

"Will do, Rhyme."

"Sit tight. I hope to have some directions for you soon."

∎

Garrett and Lydia had covered another three or four miles.

The sun was high now. It was noon maybe, or close to it, and the day was hot as a tailpipe. The bottled water that Lydia had drunk at the quarry had quickly leached from her system and she was faint from the heat and thirst.

As if he sensed this Garrett said, "We'll be there soon. It's cooler. And I got more water."

The ground was open here. Broken forests, marshes. No houses, no roads. There were many old paths branching in different directions. It would be almost impossible for anyone searching for them to figure out which way they'd gone—the paths were like a maze.

Garrett nodded down one of these narrow paths, rocks to the left, a twenty-foot drop off to the right. They walked about a half mile along this route and then he stopped. He looked back.

When he seemed satisfied that no one was nearby he stepped into the bushes and returned with a nylon string—like thin fishing line—that he ran across the path just above the ground. It was nearly impossible to see. He connected it to a stick, which in turn propped up a three- or four-gallon glass bottle, filled with a milky liquid. There was some residue on the side and she got a whiff of it—ammonia. She was horrified. Was it a bomb? she wondered. As a nurse on ER duty she'd treated several teenagers who'd been hurt making homemade explosives. She remembered how their blackened skin had actually been shattered by the detonation.

"You can't do that," she whispered.

"I don't want any shit from you." He snapped his fingernails. "I'm gonna finish up here and then we're going home."

Home?

Lydia stared, numb, at the large bottle as he covered it with boughs.

Garrett pulled her down the path once more. Despite the increasing heat of the day he was moving faster now and she struggled to keep up with Garrett, who seemed to get dirtier by the minute, covered with dust and flecks of dead leaves. It was as if he were slowly turning into an insect himself every step they got farther from civilization. It reminded her of some story she was supposed to read in school but never finished.

"Up there." Garrett nodded toward a hill. "There's a place we'll stay. Go on to the ocean in the morning."

Her uniform was soaked with sweat. The top two buttons of the white outfit were undone and the white of her bra was visible. The boy kept glancing at the rounded skin of her breasts. But she hardly cared; at the moment she wanted only to escape from the Outside, to get into some cooling shade, wherever he was taking her.

Fifteen minutes later they broke from the woods and into a clearing. In front of them was an old gristmill, surrounded by reeds, cattails, tall grass. It sat beside a stream that had largely been taken over by the swamp. One wing of the mill had burnt down. Amid the rubble stood a scorched chimney—what was called a "Sherman Monument," after the Union general who burned houses and buildings during his march to the sea, leaving a landscape of blackened chimneys behind him.

Garrett led her into the front part of the mill, the portion that had been untouched by the fire. He pushed her through the doorway and swung the heavy oak door shut, bolted it. For a long moment he stood listening. When he seemed satisfied that no one was following he handed her another bottle of water. She fought the urge to gulp down the whole container. She filled her mouth, let it sit, feeling the sting against her parched mouth, then swallowed slowly.

When she finished he took the bottle away from her, untaped her hands and retaped them behind her back. "You have to do that?" she asked angrily.

He rolled his eyes at the foolishness of the question. He eased her to the floor. "Sit there and keep your goddamn mouth shut." Garrett sat against the opposite wall and closed his eyes. Lydia cocked her head toward the window and listened for the sounds of helicopters or swamp boats or the baying of the search party's dogs. But she heard only Garrett's breathing, which she decided in her despair was really the sound of God Himself abandoning her.

. . . chapter ten

A figure appeared in the doorway, accompanying Jim Bell.

He was a man in his fifties, thinning hair and a round, distinguished face. A blue blazer was over his arm and his white shirt was perfectly pressed and heavily starched though darkened with sweat stains under the arms. A striped tie was stuck in place with a bar.

Rhyme had thought this might be Henry Davett but the criminalist's eyes were one aspect of his physical body that had come through his accident unscathed—his vision was perfect—and he read the monogram on the man's tie bar from ten feet away: WWJD.

William? Walter? Wayne?

Rhyme didn't have a clue who he might be.

The man looked at Rhyme, squinted appraisingly and nodded. Then Jim Bell said, "Henry, I'd like you to meet Lincoln Rhyme."

So, not a monogram. This *was* Davett. Rhyme nodded back to the man, concluding that the tie bar had probably been his father's. William Ward Jonathan Davett.

He stepped into the room. His fast eyes took in the equipment.

"Ah, you know chromatographs?" Rhyme asked, observing a flicker of recognition.

"My Research and Development Department has a couple of them. But this model . . ." He shook his head critically. "They don't even make it anymore. Why're you using it?"

"State budget, Henry," Bell said.

"I'll send one over."

"Not necessary."

"This is garbage," the man said gruffly. "I'll get a new one here in twenty minutes."

Rhyme said, "*Getting* the evidence isn't the problem. Interpreting it is. That's why I can use your help. This is Ben Kerr, my forensic assistant."

They shook hands. Ben seemed relieved that another able-bodied person was in the room.

"Sit down, Henry," Bell said, rolling an office chair up to him. The man sat and, leaning forward somewhat, carefully smoothed his tie. The gesture, his posture, the tiny dots of his confident eyes coalesced in Rhyme's perception and he thought: charming, smart . . . and one hell of a tough businessman.

Rhyme wondered again about WWJD. He wasn't sure he'd solved the puzzle.

"This is about those women who got kidnapped, isn't it?"

Bell nodded. "Nobody's really coming right out and saying it but in the back of our minds . . ." He looked at Rhyme and Ben. ". . . We're thinking Garrett might've already raped and killed Mary Beth, dumped her body someplace."

Twenty-four hours . . .

The sheriff continued, "But we've still got a chance to save Lydia, we're hoping. And we have to stop Garrett before he goes after somebody else."

The businessman said angrily, "And Billy, that was such a shame. I heard he was just being a Good Samaritan, trying to save Mary Beth, and got himself killed."

"Garrett crushed his head in with a shovel. It was pretty bad."

"So time's at a premium. What can I do?" Davett turned to Rhyme. "You said interpreting something?"

"We have some clues as to where Garrett's been and where he might be headed with Lydia. I was hoping you might know something about the area around here and might be able to help us."

Davett nodded. "I know the lay of the land pretty well. I have geology and chemical engineering degrees. I've also lived in Tanner's Corner all my life so I'm pretty familiar with Paquenoke County."

Rhyme nodded toward the evidence charts. "Can you look at those and give us any thoughts? We're trying to link those clues to a specific location."

Bell added, "It'll probably be someplace they could get to by foot. Garrett doesn't like cars. He won't drive."

Davett put on eyeglasses and eased his head back, looking up at the wall.

FOUND AT PRIMARY CRIME SCENE— BLACKWATER LANDING

Kleenex with Blood
Limestone Dust
Nitrates
Phosphate
Ammonia
Detergent
Camphene

FOUND AT SECONDARY CRIME SCENE— GARRETT'S ROOM

Skunk Musk
Cut Pine Needles
Drawings of Insects

Pictures of Mary Beth and Family
Insect Books
Fishing Line
Money
Unknown Key
Kerosene
Ammonia
Nitrates
Camphene

Davett scanned the list up and down, taking his time,
eyes narrowing several times. A faint frown. "Nitrates
and ammonia? You know what that could be?"

Rhyme nodded. "I think he left some explosive devices
to stop the search party. I've told them about it."

Grimacing, Davett returned to the chart. "The camphene . . . I think that was used in old lanterns. Like coal-
oil lamps."

"That's right. So we think the place he's got Mary Beth
is old. Nineteenth century."

"There must be thousands of old houses and barns
and shacks around here. . . . What else? Limestone dust.
. . . That's not going to narrow things down much.
There's a huge ridge of limestone that runs all the way
through Paquenoke County. It used to be a big money-
maker here." He rose and moved his finger diagonally
along the map from the southern edge of the Great Dismal Swamp to the southwest, from Location L-4 to C-
14. "You could find limestone anywhere along that line.
That won't do you much good. But"— he stepped
back, crossed his arms—"the phosphate's helpful.
North Carolina's a major producer of phosphate but
it's not mined around here. That's farther south. So,
combined with the detergent, I'd say he's been near
polluted water."

"Hell," Jim Bell said, "that just means he's been in the
Paquenoke."

"No," Davett said, "the Paquo's clean as well water. It's dark but it's fed by the Dismal Swamp and Lake Drummond."

"Oh, it's magic water," the sheriff said.

"What's that?" Rhyme asked.

Davett explained. "Some of us old-timers call the water from the Great Dismal magic water. It's full of tannic acid from decaying cypress and juniper trees. The acid kills bacteria so it stays fresh for a long time—before refrigeration they'd use it for drinking water on sailing ships. People used to think it had magic properties."

"So," Rhyme said, never much interested in local myths if they couldn't help him forensically, "if it's not the Paquenoke, where would the phosphates place him?"

Davett looked at Bell. "Where'd he kidnap the girl most recently?"

"Same place as Mary Beth. Blackwater Landing." Bell touched the map and then moved his finger north to Location H-9. "Crossed the river, went to a hunting blind about here then headed north a half mile. Then the search party lost the trail. They're waiting for us to give them directions."

"Oh, then there's no question," Davett said with encouraging confidence. The businessman moved his finger to the east. "He crossed Stone Creek. Here. See it? Some of the waterfalls there look like foam on beer, there's so much detergent and phosphate in the water. It starts out near Hobeth Falls up north and there's a ton of runoff. They don't know a thing about planning and zoning in that town."

"Good," Rhyme said. "Now, once he crossed the creek, any thoughts about which way he'd go?"

Davett again consulted the chart. "If you found pine needles I'd have to guess this way." Tapping the map at I-5 and J-8. "There's pine everywhere in North Carolina but around here most of the forests are oak, old-growth cedar, cypress and gum. The only big pine forest I know

of is northeast. Here. On the way to the Great Dismal."
Davett stared at the charts for a moment longer, shook
his head. "Not much else I can say, I'm afraid. How
many search parties you have out?"

"One," Rhyme said.

"What?" Davett turned to him, frowning. "Just one?
You're joking."

"No," Bell said, sounding defensive under the man's
firm cross-examination.

"Well, how big is it?"

"Four deputies," Bell said.

Davett scoffed. "That's crazy." He waved at the map.
"You've got hundreds of square miles. This's Garrett
Hanlon . . . the Insect Boy. He just about *lives* north of
the Paquo. He can outmaneuver you in a minute."

The sheriff cleared his throat. "Mr. Rhyme here thinks
it's better not to use too many people."

"You *can't* use too many people in a situation like
this," Davett said to Rhyme. "You should take fifty men,
give them rifles and have them beat the bushes till you
find him. You're doing it all wrong."

Rhyme noticed that Ben observed Davett's lecture with
a mortified expression. The zoologist would, of course,
assume that one *had* to take the kid-glove approach when
arguing with crips. The criminalist, though, said calmly,
"A big manhunt would just drive Garrett to kill Lydia
and then go to ground."

"No," Davett said emphatically, "it'd scare him into
letting her go. I've got about forty-five people working a
shift at the factory now. Well, a dozen are women. We
couldn't get them involved. But the men. . . . Let me get
them out. We'll find some guns. Turn them loose around
Stone Creek."

Rhyme could just imagine what thirty or forty amateur
bounty hunters would do in a search like this. He shook
his head. "No, this is the way to handle it."

Their eyes met and for a moment there was a thick

silence in the room. Davett shrugged and looked away first but this disengagement was not a concession that Rhyme might be correct. It was just the opposite: an emphatic protest that by ignoring his advice Rhyme and Bell were proceeding at their own peril.

"Henry," Bell said, "I agreed to let Mr. Rhyme run the show. We're pretty thankful to him."

Part of the sheriff's comments were intended for Rhyme himself—implicitly apologizing for Davett.

But for his part Rhyme was delighted to be on the receiving end of Davett's bluntness. It was a shocking admission for him but Rhyme, who believed not at all in omens, felt the man's presence now was a sign—that the surgery would go well and would have some beneficial effect on his condition. He felt this because of the brief exchange that had just occurred—in which this tough businessman had looked him in the eye and told him he was dead wrong. Davett didn't even notice Rhyme's condition; all he saw was Rhyme's actions, his decision, his attitude. His damaged body was irrelevant to Davett. Dr. Weaver's magic hands would move him a step closer to a place where more people would treat him this way.

The businessman said, "I'll pray for those girls." Then turned to Rhyme. "I'll pray for you too, sir." The glance lasted a moment longer than a valediction normally would and Rhyme sensed the last promise was meant sincerely—and literally. He walked out the door.

"Henry's a bit opinionated," Bell said when Davett had left.

"And he's got his own interests here, right?" Rhyme asked.

"The girl who died from the hornets last year. Meg Blanchard. . . ."

Got herself stung 137 times. Rhyme nodded.

Bell continued, "She worked for Henry's company. Went to the same church he and his family belong to too. He's no different from most folks here—he thinks the town'd be better off without Garrett Hanlon in it. He just tends to think *his* way is the best way to handle things."

Church . . . prayer . . . Rhyme suddenly understood something. He said to Bell, "Davett's tie bar. The *J* stands for Jesus?"

Bell laughed. "You got that right. Oh, Henry'd drive a competitor out of business without a blink but he's a deacon in church. Goes three times a week or so. One of the reasons he'd like to send an army out after Garrett is that he's thinking that the boy's probably a heathen."

Rhyme still couldn't figure out the rest of the initials. "I give up. What're the other letters?"

"Stands for 'What Would Jesus Do?' That's what all those good Christians 'round here ask themselves when they're facing a big decision. I myself don't have a clue what He'd do in a case like this. But I'll tell you what *I'm* doing: calling up Lucy and your friend and gettin' 'em on Garrett's trail."

■

"Stone Creek?" Jesse Corn said after Sachs had relayed Rhyme's message to the search party. The deputy pointed. "A half mile that way."

He started through the brush, followed by Lucy and Amelia. Ned Spoto was in the rear, his pale eyes scanning the surroundings uneasily.

In five minutes they broke out of the tangle and stepped onto a well-trod path. Jesse motioned them along it, to the right—east.

"This is the path?" Sachs asked Lucy. "The one you thought he'd gone down?"

"That's right," Lucy responded.

"You were right," Sachs said quietly, for her ears only. "But we still had to wait."

"No, *you* had to show who was in charge," Lucy said brusquely.

That's absolutely right, Sachs thought. Then added: "But now we know there's probably a bomb on the trail. We didn't know that before."

"I would've been looking for traps anyway." Lucy fell silent and she continued along the path, eyes fixed on the ground, proving that she would, in fact, have been looking.

In ten minutes they came to Stone Creek, its water milky and frothing with pollutant suds. On the bank they found two sets of footprints—sneaker prints in a small size, but deep, probably left by a heavyset woman. Lydia, undoubtedly. And a man's bare feet. Garrett had apparently discarded his remaining shoe.

"Let's cross here," Jesse said. "I know the pine woods that Mr. Rhyme mentioned. This's the shortest way to get to them."

Sachs started toward the water.

"Stop!" Jesse called abruptly.

She froze, hand on her pistol, crouching. "What's the matter?" she asked. Lucy and Ned, snickering at her reaction, were sitting on rocks, taking off their shoes and socks.

"You get your socks wet and keep walking," Lucy said, "you'll be standing in need of about a dozen bandages 'fore you go a hundred yards. Blisters."

"Don't know much 'bout hiking, do you?" Ned asked the policewoman.

Jesse Corn gave an exasperated laugh at his fellow deputy. " 'Cause she lives in the *city*, Ned. Just like I don't figure you'd be an expert on subways and skyscrapers."

Sachs ignored both the chide and the gallant defense, and pulled off her short boots and black ankle-length socks. Rolled her jeans cuffs up.

They started through the stream. The water was ice-cold and felt wonderful. She regretted when the short trek through the creek—which Jesse pronounced "crick"—was over.

They waited a few minutes on the other side for their feet to dry then pulled on socks and shoes. Then searched the shore until they found the footprints once more. The party followed the trail into the woods but, as the ground grew drier and more tangled with brush, they lost the tracks.

"The pine trees're that way," Jesse said. He pointed northeast. "Makes the most sense for them to go straight through there."

Following his general guidance, they hiked for another twenty minutes, single file, scanning the ground for trip wires. Then the oak and holly and sedge gave way to juniper and hemlock. Ahead of them, a quarter mile, was a huge line of pine trees. But there was no longer any sign of the kidnapper's or his victim's footprints—no clue as to where they'd entered the forest.

"Too damn big," Lucy muttered. "How're we going to find the trail in there?"

"Let's fan out," Ned suggested. He too looked dismayed at the tangle of flora in front of them. "If he's left a bomb here it'll be the dickens to see it."

They were about to spread out when Sachs lifted her head. "Wait. Stay here," she ordered then started slowly through the brush, eyes on the ground, looking for traps. Only fifty feet away from the deputies, in a grove of some flowering trees, now barren and surrounded by rotting petals, she found Garrett's and Lydia's footprints in the dusty earth. They led to a clear path that headed into the forest.

"They came this way!" she called. "Follow my footprints. I checked it for traps."

A moment later the three deputies joined her.

"How'd you find it?" asked infatuated Jesse Corn.

"What do you smell?" she asked.

"Skunk," Ned said.

Sachs said, "Garrett had skunk scent on the pants I

found in his house. I figured he'd come this way before. I just followed the smell here."

Jesse laughed and said to Ned, "How's *that* for a city girl?"

Ned rolled his eyes and they all started up the path, moving slowly toward the line of pine trees.

Several times along this route they passed large, barren areas—the trees and bushes were dead. Sachs felt uneasy as they trekked through these—the search party was completely exposed to attack. Halfway through the second clearing, and after another bad scare when an animal or bird rustled the brush ringing the bare dirt, she pulled out her cell phone.

"Rhyme, you there?"

"What is it? Found anything?"

"We've picked up the trail. But tell me—did any of the evidence point to Garrett doing any shooting?"

"No," he answered. "Why?"

"There're some big barren patches in the woods here—acid rain or pollution's killed all the plants. We have *zero* cover. It's a perfect place for an ambush."

"I don't see any trace that's consistent with firearms. We've got the nitrates but if that was from ammunition we'd've found burnt powder grains, cleaning solvent, grease, cordite, fulminate of mercury. There's none of that."

"Which just means he hasn't fired a weapon in a while," she said.

"True."

She hung up.

Looking around cautiously now, skittish, they walked for several miles more, surrounded by the turpentiney scent of the air. Lulled by the heat, the buzzing of insects, they were still on the path that Garrett and Lydia had started along, though their footsteps were no longer visible. Sachs wondered if they'd missed—

"Stop!" Lucy Kerr cried. She dropped to her knees.

Ned and Jesse froze. Sachs drew her pistol in a fraction of a second. Then she noticed what Lucy was referring to—the silvery glimmer of a wire across the path.

"Man," Ned said, "how'd you see that? It's full-up invisible."

Lucy didn't respond. She crawled to the side of the path, following the wire. Gently pulled aside bushes. Hot, crisp leaves rustled as she lifted them out one by one.

"Want me to get the bomb squad over here from Elizabeth City?" Jesse asked.

"Shhhh," Lucy ordered.

The deputy's careful hands moved aside the leaves a millimeter at a time.

Sachs was holding her breath. In a recent case she'd been the victim of an antipersonnel bomb. She hadn't been badly injured but she remembered that in a portion of a second the astonishing noise, the heat, the pressure wave and debris had enveloped her completely. She didn't want that to happen again. She knew too that many homemade pipe bombs were filled with BBs or ball bearings—sometimes dimes or pennies—as deadly shrapnel. Would Garrett do this too? She remembered his picture: his dim, sunken eyes. She remembered the jars of insects. Remembered the death of that woman in Blackwater Landing—stung to death. Remembered Ed Schaeffer in a wasp-venom coma. Yes, she decided, Garrett would definitely rig the most vicious trap he could think of.

She cringed as Lucy eased the last leaf off the pile.

The deputy sighed, sat back on her haunches. "It's a spider," she muttered.

Sachs saw it too. It wasn't fishing line at all, just a long string of web.

They rose to their feet.

"Spider," Ned said, laughing. Jesse chuckled too.

But their voices were humorless and, Sachs noticed, as they started down the path once more each one of them carefully lifted their feet well over the glistening strand.

■

Lincoln Rhyme, head back, eyes squinting at the chalkboard.

FOUND AT SECONDARY CRIME SCENE—
GARRETT'S ROOM

Skunk Musk
Cut Pine Needles
Drawings of Insects
Pictures of Mary Beth and Family
Insect Books
Fishing Line
Money
Unknown Key
Kerosene
Ammonia
Nitrates
Camphene

He sighed angrily. Felt completely helpless. The evidence was inexplicable to him.

His eyes focused on: *Insect Books.*

Then glanced at Ben. "So. You're a student, are you?"

"That's right, sir."

"Read a lot, I'll bet."

"How I spend most of my time—if I'm not in the field."

Rhyme was gazing at the spines of the books that Amelia had brought from Garrett's room. He mused,

"What do a person's favorite books say about them? Other than the obvious—that they're interested in the subject of the books, I mean."

"How's that?"

"Well, if a person has mostly self-help books, that says one thing about them. If he's got mostly novels, that says something else. These books of Garrett's are all nonfiction guidebooks. What do you make of that?"

"I wouldn't know, sir." The big man glanced once at Rhyme's legs—involuntarily, it seemed—then he turned his attention to the evidence chart. He mumbled, "I can't really figure out people. Animals make a lot more sense to me. They're a lot more social, more predictable, more consistent than people. Hell of a lot more clever too." Then he realized he was rambling and, with a ruddy blush, stopped talking.

Rhyme glanced again at the books. "Thom, could you get me the turning frame?" Rigged to an ECU—an environmental-control unit—that Rhyme could manipulate with his one working finger, the device used a rubber armature to turn pages of books. "It's in the van, isn't it?"

"I think so."

"I hope you packed it. I *told* you to pack it."

"I said I *think* it is," the aide said evenly. "I'll go see if it's there." He left the room.

Hell of a lot more clever too . . .

Thom returned a moment later with the turning frame.

"Ben," Rhyme called. "That book on top?"

"There?" the big man asked, staring at the books. It was the *Field Guide to Insects of North Carolina*.

"Put it in the frame." He stepped on his urgency. "If you would be so kind."

The aide showed Ben how to mount the book then plugged a different set of wires into the ECU underneath Rhyme's left hand.

He read the first page, found nothing helpful. Then his mind ordered his ring finger to move. An impulse shot from the brain, spiraled down through a tiny surviving axon in his spinal cord, past a million of its dead kin, then streaked along Rhyme's arm and into his hand.

The finger flicked a fraction of an inch.

The armature's own finger slid sideways. The page turned.

They followed the path through the forest, surrounded by the oily scent of pine and the sweet fragrance from one of the plants they passed. Lucy Kerr recognized it as a chicken grape.

As she stared at the path in front of them, looking for trip wires, she was suddenly aware that they hadn't seen any of Garrett's or Lydia's footprints for a long time. She swatted what she thought was a bug on her neck but it turned out to be just a rivulet of sweat, tickling as it ran down her skin. Lucy felt dirty today. Other times—evenings and days off—she loved to be outside, in her garden. As soon as she got home from her tour at the Sheriff's Department she would pull on her faded plaid shorts and T-shirt and navy blue running shoes that trailed stitching and would go to work in one of the three cuts of property surrounding her pale green colonial home that Bud had eagerly signed over to her outright as part of the divorce, laid low by a fever of guilt. There Lucy tended her long-spurred violets, yellow lady slippers, fringed orchids and orange bell lilies. She scooped dirt, led plants up trellises, watered them and whispered encouragements as if she were speaking to the children she'd been so certain she and Buddy would one day have.

Sometimes, after an assignment took her into the Carolina hinterland, serving a warrant or inquiring why the Honda or Toyota hidden in someone's garage happened to be owned by someone else, Lucy would notice a fledgling plant and, the police work disposed of, would uproot it and take it home with her like a foundling. She'd adopted her Solomon's seal this way. A tuckahoe plant too. And a beautiful indigo bush, which had grown six feet tall under her care.

Her eyes now slipped to what she was presently passing on this anxious pursuit of theirs: an elderberry, a mountain holly, plume grass. They passed a nice evening primrose, then some cattails and wild rice—taller than any of the search party and with leaves sharp as knives. And here was a squaw root, a parasitic herb. Which Lucy Kerr also knew by another name: cancer root. She glanced at that one once then looked back to the trail.

The path led to a steep hill—a series of rocks about twenty feet high. Lucy scaled the incline easily but at the top she stopped. Thinking, No, something's wrong here.

Beside her, Amelia Sachs climbed up to the plateau, paused. A moment later Jesse and Ned appeared. Jesse was breathing hard but Ned, a swimmer and outdoorsman, was taking the hike in stride.

"What is it?" Amelia asked Lucy, assessing the frown.

"This doesn't make any sense. For Garrett to come this way."

"We've been following the path, like Mr. Rhyme told us," Jesse said. "It's the only stretch of pine we've come across. Garrett's prints were leading this way."

"They *were*. But we haven't seen them for a while."

"Why don't you think he'd come this way?" Amelia asked.

"Look what's growing here." She pointed. "More and more swamp plants. And now we're on this rise we can see the ground better—look how marshy it's getting. Come on, think about it, Jesse. Where's this going to get Garrett? We're headed right for the Great Dismal."

"What's that?" Amelia asked her. "The Great Dismal?"

"A huge swamp, one of the biggest on the East Coast," Ned explained.

Lucy continued, "There's no cover there, no houses, no roads. The best he could do would be to slog his way into Virginia but that'd take days."

Ned Spoto added, "And this time of year, they don't *make* enough insect repellent to keep you from getting eaten alive. Not to mention snakes."

"Anyplace around here they could hide in? Caves? Houses?" Sachs looked around.

Ned said, "No caverns. Maybe a few old buildings. But what's happened is the water table's changed. The swamp's coming this way and a lot of the old houses and cabins're submerged. Lucy's right. If Garrett came this way he's heading for a dead end."

Lucy said, "I think we ought to turn around."

She thought that Amelia'd throw a hissy fit at this suggestion but the woman simply pulled out her cell phone and made a call. She said into the phone, "We're in the pine forest, Rhyme. There's a path but we can't find any sign that Garrett came along here. Lucy says it doesn't make any sense for him to come this way. She says it's mostly swamp northeast of here. There's no place for him to go."

Lucy said, "I'm thinking he'd head west. Or south, back across the river."

"That way he could get to Millerton," Jesse suggested.

Lucy nodded. "Couple of big factories around there closed when the companies took their business to Mexico. Banks foreclosed on a lot of property. There're dozens of abandoned houses he could hide in."

"Or south*east*," Jesse suggested. "That's where *I'd* go—follow Route 112 or the rail line. There's a slew of old houses and barns that way too."

Amelia repeated this to Rhyme.

As Lucy Kerr thought: What a strange man he is, so terribly afflicted and yet so supremely confident.

The policewoman from New York listened then hung up. "Lincoln says to keep going. The evidence doesn't suggest he went in those directions."

"Not like there aren't any pine trees to the west and south," Lucy snapped.

But the redhead was shaking her head. "That might be logical but it's not what the evidence shows. We keep going."

Ned and Jesse were looking from one woman to the other. Lucy glanced at Jesse's face and saw the ridiculous crush; she obviously wasn't going to get any support from him. She dug in. "No. I think we should go back, see if we can find where they turned off the path."

Amelia lowered her head, stared right into Lucy's eyes. "I'll tell you what. . . . We can call Jim Bell if you want."

A reminder that Jim had declared that that damn Lincoln Rhyme was running the operation and that *he'd* put Amelia in charge of the search party. This was crazy—a man and woman who'd probably never been in the Tar Heel State before this, two people who knew nothing of the people or the geography of the area, telling lifelong residents how to do their job.

But Lucy Kerr knew that she'd signed on to do a job where, like the army, you followed the chain of command. "All right," she muttered angrily. "But for the record I'm against going that way. It doesn't make any sense." She turned and started along the path, leaving the others behind. Her footsteps growing silent suddenly as she walked over a thick blanket of pine needles that covered the path.

Amelia's phone rang and she slowed as she took the call.

Lucy strode quickly ahead of her, over the thick bed of needles, trying to control her anger. There was no way Garrett Hanlon would come this way. It was a waste of time. They should have dogs. They should call Elizabeth City and get the state police choppers out. They should—

Then the world became a blur and she was tumbling forward, giving a short scream—her hands outstretched to catch her fall. "Jesus!"

Lucy fell hard onto the path, the breath knocked out of her, pine needles digging into her palms.

"Don't move," Amelia Sachs said, climbing to her feet after tackling the deputy.

"What the hell d'you do that for?" Lucy gasped, her hands stinging from the impact with the ground.

"Don't *move*! Ned and Jesse, you either."

Ned and Jesse froze, hands on their weapons, looking around, not sure what was going on.

Amelia, wincing as she stood, stepped cautiously off the pine needles and found a long stick in the woods, picked it up. She moved forward slowly, slipping the branch into the ground.

Two feet in front of Lucy, where she'd been about to step, the stick disappeared through a pile of pine boughs. "It's a trap."

"But there's no trip wire," Lucy said. "I was looking."

Carefully Amelia lifted away the boughs and the needles. They rested on a network of fishing line and covered a pit about two feet deep.

"The fish line wasn't a trip wire," Ned said. "It was to make that—a deadfall pit. Lucy, you nearly stepped right in it."

"And inside? There a bomb?" Jesse asked.

Amelia said to him, "Let me have your flashlight." He handed it to her. She shined the beam into the hole then backed up quickly.

"What is it?" Lucy asked.

"No bomb," Amelia responded. "Hornets' nest."

Ned looked. "Christ, what a bastard . . ."

Amelia carefully lifted off the rest of the boughs, exposing the hole and the nest, which was about the size of a football.

"Man," Ned muttered, closing his eyes, undoubtedly considering what it would have been like to find a hundred stinging wasps clustered around your thighs and waist.

Lucy rubbed her hands together—they smarted from the fall. She rose to her feet. "How'd you know?"

"*I* didn't. That was Lincoln on the phone. He was reading through Garrett's books. There was an underlined passage about some insect called an ant lion. It digs a pit and stings its enemy to death when it falls in. Garrett had circled it and the ink was just a few days old. Rhyme remembered the cut pine needles and the fishing line. He figured that the boy might dig a trap and told me to look for a bed of pine boughs on the path."

"Let's burn the nest out," Jesse said.

"No," Amelia said.

"But it's dangerous."

Lucy agreed with the policewoman. "A fire'd give away our position and Garrett'd know where we are. Just leave it uncovered so people can see it. We'll come back afterward and take care of it. Hardly anybody comes along here anyway."

Amelia nodded. She made a call on her phone. "We found it, Rhyme. Nobody got hurt. There was no bomb—he put a hornets' nest inside. . . . Okay. We'll be careful. . . . Keep reading that book. Let us know if you find anything else."

They started down the path once more and covered a good quarter mile before Lucy found it in her to say, "Thanks. Y'all were right about him coming this way. I was wrong." She hesitated for another long moment then added, "Jim made a good choice—bringing you down from New York for this. I wasn't real crazy about it at first but I won't argue with results."

Amelia frowned. "Bringing us down? What do you mean?"

"To help out."

"Jim didn't do that."

"What?" Lucy asked.

"No, no, we were over at the medical center in Avery. Lincoln's having some surgery. Jim heard we were going to be here so he came by this morning to ask if we'd look at some evidence."

A long pause. Then Lucy gave a laugh as the relief flooded through her. "I thought he'd scrounged up county money to fly y'all down here after the kidnapping yesterday."

Amelia shook her head. "The surgery's not till day after tomorrow. We had some free time. That's all."

"That boy—Jim. He never said a word about it. He *can* be the quiet one sometimes."

"You were worried he didn't think you could handle the case?"

"I guess that's exactly what I thought."

"Jim's cousin works with us in New York. He told Jim we were coming down for a couple of weeks."

"Wait, you mean Roland?" Lucy asked. "Sure, I know him. Knew his wife too, before she passed. His boys're dears."

"Had them over for a barbecue not long ago," Amelia said.

Lucy laughed again. "I guess I was being paranoid here. . . . So, you were over at Avery? The medical center?"

"That's right."

"That's where Lydia Johansson works. You know, she's a nurse there."

"I didn't."

A dozen memories flickered through Lucy Kerr's mind. Some she was warmly touched by, some she wanted to avoid like the swarm of wasps she'd nearly stirred up in Garrett's trap. She didn't know whether she wanted to tell any of this to Amelia Sachs or not. What she settled for was: "That's why I'm pretty eager to save her. I had some medical problems a few years ago and Lydia was one of my nurses. She's a good person. The best."

"We'll save her," Amelia said, and she said it with a tone that Lucy sometimes—not often, but sometimes—heard in her own voice. A tone that didn't leave any doubt.

They walked more slowly now. The trap had spooked them all. And the heat was truly excruciating.

Lucy asked Amelia, "That surgery your friend's going to have? It's for his . . . situation?"

"Yep."

"What's that look?" Lucy asked, noticing a darkness cross the woman's face.

"It probably won't do anything."

"Then why's he doing it?"

Amelia explained, "There's a chance it might help. Small chance. It's experimental. Nobody with the kind of injury he has—as serious as that—has ever improved."

"And you don't want him to go through with it?"

"I don't, no."

"Why not?"

Amelia hesitated. "Because it could kill him. Or make him even worse."

"You talked to him about it?"

"Yes."

"But it didn't do any good," Lucy said.

"Not a bit."

Lucy nodded. "I figured he's a man who's a bit muley."

Amelia said, "That's putting it mildly."

A crash sounded near them, in the brush, and by the

time Lucy's hand found her pistol Amelia had drawn a careful bead on a wild turkey's chest. The four members of the search party smiled but the amusement lasted for only a moment, replaced by edginess as adrenaline eased through their hearts.

Guns replaced in holsters, eyes scanning the path, they continued forward, conversation on hold for the time being.

■

There were several categories people fell into when it came to Rhyme's injury.

Some took the joking, in-your-face approach. Crip humor, no prisoners taken.

Some, like Henry Davett, ignored his condition completely.

Most did what Ben was doing—tried to pretend that Rhyme didn't exist and prayed that they could escape at the earliest possible moment.

It was this response that Rhyme hated the most—it was one of the most blatant reminders of how different he was. But he had no time to dwell on his surrogate assistant's attitude. Garrett was leading Lydia deeper and deeper into the wilderness. And Mary Beth McConnell might be close to dying from suffocation or dehydration or a wound.

Jim Bell walked into the room. "Maybe there's some good news from the hospital. Ed Schaeffer said something to one of the nurses. Went unconscious again right after but I'm taking it as a good sign."

"What'd he say?" Rhyme asked. "Something he'd seen on that map?"

"She said it sounded like 'important.' Then 'olive.'" Bell walked to the map. Touched a location to the southeast of Tanner's Corner. "There's a development here. They named the roads after plants and fruits and things. One of them's Olive Street. But that's way south of Stone

Creek. Should I tell Lucy and Amelia to check it out? I think we ought to."

Ah, the eternal conflict, Rhyme reflected: trust evidence or trust witnesses? If he picked wrong, Lydia or Mary Beth might die. "They should stay where they are, north of the river."

"You sure?" Bell asked doubtfully.

"Yes."

"Okay," Bell said.

The phone rang and with a firm press of his left ring finger Rhyme answered it.

Sachs's voice clattered into his headset. "We're at a dead end, Rhyme. There're four or five paths here, going in different directions, and we don't have a clue which way Garrett went."

"I don't have anything more for you, Sachs. We're trying to identify more of the evidence."

"Nothing more in the books?"

"Nothing specific. But it's fascinating—they're pretty serious reading for a sixteen-year-old. He's smarter than I would have figured. Where are you exactly, Sachs?" Rhyme looked up. "Ben! Go to the map, please."

He aimed his massive frame at the wall and took up a position beside it.

Sachs consulted someone else in the search party. Then said, "About four miles northeast of where we forded Stone Creek, pretty much in a straight line."

Rhyme repeated this to Ben, who put his hand on a part of the map. Location J-7.

Near Ben's massive forefinger was an unidentified L-shaped formation. "Ben, you have any idea what that square is?"

"Think that's the old quarry."

"Oh, Jesus," Rhyme muttered, shaking his head in frustration.

"What?" Ben asked, alarmed that he'd done something wrong.

"Why the hell didn't anybody tell me there was a quarry near there?"

Ben's round face looked even more puffed up than it had been; he was taking the accusation personally. "I didn't really . . ."

But Rhyme wasn't even listening. There was no one to blame but himself for this lapse. Someone *had* told him about the quarry—Henry Davett, when he'd said that limestone was big business in the area at one time. How else do companies produce commercial limestone? Rhyme should've asked about a quarry as soon as he'd heard that. And the nitrates weren't from pipe bombs at all but from blasting out rock—that kind of residue would last for decades.

He said into the phone, "There's an abandoned quarry not far from you. To the southwest."

A pause. Faint words. She said, "Jesse knows about it."

"Garrett *was* there. I don't know if he still is. So be careful. And remember he may not be leaving bombs but he's rigging traps. Call me when you find something."

∎

Now that Lydia was away from the Outside and wasn't as sick from heat and exhaustion, she realized that she had the Inside to contend with. And that was proving to be just as frightening.

Her captor would pace for a while, look out the window, then squat on his haunches, clicking his fingernails and muttering to himself, looking over her body, then go back to pacing. Once, Garrett glanced down at the floor of the mill and picked up something. He slipped it into his mouth, chewed hungrily. She wondered if it was an insect and the thought of this nearly made her vomit.

They were in what seemed to have been the office of the mill. From here she could look down a corridor, partly burnt in the fire, to another series of rooms—

probably the grain storage and the grinding rooms. Brilliant afternoon light flowed through the burnt-out walls and ceiling of the hallway.

Something orange caught her eye. She squinted and saw bags of Doritos. Also Cape Cod potato chips. Reese's Peanut Butter Cups. And more of those Planters peanut butter and cheese cracker packages he'd had at the quarry. Sodas and Deer Park water. She hadn't seen them when they first entered the mill.

Why all this food? How long would they be staying here? Garrett had said just for the night but there were enough provisions for a month's stay. Was he going to keep her here longer than he'd originally told her?

Lydia asked, "Is Mary Beth all right? Have you hurt her?"

"Oh, yeah, like I'm going to hurt her," he said sarcastically. "I don't think so." Lydia turned away and studied the shafts of light piercing the remains of the corridor. From beyond it came a squeaking sound—the revolving millstone, she guessed.

Garrett continued, offering: "The only reason I took her away is to make sure she's okay. She wanted to get out of Tanner's Corner. She likes it at the beach. I mean, fuck, who wouldn't? Better than shitty Tanner's Corner." Snapping his nails faster now, louder. He was agitated and nervous. With his huge hands he ripped open one of the bags of chips. He ate several handfuls, chewing them sloppily, bits falling from his mouth. He drank down an entire can of Coke at once. Ate more chips.

"This place burned down two years ago," he said. "I don't know who did it. You like that sound? The waterwheel? It's pretty cool. The wheel going round and round. Like, reminds me of this song my father used to sing around the house all the time. '*Big wheel keep on turning . . .*'" He shoveled more food into his mouth and started speaking. She couldn't understand him for a moment. He swallowed. "—here a lot. You sit here at night, listen to the cicada and the bloodnouns—you know, the bullfrogs. If I'm going all the way to the ocean—like now—I spend the night here. You'll like it at night." He stopped talking and leaned toward her suddenly. Too scared to look directly at him, she kept her eyes downcast but sensed he was studying her closely. Then, in an instant, he leapt up and crouched close beside her.

Lydia winced as she smelled his body odor. She waited for his hands to crawl over her chest, between her legs.

But he wasn't interested in her, it seemed. Garrett moved aside a rock and lifted something out from underneath.

"A millipede." He smiled. The creature was long and yellow-green and the sight of it sickened her.

"They feel neat. I like them." He let it climb over his hand and wrist. "They're not insects," he lectured. "They're like cousins. They're dangerous if you try to hurt them. Their bite is really bad. The Indians around here used to grind them up and put the poison on arrowheads. When a millipede is scared it shits poison and then escapes. A predator crawls through the gas and dies. That's pretty wild, huh?"

Garrett grew silent and studied the millipede intently, the way Lydia herself would look at her niece and nephew—with affection, amusement, almost love.

Lydia felt the horror rising in her. She knew she should stay calm, knew she shouldn't antagonize Garrett, should just play along with him. But seeing that disgusting bug slither over his arm, hearing his fingernails click, watching his blotched skin and wet, red eyes, the flecks of food on his chin, she convulsed in panic.

As the disgust and the fear boiled up in her Lydia imagined she heard a faint voice, urging, "Yes, yes, yes!" A voice that could only belong to a guardian angel.

Yes, yes, yes!

She rolled onto her back. Garrett looked up, smiling

from the sensation of the animal on his skin, curious about what she was doing. And Lydia lashed out as hard as she could with both feet. She had strong legs, used to carrying her big frame for eight-hour shifts at the hospital, and the kick sent him tumbling backward. He hit his head against the wall with a dull thud and rolled to the floor, stunned. Then he cried out, a raw scream, and grabbed his arm; the millipede must have bit him.

Yes! Lydia thought triumphantly as she rolled upright. She struggled to her feet and ran blindly toward the grinding room at the end of the corridor.

. . . chapter twelve

According to Jesse Corn's reckoning they were almost to the quarry.

"About five minutes ahead," he told Sachs. Then he glanced at her twice and after some tacit debate said, "You know, I was going to ask you. . . . When you drew your weapon, when that turkey came outa the brush. Well, and at Blackwater Landing too when Rich Culbeau surprised us. . . . That was . . . well, that was something. You know how to drive a nail, looks like."

She knew, from Roland Bell, the Southern expression meant "to shoot."

"One of my hobbies," she said.

"No foolin'!"

"Easier than running," she said. "Cheaper than joining a health club."

"You in competition?"

Sachs nodded. "North Shore Pistol Club on Long Island."

"How 'bout that," he said with a daunting enthusiasm. "NRA Bullseye matches?"

"Right."

"That's my sport too! Well, skeet and trap, course. But sidearms're my specialty."

Hers too but she thought it best not to find too much in common with adoring Jesse Corn.

"You reload your own ammo?" he asked.

"Uh-huh. Well, the .38s and .45s. Not the rimfire, of course. Getting the bubbles out of slugs—that's the big problem."

"Whoa, you're not telling me you cast your own bullets?"

"I do," she admitted, recalling that when everyone else's apartment in her building smelled of waffles and bacon on Sunday morning hers often was redolent of the unique aroma of molten lead.

"I don't do that," he said apologetically. "I buy match rounds."

They walked for another few minutes in silence, all eyes on the ground, looking for more deadfall traps.

"So," Jesse Corn said, offering a coy grin, swiping his blond hair off his damp forehead. "I'll show you mine. . . ." Sachs looked at him quizzically and he continued. "I mean, what's your best score? On the Bullseye circuit?" When she hesitated he encouraged: "Come on, you can tell me. It's only a sport. . . . And, hey, I've been competing for ten years. I got a little edge on you."

"Twenty-seven hundred," Sachs said.

Jesse nodded. "Right, that's the match I mean—the three-pistol rotation, nine hundred points max for each gun. What's your best?"

"No, that's my score," she said, wincing as a jolt of arthritic pain coursed through her stiff legs. "Twenty-seven hundred."

Jesse turned to her, looking for signs of a joke. When she didn't grin or guffaw, he exhaled a fast laugh. "But that's a perfect score."

"Oh, I don't shoot that *every* match. But you asked what my best was."

"But . . ." His eyes were wide. "I've never even *met* anybody shot a twenty-seven hundred."

"You have now," Ned said, laughing hard. "And don't feel bad, Jess—it's only a sport."

"Twenty-seven . . ." The young deputy shook his head.

Sachs decided she should have lied. With this information about her ballistic prowess it seemed that Jesse Corn's love for her was sealed.

"Say, after this is over," he said shyly, "you have some free time, maybe you and me could go out to the range, waste us some ammo."

And Sachs thought: Better a box of Winchester .38 specials than a cup of Starbucks accompanied by talk of how hard it is to meet women in Tanner's Corner.

"Let's see how things go."

"It's a date," he said, using the word she'd hoped wouldn't surface.

"There," Lucy said. "Look." They stopped at the edge of the forest and saw the quarry in front of them.

Sachs motioned them into a crouch. Damn, that hurts. She popped condroitin and glucosamine daily but this Carolina humidity and heat—it was hell on her poor joints. She gazed at the huge pit—two hundred yards across and easily a hundred feet deep. The walls were yellow, like old bone, and they dropped straight down into green, brackish water that smelled sour. The vegetation for twenty yards around the perimeter had died bad deaths.

"Keep clear of the water," Lucy warned in a whisper. "It's bad. Kids used to swim here. Not long after they shut it down. My nephew did once—Ben's younger brother. But I just showed him the coroner's picture from when they fished Kevin Dobbs out after he'd drowned and been in the water for a week. Never went back."

"I think Dr. Spock recommends that approach," Sachs said. Lucy laughed.

Sachs, thinking about children again.

Not now, not now. . . .

Her phone vibrated. As they'd gotten closer to their prey she'd turned off the ringer. She answered. Rhyme's voice crackled, "Sachs. Where are you?"

"The rim of the quarry," she whispered.

"Any sign of him?"

"We just got here. Nothing yet. We're about to start searching. All the buildings've been torn down and I don't see anywhere he could be hiding. But there're a dozen places he could've left a trap."

"Sachs. . . ."

"What is it, Rhyme?" His solemn tone chilled her.

"There's something I have to tell you. I just got the DNA and serologic results from the medical center. On that Kleenex you found at the scene this morning."

"And?"

"It was Garrett's semen all right. And the blood—it was Mary Beth's."

"He raped her," Sachs whispered.

"Be careful, Sachs, but move fast. I don't think Lydia has much time left."

■

She was hiding in a dark, filthy bin that had been used to store grain long ago.

Hands behind her, still dizzy from the heat and dehydration, Lydia Johansson had stumbled down the bright corridor away from where Garrett lay writhing and had found this hiding space on the floor below the grinding room. When she slipped inside and closed the door a dozen mice had skittered over her feet and it took every ounce of willpower within her to keep from screaming.

Now listening for Garrett's footsteps over the low-gear sound of the grinding wheel nearby.

Panic was filling her and she was starting to regret her defiant escape. But there was no going back, she decided. She'd hurt Garrett and now he was going to hurt her back if he found her. Maybe do worse. There was nothing to do but try to escape.

No, she decided, that wasn't the right way to think. One of her angel books said there was no such thing as "trying to." You either did or you didn't. She wasn't going to *try* to get away. She was *going* to escape. She just had to have faith.

Lydia looked through a crack in the bin door, listened carefully. She heard him in one of the rooms nearby, muttering to himself and ripping open bins and closet doors. She'd hoped that he'd think she'd run outside through the collapsed wall in the burnt-out corridor but it was obvious from his methodical search that he knew she was still here. She couldn't stay in the storage closet any longer. He'd find her. She glanced out through a crack in the door and, not seeing him, she slipped out of the bin and ran into an adjoining room, moving silently on her white sneakers. The only exit from this room was a stairway leading up to the second floor. She staggered up it, gasping for breath and, not having her hands for balance, bounding off the walls and the wrought-iron railing.

She heard his voice echoing in the corridor. "You made him bite me!" he cried. "It hurts, it hurts."

Wish it had stung you in the eye or crotch, she thought and struggled up the stairs. Fuck you fuck you fuck you!

She heard him ripping open closet doors in the room below. Heard his guttural moaning. Imagined she could hear the snick, snick of his nails.

That shiver of panic again. Nausea swelling.

The room at the top of the stairs was large and had a number of windows facing the burnt portion of the mill. There was one door, which was unlocked, and she pushed it open, stepped into the grinding area itself—two large millstones sat in the center. The wooden mechanism was rotted; the sound she'd heard wasn't the stones but the waterwheel, powered by the diverted stream. It still turned slowly. Rust-colored water cascaded off it into a deep, narrow pit, like a well. Lydia couldn't see the bottom. The water must've drained back into the stream somewhere below the surface.

"Stop!" Garrett cried.

She jumped in shock at the angry sound. He stood in the doorway. His eyes were red and wide and he was cradling his arm, on which was a huge black-and-yellow bruise. "You made it sting me," he muttered, staring at her with hatred. "It's dead. You made me kill it! I didn't *want* to but you made me! Now get your ass downstairs. I've gotta tape your legs up now."

He started forward.

She looked at his bony face, brows knit together, his huge hands, his angry eyes. Into her thoughts came a burst of images: a cancer patient of hers, slowly wasting to death. Mary Beth McConnell locked away somewhere. The boy madly chewing his chips. The scuttling millipede. The fingernails snapping. The Outside. Her long nights alone, waiting—desperately—for a brief phone call from her boyfriend. Taking the flowers to Blackwater Landing, even though she didn't really want to . . .

It was all too much for her.

"Wait," Lydia said placidly.

He blinked. Stopped walking.

She smiled at him—the way she'd smile at a terminal patient—and, sending a good-bye prayer to her boyfriend, Lydia, hands still bound behind her, plunged headfirst into the narrow pit of dark water.

∎

The crosshairs of the Hitech telescopic sight rested on the redheaded cop's shoulders.

That was *some* hair, Mason Germain thought.

He and Nathan Groomer were on a rise overlooking the old Anderson Rock Products quarry. About a hundred yards away from the search party.

Nathan finally stated the conclusion he must've come to a half hour ago. "This don't have anything to do with Rich Culbeau."

"No, it doesn't. Not exactly."

"What's that mean? 'Not exactly'?"

"Culbeau's out here someplace. With Sean O'Sarian—"

"*That* boy's scarier than two Culbeaus."

"No argument there," Mason said. "And Harris Tomel too. But that's not what we're doing."

Nathan looked back at the deputies and the redhead. "Guess not. Why're you sighting down on Lucy Kerr with *my* gun?"

After a moment Mason handed back the Ruger M77 and said, " 'Cause I didn't bring my fucking binoculars. And it wasn't Lucy I was looking at."

They started along the ridge. Mason was thinking about the redhead. Thinking about pretty Mary Beth McConnell. And Lydia. Thinking too how sometimes life just doesn't go the way you want it to. Mason Germain knew, for instance, that he should've advanced further than senior deputy by now. He knew he should've handled his request for promotion different. Just like he should've handled things different when Kelley left him for that trucker five years ago and, for that matter, handled his whole marriage different *before* she left him.

And should've handled the first Garrett Hanlon case a lot different too. The case where Meg Blanchard woke from her nap and found the hornets clustered on her chest and face and arms. . . . One hundred thirty-seven stings and a terrible slow death.

Now he was paying for those bad choices. His life was just a series of still days, worrying, sitting on his porch and drinking too much, not even finding the energy to put his boat in the Paquo and go after bass. Trying desperately to figure out how to fix what maybe couldn't be fixed. He—

"So you gonna tell me what we're doing?" Nathan asked.

"We're looking for Culbeau."

"But you just said . . ." Nathan's voice faded. When Mason said nothing else the deputy sighed loudly. "Culbeau's house, where we're s'posed to be, is six or seven miles away and here we are north of the Paquo, me with my deer gun and you with that zipped mouth of yours."

"I'm saying if Jim *asks,* we were out here looking for Culbeau," Mason said.

"And what we're really doing is . . . ?"

Nathan Groomer could prune trees at five hundred yards with this Ruger of his. He could charm a point-five-oh DUI out of his car in three minutes. He could carve decoys that'd sell for five hundred bucks each to collectors if he ever bothered to try to sell any. But his talents and smarts didn't go much beyond that.

"We're going to get that boy," Mason said.

"Garrett."

"Yeah, Garrett. Who else? *They're* going to flush him for us." Nodding toward the redhead and the deputies. "And *we're* going to get him."

"Whatta you mean by 'get'?"

"You're going to shoot him, Nathan. And kill him dead as a stick."

"Shoot him?"

"Yessir," Mason said.

"Hold on there. You're not ramshagging *my* career 'cause you're hot to get that boy."

"You don't have a career," Mason snapped. "You got a *job.* And if you want to keep it you'll do what I'm telling you. Listen here—I've talked to him. Garrett. During those other investigations, when he killed those people."

"Yeah. Did you? I guess you would, sure."

"And know what he told me?"

"No. What?"

Mason was trying to think if this was credible. Then recalling Nathan's dog-eyed concentration as he spent hour after hour sanding the back of a pinewood duck, lost in happy oblivion, the senior deputy continued, "Garrett said if he was standing in need to he'd kill any law tried to stop him."

"He said that? That boy?"

"Yep. Looked me right in the eye and said so. And said he was looking forward to it too. Hoped I was in the lead but he'd take any anybody happened to be handy."

"That son of a bitch. You tell Jim?"

"Course I did. You think I wouldn't? But he didn't pay it a lick of mind. I like Jim Bell. You know I do. But the truth is he's more concerned about *keeping* his cushy job than he is with *doing* it."

The deputy was nodding and a portion of Mason was astonished that Nathan had bought this so easily and never even guessed that there might be another reason he was so *hot to get that boy*.

The sharpshooter thought for a moment. "Has Garrett got a gun?"

"I don't know, Nathan. But tell me: 'Bout how hard is it to get a firearm in North Carolina? The phrase 'fallin' off a log' come to mind?"

"That's true."

"See, Lucy and Jesse—even Jim—they don't appreciate that kid like I do."

"Appreciate?"

"Appreciate the *danger*'s what I mean," Mason said.

"Oh."

"He's killed three people so far, probably Todd Wilkes too, strung that little boy up by his neck. Or at least scared him into killing himself. Which is murder all the same. And that girl got stung—Meg? You see those pictures of her face after the wasps were through with her? Then think about Ed Schaeffer. You and me were out drinking with him just last week. Now he's in the hospital and he might never wake up."

"It's not like I'm a sniper or nothing, Mase."

But Mason Germain wasn't going to give an inch. "You *know* what the courts're going to do. He's sixteen. They're gonna say, 'Poor boy. Parents're dead. Let's put him in some halfway house.' Then he's going to get out in six months or a year and do it all over again. Kill some other football player headed for Chapel Hill, some other girl in town never hurt a soul."

"But—"

"Don't *worry*, Nathan. You're doing Tanner's Corner a favor."

"That ain't what I was going to say. The thing is, we kill him, we lose any chance of finding Mary Beth. He's the only one knows where she is."

Mason gave a sour laugh. "Mary Beth? You think she's alive? No way. Garrett raped and killed her, and buried her in a shallow grave someplace. We can stop worrying about her. It's our job now to make sure that don't happen to anybody else. You with me?"

Nathan didn't say anything but the snapping sound of the deputy pressing the long copper-jacketed shells into his rifle's magazine was answer enough.

II

The White Doe

. . . chapter thirteen

Outside the window was a large hornets' nest.

Resting her head against the greasy glass of her prison, an exhausted Mary Beth McConnell stared at it.

More than anything else about this terrible place, the nest—gray and moist and disgusting—gave her a sense of hopelessness.

More than the bars that Garrett had so carefully bolted outside of the windows. More than the thick oak door, secured with three huge locks. More than the memory of the terrible trek from Blackwater Landing in the company of the Insect Boy.

The wasps' nest was in the shape of a cone, the point facing toward the earth. It rested on a forked branch that Garrett had propped up near the window. The nest must've been home to hundreds of the glossy black-and-yellow insects that oozed in and out of the hole in the bottom.

Garrett had been gone when she'd wakened this morning and after lying in bed for an hour—groggy and nause-ated from the vicious blow to her head last night—Mary

Beth had climbed unsteadily to her feet and looked out the window. The first thing that she'd noticed was the nest outside the back window, near the bedroom.

The wasps hadn't made the nest here; Garrett had placed it outside the window himself. At first, she couldn't figure out why. But then, with a feeling of despair, she understood: her captor had left it as a flag of victory.

Mary Beth McConnell knew her history. She knew about warfare, knew about armies conquering other armies. The reason for flags and standards wasn't only to identify your side; it was to remind the vanquished who now controlled them.

And Garrett had won.

Well, he'd won the *battle;* the outcome of the war had yet to be decided.

Mary Beth pressed the gash on her head. It had been a terrible blow to her temple, and had peeled away some skin. She wondered if it would become infected.

She found a rubber band in her backpack and tied her long brunette hair into a ponytail. Sweat trickled down her neck and she felt a fierce aching of thirst. She was breathless from the stifling heat in the closed rooms and thought about taking off her thick denim shirt—worried about snakes and spiders, she always wore long sleeves when she was on a dig around brush or tall grass. But despite the heat now she decided to leave the shirt on. She didn't know when her captor would return; she wore only a lacy pink bra underneath the shirt and Garrett Hanlon sure didn't need any encouragement in *that* department.

With a last glance at the nest Mary Beth stepped away from the window. Then walked around the three-room shack once more, searching futilely for a breach in the place. It was a solid building, very old. Thick walls—a combination of hand-hewn logs and heavy boards nailed together. Outside the front window was a large field of tall grass that ended in a line of trees a hundred yards away. The cabin itself was in another stand of thick trees. Looking out the back window—the hornets' nest window—she could just see through the trunks to the glistening surface of the pond they'd skirted yesterday to get here.

The rooms themselves were small but surprisingly clean. In the living room was a long brown-and-gold couch, several old chairs around a cheap dining room table, a second table on which were a dozen quart juice jars covered with mesh and filled with insects he'd collected. A second room contained a mattress and a dresser. The third room was empty, except for several half-full cans of brown paint sitting in the corner; it seemed that Garrett had painted the exterior of the cabin recently. The color was dark and depressing and she couldn't understand why he'd picked it—until she realized it was the same shade as the bark of the trees that surrounded the cabin. Camouflage. And it occurred to her again what she'd thought yesterday—that the boy was much cagier, and more dangerous, than she'd thought.

In the living room were stacks of food—junk food and rows of canned fruits and vegetables—Farmer John brand. From the label a stolid farmer smiled at her, the image as outdated as the 1950s Betty Crocker. She searched the cabin desperately for water or soda—anything to drink—but couldn't find a thing. The canned fruits and vegetables would be packed in juice but there was no opener or any sort of tool or utensil to open them. She had her backpack with her but had left her archaeological tools at Blackwater Landing. She tried banging a can on the side of the table to split it open but the metal didn't give.

Downstairs was a root cellar that you reached via a door in the floor of the shack's main room. She glanced at it once and shivered with disgust, felt her skin crawl. Last night—after Garrett had been gone for some time—Mary Beth had worked up her courage and walked down the rickety stairs into the low-ceilinged basement, looking for a way out of the horrible cabin. But there'd been no exit—just dozens of old boxes and jars and bags.

She hadn't heard Garrett return and suddenly, in a rush, he'd charged down the stairs toward her. She'd screamed and tried to flee but the next thing she remembered was lying on the dirt floor, blood spattered on her chest and clotted in her hair, and Garrett, smelling of unwashed adolescence, walking up slowly, wrapping his arms around her, his eyes fixed on her breasts. He'd lifted her and she'd felt his hard penis against her as he carried her slowly upstairs, deaf to her protests. . . .

No! she now told herself. Don't think about it.

Or about the pain. Or the fear.

And where was Garrett now?

As frightened as she'd been with him padding around the cabin yesterday she was nearly as scared now that he'd forget about her. Or would get killed in an accident or shot by the deputies looking for her. And she'd die of thirst here. Mary Beth McConnell remembered a project she and her graduate adviser had been involved in: a North Carolina State Historical Society–sponsored disinterment of a nineteenth-century grave to run DNA tests on the body inside, to see if the corpse was that of a descendant of Sir Francis Drake, as a local legend claimed. To her horror, when the top of the coffin was lifted off, the arm bones of the cadaver were upraised and there were scratch marks on the inside of the lid. The man had been buried alive.

This cabin would be her coffin. And no one—

What was that? Looking out the front window, she thought she saw motion just inside the edge of the forest in the distance. Through the brush and leaves she believed it might be a man. Because his clothes and broad-brimmed hat seemed dark and there was something confident about his posture and gait she thought: He looks like a missionary in the wilderness.

But wait. . . . Was someone really there? Or was it just the light on the trees? She couldn't tell.

"Here!" she cried. But the window was nailed shut and even if it had been open she doubted he could hear her scream, feeble from her dry throat, from this distance.

She grabbed her backpack, hoping she still had the whistle that her paranoid mother had bought her for protection. Mary Beth had laughed at the idea—a rape whistle in Tanner's Corner?—but she now searched desperately for it.

But the whistle was gone. Maybe Garrett had found it and taken it when she'd been passed out on the bloody mattress. Well, she'd scream for help anyway—scream as loudly as she could, despite her parched throat. Mary Beth grabbed one of the insect jars, intending to smash it through the window. She drew it back like a pitcher about to let fly the last ball of a no-hitter. Then her hand lowered. No! The Missionary was gone. Where he'd been was just a dark willow trunk, grass and a bay tree, swaying in the hot wind.

Maybe *that* was all she'd seen.

Maybe he hadn't been there at all.

To Mary Beth McConnell—hot, scared, racked with thirst—truth and fiction now blended together and all the legends she'd studied about this eerie North Carolina countryside seemed to become real. Maybe the Missionary was just another in the cast of imaginary characters, like the Lady of Drummond Lake.

Like the other ghosts of the Great Dismal Swamp.

Like the White Doe in the Indian legend—a tale that was becoming alarmingly like her own.

Head throbbing, dizzy in the heat, Mary Beth lay on the musty couch and closed her eyes, watching the wasps hover close, then enter the gray nest, the flag of her captor's victory.

■

Lydia felt the bottom of the stream beneath her feet and kicked to the surface.

Choking, spitting water, she found herself in a swampy pool about fifty feet downstream from the mill. Hands still taped behind her back, she kicked hard to right herself, wincing in pain. She'd either sprained or broken her ankle on the wooden paddle of the waterwheel as she'd leapt into the sluice. But the water here was six or seven feet deep and if she didn't kick she'd drown.

The pain in her ankle was astonishing but Lydia forced her way to the surface. She found that by filling her lungs and rolling on her back she could float and keep her face above water as she kicked with her good foot toward the shore.

She'd gone five feet when she felt a cold slithering on the back of her neck, curling around her head and ear, heading for her face. Snake! she realized in panic. Flashing back to a case in the emergency room last month—a man brought in with a water moccasin bite, his arm swollen nearly double; he'd been hysterical with pain. She now spun around and the muscular snake slithered across her mouth. She screamed. But with empty lungs and no buoyancy she sank beneath the surface and began to choke. She lost sight of the snake. Where is it, where? she thought furiously. A bite on the face could blind her. On the jugular or the carotid, she'd die.

Where? Was it above her? About to strike?

Please, please, help me, she thought to the guardian angel.

And maybe the angel heard. Because when she bobbed once again to the surface there was no sign of the creature. She finally touched the muck of the stream bottom with her stockinged feet—she'd lost her shoes in the dive. She paused, catching her breath, trying to calm down. Slowly she struggled toward the shore, up a steep incline of mud and slick sticks and decaying leaves that eased her back a foot for every two that she managed to stagger forward. Watch the Carolina clay, she reminded herself; it'll hold you like quicksand.

Just as she staggered out of the water a gunshot, very close, split the air.

Jesus, Garrett has a gun! He's shooting!

She dropped back into the water and sank beneath the surface. She stayed for as long as she could but finally had to surface. Gasping for breath, she broke from the water just as the beaver slapped its tail once more, making a second loud crack. The animal vanished toward its dam—a big one, two hundred feet long. She felt a hysterical laugh rise up in her from the false alarm but managed to control the urge.

Then Lydia stumbled into the sedge and mud and lay on her side, gasping, spitting water. After five minutes she'd caught her breath. She rolled into a sitting position and looked around her.

No sign of Garrett. She struggled to her feet. Tried to pull her hands apart but the duct tape held tight, despite the soaking. She could see the burnt chimney of the mill from here. She oriented herself and decided which direction to go in to find the path that would take her back south of the Paquo, back home. She wasn't that far from it; her swim in the creek hadn't taken her downstream much from the mill.

But Lydia couldn't will herself to move.

She felt paralyzed from the fear, from the hopelessness.

Then she thought of her favorite TV show—*Touched by an Angel*—and when she thought of the program she had another memory, of the last time she'd watched the show. Just as it was over and a commercial came on, the door to her town house swung open and there was her boyfriend with a six-pack. He hardly ever dropped by for surprise visits and she'd been ecstatic. They'd spent a glorious two hours together. She decided that her angel had given her this memory just now as a sign that there was hope when you least expected it.

Clutching this thought firmly in her mind, Lydia rolled awkwardly to her feet and started through the sedge and swamp grass. From nearby she heard a guttural sound. A faint growling. She knew there were bobcats here, north of the river. Bears too and wild boars. But even though she was limping painfully, Lydia moved as confidently toward the path as if she were making the rounds at work, dispensing pills and gossip and cheering up the patients under her care.

■

Jesse Corn found a bag.

"Here! Look here. I've got something. A crocus sack."

Sachs started down a rocky incline along the edge of the quarry to where the deputy stood, pointing at something on a ledge of limestone that had been blasted flat. She could see the grooves from where the drills had tapped into the dull stone to pack with dynamite. No wonder Rhyme had found so much nitrate; this place was one big demolition field.

She walked up to Jesse. He was standing in front of an old cloth bag. "Rhyme, can you hear me?" Sachs called into her phone.

"Go ahead. There's a lot of static but I can just hear you."

"We've got a bag here," she told him. Then asked Jesse, "What'd you call it?"

"Crocus sack. What they call a burlap bag down here."

She said to Rhyme, "It's an old burlap bag. Looks like there's something in it."

Rhyme asked, "Garrett leave it?"

She looked at the ground. Where the stone floor met the walls. "It's definitely Garrett's and Lydia's footprints. They lead up an incline to the rim of the quarry."

"Let's get after them," Jesse said.

"Not yet," Sachs said. "We need to examine the bag."

"Describe it," the criminalist ordered.

"Burlap. Old. About twenty-four by thirty-six inches. Not much inside. It's closed up. Not tied, just twisted."

"Open it carefully, remember the traps."

Sachs eased a corner of the bag down, peered inside.

"It's clear, Rhyme."

Lucy and Ned came down the path and all four of them stood around the bag as if it were the body of a drowned man pulled from the quarry.

"What's in it?"

Sachs pulled on her latex gloves, which were very soft because of the sun. Immediately her hands began to sweat and tingle from the heat.

"Empty water bottles. Deer Park. No store price or inventory stickers on them. Wrappers from two packages of Planters peanut butter and cheese crackers. No store stickers on them either. You want UPC codes to trace the shipments?"

"If we had a week, maybe," Rhyme muttered. "No, don't bother. More details on the bag," he ordered.

"There's a little printing on it. But it's too faded to read. Anybody make it out?" she asked the others.

No one could read the lettering.

"Any idea what was inside originally?" Rhyme asked.

She picked up the bag and smelled it. "Musty. Been inside someplace for a long time. Can't tell what was in it." Sachs turned the bag inside out and hit it hard with the flat of her hand. A few old, shriveled corn kernels fell onto the ground.

"Corn, Rhyme."

"My namesake." Jesse laughed.

Rhyme asked, "Farms around here?"

Sachs relayed the question to the search party.

"Dairy, not corn," Lucy said, looking at Ned and Jesse, who nodded.

Jesse said, "But you'd feed corn to cows."

"Sure," Ned said. "I'd guess it came from a feed-and-grain store someplace. Or a warehouse."

"You hear that, Rhyme?"

"Feed and grain. Right. I'll get Ben and Jim Bell on that. Anything else, Sachs?"

She looked at her hands. They were blackened. She turned the bag over. "Looks like there's scorch on the bag, Rhyme. It wasn't burned itself but it was sitting in something that had."

"Any idea what?"

"Bits of charcoal, looks like. So I'd guess wood."

"Okay," he said. "It's going on the list."

She glanced at Garrett's and Lydia's footprints. "We're going after them again," she told Rhyme.

"I'll call when I have some more answers."

Sachs announced to the search party, "Back up to the top." Feeling the shooting pains in her knees she gazed up to the lip of the quarry, muttering, "Didn't seem that high when we got here."

"Oh, hey, that's a rule—hills're always twice as tall going up as coming down," said Jesse Corn, the resident storehouse of aphorisms, as he politely let her precede him up the narrow path.

. . . chapter fourteen

Lincoln Rhyme, ignoring a glistening black-and-green fly that strafed nearby, was gazing at the latest evidence chart.

FOUND AT SECONDARY CRIME SCENE—QUARRY

Old Burlap Bag—Unreadable Name on It
Corn—Feed and Grain?
Scorch Marks on Bag
Deer Park Water
Planters Cheese Crackers

The most unusual evidence is the best evidence. Rhyme was never happier at a crime scene than when he found something completely unidentifiable. Because it meant that if he *could* identify it there'd be limited sources he could trace it back to.

But these items—the evidence Sachs had found at the quarry—were common. If the printing on the bag had been legible then he might have traced that to a single source. But it wasn't. If the water and crackers had price stickers they might have been traced to the stores that sold them and to a clerk who recalled Garrett and might have some information about where to find him. But they didn't. And scorched wood? That led to every barbecue in Paquenoke County. Useless.

The corn might be helpful—Jim Bell and Steve Farr were on phones right now, calling feed-and-grain outlets—but Rhyme doubted the clerks would have anything more to say than "Yeah. We sell corn. In old burlap bags. Like everybody does."

Damn! He had no sense of this place at all. He needed weeks—months—to get a feel for the area.

But, of course, they didn't have weeks or months.

Eyes moving from chart to chart, fast as the fly.

FOUND AT PRIMARY CRIME SCENE— BLACKWATER LANDING

Kleenex with Blood
Limestone Dust
Nitrates
Phosphate
Ammonia
Detergent
Camphene

Nothing more to be deduced from that one.

Back to the insect books, he decided.

"Ben, that book there—*The Miniature World*. I want to look at it."

"Yessir," the young man said absently, eyes on the evidence chart. He picked it up and held it out to Rhyme.

A moment passed as the book hovered in the air over the criminalist's chest. Rhyme cast a wry gaze at Ben, who glanced at him and, after a beat, gave a sudden jerk and reared back, realizing that he was offering something to a man who'd need divine intervention to take it.

"Oh, my, Mr. Rhyme . . . look," Ben blurted, his round face red. "I'm so sorry. I wasn't thinking, sir. Man, that was stupid. I really—"

"Ben," Rhyme said evenly, "shut the fuck up."

The huge man blinked in shock. Swallowed. The book, tiny in his massive hand, lowered. "It was an accident, sir. I said I was—"

"Shut. Up."

Ben did. His mouth closed. He looked around the room for help but there was no help on the horizon. Thom was standing against the wall, silent, arms crossed, not about to become a U.N. peacekeeper.

Rhyme continued in a low growl, "You're walking on eggshells and I'm sick of it. Quit your goddamn cringing."

"Cringing? I was just trying to be decent to somebody who's . . . I mean—"

"No, you weren't. You've been trying to figure out how to get the hell out of here without looking at me any more than you have to and without upsetting your own delicate little psyche."

The massive shoulders stiffened. "Well, now, sir, I don't think that's completely fair."

"Bullshit. It's about time I took the gloves off. . . ." Rhyme laughed viciously. "How do you like *that* metaphor? Me, taking off gloves? Something I'm not going to be able to do very fast, am I now? . . . How's *that* for a crip joke?"

Ben was desperate to escape—to flee out the door—but his massive legs were rooted like oak trunks.

"What I've got isn't contagious," Rhyme snapped. "You think it's going to rub off? Doesn't work that way. You're walking around here like you breathe the air and they're going to have to cart *you* off in a wheelchair. Hell, you're even afraid if you *look* my way you're going to end up like me!"

"That's not true!"

"Isn't it? I think it is. . . . How come I scare the hell out of you?"

"You don't!" Ben snarled. "No way!"

Rhyme raged, "Oh, yes, I do. You're *terrified* to be in the same room with me. You're a fucking coward."

The big man leaned forward, spittle flying from his lips, jaw trembling, as he shouted back, "Well, fuck you, Rhyme!" He was speechless with rage for a moment. Then continued, "I come over here as a favor to my aunt. It messes up all my plans and I'm not getting paid a penny! I listen to you boss people around like you're some kind of fucking prima donna. I mean, I don't know where the hell you get off, mister. . . ." His voice faded and he squinted at Rhyme, who was laughing hard.

"What?" Ben snapped. "What the hell're you laughing at?"

"See how easy it is?" Rhyme asked, chuckling now. Thom too was having trouble suppressing a smile.

Breathing heavily, straightening up, Ben wiped his mouth. Angry, wary. He shook his head. "What do you mean? What's easy?"

"Looking me in the eye and telling me I'm a prick." Rhyme continued in a placid voice, "Ben, I'm just like anybody else. I don't like it when people treat me like a china doll. And I know *they* sure as hell don't like to worry that they're going to break me."

"You suckered me. You said those things just to get my goat."

"Let's say: just to get through to you." Rhyme wasn't sure that Ben would ever become a Henry Davett—a man who cared only about the core, the spirit, of a human being and ignored the packaging. But Rhyme had at least managed to push the zoologist a few steps in the direction of enlightenment.

"I oughta walk out that door and not come back."

"A lot of people would, Ben. But I need you. You're

*...ung beetles are credited with giving ancient
...the idea for the wheel. ...*

*...naturalist named Réaumur observed in the
...enteen hundreds that wasps make paper nests
...m wood fiber and saliva. That gave him the
...a to make paper from wood pulp, not cloth,
...paper manufacturers had been doing up until
...n. ...*

...what among this was revealing to the case? Was
...nything that could help Rhyme find two human
...on the run somewhere in a hundred square miles
...st and swampland?

*...sects make great use of the sense of smell. For
...em it is a multidimensional sense. They actu-
...ly "feel" smells and use them for many things.
...or education, for intelligence, for communica-
...on. When an ant finds food it returns to the
...est leaving a scented trail, sporadically touch-
...g the ground with its abdomen. When other
...nts come across the line they follow it back to
...he food. They know which direction to go in
...ecause the scent is "shaped"; the narrow end of
...he smell points toward the food like a direc-
...onal arrow. Insects also use smells to warn of
...pproaching enemies. Since an insect can detect
...single molecule of scent miles away insects are
...arely surprised by their enemies. ...*

...riff Jim Bell walked quickly into the room. On his
...uered face was a smile. "Just heard from a nurse at
...spital. There's some news about Ed. Looks like he's
...g out of that coma and said something. His doc-
...onna be calling in a few minutes. I'm hoping we'll
...ut what he meant by 'olive' and if he saw anything
...c on that map in the blind."

good. You've got a flair for forensics. Now, come on. We broke the ice. Let's get back to work."

Ben began to mount *The Miniature World* in the turning frame. As he did he glanced at Rhyme and asked, "So there's really a lot of people who look you in the eye and call you a son of a bitch?"

Rhyme, staring at the cover of the book, deferred to Thom, who said, "Oh, sure. Of course that's only after they get to know him."

■

Lydia was still only a hundred feet from the mill.

She was moving as quickly as she could toward the path that would take her to freedom but her ankle throbbed in pain and hampered her progress significantly. Also, she had to move slowly—truly silent travel through brush requires the use of your hands. But, like some of the brain-lesion victims she'd worked with at the hospital, she had limited equilibrium and could only stumble from clearing to clearing, making far more noise than she wanted to.

She circled wide around the front of the mill. Pausing. No sign of Garrett. No sound at all except for the flushing of the diverted stream water into the ruddy swamp.

Five more feet, ten.

Come on, angel, she thought. Stay with me a little longer. Help me get through this. Please . . . Just a few minutes and we'll be home-free.

Oh, man alive, that hurts. She wondered if a bone was broken. Her ankle was swollen and she knew that, if it was a fracture, walking unsupported like this could make it ten times worse. The color of the skin was darkening too—which meant broken vessels. Blood poisoning was a possibility. She thought of gangrene. Amputation. If that happened what would her boyfriend say? He'd leave her, she supposed. Their relationship was casual at best—at least on his part. Besides, she knew, from her job in oncology, how people disappeared from patients' lives once they started losing body parts.

She paused and listened, looked around her. Had Garrett fled? Had he given up on her and gone to the Outer Banks to be with Mary Beth?

Lydia kept moving toward the path that led back to the quarry. Once she found it she'd have to move even more carefully—because of the ammonia trap. She didn't remember exactly where he'd rigged it.

Another thirty feet . . . and there it was—the path that led back home.

She paused again, listening. Nothing. She noticed a dark-skinned, placid snake sunning itself on the stump of an old cedar. So long, she thought to it. I'm going home.

Lydia started forward.

And then the Insect Boy's hand lashed out from underneath a lush bay tree and snagged her good ankle. Unstable anyway, hands useless, Lydia could do nothing but try to twist to the side so that her solid rump took the force of the fall. The snake awoke at the sound of her scream and vanished.

Garrett climbed on top of her, pinning her to the ground, face red with anger. He must've been lying there for fifteen minutes. Keeping silent, not moving an inch until she was within striking distance. Like a spider waiting for its next kill.

"Please," Lydia muttered, breathless from the shock and horrified that she'd been betrayed by her angel. "Don't hurt—"

"Quiet," he raged in a whisper, looking around. "I'm at the end of my row with you." He pulled her roughly to her feet. He could've taken her by the arm or rolled her onto her back and eased her up that way. But he didn't; he reached around her from behind, his hands over her breasts, and lifted her to her feet. She felt his taut body rub disgustingly against her back and butt. Finally, after

what seemed like forever, he releas[ed] bony fingers around her arm and [...] toward the mill, oblivious to her [...] only once, to examine a long line [of...] eggs across the path. "Don't hurt [...] And watched her feet carefully to ma[ke...]

■

With a sound that Rhyme had always [...] a butcher sharpening a knife, the turn[...] another page of *The Miniature World*, w[...] from its battered condition, Garrett [...] book.

*Insects are astonishingly adept at su[...]
birch moth, for example, is naturally[...]
in the areas surrounding industrial [...]
England, the species' coloring change[...]
to blend in with the soot on the [...]
trunks and appear less obvious to its e[...]*

Rhyme flipped through more pages, [...] ring finger tapping the ECU controller [...] pages, hiss, hiss, blade on steel. Reading th[...] rett had marked. The paragraph about [...] had saved the search party from falling [...] boy's traps and Rhyme was trying to dra[...] sions from the book. As fish psychologi[...] told him, animal behavior is often a g[...] human—especially when it comes to matt[...]

*Praying mantises rub their abdom[...]
their wings, producing an unear[...]
which disorients pursuers. Mantises, [...]
will eat any living creature smaller [...]
selves, including birds and mammals.[...]*

Despite his skepticism about human testimony Rhyme decided that he'd now be happy for a witness. The helplessness, the fish-on-dry-land disorientation, was wearing heavily on him.

Bell paced slowly in the lab, glancing expectantly toward the doorway every time footsteps approached.

Lincoln Rhyme stretched again, pressing his head back into the headrest of the chair. Eyes on the evidence chart, eyes on the map, eyes back to the book. And all the while the green-and-black nutshell of a fly zipped around the room with an unfocused desperation that seemed to match his own.

■

An animal nearby darted across the path and vanished.

"What was that?" Sachs asked, nodding at it. To her the creature had looked like a cross between a dog and a large alley cat.

"Gray fox," Jesse said. "Don't see 'em too often. But then I don't usually go for walks north of the Paquo."

They moved slowly as they tried to follow the frail indications of Garrett's passage. And all the while they kept their eyes out for more deadfall traps and ambush from the surrounding trees and brush.

Once again Sachs felt the foreboding that had dogged her since they'd driven past the child's funeral that morning. They'd left the pines behind and were in a different type of forest. The trees were what you'd see in a tropical jungle. When she asked about them Lucy told her they were tupelo gum, old-growth bald cypress, cedar. They were bound together with webby moss and clinging vines that absorbed sound like thick fog and accentuated her sense of claustrophobia. There were mushrooms and mold and fungus everywhere and scummy marshes all around them. The aroma in the air was that of decay.

Sachs looked at the trodden ground. She asked Jesse, "We're miles from town. Who makes these paths?"

He shrugged. "Mostly bad pay."

"What's that?" she asked, recalling that Rich Culbeau had used the phrase.

"You know, somebody who doesn't pay his debts. Basically, it just means trash. Moonshiners, kids, swamp people, PCP cookers."

Ned Spoto took a drink of water and said, "We get calls sometimes: there's been a shooting, somebody's screaming, calls for help, mysterious lights flashing signals. Stuff like that. Only by the time we get out here, there's nothing. . . . No body, no perp, no complaining witness. Sometimes we find a blood trail but it don't lead anywhere. We make the run—we have to—but nobody in the department ever comes out in these parts alone."

Jesse said, "You feel different out here. You feel that—this sounds funny—but you feel that life's different, cheaper. I'd rather be arresting a couple of armed kids pumped up on angel dust at a mini-mart than come out here on a call. At least there, there're rules. You kinda know what to expect. Out here . . ." He shrugged.

Lucy nodded. "That's true. And normal rules don't apply to *anybody* north of the Paquo. Us *or* them. You can see yourself shooting before you read anybody their rights and that'd be perfectly all right. Hard to explain."

Sachs didn't like the edgy talk. If the other deputies hadn't been so somber and unnerved themselves she would have thought they were putting on a show to scare the city girl.

Finally they stopped at a place where the path branched out into three directions. They walked about fifty feet down each but could find no sign of which one Garrett and Lydia had chosen. They returned to the crossroads.

She heard Rhyme's words echoing in her mind. *Be careful, Sachs, but move fast. I don't think we have much time left.*

Move fast. . . .

But there was no hint of where they ought to be moving *to* and as Sachs looked down the choked paths it seemed impossible that anyone, even Lincoln Rhyme, could figure out where their prey had gone.

Then her cell phone rang and both Lucy and Jesse Corn looked at her expectantly, hoping, as did Sachs, that Rhyme had come up with a new suggestion about which way to go.

Sachs answered, listened to the criminalist and then nodded. Hung up. She took a breath and looked at the three deputies.

"What?" asked Jesse Corn.

"Lincoln and Jim just heard from the hospital about Ed Schaeffer. Looks like he woke up long enough to say, 'I love my kids,' and then he died. . . . They thought he'd said something earlier about 'Olive' Street but it turned out he was just trying to say 'I love.' That's all he said. I'm so sorry."

"Oh, Jesus," Ned muttered.

Lucy lowered her head and Jesse put his arm around her shoulders. "What do we do now?" he asked.

Lucy looked up. Sachs could see tears in her eyes. "We're gonna get that boy, that's what," she said with a grim determination. "We're going to pick the most logical path and keep in that direction till we find him. And we're going to go fast. That all right with you?" she asked Sachs, who had no problem momentarily yielding command to the deputy.

"You bet it is."

. . . chapter fifteen

Lydia had seen this look in men's eyes a hundred times.

A need. A desire. A hunger.

Sometimes, a pointless itch. Sometimes, an inept expression of love.

This big girl, with stringy hair, a spotted face in her teens and a pocked face now, believed she had little to offer men. But she knew too that they would, for a few years at least, ask one thing from her and she'd decided long ago that to get by in the world she would have to exploit the little power that she had. And so Lydia Johansson was now on a playing field that was very familiar to her.

They were back in the mill, in the dark office once again. Garrett was standing over her, his scalp glistening with sweat through the patchy crew cut. His erection was obvious through his slacks.

His eyes slid over her chest, where her soaked, translucent uniform had ripped open in her fall down the sluice (or had he done it when he grabbed her on the trail?), her bra strap snapped (or had he torn it?).

Lydia eased away from him, wincing at the pain in her ankle. Pressing against the wall, sitting, legs splayed, as she studied that *look* in the boy's eyes. Feeling a cold, spidery repulsion.

And yet she thought: Should I let him?

He was young. He'd come instantly and it would be over with. Maybe afterward he'd fall asleep and she could find that knife of his and cut her hands free. Then knock him out and tape *him* up.

But those red bony hands of his, his welty face next to her cheek, his disgusting breath and body stench. . . . How could she face it? Lydia closed her eyes momentarily. Uttered a prayer as insubstantial as her Blue Sunset eye shadow. Yes or no?

But any angels in the vicinity remained silent on this particular decision.

All she'd have to do was smile at him. He'd be inside her in a minute. Or she could take him into her mouth. . . . It wouldn't mean anything.

Fuck me fast then let's watch a movie. . . .   A joke between her boyfriend and her. She'd greet him at the door, in the red teddy she'd bought mail-order from Sears. She'd throw her arms around his shoulders and whisper those words to him.

You do this, she thought to herself, and you might be able to escape.

But I can't!

Garrett's eyes were locked on to her. Coursing over her body. His prick couldn't violate her any more thoroughly than his red eyes were doing right now. Jesus, he wasn't just an insect—he was a mutation out of one of Lydia's horror books, something that Dean Koontz or Stephen King could have made up.

Fingernails clicking.

He was examining her legs now, round and smooth—her best feature, she believed.

Garrett snapped, "Why're you crying? It's your fault

you hurt yourself. You shouldn't've run. Let me see it."
Nodding toward her swollen ankle.

"It's okay," Lydia said quickly but then, almost involuntarily, she held her foot out to him.

"Some assholes at school pushed me down the hill behind the Mobil station last year," he said. "Sprained my ankle. Looked like that. Hurt like a bitch."

Get it over with, she told herself. You'll be that much closer to home.

Fuck me fast . . .

No!

But she didn't pull away when Garrett sat down in front of her. He took her leg. His long fingers—God, they were huge—were gripping her around the calf, then around the ankle. He was trembling. Looking at the holes in her white pantyhose, where her pink flesh ballooned out. He studied her foot.

"It's not cut. But it's all black. What's that all about?"

"Might be broken."

He didn't respond, didn't seem sympathetic. It was as if her pain was meaningless to him. As if he couldn't understand that a human being might be suffering. His concern was just an excuse to touch her.

She extended her leg farther, her muscles quivering from the effort of elevating the limb. Her foot touched Garrett's body near his groin.

His eyelids lowered. His breathing was fast.

Lydia swallowed.

He moved her foot. It brushed against his penis through the wet cloth. He was hard as the wooden paddle of the waterwheel that she'd smacked trying to escape.

Garrett slid his hand farther up her leg. She felt his nails snag her pantyhose.

No . . .

Yes . . .

Then he froze.

His head tilted back and his nostrils flared. He inhaled deeply. Twice.

Lydia sniffed the air too. A sour smell. It took a moment before she recognized it. Ammonia.

"Shit," he whispered, eyes wide with horror. "How'd they get here this fast?"

"What?" she asked.

He leapt up. "The trap! They've tripped it! They'll be here in ten minutes! How the fuck d'they get here so fast?" He leaned into her face and she'd never seen so much anger and hatred in anyone's eyes. "You leave anything on the trail? Send 'em a message?"

She cringed, sure he was about to kill her. He seemed completely out of control. "No! I swear! I promise."

Garrett started toward her. Lydia shrank back but he walked past her quickly. He was frantic, ripping the material as he pulled his shirt and slacks off, his underwear, socks. She stared at his lean body, the substantial erection only slightly diminished. Naked, he ran to the corner of the room. There were some other clothes, folded, resting on the floor. He put these on. Shoes too.

Lydia lifted her head and looked out the window, through which the smell of the chemical was strong. So his trap hadn't been a bomb—he'd used the ammonia as a weapon itself; it had rained down on the search party, burning and blinding them.

Garrett continued, speaking almost in a whisper, "I have to get to Mary Beth."

"I can't walk," Lydia said, sobbing. "What are you going to do with *me*?"

He pulled the folding knife from the pocket of his pants. Opened it up with a loud click. Turned toward her.

"No, no, please. . . ."

"You're hurt. Like, there's no way you can keep up with me."

Lydia stared at the blade. It was stained and nicked. Her breath came in short gasps.

Garrett walked closer. Lydia started to cry.

■

How had they gotten here so fast? Garrett Hanlon wondered again, jogging from the front door of the mill to the stream, the panic he felt so often prickling his heart the way the poison oak hurt his skin.

His enemies had covered the ground from Blackwater Landing to the mill in just a few hours. He was astonished; he'd thought it would take them at least a day, probably two, to find his trail. The boy looked toward the path leading from the quarry. No sign of them. He turned in the opposite direction and started slowly down another trail—this one led away from the quarry, downstream from the mill.

Clicking his nails, asking himself: How, how, how?

Relax, he told himself. There was plenty of time. After the ammonia bottle crashed down on the rocks the police would be moving slow as dung beetles on balls of shit, worried about other traps. In a few minutes he'd be in the bogs and they'd never be able to follow him. Even with dogs. He'd be with Mary Beth in eight hours. He—

Then Garrett stopped.

On the side of the path was a plastic water bottle, empty. It looked as if somebody had just dropped it. He sniffed the air, picked up the bottle, smelled the inside. Ammonia!

An image snapped into his mind: a fly stuck in a spider's web. He thought: Shit! They tricked me!

A woman's voice barked, "Hold it right there, Garrett." A pretty redheaded woman in jeans and a black T-shirt stepped out of the bushes. She was holding a pistol and pointing it directly at his chest. Her eyes went to the knife in his hand then back to his face.

"He's over here," the woman shouted. "I've got him." Then her voice dropped and she looked into Garrett's eyes. "Do what I say and you won't get hurt. I want you to toss the knife away and lie down on the ground, face first."

■

But the boy didn't lie down.

He merely stood still, slouching awkwardly, fingernail and thumbnail of his left hand clicking compulsively. He looked utterly scared and desperate.

Amelia Sachs glanced again at the stained knife, held firmly in his hand. She kept the sight of the Smith & Wesson on Garrett's chest.

Her eyes stung from the ammonia and the sweat. She wiped her face with her sleeve.

"Garrett. . . ." Speaking calmly. "Lie down. Nobody's going to hurt you if you do what we say."

She heard distant shouting. "I got Lydia," Ned Spoto called. "She's okay. Mary Beth's not here."

Lucy's voice was calling, "Where, Amelia?"

"On the path to the stream," Sachs shouted. "Throw the knife over there, Garrett. On the ground. Then lie down."

He stared at her cautiously. Red blotches on his skin, eyes wet.

"Come on, Garrett. There're four of us here. There's no way out."

"How?" he asked. "How'd you find me?" His voice was childlike, younger than most sixteen-year-olds'.

She didn't share with him that how they'd found the ammonia trap and the mill had been Lincoln Rhyme, of course. Just as they'd started down the center path at the crossroads in the woods the criminalist had called her. He'd said, "One of the feed-and-grain clerks Jim Bell talked to said that you don't see corn used as feed around here. He said it probably came from a gristmill and Jim knew about an abandoned one that'd burned last year. That'd explain the scorch marks."

Bell got on the phone and told the search party how to get to the mill. Then Rhyme had come back on and added, "I've got a thought about the ammonia too."

Rhyme had been reading Garrett's books and found an underlined passage about insects' using smells to communicate warnings. He'd decided that since the ammonia wasn't found in commercial explosives, like the kind used at the quarry, Garrett had possibly rigged some ammonia on a fishing-line trip wire. This was so that when the pursuers spilled it the boy could smell that they were close and could escape.

After they found the trap it'd been Sachs's idea to fill one of Ned's water bottles with ammonia, quietly surround the mill and pour the chemical on the ground outside the mill—to flush the boy.

And flush him it had.

But he still wasn't listening to her instructions. Garrett looked around and then studied her face, as if trying to decide if she really would shoot him.

He scratched at a rash on his face and wiped sweat, then adjusted his grip on the knife, looking right and left, eyes filling with despair and panic.

Afraid to startle him into running—or attacking her— Sachs tried to sound like a mother coercing her child to sleep. "Garrett, do what I'm asking. Everything'll be fine. Just do what I'm asking. Please."

■

"You got a shot? Take it," Mason Germain was whispering.

A hundred yards away from where that bitchy redhead from New York was confronting the killer, Mason and Nathan Groomer were on the crest of a bald hill.

Mason was standing. Nathan was prone on the hot ground. He'd sandbagged the Ruger on a low rise of helpful rocks and was concentrating on controlling his breathing, the way hunters of elks and geese and human beings are supposed to do before they shoot.

"Go on," Mason urged. "There's no wind. You got a clear view. Take the shot!"

"Mason, the boy's not *doing* anything."

They saw Lucy Kerr and Jesse Corn walk into the clearing, joining the redhead, their guns also pointed at the boy. Nathan continued, "Everybody's got him covered and it's only a knife he's got. A little pissant knife. It looks like he's going to give up."

"He's *not* going to give up," spat out Mason Germain, who shifted his slight weight from one foot to the other in impatience. "I told you—he's faking. He's gonna kill one of 'em as soon as their guard's down. It don't mean anything to you that Ed Schaeffer's dead?" Steve Farr had called with this sad news a half-hour ago.

"Come on, Mason. I'm as tore up about that as anybody. That doesn't have a thing to do with the rules of engagement. Besides, look, will you? Lucy and Jesse're six feet away from him."

"You worried about hitting *them*? Fuck, you could hit a dime at this range, Nathan. Nobody shoots better'n you. Take it. Take your shot."

"I—"

Mason was watching the curious little play going on in the clearing. The redhead lowered her gun and took a step forward. Garrett was still holding the knife. Head swiveling back and forth.

The woman took another step toward him.

Oh, that's *helpful*, bitch.

"She in your line of fire?"

"No. But, I mean," Nathan said, "we're not even supposed to *be* here."

"That's not the issue," Mason muttered. "We *are* here.

I authorized backup to protect the search party and I'm ordering you to take a shot. Your safety off?"

"Yeah, it's off."

"Then shoot."

Peering through the 'scope.

Mason watched the gun barrel of the Ruger freeze, as Nathan grew into his weapon. Mason had seen this before—when he hunted with friends who were far better sportsmen than he was. It was an eerie thing that he didn't quite understand. Your weapon becomes part of you just before the gun fires, almost by itself.

Mason waited for the booming report of the long gun.

Not a breath of wind. A clean target. A clear backdrop.

Shoot, shoot, shoot! was Mason's silent message.

But instead of the crack of a rifle shot he heard a sigh. Nathan lowered his head. "I can't."

"Gimme the fucking gun."

"No, Mason. Come on."

But the expression in the senior deputy's eyes silenced the marksman and he handed over the rifle and rolled aside.

"How many in the clip?" Mason snapped.

"I—"

"How many rounds in the clip?" Mason said as he dropped to his belly and took up a position identical to his colleague's a moment before.

"Five. But nothing personal, Mason, you ain't the best rifle shot in the world and there're three innocents in the field of target and if you . . ." But his voice faded. There was only one place for this sentence to go and Nathan didn't want to accompany it there.

True, Mason knew, he wasn't the best shot in the world. But he'd killed a hundred deer. And he'd fired high scores on the state police range in Raleigh. Besides, good shot or bad, Mason knew that the Insect Boy had to die and had to die now.

He too breathed steadily, curled his finger around the

ribbed trigger. And found that Nathan had been lying; he'd never unsafetied the rifle. Mason now angrily pushed the button and started controlling his breathing once more.

In, out.

He rested the crosshairs on the boy's face.

The redhead moved closer to Garrett and for a moment her shoulder was in the line of fire.

Jesus my Lord, you *are* making it difficult, lady. She swayed back out of view. Then her neck appeared in the center of the scope. She swayed to the left but remained close to the center of the crosshairs.

Breathe, breathe.

Mason, ignoring the fact that his hands were shaking far more than they ought to, concentrated on the blotchy face of his target.

Lowered the crosshairs to Garrett's chest.

The redhead cop swayed once more into the line of fire. Then she eased out again.

He knew he should squeeze the trigger gently. But, as so often in his life, anger took over and made the decision for him. He pulled the sliver of metal with a jerk.

chapter sixteen

Behind Garrett a plug of dirt shot into the air and he slapped his hand to his ear, where he, like Sachs, had felt the zip of a bullet streak past.

An instant later the booming sound of the gun filled the clearing.

Sachs spun around. From the delay between the sound of the bullet itself and the muzzle report she knew the shot hadn't come from Lucy or Jesse but from a hundred yards or so behind them. The deputies too were looking back, guns raised, trying to spot the shooter.

Crouching, Sachs glanced at Garrett's face and she saw his eyes—the terror and confusion in them. For a moment, only an instant, he wasn't a killer who'd crushed a boy's skull or a rapist who'd bloodied Mary Beth McConnell and invaded her body. He was a scared little boy, whimpering, "No, no!"

"Who is it?" Lucy Kerr called. "Culbeau?" They took cover in some bushes.

"Get down, Amelia," Jesse called. "We don't know who they're shooting at. Might be a friend of Garrett's, aiming for us."

But Sachs didn't think so. The bullet was meant for Garrett. She scanned the hilltops nearby, looking for signs of the sniper.

Another shot snapped past. This one was a wider miss.

"Holy Mary," Jesse Corn said, swallowing the apparently unaccustomed blasphemy. "Look, up there—it's *Mason*! And Nathan Groomer. On that rise."

"It's *Germain*?" Lucy asked bitterly, squinting. She furiously pressed the transmit button on her Handi-talkie and shouted, "Mason, what the hell're you doing? Are you there? Are you receiving? . . . Central. Come in, Central. Goddamn, I can't get reception."

Sachs pulled out her cell phone and called Rhyme. He answered a moment later. She heard his voice, hollow, through the speakerphone. "Sachs, have you—?"

"We've got him, Rhyme. But that deputy, Mason Germain, he's on a hill nearby, firing at the boy. We can't get him on the radio."

"No, no, no, Sachs! He *can't* kill him. I checked the degradation of the blood on the tissue—Mary Beth was alive as of last night! If Garrett dies we'll never find her."

She shouted this to Lucy but the deputy still couldn't raise Mason on the radio.

Another shot. A rock shattered, spraying them with dust.

"Stop it!" Garrett sobbed. "No, no . . . I'm scared. Make him stop!"

Sachs said to Rhyme, "Ask Bell if Mason's got a cell phone and have him call, tell him to stop the shooting."

"Okay, Sachs . . ."

Rhyme hung up.

If Garrett dies we'll never find her . . .

Amelia Sachs made a fast decision and tossed her gun on the ground behind her then stepped forward, facing Garrett, a foot from him, directly in between Mason's gun and the boy. Thinking: In the time it took to do this Mason might've pulled the trigger, and the bullet, preceding the sound wave of the gunshot, might be headed directly toward my back.

She stopped breathing. Imagining she could feel the slug streaking at her.

A moment passed. There was no shot.

"Garrett, you've got to put the knife down."

"You tried to kill me! You tricked me!"

She wondered if he'd stab her—in anger or panic. "No. We didn't have anything to do with it. Look, I'm in front of you. I'm protecting you. He won't shoot again."

Garrett studied her face carefully with his twitchy eyes.

She wondered if Mason was waiting for her to move aside just enough so that he could sight on Garrett. He was obviously a bad shot and she imagined a bullet shattering her spine.

Ah, Rhyme, she thought, you're here for your operation to try to be more like me; maybe today I'll become more like you. . . .

Jesse Corn was sprinting through the brush up the hill, waving his arms and calling, "Mason, stop shooting! Stop shooting!"

Garrett continued to examine Sachs closely. Then he tossed the knife aside and started compulsively clicking his fingernails over and over.

As Lucy ran forward and cuffed Garrett, Sachs turned to the hill where Mason had been shooting from. She saw him stand, speaking on his phone. He glanced directly at her, it seemed, then shoved the phone into his pocket and started down the hill.

■

"What the hell were you thinking of?" Sachs raged at Mason. She walked straight up to him. They stood only a foot apart and she was an inch taller than he was.

"Saving your ass, lady," Mason replied harshly. "Didn't you happen to notice he had a weapon?"

"Mason"—Jesse Corn tried to diffuse the situation—"she was trying to calm things down is all. She got him to give up."

But Amelia Sachs didn't need any big brothers. She said, "I've been doing takedowns for years. He wasn't going to move on me. The only threat was from *you*. You could've hit one of *us*."

"Oh, bullshit." Mason leaned close to her and she could smell the musky aftershave he seemed to have poured on.

She eased away from the cloud of scent and said, "And if you'd killed Garrett, Mary Beth probably would've starved or suffocated to death."

"She's dead," Mason snapped. "That girl is lying in a grave somewhere and we'll never find her body."

"Lincoln got a report on her blood," Sachs responded. "She was alive as of last night."

This gave him a moment's pause. He muttered, "Last night ain't now."

"Come on, Mason," Jesse said. "It worked out okay."

But he wasn't calming. He lifted his arms and slapped his thighs. He looked into Sachs's eyes, said, "I don't know what the fuck we need you down here for anyway."

"Mason," Lucy Kerr cut in, "it's over with. We wouldn't've found Lydia, it hadn't been for Mr. Rhyme and Amelia here. We have them to thank. Let it go."

"*She's* the one not letting it go."

"When somebody puts me in the line of fire there better be a pretty good reason," Sachs said evenly. "And it's no reason at all that you're gunning for that boy because *you* haven't been able to make a case against him."

"You got no business talking about how I do my job. I—"

"Okay, we got to wrap this up here," Lucy said, "and get back to the office. We're still working on the assumption that Mary Beth *isn't* dead and we've got to find her."

"Hey," Jesse Corn called. "There's the chopper."

A helicopter from the medical center landed in a clearing near the mill and the medics brought Lydia out on a stretcher; she was suffering from minor heatstroke and had a badly sprained ankle. The woman had been hysterical at first—Garrett had come at her with a knife and even though it turned out he had used it just to cut a piece of duct tape to gag her she was still very shaken. She managed to calm down enough to tell them that Mary Beth wasn't anywhere near the mill. Garrett had her hidden near the ocean somewhere, on the Outer Banks. She didn't know where exactly. Lucy and Mason had tried to get Garrett to say but he'd remained mute and sat, hands cuffed behind him, staring morosely at the ground.

Lucy said to Mason, "You, Nathan and Jesse walk Garrett over to Easedale Road. I'll have Jim send a car there. The Possum Creek turnoff. Amelia wants to search the mill. I'll help her. Send another car over to Easedale in a half hour or so for us."

Sachs was happy to hold Mason's eyes for as long as he wanted to have a pissing contest. But he turned his attention to Garrett, looking the scared boy up and down like a guard studying a death-row prisoner. Mason nodded to Nathan. "Lessgo. Those cuffs on tight, Jesse?"

"They're tight, sure," Jesse said.

Sachs was glad Jesse would be with them to keep Mason on his good behavior. She'd heard stories about "escaping" prisoners being beaten by their transporting officers. Occasionally they ended up dead.

Mason gripped Garrett roughly by the arm and pulled him to his feet. The boy cast a hopeless look at Sachs. Then Mason led him down the path.

Sachs said to Jesse Corn, "Keep an eye on Mason. You may need all of Garrett's cooperation to find Mary Beth. And if he's too scared or mad you won't get anything out of him."

"I'll make sure of it, Amelia." A glance her way. "That was gutsy, what you did. Stepping in front of him. I wouldn't've done that."

"Well," she said, not in the mood for any more adoration. "Sometimes you just act and don't think."

He nodded brightly as if adding that expression to his repertoire. "Oh, hey, I was gonna ask—you have a nickname you go by?"

"Not really."

"Good. I like 'Amelia' just the way it is."

For a ridiculous moment she thought he was going to kiss her to celebrate the capture. Then he started off after Mason, Nathan and Garrett.

Brother, thought exasperated Amelia Sachs, watching Jesse turn to give her a cheerful wave: One of the deputies wants to shoot me and one of them's just about got the church reserved and the caterer lined up.

■

Sachs walked the grid carefully inside the mill—concentrating on the room where Garrett had kept Lydia. Walking back and forth, one step at a time.

She knew there were *some* clues here as to where Mary Beth McConnell was being held. Yet sometimes the connection between a perp and a location was so tenuous that it existed only microscopically and as Sachs traversed the room she found nothing helpful—only dirt, bits of hardware and burnt wood from the walls that had collapsed during the mill fire, food, water, empty wrappers and the duct tape that Garrett had brought (all without store labels). She found the map that poor Ed Schaeffer had gotten a look at. It showed Garrett's route to the mill but no destinations beyond that were marked.

Still, she searched twice. Then once more. Part of this was Rhyme's teaching, part of it was her own nature. (And was part of it, she wondered, a delaying tactic? To postpone as long as possible Rhyme's appointment with Dr. Weaver?)

Then Lucy's voice called, "I've got something."

Sachs had suggested that the deputy search the grinding room. That was where Lydia had told them she'd tried to escape from Garrett and Sachs had reasoned that if there'd been a struggle something might have fallen from Garrett's pockets. She'd given the deputy a fast course in walking the grid, told her what to look for and how to properly handle evidence.

"Look," Lucy said enthusiastically as she carried a cardboard box over to Sachs. "Found this hidden behind the millstone."

Inside was a pair of old shoes, a waterproof jacket, a compass and a map of the North Carolina coastline. Sachs also noticed a dusting of white sand in the shoes and in the folds of the map.

Lucy started to open up the map.

"No," Sachs said. "There could be some trace inside. Wait till we're back with Lincoln."

"But he could've marked the place where he's got her."

"He might've. But it'll still be marked when we get back to the lab. We lose trace now, we lose it forever." Then she said, "You keep searching inside. I want to check out the path he was going down when we stopped him. It led to the water. Maybe he had a boat hidden there. There might be another map or something."

Sachs left the mill and hiked down toward the stream. As she passed the rise where Mason had been shooting from she turned the corner and found two men staring at her. They carried rifles.

Oh, no. Not them.

"Well," Rich Culbeau said. Brushed away a fly that landed on his sunburnt forehead. He tossed his head and his thick, shiny braid swung like a horse's tail.

"Thanks loads, ma'am," the other one said to her with mild sarcasm.

Sachs recalled his name: Harris Tomel—the one who resembled a Southern businessman as much as Culbeau looked like a biker.

"No reward for us," Tomel continued. "And out all day in the hot sun."

Culbeau said, "The boy tell you where Mary Beth is?"

"You'll have to talk to Sheriff Bell about that," Sachs said.

"Just thought he might've said."

Then she wondered: How had they found the mill? They might've followed the search party but they might also have had a tip—from Mason Germain maybe, hoping for a little backup for his renegade sniper operation.

"I was right," Culbeau continued.

"What's that?" Sachs asked.

"Sue McConnell upped the reward to two thousand." He shrugged.

Tomel added, "So near yet so far."

"You'll excuse me, I've got some work to do." Sachs started past them, thinking, And where's the other one of this gang? The skinny—

A fast noise behind her and she felt her pistol being lifted out of her holster. She spun around, crouching, as the gun disappeared into the hand of scrawny, freckled Sean O'Sarian, who danced away from her, grinning like the class cutup.

Culbeau shook his head. "Sean, come on."

She held her hand out. "I'd like that back."

"Just looking. Fine piece. Harris here collects guns. This's a nice one, don't you think, Harris?"

Tomel said nothing, just sighed and wiped sweat off his forehead.

"You're borrowing trouble," Sachs said.

Culbeau said, "Give it back t'her, Sean. Too hot for your pranking."

He pretended to hand it to her, butt first, then grinned and pulled his hand away. "Hey, honey, where you from exactly? New York, I heard. What's it like there? Wild place, I'll bet."

"Quit fooling with the goddamn gun," Culbeau muttered. "We're out the money. Let's just live with it and get back to town."

"Give me back the weapon now," Sachs muttered.

But O'Sarian was dancing around, sighting on trees as if he were a ten-year-old playing cops and robbers. "Pow, pow . . ."

"Okay, forget about it." Sachs shrugged. "It's not mine anyway. When you're through playing just take it back to the Sheriff's Department." She turned to walk past O'Sarian.

"Hey," he said, frowning with disappointment that she didn't want to play anymore. "Don't you—"

Sachs dodged to his right, ducked and came up behind him fast, catching him in a one-armed neck lock. In half a second the switchblade was out of her pocket, the blade open and the point tapping out red dots on the underside of his chin.

"Oh, Jesus, what the hell're you doing?" he blurted then realized that speaking pushed his throat against the tip of the knife. He shut up.

"Okay, okay," Culbeau said, holding up his hands. "Let's not—"

"Drop your weapons on the ground," Sachs said. "All of you."

"*I* didn't do anything," Culbeau protested.

"Listen, miss," Tomel said, trying to sound reasonable, "we didn't mean any trouble. Our friend here is—"

The knife tip poked his stubbly chin.

"Ahh, do it, do it!" O'Sarian said desperately, teeth together. "Put the fucking guns down."

Culbeau eased his rifle to the ground. Tomel too.

Repulsed by O'Sarian's unclean smell, Sachs slid her hand along his arm and seized her gun. He released it. She stepped back, shoved O'Sarian away, kept the pistol pointed at him.

"I was just pranking," O'Sarian said. "I do that. I fool around. I don't mean nothing. Tell her I fool around—"

"What's going on here?" Lucy Kerr said, walking down the path, hand on her pistol grip.

Culbeau shook his head. "Sean was being an asshole."

"Which is gonna get him killed someday," Lucy said.

Sachs closed the switchblade one-handed and put it back into her pocket.

"Look, I'm cut. Look, blood!" O'Sarian held up a stained finger.

"Damn," Tomel said reverently, though Sachs had no idea what he was referring to.

Lucy looked at Sachs. "You want to do anything about this?"

"Take a shower," she responded.

Culbeau laughed.

Sachs added, "We don't have time to waste on them."

The deputy nodded to the men. "This is a crime scene. You boys're out your reward." She nodded at the rifles. "You want to hunt, do it elsewhere."

"Oh, like anything's in season," O'Sarian asked sarcastically, dishing on Lucy for the stupidity of her comment. "I mean, hell-*ohhh*."

"Then head back to town—'fore you bollix up your lives any more'n you already have."

The men picked up their guns. Culbeau lowered his head to O'Sarian's ear and spoke quiet, angry words to him. O'Sarian gave a shrug and grinned. For a moment Sachs thought Culbeau was going to hit him. But then the tall man calmed and turned back to Lucy. "You find Mary Beth?"

"Not yet. But we got Garrett and he'll tell us."

Culbeau said, "Wish we got the reward but I'm glad he's caught. That boy's trouble."

When they were gone Sachs asked, "You find anything else in the mill?"

"No. Thought I'd come down here to help you look for a boat."

As they continued down the path Sachs said, "One thing I forgot about. We ought to send somebody back to that trap—the hornets' nest. Kill 'em and fill in the hole."

"Oh, Jim sent Trey Williams, one of our deputies, over there with a can of wasp spray and a shovel. But there weren't any wasps. It was an old nest."

"Empty?"

"Right."

So it wasn't a trap at all, just a trick to slow them down. Sachs reflected too that the ammonia bottle wasn't intended to hurt anybody either. Garrett *could* have rigged it to spill on his pursuers, blinding them. But he'd perched it on the side of a small cliff. If they hadn't found the fishing line first and tripped it, the bottle would've fallen onto rocks ten feet below the path, warning Garrett with the smell of the ammonia but not hurting anyone.

She had an image of Garrett's wide, frightened eyes once more.

I'm scared. Make him stop!

Sachs realized Lucy was talking to her.

"I'm sorry?"

The deputy said, "Where'd you learn how to use that toad sticker of yours—that knife?"

"Wilderness training."

"Wilderness? Where?"

"Place called Brooklyn," Sachs responded.

■

Waiting.

Mary Beth McConnell stood beside the grimy window. She was edgy and dizzy—from the close heat of her prison and the bristling thirst. She hadn't found a drop of any liquid to drink in the entire house. Glancing out the back window of the cabin, past the wasps' nest, she could see empties of bottled water in a trash heap. They taunted her and the sight made her feel all the more thirsty. She knew she couldn't last more than a day or two in this heat without something to drink.

Where are you? Where? She spoke silently to the Missionary.

If there *had* been a man there—and he wasn't just a creation of her desperate, thirst-crazed imagination.

She leaned against the hot wall of the shack. Wondered if she'd faint. Tried to swallow but there wasn't a bit of moisture in her mouth. The air enwrapped her face, stifling as hot wool.

Then thinking angrily: Oh, Garrett . . . I knew you'd be trouble. She remembered the old saw: No good deed goes unpunished.

I should never have helped him out. . . . But how could I *not*? How could I not save him from those high school boys? She recalled seeing the four of them, watching Garrett on the ground after he'd fainted on Maple Street last year. One tall, sneering boy, a friend of Billy Stail's from the football team, unzipped his Guess! jeans, pulled out his penis and was about to urinate on Garrett. She'd stormed up to them, given them hell and snatched one boy's cell phone to call an ambulance for Garrett.

I *had* to do it, of course.

But once I'd saved him, I was his. . . .

At first, after that incident, Mary Beth was amused that he would shadow her like a shy admirer. Calling her at home to tell her things he'd heard on the news, leaving presents for her (but *what* presents: a glistening green beetle in a tiny cage; clumsy drawings of spiders and centipedes; a dragonfly on a string—a live one!).

But then she began to notice him nearby a little too often. She'd hear footsteps behind her as she walked from the car to the house, late at night. See a figure in the trees near her house in Blackwater Landing. Hear his high, eerie voice muttering words she couldn't make out, talking or singing to himself. He'd spot her on Main Street and make a beeline to her, rambling on, taking up precious time, making her feel more and more uneasy. Glancing—both embarrassed and desirous—at her breasts and legs and hair.

"Mary Beth, Mary Beth . . . did you know that if a spiderweb was, like, stretched all around the world it'd weigh less than an ounce. . . . Hey, Mary Beth, you know that a spiderweb is something like five times stronger than steel? And it's way more elastic than nylon? Some webs are really cool—they're like hammocks. Flies lie down in them and never wake up."

(She should have noticed, she now reflected, that much of his trivia was about spiders and insects snaring prey.)

And so she rearranged her life to avoid running into him, finding new stores to shop in, different routes home, different paths to ride her mountain bike on.

But then something happened that would negate all her efforts to distance herself from Garrett Hanlon: Mary Beth made a discovery. And it happened to be on the banks of the Paquenoke River right in the heart of Blackwater Landing—a place that the boy had staked out as his personal fiefdom. Still, it was a discovery so important that not even a gang of moonshiners, let alone a skinny boy obsessed with insects, could keep her away from the place.

Mary Beth didn't know why history excited her so much. But it always had. She remembered going to Colonial Williamsburg when she was a little girl. It was only a two-hour drive from Tanner's Corner and the family went there often. Mary Beth memorized the roads near the town so that she'd know when they were almost to their destination. Then she'd close her eyes and after her father had parked the Buick she made her mother lead her by the hand into the park so that she could open her eyes and pretend that she was actually back in Colonial America.

She'd felt this same exhilaration——only a hundred times greater——when she'd been walking along the banks of the Paquenoke in Blackwater Landing last week, eyes on the ground, and noticed something half buried in the muddy soil. She'd dropped to her knees and started moving aside dirt with the care of a surgeon exposing an ailing heart. And, yes, there they were: old relics——the evidence that a stunned twenty-three-year-old Mary Beth McConnell had been searching desperately for. Evidence that could prove her theory——which would rewrite American history.

Like all North Carolinians——and most schoolchildren in America——Mary Beth McConnell had studied the Lost Colony of Roanoke in history class: In the late 1500s a settlement of English colonists landed on Roanoke Island, between the mainland of North Carolina and the Outer Banks. After some mostly harmonious contact between the settlers and the local Native Americans, relations deteriorated. With winter approaching and the colonists running short on food and other provisions Governor John White, who'd founded the colony, sailed back to England for relief. But by the time he returned to Roanoke the colonists——more than a hundred men, women and children——had disappeared.

The only clue as to what had happened was the word "Croatoan" carved in tree bark near the settlement. This was the Indian name for Hatteras, about fifty miles south of Roanoke. Most historians believed the colonists died at sea en route to Hatteras or were killed when they arrived, though there was no record of them ever landing there.

Mary Beth had visited Roanoke Island several times and had seen the reenactment of the tragedy performed at a small theater there. She was moved——and chilled——by the play. But she never thought much about the story until she was older and studying at the University of North Carolina in Avery, where she read about the Lost

Colony in depth. One aspect of the story that raised unanswered questions about the fate of the colonists involved a girl named Virginia Dare and the legend of the White Doe.

It was a story that Mary Beth McConnell—an only child, a bit of a renegade, single-minded—could understand. Virginia Dare was the first English child born in America. She was Governor White's granddaughter and was one of the Lost Colonists. Presumably, the history books reported, she died with them at, or on the way to, Hatteras. But as Mary Beth continued her research she learned that not long after the disappearance of the colonists, when more British began to settle on the Eastern Seaboard, local legends about the Lost Colony began to spring up.

One tale was that the colonists weren't killed right away but survived and continued to live among the local tribes. Virginia Dare grew into a beautiful young woman—blond and fair-skinned, strong-willed and independent. A medicine man fell in love with her but she rejected him and not long after that she disappeared. The medicine man claimed he hadn't harmed her but, because she rejected his love, he'd turned her into a white deer.

No one believed him, of course, but soon people in the area began seeing a beautiful white doe who seemed to be the leader of all the animals in the woods. The tribe, frightened by the doe's apparent powers, held a contest to capture her.

One young brave managed to track her down and made a nearly impossible shot with a silver-tipped arrow. It pierced her chest and as she lay dying the doe looked up at the hunter with chillingly human eyes.

He stammered, "Who are you?"

"Virginia Dare," the deer whispered and died.

Mary Beth had decided to look into the story of the White Doe in earnest. Spending long days and nights in academic archives at UNC at Chapel Hill and at Duke

University, reading old diaries and journals from the sixteenth and seventeenth centuries, she found a number of references to "white deer" and mysterious "white beasts" in northeastern North Carolina. But the sightings weren't on either Roanoke or Hatteras. The creatures were seen along the "Black-water banks where the Serpentine river flowes west from the Great Swamp."

Mary Beth knew the power of legend and how there is often truth in even the most fanciful tales. She reasoned that maybe the Lost Colonists, afraid of attack by the local tribes, had left the word "Croatoan" to lead off their attackers and escaped not south but west, where they settled along the banks of the, yes, *serpentine* Paquenoke River—near Tanner's Corner in what was now called Blackwater Landing. There the Lost Colonists grew more and more powerful and the Indians—fearful of the threat—attacked and killed them. Virginia Dare, Mary Beth allowed herself to speculate, interpreting the legend of the White Doe, might have been one of the last settlers alive, fighting to the death.

Well, this was her theory but Mary Beth had never found any proof to support it. She'd spent days prowling around Blackwater Landing with ancient maps, trying to figure out exactly where the colonists might've landed and where their settlement had been. Then finally last week, walking along the banks of the Paquo, she found evidence of the Lost Colony.

She remembered her mother's horror when the girl had told her that she was going to be doing some archaeological work at Blackwater Landing.

"Not *there*," the doughy woman had said bitterly, as if she herself were in danger. "That's where the Insect Boy kills people. He'll find you, he'll hurt you."

"Mother," she'd snapped back, "you're like those assholes at school who tease him."

"You said that word again. I asked you not to. The 'A' word."

"Mom, come on—you sound like a hard-shell Baptist sitting on the anxious bench." Meaning the front row in church, where sat those parishioners particularly worried about their own, or—more likely—someone else's, moral standing.

"Even the name is scary," Sue McConnell muttered. "Blackwater."

And Mary Beth explained that there were dozens of Blackwaters in North Carolina. Any river that flowed from marshlands was referred to as a blackwater river because it was darkened by deposits of decaying vegetation. The Paquenoke was fed by the Great Dismal Swamp and surrounding bogs.

But this information didn't relieve her mother one bit. "Please, don't go, honey." Then the woman fired her own silver-tipped arrow of guilt: "Now that your father's gone, if anything happened to you I wouldn't have anyone. . . . I'd be alone. I wouldn't know what to do. You don't want that, do you?"

But Mary Beth, fired by the adrenaline that had excited explorers and scientists forever, had packed up her brushes and collection jars and bags and gardener's spade and headed off yesterday morning in the wet, yellow heat to continue her archaeological work.

And what had happened? She'd been assaulted and kidnapped by the Insect Boy. Her mother had been right.

Now, sitting in this hot, disgusting cabin, in pain, sick and half delirious with thirst, she thought about her mother. Having lost her husband to wasting cancer, the woman's life was falling apart. She'd given up her friends, her volunteer work at the hospital, any semblance of routine and normalcy in her life. Mary Beth found herself assuming the role of parent, while her mother slipped into the world of daytime TV and junk food. Pudgy and insensate and needy, she was nothing more than a pathetic child.

But one of the things her father had taught Mary

the Outer Banks would probably find her within several days. And Rhyme was now ready for the operation. He clung, of all things, to a bizarre good-luck charm—the memory of Henry Davett's gruff argument with him, the man's tempered-steel gaze. The image of the businessman prodded him to return to the hospital, to finish the tests and to go under the knife. He glanced at Ben and was about to instruct him on how to pack up the forensic equipment when Sachs took up Bell's cause. "We found some evidence at the mill, Rhyme. Lucy did, actually. Good evidence."

Rhyme said sourly, "If it's *good* evidence then somebody else'll be able to figure out where it leads to."

"Look, Lincoln," Bell began in his reasonable Carolinian accent, "I'm not going to push it but you're the only one 'round here's got experience at major crimes like this. We'd be at sea trying to figure out what *that's* telling us, for instance." He nodded at the chromatograph. "Or whether this bit of dirt or that footprint means anything."

Head rubbing against the Storm Arrow's pillowy rest, Rhyme glanced at Sachs's imploring face. Sighing, he finally asked, "Garrett's not saying *anything*?"

"He's talking," Farr said, tugging at one of his flaglike ears. "But he's denying killing Billy and he's saying he got Mary Beth away from Blackwater Landing for her own good. That's it. Won't say a word about where she is."

Sachs said, "In this heat, Rhyme, she could die first."

"Or starve to death," Farr pointed out.

"Oh, for God's sake . . .

"Thom," Rhyme snapped, "call Dr. Weaver. Tell her be here for a little longer. Emphasize 'little.' "

"That's all we're asking, Lincoln," Bell said, relief in his face. "An hour or two. We sure appreciate it—we'll you an honorary resident of Tanner's Corner," the ff joked. "We'll give you the key to the town."

Beth—by his life as well as by his arduous death—was that you do what you're destined for and don't alter your course for anyone. Mary Beth hadn't dropped out of school as her mother had begged and gotten a job close to home. She balanced her mother's need for support with her own—the need to get her grad degree and, when she graduated next year, to find a job doing serious fieldwork in American anthropology. If that happened to be nearby, fine. But if it was conducting Native American digs in Santa Fe, or Eskimo in Alaska, or African American in Manhattan, then that was where she'd go. She'd always be there for her mother but she had her own life to look forward to.

Except that now when she should be unearthing and collecting more evidence at Blackwater Landing, conferring with her grad adviser and writing proposals, running tests on the relics she'd found, she was trapped in a psychotic teenager's love nest.

A wave of hopelessness coursed through her.

She felt the tears.

But then she stopped them cold.

Stop it! . . . Be strong. Be your *father's* daughter, fighting his illness every single minute of the day, never resting. Not your mother's.

Be Virginia Dare, who rallied the Lost Colonists.

Be the White Doe, the queen of all the animals in the forest.

And then, just as she was thinking of an illustration of the majestic deer in a book about North Carolina legends, there was another flash of motion at the edge of the forest. The Missionary came out of the woods, a large backpack over his shoulder.

He *was* real!

Mary Beth grabbed one of Garrett's jars, which held a dinosaur-like beetle, and slammed it against the window. The jar crashed through the glass and shattered on the iron bars outside.

"Help me!" she screamed in a voice barely audible because of her sand-dry throat. "Help!"

A hundred yards away the man paused. Looked around.

"Please! Help me!" A long wail.

He looked behind him. Then into the woods.

She took a deep breath and tried to call again but her throat seized. She started choking, spit some blood.

And across the field the Missionary kept on walking into the woods. He disappeared from view a moment later.

Mary Beth sat heavily in the musty couch and leaned her head hopelessly against the wall. She glanced up suddenly; some motion had caught her eye again. It was nearby—in the cabin. The beetle in the jar—the miniature triceratops—had survived the trauma of losing his home. Mary Beth watched him troop doggedly up a summit of broken glass, open one set of wings, then spread a second set, which fluttered invisibly and lifted him off the windowsill to freedom.

. . . chapter seventeen

"We've caught him," Rhyme said to Jim Bell and brother-in-law, Deputy Steve Farr. "Amelia and me. was the bargain. Now we have to get back to Avery."

"Well, Lincoln," Bell began delicately, "it's jus Garrett's not talking. He's not telling us anything where Mary Beth is."

Ben Kerr stood nearby uncertainly, beside the mountain range on the computer screen connect chromatograph. His initial hesitancy had vanish now seemed to regret the end of his assignme Sachs was in the lab too. Mason Germain wa was just as well—Rhyme was furious that gered Sachs's life with the sniping at the m angrily ordered the deputy to stay out of th time being.

"I appreciate that," Rhyme said dismiss ing to Bell's implicit request for more he that she's in immediate danger." Lydia h Mary Beth was alive and had told them tion where she was being held. A con

All the faster to unlock the door and get the hell out of here, Rhyme thought cynically. He asked Bell, "Where's Lydia?"

"In the hospital."

"She all right?"

"Nothing serious. They're keeping her in for observation for a day."

"What'd she say—*exactly*?" Rhyme demanded.

Sachs said, "That Garrett told her he's got Mary Beth east of here, near the ocean. On the Outer Banks. He also said that he didn't really kidnap her. She went along willingly. He was just looking out for her and she was happy to be where she was. She also told me that we caught Garrett completely off guard. He never thought we'd get to the mill so fast. When he smelled the ammonia he panicked, changed his clothes, gagged her and ran out the door."

"Okay . . . Ben, we've got some things to look at."

The zoologist nodded, pulled on his latex gloves once more—without Rhyme's having to instruct him to do so, the criminalist observed.

Rhyme asked about the food and water found at the mill. Ben held them up. The criminalist observed, "No individual store labels. Like the others. Won't do us any good. See if there's anything adhering to the sticky sides of the duct tape."

Sachs and Ben bent over the roll and spent ten minutes examining it with a hand glass. She pulled fragments of wood from the side and Ben once again held the instrument so Rhyme could peer into the eyepieces. But under the microscope it was clear that they matched the wood in the mill. "Nothing," she said.

Ben then picked up the map that showed Paquenoke County. It was marked with *X*'s and arrows, indicated Garrett's path to the mill from Blackwater Landing. There was no price sticker on this either. And it gave no indication of where the boy had been headed once he'd left the mill.

Rhyme said to Bell, "You have an ESDA?"

"A what?"

"Electrostatic Detection Apparatus."

"Don't even know what that is."

"Picks up indented writing on paper. If Garrett had written something on top of the map, a town or address, we could see it."

"Well, we don't have one. Should I call the state police?"

"No. Ben, just shine a flashlight on the map at a low angle. See if there're any indentations."

Ben did this and though they searched every inch of the map they could see no evidence of writing or other marking.

Rhyme ordered Ben to examine the second map, the one Lucy had found in the gristmill. "Let's see if there's any trace in the folds. It's too big for magazine subscription cards. Open it over a newspaper."

More sand poured out. Rhyme noticed immediately that it was in fact ocean sand, the sort that would be found on the Outer Banks—the grains were clear, not opaque, as would have been the case with inland sand.

"Run a sample through the chromatograph. Let's see if there's any other trace that'll be helpful."

Ben started the noisy machine.

As they waited for the results he spread the map out on the table. Bell, Ben and Rhyme examined it carefully. It depicted the eastern shore of the U.S. from Norfolk, Virginia, and the Hampton Roads shipping lanes all the way down to South Carolina. They looked over every inch but Garrett hadn't circled or marked any location.

Of *course* not, Rhyme thought; it's never that easy. They used the flashlight on this map too. But found no indented writing.

The chromatograph results flashed up onto the screen. Rhyme glanced at it quickly. "Not much help. Sodium chloride—salt—along with iodine, organic material. . . .

All consistent with seawater. But there's hardly any other trace. Doesn't do us much good for tying the sand to a specific location." Rhyme nodded at the shoes that had been in the box with the map. He asked Ben, "Any other trace in those?"

The young man examined them carefully, even unlacing them—just as Rhyme was about to ask him to do. This boy has good criminalist potential, Rhyme thought. He shouldn't be wasting his talent on neurotic fish.

The shoes were old Nikes—so common that tracing them to a particular store where Garrett might have bought them was impossible.

"Flecks of dried leaves, looks like. Maple and oak. If I had to guess."

Rhyme nodded. "Nothing else in the box?"

"Nothing."

Rhyme looked up at the other evidence charts. His eye paused at the references to camphene.

"Sachs, in the mill, were there old-fashioned lamps on the walls? Or lanterns?"

"No," Sachs answered. "None."

"Are you sure," he persisted gruffly, "or did you just not notice?"

She crossed her arms and said evenly, "The floors were ten-inch-wide chestnut, the walls plaster and lath. There was graffiti on one of the walls in blue spray paint. It said, 'Josh and Brittany, luv always,' love spelled L-U-V. There was one Shaker-style table, cracked down the middle and painted black, three bottles of Deer Park water, a pack of Reese's Peanut Butter Cups, five bags of Doritos, two bags of Cape Cod potato chips, six cans of Pepsi, four cans of Coke, eight packets of Planters peanut butter and cheese crackers. There were two windows in the room. One was boarded over. In the unboarded window there was only one pane that was unbroken—the others had been smashed—and every doorknob and window latch in the place was stolen. There were old-fashioned raised electric switches on the walls. And, yes, I'm sure there were no old-fashioned lamps."

"Whoa, she got you there, Lincoln," Ben said, laughing.

Now being one of the gang, the young man was rewarded with a glower from Rhyme. The criminalist stared once more at the evidence then shook his head, said to Bell, "I'm sorry, Jim, the best I can tell you is that she's probably being held in a house not far from the ocean but—if the deciduous leaves are near the place— not *on* the water. Because oak and maple wouldn't grow in sand. And it's old—because of the camphene lamps. Nineteenth century. That's the best I can do, I'm afraid."

Bell was looking at the map of the Eastern shore, shaking his head. "Well, I'm going to talk to Garrett again, see if he'll cooperate. If not I'm gonna give the D.A. a call and think about trading a plea for information. Worse comes to worst I'll fix up a search of the Outer Banks. I tell you, Lincoln, you're a lifesaver. I can't thank you enough. You'll be here for a spell?"

"Only long enough to show Ben how to pack up the equipment."

Rhyme spontaneously thought again of his mascot, Henry Davett. But he found to his surprise that his elation that his job was now finished was tainted by his frustration that the ultimate answer to the puzzle of finding Mary Beth McConnell still eluded him. But, as his ex-wife used to say to him as he walked out the door of their apartment at one or two A.M. to run a crime scene, you can't save the entire world. "I wish you luck, Jim."

Sachs said to Bell, "You mind if I come with you? To see Garrett?"

"Feel free," the sheriff said. He seemed to want to add something—maybe about female charm helping them get some information out of the boy. But he then apparently—and wisely, Rhyme reflected—thought better of it.

"Let's get to work, Ben," Rhyme said. He wheeled to

the table that held the density gradient tubes. "Now listen carefully. A criminalist's tools are like a tactical officer's weapons. They have to be packed and stored just right. You treat them as if somebody's life will depend on them because, believe me, it will. Are you listening, Ben?"

"I'm listening."

The Tanner's Corner lockup was a structure two long blocks away from the Sheriff's Department.

Sachs and Bell walked along the blistering sidewalk toward the place. Again she was struck by the ghost-town quality of Tanner's Corner. The sickly drunks they'd noticed when they first arrived were still downtown, sitting on a bench, silent. A skinny, coiffed woman parked her Mercedes in an empty row of parking spaces, climbed out and walked into the nail salon. The glitzy car seemed completely out of place in the small town. There was no one else on the street. Sachs noticed a half-dozen businesses had gone under. One of them had been a toy store. A mannequin of a baby wearing a sun-bleached jumper lay in the window. Where, she thought again, were all the children?

Then she looked across the street and saw a face watching her from the dim recesses of Eddie's bar. She squinted. "Those three guys?" she said, nodding.

Bell looked. "Culbeau and his buddies?"

"Uh-huh. They're trouble. They got my weapon away from me," Sachs said. "One of them did. O'Sarian."

The sheriff frowned. "What happened?"

"I got it back," she answered shortly.

"You want me to bring him in?"

"No. Just thought you should know: they're upset about losing out on the reward. If you ask me, though, it's more than that. They're gunning for that boy."

"Them and the rest of the town."

Sachs said, "But the rest of the town doesn't carry around loaded weapons."

Bell chuckled and said, "Well, not all of 'em, anyway."

"I'm also a little curious how they happened to end up at the mill."

The sheriff thought about this for a moment. "Mason, you thinking?"

"Yep," Sachs said.

"Wish he'd take his vacation this week. But there's no chance of that happening. Well, here we are. Not much of a jail. But it works."

They walked inside the single-story cinder-block building. The groaning air conditioner kept the rooms mercifully cool. Bell told her to drop her gun in the lock-box. He did the same and they walked into the interrogation room. He closed the door.

Wearing a blue jumpsuit, courtesy of the county, Garrett Hanlon sat at a fiberboard table, across from Jesse Corn. The deputy smiled at Sachs and she gave him a smaller smile in return. She then looked at the boy and was struck again at how sad and desperate he seemed.

I'm scared. Make him stop!

On his face and arms were welts that hadn't been there earlier. She asked, "What happened to your skin?"

He looked down at his arm and rubbed self-consciously. "Poison oak," he muttered.

In a kind voice Bell said, "You heard your rights, didn't you? Did Deputy Kerr read them to you?"

"Yeah."

"And you understand them?"

"I guess."

"There's a lawyer on his way. Mr. Fredericks. He's coming from a meeting in Elizabeth City and he'll be here pretty soon. You don't have to say anything until he gets here. You understand that?"

He nodded.

Sachs glanced at the one-way mirror. Wondered who was on the other side, manning the video camera.

"But we hope you'll talk to us, Garrett," Bell continued. "We have some real important things to ask you about. First of all, it's true? Mary Beth's alive?"

"Sure she is."

"Did you rape her?"

"Like, I'd *never* do that," he said, and the pathos momentarily gave way to indignation.

"But you kidnapped her," Bell said.

"Not really."

"Not *really*?"

"She, like, didn't get it that Blackwater Landing's dangerous. I had to get her away or she wouldn't be safe. That's all. I saved her. Like, sometimes you gotta make somebody do things they don't want to. For their own good. And, you know, then they catch on."

"She's near the beach somewhere, isn't she? The Outer Banks, right?"

He blinked at this, red eyes narrowing. He'd be realizing that they'd found the map and talked to Lydia. He looked down at the fiberboard table. Didn't say anything else.

"Where is she exactly, Garrett?"

"I can't tell you."

"Son, you're in serious trouble. You got a murder conviction staring you in the face."

"I didn't kill Billy."

"How'd you know it was Billy I was talking about?"

Bell asked quickly. Jesse Corn lifted an eyebrow to Sachs, impressed at his boss's cleverness.

Garrett's fingernails clicked together. "Whole world knows Billy got killed." His fast eyes circled the room. Resting inevitably on Amelia Sachs. She could endure the imploring look for only a moment then had to look away.

"We got your fingerprints on the shovel that killed him."

"The shovel? That killed him?"

"Yep."

He seemed to think back to what had happened. "I remember seeing it lying there on the ground. I guess maybe I picked it up."

"Why?"

"I don't know. I wasn't thinking. I felt all weird seeing Billy lying there, like, all bloody and everything."

"Well, you have any idea who *did* kill Billy?"

"This man. Mary Beth told me that she was, like, doing this project for school there, by the river, and Billy stopped to talk to her. And then this man came up. He'd been following Billy and they started arguing and fighting and this guy grabbed the shovel and killed him. Then I came by and he ran off."

"You saw him?"

"Yessir."

"What were they arguing about?" Bell asked skeptically.

"Drugs or something, Mary Beth said. Sounded like Billy was selling drugs to the kids on the football team. Like, those steroid things?"

"Jeeez," said Jesse Corn, giving a sour laugh.

"Garrett," Bell said. "Billy wasn't into drugs. I knew him. And we never had any reports about steroids at the high school."

"I understand that Billy Stail ragged on you a lot," Jesse said. "Billy and a couple other boys on the team."

Sachs thought this wasn't right—two big deputies double-teaming him.

"That they made fun of you. Called you Bug Boy. You took a swing at Billy once and he and his friends beat you up bad."

"I don't remember."

"Principal Gilmore told us," Bell said. "They had to call security."

"Maybe. But I didn't kill him."

"Ed Schaeffer died, you know. He got stung to death by those wasps in the blind."

"I'm sorry that happened. That wasn't *my* fault. I didn't put the nest there."

"It wasn't a trap?"

"No, it was just there, in the hunting blind. I went there all the time—even slept there—and they didn't bother me. Yellow jackets only sting when they're afraid you're going to hurt their family."

"Well, tell us about this man you say killed Billy," the sheriff said. "You ever see him around here before?"

"Yessir. Two or three times the last couple years. Walking through the woods around Blackwater Landing. Then once I saw him near the school."

"White, black?"

"White. And he was tall. Maybe about as old as Mr. Babbage—"

"His forties?"

"Yeah, I guess. He had blond hair. And he was wearing overalls. Tan ones. And a white shirt."

"But it was just your and Billy's fingerprints on the shovel," Bell pointed out. "Nobody else's."

Garrett said, "Like, I think he was wearing gloves."

"Why'd he be wearing gloves this time of year?" Jesse said.

"Probably so he *wouldn't* leave fingerprints," Garrett shot back.

Sachs thought back to the friction-ridge prints on the shovel. She and Rhyme hadn't done the printing themselves. Sometimes it's possible to image grain prints from leather gloves. Cotton or wool glove prints were much less detectable although fabric fibers could slough off and get caught in the tiny splinters in a wooden surface like a tool handle.

"Well, what you say could've happened, Garrett," Bell said. "But it just doesn't seem like the truth to anybody."

"Billy was dead! I just picked up the shovel and looked at it. Which I shouldn't have. But I did. That's all that happened. I knew Mary Beth was in danger so I took her away to be safe." He said this to Sachs, gazing at her with imploring eyes.

"Let's get back to her," Bell said. "Why was she in danger?"

"Because she was in Blackwater Landing." He snapped his nails again. . . . *Different from my habit,* Sachs reflected. *I dig into my flesh, he clicks nail against nail. Which is worse?* she wondered. *Mine,* she decided; *it's more destructive.*

He turned his damp, ruddy eyes back to Sachs.

Stop it! I can't take that look! she thought, glancing away.

"And Todd Wilkes? The boy who hung himself? Did you threaten him?"

"No!"

"His brother saw you shouting at him last week."

"He was dropping lit matches on anthills. That's shitty and mean and I told him to stop it."

"What about Lydia?" Bell said. "Why'd you kidnap *her*?"

"I was worried about her too."

"Because she was in Blackwater Landing?"

"Right."

"You were going to rape her, weren't you?"

"No!" Garrett started to cry. "I wasn't going to hurt her. Or anybody! And I didn't kill Billy! Everybody's trying to get me to say I did something that I didn't!"

Bell dug up a Kleenex and handed it to the boy.

The door swung open fast and Mason Germain walked in. He'd probably been the one watching through the one-way mirror and from the look on his face it was clear he'd lost patience. Sachs smelled his raw cologne; she'd come to detest the cloying scent.

"Mason—" Bell began.

"Listen to me, boy, you tell us where that girl is and you tell us now! 'Cause if you don't you're going to Lancaster and you're going to stay there till they put your ass on trial. . . . You heard about Lancaster, haven't you? Case you haven't, let me tell—"

"All right, that's enough," a high-pitched voice commanded.

A bantam strode into the room—a man even shorter than Mason, with razor-trimmed hair perfectly sprayed into place. A gray suit, all buttons snug, a baby blue shirt and striped tie. He wore shoes with three-inch heels.

"Don't say another word," he said to Garrett.

"Hello, Cal," Bell said, not pleased the visitor was here. The sheriff introduced Sachs to Calvin Fredericks, Garrett's lawyer.

"What the hell're you doing interrogating my client without me being here?" He nodded at Mason. "And what the hell was that Lancaster stuff about? I should have *you* put away for talking to him like that."

"He knows where the girl is, Cal," Mason muttered. "He's not telling us. He had his rights read to him. He—"

"A sixteen-year-old boy? Well, I'm inclined to get this case thrown out right now and get on to an early supper." He turned to Garrett. "Hey, young man, how you doing?"

"My face itches."

"They Mace you?"

"Nosir, just happens."

"We'll get it taken care of. Get some cream or something. Now, I'm going to be your lawyer. The state appointed me. You don't have to pay. They read you your rights? Told you you didn't have to say anything?"

"Yessir. But Sheriff Bell wanted to ask me some questions."

He said to Bell, "Oh, this's cute, Jim. What *were* you thinking of? Four deputies in here?"

Mason said, "We were thinking of Mary Beth McConnell. Who he kidnapped."

"Allegedly."

"And raped," Mason muttered.

"I didn't!" Garrett shouted.

"We got a bloody tissue with his come all over it," Mason snapped.

"No, no!" the boy said, his face growing alarmingly red. "Mary Beth hurt herself. That's what happened. She hit her head and I, like, wiped off the blood with a Kleenex I had in my pocket. And about the other . . . sometimes I just, you know, touch myself . . . I know I shouldn't. I know it's wrong. But I can't help it."

"Shhhh, Garrett," Fredericks said, "you don't have to explain a single thing to anybody." To Bell he said, "Now, this interrogation is over with. Take him back to the cell."

As Jesse Corn was leading him out the door Garrett stopped suddenly and turned to Sachs. "Please, you have to do something for me. Please! My room at home—it's got some jars."

"Go on, Jesse," Bell commanded. "Take him out."

But Sachs found herself saying, "Wait." To Garrett: "The jars? With your insects?"

The boy nodded. "Will you put water in them? Or at least let them go—outside—so they have a chance. Mr. and Mrs. Babbage, they won't do anything to keep them alive. Please. . . ."

She hesitated, sensing everyone's eyes upon her. Then nodded. "I'll do it. I promise."

Garrett gave her a faint smile.

Bell looked at Sachs with a cryptic gaze then nodded toward the door and Jesse led the boy out. The lawyer started after him but Bell stuck a finger in his chest. "You're not going anywhere, Cal. We're sitting here till McGuire shows up."

"Don't touch me, Bell," he muttered. But he sat as ordered. "Jesus Lord, what's all this folderol here, you talking to a sixteen-year-old without—"

"Shut the hell up, Cal. I wasn't fishing for a confession, which he didn't give us and I wouldn't use if he did. We got more evidence than we need to put him away forever. All I care about is finding Mary Beth. She's on the Outer Banks somewhere and that's a hell of a big haystack to find somebody in without some help."

"No way. He's not saying another word."

"She could die of thirst, Cal, she could starve to death. Heatstroke, get sick . . ."

When the lawyer gave no response, the sheriff said, "Cal, that boy's a menace. He's got a slew of incident reports against him—"

"Which my secretary read to me on the way over here. Hell, they're mostly for truancy. Oh, and for peeping— when he, funnily enough, wasn't even on the property of the complaining party, just hanging out on the sidewalk."

"The hornets' nest a few years ago," Mason said angrily. "Meg Blanchard."

"You released him," the lawyer pointed out happily. "Not even indicted."

Bell said, "This one's different, Cal. We got eyewitnesses, we got hard evidence and now Ed Schaeffer's dead. We can do to this boy pretty much what we feel like."

A slim man in a wrinkled blue seersucker suit walked into the interrogation room. Thinning gray hair, a lined fifty-five-year-old face. He glanced at Amelia with a vacant nod and at Fredericks with a darker expression. "I heard enough of that to make me think this's one of the easiest cases of murder one, kidnapping and sexual assault I've had in years."

Bell introduced Sachs to Bryan McGuire, the Paquenoke County prosecutor.

"He's sixteen," Fredericks said.

In an unflappable voice the D.A. said, "Isn't a venue in this state wouldn't try him as an adult and put him away for two hundred years."

"So, giddyap, McGuire," Fredericks said impatiently. "You're fishing for a bargain. I know that tone."

McGuire nodded to Bell and Sachs deduced that a conversation between the sheriff and the district attorney had occurred earlier about this very subject.

"Of *course* we're bargaining," Bell continued. "There's a good chance that girl's alive and we want to find her 'fore she's *not* alive anymore."

McGuire said, "We got so many charges on this one, Cal, you'd be amazed at how flexible we can be."

"Amaze me," the cocky defense lawyer said.

"I could go with two counts unlawful detention and assault and two counts first-degree manslaughter—one for Billy Stail, one for the deputy who died. Yessir, I'm willing to do that. All conditioned on finding the girl alive."

"Ed Schaeffer," the lawyer countered. "That was accidental."

Mason raged, "It was a fucking trap the boy set."

"I'll give you first manslaughter for Billy," McGuire offered, "and negligent homicide for the deputy."

Fredericks chewed on this for a moment. "Lemme see what I can do." His heels tapping noisily, the lawyer vanished in the direction of the cells to consult with his client. He returned five minutes later and he wasn't happy.

"Whatsa story?" Bell asked, discouraged as he read the lawyer's expression.

"No luck."

"Stonewalling?"

"Completely."

Bell muttered, "If you know something and you're not telling us, Cal, I don't give a shit about attorney-client privilege—"

"No, no, Jim, for real. He says he's protecting the girl. He says she's happy where she is and you oughta go looking for this guy in tan overalls and a white shirt."

Bell said, "He doesn't even have a good description and if he gave us one it'd change tomorrow because he's making it up."

McGuire slicked back his already-slicked-back hair. The defense used Aqua Net, Sachs could smell. The prosecution, Brylcreem. "Listen, Cal, this's your problem. I'm offering you what I'm offering. You get us the girl's whereabouts and she's alive, I'll go with reduced counts. You don't, I'll take it to trial and go for the moon. That boy'll never see the outside of a prison again. We both know it."

Silence for a moment.

Fredericks said, "I've got a thought."

"Uh-huh," McGuire said skeptically.

"No, listen . . . I had a case in Albemarle a spell back, a woman claimed her boy'd run away from home. But it seemed fishy."

"The *Williams* case?" McGuire asked. "That black woman?"

"That was it."

"I heard of that one. You represented her?" Bell asked.

"Right. She was giving us pretty odd stories and had a history of mental problems. I hired this psychologist over in Avery, hoping he could give me an insanity opinion. He ran some tests on her. During one of 'em she opened up and told us what had happened."

"Hypnosis—that recovered-memory crap?" McGuire asked.

"No, it's something else. He called it empty chair therapy. I don't exactly know how it works but it really started her talking. Like all she needed was a little push.

Let me give this guy a call and have him come over and talk to Garrett. The boy might see reason. . . . But"—now the defense got to poke a finger in Bell's chest—"everything they talk about's privileged and you don't get diddly unless the guardian ad litem and I say so first."

Bell caught McGuire's eye and nodded. The D.A. said, "Call him."

"Okay." Fredericks stepped toward the phone in the corner of the interrogation room.

Sachs said, "Excuse me?"

The lawyer turned to her.

"That case the psychologist helped you with? The Williams case?"

"Yeah?"

"What happened with her child? Did he run away?"

"Naw, the mother killed him. Baled him up in chicken wire and a cinder block and drowned him in a pond behind the house. Hey, Jim, how do I get an outside line?"

∎

The scream was so loud that it stung her dry throat like fire and for all Mary Beth knew permanently damaged her vocal cords.

The Missionary, walking by the edge of the woods, paused. His backpack was over one shoulder, a tank like a weed sprayer in his hand. He glanced around himself.

Please, please, please, Mary Beth was thinking. Ignoring the pain, she tried again. "Over here! Help me!"

He looked at the cabin. Started to walk away.

She took a deep breath, thought of Garrett Hanlon's clicking fingernails, his wet eyes and hard erection, thought of her father's brave death, of Virginia Dare. . . . And she gave the loudest scream she ever had.

This time the Missionary stopped, looked toward the cabin again. He pulled off his hat, left the rucksack and tank on the ground and started running toward her.

Thank you. . . . She started to sob. Oh, thank you!

He was thin and well-tanned. In his fifties but in good shape. Clearly an outdoorsman.

"What's wrong?" he called, gasping, when he was fifty feet away, slowing to a trot. "Are you all right?"

"Please!" she rasped. The pain in her throat was overwhelming. She spit more blood.

He walked cautiously up to the broken window, looking at the shards of glass on the ground.

"You need some help?"

"I can't get out. Somebody's kidnapped me—"

"Kidnapped?"

Mary Beth wiped her face, which was wet with tears of relief and sweat. "A high school kid from Tanner's Corner."

"Wait . . . I heard about that. Was on the news. *You're* the one he kidnapped?"

"That's right."

"Where is he now?"

She tried to speak but her throat hurt too much. She breathed deeply and finally responded, "I don't know. He left last night. Please . . . do you have any water?"

"A canteen, with my gear. I'll get it."

"And call the police. You have a phone?"

"Not with me." He shook his head and grimaced. "I'm doing contract work for the county." He nodded toward the backpack and tank. "We're killing marijuana, you know, that kids plant out here. The county gives us those cell phones but I never bother with mine. You hurt bad?" He studied her head, the crusted blood.

"It's okay. But . . . water. I need water."

He trotted back to the woods and for a terrible moment she was afraid he'd keep going. But he picked up an olive drab canteen and ran back. She took it with trembling hands and forced herself to drink slowly. The water was hot and musty but she'd never had as wonderful a drink as this.

"I'm going to try and get you out," the man said. He walked to the front door. A moment later she heard a faint thud as he either kicked the door or tried to break it with his shoulder. Another. Two more. He picked up a rock and slammed it into the wood. It had no effect. He returned to the window. "It's not budging." He wiped sweat from his forehead as he examined the bars on the windows. "Man, he built himself a prison here. Hacksaw'd take hours. Okay, I'll go for help. What's your name?"

"Mary Beth McConnell."

"I'm going to call the police then come back and get you out."

"Please, don't be long."

"I got a friend isn't too far away. I'll call nine-one-one from his place and we'll come back. That boy . . . does he have a gun?"

"I don't know. I didn't see one. But I don't know."

"You sit tight, Mary Beth. You're gonna be okay. I don't run as a rule but I'll do some running today." He turned and started through the field.

"Mister . . . thank you."

But he didn't acknowledge her gratitude. He sprinted through the sedge and tall grass and disappeared in the woods, not even pausing to collect his gear. Mary Beth remained standing in front of the window, cradling the canteen as if it were a newborn baby.

. . . chapter nineteen

On the street across from the lockup Sachs saw Lucy Kerr sitting on a park bench in front of a deli, drinking an Arizona iced tea. She crossed the street. The women nodded to each other.

Sachs noticed a sign on the front of the place. COLD BEER. She asked Lucy, "You have an open-container law in Tanner's Corner?"

"Yeah," Lucy said. "And we take it pretty serious. The law is if you're going to drink from a container it's got to be open."

Took just a second for the joke to register. Sachs laughed. She said, "You want something stronger?"

Lucy nodded at the iced tea. "This'll do fine."

Sachs came out a minute later with a Sam Adams ale foaming excessively in a large Styrofoam cup. She sat down next to the deputy. She told Lucy about the discussion between McGuire and Fredericks, about the psychologist.

"Hope that works," Lucy said. "Jim was figuring there's gotta be thousands of old houses on the Outer Banks. We'll have to narrow down the search some."

They said nothing for a few minutes. A lone teenager clattered past on a noisy skateboard and vanished. Sachs commented on the absence of children in town.

"True," Lucy said. "Hadn't thought about it but there aren't a lot of kids here. I think most of the young couples've moved away, places closer to the interstate maybe or bigger towns. Tanner's Corner's not the sort of place for anybody on the way up."

Sachs asked, "You have any? Children?"

"No. Buddy and I never did. Then we split up and I never met anybody after that. My big regret, I'll have to say. No kids."

"How long you been divorced?"

"Three years."

Sachs was surprised the woman hadn't remarried. She was very attractive—especially her eyes. When Sachs had been a professional model in New York, before she'd decided to follow in her father's law enforcement career, she'd spent a lot of time with many gorgeous people. But so often their gazes were vacant; if the eyes aren't beautiful, Amelia Sachs had concluded, neither is the person.

Sachs told Lucy, "Oh, you'll meet somebody, have a family."

"I've got my job," Lucy said quickly. "Don't have to do everything in life, you know."

Something was going unsaid here—something that she felt Lucy wanted to divulge. Sachs wondered whether she should push it or not. She tried the oblique approach. "Must be a thousand men in Paquenoke County dying to go out with you."

After a moment Lucy said, "Fact is, I don't date much."

"Really?"

Another pause. Sachs looked up and down the dusty, deserted street. The skateboarder was long gone. Lucy took a breath to say something, opted for a long sip of iced tea instead. Then, on impulse, it seemed, the police-woman said, "You know that medical problem I told you about?"

Sachs nodded.

"Breast cancer. Wasn't too advanced but the doctor said they probably should do a double radical. And that's what they did."

"I'm sorry," Sachs said, frowning with sympathy. "You go through the treatments?"

"Yup. Was bald for a while. Interesting look." She sipped more of the iced tea. "I'm three and a half years in remission. So far, so good." Lucy continued, "Really threw me for a loop, that happening. No history of it in my family. Grandmother's healthy as a horse. My mom's still working five days a week at the Mattamuskeet National Wildlife Reserve. She and my dad hike the Appalachian two, three times a year."

Sachs asked, "You can't have kids because of the radiation?"

"Oh, no, they used a shield. It's just . . . I guess I'm not inclined to date much. You know where a man's hand goes right after you kiss serious for the first time. . . ."

Sachs couldn't argue with *that*.

"I'll meet some nice guy and we'll have coffee or something but in ten minutes I start to worry about what he's going to think when he finds out. And I end up not returning his phone calls."

Sachs said, "So you've given up on a family?"

"Maybe, when I'm older, I'll meet a widower with a couple grown kids. That'd be nice."

She said this casually but Sachs could hear in her voice that she'd repeated it to herself often. Maybe every day.

Lucy lowered her head, sighed. "I'd give up my badge in a minute to have children. But, hey, life doesn't always go in the direction we want."

"And your ex left you after the operation? What's his name again?"

"Bud. Not *right* after. But eight months later. Hell, I can't blame him."

"Why do you say that?"

"What?"

"That you can't blame him?" Sachs asked.

"Just, I can't. I changed and ended up being different. I turned into something he hadn't bargained for."

Sachs said nothing for a moment then she offered, "Lincoln's different. About as different as they come."

Lucy considered this. "So there's more to you two than just being, what would you say, colleagues?"

"That's right," Sachs said.

"Thought that might be the case." Then she laughed. "Hey, you're a tough cop from the big city. . . . How do *you* feel about children?"

"I'd like some. Pop—my father—wanted grandkids. He was a cop too. Liked the idea of three generations on the force. Thought *People* magazine might do a story on us or something. He loved *People*."

"Past tense?"

"Died a few years ago."

"Killed on his beat?"

Sachs debated but finally answered, "Cancer."

Lucy said nothing for a moment. Looked at Sachs in profile, back to the lockup. "Can he have children? Lincoln?"

The foam was down in the cup of beer and she sipped in earnest. "Theoretically, yes."

And chose not to tell Lucy that this morning, when they were at the Neurologic Research Institute in Avery, the reason that Sachs had slipped out of the room with Dr. Weaver was to ask if the operation would affect Rhyme's chances of having children. The doctor had said that it wouldn't and had started to explain about the intervention necessary that would enable her to get pregnant. But just then Jim Bell had showed up with his plea for help.

Nor did she tell the deputy that Rhyme had deflected the subject of children every time it came up and she was left to speculate why he was so reluctant to consider the matter. It could have been any number of reasons, of course: his fear that having a family might interfere with his practice of criminalistics, which he needed to keep his sanity. Or his knowledge that quadriplegics, statistically at least, have a shorter life span than the nondisabled. Or maybe he wanted to have the freedom to wake up one day and decide that he'd had enough and that he didn't want to live any longer. Perhaps it was all of these, coupled with the belief that he and Sachs would hardly be the most normal of parents (though she would have countered: And what exactly *is* normal nowadays?).

Lucy mused, "I always wondered if I had kids would I keep working? How 'bout you?"

"I carry a weapon but I'm mostly crime scene. I'd cut out the risky stuff. Have to drive slower too. I've got a Camaro that'll churn three hundred sixty horses sitting in my garage in Brooklyn right now. Can't really see having one of those baby seats in it." A laugh. "I guess I'd have to learn how to drive a Volvo station wagon with an automatic. Maybe I could take lessons."

"I can see you laying rubber pulling out of the Food Lion parking lot."

Silence fell between them, that odd silence of strangers who've shared complicated secrets and realize they can go no further with them.

Lucy looked at her watch. "I should get back to the station house. Help Jim make calls about the Outer Banks." She tossed the empty bottle into the trash. Shook her head. "I keep thinking about Mary Beth. Wondering where she is, if she's okay, if she's scared."

As she said this, though, Amelia Sachs was thinking not about the girl but about Garrett Hanlon. Because they'd been talking about children Sachs was imagining how she'd feel if *she* had a son who was accused of murder and kidnapping. Who was looking at the prospect of spending the night in jail. Maybe a hundred nights, maybe thousands.

Lucy paused. "You headed back?"

"In a minute or two."

"Hope to see you 'fore you leave." The deputy disappeared up the street.

A few minutes later the door to the lockup opened and Mason Germain walked out. She'd never once seen him smile and he wasn't smiling now. He looked around the street but didn't notice her. He strode over the broken sidewalk and disappeared into one of the buildings—a store or bar—on the way to the County Building.

Then a car pulled up across the street and two men got out. Garrett's lawyer, Cal Fredericks, was one and the other was a heavyset man in his forties. He was in a shirt and tie—the top button undone and the sloppy knot of his striped tie pulled down a few inches from his throat. His sleeves were rolled up and his navy sports jacket was draped over his arm. His tan slacks were savagely wrinkled. His face had the kindness of a grade-school teacher. They walked inside.

Sachs tossed the cup in an oil drum outside the deli. She crossed the empty street and followed them into the lockup.

. . . chapter twenty

Cal Fredericks introduced Sachs to Doctor Elliott Penny.

"Oh, you're working with Lincoln Rhyme?" the doctor asked, surprising Sachs.

"That's right."

"Cal told me it was mostly because of you two they caught Garrett. Is he here? Lincoln?"

"He's at the County Building right now. Probably won't be there long."

"We have a friend in common. I'd like to say hi. I'll stop by if I get a chance."

Sachs said, "He should be there for another hour or so." She turned to Cal Fredericks. "Can I ask you something?"

"Yes'm," the defense lawyer said cautiously; Sachs was, in theory, working for the enemy.

"Mason Germain was talking to Garrett in the lockup earlier. He mentioned Lancaster. What's that?"

"The Violent Felony Detention Center. He'll be transferred there after the arraignment. Held there until the trial."

"It's juvenile?"

"No, no. Adult."

"But he's sixteen," Sachs said.

"Oh, McGuire'll try him as an adult—if we can't work out a plea."

"How bad is it?"

"What, Lancaster?" The lawyer shrugged his narrow shoulders. "He'll get hurt. No getting around that. I don't know how bad. But he *will* get hurt. A boy like him's gonna be at the bottom of the food chain at VFDC."

"Can he be segregated?"

"Not there. It's all general population. Just a big holding pen, basically. The best we can do is hope the guards look out for him."

"How 'bout bail?"

Fredericks laughed. "There's no judge in the world'd set bail in a case like this. He's a bond-jumper waiting to happen."

"Is there anything we can do to get him into a different facility? Lincoln's got friends in New York."

"New York?" Fredericks gave her a genteel but wry Southern smile. "I don't think that carries much weight south of the Mason-Dixon line. Probably not even west of the Hudson." He nodded toward Dr. Penny. "No, our best bet is to get Garrett to cooperate then work out a plea."

"Shouldn't his foster parents be here?"

"Should be, yep. I called them but Hal said the boy's on his own. He wouldn't even let me talk to Maggie—his mother."

"But Garrett can't be making decisions on his own," Sachs said. "He's just a boy."

"Oh," Fredericks explained, "before the arraignment or plea deal's agreed to the court'll appoint a guardian ad litem. Don't worry, he'll be looked out for."

Sachs turned to the doctor. "What're you going to do? This empty chair test?"

Dr. Penny glanced at the lawyer, who nodded his okay to explain. "It's not a test. It's a type of Gestalt therapy— a behavioral technique that's known for getting very fast results in understanding certain types of behavior. I'm going to have Garrett imagine that Mary Beth is sitting in a chair in front of him and have him talk to her. Explain to her why he kidnapped her. I hope to get him to understand that she's upset and frightened and that what he did was wrong. That she'll be better off if he tells us where she is."

"And this'll work?"

"It's not really intended for this type of situation but I think it could get results."

The lawyer glanced at his watch. "You ready, Doctor?" He nodded.

"Let's go." The doctor and Fredericks disappeared into the interrogation room.

Sachs hung back, got a cup of water from the cooler. Sipped it slowly. When the deputy at the front desk turned his attention back to his newspaper Sachs quickly stepped through the door of the observation room, where the video camera sat for taping suspects. The room was empty. She pulled the door shut and sat down, peered into the interrogation room. She could see Garrett in one chair in the middle of the room. The doctor sat at the table. Cal Fredericks was in the corner, his arms folded, ankle resting on a knee, revealing the height of his shoes' stubby heels.

A third chair, unoccupied, sat facing Garrett.

Cokes were on the table. The cans sweated with condensation.

Through the cheap, clattering speaker above the mirror Sachs heard their voices.

"Garrett, I'm Doctor Penny. How're you?"

No answer.

"It's a little warm in here, isn't it?"

Still Garrett said nothing. He looked down. Clicked

the nails on his finger and thumb. Sachs couldn't hear the sound. She found her own thumbnail digging into the flesh of her index finger. Felt moisture, saw the blood. Stop it stop it stop it, she thought and forced herself to lower her hands to her sides.

"Garrett, I'm here to help you. I'm working with your lawyer, Mr. Fredericks here, and we're trying to get you a reduced sentence for what's happened. We can help you but we need your cooperation."

Fredericks said, "The doctor's going to talk to you, Garrett. We're going to try to find out a few things. But everything you say is going to be just between us. We won't tell anybody else without your permission. You understand that?"

He nodded.

"Remember, Garrett," the doctor said, "we're the good guys. We're on your side. . . . Now, I want to try something."

Her eyes were on the boy's face. He scratched at a welt. He said, "I guess."

"See that chair there?"

Dr. Penny nodded toward the chair and the boy glanced at it. "I see it."

"We're going to play sort of a game. You're going to pretend there's somebody real important in that chair."

"Like the President?"

"No, I mean, somebody important to you. Somebody you know in real life. You're going to pretend they're sitting there in front of you. I want you to talk to them. And I want you to be real honest with them. You tell them whatever you want to say. Share your secrets with them. If you're mad at them you tell them that. If you love them tell them so. If you want them—like you'd want a girl—tell them. Remember it's okay to say anything at all. Nobody's going to be upset with you."

"Just talk to the chair?" Garrett asked the doctor. "Why?"

"Go on."

"This is . . . it's kinda hard."

Cal Fredericks was sitting forward, pen held over a pad of paper.

Dr. Penny said softly, "Let's set the scene. . . . Mary Beth's right there. She's waiting. She wants you to say it."

Garrett asked, "She does? You think so?"

"I do," the doctor reassured him. "Do you want to tell her something about where she is now? Where you took her? What it's like? Maybe why you took her to that particular place?"

"No," Garrett said. "I don't want to say anything about that."

"Then what do you want to say?"

"I . . ." His voice faded. His nails clicked.

"I know it's difficult."

Sachs too was sitting forward in her chair. Come on, she found herself thinking, come on, Garrett. We want to help you. Meet us halfway.

Dr. Penny continued, his voice hypnotic. "Go ahead, Garrett. There's Mary Beth right there in the chair. She's waiting. She's wondering what you're going to say. Talk to her." The doctor pushed the soft drink closer to Garrett and he took several long drinks, the cuffs ringing against the can as he lifted it with both hands. After this momentary break the doctor continued. "What is there that you really want to say to her? That one important thing? I can see that you want to say it. I can see that you need to say it. And I think that she needs to hear it."

The doctor pushed the empty chair closer. "There she is, Garrett, sitting there right in front of you, looking at you. What's that one thing you'd say to her that you haven't been able to? Now's your chance. Go ahead."

Another swallow of Coke. Sachs noticed that the boy's hands were shaking. What was coming? she wondered. What was he about to say?

Suddenly, startling both the men in the room, Garrett

leaned forward and blurted to the chair, "I really, really like you, Mary Beth. And . . . and I think I love you." He took several deep breaths, clicked his fingernails a few times then gripped the arms of the chair nervously and lowered his head, his face red as sunset.

"That's what you wanted to say?" the doctor asked.

Garrett nodded.

"Anything else?"

"Uhm, no."

This time it was the doctor who glanced at the lawyer and shook *his* head.

"Mister," Garrett began. "Doctor . . . I've, like, got this question?"

"Go ahead, Garrett."

"Okay . . . there's this book of mine I'd really like to have from my house. It's called *The Miniature World*. Would that be okay?"

"We'll see if that can be arranged," the doctor said. He looked past Garrett to Fredericks, who rolled his eyes in frustration. The men rose, pulled on their jackets.

"That'll be it for now, Garrett."

The boy nodded.

Sachs quickly rose and stepped outside into the lockup office. The desk deputy hadn't noticed her eavesdropping.

Fredericks and the doctor stepped outside as Garrett was led back into the cell.

Jim Bell pushed through the doorway. Fredericks introduced him to the doctor, and the sheriff asked, "Anything?"

Fredericks shook his head. "Not a thing."

Bell said grimly, "Was just over with the magistrate. They're gonna arraign him at six and get him over to Lancaster tonight."

"*Tonight?*" Sachs said.

"Better to get him out of town. There're a few people around here'd like to take matters into their own hands."

Dr. Penny said, "I can try again later. He's very agitated right now."

" 'Course he's agitated," Bell muttered. "He just got himself arrested for murder and kidnapping. That'd make me agitated too. Do whatever you want in Lancaster but McGuire's slapping the charges on him and we're shipping him out 'fore dark. And by the way, Cal, I have to tell you: McGuire's going for murder one."

■

In the County Building, Amelia Sachs found Rhyme as ornery as she'd thought he'd be.

"Come on, Sachs, help poor Ben with the equipment and let's get on our way. I told Dr. Weaver I'd be at the hospital sometime this *year*."

But she just stood at the window, looking out. Finally she said, "Rhyme."

The criminalist looked up, squinted as he studied her the way he'd study a bit of trace evidence he couldn't identify. "I don't like that, Sachs."

"What?"

"I don't like it one bit. Ben, no, you have to take the armature off before you pack it up."

"Armature?" Ben was struggling to close up the boxy ALS—alternative light source, used to image substances invisible to the unaided eye.

"The wand," Sachs explained and took over packing up the device.

"Thanks." Ben began to coil computer wire.

"That look of yours, Sachs. *That's* what I don't like. Your look and the tone of your voice."

"Ben," she asked, "could you give us a few minutes alone?"

"No, he couldn't," Rhyme snapped. "We don't have time. We've got to get packed up and out of here."

"Five minutes," she said.

Ben looked from Rhyme to Sachs and because Sachs stared at him with an imploring gaze, not an angry gaze, she won the contest and the big man stepped out of the room.

Rhyme tried to preempt her. "Sachs, we've done all we can do. We saved Lydia. We've caught the perp. He'll take a plea and tell them where Mary Beth is."

"He's not going to tell where she is."

"But that's not our problem. There's nothing more—"

"I don't think he did it."

"Killed Mary Beth? I agree. The blood shows she's probably alive but—"

"I mean, killed Billy."

Rhyme tossed his head, to flick an infuriating tail of hair off his forehead. "You believe that man in the tan overalls story that Jim mentioned?"

"Yes, I do."

"Sachs, he's a troubled boy and you feel sorry for him. *I* feel sorry for him. But—"

"That doesn't have anything to do with it."

"You're right, it doesn't," he snapped. "The *only* thing that's relevant is the evidence. And the evidence shows there's no man in overalls and that Garrett's guilty."

"The evidence *suggests* he's guilty, Rhyme. It doesn't prove it. Evidence can be interpreted in a lot of different ways. Besides, I've got some evidence of my own."

"Such as?"

"He asked me to take care of his insects for him."

"So?"

"Doesn't it seem a little odd that a cold-blooded killer would care what happened to some goddamn insects?"

"That's not evidence, Sachs. That's his strategy. It's psychological warfare, trying to break down our defenses. The boy's smart, remember. High IQ, good grades. And look at his reading matter. It's heady stuff—he's learned a lot from the insects. And one thing about them is that they have no moral code. All they care about is surviving. *Those* are the lessons he's learned. *That's* been his child development. It's sad, but it's not our problem."

"You know that trap he set. The pine-bough trap?"

Rhyme nodded.

"It was only two feet deep. And the hornets' nest inside? It was empty. No wasps. And the ammonia bottle wasn't rigged to hurt anybody. It was just so he'd have some warning when a search party was getting close to the mill."

"That's not empirical evidence, Sachs. Like the bloody tissue, for instance."

"He said he had been masturbating. And that Mary Beth hit her head and he wiped the wound with it. Anyway, if he raped her what would be the point of a tissue?"

"To clean up afterward."

"Doesn't fit any rape profile I know."

Rhyme quoted himself, from the foreword of his criminalistics textbook, " 'A profile is a *guide*. Evidence is—' "

"—'God,' " she completed the quotation. "Okay, then—there were plenty of footprints at the scene. Remember, it was trampled. Some of those might've been the overall man's."

"There are no other prints on the murder weapon."

"He claims the man wore gloves," she countered.

"But no leather grain prints either."

"Could've been cloth. Let me test it and—"

" '*Could* have, *could* have. . . .' Come on, Sachs, this is pure speculation."

"But you should've heard him when he was talking about Mary Beth. He was *concerned* about her."

"He was acting. What's my number one rule?"

"You have a lot of number one rules," she muttered.

He continued unfazed, "You can't trust witnesses."

"He thinks he loves her, he cares for her. He really believes he's protecting her."

A man's voice interrupted. "Oh, he *is* protecting her." Sachs and Rhyme looked to the doorway. It was Dr. Elliott Penny. He added, "Protecting her from himself."

Sachs introduced them.

"I wanted to meet you, Lincoln," Dr. Penny said. "I specialize in forensic psychology. Bert Markham and I were on a panel together at the AALEO last year and he speaks highly of you."

"Bert's a good friend," Rhyme said. "Just appointed head of Chicago PD Forensics."

Dr. Penny nodded toward the corridor. "Garrett's lawyer's in there with the D.A. right now but I don't think the outcome's going to be very good for the boy."

"What did you mean just then, about protecting her from himself?" Sachs asked cynically. "Some kind of multiple personality crap?"

"No," replied the doctor, not at all troubled by her abrasive skepticism. "There's definitely some mental or emotion disturbance at work but it's nothing as exotic as multiple personalities. Garrett knows *exactly* what he did to Mary Beth and Billy Stail. I'm pretty sure he's hidden her someplace to keep her away from Blackwater Landing, where he probably *did* kill those other people over the past couple of years. And scared—what was his name?—the Wilkes boy into killing himself. I think he was planning to rape and kill Mary Beth at the same time he killed Billy but that the part of him that quote *loves* her wouldn't let him. He got her away from Blackwater Landing as fast as he could to keep from hurting her. I think he *did* rape her, though to him it's not rape, just the consummation of what he sees as their quote *relationship*. As normal to him as a husband and wife on their honeymoon. But he still felt the urge to kill her and so he went back to Blackwater Landing the next day and got a substitute victim, Lydia Johansson. He was undoubtedly going to murder her in place of Mary Beth."

"I hope you're not billing the defense," Sachs said acerbically, "if that's your sympathetic testimony."

Dr. Penny shook his head. "Based on the evidence I've

heard that boy's going to jail with or without expert witnesses."

"I don't think he killed the boy. And I think the kidnapping's not as black and white as we're making it."

Dr. Penny shrugged. "My professional opinion is that he did. Obviously I haven't run all the tests but he exhibits clear dissocial and sociopathic behavior—and I'm thinking of all *three* major diagnostic systems. *The International Classification of Diseases, the DSM-IV* and *the Revised Psychopathy Checklist.* Would I have to run the complete battery of tests? Of course. But he clearly presents with an affect-less antisocial/criminal personality. He's got a high IQ, he exhibits strategic thinking patterns and organized-offender behavior, considers revenge acceptable, displays no remorse . . . he's a very dangerous person."

"Sachs," Rhyme said, "what's the point? This isn't our game anymore."

She ignored him and his piercing eyes. "But, Doctor—"

The doctor held up a hand. "Can I ask *you* a question?"

"What?"

"Do you have children?"

A hesitation. "No," she responded. "Why?"

"You understandably feel sympathy for him—I think we all do—but you might be confusing that with some latent maternal sense."

"What does that mean?"

The doctor continued, "I mean that if you have some desire to have children yourself you might not be able to take an objective view about a sixteen-year-old boy's innocence or guilt. Especially one who's an orphan and has had a tough time in life."

"I can take a perfectly objective role," she snapped. "There's just too much that doesn't add up. Garrett's motives don't make sense, he—"

"Motives are the weak leg of the evidentiary stool, Sachs, you know that."

"I don't need any more maxims, Rhyme," she snapped.

The criminalist sighed in frustration, glanced at the clock.

Dr. Penny continued. "I heard you asking Cal Fredericks about Lancaster, about what was going to happen to the boy."

She lifted an eyebrow.

"Well, I think you can help him," the doctor said. "The best thing you can do is to just spend some time with him. The county'll assign a caseworker to liaise with the guardian the court appoints and you'll have to get their approval but I'm sure it can be arranged. He might even open up with you about Mary Beth."

As she was considering this Thom appeared in the doorway. "Van's outside, Lincoln."

Rhyme glanced at the map one last time and then turned toward the doorway. "'Once more into the breach, dear friends. . . .'"

Jim Bell walked into the room and rested his hand on Rhyme's insensate arm. "We're organizing a search of the Outer Banks. With a little luck we'll have her in a few days. Listen, I can't thank you enough, Lincoln."

Rhyme deflected the gratitude with a nod and wished the sheriff good luck.

"I'll come visit you at the hospital, Lincoln," Ben said. "I'll bring some scotch. When're they going to let you start drinking again?"

"Not soon enough."

"I'll help Ben finish up," Sachs told him.

Bell said to her, "We'll get you a ride over to Avery."

She nodded. "Thanks. I'll be there soon, Rhyme."

But the criminalist had, it seemed, already departed from Tanner's Corner, mentally if not physically, and he said nothing. Sachs heard only the vanishing whine as the Storm Arrow steamed down the corridor.

∎

Fifteen minutes later they had most of the forensic equipment put away and Sachs sent Ben Kerr home, thanking him for his volunteer efforts.

In his wake Jesse Corn had appeared at Sachs's side. She wondered if he'd been staking out the corridor, waiting for a chance to catch her alone.

"He's quite somebody, isn't he?" Jesse asked. "Mr. Rhyme." The deputy began stacking boxes that didn't need to be stacked.

"That he is," she said noncommittally.

"That operation he's talking about. Will it fix him?"

It'll kill him. It'll make him worse. It'll turn him into a vegetable.

"No."

She thought Jesse would ask, Then why's he doing it? But the deputy offered another one of his sayings: "Sometimes you just find yourself standing in need to do *something*. No matter it seems hopeless."

Sachs shrugged, thinking: Yeah, sometimes you just do.

She snapped the locks on a microscope case and coiled the last of the electrical cords. She noticed a stack of books on the table, the ones she'd found in Garrett's room in his foster parents' house. She picked up *The Miniature World,* the book that the boy had asked Dr. Penny for. She opened it. Flipped through the pages, read a passage.

> There are 4,500 known species of mammals in the world but 980,000 known species of insects and an estimated two to three million more not yet discovered. The diversity and astonishing resilience of these creatures arouses more than simple admiration. One thinks of Harvard biologist and entomologist E. O. Wilson's coined term "Biofilia," by which he means the emotional affiliation humans feel toward other living organisms. There is certainly as great an

opportunity for such a connection with insects as there is for a pet dog or prize racehorse, or indeed, other humans.

She glanced out into the corridor, where Cal Fredericks and Bryan McGuire were still engaged in their complicated verbal fencing match. Garrett's lawyer was clearly losing.

Sachs snapped the book shut. Hearing in her mind the doctor's words.

The best thing you can do is to just spend some time with him.

Jesse said, "Say, might be a little hectic to go out to the pistol range. But you interested in some coffee?"

Sachs laughed to herself. So she'd got the Starbucks invite after all. "Probably shouldn't. I'm going to drop this book over at the lockup. Then I have to go over to the hospital in Avery. How 'bout a rain check?"

"You got it."

In Eddie's, the bar a block from the lockup, Rich Culbeau said sternly, "This ain't no game."

"I don't think it's a game," Sean O'Sarian said. "I only *laughed*. I mean, shit, was just a laugh. I was looking at that commercial there." Nodding at the greasy TV screen above the Beer Nuts rack. "Where this guy's trying to get to the airport and his car—"

"You do that too much. You prank around. You don't pay attention."

"All right. I'm listening. We're going in the back. The door'll be open."

"That's what I was gonna ask," Harris Tomel said. "The back door to the lockup's never open. It's always locked and it's got that, you know, bar on the inside."

"The bar'll be off and the door'll be *un*locked. Okay?"

"You say so," Tomel said skeptically.

"It'll be open." Culbeau continued, "We go in. There'll be a key to his cell on the table, that little metal one. You know it?"

Of course they knew the table. Anybody who'd spent a night in the Tanner's Corner lockup had to've barked his shins on that fucking table bolted to the floor near the door, especially if they were drunk.

"Yeah, go ahead," O'Sarian said, now paying attention.

"We unlock the cell and go in. I'm going to hit the kid with the pepper spray. Put a bag over him—I got a crocus sack like I use for kittens in the pond, just put that over his head and get him out the back. He can shout if he wants but won't nobody hear him. Harris, you be waiting with the truck. Back it right up near the door. Keep it in gear."

"Where we gonna take him to?" O'Sarian asked.

"None of our places," Culbeau said, wondering if O'Sarian was thinking they *were* going to take a kidnapped prisoner to one of their houses. Which, if he did, meant the skinny kid was even more stupid than Culbeau thought he was. "The old garage, near the tracks."

"Good," O'Sarian offered.

"We get him out there. I got my propane torch. And we start on him. Five minutes is all it'll take, I figure, and he'll tell us where Mary Beth is."

"And then do we . . ." O'Sarian's voice faded.

"What?" Culbeau snapped. Then whispered, "You gonna say something you maybe don't want to say out loud in public?"

O'Sarian whispered back, "*You* were just talking 'bout using a torch on the boy. Doesn't seem to me that's any worse than what I'm asking—about afterward."

Which Culbeau had to agree with, though of course he didn't tell O'Sarian he may have a point. Instead he said only, "Accidents happen."

"They do," Tomel agreed.

O'Sarian toyed with a beer-bottle cap, dug some crud out from under his nails with it. He'd turned moody.

"What?" Culbeau asked.

"This's getting risky. Woulda been easier to take the boy in the woods. At the mill."

"But he's *not* in the woods at the mill anymore," Tomel said.

O'Sarian shrugged. "Just wondering if it's worth the money."

"You wanta back out?" Culbeau scratched his beard, thinking it was so hot he ought to shave it but then you could see his triple chin more. "I'd rather split it two ways than three."

"Naw, you know I don't want to. Ever-thing's fine." O'Sarian's eyes strayed to the TV again. A movie caught his attention and he shook his head, eyes wide, looking at one of the actresses.

"Hold on here," Tomel said, eyes out the window. "Take a look." He was nodding outside.

That redheaded policewoman from New York, the one so damn fast with the knife, was walking up the street, carrying a book.

Tomel said, "Nice-looking lady. I could use a little of that."

But Culbeau remembered her cold eyes and the steady point of the knife under O'Sarian's chin. He said, "Juice ain't worth the squeeze."

The redhead walked into the lockup.

O'Sarian was looking too. "Well, that fucks things up a bit."

Culbeau said slowly, "No, it don't. Harris, get that truck over there. And keep the motor running."

"But what about *her*?" Tomel asked.

Culbeau said, "I got plenty of pepper spray."

■

Inside the lockup Deputy Nathan Groomer leaned back in the rickety chair and nodded at Sachs.

Jesse Corn's infatuation had grown tedious; Nathan's formal smile was a relief to her. "Hello, miss."

"It's Nathan, right?"

"Right."

"That's some decoy there." Sachs looked down at his desk.

"This old thing?" he asked humbly.

"What is it?"

"Female mallard. About a year old. The duck. Not the decoy."

"You make that yourself?"

"Hobby of mine. Have a couple others at my desk in the main building. Check 'em out, you want. Thought you were leaving."

"Will be soon. How's he doing?"

"He who? Sheriff Bell?"

"No, I mean Garrett."

"Oh, I dunno. Mason went back to see him, had a talk. Tried to get him to tell where the girl was. But he wouldn't say anything."

"Mason's back there now?"

"No, he left."

"How about Sheriff Bell and Lucy?"

"Nope, they're all gone. Back at the County Building. Anything I can help you with?"

"Garrett wanted this book." She held it up. "Is it okay if I give it to him?"

"What is it, a Bible?"

"No, it's about insects."

Nathan took it and searched it carefully—for weapons, she supposed. Then he handed it back. "Creepy, that boy is. Somethin' out of a horror movie. You *oughta* give him a Bible."

"I think this is all he's interested in."

"I guess you're right about that. Slip your weapon in the lockbox there and I'll let you in."

Sachs put the Smith & Wesson inside and stepped to the door but Nathan was looking at her expectantly. She lifted an eyebrow.

"Well, miss, I understand you got a knife too."

"Oh, sure. I forgot about it."

"Rules is rules, you know."

She handed over the switchblade. He dropped it in beside the gun.

"You want the cuffs too?" She touched her handcuff case.

"Nope. Can't get into much trouble with those. Course, we had us a reverend who did once. But that was only 'cause his wife come home early and found him hitched to the bedpost with Sally Anne Carlson atop him. Come on, I'll let you in."

■

Rich Culbeau, flanked by nervous Sean O'Sarian, stood beside a dying lilac bush at the back of the lockup.

The back door to the place overlooked a large field, filled with grass and trash and parts of old cars and appliances. More than a few limp condoms too.

Harris Tomel drove his sparkling Ford F-250 up over the curb and backed around. Culbeau thought he should've come the other way because this looked a little obvious but there was nobody out on the street and, besides, after the custard stand closed, there was no reason for anybody to come down here. At least the truck was new and had a good muffler; it was quiet.

"Who's in the front office?" O'Sarian asked.

"Nathan Groomer."

"That girl cop with him?"

"I don't know. How the hell do I know? But if she is she'll have her gun and that knife she was tattooing you with in the lockbox."

"Won't Nathan hear if the girl screams?"

Recalling the redhead's eyes and the flash of the blade once more, Culbeau said, "The boy'll be more likely to scream than her."

"Well, then, what if *he* does?"

"We'll get the bag over him fast. Here." Culbeau handed O'Sarian a red-and-white canister of pepper spray. "Aim low 'cause people duck."

"Does it? . . . I mean, will it get on us? The spray?"

"Not if you don't shoot yourself in the fucking face. It's a stream. Not like a cloud."

"Which of 'em should I take?"

"The boy."

"What if the girl's closer to me?"

Culbeau muttered, "She's mine."

"But—"

"She's mine."

"Okay," O'Sarian agreed.

They dipped their heads as they went past a filthy window in the back of the lockup and paused at the metal door. Culbeau noticed that it was open a half inch. "See, it's unlocked," he whispered. Feeling he'd scored some kind of point against O'Sarian. Then wondering why he felt he needed to. "Now, I'll nod. Then we go in fast, spray 'em both—and be generous with that shit." He handed O'Sarian a thick bag. "Then throw that over his head."

O'Sarian gripped the canister firmly, nodded at the second bag, which had appeared in Culbeau's hand. "So we're taking the girl too."

Culbeau sighed, said an exasperated, "Yeah, Sean. We are."

"Oh. Okay. Just wondered."

"When they're down just drag 'em out fast. Don't stop for nothing."

"Okay. . . . Oh, I was meaning to say. I got my Colt."

"What?"

"I got my .38. I brought it." He nodded toward his pocket.

Culbeau paused for a moment. Then he said, "Good." He closed his big hand around the door handle.

chapter twenty-two

Would this be his last view? he wondered.

From his hospital bed Lincoln Rhyme could see a park on the grounds of the University Medical Center in Avery. Lush trees, a sidewalk meandering through a rich, green lawn, a stone fountain that a nurse had told him was a replica of some famous well on the UNC campus at Chapel Hill.

From the bedroom in his town house on Central Park West in Manhattan, Rhyme could see sky and some of the buildings along Fifth Avenue. But the windows there were high off the floor and he couldn't see Central Park itself unless his bed was shoved right against the pane, which let him look down onto the grass and trees.

Here, perhaps because the facility had been built with SCI and neuro patients in mind, the windows were lower; even the views here were accessible, he thought wryly to himself.

Then wondered again whether or not the operation would have any success. Whether he'd even survive it.

Lincoln Rhyme knew that it was the inability to do the simple things that was the most frustrating.

Traveling from New York to North Carolina, for instance, had been such a project, so long anticipated, so carefully planned, that the difficulty of the journey had not troubled Rhyme at all. But the overwhelming burden of his injury was the heaviest when it came to the small tasks that a healthy person does without thinking. Scratching an itch on your temple, brushing your teeth, wiping your lips, opening a soda, sitting up in a chair to look out the window and watch sparrows bathe in the dirt of a garden. . . .

He wondered again how foolish he was being.

He'd had the best neurologists in the country and was a scientist himself. He'd read, and understood, the literature about the near impossibility of neuro improvement in a patient with a C4 spinal cord injury. Yet he was determined to go ahead with Cheryl Weaver's operation—despite the chance that this bucolic setting outside his window in a strange hospital in a strange town might be the very last image of nature he ever saw in this life.

Of course there are risks.

So why was he doing it?

Oh, there was a very good reason.

Yet it was a reason that the cold criminalist in him had trouble accepting and one that he'd never dare utter out loud. Because it had nothing to do with being able to prowl over a crime scene searching for evidence. Nothing to do with brushing his teeth or sitting up in bed. No, no, it was exclusively because of Amelia Sachs.

Finally he'd admitted the truth: that he'd grown terrified of losing her. He'd brooded that sooner or later she'd meet another Nick—the handsome undercover agent who'd been her lover a few years ago. This was inevitable, he figured, as long as he remained as immobile as he was. She wanted children. She wanted a normal life. And so Rhyme was willing to risk death, to risk making his condition worse, in the hope that he could improve.

He knew of course that the operation wouldn't allow him to stroll down Fifth Avenue with Sachs on his arm. He was simply hoping for a minuscule improvement—to move slightly closer to a normal life. Slightly closer to her. But summoning up his astonishing imagination, Rhyme could picture himself closing his hand on hers, squeezing it and feeling the faint pressure of her skin.

A small thing to everyone else in the world, but to Rhyme, a miracle.

Thom walked into the room. After a pause he said, "An observation."

"I don't want one. Where's Amelia?"

"I'm going to tell you anyway. You haven't had a drink in five days."

"I know. It pisses me off."

"You're getting in shape for the operation."

"Doctor's orders," Rhyme said testily.

"When have *those* ever meant anything to you?"

A shrug. "They're going to be pumping me full of who knows what kind of crap. I didn't think it would be *smart* to add to the cocktail in my bloodstream."

"It wouldn't've been. You're right. But you paid attention to your doctor. I'm proud of you."

"Oh, pride—now there's a *helpful* emotion."

But Thom was a waterfowl to Rhyme's rain. He continued, "But I want to say something."

"You're going to anyway whether *I* want you to or not."

"I've read a lot about this, Lincoln. The procedure."

"Oh, have you? On *your* time, I hope."

"I just want to say that if it doesn't work this time, we'll come back. Next year. Two years. Five years. It'll work then."

The sentiment within Lincoln Rhyme was as dead as

his spinal cord but he managed: "Thank you, Thom. Now, where the hell is that doctor? I've been hard at work catching psychotic kidnappers for these people. I think they'd be treating me a little better than this."

Thom said, "She's only ten minutes late, Lincoln. And we did change the appointment twice today."

"It's closer to twenty minutes. Ah, here we go."

The door to the hospital room swung open. And Rhyme looked up, expecting to see Dr. Weaver. But it wasn't the surgeon.

Sheriff Jim Bell, his face dotted with sweat, walked inside. In the corridor behind him was his brother-in-law, Steve Farr. Both men were clearly upset.

The criminalist's first thought was that they'd found Mary Beth's body. That the boy had in fact killed her. And his next thought was how badly Sachs would react to this news, having had her faith in the boy shattered.

But Bell had different news. "I'm sorry to have to tell you this, Lincoln." And Rhyme knew the message was something closer to him personally than just Garrett Hanlon and Mary Beth McConnell. "I was going to call," the sheriff said. "But then I figured you should hear it from somebody in person. So I came."

"What, Jim?" he asked.

"It's Amelia."

"What?" Thom asked.

"What about her?" Rhyme couldn't, of course, feel his heart pounding in his chest but he could sense the blood surge through his chin and temples. "What? Tell me!"

"Rich Culbeau and those buddies of his went by the lockup. I don't know what they had in mind exactly—probably no good—but anyway, what they found was my deputy, Nathan, cuffed, in the front office. And the cell was empty."

"Cell?"

"Garrett's cell," Bell continued, as if this explained everything.

Rhyme still didn't understand the significance. "What—"

In a gruff voice the sheriff said, "Nathan said that your Amelia trussed him up at gunpoint and broke Garrett outa jail. It's a felony escape. They're on the run, they're armed and nobody has a clue where they are."

III

Knuckle Time

chapter twenty-three

Running.

As best she could. Her legs ached from the waves of arthritic pain coursing through her body. She was drenched in sweat and was already dizzy from the heat and dehydration.

And she was still in shock at the thought of what she'd done.

Garrett was beside her, jogging silently through the forest outside Tanner's Corner.

This is way past stupid, lady. . . .

When Sachs had gone into the cell to give Garrett *The Miniature World* she'd watched the boy's happy face as he'd taken the book from her. A moment or two passed and, almost as if someone else were forcing her to, she'd reached through the bars, taken the boy by the shoulders. Flustered, he'd looked away. "No, look at me," she'd instructed. "Look."

Finally he had. She'd studied his blotched face, his twitching mouth, the dark pits of eyes, the thick brows. "Garrett, I need to know the truth. This is only between you and me. Tell me—did you kill Billy Stail?"

"I swear I didn't. I swear! It was that man—the one in the tan overalls. *He* killed Billy. That's the truth!"

"It's not what the facts show, Garrett."

"But people can see the same thing different," he'd responded in a calm voice. "Like, the way *we* can look at the same thing a fly sees but it doesn't look the same."

"What do you mean?"

"*We* see something moving—just a blur when somebody's hand's trying to swat the fly. But the way a *fly's* eyes work is he sees a hand stopping in midair a hundred times on its way down. Like a bunch of still pictures. It's the same hand, same motion, but the fly and us see it way different. And colors. . . . We look at something that's just solid red to us but some insects see a dozen different types of red."

The evidence suggests he's guilty, Rhyme. It doesn't prove it. Evidence can be interpreted in a lot of different ways.

"And Lydia," Sachs had persisted, gripping the boy even more firmly, "why'd you kidnap her?"

"I *told* everybody why. . . . 'Cause she was in danger too. Blackwater Landing . . . it's a dangerous place. People die there. People disappear. I was just protecting her."

Of course it's a dangerous place, she'd thought. But is it dangerous because of *you?*

Sachs had then said, "She said you were going to rape her."

"No, no, no. . . . She jumped into the water and her uniform got wet and torn. I saw her, you know, on top. Her chest. And I got kind of . . . turned on. But that's all."

"And Mary Beth. Did you hurt her, rape her?"

"No, no, no! I told you! She hit her head and I cleaned it off with that tissue. I'd never do that, not to Mary Beth."

Sachs had stared at him a moment longer.

Blackwater Landing . . . it's a dangerous place.

Finally she'd asked, "If I get you out of here will you take me to Mary Beth?"

Garrett had frowned. "I do that, then you'd bring her back to Tanner's Corner. And she might get hurt."

"It's the only way, Garrett. I'll get you out if you take me to her. We can make sure she'll be safe, Lincoln Rhyme and I."

"You can do that?"

"Yes. But if you don't agree you'll stay in jail for a long time. And if Mary Beth dies because of you it'll be murder, same as if you shot her. And you'll never get out of jail."

He'd looked out the window. It seemed that his eyes were following the flight of an insect. Sachs couldn't see it. "All right."

"How far away is she?"

"On foot, it'll take us eight, ten hours. Depending."

"On what?"

"On how many they got coming after us and how careful we are getting away."

Garrett said this quickly and his assured tone troubled Sachs—it was as if he'd been anticipating that someone would break him out or that he'd escape and he'd already considered avoiding pursuit.

"Wait here," she'd told him. And stepped back into the office. She'd reached into the lockbox, pulled out her gun and knife and, against all training and sense, turned the Smith & Wesson on Nathan Groomer.

"I'm sorry to do this," she whispered. "I need the key to his cell and then I need you to turn around and put your hands behind your back."

Wide-eyed, he'd hesitated, perhaps debating whether or not to go for his sidearm. Or—she realized now—probably not even thinking at all. Instinct or reflex or just plain anger might've driven him to pull the weapon from his holster.

"This is way past stupid, lady," he'd said.

"The key."

He opened the drawer and tossed it on the desk. He put his hands behind his back. She cuffed him with his own handcuffs and ripped the phone from the wall.

She'd then freed Garrett, cuffed him too. The back door to the lockup seemed to be open but she thought she heard footsteps and a running car engine outside. She opted for the front door. They'd made a clean escape, undetected.

Now, a mile from downtown, surrounded by brush and trees, the boy directed her along an ill-defined path. The chains of the cuffs clinked as he pointed in the direction they should go.

She was thinking: But, Rhyme, there was nothing I could do! Do you understand? I had no choice. If the detention center in Lancaster was like what she expected he'd be raped and beaten his first day there and perhaps killed before a week passed. Sachs knew too that this was the only way to find Mary Beth. Rhyme had exhausted the possibilities with the evidence and the defiance in Garrett's eyes told her that he'd never cooperate.

(No, I'm *not* confusing being maternal with being concerned, Dr. Penny. All I know is that if Lincoln and I had a son he'd be as single-minded and stubborn as we are and that if anything happened to us I'd pray for someone to look out for him the way I'm looking out for Garrett. . . .)

They moved quickly. Sachs was surprised at how elegantly the boy slipped through the woods, despite having his hands cuffed. He seemed to know exactly where to put his feet, what plants you could easily push through and which offered resistance. Where the ground was too soft to walk on.

"Don't step there," he said sternly. "That's clay from a Carolina bay. It'll hold you like glue."

They hiked for a half hour until the ground grew soupy and the air became fragrant with the smells of methane and decay. The route finally became impassable—the path ended in a thick bog—and Garrett led them to a two-lane asphalt road. They started through the brush beside the shoulder.

Several cars drove by leisurely, their drivers oblivious to the felony they were passing.

Sachs watched them enviously. On the lam for only twenty minutes, she reflected, and already she felt a heart-wrenching tug at the normalcy of everyone else's life—and at the dark turn hers had taken.

This is way past stupid, lady.

■

"Hey there!"

Mary Beth McConnell jerked awake.

With the heat and oppressive atmosphere in the cabin she'd fallen asleep on the smelly couch.

The voice, nearby, called again. "Miss, are you all right? Hello? Mary Beth?"

She leapt from the bed and walked quickly toward the broken window. She felt dizzy, had to lower her head for a minute, steady herself against the wall. The pain in her temple throbbed ferociously. She thought: Fuck you, Garrett.

The pain subsided, her vision cleared. And she continued to the window.

It was the Missionary. He had his friend with him, a tall, balding man in gray slacks and a work shirt. The Missionary carried an ax.

"Thank you, thank you!" she whispered.

"Miss, you all right?"

"I'm fine. He hasn't come back." Her voice was still painfully raw. He handed her another canteen of water and she drank the whole container down.

"I called the town police," he told her. "They're on their way. They'll be here in fifteen, twenty minutes. But we aren't gonna wait for them. We're gonna get you out now, the two of us."

stumbled backward as it sailed into the room, missing her by a scant foot. She sank onto the couch, sobbing.

As they walked toward the woods she heard Tom call again, "Get yourself ready!"

■

They were at Harris Tomel's house, a nice five-bedroom colonial on a good-sized cut of grass the man'd never done a lick of work to. Tomel's idea of lawn decorations was parking his F-250 in the front yard and his Suburban in the back.

He did this because, being the sort-of college boy of the trio and owning more sweaters than plaid shirts, Tomel had to try a little harder to seem like a shit-kicker. Oh, sure, he'd done fed time but it was for some crappy scam in Raleigh where he sold stocks and bonds in companies whose only problem was that they didn't exist. He could shoot good as a sniper but Culbeau'd never known him to whale on anybody by himself, skin on skin, at least nobody who wasn't tied up. Tomel also *thought* about things too much, spent too much time on his clothes, asked for call liquor, even at Eddie's.

So unlike Culbeau, who worked hard on his own split-level, and unlike O'Sarian, who worked hard picking up waitresses who'd keep his trailer nice, Harris Tomel just let the house and yard go. Hoping, Culbeau assumed, that it'd goose the impression that he was a mean fuck.

But that was Tomel's business and the three men weren't at the house with its scruffy yard and Detroit lawn ornaments to discuss landscaping; they were here for one reason only. Because Tomel had inherited the gun collection to end all gun collections when his father went into Spivy Pond ice fishing on New Year's Eve a few years ago and didn't surface till the next tax day.

They stood in the man's paneled den, looking over the gun cases the same way Culbeau and O'Sarian had stood at the penny candy rack in Peterson's Drugs on Maple Street twenty years ago, deciding what to steal.

O'Sarian picked the black Colt AR-15, the civvy version of the M-16, because he was always yammering on and on about Vietnam and watched every war movie he could find.

Tomel took the beautiful Browning shotgun with the inlay, which Culbeau coveted as much as he coveted any woman in the county, even though he himself was a rifle man and would rather drill a hole in a deer's heart from three hundred yards than blow a duck into a dust of feathers. For himself, today, he chose Tomel's nifty Winchester .30-06 with a 'scope the size of Texas.

They packed plenty of ammo, water, Culbeau's cell phone and food. 'Shine of course.

Sleeping bags, too. Though none of them expected the hunt to last very long.

chapter twenty-four

A grim Lincoln Rhyme wheeled into the dismantled forensic lab in the Paquenoke County Building.

Lucy Kerr and Mason Germain stood beside the fiberboard table that had held the microscopes. Their arms were crossed and, as Thom and Rhyme entered, both deputies regarded the criminalist and his aide with a blend of contempt and suspicion.

"How the hell could she do it?" Mason asked. "What was she thinking of?"

But these were two of many questions about Amelia Sachs and what she'd done that couldn't be answered, not yet, and so Rhyme asked merely, "Was anybody hurt?"

"No," Lucy said. "But Nathan was pretty shook up, looking down the barrel of that Smith and Wesson. Which *we* were crazy enough to give her."

Rhyme struggled to remain outwardly calm, yet his heart was pierced with fear for Sachs. Lincoln Rhyme trusted evidence before all else and the evidence showed clearly that Garrett Hanlon was a kidnapper and killer. Sachs, tricked by his calculated facade, was as much at risk as Mary Beth or Lydia.

Jim Bell entered the room.

"Did she take a car?" Rhyme continued.

"I don't think so," Bell said. "I asked around. No vehicles missing yet."

Bell looked at the map, still taped to the wall. "This isn't an easy area to get out of and not get seen. Lot of marshland, not many roads. I've—"

Lucy said, "Get some dogs, Jim. Irv Wanner runs a couple hounds for the state police. Call Captain Dexter in Elizabeth City and get Irv's number. He'll track 'em down."

"Good idea," Bell said. "We'll—"

"I want to propose something," Rhyme interrupted.

Mason gave a cold laugh.

"What?" Bell asked.

"I'll make a deal with you."

"No deals," Bell said. "She's a fleeing felon. And armed, to boot."

"She's not going to shoot anybody," Thom said.

Rhyme continued, "Amelia's convinced there's no other way to find Mary Beth. That's why she did it. They're going to where she's being held."

"Doesn't matter," Bell said. "You can't go breaking murderers out of jail."

"Give me twenty-four hours before you call the state police. I'll find them for you. We can work something out with the charges. But if troopers and dogs get involved we all know they'll play it by the book and that means there's a good chance of people getting hurt."

"That's a hell of a deal, Lincoln," Bell said. "Your friend busts out our prisoner—"

"He wouldn't *be* your prisoner if it weren't for me. You never would've found him on your own."

"No damn way," Mason said. "We're wasting time and they're getting farther away every minute we've wasted talking. I'm of a mind to get every man in town out looking for 'em now. Deputize the lot. Do what Henry Davett suggested. Pass out rifles and—"

Bell interrupted him and asked Rhyme, "If we give you your twenty-four hours then what's in it for us?"

"I'll stay and help you find Mary Beth. However long it takes."

Thom said, "The operation, Lincoln . . ."

"Forget the operation," he muttered, feeling the despair as he said this. He knew that Dr. Weaver's schedule was so tight that if he missed his appointed date on the table he'd have to go back on the waiting list. Then it crossed his mind that one reason Sachs had done this was to keep Rhyme from having the surgery. To buy a few more days and give him a chance to change his mind. But he pushed this thought aside, raging to himself: Find her, save her. Before Garrett adds her to the list of his victims.

Stung 137 times.

Lucy said, "We're looking at a bit of, what would you say, divided loyalty here, aren't we?"

Mason: "Yeah, how do we know you aren't gonna send us 'round Robin Hood's barn and let her get away?"

"Because," Rhyme said patiently, "Amelia's wrong. Garrett *is* a murderer and he just used her to break out of jail. Once he doesn't need her he'll kill her."

Bell paced for a moment, gazing up at the map. "Okay, we'll do it, Lincoln. You've got twenty-four hours."

Mason sighed. "And how the hell're you going to find her in that wilderness?" He motioned toward the map. "You just going to call her up and ask where she is?"

"That's exactly what I'm going to do. Thom, let's get the equipment set up again. And somebody get Ben Kerr back here!"

■

Lucy Kerr stood in the office adjacent to the war room, on the phone.

"North Carolina State Police, Elizabeth City," the woman's crisp voice answered. "How can I help you?"

"Detective Gregg."

"Hold, please."

" 'Lo?" asked a man's voice after a moment.

"Pete, s'Lucy Kerr over in Tanner's Corner."

"Hey, Lucy, how's it going? What's with those missing girls?"

"Got that under control," she said, her voice calm, though she was enraged that Bell had insisted she recite the words Lincoln Rhyme had dictated to her. "But we do have another little problem."

Little problem . . .

"Whatcha need? A couple troopers?"

"No, just a cell phone trace."

"Got a warrant?"

"Magistrate's clerk's faxing it to you right now."

"Gimme the phone and serial numbers."

She gave him the information.

"What's that area code, two one two?"

"It's a New York number. Party's roaming now."

"Not a problem," Gregg said. "You want a tape of the conversation?"

"Just location."

And a clear line of sight to the target . . .

"When . . . wait. Here's the fax. . . ." A pause as he read. "Oh, just a missing person?"

"That's all," she said reluctantly.

"You know it's expensive. We'll have to bill you."

"I understand."

"Okay, hold the line, I'll call my tech people." There was a faint click.

Lucy sat on the desk, shoulders slumped, flexing her left hand, staring at fingers ruddy from years of gardening, an old scar from the metal strap on a pallet of mulch, the indentation in her ring finger from five years of wedding band.

Flex, straighten.

Watching the veins and muscles beneath the skin, Lucy

Kerr realized something. That Amelia Sachs's crime had tapped into an anger within her that was more intense than anything she'd ever felt.

When they took part of her body away she'd felt ashamed and then forlorn. When her husband left she'd felt guilty and resigned. And when she finally grew mad at those events she was angry in a way that suggested embers—an anger that radiates immense heat but never bursts into flames.

But for a reason she couldn't understand, this woman cop from New York had let the simple white-hot fury burst from Lucy's heart—like the wasps that had streamed out of the nest and killed Ed Schaeffer so horribly.

White-hot fury at the betrayal of Lucy Kerr, who never intentionally caused a soul pain, who was a woman who loved plants, a woman who'd been a good wife to her man, a good daughter to her parents, a good sister, a good policewoman, a woman who wanted only the harmless pleasures life gave freely to everyone else but seemed determined to withhold from her.

No more shame or guilt or resignation or sorrow.

Simple fury—at the betrayals in her life. The betrayal by her body, by her husband, by God.

And now by Amelia Sachs.

"Hello, Lucy?" Pete asked from Elizabeth City. "You there?"

"Yes, I'm here."

"You . . . are you okay? You sound funny."

She cleared her throat. "Fine. You set up?"

"You're good to go. When's the subject going to be making a call?"

Lucy looked into the other room. Called, "Ready?"

Rhyme nodded.

Into the phone she said, "Any time now."

"Stay on the line," Gregg said. "I'll liaise."

Please let this work, Lucy thought. Please . . .

Then she added a footnote to her prayer: And, dear Lord, give me one clear shot at my Judas.

■

Thom fitted the headset over Rhyme's head. The aide then punched in a number.

If Sachs's phone was shut off it would ring only three times and the pleasant lilt of the voice-mail lady would start to speak.

One ring . . . two . . .

"Hello?"

Rhyme didn't believe he'd ever felt such relief, hearing her voice. "Sachs, are you all right?"

A pause. "I'm okay."

In the other room he saw Lucy Kerr's sullen face nod.

"Listen to me, Sachs. Listen to me. I know why you did it but you have to give yourself up. You . . . are you there?"

"I'm here, Rhyme."

"I know what you're doing. Garrett's agreed to take you to Mary Beth."

"That's right."

"You can't trust him," Rhyme said. (Thinking in despair: Or me either. He saw Lucy moving her finger in a circle, meaning: Keep her on the line.) "I've made a deal with Jim. If you bring him back in they'll work something out with the charges against you. The state's not involved yet. And I'll stay here as long as it takes to find Mary Beth. I've postponed the operation."

He closed his eyes momentarily, pierced with guilt. But he had no choice. He pictured what the death of that woman in Blackwater Landing had been like, the death of Deputy Ed Schaeffer. . . . Imagining the hornets swarming over Amelia's body. He had to betray her in order to save her.

"Garrett's innocent, Rhyme. I know he is. I couldn't let him go to the detention center. They'd kill him there."

"Then we'll arrange for him to be held someplace else. And we'll look at the evidence again. We'll find *more* evidence. We'll do it together. You and me. That's what we say, Sachs, right? You and me. . . . Always you and me. There's *nothing* we can't find."

There was a pause. "There's nobody on Garrett's side. He's all by himself, Rhyme."

"We can protect him."

"You can't protect somebody from a whole town, Lincoln."

"No first names," Rhyme said. "That's bad luck, remember?"

"This whole thing has been bad luck."

"Please, Sachs. . . ."

She said, "Sometimes you just have to go on faith."

"Now who's dispensing maxims?" He forced himself to laugh—in part to reassure her. In part, himself.

Faint static.

Come home, Sachs, he was thinking. Please! We can still salvage something from this. Your life is as precarious as the thread of the nerve in my neck—the tiny fiber that still works.

And as precious to me.

She said, "Garrett tells me we can get to Mary Beth by tonight or tomorrow morning. I'll call you when we have her."

"Sachs, don't hang up yet. One thing. Let me say one thing."

"What?"

"Whatever you think about Garrett, don't trust him. You think he's innocent. But just accept that maybe he isn't. You know how we approach crime scenes, Sachs."

"With an open mind," she recited the rule. "No preconceptions. Believing that anything's possible."

"Right. Promise me you'll remember that."

"He's cuffed, Rhyme."

"Keep him that way. And don't let him near your weapon."

"I won't. I'll call you when we have Mary Beth."

"Sachs—"

The line went dead.

"Damn," the criminalist muttered. He closed his eyes, tried to shake off the headset in fury. Thom reached forward and lifted the unit off his head. With a brush he smoothed Rhyme's dark hair.

Lucy hung up the phone in the other room and stepped inside. Rhyme could tell from her expression that the trace hadn't worked.

"Pete said they're within three miles of downtown Tanner's Corner."

Mason muttered, "They can't do any better than that?"

Lucy said, "If she'd been on the line a few minutes longer they could've pinpointed her down to fifteen feet."

Bell was examining the map. "Okay, three miles outside of downtown."

"Would he go back to Blackwater Landing?" Rhyme asked.

"No," Bell said. "We know they're headed for the Outer Banks and Blackwater Landing'd take him in the opposite direction."

"What's the best way to get to the Banks?" the criminalist asked.

"They can't do it on foot," Bell said, walking to the map. "They'll have to take a car or car and a boat. There're two ways to get there. They could go Route 112 south to 17. That'll take them to Elizabeth City and they could get a boat or keep on 17 all the way to 158 and drive to the beaches. Or they could take Harper Road. . . . Mason, you take Frank Sturgis and Trey and get over to 112. Set up a roadblock at Belmont."

Rhyme noticed this was Location M-10 on the map.

The sheriff continued, "Lucy, you and Jesse take Harper down to Millerton Road. Set up there." This was H-14.

Bell called his brother-in-law into the room. "Steve, you coordinate communications and get everybody Handi-talkies if they don't already have them."

"Sure thing, Jim."

Bell said to Lucy and Mason, "Tell everybody that Garrett's in one of our detention jumpsuits. They're blue. What's your girl wearing? I don't remember."

"She's not my girl," Rhyme said.

"Sorry."

Rhyme said, "Jeans, black T-shirt."

"She have a hat?"

"No."

Lucy and Mason headed out the door.

A moment later the room was empty except for Bell, Rhyme and Thom.

The sheriff called the state police and told the detective who'd helped them with the mobile locator to keep somebody on that frequency, that the missing person might call in later.

Rhyme noticed Bell pause. He glanced at Rhyme and said into the phone, "Appreciate the offer, Pete. But so far it's just a missing person. Nothing serious."

He hung up. Muttered, "Nothing serious. Jesus, our Lord . . ."

■

Fifteen minutes later Ben Kerr walked into the office. He actually seemed glad to be back though he was visibly upset at the news that necessitated his return.

Together he and Thom finished unpacking the state police's forensic equipment while Rhyme stared up at the map and the evidence charts on the wall.

FOUND AT PRIMARY CRIME SCENE—
BLACKWATER LANDING

Kleenex with Blood
Limestone Dust
Nitrates
Phosphate
Ammonia
Detergent
Camphene

FOUND AT SECONDARY CRIME SCENE—
GARRETT'S ROOM

Skunk Musk
Cut Pine Needles
Drawings of Insects
Pictures of Mary Beth and Family
Insect Books
Fishing Line
Money
Unknown Key
Kerosene
Ammonia
Nitrates
Camphene

FOUND AT SECONDARY CRIME SCENE—
QUARRY

Old Burlap Bag—Unreadable Name on It
Corn—Feed and Grain?
Scorch Marks on Bag
Deer Park Water
Planters Cheese Crackers

Found at Secondary Crime Scene—Mill

Map of Outer Banks
Ocean Beach Sand
Oak/Maple Leaf Residue

As Rhyme gazed at the last chart he realized how little evidence Sachs had found at the mill. This was always a problem when you locate obvious clues at crime scenes— like the map and the sand. Psychologically your attention flags and you search less diligently. He now wished they had more evidence from the scene.

Then Rhyme recalled something. Lydia had said that Garrett'd changed his clothes at the mill when the search party was closing in. Why? The only reason was that he knew that the clothes he'd hidden there could reveal where he'd hidden Mary Beth. He glanced at Bell. "Did you say Garrett was wearing a prison jumpsuit?"

"That's right."

"You have what he was wearing when he was arrested?"

"It'd be over at the lockup."

"Could you have them sent over here?"

"The clothes? Right away."

"Have them put in a paper bag," he ordered. "Don't unfold them."

The sheriff called the lockup, told a deputy to bring them over. From the one-sided conversation Rhyme deduced that the deputy was more than happy to participate in helping to find the woman who'd hog-tied and shamed him.

Rhyme stared at the map of the Eastern shore. They could narrow the search to old houses—because of the camphene lamp—and to ones set back from the beach itself—because of the maple and oak leaf trace. But the sheer size of the place was daunting. Hundreds of miles.

Bell's phone rang. He answered and spoke for a minute

then hung up. Walked to the map. "They've got the road-blocks set up. Garrett and Amelia might move inland here to get around them"—he tapped Location M-10—"but from where Mason and Frank are they've got a good view of this field and they'd be seen."

Rhyme asked, "What about that railroad line south of town?"

"Not used for passenger travel. It's a freight line and there's no set schedule for the trains. But they could hike along it. That's why I set up the block at Belmont. My bet is they'll go that way. I'm also thinking Garrett might hide out for a while in the Manitou Falls Wildlife Preserve—with his interest in bugs and nature and stuff. He probably spends a lot of time there." Bell tapped spot T-10.

Farr asked, "What about that airport?"

Bell looked at Rhyme. "Can she hot-wire an airplane?"

"No, she doesn't fly."

Rhyme noticed a reference on the map. He asked, "What's that military base?"

"Used it to store weapons in the sixties and seventies. It's been closed for years. But there're tunnels and bunkers all over the place. We'd need two dozen men to search the place and he could still probably find a nook to hide in."

"Is it patrolled?"

"Not anymore."

"What's that square area? At spot E-5 and E-6?"

"That? Probably that old amusement park," Bell said, looking at Farr and Ben.

"Right," said Ben. "My brother and I used to go there when I was a kid. It was called, what? Indian Ridge or something."

Bell nodded. "It was a re-creation of an Indian village. Went outa business a few years ago—nobody went. Williamsburg and Six Flags were a lot more popular. Good place to hide but it's in the opposite direction of the Outer Banks. Garrett wouldn't go there."

Bell touched spot H-14. "Lucy's here. And Garrett and Amelia'd have to stick to Harper Road in those parts. They go off the road and it's swampland filled with clay. Take 'em days to get through it—if they survived, which they probably wouldn't. So. . . . I guess we just wait and see what happens."

Rhyme nodded absently, his eyes moving like his friend—the skittish fly, now departed—from one topographical landmark in Paquenoke County to another.

chapter twenty-five

Garrett Hanlon led Amelia down a wide asphalt road. They were walking slower than before, exhausted from the exertion and the heat.

There was a familiarity about the area and she realized this was Canal Road—the one that they'd taken from the County Building that morning to search the crime scenes at Blackwater Landing. Ahead she could see the dark rippling of the Paquenoke River. Across the canal were those large, beautiful houses she'd commented on earlier to Lucy.

She looked around. "I don't get it. This is the main road into town. Why aren't there any roadblocks?"

"They think we're going a different way. They've set up the roadblocks south and east of here."

"How do you know that?"

Garrett answered, "They think I'm fucked-up. They think I'm stupid. When you're different that's what people think. But I'm not."

"But we *are* going to Mary Beth?"

"Sure. Just not the way they think."

Once again Garrett's confidence and caginess troubled her but her attention slipped back to the road and they continued on in silence. In twenty minutes they were within a half mile of the intersection where Canal Road ended at Route 112—the place where Billy Stail had been killed.

"Listen!" he whispered, gripping her arm with his cuffed hands.

She cocked her head but heard nothing.

"Into the bushes." They slipped off the road into a stand of scratchy holly trees.

"What?" she asked.

"Shhhh."

A moment later a large flatbed truck came into view behind them.

"That's from the factory," he whispered. "Up ahead there."

The sign on the truck was for Davett Industries. She recognized the name of the man who'd helped them with the evidence. When it was past they returned to the road.

"How did you hear that?"

"Oh, you gotta be cautious all the time. Like moths."

"Moths? What do you mean?"

"Moths're pretty cool. They, like, sense ultrasound waves. They have these radar detector things. When a bat shoots out a beam of sound to find them, moths fold their wings and drop to the ground and hide. Magnetic and electronic fields too—insects can feel them. Like, things we aren't even aware of. You know you can lead some insects around with radio waves? Or make 'em go away too, depending on the frequency." He fell silent, head turned away, frozen in position. Then he looked back at her. He said, "You have to listen all the time. Otherwise they can sneak up on you."

"Who?" she asked uncertainly.

"You know, everybody." Then he nodded up the road, toward Blackwater Landing and the Paquenoke. "Ten minutes and we'll be safe. They'll never find us."

She was wondering what, realistically, would happen to Garrett when they found Mary Beth and returned to Tanner's Corner. There would still be some charges against him. But if Mary Beth corroborated the story of the real murderer—the man in the tan overalls—then the D.A. might accept that Garrett *had* kidnapped her for her own good. Defense of others was recognized by all criminal courts as a justification. And he'd probably drop the charges.

And who *was* the man in the overalls? Why was he prowling the forests of Blackwater Landing? Had he been the one who'd killed those other residents over the past few years and was trying to blame Garrett for the deaths? Had *he* scared young Todd Wilkes into killing himself? Was there a drug ring that Billy Stail had been involved in? She knew that drug problems in small towns were as serious as in the city.

Then something else occurred to her: that Garrett could identify Billy Stail's real murderer—the man in the overalls, who by now might've heard about the escape and be out looking for Garrett and for her too. To silence them. Maybe they should—

Suddenly Garrett froze, an alarmed look on his face. He spun around.

"What?" she whispered.

"Car, moving fast."

"Where?"

"Shhh."

A flash of light from behind them caught their eyes.

You have to listen all the time. Otherwise they can sneak up on you.

"No!" Garrett cried in dismay and pulled her into a stand of sedge.

Two Paquenoke County squad cars were racing along Canal Road. She couldn't see who was driving the first one but the deputy in the passenger seat—the black deputy who'd set up the chalkboard for Rhyme—was squinting as he scanned the woods. He held a shotgun. Lucy Kerr was driving the second car. Jesse Corn sat beside her.

Garrett and Sachs lay flat, hidden by broom grass.

Moths fold their wings and drop to the ground. . . .

The cars sped past and skidded to a stop where Canal Road met Route 112. They parked perpendicular to the road, blocking both lanes, and the deputies got out, weapons ready.

"Roadblock," she muttered. "Hell."

"No, no, no," Garrett muttered, dumbfounded. "They were supposed to think we were going the *other* way— east. They *had* to think that!"

A passenger car passed them, slowing at the end of the road. Lucy flagged down the car and questioned the driver. Then they made him get out of the vehicle and open the trunk, which they searched carefully.

Garrett huddled in the nest of grass. "How the fuck d'they figure out we were coming this way?" he whispered. "*How?*"

Because they've got Lincoln Rhyme, Sachs answered silently.

■

"They don't see anything yet, Lincoln," Jim Bell told him.

"Amelia and Garrett aren't going to be walking down the middle of Canal Road," Rhyme said testily. "They'll be in the bushes. Keeping a low profile."

"There's a roadblock set up and they're searching every car," Jim Bell said. "Even if they know the drivers."

Rhyme looked again at the map on the wall. "There's no other way for them to go west from Tanner's Corner?"

"From the lockup the only way through the marshes is Canal Road to Route 112." But Bell sounded doubtful. "I gotta say, though, this's a big risk, Lincoln—committing everybody to Blackwater Landing. If they really *are* headed east to the Outer Banks they're gonna get past us now and we'll never find them. This idea of yours, well, it's a little far-fetched."

But Rhyme believed it was right. As he'd stared at the map twenty minutes before, tracing the route the boy had taken with Lydia—which led toward the Great Dismal Swamp and very little else—he had started wondering about Lydia's abduction. He had remembered what Sachs had told him when they were in the field pursuing Garrett this morning.

Lucy says it doesn't make any sense for him to come this way.

And that had made him ask a question that no one had yet answered satisfactorily. *Why* exactly did Garrett kidnap Lydia Johansson? To kill her as a substitute victim was Dr. Penny's answer. But, as it turned out, he *hadn't* killed her even though he'd had plenty of time to. Or raped her. Nor was there any other motive for abducting her. They were strangers, she'd never taunted him, he didn't seem to have an obsession with her, she wasn't a witness to Billy's murder. What could his point have been?

Then he had recalled how Garrett had willingly told Lydia that Mary Beth was being held on the Outer Banks—and how she was happy, how she didn't need to be rescued. Why would he volunteer that information? And the evidence at the mill—the ocean sand, the map of the Outer Banks . . . Lucy had found it easily, according to Sachs. Too easily. The scene, he had decided, had been staged, as forensic scientists call evidence planted to lead investigators off.

Rhyme had shouted bitterly, "We've been set up!"

"What do you mean, Lincoln?" Ben had asked.

"He tricked us," the criminalist had said. A sixteen-year-old boy had fooled them all. From the beginning. Rhyme had explained that Garrett had intentionally kicked off one shoe at the scene when he kidnapped Lydia. He'd filled it with limestone dust, which would lead anyone with knowledge of the area—Davett, for instance—to think of the quarry, where he'd planted the other evidence, the scorched bag and corn—that in turn led to the mill.

The searchers were *supposed* to find Lydia, along with the rest of the planted evidence—to convince them that Mary Beth was being held in a house on the Outer Banks.

Which meant of course that she was being held in the opposite direction—west of Tanner's Corner.

Garrett's plan was brilliant but he had made one mistake—assuming that it would take the search party several days to find Lydia (which is why he'd left all the food for her). By then he'd have been with Mary Beth in the real hiding place and the searchers would be combing the Outer Banks.

And so Rhyme had asked Bell what was the best route west from Tanner's Corner. "Blackwater Landing," the sheriff had answered. "Route 112." And Rhyme had ordered Lucy and the other deputies there as fast as possible.

There was a chance that Garrett and Sachs had been through the intersection already and were on their way west. But Rhyme had calculated distances and didn't think that on foot—and keeping under cover—they could have gotten that far in so little time.

Lucy now called in from the roadblock. Thom put the call on the speakerphone. The policewoman, undoubtedly still suspicious and wondering whose side Rhyme was really on, said skeptically, "I don't see any sign of them here and we've checked every car that's come by. Are you sure about this?"

"Yes," he announced. "I'm sure."

And whatever she chose to think of this arrogant response she said nothing other than "Let's hope you're right. There's a chance for some real sorrow here." She hung up.

A moment later Bell's phone rang. He listened. Looked up at Rhyme. "Three more deputies just got to Canal

Road, about a mile south of 112. They're going to do a sweep north on foot toward Lucy and the others and pin Garrett and Sachs in." He listened into the phone for a moment longer. Glanced at Rhyme, then away, and continued into the phone: "Yeah, she's armed . . . And, yeah, I hear tell she's a good shot."

■

Sachs and Garrett crouched in the bushes, watching the passenger cars waiting to get through the roadblock.

Then, behind them, another sound that even without a moth's sensitive hearing Sachs could detect: sirens. They saw a second set of flashing lights—coming from the other—the southern—end of Canal Road. Another squad car parked and three more deputies got out, also armed with shotguns. They started slowly through the bushes, moving toward Garrett and Sachs. In ten minutes they'd walk right through the nest of sedge where the fugitives were hiding.

Garrett looked at her expectantly.

"What?" she asked.

He glanced at her gun.

"Aren't you going to use that?"

She stared at him in shock. "No. Of course not."

Garrett nodded toward the roadblock. "*They* will."

"Nobody's going to be doing any shooting!" she whispered fiercely, horrified that he'd even consider it. She looked behind her into the woods. It was marshy and impossible to get through without being seen or heard. Ahead of them was the chain-link fence surrounding Davett Industries. Through the mesh she saw the cars in the parking lot.

Amelia Sachs had worked street crimes for a year. That experience, combined with what she knew about cars, meant that she could break into and hot-wire a vehicle in under thirty seconds.

But even if she boosted wheels how could they get out of the factory grounds? There was a delivery and shipping entrance to the factory but it too opened onto Canal Road. They'd still have to drive past the roadblock. Could they steal a four-by-four or pickup and make it through the fence where nobody could see them then drive off the road to Route 112? There were steep hills and sharp drop-offs into marshes everywhere around Blackwater Landing; could they escape without rolling a truck and killing themselves?

The deputies on foot were now only two hundred feet away.

Whatever they were going to do, now was the time. Sachs decided they had no choice. "Come on, Garrett. We've got to get over the fence."

Crouching, they moved forward toward the parking lot.

"Are you thinking of a car?" he said, noticing where they were headed.

Sachs glanced back. The deputies were a hundred yards away.

Garrett continued, "I don't like cars. They scare me."

But she wasn't paying attention. She kept hearing his earlier words, circulating through her thoughts.

Moths fold their wings and drop to the ground.

■

"Where are they now?" Rhyme demanded. "The deputies making the sweep?"

Bell relayed the question into his phone, listened then touched a spot on the map about halfway up square G-10. "They're close to here. That's the entrance to Davett's company. Eighty, a hundred yards, moving north."

"Can Amelia and Garrett get around the factory to the east?"

"Naw, Davett's property's all fenced. Beyond that it's serious swamp. If they went west they'd have to swim the canal and they probably couldn't climb the banks. Anyway there's no cover there. Lucy and Trey'd spot 'em for sure."

Waiting was so hard. Rhyme knew that Sachs would scratch and pick at her flesh in an attempt to relieve the anxiety that was a dark corollary to her drive and talent. Destructive habits, yes, but how he envied her them. Before the accident Rhyme himself would bleed off tension by pacing and walking. Now he had nothing to do but stare at the map and obsess about how much at risk she was.

A secretary stuck her head in the door.

"Sheriff Bell, state police on line two."

Jim Bell stepped into the office across the hall and took the call. He spoke for a few minutes then trotted back into the lab. He said excitedly, "We've got 'em! They pinpointed her cell phone signal. She's on the move, going west on Route 112. They got past the roadblock."

Rhyme asked, "How?"

"Looks like they snuck into Davett's parking lot and stole a truck or four-by-four then drove off the road for a while and got back on the highway. Man, that took some serious driving."

That's my Amelia, Rhyme thought. That woman can drive up walls. . . .

Bell continued, "She's going to ditch the car and get another one."

"How do you know?"

"She's on the phone with a car rental company in Hobeth Falls. Lucy and the others're after her, silent pursuit. We're talking to Davett's people to see who's missing a vehicle from the lot. But we don't need a description if she just stays on the line a little longer. Another few minutes and the tech people'll have the exact location."

Lincoln Rhyme stared at the map—though it was by now imprinted on his mind. After a moment he sighed then muttered, "Good luck."

But whether that wish was directed toward predator or toward prey, he couldn't have said.

. . . chapter twenty-six

Lucy Kerr nudged the Crown Victoria up to eighty.

You drive fast, Amelia?

Well, so do I.

They were speeding along Route 112, the gumball machine on top of the car spinning madly with its red, white and blue lights. The siren was off. Jesse Corn was beside her, on the phone with Pete Gregg in the Elizabeth City state police office. In the squad car directly behind them were Trey Williams and Ned Spoto. Mason Germain and Frank Sturgis—a quiet man and a recent grandfather—were in the third car.

"Where are they now?" Lucy asked.

Jesse asked the state police this question and nodded as he received an answer. He said, "Only five miles away. They turned off the highway, heading south."

Please, Lucy offered yet another prayer, please, stay on the phone just a minute more.

She nudged the accelerator closer to the floor.

You drive fast, Amelia. I drive fast.

You're a good shot.

But I'm a good shot too. I don't make a show of it like you do, what with all that fancy quick-draw crap, but I've lived with guns all my life.

Recalling that when Buddy left her she took every round of live ammo in the house and pitched them into the murky waters of Blackwater Canal. Worrying that she might wake up one night, glance at his empty side of the bed and then wrap her lips around the oily barrel of her service revolver and send herself to the place where her husband, and nature, seemed to want her to be.

Lucy had gone around for three and a half months with an unloaded service pistol, collaring 'shiners and militiamen and big, snotty teens huffed to oblivion on butane. And she'd handled them all on bluff alone.

Then she woke up one morning and, as if a fever had passed, had gone to Shakey's Hardware on Maple Street and bought a box of Winchester .357 shells. ("Jeez, Lucy, the county's in worser shape than I thought, making you buy your own ammo.") She'd gone home and loaded her weapon and kept it that way ever since.

It was a significant event for her. The reloaded gun was an emblem of survival.

Amelia, I shared my darkest moments with you. I told you about the surgery—which is the black hole of my life. I told you about my shyness with men. About my love for children. I backed you up when Sean O'Sarian got your gun. I apologized when you were right and I was wrong.

I trusted you. I—

A hand touched her shoulder. She glanced at Jesse Corn. He was giving her one of his gentle smiles. "The highway curves up ahead," he said. "I'd just as soon *we* made that curve too."

Lucy exhaled slowly and sat back in the seat, let her shoulders slump. She eased off on the speed.

Still, when they made the curve Jesse'd mentioned, which was posted forty, she was doing sixty-five.

■

"A hundred feet up the road," Jesse Corn whispered.

They were out of their cars, the deputies, and were clustered around Mason Germain and Lucy Kerr.

The state police had finally lost the signal from Amelia's cell phone but only after it'd been stationary for about five minutes at the location they were now looking at: a barn fifty feet from a house in the woods—a mile off Route 112. It was, Lucy noted, *west* of Tanner's Corner. Just as Lincoln Rhyme had predicted.

"You don't think Mary Beth's in *there*, do you?" asked Frank Sturgis, brushing at his yellow-stained moustache. "I mean, it's all of seven miles from downtown. I'd feel pretty foolish, he's been keeping the girl that close to town."

"Naw, they're just waiting for us to go past," Mason said. "Then they're gonna go on to Hobeth Falls and pick up the rental car."

"Anyway," Jesse said, "somebody lives here." He'd called in the address of the house. "Pete Hallburton. Anybody know him?"

"Think so," said Trey Williams. "Married. No connection to Garrett that I know of."

"They have kids?"

Trey shrugged. "Think they might. Seem to recall a soccer game last year . . ."

"It's summer. The youngsters might be home," Frank muttered. "Garrett might've taken 'em hostage inside."

"Maybe," Lucy said. "But the triangulation on Amelia's phone signal placed them in the barn, not the house. They *could've* gone inside but I don't know . . . I can't see 'em takin' hostages. Mason's right, I think: They're just hiding out here until they think it's safe to get up to Hobeth for that rental car."

"Whatta we do?" Frank asked. "Block the drive with our cars?"

"We pull up, do that, they'll hear us," Jesse said.

Lucy nodded. "I think we should just hit the barn on foot—fast—from two directions."

"I've got CS gas," Mason said. CS-38—a powerful military tear gas kept under lock and key in the Sheriff's Department. Bell hadn't distributed any and Lucy wondered how Mason had gotten his hands on some.

"No, no," Jesse protested. "Might make 'em panic."

Lucy believed that wasn't his concern at all. She bet he didn't want to expose his new girlfriend to the vicious gas. Still, she agreed, feeling that, since the deputies didn't have masks, gas might work against *them*. "No gas," she said. "I'll go in the front. Trey, you take the—"

"No," Mason said evenly. "I go in the front."

Lucy hesitated then said, "Okay. I'll go in the side door. Trey and Frank, you're on the back and far side." She looked at Jesse. "I want you and Ned to keep an eye on the front and back doors of the house. There."

"Got it," Jesse said.

"And the windows," Mason said sternly to Ned. "I don't want anybody sighting down on our backs from inside."

Lucy said, "If they come out driving, just take out the tires or if you've got a Magnum like Frank there aim for the engine block. Don't shoot Garrett or Amelia unless you have to. You all know the rules of engagement." She was looking at Mason when she said this, thinking of his sniper attack at the mill. But the deputy seemed not to hear her. She called in on her Handi-talkie and told Jim Bell they were about to storm the barn.

"I've got the ambulance standing by," he said.

"This isn't a SWAT operation," Jesse said, overhearing the transmission. "We've gotta be damn careful about any shooting."

Lucy clicked off the radio. She nodded toward the building. "Let's move out."

They ran, crouching, using the oaks and pine for cover.

Her eyes were fastened on the dark windows of the barn. Twice she was sure she saw movement inside. It might have been the reflection of trees and clouds as she ran but she couldn't be sure. As they approached she paused and switched her gun to her left hand, wiped her palm. Took the weapon once more in her shooting hand.

The deputies clustered at the windowless back of the barn. Lucy was thinking that she'd never done anything like this.

This isn't a SWAT operation. . . .

But you're wrong, Jesse—that's exactly what it is.

Dear Lord, give me one clear shot at my Judas.

A fat dragonfly strafed her. She brushed it away with her left hand. It returned and hovered nearby ominously, as if Garrett had sent the creature out to distract her.

Stupid thought, she told herself. Then swatted furiously at the bug again.

The Insect Boy . . .

You're going down, Lucy thought—the message meant for both fugitives.

"I'm not going to say anything," Mason said. "I'm just going in. When you hear me kick in the door, Lucy, you go through the side."

She nodded. And as concerned as she was about Mason being too eager, as desirous as she was to get Amelia Sachs, she was still happy to share some of the burden of this hard job.

"Let me make sure the side door's open," she whispered.

They dispersed, jogging into position. Lucy ducked under one of the windows and hurried to the side door. It wasn't locked and was open a crack. She nodded to Mason, who stood at the corner, watching her. He nodded back and held up ten fingers, meaning, she assumed, to count the seconds down until he went through the door, and then disappeared.

Ten, nine, eight . . .

She turned to the door, smelling the musty wood scent laced with the sweet aroma of gasoline and oil that flowed from inside the barn. She listened carefully. She heard a tapping—the noise of the engine of the car or truck Amelia had stolen.

Five, four, three . . .

She took a deep breath to calm herself. Another.

Ready, she told herself.

Then there was a loud crash from the front of the building as Mason kicked inside. "Sheriff's office!" he cried. "Nobody move!"

Go! she thought.

Lucy kicked the side door. But it moved only a few inches and stopped fast—hitting a large riding lawn mower parked just inside the door. It wouldn't go any farther. She slammed into it with her shoulder twice but the door held.

"Shit," she whispered and ran around to the front of the barn.

Before she got halfway there she heard Mason call out, "Oh, Jesus."

And then she heard a gunshot.

Followed a moment later by a second one.

■

"What's going on?" Rhyme demanded.

"Okay," Bell said uncertainly, holding the phone. There was something about his stance that alarmed Rhyme; the sheriff stood with the phone pressed hard against his ear, his other fist clenched and away from his body. He nodded as he listened. Looked at Rhyme. "There've been shots."

"Shots?"

"Mason and Lucy went into the barn. Jesse said there were two shots." He looked up, shouted into the other room. "Get the ambulance over to the Hallburton place. Badger Hollow Road, off Route 112."

Steve Farr called, "It's on its way."

Rhyme pressed his head back into the headrest of the chair. Glanced at Thom, who said nothing.

Who was shooting? Who'd been hit?

Oh, Sachs . . .

An edge in his voice, Bell said, "Well, find out, Jesse! Is anybody down? What the hell's going on?"

"Is Amelia all right?" Rhyme shouted.

"We'll know in a minute," Bell said.

But it felt more like days.

Finally Bell stiffened again as Jesse Corn or somebody came on the phone. He nodded. "Jesus, he did what?" He listened a moment longer then looked at Rhyme's alarmed face. "It's all right. Nobody's hurt. Mason kicked his way into the barn and saw some overalls hung up on the wall. A rake or shovel or something in front of it. It was real dark. He thought it was Garrett with a gun. He fired a couple times. That's all."

"Amelia's all right?"

"They weren't even there. It was just the truck they stole that was inside. Garrett and Amelia must've been in the house but they probably've heard the shots and took off into the woods. They can't get too far. I know the property—it's all surrounded by bogs."

Rhyme said angrily, "I want Mason off the case. That was no mistake—he shot on purpose. I *told* you he was too hotheaded."

Bell obviously agreed. Into the phone he said, "Jesse, put Mason on. . . ." There was a short pause. "Mason, what the hell is this all about? . . . Why'd you fire? . . . Well, what if it'd been Pete Hallburton standing there? Or his wife or one of his kids? . . . I don't care. You head back here right now. That's an order. . . . Well, let *them* search the house. Get in your cruiser and head back. . . . I'm not telling you again. I—"

"Shit." Bell hung up. A moment later the phone rang again. "Lucy, what's going on? . . ." The sheriff listened,

frowning, eyes on the floor. He paced. "Oh, Jesus. . . .
You're sure?" He nodded then said, "Okay, stay there.
I'll call you back." He hung up.

"What happened?"

Bell shook his head. "I don't believe it. We got suckered. She did a number on us, your friend."

"What?"

Bell said, "Pete Hallburton's *there.* He's home—in his
house. Lucy and Jesse just talked to him. His wife works
the three-to-eleven shift over at Davett's company and
she forgot her supper so he dropped it off a half hour ago
and drove home."

"*He* drove home? Were Amelia and Garrett hiding in
the trunk?"

Bell gave a disgusted sigh. "He's got a pickup. No place
to hide. Not for them anyway. But there was plenty of
room for her cell phone. Behind a cooler he had in the
back."

Rhyme too now barked a cynical laugh. "She called the
rental company, got put on hold and hid the phone in the
truck."

"You got that right," Bell muttered.

Thom said, "Remember, Lincoln, she called that rental
place this morning. She was mad because she was on hold
for so long."

"She *knew* we'd have a locator on the phone," Bell
said. "They waited till Lucy and the squad cars left Canal
Road and then went on their merry goddamn way." He
looked at the map. "They've got forty minutes on us.
They could be anywhere."

. . . chapter twenty-seven

After the police cruisers had abandoned the roadblock and disappeared west down Route 112, Garrett and Sachs jogged to the end of Canal Road and crossed the highway.

They skirted the Blackwater Landing crime scenes then turned left and moved quickly through brush and an oak forest, following the Paquenoke River.

A half mile into the forest they came to a tributary of the Paquo. It was impossible to go around and Sachs had no desire to swim across the dark water, dotted with insects and slime and trash.

But Garrett had made other arrangements. He pointed his cuffed hands to a place on the shore. "The boat."

"Boat? Where?"

"There, there." He pointed again.

She squinted and could just make out the shape of a small boat. It was covered with brush and leaves. Garrett walked to it, and working as best he could with the handcuffs on, began stripping off the foliage hiding the vessel. Sachs helped him.

"Camouflage," he said proudly. "I learned it from insects. There's this little cricket in France—the truxalis. This is totally cool—it changes its color three times a summer to match the different greens of grass during the season. Predators can hardly see it."

Well, Sachs too had used some of the boy's esoteric knowledge about insects. When Garrett had commented on the moths—their ability to sense electronic and radio signals—she'd realized that of course Rhyme had set up a locator on her cell phone. She'd remembered that she'd been on hold for a long time at Piedmont-Carolina Car Rental that morning. Then she'd snuck into the Davett Industries parking lot, called the rental company and slipped the phone, playing interminable Muzak, into the back of an unoccupied pickup truck whose motor'd been running, parked in front of the employee entrance to the building.

The trick had apparently worked. The deputies took off after the truck when it left the grounds.

As they uncovered the boat Sachs now asked Garrett, "The ammonia? And the pit with the wasps' nest. You learned those from the insects too?"

"Yeah," he said.

"You weren't going to hurt anybody, were you?"

"No, no, the ant-lion pit was just to scare you, to slow you up. I put an empty nest in there on purpose. The ammonia was to warn me if you got close. That's what insects do. Smells're, like, an early warning system or something for them." His red, watery eyes shone with a curious admiration. "That was pretty cool, what you did, finding me at the mill. I, like, never thought you'd get there fast as you did."

"And you left that fake evidence in the mill—the map and the sand—to lead us off."

"Yeah, I told you—insects're smart. They've gotta be."

They finished uncovering the battered boat. It was painted dark gray, was about ten feet long and had a small outboard motor on it. Inside were a dozen plastic gallon bottles of spring water and a cooler. Sachs tore open one of the waters and drank a dozen mouthfuls. She handed the bottle to Garrett and he drank too. Then he opened the cooler. Inside were boxes of crackers and chips. He looked them over carefully to make sure everything was accounted for and undamaged. He nodded then climbed into the boat.

Sachs followed, sat with her back to the bow, facing him. He gave her a knowing grin, as if acknowledging that she didn't trust him enough to turn her back on him, and pulled the starter rope. The engine sputtered to life. He pushed off from the shore and, like modern Huck Finns, they started down the river.

Sachs reflecting: This is knuckle time.

A phrase her father had used. The trim, balding man, a beat patrolman in Brooklyn and Manhattan most of his life, had had a serious talk with his daughter when she'd told him she wanted to give up modeling and get into police work. He'd been all for the decision but had said this about the profession: "Amie, you have to understand: sometimes it's a rush, sometimes you get to make a difference, sometimes it's boring. And sometimes, not too often, thank God, it's knuckle time. Fist to fist. You're all by your lonesome, with nobody to help you. And I don't mean just against the perps. Sometimes it'll be you against your boss. Sometimes against *their* bosses. Could be you against your buddies too. You gonna be a cop, you got to be ready to go it alone. There's no getting around it."

"I can handle it, Pop."

"That's my girl. Let's go for a drive, honey."

Sitting in this rickety boat, being piloted by a troubled young man, Sachs had never felt so alone in her life.

Knuckle time . . . fist to fist.

"Look there," Garrett said quickly. Pointing to an insect of some kind. "It's my favorite of all. The water boatman. It flies under the water." His face lit up with unbridled enthusiasm. "It really does! Hey, that'd be pretty neat, wouldn't it? To fly underwater. I like water. It feels good on my skin." The smile faded and he rubbed his arm. "This fucking poison oak . . . I get it all the time. It itches bad sometimes."

They began threading their way through small inlets, around islands, roots and gray trees, half-submerged, always returning to a westerly course, toward the lowering sun.

A thought came to Sachs, an echo of something that had occurred to her earlier, in the boy's cell just before she broke him out of jail: By hiding a boat filled with provisions, gassed up, Garrett had anticipated that he would somehow escape from jail. And that her role in this journey was part of an elaborate, premeditated plan.

"Whatever you think about Garrett, don't trust him. You think he's innocent. But just accept that maybe he isn't. You know how we approach crime scenes, Sachs."

"With an open mind. No preconceptions. Believing that anything's possible."

But then she looked at the boy once again. His eyes bright and skipping happily from sight to sight as he guided the boat through the channels, looking nothing at all like an escaped criminal but for all the world like an enthusiastic teenager on a camping trip, content and excited about what he might find around the next bend in the river.

■

"She's good, Lincoln," Ben said, referring to the cell phone trick.

She *is* good, the criminalist thought. Adding, to himself: She's as good as I am. Though he conceded grimly—and to himself alone—that she'd been *better* than he this time.

Rhyme was furious with himself for not anticipating it. This isn't a game, he thought, an exercise—like the way he'd challenge her sometimes when she was walking the grid or when they were analyzing evidence back in his lab in New York. Her life was in danger. She had perhaps only hours before Garrett assaulted or killed her. He couldn't afford to slip up again.

A deputy appeared in the doorway, carrying a paper Food Lion bag. It contained Garrett's clothes from the lockup.

"Good!" Rhyme said. "Do a chart, somebody. Thom, Ben . . . do a chart. 'Found at the Secondary Crime Scene—the Mill.' Ben, write, write!"

"But we've got one," Ben said, pointing to the chalkboard.

"No, no, no," Rhyme snapped. "Erase it. Those clues were *fake*. Garrett planted them to lead us off. Just like the limestone in the shoe he left behind when he snatched Lydia. If we can find some evidence in his clothes"—nodding at the bag—"that'll tell us where Mary Beth *really* is."

"If we're lucky," Bell said.

No, Rhyme thought, if we're skillful. He said to Ben, "Cut a piece of the pants—near the cuff—and run it through the chromatograph."

Bell stepped out of the office to talk to Steve Farr about getting priority frequencies on the radios without tipping the state police about what was happening, which Rhyme had insisted he do.

Now the criminalist and Ben waited for the results from the chromatograph. As they did, Rhyme asked, "What else do we have?" Nodding toward the clothes.

"Brown paint stains on Garrett's pants," Ben reported as he examined them. "Dark brown. Looks recent."

"Brown," Rhyme repeated, examining them. "What's the color of Garrett's parents' house?"

"I don't know," Ben began.

"I didn't *expect* you to be a storehouse of Tanner's Corner trivia," Rhyme grumbled. "I meant: Call them."

"Oh." Ben found the number in the case file and called. He spoke to someone for a moment then hung up. "That's one uncooperative son of a bitch. . . . Garrett's foster dad. Anyway, their house is white and there's nothing painted dark brown on the property."

"So, it's probably the color of the place where he's got her."

The big man asked, "Is there a paint database somewhere we can compare it to?"

"Good idea," Rhyme responded. "But the answer's no. I have one in New York but that won't do us any good here. And the FBI database is automotive. But keep going. What's in the pockets, anything? Put on—"

But Ben was already pulling on the latex gloves. "This what you were going to say?"

"It was," Rhyme muttered.

Thom said, "He hates to be anticipated."

"Then I'll try to do it more," Ben said. "Ah, here's something." Rhyme squinted at several small white objects the young man dug out of Garrett's pocket.

"What are they?"

Ben sniffed. "Cheese and bread."

"More food. Like the crackers and—"

Ben was laughing.

Rhyme frowned. "What's funny?"

"It's food—but it's not for Garrett."

"What do you mean?"

"Haven't you ever fished?" Ben asked.

"No, I've never fished," Rhyme grumbled. "If you want fish you buy it, you cook it, you eat it. What the hell does fishing have to do with cheese sandwiches?"

"They're not from sandwiches," Ben explained. "They're stinkballs. Bait for fishing. You wad up bread and cheese and let 'em get good and sour. Bottom feeders love 'em. Like catfish. The smellier the better."

Rhyme's eyebrow lifted. "Ah, now *that's* helpful."

Ben examined the cuffs. He brushed a small amount out onto a *People* magazine subscription card and then looked at it under the microscope. "Nothing much distinctive," he said. "Except little flecks of something. White."

"Let me see."

The zoologist carried the large Bausch & Lomb microscope over to Rhyme, who looked through the eyepieces. "Okay, good. They're paper fibers."

"They are?" Ben asked.

"It's *obvious* they're paper. What else would they be? Absorbent paper too. Don't have a clue what the source is, though. Now, that dirt is very interesting. Can you get some more? Out of the cuffs?"

"I'll try."

Ben cut the stitching securing the cuff and unfolded it. He brushed more dirt out onto the card.

" 'Scope it," Rhyme ordered.

The zoologist prepared a slide and slipped it onto the stage of the compound microscope, which he again held rock steady for Rhyme, who peered into the eyepieces. "There's a lot of clay. I mean, a *lot.* Feldspathic rock, probably granite. And—what's that? Oh, peat moss."

Impressed, Ben asked, "How d'you know all this?"

"I just do." Rhyme didn't have time to go into a discussion of how a criminalist must know as much about the physical world as he does about crime. He asked, "What else was in the cuffs? What's *that*?" Nodding toward something resting on the subscription card. "That little whitish-green thing?"

"It's from a plant," Ben said. "But that's not my expertise. I studied marine botany but it wasn't my favorite subject. I'm more into life forms that've got a chance to get away when you're collecting them. Seems more sporting."

Rhyme ordered, "Describe it."

Ben looked it over with a magnifying glass. "A reddish stalk and a dot of liquid on the end. It looks viscous. There's a white, bell-shaped flower attached to it. . . . If I had to guess—"

"You do," Rhyme snapped. "And quickly."

"I'm pretty sure it's from a sundew."

"What the hell's that? Sounds like dish soap."

Ben said, "It's like a Venus flytrap. They eat insects. They're fascinating. When I was a kid we'd sit and watch 'em for hours. The way they eat is—"

"*Fascinating*," Rhyme repeated sarcastically. "I'm not interested in their dining habits. Where're they *found*? That's what would be *fascinating* to me."

"Oh, all over the place here."

Rhyme scowled. "Useless. Shit. All right, run a sample of that dirt through the chromatograph after the cloth sample's done." He then looked at Garrett's T-shirt, which was lying, spread open, on a table. "What're those stains?"

There were several reddish blotches on the shirt. Ben studied them closely and shrugged, shook his head.

The criminalist's thin lips curved into a wry smile. "You game to taste it?"

Without hesitation Ben lifted the shirt and licked a small portion of the stain.

Rhyme called, "Good man."

Ben lifted an eyebrow. "I assumed that was standard procedure."

"No way in hell would I have done that," Rhyme responded.

"I don't believe that for a minute," Ben said. He licked it again. "Fruit juice, I'd guess. Can't tell what flavor."

"Okay, add that to the list, Thom." Rhyme nodded at

the chromatograph. "Let's get the results from the scraps of pants' cloth and then run the dirt from the cuffs."

Soon the machine had told them what trace substances were embedded in Garrett's clothes and what had been found in the dirt in his cuffs: sugar, more camphene, alcohol, kerosene and yeast. The kerosene was in significant amounts. Thom had added these to the list and the men examined the chart.

FOUND AT THE SECONDARY CRIME SCENE—
MILL

Brown Paint on Pants
Sundew Plant
Clay
Peat Moss
Fruit Juice
Paper Fibers
Stinkball Bait
Sugar
Camphene
Alcohol
Kerosene
Yeast

What did all this mean? Rhyme wondered. There were too many clues. He couldn't see any relationships among them. Was the sugar from the fruit juice or from a separate location the boy had been to? Had he *bought* the kerosene or had he just happened to hide in a gas station or barn where the owner stored it? Alcohol was found in more than three thousand common household and industrial products—from solvents to aftershave. The yeast had undoubtedly been picked up in the gristmill, where grain had been ground into flour.

After a few minutes Lincoln Rhyme's eyes flicked to another chart.

FOUND AT SECONDARY CRIME SCENE—
GARRETT'S ROOM

Skunk Musk
Cut Pine Needles
Drawings of Insects
Pictures of Mary Beth and Family
Insect Books
Fishing Line
Money
Unknown Key
Kerosene
Ammonia
Nitrates
Camphene

Something that Sachs had mentioned when she was searching the boy's room came back to him.

"Ben, could you open that notebook there, Garrett's notebook? I want to look at it again."

"You want me to put it in the turning frame?"

"No, just thumb through it," Rhyme told him.

The boy's stilted drawings of the insects flipped past: a water boatman, a diving bell spider, a water strider.

He remembered that Sachs had told him that, except for the wasp jar—Garrett's safe—the insects in his collection were in jars containing water. "They're all aquatic."

Ben nodded. "Seem to be."

"He's attracted to water," Rhyme mused. He looked at Ben. "And that bait? You said it's for bottom feeders."

"Stinkballs? Right."

"Saltwater or fresh?"

"Well, fresh. Of course."

"And the kerosene—boats run on that, right?"

"White gas," Ben said. "Small outboards do."

Rhyme said, "How's this for a thought? He's going west by boat on the Paquenoke River?"

Ben said, "Makes sense, Lincoln. And I'll bet there's so much kerosene because he's been refueling a lot—making runs back and forth between Tanner's Corner and the place he's got Mary Beth. Getting it ready for her."

"Good thinking. Call Jim Bell in here, would you?"

A few minutes later Bell returned and Rhyme explained his theory.

Bell said, "Water bugs gave you that idea, huh?"

Rhyme nodded. "If we know insects, we'll know Garrett Hanlon."

"It's no crazier than anything else I've heard today," Jim Bell said.

Rhyme asked, "Have you got a police boat?"

"No. But it wouldn't do us any good anyway. You don't know the Paquo. From the map it looks like any other river—with banks and all. But it's got a thousand inlets and branches flowing into and out of marshes. If Garrett's on it he's not staying to the main channel. I guarantee you that. It'd be impossible to find him."

Rhyme's eyes followed the Paquenoke west. "If he was moving supplies to the place where he's got Mary Beth that means it's probably not too far off the river. How far west would he have to go to be in an area that was habitable?"

"Have to be a ways. See up there?" Bell touched a spot around Location G-7. "That's north of the Paquo; nobody'd live there. South of the river it gets pretty residential. He'd be seen for sure."

"So at least ten miles or so west?"

"You got that right," Bell said.

"That bridge?" Rhyme nodded toward the map. Looking at spot E-8.

"The Hobeth Bridge?"

"What're the approaches to it like? The highway?"

"Just landfill. But there's a lot of it. The bridge's about forty feet high so the ramps leading up to it are long. Oh, wait. . . . You're thinking Garrett'd have to sail back to the main channel to get under the bridge."

"Right. Because the engineers would've filled in the smaller channels on either side when they built the approaches."

Bell was nodding. "Yep. Makes sense to me."

"Get Lucy and the others there now. To the bridge. And, Ben, call that fellow—Henry Davett. Tell him we're sorry but we need his help again."

WWJD . . .

Thinking once again of Davett, Rhyme now offered a prayer—though not to any deities. It was directed to Amelia Sachs: Oh, Sachs, be careful. It's only a matter of time until Garrett comes up with an excuse for you to take the cuffs off him. Then to lead you to someplace deserted. Then he'll manage to get a hold of your gun. . . . Don't let the passing hours lull you into trusting him, Sachs. Don't let your guard down. He's got the patience of a mantis.

. . . . chapter twenty-eight

Garrett knew the waterways like an expert river pilot and steered the boat up what seemed to be dead ends yet he always managed to find creeks, thin as spiderweb strands, that led them steadily west through the maze.

He pointed out river otter, muskrat and beaver to Sachs—sightings that might have excited amateur naturalists but left her cold. Her wildlife was the rats and pigeons and squirrels of the city—and only to the extent they were useful in helping her and Rhyme in their forensic work.

"Look there!" he cried.

"What?"

He was pointing to something she couldn't see. He stared at a spot near the shore, lost in whatever tiny drama was being played out on the water. All Sachs could see was some bug skipping over the surface.

"Water strider," he told her then sat back as they eased past. His face grew serious. "Insects're, like, a lot more important than us. I mean, when it comes to keeping the planet going. See—I read this someplace—if all the people on earth disappeared tomorrow the world'd keep going just fine. But if the *insects* all went away then life'd be over with way fast—like, one generation. The plants'd die then the animals and the earth'd turn into this big rock again."

Despite his adolescent vernacular Garrett spoke with the authority of a professor and the verve of a revivalist. He continued, "Yeah, some insects're a pain in the ass. But that's only a few of them, like one or two percent." His face grew animated and he said proudly, "And the ones that eat crops and stuff, well, I have this idea. It's pretty cool. I want to breed this special kind of golden lacewing to control the bad ones, instead of poisons—so the good insects and other animals don't die. The lacewing'd be the best. Nobody's done that yet."

"You think you can, Garrett?"

"I don't exactly know how yet. But I'm gonna learn."

She recalled what she'd read in his book, E. O. Wilson's term, biofilia—the affection people have for other types of life on the planet. And as she listened to him telling her this trivia—all proof of a love of nature and learning—foremost in her thoughts was this: anyone who could be so fascinated by living creatures and, in his odd way, could love them couldn't possibly be a rapist and killer.

Amelia Sachs held on tightly to this thought and it sustained her as they navigated the Paquenoke, escaping from Lucy Kerr and from the mysterious man in the tan overalls and from the simple, troubled town of Tanner's Corner.

Escaping from Lincoln Rhyme too. And from his impending operation and the terrible consequences it might have for both of them.

The narrow boat eased through the tributaries, no longer black water but golden, camouflaged—reflecting the low sunlight—just like that French cricket Garrett had told her about. Finally the boy steered out of the back routes and into the main channel of the river, hugging the shore. Sachs looked behind them, to the east, to see if there were police boats in pursuit. She saw nothing except one of the big Davett Industries barges, headed upstream—away from them. Garrett throttled back on the motor and eased into a little cove. He peered through an overhanging willow branch, looking west toward a bridge that ran across the Paquenoke.

"We have to go under it," he said. "We can't get around." He studied the span. "You see anybody?"

Sachs looked. She saw a few flashes of light. "Maybe. I can't tell. There's too much glare."

"That's where the assholes'd be waiting for us," he said uneasily. "I always worry about the bridge. People looking for you."

Always?

Garrett beached the boat and shut the motor off. He climbed out and unscrewed a turn-bolt securing the outboard, which he pulled off and hid in the grass, along with the gas tank.

"What're you doing?" she asked.

"Can't take a chance of getting spotted."

Garrett took the cooler and the water jugs out of the boat and lashed the oars to the seats with two pieces of greasy rope. He poured the water out of a half dozen of the jugs and recapped them, set them aside. He nodded toward the bottles. "Too bad about the water. Mary Beth doesn't have any. She'll need some. But I can get some for her from this pond near the cabin." Then he waded into the river and gripped the boat by the side. "Help me," he said. "We've got to capsize it."

"We're going to sink it?"

"No. Just turn her upside down. We'll put the jugs underneath. She'll float fine."

"Upside down?"

"Sure."

Sachs realized what Garrett had in mind. They'd get up underneath the boat and float past the bridge. The dark hull, low in the water, would be almost impossible to see from the bridge. Once they were past they could right the boat and row the rest of the way to where Mary Beth was.

He opened the cooler and found a plastic bag. "We can put our things in it that we don't want to get wet." He dropped his book, *The Miniature World,* inside it. Sachs added her wallet and the gun. She tucked her T-shirt into her jeans and slipped the bag down the front of her shirt.

Garrett said, "Can you take my cuffs off?" He held his hands out.

She hesitated.

"I don't want to drown," he said, eyes imploring.

I'm scared. Make him stop!

"I won't do anything bad. I promise."

Reluctantly Sachs fished the key from her pocket and undid the cuffs.

■

The Weapemeoc Indians, native to what is now North Carolina, were, linguistically, part of the Algonquin nation and were related to the Powhatans, the Chowans and the Pamlico tribes in the Mid-Atlantic portion of the United States.

They were excellent farmers and were envied among their fellow Native Americans for their fishing prowess. They were peaceful to an extreme and had little interest in arms. Three hundred years ago the British scientist Thomas Harriot wrote, "Those weapons that they have, are onlie bowes made of Witch hazle, and arrows of reeds; neither have they anything to defend themselves but targets made of barcks; and some armours made of sticks wickered together with thread."

It took British colonists to turn these people militant and they did so quite efficiently by, simultaneously, threatening them with God's wrath if they didn't convert immediately to Christianity, decimating the population by importing influenza and smallpox, demanding food and shelter they were too lazy to provide for themselves and murdering one of the tribe's favorite chiefs, Wingina, who, the colonists were convinced, erroneously, as it happened, was plotting an attack on the British settlements.

To the colonists' indignant surprise, rather than accepting the Lord Jesus Christ into their hearts, the Indians declared allegiance to their own deities—spirits called Manitous—and then war against the British, the opening action of which (according to history as writ by young Mary Beth McConnell) was the assault on the Lost Colonists at Roanoke Island.

After the settlers fled, the tribe—anticipating British reinforcements—took a new look at weaponry and began to use copper, which had been used only for decoration, in making arms. Metal arrowheads were much sharper than flint and easier to make. However, unlike in the movies, an arrow fired by an unpulleyed bow usually won't penetrate very far into the skin and is rarely fatal. To finish off his wounded adversary the Weapemeoc warrior would apply the coup de grâce—a blow to the head with a club called, appropriately, a "coup stick," which the tribe became very talented in making.

A coup stick is nothing more than a large, rounded rock bound into the split end of a stick and lashed into place with a leather thong. It's a very efficient weapon, and the one that Mary Beth McConnell was now making, based on her knowledge of Native American archaeology, was surely as deadly as the ones that—in her theory—had crushed the skulls and snapped the spines of the Roanoke settlers as they fought their last battle on the shores of the Paquenoke at what was now called Blackwater Landing.

She'd made hers out of two curved support rods from the old dinner table chair in the cabin. The rock was the one that Tom, the Missionary's friend, had flung at her.

She'd mounted it in between the two rods and bound it with long strips of denim torn from her shirttail. The weapon was heavy—six or seven pounds—but it wasn't too heavy for Mary Beth, who regularly lifted thirty- and forty-pound rocks at archaeological digs.

She now rose from the bed and swung the weapon several times, pleased with the power the club gave her. A skittish sound registered in her hearing—the insects in the jars. It made her think of Garrett's disgusting habit of snapping his fingernails together. She shivered in rage and lifted the coup stick to bring it down on the jar closest to her.

But then she paused. She hated the insects, yes, but her anger wasn't really directed at them. It was Garrett she was furious with. She left the jars alone and walked to the door then slammed the stick into it several times—near the lock. The door didn't budge. Well, she hadn't expected it to. But the important thing was that she'd tied the rock to the head of the club very firmly. It hadn't slipped.

Of course if the Missionary and Tom returned with a gun, the club wouldn't do much good against them. But she decided that if they got inside she'd keep the stick hidden behind her and the first one who touched her would get a broken skull. The other might kill her but she'd take one of them with her. (She imagined that this was how Virginia Dare had died.)

Mary Beth sat down and looked out the window, at the low sun on the line of trees where she'd first seen the Missionary.

What was the feeling coursing through her? Fear, she supposed.

But then she decided that it wasn't fear at all. It was impatience. She wanted her enemies to return.

Mary Beth lifted the coup stick into her lap.

Get yourself ready, Tom had told her.

Well, that she had.

■

"There's a boat."

Lucy leaned forward through the leaves of a pungent bay tree on the shore near the Hobeth Bridge. Her hand was on her weapon.

"Where?" she asked Jesse Corn.

"There." Pointing upstream.

She could vaguely see a slight darkness on the water, a half mile away. Moving in the current.

"What do you mean, boat?" she asked. "I don't see—"

"No, look. It's upside down."

"I can hardly see it," she said. "You've got good eyes."

"Is it them?" Trey asked.

"What happened? Did it capsize?"

But Jesse Corn said, "Naw, they're underneath it."

Lucy squinted. "How do you know?"

"Just have a feeling," he said.

"There's enough air under there?" Trey asked.

Jesse said, "Sure. It's high enough in the water. We used to do that with canoes on Bambert Lake. When we were kids. We'd play submarine."

Lucy said, "What do we do? We need a boat or something to get to them." She looked around.

Ned pulled his police utility belt off, handed it to Jesse Corn. "Hell, I'll just go out and kick it back into shore."

"You can swim that?" she asked.

The man took his boots off. "I swum this river a million times."

"We'll cover you," Lucy said.

"They're underwater," Jesse said. "I wouldn't worry too much about them shooting anybody."

Trey pointed out, "A little grease on the shells and they'll last for weeks underwater."

"Amelia's not gonna shoot," said Jesse Corn, Judas's defender.

"But we're not taking any chances," Lucy said. Then

to Ned: "Don't flip it over. Just swim out and steer it over this way. Trey, you go over there, by the willow, with the scattergun. Jesse and I'll be over there on the shore. We'll have 'em in a cross fire if anything happens."

Ned, barefoot and shirtless, walked gingerly on the rocky embankment down to the mud beach. He looked around carefully—for snakes, Lucy supposed—and then eased into the water. Ned breaststroked out toward the boat, swimming very quietly, keeping his head above water. Lucy pulled her Smith & Wesson from the holster. Cocked the hammer. Glanced at Jesse Corn, who looked at her weapon uneasily. Trey was standing beside a tree, holding the shotgun, muzzle up. He noticed her cocked pistol and he racked a round into the chamber of the Remington.

The boat was thirty feet from them, near midstream.

Ned was a strong swimmer and he was closing the distance quickly. He'd be there in—

The gunshot was loud and close. Lucy jumped as a spume of water shot into the air a few feet from Ned.

"Oh, no!" Lucy called, bringing up her weapon, looking for the shooter.

"Where, where?" Trey called, crouching and adjusting his grip on the shotgun.

Ned dove under the surface.

Another shot. Water flew into the air. Trey lowered the scattergun and started firing at the boat. Panic fire. The twelve-gauge didn't have a plugged tube; it was loaded with seven rounds. The deputy emptied it in seconds, hitting the boat squarely with every round, sending splinters of wood and water flying everywhere.

"No!" Jesse cried. "There're people under there!"

"Where're they shooting from?" Lucy called. "Under the boat? The other side of it? I can't tell. Where *are* they?"

"Where's Ned?" Trey asked. "Is he hit? Where's Ned?"

"I don't know," Lucy shouted, voice raw with panic. "I can't see him."

Trey reloaded and aimed at the boat once more.

"No!" Lucy ordered. "Don't fire. Cover me!"

She ran down the embankment and waded into the water. Suddenly, near the shore, she heard a choking gasp as Ned bobbed to the surface. "Help me!" He was terrified, looking behind him, scrabbling out of the water.

Jesse and Trey aimed their weapons at the far shore and stepped slowly down the incline to the river. Jesse's dismayed eyes were fixed on the riddled vessel—the terrible, ragged holes in the hull.

Charging into the water, Lucy holstered her gun and grabbed Ned's arm, dragged him to the shore. He'd stayed under as long as he dared and was pale and weak from lack of oxygen.

"Where are they?" he struggled to ask, choking.

"Don't know," she said, pulling him into a stand of bushes. He collapsed on his side, spitting and coughing. She looked him over carefully. He hadn't been hit.

They were joined by Trey and Jesse, both of them crouching, eyes gazing across the river, looking for their attackers.

Ned was still choking. "Fucking water. Tastes like shit."

The boat was slowly easing toward them, half submerged now.

"They're dead," whispered Jesse Corn, staring at the boat. "They have to be."

The boat floated closer. Jesse slipped his utility belt off and started forward.

"No," Lucy said, eyes on the far shore. "Let it come to us."

. . . chapter twenty-nine

The capsized boat floated into an uprooted cedar, extending into the river, and stopped.

The deputies waited a few moments. There was no movement other than the rocking of the shattered vessel. The water was ruddy but Lucy couldn't tell if the color was due to blood or was from the fiery sunset.

Pale, troubled Jesse Corn glanced at Lucy, who nodded. All three of the other deputies kept their guns on the boat as Jesse waded out and flipped it over.

The remnants of several torn water jugs bobbed out and floated leisurely downstream. There was no one underneath.

"What happened?" Jesse asked. "I don't get it."

"Hell," Ned muttered bitterly. "They set us up. It was a goddamn ambush."

Lucy hadn't believed that her anger could get any more consuming. But it now seized her like raw electric current. Ned was right; Amelia had used the boat like one of Nathan Groomer's decoys and ambushed them from the far shore.

"No," Jesse protested. "She wouldn't do that. If she shot it was just to scare us. Amelia knows her way 'round firearms. She could've hit Ned, she'd wanted to."

"Goddamnit, Jesse, open your eyes, will you?" Lucy snapped. "Firing from heavy cover like that? Doesn't matter how good a shot you are; she still could've missed. And on water? There could've been a ricochet. Or Ned might've panicked and swum into a bullet."

Jesse Corn had no response for that. He rubbed his face with his palms and stared out over the far shore.

"Okay, here's what we're doing," Lucy said in a low voice. "It's getting late. We're going as far as we can while there's still some light. Then we'll have Jim bring us some supplies for the night. We'll be camping out. We're going to assume they're gunning for us and we're going to act accordingly. Now, let's get across the bridge and look for their trail. Everybody locked and loaded?"

Ned and Trey said they were. Jesse Corn stared at the shattered boat for a moment then slowly nodded.

"Then let's go."

The four deputies started over the fifty yards of unprotected bridge—but they didn't walk in a cluster. They were in a long line so that if Amelia Sachs were to shoot again she couldn't hit more than one of them before the others got to cover and could return fire. The formation was Trey's idea, one that he got from a World War II movie, and because he'd thought of it he assumed he'd take the point position. But that was the spot Lucy Kerr insisted on taking for herself.

■

"You came damn close to hitting him."

Harris Tomel said, "No way."

But Culbeau persisted. "I said, *scare* 'em. You'd hit Ned, you know what kinda shit we'd be in?"

"I know what I'm doing, Rich. Give me a little credit, okay?"

Fucking schoolboy, Culbeau thought.

The three men were on the north shore of the Paquo, trekking along a path that followed the river.

In fact, while Culbeau *was* pissed that Tomel had fired too close to the deputy swimming out to the boat, he was sure the sniping had worked. Lucy and the other deputies'd be skittish as sheep now and would move nice and slow.

The shooting also had another beneficial effect—Sean O'Sarian was spooked and was being quiet for a change.

They walked for twenty minutes then Tomel asked Culbeau, "You know the boy's going in this direction?"

"Yep."

"But you don't have any idea where he's gonna end up."

" 'Course not," Culbeau said. "If I did we could just go there direct, right?"

Come on, schoolboy. Use your fucking noggin.

"But—"

"Don't worry. We're gonna find him."

"Can I have some water?" O'Sarian finally asked.

"Water? You want water?"

O'Sarian said complacently, "Yeah, that's what I'd like."

Culbeau glanced at him suspiciously and handed him a bottle. He'd never known the scrawny young man to actually drink something that wasn't beer, whisky or 'shine. He drank it down, wiped a mouth surrounded by freckles and tossed the bottle aside.

Culbeau sighed. He said sarcastically, "Hey now, Sean, you sure you want to leave something with your finger-prints on the trail?"

"Oh, right." The skinny man scurried into the brush and retrieved it. "Sorry."

Sorry? Sean O'Sarian apologizing? Culbeau stared for

a moment in disbelief then nodded them all forward again.

They came to a bend in the river and, being on high ground, they could see for miles downstream.

Tomel said, "Hey, look up there. There's a house. Bet the boy and the redhead've headed that way."

Culbeau sighted through the 'scope of his deer rifle. About two miles down the valley was an A-frame vacation house, just about on the river. It'd be a logical hiding place for the boy and the woman cop to hole up. He nodded. "Bet they are. Let's go."

∎

Downstream from the Hobeth Bridge, the Paquenoke River makes a sharp bend to the north.

It's shallow here, near the shore, and the muddy shoals are piled high with driftwood and vegetation and trash.

Like skiffs adrift, two human forms floating in the water now missed the turn and were eased by the current into this refuse heap.

Amelia Sachs let go of the plastic water jug—her improvised flotation device—and reached out a wrinkled hand to grip a branch. She then realized that this wasn't a very smart thing to do because her pockets were filled with rocks for ballast and she felt herself being tugged downward into the dusky water. But she straightened her legs and found the river bottom only four feet below the surface. She stood unsteadily and slogged forward. Garrett appeared beside her a moment later and helped her out of the water onto the muddy ground.

They crawled up a slight incline, through a tangle of bushes, and collapsed in a grassy clearing, lay there for a few minutes, caught their breath. She pulled the plastic bag out of her shirt. It had leaked slightly but there wasn't any serious water damage. She handed him his insect book and opened the cylinder of her gun then rested it on a clump of brittle, yellow grass to dry.

She'd been wrong about what Garrett had planned. They *had* slipped empty water jugs under the overturned boat for buoyancy but then he'd shoved it into midstream without getting underneath it. He'd told her to fill her pockets with rocks. He'd done the same and they hurried downstream past the boat, fifty feet or so, and slipped into the water, each holding a half-full water jug for flotation. Garrett showed her how to lean her head back. With the rocks for ballast only their faces were above the water. They'd float downstream on the current ahead of the boat.

"The diving bell spider does this," he'd told her. "Like a scuba diver. Carries his air around with him." He'd done this several times in the past to "get away," though—just like earlier—he didn't elaborate on why he'd been escaping and from whom. Garrett had explained that if the police weren't at the bridge they'd swim over to the boat, beach it, drain out the water and continue on their way, rowing with the oars. If the deputies were on the bridge their attention would be on the boat and they wouldn't notice Garrett and Amelia floating ahead of it. Once past the bridge they'd kick to shore and continue their journey on foot.

Well, he'd been right about that part; they'd gotten under the bridge undetected. But Sachs was still shocked at what had happened next—unprovoked, the deputies had fired round after round at the overturned boat.

Garrett too was badly shaken by the gunshots. "They thought we were under there," he whispered. "Fuckers tried to kill us."

Sachs said nothing.

He added, "I've done some bad things . . . but I'm no *phymata.*"

"What's that?"

"An ambush bug. Lies in wait and kills. That's what

they were going to do with us. Just, like, shoot us. Not give us any chance at all."

Oh, Lincoln, she thought, what a mess this is. Why did I do it? I should just surrender now. Wait here for the deputies, give it up. Go back to Tanner's Corner and try to make amends.

But she looked over at Garrett, hugging himself, shivering with fear. And she knew she couldn't turn back now. She'd have to keep going, play this crazy game out.

Knuckle time . . .

"Where do we go now?"

"See that house there?"

A brown A-frame.

"Is Mary Beth there?"

"Naw, but they've got a little trolling boat we can borrow. And we can get dry and get some food."

Well, what did a count of breaking and entering matter after tallying up her criminal charges today?

Garrett suddenly picked up her pistol. She froze, watching the blue-black gun in his hands. Knowingly he looked in the chambers and saw it was loaded with six rounds. He clicked the cylinder into the frame of the gun and balanced it in his hand with a familiarity that unnerved her.

Whatever you think about Garrett, don't trust him . . .

He glanced at her and gave a grin. Then he handed her the gun butt first. "Let's go this way." Nodding toward a path.

She replaced the weapon in her holster, feeling the flutter of her heart from the scare.

They walked toward the house. "It's empty?" Sachs asked, nodding toward the structure.

"Nobody's there now." Garrett paused and looked back. After a moment he muttered, "They're pissed now, the deputies. And they're after us. With all their guns and things. Shit." He turned and led her along a path to the house. He was silent for a few minutes. "You wanta know something, Amelia?"

"What?"

"I was thinking about this moth—the grand emperor moth?"

"What about it?" she asked absently, hearing in her memory the terrible shotgun blasts, meant for her and this boy. Lucy Kerr, trying to kill her. The echoes of the shots obscured everything else in her mind.

"The coloring on its wings?" Garrett told her. "Like, when they're open, they look just like an animal's eyes. I mean, it's pretty cool—there's even a white dot in the corner like a reflection of light in the pupil. Birds see that and think it's a fox or a cat and it scares them off."

"Can't the birds smell that it's a moth and not an animal?" she asked, not concentrating on the conversation.

He looked at her for a moment to see if she was joking. He said, "Birds can't smell," as if she'd just asked if the world was flat. He looked behind them, up the river again. "We'll have to slow 'em down. How close you think they are?"

"Very close," she said.

With all their guns and things.

■

"It's them."

Rich Culbeau was looking at the footprints in the mud of the shore. "The trail's only ten, fifteen minutes old."

"And they're heading for the house," Tomel said.

They moved cautiously up a path.

O'Sarian still wasn't acting weird. Which for him actually *was* weird. And scary. He hadn't snuck any hits of 'shine, hadn't been pranking, hadn't even been talking—and Sean was the number one motormouth in Tanner's Corner. The shooting at the river had really shaken him. Now, as they walked through the woods, he swung the muzzle of the black soldier rifle around fast at every sound from the brush. "Did you see that nigger shoot?"

he said finally. "Must've put ten slugs in that boat in less than a minute."

"Was pellets," Harris Tomel corrected.

And instead of challenging him and trying to impress them with what he knew about guns (and acting like the all-purpose asshole he was), O'Sarian just said, "Oh, buckshot. Right. I should've thought of that." And nodded like a kid in school who'd just learned something new and interesting.

They moved closer to the house. It looked like a nice place, Culbeau thought. A vacation house probably—maybe some lawyer's or doctor's from Raleigh or Winston-Salem. A good hunting lodge, full bar, nice bedrooms, a freezer for venison.

"Hey, Harris," O'Sarian asked.

Culbeau'd never known the boy to use anybody's first name.

"What?"

"This thing shoot high or low?" Holding up the Colt.

Tomel glanced at Culbeau, probably also trying to figure out where the weird part of O'Sarian had gone.

"First one's right on the money but it'll kick higher than you're used to. Drop the muzzle for the next shots."

"Because the stock's plastic," O'Sarian asked, "so it's lighter than wood?"

"Yeah."

He nodded again, his face even more serious than earlier. "Thanks."

Thanks?

The woods ended and the men could see a large clearing around the house—easily fifty yards in all directions without even a sapling for cover. The approach'd be tough.

"Think they're inside?" Tomel asked, kneading his gorgeous shotgun.

"I don't— Wait, get down!"

The three men crouched fast.

"I saw something downstairs. Through that window to the left." Culbeau looked through the 'scope on the deer rifle. "Somebody's moving around. On the ground floor. I can't see too good, with the blinds. But there's definitely somebody there." He scanned the other windows. "Shit!" A panicked whisper. He dropped to the ground.

"What?" O'Sarian asked, alarmed, gripping his gun and spinning around.

"Get down! One of 'em's got a rifle with a 'scope. They're sighting right at us. Upstairs window. Damn."

"Gotta be the girl," Tomel said. "That boy's too much of a faggot to know which end the bullet comes out."

"Fuck that bitch," Culbeau muttered. O'Sarian was easing behind a tree, hugging his 'Nam gun close to his cheek.

"She's got the whole field covered from here," Culbeau said.

"We wait till it's dark?" Tomel asked.

"Oh, with little miss tit-less deputy coming up behind us? I don't think that'll work, now, Harris, will it?"

"Well, can you hit her from here?" Tomel nodded toward the window.

"Probably," Culbeau said, sighing. He was about to start ragging on Tomel when O'Sarian said in a weirdly normal voice, "But if Rich shoots, then Lucy and th'others'll hear. I think we oughta flank 'em. Go around the side and try and get inside. A shot'd be a lot quieter in there."

Which was just what Culbeau was about to say.

"That'll take a half hour," Tomel snapped, probably pissed at being outthought by O'Sarian.

Who remained at the top of his uncrazy form. The young man clicked the safety off his gun and squinted toward the house. "Well, I'd say we gotta make it take *less* than half an hour. Whatta *you* think, Rich?"

. . . chapter thirty

Steve Farr led Henry Davett into the lab once again. The businessman thanked Farr, who left, and nodded to Rhyme.

"Henry," Rhyme said, "thank you for coming."

As before, the businessman paid no attention to Rhyme's condition. This time, though, Rhyme took no comfort from his attitude. His concern for Sachs was consuming him. He kept hearing Jim Bell's voice.

You usually have twenty-four hours to find the victim; after that they become dehumanized in the kidnapper's eyes and he doesn't think anything about killing them.

This rule, which had applied to Lydia and Mary Beth, now encompassed Amelia Sachs's fate too. The difference was, Rhyme believed, that Sachs might have far fewer than twenty-four hours.

"I thought you'd caught that boy. That's what I heard."

Ben said, "He got away from us."

"No!" Davett frowned.

"Sure did," Ben offered. "Old-fashioned jailbreak."

Rhyme: "I've got some more evidence but I don't know what to make of it. I was hoping you could help again."

The businessman sat down. "I'll do what I can."

A glance at his WWJD tie bar.

Rhyme nodded toward the chart, said, "Could you look that over? The list on the right."

"The mill—is *that* where he was? That old mill north-east of town?"

"Right."

"I *knew* about the place." Davett grimaced angrily. "I should've thought of it."

Criminalists can't let the verb "should have" creep into their vocabulary. Rhyme said, "It's impossible to think of everything in this business. But take a look at the chart. Does anything on it seem familiar to you?"

Davett read carefully.

FOUND AT THE SECONDARY CRIME SCENE—
MILL

Brown Paint on Pants
Sundew Plant
Clay
Peat Moss
Fruit Juice
Paper Fibers
Stinkball Bait
Sugar
Camphene
Alcohol
Kerosene
Yeast

As he gazed at the list he said in a distracted voice, "It's like a puzzle."

"That's the nature of my job," Rhyme said.

"How much can I speculate?" the businessman asked.

"As much as you'd like," Rhyme said.

"All right," Davett said. He thought for a moment then said, "A Carolina bay."

Rhyme asked, "What's that? A horse?"

Davett glanced at Rhyme to see if he was joking. Then said, "No, it's a geologic structure you see on the Eastern Seaboard. Mostly, though, they're found in the Carolinas. North and South. They're basically oval ponds, about three or four feet deep, freshwater. They could be a half acre big or a couple of hundred. The bottom of them is mostly clay and peat. Just what's on the chart there."

"But clay and peat—they're pretty common around here," Ben said.

"They are," Davett agreed. "And if you'd found just those two things I wouldn't have a clue where they came from. But you found something else. See, one of the most interesting characteristics about Carolina bays is that insect-killer plants grow around them. You see hundreds of Venus flytraps, sundews and pitcher plants around bays—probably because the ponds promote insects. If you found a sundew along with clay and peat moss then there's no doubt the boy's spent time around a Carolina bay."

"Good," Rhyme said. Then, gazing at the map, asked, "What does 'bay' mean? An inlet of water?"

"No, it refers to bay trees. They grow around the ponds. There're all sorts of myths about them. Settlers used to think they were carved out of the land by sea monsters or witches casting spells. Meteorites were a theory for a few years. But they're really just natural depressions caused by wind and currents of water."

"Are they unique to a particular area around here?" Rhyme asked, hoping that they'd help narrow down the search.

"To some extent." Davett rose and walked to the map. With his finger he circled a large area to the west of Tanner's

Corner. Location B-2 to E-2 and F-13 to B-12. "You'll find them mostly here, in this area, just before you get to the hills."

Rhyme was discouraged. What Davett had circled must have included seventy or eighty square miles.

Davett saw Rhyme's reaction. He said, "Wish I could be more helpful."

"No, no, I appreciate it. It *will* be helpful. We just need to narrow down more of the clues."

The businessman read, "Sugar, fruit juice, kerosene . . ." He shook his head, unsmiling. "You have a difficult job, Mr. Rhyme."

"These are the tough cases," Rhyme explained. "When you have no clues you're free to speculate. When you have a lot of them you can usually get the answer pretty quickly. But having a few clues, like this . . ." Rhyme's voice faded.

"We're hog-tied by the facts," Ben muttered.

Rhyme turned to him. "Exactly, Ben. Exactly."

"I should be getting home," Davett said. "My family's expecting me." He wrote a phone number on a business card. "You can call me anytime."

Rhyme thanked him again and turned his gaze back to the evidence chart.

Hog-tied by the facts . . .

■

Rich Culbeau sucked the blood off his arm from where the brambles had scratched it deeply. He spit against a tree.

It had taken them twenty minutes of hard slogging through the brush to get to the side porch of the A-frame vacation house without being seen by the bitch with the sniper gun. Even Harris Tomel, who normally looked like he'd just stepped off a country club patio, was bloody and dust-stained.

The new Sean O'Sarian, quiet and thoughtful and, well, *sane,* was waiting back on the path, lying on the ground with his black gun like an infantry grunt at Khe Sahn, ready to slow up Lucy and the other Vietcong with a few shots over their heads in case they came up the trail toward the house.

"You ready?" Culbeau asked Tomel, who nodded.

Culbeau eased open the knob of the mudroom door and pushed the door inside, his gun up and ready. Tomel followed. They were skittish as cats, knowing that the redheaded cop with the deer rifle she surely knew how to use could be waiting for them anywhere in the house.

"You hear anything?" Culbeau whispered.

"Just music." It was soft rock—the sort Culbeau listened to because he hated country-western.

The two men moved slowly down the dim hallway, guns up and cocked. They slowed. Ahead of them was the kitchen, where Culbeau had seen somebody—probably the boy—moving when he'd sighted on the house through the rifle 'scope. He nodded toward the room.

"Don't think they heard us," Tomel said. The music was up pretty high.

"We go in together. Shoot for their legs or knees. Don't kill him—we still gotta get him to tell us where Mary Beth is."

"The woman too?"

Culbeau thought for a moment. "Yeah, why not? We might want to keep her alive for a while. You know what for."

Tomel nodded.

"One, two . . . three."

They pushed fast into the kitchen and found themselves about to shoot a weatherman on a big-screen TV. They crouched and spun around, looking for the boy and the woman. Didn't see them. Then Culbeau looked at the set. He realized it didn't belong here. Somebody'd rolled it in from the living room and set it up in front of the stove, facing the windows.

Culbeau peered out through the blinds. "Shit. They put the set here so we'd see it from across the field, from the path. And think there was somebody in the house." He took off up the stairs, taking them two at a time.

"Wait," Tomel called. "She's up there. With the gun."

But of course the redhead wasn't up there at all. Culbeau kicked into the bedroom where he'd seen the rifle barrel and the telescopic sight aiming at them and he now found pretty much what he expected to find: a piece of narrow pipe on top of which was taped the ass end of a Corona bottle.

In disgust he said, "*That's* the gun and 'scope. Jesus Christ. They rigged it to bluff us out. It cost us a half fucking hour. And the goddamn deputies're probably five minutes away. We gotta get outa here."

He stormed past Tomel, who started to say, "Pretty smart of her . . ." But, seeing the fire in Culbeau's eyes, he decided not to finish his sentence.

■

The battery ran down and the tiny electric trolling engine fell silent.

Their narrow skiff they'd stolen from the vacation house drifted on the current of the Paquenoke, through the oily mist covering the river. It was dusk. The water was no longer golden but moody gray.

Garrett Hanlon picked up a paddle in the bottom of the boat and headed toward shore. "We gotta land someplace," he said. "Before it's, like, totally dark."

Amelia Sachs noticed that the landscape had changed. The trees had thinned and large pools of marsh met the river. The boy was right; a wrong turn would take them into a back alley of some impenetrable bog.

"Hey, what's wrong?" he asked, seeing her troubled expression.

"I'm a hell of a long way from Brooklyn."

"That's in New York?"

"Right," she said.

He clicked his nails. "And it bothers you not being there?"

"You bet it does."

Steering toward the shore, he said, "That's what scares insects the most."

"What's that?"

"Like, it's weird. They don't mind working and they don't mind fighting. But they get all freaked out in an unfamiliar place. Even if it's safe. They hate it, don't know what to do."

Okay, Sachs thought, I guess I'm a card-carrying insect. She preferred the way Lincoln phrased it: Fish out of water.

"You can always tell when an insect's really upset. They clean their antennas over and over again. . . . Insects' antennas show their moods. Like our faces. Only the thing is," he added cryptically, "*they* don't fake it. Like we do." He laughed in an odd way—a sound she hadn't heard before.

He eased over the side of the boat into the water and pulled the boat onto the land. Sachs climbed out. He directed her through the woods and seemed to know exactly where he was going despite the darkness of dusk and the absence of any path that she could see.

"How do you know where to go?" she asked.

Garrett said, "I guess I'm like the monarchs. I just know directions pretty good."

"Monarchs?"

"You know, the butterflies. They migrate a thousand miles and know exactly where they're going. It's really, really cool—they navigate by the sun and, like, change course automatically depending on where it is on the horizon. Oh, and when it's overcast or dark they use this other sense they have—they can feel the earth's magnetic fields."

When a bat shoots out a beam of sound to find them, moths fold their wings and drop to the ground and hide.

She was smiling at his enthusiastic lecture when she stopped suddenly and crouched. "Look out," she whispered. "There! There's a light."

Faint illumination reflecting off a murky pond. An eerie yellow light like a failing lantern.

But Garrett was laughing.

She looked at him quizzically.

He said, "Just a ghost."

"What?" she asked.

"It's the Lady of the Swamp. Like, this Indian maiden who died the night before her wedding. Her ghost still paddles through the Dismal Swamp looking for the guy she was going to marry. We're not in the Great Dismal but it's near here." He nodded toward the glow. "What it is really is just fox fire—this gross fungus that glows."

She didn't like the light. It reminded her of the uneasiness she felt as they drove into Tanner's Corner that morning, seeing the small coffin at the funeral.

"I don't like the swamp, with or without ghosts," Sachs said.

"Yeah?" Garrett said. "Maybe you'll get to like it. Someday."

He led her along a road and after ten minutes he turned down a short, overgrown driveway. There was an old trailer sitting in a clearing. In the gloom she couldn't see clearly but it seemed to be a ramshackle place, leaning to the side, rusted, tires flat and overgrown with ivy and moss.

"This is yours?"

"Well, nobody's lived here for years so I *guess* it's mine. I have a key but it's at home. I didn't have a chance to get it." He went around to the side and managed to open a window, boosted himself up and through it. A moment later the door opened.

She walked inside. Garrett was rummaging through a cabinet in the tiny kitchen. He found some matches and lit a propane lantern. It gave off a warm, yellow glow. He opened another cabinet, peered inside.

"I had some Doritos but the mice got 'em." He pulled out some Tupperware and examined it. "Chewed right through. Shit. But I've got Farmer John macaroni. It's good. I eat it all the time. And some beans too." He started opening cans as Sachs looked around the trailer. A few chairs, a table. In the bedroom she could see a dingy mattress. There was a thick mat and a pillow on the living room floor. The trailer itself radiated poverty: broken doors and fixtures, bullet holes in the walls, windows broken, carpet stained beyond cleaning. In her days as a patrol officer for the NYPD she'd seen many sad places like this—but always from the outside; now this was *her* temporary home.

Thinking of Lucy's words from that morning.

Normal rules don't apply to anybody north of the Paquo. Us or them. You can see yourself shooting before you read anybody their rights and that'd be perfectly all right.

Remembering the stunning blasts of the shotgun, intended for her and Garrett.

The boy hung pieces of greasy cloth over the windows to keep anyone from seeing the light inside. He stepped outside for a moment then came back with a rusty cup, filled, presumably, with rainwater. He held it out to her. She shook her head. "Feel like I drank half the Paquenoke."

"This's better."

"I'm sure it is. I'll still pass."

He drank the contents of the cup and then stirred the food as it heated on the small propane stove. In a soft voice he sang an eerie tune over and over, "*Farmer John, Farmer John. Enjoy it fresh from Farmer John. . . .*" It was nothing more than an advertising jingle but the chant was unsettling and she was glad when he stopped.

Sachs was going to pass on the food but she realized suddenly that she was famished. Garrett poured the contents into two bowls and handed her a spoon. She spit on the utensil and wiped it on her shirt. They ate for a few minutes in silence.

Sachs noticed a sound outside, a raucous, high-pitched noise. "What's that?" she asked. "Cicadas?"

"Yeah," he said. "It's just the males make that noise. Only the males. Make all that noise just from these little plates on their body." He squinted, reflected for a moment. "They live this totally weird life. . . . The nymphs dig into the ground and stay there for, like, twenty years before they hatch. Then they come out and climb a tree. Their skin splits down the back and the adult crawls out. All those years in the ground, just hiding, before they come out and become adults."

"Why do you like insects so much, Garrett?" Sachs asked.

He hesitated. "I don't know. I just do."

"Haven't you ever wondered about it?"

He stopped eating. Scratched one of his poison oak welts. "I guess I got interested in them after my parents died. After that happened I was pretty unhappy. I felt funny in my head a lot. Confused and, I don't know, just different. The counselors at school just said it was because Mom and Dad and my sister died and they, like, told me I should work harder to get over it. But I couldn't. I just felt like I wasn't a real person. I didn't care about anything. All I did was lie in bed or go into the swamp or the woods and read. For a year that's all I did. Like, I hardly saw anybody. Just moved from foster home to foster home. . . . But then I read something neat. In that book there."

Flipping open *The Miniature World,* he found a page. He showed it to her. He'd circled a passage headed Characteristics of Healthy Living Creatures. Sachs scanned it, read several of the list of eight or nine entries.

—*A healthy creature strives to grow and develop.*
—*A healthy creature strives to survive.*
—*A healthy creature strives to adapt to its environment.*

Garrett said, "I read that and it was like, wow, I could be like that. I could be healthy and normal again. I tried totally hard to follow the rules it said. And that made me feel better. So I guess I felt close to them—insects, I mean."

A mosquito landed on her arm. She laughed. "But they also drink your blood." She slapped it. "Got him."

"*Her,*" Garrett corrected. "It's just the females drink blood. The males drink nectar."

"Really?"

He nodded then grew quiet for a moment. Looked at the dot of blood on her arm. "Insects never go away."

"What do you mean?"

He found another passage in the book and read aloud, " 'If any creature could be called immortal it is the insect, which inhabited the earth millions of years before the advent of mammals and which will be here on earth long after intelligent life has vanished.' " Garrett put the book down and looked up at her. "See, the thing is, if you kill one there're always more. If my mom and dad and sister were insects and they died there'd be others just like them and I wouldn't be alone."

"Don't you have any friends?"

Garrett shrugged. "Mary Beth. She's sort of the only one."

"You really like her, don't you?"

"Totally. She saved me from this kid who was going to do something shitty to me. And, I mean, she *talks* to me. . . ." He thought for a moment. "I guess *that's* what I like about her. Talking. I was thinking, like, maybe in a few years, when I'm older, she might wanta go out with me. We could do things like other people do. You know, go to movies. Or go on picnics. I was watching her on a picnic once. She was with her mother and some friends. They were having fun. I watched for, like, hours. I just sat under a holly bush with some water and Doritos and pretended I was with them. You ever go on a picnic?"

"I have, sure."

"I went with my family a lot. I mean, my real family. I liked it. Mom and Kaye'd set the table and cook stuff on this little grill from Kmart. Dad and me'd take our shoes and socks off and stand in the water to fish. I remember what the mud felt like and the cold water."

Sachs wondered if that was why he liked water and water insects so much. "And you thought you and Mary Beth would go on picnics?"

"I don't know. Maybe." Then he shook his head and offered a sad smile. "I guess not. Mary Beth's pretty and smart and a bunch older than me. She'll end up with somebody who's handsome and smart. But maybe we could be friends, her and me. But even if not, all I really care about is she's okay. She'll stay with me till it's safe. Or you and your friend, that man in the wheelchair everybody was talking about, you can help her go someplace where she'd be safe." He looked out the window and fell silent.

"Safe from the man in the overalls?" she asked.

He didn't answer for a moment then nodded. "Yeah. That's right."

"I'm going to get some of that water," Sachs said.

"Wait," he said. He tore some dry leaves off a small branch resting on the kitchen counter, told her to rub her bare arms and neck and cheeks with it. It gave off a strong herbal smell. "Citronella plant," he explained. "Keeps the mosquitoes away. You won't have to swat 'em anymore."

Sachs picked up the cup. She went outside, looked at

the rainwater barrel. It was covered with a fine screen.
Lifted it, filled the cup and drank. The water seemed
sweet. She listened to the creaks and zips of the insects.

*Or you and your friend, that man in the wheelchair
everybody was talking about, you can help her go someplace where she'd be safe.*

*The phrase echoed in her head: The man in the wheel-
chair, the man in the wheelchair.*

She returned to the trailer. Set down the cup. Looked
around the tiny living room. "Garrett, would you do me
a favor?"

"I guess."

"You trust me?"

"I guess."

"Go sit over there."

He looked at her for a moment then stood and walked
to the old armchair she was nodding at. Sachs walked
across the tiny room and picked up one of the rattan
chairs in the corner. She carried it to where the boy sat
and placed it on the floor, facing him.

"Garrett, you remember what Dr. Penny was telling
you to do in jail? About the empty chair?"

"Talk to the chair?" he asked, eyeing it uncertainly. He
nodded. "That game."

"That's right. I want you to do it again. Will you?"

He hesitated, wiped his hands on the legs of his pants.
Stared at the chair for a moment. Finally he said, "I
guess."

. . . chapter thirty-one

Amelia Sachs was thinking back to the interrogation room and the session with the psychologist.

From her vantage point Sachs had watched the boy closely through the one-way mirror. She remembered how the doctor had tried to get him to imagine that Mary Beth was in the chair but that, while Garrett hadn't wanted to say anything to her, he did want to talk to *somebody*. She'd seen a look in his face, a longing, disappointment—and anger too, she believed—when the doctor turned him away from where he wanted to go.

Oh, Rhyme, I understand that you like hard, cold evidence. That we can't depend on those "soft" things—on words and expressions and tears and the look in someone's eyes as we sit across from them and listen to their stories. . . . But that doesn't mean those stories are *always* false. I believe there's more to Garrett Hanlon than the evidence tells us.

"Look at the chair," she said. "Who do you want to imagine sitting there?"

He shook his head. "I don't know."

She pushed the chair closer. Smiled to encourage him. "Tell me. It's okay. A girl? Somebody at school?"

He shook his head once more.

"Tell me."

"Well, I don't know. Maybe . . ." After a pause he blurted: "Maybe my father."

Sachs remembered, with irritation, the cold eyes and crude manners of Hal Babbage. She supposed that Garrett would have a lot to say to him.

"Just your father? Or both him and Mrs. Babbage?"

"No, no, not him. I mean, my real father."

"Your real father?"

Garrett nodded. He was agitated, nervous. Clicking his nails frequently.

Insects' antennas show their moods . . .

Looking at his troubled face, Sachs realized with concern that she had no idea what she was doing. There were surely all sorts of things psychologists did to draw patients out, to guide them, to protect them when they practiced any type of therapy. Was there a chance that she would make Garrett worse? Push him over a line so that he actually *would* do something violent and hurt himself or someone else? Nonetheless, she was going to try it. Sachs's nickname in the New York City Police Department was P.D.—for "the portable's daughter," the child of a beat patrolman—and she definitely took after her old man: his love of cars, love of police work, impatience with bullshit and especially his talent for street-cop psychology. Lincoln Rhyme disparaged her being a "people cop" and warned that it would be her downfall. He extolled her talent as a criminalist and, though she *was* a talented forensic scientist, in her heart she was just like her father; for Amelia Sachs the best type of evidence was that found in the human heart.

Garrett's eyes strayed to the window, where bugs thumped suicidally against the rusty screen.

"What was your father's name?" Sachs asked.

"Stuart. Stu."

"What did *you* call him?"

" 'Dad' mostly. 'Sir' sometimes." Garrett smiled sadly. "If I'd done something wrong and thought I better be, like, on good behavior."

"You two got along?"

"Better'n most of my friends and their dads. They got whipped some and their dads were always yelling at them. You know: 'Why'd you miss that goal?' 'Why's your room so messy?' 'Why didn't you get your homework done?' But Dad was okay to me. Until . . ." His voice bled out.

"Go on."

"I don't know." Another shrug.

Sachs persisted. "Until what, Garrett?"

Silence.

"Say it."

"I don't want to tell you. It's stupid."

"Well, don't tell *me*. Tell *him*, your dad." She nodded toward the chair. "There's your father right there in front of you. Imagine it." The boy edged forward, staring at the chair, almost fearfully. "There's Stu Hanlon sitting there. Talk to him."

For an instant there was such a look of longing in the boy's eyes that Sachs wanted to cry. She knew they were close to something important and she was afraid he'd balk. "Tell me about him," she said, changing tack slightly. "Tell me what he looked like. What he wore."

After a pause the boy said, "He was tall and pretty thin. He had dark hair and it stuck up right after he'd get his hair cut. He had to put this stuff on that smelled good to keep it down for a couple days afterward. He always wore pretty nice clothes. He didn't even have a pair of jeans, I don't think. He always wore shirts with, you know, collars on them. And pants with cuffs." Sachs recalled noting when she searched his room that he had no jeans, only cuffed slacks. A faint smile bloomed on

Garrett's face. "He used to drop a quarter down the side of his pants and try and catch it in his cuff and if he did then my sister or me could have it. It was, like, this game we played. On Christmas he'd bring home silver dollars for us and he'd keep sliding them down his pants until we got them."

The silver dollars in the wasp jar, Sachs recalled.

"Did he have any hobbies? Sports?"

"He liked to read. He'd take us to bookstores a lot and he read to us. A lot of history and travel books. And stuff about nature. Oh, and he fished. Almost every weekend."

"Well, imagine that he's sitting there in the empty chair and he's wearing his nice slacks and a shirt with a collar. And he's reading a book. Okay?"

"I guess."

"He puts the book down—"

"No, first he'd, like, mark the place he was reading. He had a ton of bookmarks. He sort of collected them. My sister and me got him one the Christmas before the accident."

"Okay, he marks his place and puts the book down. He's looking at you. Now you've got a chance to say something to him. What would you say?"

He shrugged, shook his head. Looked around the dim trailer nervously.

But Sachs wasn't going to let it go.

Knuckle time . . .

She said, "Let's think about a specific thing you'd like to talk to him about. An incident. Something you're unhappy about. Was there anything like that?"

But Dad was okay to me. Until . . .

The boy was gripping his hands, rubbing them together, clicking his nails.

"Tell him, Garrett."

"Okay, I guess there was something."

"What?"

"Well, that night . . . the night they died."

Sachs felt a faint shudder. Knew they were probably going very hard places with this. She thought for a moment about pulling back. But it wasn't in Amelia Sachs's nature to pull back and she didn't now. "What about that night? You want to talk to your father about something that happened?"

He nodded. "See, they were in the car going to dinner. It was Wednesday. Every Wednesday we went to Bennigan's. I liked the chicken fingers. I'd have the chicken fingers and fries and a Coke. And Kaye, my sister'd get onion rings and we'd split the fries and the rings and sometimes we drew pictures on an empty plate with the squeeze bottle of ketchup."

His face was pale and drawn. There was so much sorrow in his eyes, Sachs thought. She fought down her own emotions. "What do you remember about that night?"

"It was outside the house. In the driveway. They were in the car, Dad and Mom and my sister. They were going to dinner. And"—he swallowed—"what it was they were going to leave without me."

"They were?"

He nodded. "I was late. I'd been in the woods in Blackwater Landing. And I'd kinda lost track of time. I ran, like, a half mile or something. But my father wouldn't let me in. He must've been mad because I was late. I wanted to get in so bad. It was really cold. I remember I was shivering and they were shivering. I remember there was frost on the windows. But they wouldn't let me in."

"Maybe your father didn't see you. Because of the frost."

"No, he saw me. I was right beside his side of the car. I was banging on the window and he saw me but he didn't open the door. He just kept frowning and shouting at me. And I kept thinking, He's mad at me and I'm cold and I'm not going to get my chicken fingers and French fries. I'm not going to have dinner with my family." Tears ran down his cheeks.

Sachs wanted to put her arm around the boy's shoulders but she remained where she was. "Go on." Nodding toward the chair. "Talk to your father. What do you want to say to him?"

He looked at her but she pointed toward the chair. Finally Garrett turned to it. "It's so cold!" he said, gasping. "It's cold and I want to get in the car. Why won't he let me in the car?"

"No, tell *him*. Imagine he's there."

Sachs was thinking: This is the same way Rhyme urged her to imagine herself as the perp at crime scenes. It was utterly harrowing and she now felt the boy's fear all too clearly. Still, she didn't let up. "Tell him—tell your *father*."

Garrett looked at the old chair uneasily. He leaned forward. "I . . ."

Sachs whispered, "Go ahead, Garrett. It's okay. I won't let anything happen to you. Tell him."

"I just wanted to go to Bennigan's with you!" he said, sobbing. "That's all. Like, just to have dinner, all of us. I just wanted to go with you. Why wouldn't you let me in the car? You saw me coming and you locked the door. I wasn't *that* late!" Then Garrett grew angry. "You locked me out! You were mad at me and it wasn't fair. What I did, being late . . . it wasn't *that* bad. I must've done something else to make you mad. What? Why didn't you want me to go with you? Tell me what I did." His voice was choked. "Come back and tell me. Come back! I want to know! What did I do? Tell me, tell me, tell me!"

Sobbing, he jumped up and kicked the empty chair hard. It sailed across the room and fell on its side. He grabbed the chair and, screaming in fury, smashed it into the floor of the trailer. Sachs pushed back, blinking in shock at the anger she'd unleashed. He slammed the chair down a dozen times until it was nothing but a shattered mass of wood and rattan. Finally Garrett collapsed on the floor, hugging himself. Sachs rose and put her arms around him as he sobbed and shook.

After five minutes the crying ended. He stood up, wiped his face on his sleeve.

"Garrett," she began in a whisper.

But he shook his head. "I'm going outside," he said. Then rose and pushed out the door.

She sat for a moment, wondering what to do. Sachs was utterly exhausted but she didn't lie down on the mat he'd left for her and try to sleep. She shut the lantern off and pulled the cloth off the window then sat in the musty armchair. She leaned forward, smelling the pungent aroma of the citronella plant, and watched the hunched-over silhouette of the boy, sitting outside on an oak stump and gazing intently at the moving constellations of lightning bugs that filled the forest around him.

. . . chapter thirty-two

Lincoln Rhyme muttered, "I don't believe it."

He'd just spoken with a furious Lucy Kerr and had learned that Sachs had taken several shots at a deputy under the Hobeth Bridge.

"I don't believe it," he repeated in a whisper to Thom.

The aide was a master of dealing with broken bodies and spirits broken *because* of broken bodies. But this was a different matter, far worse, and the best he could do was offer, "It's a mix-up. It has to be. Amelia wouldn't do that."

"She *wouldn't*," Rhyme muttered. This time offering the denial to Ben. "There's no way. Not even to scare them off." He told himself that she'd *never* shoot at a fellow officer, even just to scare them. Yet he was also thinking about what desperate people did. The crazy risks they took. (Oh, Sachs, why do you have to be so impulsive and stubborn? Why do you have to be so much like me?)

Bell was in the office across the hall. Rhyme could hear him as he spoke endearments over the phone. He supposed that the sheriff's wife and family weren't used to late night absences; law enforcement in a town like Tanner's Corner probably didn't require as many hours as the Garrett Hanlon case had taken.

Ben Kerr sat beside one of the microscopes, his huge arms crossed over his chest. He was gazing at the map. Unlike the sheriff he hadn't made any calls home and Rhyme wondered if he had a wife or girlfriend or if the shy man's life was wholly consumed with science and the mysteries of the ocean.

The sheriff hung up. He walked back into the lab. "You have any more ideas, Lincoln?"

Rhyme nodded at the evidence chart.

FOUND AT THE SECONDARY CRIME SCENE— MILL

Brown Paint on Pants
Sundew Plant
Clay
Peat Moss
Fruit Juice
Paper Fibers
Stinkball Bait
Sugar
Camphene
Alcohol
Kerosene
Yeast

He reiterated what they knew about the house where Mary Beth was being kept. "There's a Carolina bay on the way to or near the place. Half the marked passages in his insect books are about camouflage and the brown paint on his pants's the color of tree bark so the place is probably in or next to a forest. The camphene lamps are from the 1800s so the place is old, probably Victorian era.

But the rest of the trace isn't much help. The yeast would be from the mill. The paper fibers could be from anywhere. The fruit juice and sugar? From food or drinks Garrett had with him. I just can't—"

The phone rang.

Rhyme's left ring finger twitched on the ECU and he answered the call.

"Hello?" he said into the speakerphone.

"Lincoln."

He recognized the soft, exhausted voice of Mel Cooper.

"What do you have, Mel? I need some good news."

"I hope it's good. That key you found? We've been looking through sourcebooks and databases all night. Finally tracked it down."

"What is it?"

"It's to a trailer made by the McPherson Deluxe Mobile Home Company. The trailers were manufactured from 1946 through the early '70s. Company's out of business but according to the guide, the serial number on the key you've got fits a trailer that was made in '69."

"Any description?"

"No pictures in the guide."

"Hell. Tell me, does one live in these things in a trailer park? Or drive 'em around like a Winnebago?"

"Live in them, I'd guess. They measure eight by twenty. Not the sort of thing you'd cruise around in. Anyway, they're not motorized. You have to tow it."

"Thanks, Mel. Get some sleep."

Rhyme shut the phone off. "What do you think, Jim? Any trailer parks around here?"

The sheriff seemed doubtful. "There're a couple along Route 17 and 158. But they aren't even close to where Garrett and Amelia were headed. And they're crowded. Hard to hide out in a place like that. Should I send somebody to check them out?"

"How far?"

"Seventy, eighty miles."

"No. Garrett probably found a trailer abandoned someplace in the woods and took it over." Rhyme glanced at the map. Thinking: And it's parked somewhere in a hundred square miles of wilderness.

Wondering too: Had the boy gotten out of the handcuffs? Did he have Sachs's gun? Was she falling asleep just now, her guard down, Garrett waiting for the moment when she slipped into unconsciousness. He'd rise, crawl closer to her with a rock or a hornets' nest. . . .

The anxiety racing through him, he stretched his head back, heard a bone pop. He froze, worried about the excruciating contractures that occasionally racked the muscles that were still connected to extant nerves. It seemed completely unfair that the same trauma that made most of your body numb also subjected the sensate part to agonizing tremors.

There was no pain this time but Thom noticed the alarm on his boss's face.

The aide said, "Lincoln, that's it . . . I'm taking your blood pressure and you're going to bed. No argument."

"All right, Thom, all right. Only we have to make one phone call first."

"Look at what time it is. . . . Who's awake now?"

"It's not a matter of who's awake now," Rhyme said wearily. "It's a matter of who's *about* to be awake."

■

Midnight, in the swamp.

The sounds of insects. The fast shadows of bats. An owl or two. The icy light of the moon.

Lucy and the other deputies hiked four miles over to Route 30, where a camper awaited. Bell had pulled strings and "requisitioned" the vehicle from Fred Fisher Winnebagos. Steve Farr had driven it over here to meet the search party and give them a place to stay for the night.

They stepped inside the cramped quarters. Jesse, Trey and Ned hungrily ate the roast beef sandwiches that Farr had brought. Lucy drank a bottle of water, passed on the food. Farr and Bell—bless their hearts—had also dug up clean uniforms for the searchers.

She called in and told Jim Bell that they'd tracked the pair to an A-frame vacation house, which had been broken into. "Looked like they'd been watching TV, you can believe *that*."

But it had been too dark to follow the trail and they'd decided to wait until dawn to resume the search.

Lucy picked up the clean clothes and stepped inside the bathroom. In the tiny shower stall she let the weak stream of water course over her body. Her hands started with her hair and face and neck and then, as always, tentatively washed her flat chest, feeling the ridges of scar, then grew more certain as they moved to her belly and thighs.

She wondered again why she had such an aversion to silicone or the reconstructive surgery that, the doctor explained, took fat from her thighs or butt and remade the breasts. Even nipples could be reconstructed—or tattooed on.

Because, she told herself, it was fake. Because it wasn't real.

And, so, why bother?

But then, Lucy thought, look at that Lincoln Rhyme. He was only a partial man. His legs and arms were fake— a wheelchair and an aide. But thinking about him reminded her of Amelia Sachs and anger seared her again. She pushed those thoughts aside, dried herself and pulled on a T-shirt, thinking absently about the drawer of bras in the dresser in the guest room of her house—and recalled that she'd been meaning to throw them out for two years. But, for some reason, never had. Then she put on her uniform blouse and slacks. She stepped out of the bathroom. Jesse was hanging up the phone.

"Anything?"

"No," he said. "They're still working on the evidence, Jim and Mr. Rhyme."

Lucy shook her head at the food Jesse offered her then sat down at the table, pulled her service revolver out of its holster. "Steve?" she asked Farr.

The crew-cut young man looked up from the newspaper he was reading, lifted an eyebrow.

"You bring what I asked for?"

"Oh, yeah." He dug in the glove compartment and handed her a yellow-and-green box of Remington bullets. She ejected the round-point cartridges from her pistol and Speedloaders and replaced them with the new bullets—hollow points, which have more stopping power and cause much more damage to soft tissue when they hit a human being.

Jesse Corn watched her closely but it was a moment before he spoke, as she knew he'd do. "Amelia's not dangerous," he said, in a low voice, the words meant for her only.

Lucy set the gun down and looked into his eyes. "Jesse, everybody said Mary Beth was at the ocean but turns out she's in the opposite direction. Everybody said Garrett was just a stupid kid but he's smart as a snake and's conned us a half-dozen times. We don't know *anything* anymore. Maybe Garrett's got a store of weapons someplace and has some plan or another to take us out when we walk into his trap."

"But Amelia's with him. She wouldn't let that happen."

"Amelia's a damn traitor and we can't trust her an inch. Listen, Jesse, I saw that look on your face when you saw she wasn't under the boat. You were relieved. I know you think you like her and you're hoping she likes you. . . . No, no, let me finish. But she busted a killer outa jail. And if you'd been the one out there in the river instead of Ned, Amelia'd have shot at you just as fast."

He began to protest but the chill look in her eyes kept him quiet.

"It's easy to get infatuated with somebody like that," Lucy continued. "She's pretty and she's from someplace else, someplace exotic. . . . But she doesn't understand life down here. And she doesn't understand Garrett. You know him—that's one sick boy and it's just a fluke that he's not doing life right now."

"I *know* Garrett's dangerous. I'm not arguing there. It's Amelia I'm thinking of."

"Well, it's us that *I'm* thinking of and everybody else in Blackwater Landing that boy could be planning on killing tomorrow or next week or next year if he gets away from us. Which he might just do, thanks to her. Now, I need to know if I can count on you. If not, you can go on home and we'll have Jim send somebody else in your place."

Jesse glanced at the box of shells. Then back to her. "You can, Lucy. You can count on me."

"Good. You better mean that. 'Cause at first light I'm tracking them down and bringing 'em both back. I hope alive but, I tell you, that's become optional."

•

Mary Beth McConnell sat alone in the cabin, exhausted but afraid to sleep.

Hearing noises everywhere.

She'd given up on the couch. She was afraid that if she remained there she'd stretch out and fall asleep then wake to find the Missionary and Tom gazing at her through the window, about to break in. So she was perched at a dining room chair, which was about as comfortable as brick.

Noises . . .

On the roof, on the porch, in the woods.

She didn't know what time it was. She was afraid to even push the light button on her wristwatch to glimpse the face—out of the crazy fear that the flash would some-how beckon to her attackers.

Exhausted. Too tired even to wonder again why this had happened to her, what she might have done to prevent it.

No good deed goes unpunished . . .

She stared out at the field in front of the cabin, now completely black. The window was like a frame around her fate: Whom would it show approaching through the field? Her killers or her rescuers?

She listened.

What was *that* noise: A branch on bark? Or the rasp of a match?

What was that dot of light in the woods: A firefly, or a campfire?

That motion: A deer goaded to run by the scent of bobcat or the Missionary and his friend settling in around the fire to drink beer and eat food then prowl through the woods to come for her and satisfy their bodies in other ways?

Mary Beth McConnell couldn't tell. Tonight, as in so much of life, she sensed only ambiguity.

You find relics of long-dead settlers but you wonder if maybe your theory is completely wrong.

Your father dies of cancer—a long, wasting death that the doctors say is inevitable but you think: Maybe it wasn't.

Two men are out there in the woods, planning to rape and kill you.

But maybe not.

Maybe they've given up. Maybe they're passed out on moonshine. Or were scared off at the thought of the con-sequences, deciding that their fat wives or callused hands are safer, or easier, than what they had planned with her.

Spread-eagle at your place . . .

A sharp crack filled the night. She jumped at the sound. A gunshot. It seemed to come from where she'd seen the firelight. A moment later there was a second shot. Closer.

Breathing heavily in fear, gripping the coup stick. Unable to look out the black window, unable not to. Terrified that she'd see Tom's pasty face appearing slowly in the frame, grinning. *We'll be back.*

The wind was up, bending the trees, the brush, the grass.

She thought she heard a man laughing, the sound soon lost in the hollow wind like the call of one of the Manitou spirits of the Weapemeocs.

She thought she heard a man calling, "Get yourself ready, get yourself ready. . . ."

But maybe not.

■

"You hear shots?" Rich Culbeau asked Harris Tomel.

They sat around a dying campfire. They were uneasy and not nearly as drunk as if this'd been a normal hunting trip, not nearly as drunk as they *wanted* to be. The 'shine just wasn't taking.

"Pistol," Tomel said. "Large caliber. Ten millimeter or a .44, .45. Automatic."

"Bullshit," Culbeau said. "You can't tell it's an automatic or not."

"Can," Tomel lectured. "A revolver's louder—because of the gap between the cylinder and the barrel. Logical."

"Bullshit," Culbeau repeated. Then asked, "How far?"

"Humid air. It's night . . . I make it four, five miles." Tomel sighed. "I want this thing to be over with. I'm sick of it."

"I hear that," Culbeau said. "Was easier in Tanner's Corner. Getting complicated now."

"Damn bugs," Tomel said, swatting a mosquito.

"Whatta you think somebody's shooting for this time of night? It's almost one."

"Raccoon in the garbage, black bear in a tent, man humping somebody else's wife."

Culbeau nodded. "Look—Sean's asleep. That man sleeps anytime, anyplace." He kicked through the embers to cool them.

"He's on fucking medication."

"He is? I didn't know that."

"That's *why* he sleeps anytime, anyplace. He's acting funny, don'tcha think?" Tomel asked, glancing at the skinny man as if he were a snoozing snake.

"Liked him better when you couldn't figure him out. Now he's all serious, it scares the shit outa me. Holding that gun like it's his dick and all."

"You're right 'bout that," Tomel muttered then stared into the murky forest for several minutes. He sighed then said, "Hey, you got the Six-Twelve? I'm getting eaten alive here. And hand me that bottle of 'shine while you're at it."

■

Amelia Sachs opened her eyes at the sound of the pistol shot.

She looked into the bedroom of the trailer, where Garrett was asleep on the mattress. He hadn't heard the noise.

Another shot.

Why was somebody shooting this late? she wondered.

The shots reminded her of the incident on the river— Lucy and the others firing at the boat they thought Sachs and Garrett were under. She pictured the geysers of water flying into the air from the stunning shotgun blasts.

She listened carefully but heard no more shots. Heard nothing other than the wind. And the cicadas, of course.

They live this totally weird life. . . . The nymphs dig into the ground and stay there for, like, twenty years before they hatch. . . . All those years in the ground, just hiding, before they come out and become adults.

But soon her mind was occupied once again with what she'd been considering before the gunshots interrupted her thoughts.

Amelia Sachs had been thinking of an empty chair.

Not Dr. Penny's therapy technique. Or what Garrett had told her about his father and that terrible night five years ago. No, she was thinking of a different chair—Lincoln Rhyme's red Storm Arrow wheelchair.

That's what they were doing down here in North Carolina, after all. Rhyme was risking everything, his life, what was left of his health, his and Sachs's life together, so that he could move closer to climbing out of that chair. Leaving it behind him, empty.

And, lying here in this foul trailer, a felon, alone in her own knuckle time, Amelia Sachs finally admitted to herself what had troubled her so about Rhyme's insistence on the operation. Of course, she was worried that he'd die on the table. Or that the operation would make him worse. Or that it wouldn't work at all and he'd be plunged into depression.

But those weren't her main fears. That wasn't why she'd done everything she could to stop him from having the operation. No, no—what scared her the most was that the operation *would* succeed.

Oh, Rhyme, don't you understand? I don't *want* you to change. I love you the way you are. If you were like everyone else what would happen to us?

You say, "It'll always be you and me, Sachs." But the you and me is based on who we are *now*. Me and my bloody nails and my itchy need to move, move, move.... You and your damaged body and elegant mind that roams faster and further than I ever could in my stripped and rigged Camaro.

That mind of yours that holds me tighter than the most passionate lover ever could.

And if you become *normal* again? When you're your own arms and legs, Rhyme, then why would you want me? Why would you need me? I'd become just another portable, a beat cop with some talent for forensics. You'll meet another one of the treacherous women who've derailed your life in the past—another selfish wife, another married lover—and you'll fade away from me the way Lucy Kerr's husband left after *her* surgery.

I want you the way you are. . . .

She actually shuddered at how appallingly selfish this thought was. Yet she couldn't deny it.

Stay in your chair, Rhyme! I don't want it empty. . . . I want a life with you, a life the way it's always been. I want children with you, children who'll grow up to know you exactly the way you are.

Amelia Sachs found she was staring at the black ceiling. She closed her eyes. But it was an hour later before the sound of the wind and the cicadas, their thoracic plates singing like monotonous violins, finally seduced her to sleep.

. . . chapter thirty-three

Sachs woke just after dawn to the droning noise—which in her dream had been placid locusts but turned out to be her Casio wristwatch's alarm. She clicked it off.

Her body was in agony, an arthritic's response to sleeping on a thin pad over a riveted, metal floor.

But she felt oddly buoyant. Low sunlight streamed through the windows of the trailer and she took this as a good omen. Today they were going to find Mary Beth McConnell and return to Tanner's Corner with her. She'd confirm Garrett's story and Jim Bell and Lucy Kerr could start the search for the real killer—the man in the tan overalls.

She watched Garrett awaken in the bedroom and roll upright on the saggy mattress. With his lengthy fingers he combed his mussed hair into place. He looks just like any other teenager in the morning, she thought. Gangly and cute and sleepy. About to get dressed, about to take the bus to school and see his friends, to learn things in class, to flirt with girls, toss footballs. Watching him look around groggily for his shirt, she noticed his skinny frame and worried about getting him some good food—cereal, milk, fruit—and washing his clothes, making sure he took a shower. This, she thought, is what it would be like to have children of your own. Not to borrow youngsters from friends for a few hours—like her goddaughter, Amy's girl. But to be there every day when they wake up, with their messy rooms and difficult adolescent attitudes, to fix them meals, to buy them clothes, to argue with them, to take care of them. To be the hub of their lives.

"Morning." She smiled.

He smiled back. "We gotta go," he said. "Gotta get to Mary Beth. Been away from her for too long. She's got to be totally scared and thirsty."

Sachs climbed unsteadily to her feet.

He glanced at his chest, at the poison oak splotches, and seemed embarrassed. He pulled his shirt on quickly. "I'm going outside. Have to, you know, take care of business. And I'm gonna leave a couple of empty hornets' nests around. Might slow 'em up—if they come this way." Garrett stepped outside but returned just a moment later. He left a cup of water on the table beside her. Said shyly: "This's for you." He stepped out again.

She drank it down. Longing for a toothbrush and time for a shower. Maybe when they got to—

"It's *him!*" a man's voice called in a whisper.

Sachs froze, looked out the window. She saw nothing. But from a tall stand of bushes near the trailer the forced whisper continued, "I've got him in my sights. I've got a clear shot."

The voice was familiar and she decided it sounded like Culbeau's friend, Sean O'Sarian. The skinny one. The redneck trio had found them—they were going to kill the boy or torture him into telling where Mary Beth was so they could get the reward.

Garrett hadn't heard the voice. Sachs could see him—he was about thirty feet away, setting an empty hornets' nest on the trail. She heard footsteps in the bushes pushing forward toward the clearing where the boy was.

She grabbed the Smith & Wesson and stepped quietly outside. She crouched, motioning desperately to Garrett. He didn't see her.

The footsteps in the bushes grew closer.

"Garrett," she whispered.

He turned, saw Sachs motioning for him to join her. He frowned, seeing the urgency in her eyes. Then he glanced to his left, into the bushes, and she saw terror blossom in his face. He held his hands out, a defensive gesture. He cried, "Don't hurt me, don't hurt me, don't hurt me!"

Sachs dropped into a crouch, curled her finger around the trigger, cocked the pistol and aimed toward the bushes.

It happened so quickly . . .

Garrett falling to his belly in fear, crying out, "Don't, don't!"

Amelia lifting her pistol, two-handed combat stance, pressure on the trigger, waiting for a target to present. . . .

The man bursting from the bushes into the clearing, gun raised toward Garrett. . . .

Just as Deputy Ned Spoto turned the corner of the trailer right beside Sachs, blinked in surprise and leapt toward her, arms outstretched. Startled, Sachs stumbled away from him. Her weapon fired, bucking hard in her hand.

And thirty feet away—beyond the faint cloud of smoke from the muzzle—she saw the bullet from her gun strike the forehead of the man who'd been in the bushes—not Sean O'Sarian at all but Jesse Corn. A black dot appeared above the young deputy's eye and, as his head jerked back, a horrible pink cloud puffed out behind him. Without a sound he dropped straight to the ground.

Sachs gasped, staring at the body, which twitched once and then lay completely still. She was breathless. She dropped to her knees, the gun tumbling from her hand.

"Oh, Jesus," Ned muttered, also staring in shock at the body. Before the deputy could recover and draw his gun, Garrett rushed him. The boy snagged Sachs's pistol from the ground and pointed it at Ned's head, then took the deputy's weapon and flung it into the bushes.

"Lie down!" Garrett raged at him. "On your face!"

"You killed him, you killed him," Ned muttered.

"Now!"

Ned did as he was told, tears running down his tanned cheeks.

"Jesse!" Lucy Kerr's voice called from nearby. "Where are you? Who's shooting?"

"No, no, no . . ." Sachs moaned. Watching an astonishing amount of blood pour from the dead deputy's shattered skull.

Garrett Hanlon glanced at Jesse's body. Then past it—toward the sound of approaching feet. He put his arm around Sachs. "We have to go."

When she didn't answer, when she simply stared, completely numb, at the scene in front of her—the end of the deputy's life, and the end of her own—Garrett helped her to her feet then took her hand and pulled her after him. They vanished into the woods.

IV

Hornets' Nest

chapter thirty-four

What was happening now? a frantic Lincoln Rhyme wondered.

An hour ago, at five-thirty A.M., he'd finally gotten a call from a very put-out drone in the Real Estate Division of the North Carolina Department of Taxation. The man had been awakened at one-thirty and given the assignment of tracking down delinquent taxes on any land on which a claimed residence was a McPherson trailer. Rhyme had first checked to see if Garrett's parents had owned one and—when he learned they hadn't—reasoned that if the boy was using the place as a hideout it was abandoned. And if it was abandoned the owner had defaulted on the taxes.

The assistant director told him there'd been two such properties in the state. In one case, near the Blue Ridge, to the west, the land and trailer had been sold at a tax lien foreclosure to a couple who currently lived there. The other, on an acre in Paquenoke County, wasn't worth the time or money to foreclose on. He'd given Rhyme the address, an RFD route about a half mile from the Paquenoke River. Location C-6 on the map.

Rhyme had called Lucy and the others and sent them there. They were going to approach at first light and, if Garrett and Amelia were inside, surround them and talk them into surrendering.

The last Rhyme had heard they'd spotted the trailer and were moving in slowly.

Unhappy that his boss had gotten virtually no sleep, Thom sent Ben out of the room and went through the morning ritual carefully. The four *B*s: bladder, bowel, brushing teeth and blood pressure.

"It's high, Lincoln," Thom muttered, putting away the sphygmomanometer. Excessive blood pressure in a quad could lead to an attack of dysreflexia, which in turn could result in a stroke. But Rhyme didn't pay any attention. He was riding on pure energy. He wanted desperately to find Amelia. He wanted—

Rhyme looked up. Jim Bell, an alarmed expression on his face, walked through the doorway. Ben Kerr, equally upset, entered behind him.

"What happened?" Rhyme asked. "Is she all right? Is Amelia—"

"She killed Jesse," Bell said in a whisper. "Shot him in the head."

Thom froze. Glanced at Rhyme. The sheriff continued, "He was about to arrest Garrett. She shot him. They took off."

"No, it's impossible," Rhyme whispered. "There's a mistake. Somebody else did it."

But Bell was shaking his head. "No. Ned Spoto was there. He saw the whole thing. . . . I'm not saying she did it on purpose—Ned went for her and her gun went off—but it's still felony murder."

Oh, my God . . .

Amelia . . . second-generation cop, the Portable's Daughter. And now she'd killed one of her own. The worst crime a police officer could commit.

"This's way past us now, Lincoln. I've got to get the state involved."

"Wait, Jim," Rhyme said urgently. "Please. . . . She's desperate now, she's scared. So's Garrett. You call in troopers, a lot more people're going to get hurt. They'll be gunning for them both."

"Well, apparently they *oughta* be gunning for them," Bell spat back. "And looks like they shoulda been from the git-go."

"I'll find them for you. I'm close." Rhyme nodded toward the evidence chart and map.

"I gave you one chance and look what happened."

"I'll find them and I'll talk her into surrendering. I know I can. I'll—"

Suddenly Bell was jostled aside and a man rushed into the room. It was Mason Germain. "You fucking son of a bitch!" he cried and made right for Rhyme. Thom stepped in the way but the deputy flung aside the thin man. He rolled to the floor. Mason grabbed Rhyme by the shirt. "You fucking freak! You come down here and play your little—"

"Mason!" Bell started forward but the deputy shoved him aside again.

"—play your little games with the evidence—your little puzzles. And now a good man's dead because of you!" Rhyme smelled the man's potent aftershave as the deputy drew his fist back. The criminalist cringed and turned his face away.

"I'm going to kill you. I'm going to—" But Mason's voice was choked off as a huge arm wrapped around his chest and he was lifted clean off the floor.

Ben Kerr carried the deputy away from Rhyme.

"Kerr, goddamn it, let go of me!" Mason gasped. "You asshole! You're under arrest!"

"Calm yourself down, Deputy," the big man said slowly.

Mason was reaching for his pistol but with his other hand Ben clamped down hard on the man's wrist. Ben looked at Bell, who waited a moment then nodded. Ben released the deputy, who stood back, fury in his eyes. He said to Bell, "I'm going out there and I'm finding that woman and I'm—"

"You are not, Mason," Bell said. "You want to keep working in this department you'll do what I tell you. We're going to handle it my way. You're staying in the office here. You understand?"

"Son of a bitch, Jim. She—"

"Do you understand me?"

"Yeah, I fucking understand you." He stormed out of the lab.

Bell asked Rhyme, "You all right?"

Rhyme nodded.

"And you?" He glanced at Thom.

"I'm fine." The aide adjusted Rhyme's shirt. And despite the criminalist's protest he took the blood pressure again. "The same. Too high but not critical."

The sheriff shook his head. "I've got to call Jesse's parents. Lord, I don't want to do that." He walked to the window and stared outside. "First Ed, now Jesse. What a nightmare this whole thing's been."

Rhyme said, "Please, Jim. Let me find them and give me a chance to talk to her. If you don't, it's going to escalate. You know that. We'll end up with more people dead."

Bell sighed. Glanced at the map. "They've got a twenty-minute lead. You think you can find them?"

"Yes," Rhyme answered. "I can find them."

■

"That direction," Sean O'Sarian said. "I'm positive."

Rich Culbeau was looking west, where the young man was pointing—toward where they'd heard the gunshot and the shouting fifteen minutes ago.

Culbeau finished peeing against a pine tree and asked, "What's over that way?"

"Swamp, a few old houses," said Harris Tomel, who had hunted probably every square foot of Paquenoke County. "Not much else. Saw a gray wolf there a month ago." The wolves had supposedly been extinct but were making a comeback.

"No fooling," Culbeau said. He'd never seen one, always wanted to.

"You shoot it?" O'Sarian asked.

"You don't shoot 'em," Tomel said.

Culbeau added, "They're protected."

"So?"

And Culbeau realized he didn't have an answer for that.

They waited a few minutes longer but there were no more gunshots, no more shouts. "May as well keep going," Culbeau said, pointing toward where the shot had come from.

"May as well," said O'Sarian as he took a hit from a bottle of water.

"Hot again today," Tomel offered, looking at the low disk of radiant sun.

"It's hot every day," Culbeau muttered. He picked up his gun and started along the path, his army of two trudging along behind him.

■

Thunk.

Mary Beth's eyes shot open, pulling her from a deep, unwanted sleep.

Thunk.

"Hey, Mary Beth," a man's voice called cheerfully. Like an adult speaking to a child. In her grogginess she thought: It's my father! What's he doing back from the hospital? He's in no shape to chop wood. I'll have to get him back to bed. Has he had his medicine?

Wait!

She sat up, dizzy, head throbbing. She'd fallen asleep in the dining room chair.

Thunk.

Wait. It's not my father. He's dead. . . . It's Jim Bell. . . .

Thunk.

"Mareeeeeeee Bayeth . . ."

She jumped as the leering face looked in the window. It was Tom.

Another slam on the door as the Missionary's ax bit into the wood.

Tom leaned inside, squinting into the gloom. "Where are you?"

She stared at him, paralyzed.

Tom continued, "Oh, hey, there you are. My, you're prettier'n I remembered." He held up his wrist, showed her thick bandages. "I lost a pint of blood, thanks to you. I think it's only fair I get a little back."

Thunk.

"I have to tell you, honey," he said. "I fell asleep last night thinking about feeling up your titties yesterday. Thank you much for that sweet thought."

Thunk.

With this blow the ax broke through the door. Tom disappeared from the window and joined his friend.

"Keep going, boy," he called encouragingly. "You're on a roll."

Thunk.

. . . chapter thirty-five

His worry now was that she'd hurt herself.

Since he'd known Amelia Sachs, Lincoln Rhyme had watched her hands disappear into her scalp and return bloody. He'd watched her worry nails with teeth, and skin with nails. He'd seen her drive at a hundred fifty miles per hour. He didn't know exactly what pushed her but he knew there was something within her that made Amelia Sachs live on the edge.

Now that this had happened, now that she'd killed, the anxieties might push her over the line. After the accident that left Rhyme a broken man, Terry Dobyns, the NYPD psychologist, had explained to him that, yes, he would feel like killing himself. But it wasn't depression that would motivate him to act. Depression depleted your energy; the main cause of suicide was a deadly fusion of hopelessness, anxiety and panic.

Which would be exactly what Amelia Sachs—hunted, betrayed by her own nature—would be feeling right now.

Find her! was his only thought. Find her fast.

But where was she? The answer to that question still eluded him.

He looked at the chart again. There was no evidence from the trailer. Lucy and the other deputies had searched it fast—too fast, of course. They were under the spell of hunt lust—even immobilized Rhyme often felt this—and the deputies were desperate to get on the trail of the enemy who'd killed their friend.

The only clues he had to Mary Beth's location—to where Garrett and Sachs were now headed—were right in front of him. But they were as enigmatic as any set of clues he'd ever analyzed.

FOUND AT THE SECONDARY CRIME SCENE— MILL

Brown Paint on Pants
Sundew Plant
Clay
Peat Moss
Fruit Juice
Paper Fibers
Stinkball Bait
Sugar
Camphene
Alcohol
Kerosene
Yeast

We need more evidence! he raged to himself.

But we don't *have* any more goddamn evidence.

When Rhyme was mired smack in the denial stage of grief, after the accident, he had tried to summon superhuman willpower to make his body move. He had recalled the stories of the people who lifted cars off children or had run at impossible speeds to find help in emergencies.

But he'd finally accepted that those types of strength were no longer available to him.

But he did have one type of strength left—mental strength.

Think! All you have is your mind and the evidence that's in front of you. The evidence isn't going to change.

So change the way you're thinking.

All right, let's start over. He went through the chart once more. The trailer key had been identified. The yeast would be from the mill. The sugar, from food or juice. The camphene, from an old lamp. The paint, from the building where she was being held. The kerosene, from the boat. The alcohol could be from anything. The dirt in the boy's cuffs? It exhibited no particularly unique characteristics and was—

Wait . . . the dirt.

Rhyme recalled that he and Ben had run the density gradient test of the dirt sampled from in the shoes and car-floor mats of county workers yesterday morning. He'd ordered Thom to photograph each tube and note which employee it had come from on the back of the Polaroid.

"Ben?"

"What?"

"Run the dirt you found in Garrett's cuffs at the mill through the density gradient unit."

After the dirt had settled in the tube the young man said, "Got the results."

"Compare it with the pictures of the samples you did yesterday morning."

"Good, good." The young zoologist nodded, impressed with the idea. He flipped through the Polaroids, paused. "I've got a match!" he said. "One's almost identical."

The zoologist was no longer hesitant to give opinions, Rhyme was pleased to note. And he wasn't hedging either.

"Whose shoes was it from?"

Ben looked at the notation on the back of the Polaroid. "Frank Heller. He works in the Department of Public Works."

"Is he in yet?"

"I'll find out." Ben vanished. He returned a few minutes later, accompanied by a heavyset man in a white short-sleeved shirt. He eyed Rhyme uncertainly. "You're the fellow from yesterday. Making us clean off our shoes." He laughed but the sound was uneasy.

"Frank, we need your help again," Rhyme explained. "Some of the dirt on your shoes matches dirt we found on the suspect's clothes."

"The boy who kidnapped those girls?" Frank muttered, red-faced and looking completely guilty.

"That's right. Which means he might—this is pretty far-fetched but he *might*—have the girl maybe two or three miles from where you live. Could you point out on the map exactly where that is?"

He said, "It's not like I'm a suspect or anything, am I?"

"No, Frank. Not at all."

" 'Cause I got people'll vouch for me. I'm with the wife every night. We watch TV. *Jeopardy!* and *Wheel of Fortune.* Like clockwork. Then WWF. Sometimes her brother comes over. I mean, he owes me money but he'd back me up even if he didn't."

"That's okay," Ben reassured him. "We just need to know where you live. On that map there."

"That'd be here." He stepped to the wall and touched a spot. Location D-3. It was north of the Paquenoke—north of the trailer where Jesse had been killed. There were a number of small roads in the area but no towns marked.

"What's the area like around you?"

"Forests and fields mostly."

"You know anywhere that somebody might hide a kidnap victim?"

Frank seemed to be considering this question earnestly. "I don't, no."

Rhyme: "Can I ask you a question?"

"On top of the ones you already asked?"

"That's right."

"I suppose you can."

"You know about Carolina bays?"

"Sure. Everybody does. Meteors made 'em. Long time ago. When the dinosaurs got themselves killed."

"Are there any near you?"

"Oh, you bet there are."

Which was something that Rhyme was hoping the man would say.

Frank continued. "Must be close to a hundred of 'em."

Which was something he was hoping he *wouldn't*.

■

Head back, eyes closed, reviewing the evidence charts in his mind.

Jim Bell and Mason Germain were back in the evidence room, along with Thom and Ben, but Lincoln Rhyme was paying them no mind. He was in his own world, an orderly place of science and evidence and logic, a place where he needed no mobility, a place where his feelings for Amelia and what she'd done were mercifully forbidden entry. He could see the evidence in his mind as clearly as if he were staring at the notations on the chalkboard. In fact, he was able to see them *better* with his eyes shut.

Paint sugar yeast dirt camphene paint dirt sugar . . . yeast . . . yeast . . .

A thought slipped into his mind, fished away. Come back, come back, come back. . . .

Yes! He snagged it.

Rhyme's eyes snapped open. He looked into the empty corner of the room. Bell followed his eyes.

"What is it, Lincoln?"

"You have a coffee machine here?"

"Coffee?" Thom asked, not pleased. "No caffeine. Not with your blood pressure the way—"

"No, I don't want a goddamn cup of coffee! I want a coffee *filter*."

"Filter? I'll dig one up." Bell disappeared and returned a moment later.

"Give it to Ben," Rhyme ordered. Then said to the zoologist, "See if the paper fibers from the filter match the ones we found on Garrett's clothes at the mill."

Ben rubbed some fibers off the filter onto a slide. He gazed through the eyepieces of the comparison microscope, adjusted the focus and then moved the stages so the samples were next to each other in the split-screen viewfinder.

"The colors're a little different, Lincoln, but the structure and size of the fibers're pretty much the same."

"Good," Rhyme said, his eyes now on the T-shirt with the stain on it.

He said to Ben, "The juice, the fruit juice on the shirt. Taste it again. Is it a little sour? Tart?"

Ben did. "Maybe a little. Hard to tell."

Rhyme's eyes strayed to the map, imagining that Lucy and the others were closing in on Sachs somewhere in that green wilderness, eager to shoot. Or that Garrett had Sachs's gun and might be turning it on her.

Or that *she* was holding her gun to her own scalp, squeezing the trigger.

"Jim," he said, "I need you to get something for me. For a control sample."

"Okay. Where?" He fished his keys from his pocket.

"Oh, you won't need your car."

■

Many images revolved in Lucy Kerr's thoughts: Jesse Corn, on his first day in the Sheriff's Department, standard-issue shoes polished perfectly but his socks mismatched; he'd gotten dressed before light to make sure he wasn't late.

Jesse Corn, hunkered down behind a cruiser, shoulder touching hers, while Barton Snell—his mind on fire from PCP—took potshots at the deputies. It was Jesse's easygoing banter that got the big man to put down his Winchester.

Jesse Corn, proudly driving his new cherry-red Ford pickup over to the County Building on his day off and giving some kids a ride in the bed, up and down the parking lot. They shouted, "Wheeee," in unison as he rolled over the speed bumps.

These thoughts—and a dozen others—stayed with her now as she, Ned and Trey pushed through a large oak forest. Jim Bell had told them to wait at the trailer and he'd send Steve Farr, Frank and Mason to take over the pursuit. He wanted her and the other two deputies to return to the office. But they hadn't even bothered to vote on the matter. As reverently as possible they'd moved Jesse's body into the trailer, covered it with a sheet. Then she'd told Jim that they were going after the fugitives and that nothing on God's earth was going to stop them.

Garrett and Amelia were fleeing fast and were making no effort to cover their tracks. They moved along a path that bordered marshland. The ground was soft and their footprints were clearly visible. Lucy remembered something that Amelia had told Lincoln Rhyme about the crime scene at Blackwater Landing as the redhead had gazed at the footprints there: Billy Stail's weight had been on the toes, which meant that he'd been running toward Garrett to rescue Mary Beth. Lucy now noticed this same thing about the prints of the two people they pursued. They were sprinting.

And so Lucy said to her two fellow deputies, "Let's jog." And despite the heat and their exhaustion they trotted forward together.

They continued this way for a mile until the ground grew drier and they could no longer see the footprints. Then the trail ended in a large grassy clearing and they had no idea where their prey had gone.

"Damn," Lucy muttered, gasping for breath and furious that they'd lost the trail. "Goddamn!"

They ringed the clearing, studying every foot of the ground, but could find no path or any other clue as to which way Garrett and Amelia Sachs had gone.

"What do we do?" Ned asked.

"Call in and wait," she muttered. She leaned against a tree, caught the bottled water that Trey tossed to her and drank it down.

Recalling:

Jesse Corn, shyly showing off a glistening silver pistol he was planning on using in his NRA competition matches. Jesse Corn, accompanying his parents to First Baptist Church on Locust Street.

The images kept looping through her mind. They were painful for her to picture and stoked her anger. But Lucy made no effort to force them away; when she found Amelia Sachs she wanted her fury to be unrelenting.

■

With a squeak, the door to the cabin eased open a few inches.

"Mary Beth," Tom sang. "You come on out now, come out and play."

He and the Missionary whispered to each other. Then Tom spoke again. "Come on, come on, honey. Make it easy on yourself. We won't hurt you. We were just pulling your leg yesterday."

She stood upright, against the wall, behind the front door. Didn't say a word. Gripped the coup stick in both hands.

The door eased open farther, the hinges giving another

squeal. A shadow fell onto the floor. Tom stepped inside, cautious.

"Where is she?" the Missionary whispered from the porch.

"There's a cellar," Tom said. "She's down there, I'll bet."

"Well, get her and let's go. I don't like it here."

Tom took another step inside. He was holding a long skinning knife.

Mary Beth knew about the philosophy of Indian warfare and one of the rules is that if the parlays fail and war is inevitable you don't banter or threaten; you attack with all your force. The point of battle isn't to talk your enemy into submission or explain or chide; it's to annihilate them.

And so she stepped calmly out from behind the door, screamed like a Manitou spirit and swung the club with both hands as Tom spun around, eyes wide in terror. The Missionary cried, "Look out!"

But Tom didn't have a chance. The coup stick caught him solidly in front of his ear, shattering his jaw and closing down half his throat. He dropped the knife and grabbed his neck, falling to his knees, choking. He crawled back outside.

"Hehf . . . hehf meh," he gasped.

But there was no help forthcoming—the Missionary simply reached down and pulled him off the porch by his collar, letting him fall to the ground, holding his shattered face, as Mary Beth watched from the window. "You asshole," the Missionary muttered to his friend and then drew a pistol from his back pocket. Mary Beth swung the door shut, took her place behind it again, wiping her sweating hands and getting a better grip on the stick. She heard the double click of a gun cocking.

"Mary Beth, I got a gun here and, you probably figured out, under the circumstances I got no problem using it. Just come on out. You don't, I'll shoot inside and I'll probably hit you."

She crouched down against the wall behind the door, waiting for the gunshot.

But he never fired. It was a trick; he kicked the door hard and it swung into her, stunning her for an instant, knocking her down. But as he started inside she kicked the door closed just as hard as he'd shoved it open. He wasn't expecting any more resistance and the heavy wooden slab caught him on the shoulder, knocking him off balance. Mary Beth stepped toward him and swung the coup stick at the only target on him she could reach— his elbow. But he dropped to the floor just as the rock would have struck him and she missed. The momentum of her fierce swing pulled the stick from her sweaty hands and it skidded along the floor.

No time to get it. Just run! Mary Beth jumped past the Missionary before he could turn and fire and she sprinted out the door.

At last!

Free of this hellhole at last!

She ran to the left, heading back toward the path that her captor had brought her down two days ago, the one that led past a big Carolina bay. At the corner of the cabin she turned toward the pond.

And ran right into the arms of Garrett Hanlon.

"No!" she cried. "No!"

The boy was wild-eyed. He held a gun. "How'd you get out? How?" He grabbed her wrist.

"Let me go!" She tried to pull away from him but his grip was like steel.

There was a grim-faced woman with him, pretty, with long red hair. Her clothes, like Garrett's, were filthy. The woman was silent, her eyes dull. She didn't seem the least bit startled by the girl's sudden appearance. She looked drugged.

"Goddamn," the Missionary's voice called. "You fucking bitch!" He turned the corner and found Garrett aiming the pistol at his face. The boy screamed, "Who're you? What'd you do to my house? What'd you do to Mary Beth?"

"She attacked us! Look at my friend. Look at—"

"Throw that away," Garrett raged. Nodding at the man's pistol. "Throw it away or I'll kill you! I will. I'll blow your fucking head off!"

The Missionary looked at the boy's face and the gun. Garrett cocked his pistol. "Jesus . . ." The man pitched the revolver into the grass.

"Now get outa here! Move."

The Missionary backed away then helped Tom to his feet and they staggered off toward the trees.

Garrett walked toward the front door of the cabin, pulling Mary Beth after him. "Into the house! We have to get in. They're after us. We can't let them see us. We'll hide in the cellar. Look what they did to the locks! They broke my door!"

"No, Garrett!" Mary Beth said in a rasping voice. "I'm not going back in there."

But he said nothing and pulled her into the cabin. The silent redhead walked unsteadily inside. Garrett shoved the door closed, looking at the shattered wood, the broken locks, dismay on his face. "No!" he cried, seeing shards of glass on the floor—from the jar that had held the dinosaur beetle.

Mary Beth, appalled that the boy seemed the most upset that one of his bugs had escaped, strode up to Garrett and slapped him hard on the face. He blinked in surprise and staggered backward. "You prick!" she screamed. "They could've killed me."

The boy was flustered. "I'm sorry!" His voice cracked. "I didn't know about them. I thought there was nobody around here. I didn't mean to leave you this long. I got arrested."

He shoved splinters under the door to wedge it shut.

"Arrested?" Mary Beth asked. "Then what're you doing here?"

Finally the redhead spoke. In a mumbling voice she said, "I got him out of jail. So we could find you and bring you back. And you could back up his story about the man in the overalls."

"What man?" Mary Beth asked, confused.

"At Blackwater Landing. The man in the tan overalls, the one who killed Billy Stail."

"But . . ." She shook her head. "*Garrett* killed Billy. He hit him with a shovel. I saw him. It happened right in front of me. Then he kidnapped me."

Mary Beth had never seen such an expression on another human being. Complete shock and dismay. The redhead started to turn toward Garrett but then something caught her eye: the rows of Farmer John canned fruits and vegetables. She walked slowly toward the table, as if she were sleepwalking, and picked one up. Stared at the picture on the label—a cheerful blond farmer wearing tan overalls and a white shirt.

"You made it up?" she whispered to Garrett, holding the can up. "There was no man. You lied to me."

Garrett stepped forward, fast as a grasshopper, and pulled a pair of handcuffs off the redhead's belt. He ratcheted them onto her wrists.

"I'm sorry, Amelia," he said. "But if I'd told you the truth you never would've got me out. It was the only way. I had to get back here. I had to get back to Mary Beth."

. . . chapter thirty-six

FOUND AT THE SECONDARY CRIME SCENE—
MILL

Brown Paint on Pants
Sundew Plant
Clay
Peat Moss
Fruit Juice
Paper Fibers
Stinkball Bait
Sugar
Camphene
Alcohol
Kerosene
Yeast

Obsessively Lincoln Rhyme's eyes scanned the evidence chart. Top to bottom, bottom to top.

Then again.

Why the hell was the damn chromatograph taking so long? he wondered.

Jim Bell and Mason Germain sat nearby, both silent. Lucy had called in a few minutes before to say that they'd lost the trail and were waiting north of the trailer—at Location C-5.

The chromatograph rumbled and everyone in the room remained still, waiting for the results.

Silence for long minutes, finally broken by Ben Kerr's voice. He spoke to Rhyme in a soft voice. "They used to call me it, you know. What you're probably thinking."

Rhyme looked over at him.

" 'Big Ben.' Like the clock in England. You were probably wondering."

"I wasn't. In school, you mean?"

A nod. "High school. I hit six-three and two-fifty when I was sixteen. I got made fun of a lot. 'Big Ben.' Other names too. So I never felt real comfortable with the way I looked. Think maybe that was why I acted kinda funny seeing you at first."

"Kids gave you a tough time, did they?" Rhyme asked, both acknowledging and deflecting the apology.

"They sure did. Until I took up junior varsity wrestling and pinned Darryl Tennison in three-point-two seconds and it took him a lot longer than that to get his wind back."

"I skipped P.E. class a lot," Rhyme told him. "I forged excuses from my doctor, my parents—pretty good ones, I will say—and snuck into the science lab."

"You did that?"

"Twice a week at least."

"And you did experiments?"

"Read a lot, played around with the equipment. . . . A few times, I played around with Sonja Metzger."

Thom and Ben laughed.

But Sonja, his first girlfriend, put him in mind of Amelia Sachs and he didn't like where those thoughts were headed.

"Okay," Ben said. "Here we go." The computer screen

had burst to life with the results of the control sample Rhyme had asked Jim Bell to procure. The big man nodded. "Here's what we've got: Solution of fifty-five percent alcohol. Water, lot of minerals."

"Well water," Rhyme said.

"Most likely." The zoologist continued, "Then there're traces of formaldehyde, phenol, fructose, dextrose, cellulose."

"That's good enough for me," Rhyme announced. Thinking: The fish may still be out of water but it's just grown lungs. He announced to Bell and Mason, "I made a mistake. A big one. I saw the yeast and I assumed it'd come from the mill, not the place where Garrett really has Mary Beth. But why would a *mill* have supplies of yeast? You'd only find those in a bakery . . . Or"—he lifted his eyebrow to Bell—"someplace they're brewing that." He nodded at the bottle that sat on the table. The liquid inside was what Rhyme had just asked Bell to collect from the basement of the Sheriff's Department. It was 110-proof moonshine—from one of the juice bottles that Rhyme had seen a deputy clear away when he'd taken over the evidence room and turned it into a lab. This is what Ben had just sampled in the chromatograph.

"Sugar and yeast," the criminalist continued. "Those're ingredients in liquor. And the cellulose in that batch of moonshine," Rhyme continued, looking at the computer screen, "is probably from the paper fibers—I assume when you make moonshine, you have to filter it."

"Yep," Bell confirmed. "And most 'shiners use off-the-shelf coffee filters."

"Just like the fiber we found on Garrett's clothes. And the dextrose and fructose—complex sugars found in fruit. That's from the fruit juice left over in the jar. Ben said it was tart—like cranberry juice. And you told me, Jim, that's the most popular container for moonshine. Right?"

"Ocean Spray."

"So," Rhyme summarized, "Garrett's holding Mary

Beth in a moonshiner's cabin—presumably one that's been abandoned since the raid."

"What raid?" Mason asked.

"Well, it's like the trailer," Rhyme replied shortly, hating as always to have to explain the obvious. "If Garrett's using the place to hide Mary Beth then it has to be abandoned. And what's the only reason anybody'd abandon a working still?"

"Department of revenue busted it," Bell said.

"Right," Rhyme said. "Get on the phone and find out the location of any stills that've been raided in the past couple of years. It'll be a nineteenth-century building in a stand of trees and painted brown—though it may not have been when it got raided. It's four or five miles from where Frank Heller lives and it'll be on a Carolina bay or you'll have to go around a bay to get there from the Paquo."

Bell left to call the revenue department.

"That's pretty good, Lincoln," Ben said. Even Mason Germain seemed impressed.

A moment later Bell hurried back into the room. "Got it!" He examined the sheet of paper in his hand then began tracing directions on the map, ending at Location B-4. He circled a spot. "Right here. Head of investigations at revenue said it was a big operation. They raided it a year ago and busted up the still. One of his agents checked out the place a couple, three months ago and saw that somebody'd painted it brown so he looked it over good to see if it was being used again. But he said it was empty so he didn't pay any more mind. Oh, and it's about twenty yards from a good-sized Carolina bay."

"Is there any way to get a car in there?" Rhyme asked.

"Has to be," Bell said. "All stills're near roads—to bring the supplies in and get the finished 'shine out."

Rhyme nodded and said firmly, "I need an hour alone with her—to talk her out. I know I can do it."

"It's risky, Lincoln."

"I want that hour," Rhyme said, holding Bell's eye.

Finally Bell said, "Okay. But if Garrett gets away this time it's gonna be a full-out manhunt."

"Understood. You think my van can make it there?"

Bell said, "Roads aren't great but—"

"I'll get you there," Thom said firmly. "Whatever it takes, I'll get you there."

■

Five minutes after Rhyme had wheeled out of the County Building, Mason Germain watched Jim Bell return to his office. He waited a moment and, making sure no one saw him, he stepped into the corridor and headed toward the front door of the building.

There were dozens of phones in the County Building Mason could have used to make his call but instead he pushed outside into the heat and walked quickly across the quadrangle to a bank of pay phones on the sidewalk. He fished into his pockets and dug out some coins. He looked around and when he saw he was alone he dropped them in, looked at a number on a slip of paper and punched in the digits.

■

Farmer John, Farmer John. Enjoy it fresh from Farmer John. . . . Farmer John, Farmer John. Enjoy it fresh from Farmer John. . . .

Staring at the row of cans in front of her, a dozen overall-clad farmers staring back with mocking smiles, Amelia Sachs's mind was clogged with this inane jingle, the anthem for her foolishness.

Which had cost Jesse Corn his life. And had ruined hers as well.

She was only vaguely aware of the cabin where she now sat, a prisoner of the boy she'd risked her life to save. And of the angry exchange now going on between Garrett and Mary Beth.

No, all she could see was that tiny black dot appearing in Jesse's forehead.

All she could hear was the singsong jingle. *Farmer John . . . Farmer John . . .*

Then suddenly Sachs understood something: Occasionally Lincoln Rhyme would, mentally, go away. He might converse but his words were superficial, he might smile but it was false, he might appear to listen but he wasn't hearing a word. At moments like that, she knew, he was considering dying. He'd be thinking about finding someone from an assisted-suicide group like the Lethe Society to help him. Or even, as some severely disabled people had done, actually hiring a hit man. (Rhyme, who'd contributed to the jailing of a number of OC—organized crime—mobsters, obviously had some connections there. In fact, there were probably a few who'd gladly do the job for free.)

But until this moment—with her own life now as shattered as Rhyme's, no, *more* shattered—she'd always thought he was wrong in that thinking. Now, though, she understood how he felt.

"No!" Garrett called, leaping up and cocking his ear toward the window.

You have to listen all the time. Otherwise they can sneak up on you.

Then Sachs heard it too. A car was slowly approaching.

"They've found us!" the boy cried, gripping the pistol. He ran to the window, stared out. He seemed confused. "What's that?" he whispered.

A door slammed. Then there was a long pause.

And she heard, "Sachs. It's me."

A faint smile crossed her face. No one else in the universe could have found this place except Lincoln Rhyme.

"Sachs, are you there?"

"No!" Garrett whispered. "Don't say anything!"

Ignoring him, Sachs rose and walked to a broken window. There, in front of the cabin, resting unevenly on a dirt driveway, was the black Rollx van. Rhyme, in the Storm Arrow, had maneuvered close to the cabin—as far as he could get until a hillock of dirt near the porch stopped him. Thom stood beside him.

"Hello, Rhyme," she said.

"Quiet!" the boy whispered harshly.

"Can I talk to you?" the criminalist called.

What was the point? she wondered. Still, she said, "Yes."

She walked to the door and said to Garrett, "Open it. I'm going outside."

"No, it's a trick," the boy said. "They'll attack—"

"Open the door, Garrett," she said firmly, her eyes boring into his. He looked around the room. Then bent down and pulled the wedges out from the doorjamb. Sachs opened the door, the cuffs on her stiff wrists jingling like sleigh bells.

■

"He did it, Rhyme," she said, sitting down on the porch steps in front of him. "He killed Billy. . . . I got it wrong. Dead wrong."

The criminalist closed his eyes. What horror she must be feeling, he thought. He looked at her carefully, her pale face, her stony eyes. He asked, "Is Mary Beth okay?"

"She's fine. Scared but fine."

"She saw him do it?"

Sachs nodded.

"There wasn't any man in overalls?" he asked.

"No. Garrett made that up. So I'd break him out. He had it all planned from the beginning. Leading us off to the Outer Banks. He had a boat hidden, supplies. He'd planned what to do if the deputies got close. Even had a safe house—that trailer you found. The key, right? That I found in the wasp jar? That's how you tracked us down."

"It was the key," Rhyme confirmed.

"I should've thought of that. We should've stayed someplace else."

He saw she was cuffed and noticed Garrett in the window, peering out angrily, holding a pistol. This was now a hostage situation; Garrett wasn't going to come out willingly. It was time to call the FBI. Rhyme had a friend, Arthur Potter, now retired, but still the best hostage negotiator the bureau ever had. He lived in Washington, D.C., and could be here in a few hours.

He turned back to Sachs. "And Jesse Corn?"

She shook her head. "I didn't know it was him, Rhyme. I thought it was one of Culbeau's friends. A deputy jumped me and my weapon went off. But it was my fault—I acquired an unidentified target with an unsafetied weapon. I broke rule number one."

"I'll get you the best lawyer in the country."

"It doesn't matter."

"It matters, Sachs. It matters. We'll get something worked out."

She shook her head. "There's nothing *to* work out, Rhyme. It's felony murder. Open-and-shut case." Then she was looking up, past him. Frowning. She stood. "What's—?"

Suddenly a woman's voice called, "Hold it right there! Amelia, you're under arrest."

Rhyme tried to turn but couldn't rotate his head far enough. He puffed into the controller and backed up in a semicircle. He saw Lucy and two other deputies, crouching as they ran from the woods. Their weapons were in their hands and they kept their eyes on the windows of the cabin. The two men used trees for cover. But Lucy walked boldly toward Rhyme, Thom and Sachs, her pistol leveled at Sachs's chest.

How had the search party found the cabin? Had they heard the van? Had Lucy picked up Garrett's trail again?

Or had Bell reneged on his deal and told them?

Lucy walked right up to Sachs and without a moment's pause hit her hard in the face, her fist connecting with the policewoman's chin. Sachs gave a faint wheeze at the pain and stepped back. She said nothing.

"No!" Rhyme cried. Thom stepped forward but Lucy grabbed Sachs by the arm. "Is Mary Beth in there?"

"Yes." Blood trickled from her chin.

"Is she all right?"

A nod.

Eyes on the cabin window, Lucy asked, "Does he have your weapon?"

"Yes."

"Jesus." Lucy called to the other deputies, "Ned, Trey, he's inside. And he's armed." Then she snapped at Rhyme, "I'd suggest you get under cover." And she pulled Sachs roughly back behind the van on the side opposite the cabin.

Rhyme followed the women, Thom holding the chair for stability as it crossed the uneven ground.

Lucy turned to Sachs, grabbed her by the arms. "He did it, didn't he? Mary Beth told you, right? Garrett killed Billy."

Sachs looked down at the ground. Finally she said, "Yes. . . . I'm sorry. I—"

"Sorry doesn't mean a damn thing to me or anybody else. Least of all to Jesse Corn. . . . Does Garrett have any other weapons in there?"

"I don't know. I didn't see any."

Lucy turned back to the cabin, shouted, "Garrett, can you hear me? It's Lucy Kerr. I want you to put that gun down and walk outside with your hands on your head. You do that now, okay?"

The only response was the door slamming shut. A faint pounding filled the clearing as Garrett hammered or wedged the door shut. Lucy pulled out her cell phone and started to make a call.

"Hey, Deputy," a man's voice interrupted, "you need some help?"

Lucy turned. "Oh, no," she muttered.

Rhyme too glanced toward the voice. A tall, pony-tailed man, carrying a hunting rifle, was trooping through the grass toward them.

"Culbeau," she snapped, "I got a situation here and I can't deal with you too. Just go on, get out of here." Her eyes noticed something in the field. There was another man walking slowly toward the cabin. He carried a black army rifle and squinted thoughtfully as he surveyed the field and cabin. "Is that Sean?" Lucy asked.

Culbeau said, "Yeah, and Harris Tomel's over there."

Tomel was walking up to the tall African-American deputy. They were chatting casually, as if they knew each other.

Culbeau persisted, "If the boy's in the cabin you might need some help getting him out. What can we do?"

"This is police business, Rich. The three of you, clear on outa here. Now. Trey!" she called to the black deputy. "Get 'em out."

The third deputy, Ned, walked toward Lucy and Culbeau. "Rich," he called, "there's no reward anymore. Forget about it and—"

The shot from Culbeau's powerful rifle poked a hole in the front of Ned's chest and the impact flung him several feet onto his back. Trey stared at Harris Tomel, only ten feet away. Each man looked about as shocked as the other and neither moved for a moment.

Then there was a whoop like a hyena's cry from Sean O'Sarian, who lifted his soldier gun and shot Trey three times in the back. Cackling with laughter, he vanished into the field.

"No!" Lucy screamed and lifted her pistol toward Culbeau, but by the time she fired, the men had gone for cover in the tall grass surrounding the cabin.

chapter thirty-seven

Rhyme felt the instinctive urge to drop to the ground but, of course, remained upright in the Storm Arrow wheelchair. More bullets slammed into the van where Sachs and Lucy, now face down on the grass, had been standing a moment before. Thom was on his knees, trying to work the heavy wheelchair out of the depression of soft earth where it was lodged.

"Lincoln!" Sachs cried.

"I'm okay. Move! Get to the other side of the van. Under cover."

Lucy said, "But Garrett can target us from there."

Sachs snapped back, "But he's not the one who's goddamn shooting!"

Another shotgun blast missed them by a foot and the pellets rattled along the porch. Thom put the wheelchair in neutral and muscled it toward the cabin side of the van. "Stay low," Rhyme said to the aide, who ignored a shot that zipped past them and shattered a side window of the vehicle.

Lucy and Sachs followed the two men to the shadowy area between the cabin and the van.

"Why the hell're they doing this?" Lucy cried. She fired several shots, sending O'Sarian and Tomel scrabbling for cover. Rhyme couldn't see Culbeau but knew that the big man was directly in front of them somewhere. The rifle that he'd been carrying was high powered and fitted with a large telescopic sight.

"Take the cuffs off and give me the gun," Sachs shouted.

"Give it to her," Rhyme said. "She's a better shot than you."

"No goddamn way!" The deputy shook her head, her expression one of astonishment at this suggestion. More bullets slapped the metal of the van, dug out chunks of wood from the porch.

"They've got fucking rifles!" Sachs raged. "You're no match for them. Give me the gun!"

Lucy rested her head against the side of the van and stared in shock at the slain deputies lying in the grass. "What's going on?" she muttered, crying. "What's happening?"

Their cover—the van—wasn't going to last much longer. It protected them from Culbeau and his rifle but the other two were flanking them. In a few minutes they'd set up a cross fire.

Lucy fired twice more—into the grass where a shotgun blast had erupted a moment before.

"Don't waste your ammunition," Sachs ordered. "Wait till you have a clear shot. Otherwise—"

"Shut the hell up," Lucy raged. She patted her pockets. "Lost the goddamn phone."

"Lincoln," Thom said, "I'm taking you out of the chair. You're too much of a target."

Rhyme nodded. The aide undid the harness, got his arms around Rhyme's chest and pulled him out, laid him on the ground. Rhyme tried to lift his head to see what was going on but a contracture—a merciless cramp—gripped his neck muscles and he had to lower his head to the grass until the pain passed. He'd never felt as stabbed by his helplessness as at this moment.

More shots. Closer. And more insane laughter from O'Sarian. "Hey, knife lady, where are you?"

Lucy muttered, "They're almost in position."

"Ammo?" Sachs asked.

"I've got three left in the chamber, one Speedloader."

"Loaded six?"

"Yeah."

A shot slammed into the back of the Storm Arrow and knocked it on its side. A cloud of dust rose up around it.

Lucy fired at O'Sarian but his giggling and the staccato response from the Colt told them that she'd missed.

The rifle fire also told them that in only a minute or two they'd be completely flanked.

They'd die here, shot to death, trapped in this dim valley between the shattered van and the cabin. Rhyme wondered what he would feel when the bullets tore into his body. No pain, of course, not even any pressure in his numb flesh. He glanced at Sachs, who was looking at him with a hopeless expression on her face.

You and me, Sachs. . . .

Then he glanced at the front of the cabin.

"Look," he called.

Lucy and Sachs followed his eyes.

Garrett had opened the front door.

Sachs said, "Let's get inside."

"Are you crazy?" Lucy called. "Garrett's *with* them. They're all together."

"No," Rhyme said. "He's had a chance to shoot from the window. He didn't."

Two more shots, very close. The bushes rustled nearby. Lucy lifted the pistol.

"Don't waste it!" Sachs called. But Lucy rose and fired two fast shots at the sound. The rock one of the men had thrown to shake the bushes and trick her into presenting a target rolled into view. Lucy jumped aside just as

Tomel's shotgun blast, meant for her back, streaked past, puncturing the side of the van.

"Shit," the deputy cried. Ejecting the empty cartridges and reloading with the Speedloader.

"Inside," Rhyme said. "Now."

Lucy nodded. "Okay."

Rhyme said, "Fireman's carry." This was a bad position to carry a quad in—it put stress on parts of the body that weren't used to stress, but it was faster and would expose Thom to the gunshots for the least amount of time. Rhyme was also thinking that his own body would protect Thom's.

"No," Thom said.

"Do it, Thom. No argument."

Lucy said, "I'll cover you. The three of you go together. Ready?"

Sachs nodded. Thom lifted Rhyme, cradling him like a child in his strong arms.

"Thom—" Rhyme protested.

"Quiet, Lincoln," the aide snapped. "We're doing this my way."

"Go," Lucy called.

Rhyme's hearing was stunned by several loud gunshots. Everything blurred as they ran up the few stairs into the cabin.

Another several bullets cracked into the wood of the cabin as they pushed inside. A moment later Lucy rolled into the room after them and slammed the door shut. Thom set Rhyme gently on a couch.

Rhyme had a glimpse of a terrified young woman sitting in a chair, staring at him. Mary Beth McConnell.

Garrett Hanlon, with his red, blotched face, eyes wide with fear, sat manically clicking the fingernails of one hand and holding a pistol awkwardly in the other, as Lucy aimed the gun right in his face.

"Give me the weapon!" she cried. "Now, now!"

He blinked and immediately handed the gun to her.

She put it in her belt and called out something. Rhyme didn't hear what; he was staring at the boy's bewildered and frightened eyes, a child's eyes. And he thought: I understand why you had to do it, Sachs. Why you believed him. Why you had to save him.

I understand. . . .

He said, "Everybody okay?"

"Fine," Sachs said.

Lucy nodded.

"Actually," Thom said, almost apologetically. "Not really."

He lifted his hand away from his trim belly, revealing the bloody exit wound. Then the aide went down on his knees, hard, ripping the slacks that he'd ironed with such care just that morning.

. . . chapter thirty-eight

Search the wound for severe hemorrhage, stop the bleeding. If possible, check the patient for shock.

Amelia Sachs, trained in the basic NYPD first-aid course for patrol officers, bent over Thom, examining the wound.

The aide lay on his back, conscious but pale, sweating fiercely. She clamped one hand over the wound.

"Get these cuffs off me!" she cried. "I can't take care of him this way."

"No," Lucy said.

"Jesus," Sachs muttered and examined Thom's stomach as best she could with the restraints on.

"How are you, Thom?" Rhyme blurted. "Talk to us."

"It feels numb. . . . It's feeling . . . It's funny . . ." His eyes rolled back under the lids and he passed out.

A crash above their heads. A bullet tore through the wall. Followed by a thud of a shotgun blast hitting the door. Garrett handed Sachs a wad of napkins. She pressed them against the rip in Thom's belly. She slapped him gently on the face. He gave no response.

"Is he alive?" Rhyme asked hopelessly.

"He's breathing. Shallow. But he's breathing. Exit wound isn't too bad but I don't know what kind of damage there is inside."

Lucy looked out the window fast, ducked. "Why're they doing this?"

Rhyme said, "Jim said they were into moonshine. Maybe they had their eye on this place and didn't want it found. Or maybe there's a drug lab nearby."

"There were two men earlier—they tried to break in," Mary Beth told them. "They said they were killing marijuana fields but I guess they were *growing* it. They might all be working together."

"Where's Bell?" Lucy asked. "And Mason?"

"He'll be here in a half hour," Rhyme said.

Lucy shook her head in dismay at this information. Then looked again out the window. She stiffened as, it seemed, she sighted a target. She lifted the pistol, aimed quickly.

Too quickly.

"No, let me!" Sachs cried.

But Lucy fired twice. Her grimace told them she had missed. She squinted. "Sean's just found a can. A red can. What is that, Garrett? Gas?" The boy huddled on the floor, frozen in panic. "Garrett! Talk to me!"

He turned toward her.

"The red can? What's in it?"

"It's, like, kerosene. For the boat."

Lucy muttered, "Hell, they're going to burn us out."

"Shit," Garrett cried. He rolled to his knees, staring at Lucy, eyes frantic.

Sachs, alone among them, it seemed, knew what was coming. "No, Garrett, don't—"

The boy ignored her and flung the door open and, half running, half crawling, skittered along the porch. Bullets cracked into the wood, following him. Sachs had no idea if he'd been hit.

Then there was silence. The men moved closer to the cabin with the kerosene.

Sachs looked around the room, filled with dust from the impact of the bullets. She saw:

Mary Beth, hugging herself, crying.

Lucy, her eyes filled with the devil's own hatred, checking her pistol.

Thom, slowly bleeding to death.

Lincoln Rhyme, on his back, breathing hard.

You and me . . .

In a steady voice Sachs said to Lucy, "We've got to go out there. We've got to stop them. The two of us."

"There're three of them, they've got rifles."

"They're going to set fire to the place. And either burn us alive or shoot us when we run outside. We don't have any choice. Take the cuffs off." Sachs held out her wrists. "You have to."

"How can I trust you?" Lucy whispered. "You ambushed us at the river."

Sachs asked, "Ambushed? What're you talking about?"

Lucy scowled. "What am I talking about? You used that boat as a lure and shot at Ned when he went out to get it."

"Bullshit! *You* thought we were under the boat and shot at *us.*"

"Only after you . . ." Then Lucy's voice faded, and she nodded knowingly.

Sachs said to the deputy, "It was *them.* Culbeau and the others. One of them shot first. To scare you and slow you up probably."

"And we thought it was you."

Sachs held her wrists out. "We don't have any choice."

The deputy looked at Sachs carefully then slowly reached into her pocket and found her cuff key. She undid the chrome bracelets. Sachs rubbed her wrists. "What's the ammunition situation?"

"I've got four left."

"I've got five in mine," Sachs said, taking her long-barreled Smith & Wesson from Lucy and checking the cylinder.

Sachs looked down at Thom. Mary Beth stepped forward. "I'll take care of him."

"One thing," Sachs said. "He's gay. He's been tested but ..."

"Doesn't matter," the girl responded. "I'll be careful. Go on."

"Sachs," Rhyme said. "I ..."

"Later, Rhyme. No time for that now." Sachs eased to the door, looked out quickly, eyes taking in the topography of the field, what would make good cover and shooting positions. Her hands free again, gripping a hefty gun in her palm, she felt confident once more. This was her world: guns and speed. She couldn't think about Lincoln Rhyme and his operation, about Jesse Corn's death, about Garrett Hanlon's betrayal, about what awaited her if they got out of this terrible situation.

When you move they can't getcha ...

She said to Lucy, "We go out the door. You go left behind the van but *don't* stop, no matter what. Keep moving till you get to the grass. I'm going right—for that tree over there. We get into the tall grass and stay down, move forward, toward the forest, flank them."

"They'll see us go out the door."

"They're *supposed* to see us. We want them to know there're two of us out there somewhere in the grass. It'll keep 'em edgy and looking over their shoulders. Don't shoot unless you have a clear, no-miss target. Got that? ... Do you?"

"I've got it."

Sachs gripped the doorknob with her left hand. Her eyes met Lucy's.

One of them—O'Sarian, with Tomel beside him—was lugging the kerosene can toward the cabin, not paying attention to the front door. So that when the two women charged outside, splitting up and sprinting for cover, neither of them got his weapon up in time for a clear shot.

Culbeau—back a ways so he could cover the front and sides of the cabin—must not have been expecting anybody to run either because by the time his deer rifle boomed, both Sachs and Lucy were rolling into the tall grass surrounding the cabin.

O'Sarian and Tomel disappeared into the grass too and Culbeau shouted, "You let 'em get out. What the fuck you doing?" He fired one more shot toward Sachs—she hugged the earth—and when she looked again Culbeau too had dropped into the grass.

Three deadly snakes out there in front of them. And no clue where they might be.

Culbeau called, "Go right."

One of the others responded, "Where?" She thought it was Tomel.

"I think . . . wait."

Then silence.

Sachs crawled toward where she'd seen Tomel and O'Sarian a moment ago. She could just make out a bit of red and she steered in that direction. The hot breeze pushed the grass aside and she saw it was the kerosene can. She moved a few feet closer and, when the wind cooperated again, aimed low and fired a bullet squarely into the bottom of the can. It shivered under the impact and bled clear liquid.

"Shit," one of the men called and she heard a rustle of grass as, she supposed, he fled from the can, though it didn't ignite.

More rustling, footsteps.

But coming from where?

Then Sachs saw a flash of light about fifty feet into the field. It was near where Culbeau had been and she realized it would be the 'scope or the receiver of his big gun. She lifted her head cautiously and caught Lucy's eye, pointed to herself and then toward the flash. The deputy nodded then gestured around to the flank. Sachs nodded.

But as Lucy started through the grass on the left side of the cabin, running in a crouch, O'Sarian rose and, laughing again madly, began firing with his Colt. Sharp cracks filled the field. Lucy was, momentarily, a clear target and it was only because O'Sarian was an impatient marksman that he missed. The deputy dove prone, as the dirt kicked up around her, then rose and fired one shot at him, a near hit, and the small man dropped to cover, giving a whoop and calling, "Nice try, baby!"

Sachs started forward again, toward Culbeau's sniper's nest. She heard several other shots. The pops of a revolver, then the staccato cracks of the soldier rifle, then the stunning detonation of the shotgun.

She was worried that they'd hit Lucy but a moment later she heard the woman's voice call, "Amelia, he's coming at you."

The pounding of feet in the grass. A pause. Rustling.

Who? And where was he? She felt panicked, looking around dizzily.

Then silence. A man's voice calling something indistinct.

The footsteps receded.

The wind parted the grass again and Sachs saw the glint of Culbeau's telescopic sight. He was nearly in front of her, fifty feet away, on a slight rise—a good spot for him to shoot from. He could pop up out of the grass with his big gun and cover the entire field. She crawled faster, convinced that he was sighting through the powerful 'scope at Lucy—or into the cabin and targeting Rhyme or Mary Beth through the window.

Faster, faster!

She climbed to her feet and started to run in a crouch. Culbeau was still thirty-five feet away.

But Sean O'Sarian, it turned out, was much closer than that—as Sachs found out when she sprinted into the clearing and tripped over him. He gasped as she rolled past him and fell onto her back. She smelled liquor and sweat.

His eyes were manic; he looked as disconnected as a schizophrenic.

There was an immeasurable beat and Sachs lifted her pistol as he swung the Colt toward her. She kicked backward into the grass and they fired simultaneously. She felt the muzzle blast of the three shots as he emptied the clip, all the long rounds missing. Her single shot missed too; when she rolled prone and looked for a target he was leaping through the grass, howling.

Don't miss the opportunity, she told herself. And risked a shot from Culbeau as she rose from the grass and aimed at O'Sarian. But before she could fire, Lucy Kerr stood and shot him once as he ran directly toward her. The man's head lifted and he touched his chest. Another laugh. Then he spiraled down into the grass.

The look on Lucy's face was shock and Sachs wondered if this had been her first kill in the line of duty. Then the deputy dropped into the grass. A moment later several shotgun blasts chewed up the vegetation where she'd been standing.

Sachs continued on toward Culbeau, moving very fast now; it was likely that he knew Lucy's position and when she stood again he'd have a clear shot at her.

Twenty feet, ten.

The glint from the 'scope flashed more brightly and Sachs ducked. Cringing, waiting for his shot. But apparently the big man hadn't seen her. There was no shot and she continued on her belly, easing around to the right to flank him. Sweating, the arthritis pinching her joints hard.

Five feet.

Ready.

It was a bad shooting situation. Because he was on a hill, in order to acquire a clear target she'd have to roll into the clearing on Culbeau's right, and stand. There'd be no cover. If she didn't cap his ass immediately he'd have a clear shot at her. And even if she did hit him, Tomel would have several long seconds to hit her with the scattergun.

But there was nothing to be done.

When you move . . .

Smittie up, pressure on the trigger.

A deep breath . . .

. . . *they can't getcha.*

Now!

She leapt forward and rolled into the clearing. She went up on one knee, aiming the gun.

And gave a gasp of dismay.

Culbeau's "gun" was a pipe from an old still and the 'scope was a part of a bottle resting on top. Exactly the same trick she and Garrett had used at the vacation house on the Paquenoke.

Suckered. . . .

The grass rustled nearby. A footstep. Amelia Sachs dropped to the ground like a moth.

■

The footsteps were getting closer to the cabin, powerful footsteps, first through brush then on dirt then on the wooden steps leading up to the cabin. Moving slowly. To Rhyme they seemed more leisurely than cautious. Which meant they were confident too. And therefore dangerous.

Lincoln Rhyme struggled to lift his head from the couch but couldn't see who was approaching.

A creak of floorboards, and Rich Culbeau, holding a long rifle, looked inside.

Rhyme felt another jolt of panic. Was Sachs all right?

Had one of the dozens of shots he'd heard struck her? Was she lying somewhere injured in the dusty field? Or dead?

Culbeau looked at Rhyme and Thom and concluded they weren't a threat. Still standing in the doorway, he asked Rhyme, "Where's Mary Beth?"

Rhyme held the man's eyes and said, "I don't know. She ran outside to get help. Five minutes ago."

Culbeau glanced around the room then his eyes settled on the root cellar door.

Rhyme said quickly, "Why're you doing this? What're you after?"

"Ran outside, did she? I didn't see her do that." Culbeau stepped farther into the cabin, his eyes on the root cellar door. Then he nodded behind him, toward the field. "They shouldn't've left you here alone. That was their mistake." He was studying Rhyme's body. "What happened to you?"

"I was hurt in an accident."

"You're that fellow from New York everybody was talking 'bout. You're the one figured out she was here. You really can't move?"

"No."

Culbeau gave a faint laugh of curiosity, as if he'd caught a kind of fish he'd never known existed.

Rhyme's eyes slipped to the cellar door then back to Culbeau.

The big man said, "You sure got yourself into a mess here. More than you bargained for."

Rhyme said nothing in response and finally Culbeau started forward, aiming his gun, one-handed, at the cellar door. "Mary Beth left, did she?"

"She ran out. Where are you going?" Rhyme asked.

Culbeau said, "She's down there, ain't she?" He pulled the door open fast and fired, worked the bolt, fired again. Three times more. Then he peered into the smoky darkness, reloading.

It was then that Mary Beth McConnell, brandishing her primitive club, stepped out from behind the front door, where she'd been waiting. Squinting with determination, she swung the weapon hard. It slammed into the side of Culbeau's head, ripping part of his ear. The rifle fell from his hands and down the stairs into the darkness of the cellar. But he wasn't badly hurt and lashed out with a huge fist, striking Mary Beth squarely in the chest. She gasped and dropped to the floor, the wind knocked out of her. She lay on her side, keening.

Culbeau touched his ear and examined the blood. Then he looked down at the young woman. From a scabbard on his belt he took a folding knife and opened it with a click. He gripped her brunette hair, pulled it up, exposing her white throat.

She grabbed his wrist and tried to hold it back. But his arms were huge and the dark blade moved steadily toward her skin.

"Stop," a voice from the doorway commanded. Garrett Hanlon stood just inside the cabin. He was holding a large gray rock in his hand. He walked close to Culbeau. "Leave her alone and get the fuck out of here."

Culbeau released Mary Beth's hair; her head dropped to the floor. The big man stepped back. He touched his ear again and winced. "Hey, boy, who're you to be cussing at me."

"Go on, get out."

Culbeau laughed coldly. "Why'd you come back here? I got close to a hundred pounds of weight on you. And I got a Buck knife. All you got's that rock. Well, come on over here. Let's mix it up, get it over with."

Garrett clicked his fingernails twice. He crouched like a wrestler, walked forward slowly. His face showed eerie determination. He pretended to throw the rock several times and Culbeau dodged, backed up. Then the big man laughed, sizing up his adversary and probably concluding that the boy wasn't much of a threat. He lunged forward and swung the knife toward Garrett's narrow belly. The boy jumped back fast and the blade missed. But Garrett had misjudged the distance and hit the wall hard. He dropped to his knees, stunned.

Culbeau wiped his hand on his pants and gripped the knife again matter-of-factly, surveying Garrett with no emotion, as if he were about to dress a deer. He stepped toward the boy.

Then there was a blur of motion from the floor. Mary Beth, still lying on the floor, grabbed the club and swung it into Culbeau's ankle. He cried out as it connected and turned toward her, lifting the knife. But Garrett lunged forward and pushed the man hard on the shoulder. Culbeau was off balance and he slid on his knees down the cellar stairs. He caught himself halfway down. "You little shit," he growled.

Rhyme saw Culbeau grope in the dark cellar stairway for his rifle. "Garrett! He's going for the gun!"

The boy just walked slowly to the cellar and lifted the rock. But he didn't throw it. What was he doing? Rhyme wondered. He watched Garrett pull a wad of cloth out of a hole in the end. He looked down at Culbeau, said, "It's not a rock." And, as the first few yellow jackets flew out of the hole, he flung the nest into Culbeau's face and slammed the root cellar door shut. He hooked the clasp on the lock and stood back.

Two bullets snapped through the wood of the cellar door and disappeared through the ceiling.

But there were no more shots. Rhyme thought Culbeau would have fired more than twice.

But then he also thought the screams from the basement would last longer than they did.

■

Harris Tomel knew it was time to get the hell out, back to Tanner's Corner.

O'Sarian was dead—okay, no loss there—and Culbeau had gone down to the cabin to take care of the rest of them. So it was Tomel's job to find Lucy. But he didn't mind. He was still stung with shame that he'd clenched when he'd faced down Trey Williams and it had been that psycho little shit O'Sarian who'd saved his life.

Well, he wasn't going to freeze again.

Then, beside a tree some distance away, he saw a flash of tan. He looked. Yeah, there—through the crook of a tree—he could just make out Lucy Kerr's tan uniform blouse.

Holding the two-thousand-dollar shotgun, he moved a little closer. It wasn't a great shot—there wasn't much target presenting. Just part of her chest, visible through the crook of the tree. A hard shot with a rifle. But doable with the shotgun. He set the choke on the end of the muzzle so that the pellets would scatter wider and he'd have a better chance of hitting her.

He stood fast, dropped the bead sight right on the front of her blouse and squeezed the trigger.

A huge kick. Then he squinted to see if he'd hit his target.

Oh, Christ. . . . Not again! The blouse was floating in the air—launched by the impact of the pellets. She'd hung it on the tree to lure him into giving away his position.

"Hold it right there, Harris," Lucy's voice called, behind him. "It's over with."

"That was good," he said. "You fooled me." He turned to face her, holding the Browning at waist level, hidden in the grass, the shotgun pointed in her direction. She was in a white T-shirt.

"Drop your gun," she ordered.

"I did already," he said.

He didn't move.

"Let me see your hands. In the air. Now, Harris. Last warning."

"Look, Lucy. . . ."

The grass was four feet high. He'd drop down, fire to take out her knees. Then finish her off from close range. It'd be a risk, though. She could still get off a shot or two.

Then he noticed something: a look in her eyes. A look of uncertainty. And it seemed to him that she held her gun too threateningly.

She was bluffing.

"You're out of ammo," Tomel said, smiling.

There was a pause and the expression on her face confirmed it. He lifted the shotgun with both hands and aimed it at her. She gazed back hopelessly.

"But *I'm* not," came a voice nearby. The redhead! He looked her over, and his instinct told him: She's a woman. She'll hesitate. I can get her first. He swung toward her.

The pistol in her hands bucked and the last thing Tomel felt was an itchy tap on the side of his head.

■

Lucy Kerr saw Mary Beth stagger onto the porch and call out that Culbeau was dead and that Rhyme and Garrett were all right.

Amelia Sachs nodded then walked toward Sean O'Sarian's body. Lucy turned her own attention to Harris Tomel's. She bent down and closed her shaking hands around the Browning shotgun. She thought that while she should be horrified to be prying this elegant weapon from a dead man's hands, in fact all she thought about was the gun itself. She wondered if it was still loaded.

She answered that question by racking the gun—losing one shell, but making sure that another was chambered.

Fifty feet away Sachs was bending down over O'Sarian's body as she searched it, keeping her pistol pointed at the corpse. Lucy wondered why she was bothering then decided, wryly, that it must be standard procedure.

She found her blouse and put it back on. It was torn apart by the shotgun pellets but she was self-conscious about her body in the tight T-shirt. Lucy stood by the tree, breathing heavily in the heat and watching Sachs's back.

Simple fury—at the betrayals in her life. The betrayal by her body, by her husband, by God.

And now by Amelia Sachs.

She glanced behind her, where Harris Tomel lay. It was a straight line of sight from where he'd been standing to Amelia's back. The scenario was plausible: Tomel had been hiding in the grass. He rose, shot Sachs in the back with his shotgun. Lucy then grabbed Sachs's gun and killed Tomel. Nobody'd know different—except Lucy herself and, maybe, Jesse Corn's spirit.

Lucy lifted the shotgun, which felt weightless as a larkspur blossom in her hands. Pressing the smooth, fragrant stock against her cheek, reminding her of the way she'd pressed her face against the chrome guard of the hospital bed after her mastectomy. She sighted down the smooth barrel at the woman's black T-shirt, resting the sight on the woman's spine. She'd die painlessly. And fast.

As fast as Jesse Corn had died.

This was simply trading a guilty life for an innocent one.

Dear Lord, give me one clear shot at my Judas. . . .

Lucy looked around. No witnesses.

Her finger curled around the trigger, tightened.

Squinted, held the brass dot of the bead sight rock steady thanks to arms strengthened by years of gardening, years of managing a house—and a life—on her own. Aiming at the exact center of Amelia Sachs's back.

The hot breeze whistled through the grass around her. She thought about Buddy, about her surgeon, about her house and her garden.

Lucy lowered the gun.

She racked the weapon until it was empty and, padded butt resting on her hip, muzzle skyward, she carried it back to the van in front of the cabin. She set it on the ground and found her cell phone then called the state police.

The medevac chopper was the first to arrive and the medics quickly bundled Thom up and flew him off to the medical center. One stayed to look after Lincoln Rhyme, whose blood pressure was edging critical.

When the troopers themselves showed up in a second helicopter a few minutes later it was Amelia Sachs they arrested first and left hog-tied, hands behind her, lying in the hot dirt outside the cabin, while they went inside to arrest Garrett Hanlon and read him his rights.

chapter thirty-nine

Thom would survive.

The doctor in the Emergency Medicine Department of the University Medical Center in Avery had said laconically, "The bullet? It came and went. Missed the important stuff." Though the aide would be off duty for a month or two.

Ben Kerr had volunteered to cut class and stay around Tanner's Corner for a few days to assist Rhyme. The big man had grumbled, "You don't really deserve my help, Lincoln. I mean, hell, you never even pick up after yourself."

Still not quite comfortable with crip jokes he glanced quickly at Rhyme to see if this type of banter was within the rules. The criminalist's sour grimace was a reverse affirmation that it was. But Rhyme added that, as much as he appreciated the offer, the care and feeding of a quad is a full-time, and tricky, job. Largely thankless too—if the patient is Lincoln Rhyme. And so Dr. Cheryl Weaver was arranging for a professional caregiver from the medical center to help Rhyme.

"But hang around, Ben," he said. "I still might need you. Most aides don't last more than a few days."

The case against Amelia Sachs was bad. Ballistics tests had proved that the bullet that killed Jesse Corn had come from her gun and, though Ned Spoto was dead, Lucy Kerr had given a statement describing what Ned had told her about the incident. Bryan McGuire had already announced that he was going for the death penalty. Good-natured Jesse Corn had been a popular figure around town and, since he'd died trying to arrest the Insect Boy, there was considerable outcry for making this a capital case.

Jim Bell and the state police had looked into why Culbeau and his friends would attack Rhyme and the deputies. An investigator from Raleigh had found tens of thousands of dollars in cash hidden in their houses. "More than moonshine money," the detective had said. Then echoed Mary Beth's thought: "That cabin must've been near a marijuana farm—those three were probably working it with the men who attacked Mary Beth. Garrett must've stumbled on their operation."

Now, a day after the terrible events at the 'shiners' cabin, Rhyme sat in the Storm Arrow—drivable despite the stigmata of a bullet hole—in the improvised lab, waiting for the new aide to arrive. Morose, he was brooding about Sachs's fate when a shadow appeared in the doorway.

He looked up and saw Mary Beth McConnell. She stepped into the room. "Mr. Rhyme."

He noted how pretty she was, what confident eyes she had, what a ready smile. He understood how Garrett could have become ensnared by her. "How's your head?" Nodding at the bandage on her temple.

"I'll have a pretty spectacular scar. Won't be wearing my hair pulled back too much, I don't think. But no serious damage."

Like everyone else, Rhyme had been relieved to learn that Garrett hadn't in fact raped Mary Beth. He'd been telling the truth about the bloody tissue: Garrett had startled her in the root cellar of the cabin and she'd stood quickly, hitting her head on a low beam. He'd been visibly aroused, true, but that was due only to a sixteen-year-old's hormones, and Garrett hadn't touched her other than to carry her carefully upstairs, clean the wound and bandage it. He'd apologized profusely that she'd been hurt.

The girl now said to Rhyme, "I just wanted to say thank you. I don't know what I would've done if it hadn't been for you. I'm sorry about your friend, that policewoman. But if it wasn't for her I'd be dead now. I'm sure of it. Those men were going to . . . well, you can figure that out. Thank her for me."

"I will," Rhyme told her. "Would you mind answering something?"

"What?"

"I know you gave a statement to Jim Bell but I only know what happened at Blackwater Landing from the evidence. And some of that wasn't clear. Could you tell me?"

"Sure. . . . I was down by the river, dusting off some of the relics I'd found, and I looked up and there was Garrett. I was upset. I didn't want to be bothered. Whenever he saw me he just came right up and started talking like we were best friends.

"That morning he was agitated. He was saying things like 'You shouldn't've come here by yourself, it's dangerous, people die in Blackwater Landing.' That sort of thing. He was freaking me out. I told him to leave me alone. I had work to do. He grabbed my hand and tried to make me leave. Then Billy Stail comes out of the woods and he goes, 'You son of a bitch,' or something, and he starts to hit Garrett with a shovel but he got it away from Billy and killed *him*. Then he grabbed me again and made me get into this boat and brought me to the cabin."

"How long had Garrett been stalking you?"

Mary Beth laughed. "Stalking? No, no. You've been talking to my mother, I'll bet. I was downtown about six months ago and some of the kids from his school were picking on him. I scared them off. That made me his girlfriend, I guess. He followed me around a lot but that was all. Admired me from afar, that sort of thing. I was sure he was harmless." Her smile faded. "Until the other day." Mary Beth glanced at her watch. "I should go. But I wanted to ask you—the other reason I came by—if you don't need them anymore for evidence would it be okay if I took the rest of the bones?"

Rhyme, whose eyes were now gazing out his window as thoughts of Amelia Sachs slipped back into his mind, turned slowly to Mary Beth.

"What bones?" he asked.

"At Blackwater Landing? Where Garrett kidnapped me?"

Rhyme shook his head. "What do you mean?"

Mary Beth's face furrowed with concern. "The bones—those were the relics I found. I was digging up the rest of them when Garrett kidnapped me. They're very important. . . . You don't mean they're missing?"

"Nobody recovered any bones at the crime scene," Rhyme said. "They weren't in the evidence report."

She shook her head. "No, no . . . They *can't* be gone!"

"What kind of bones?"

"I found the remains of some of the Lost Colonists of Roanoke. From the late fifteen hundreds."

Rhyme's knowledge of history was pretty much limited to New York City. "I'm not too familiar with that."

Though when she explained about the settlers on Roanoke Island and their disappearance he nodded. "I do remember something from school. Why do you think it was their remains?"

"The bones were really old and decayed and they weren't in an Algonquin burial site or a colonial graveyard. They were just dumped in the ground without any markings. That was typical of what the warriors did with the bodies of their enemies. Here . . ." She opened her backpack. "I'd already packed up a few of them before Garrett took me off." She lifted several of them out, wrapped in Saran Wrap, blackened and decomposed. Rhyme recognized a radius, a portion of a scapula, a hip-bone and several inches of femur.

"There were a dozen more," she said. "This is one of the biggest finds in U.S. archaeological history. They're very valuable. I *have* to find them."

Rhyme stared at the radius—one of the two forearm bones. After a moment he looked up.

"Could you go up the hallway there to the Sheriff's Department? Ask for Lucy Kerr and have her come down here for a minute."

"Is this about the bones?" she asked.

"It might be."

■

It had been an expression of Amelia Sachs's father's: "When you move they can't getcha."

The expression meant many things. But most of all it was a statement of their shared philosophy, father and daughter. Both of them were admirers of fast cars, lovers of police work on the street, fearful of closed spaces and lives that were going nowhere.

But now they *had* got her.

Got her for good.

And her precious cars, her precious life as a police-woman, her life with Lincoln Rhyme, her future with children . . . all that was destroyed.

Sachs, in her cell in the lockup, had been ostracized. The deputies who brought her food and coffee said nothing to her, just stared coldly. Rhyme was having a lawyer flown down from New York but, like most

police officers, Sachs knew as much about criminal law
as most attorneys. She knew that, whatever horse-trad-
ing went on between the hired gun from Manhattan and
the Paquenoke County D.A., her life as she'd lived it
was over with. Her heart was as numb as Lincoln
Rhyme's body.

On the floor an insect of some kind made a diligent
trek from one wall to the other. What was its mission? To
eat, to mate, to find shelter?

*If all the people on earth disappeared tomorrow the
world'd keep going just fine. But if the insects all went
away then life'd be over with way fast—like, one generation. The plants'd die then the animals and the earth'd turn
into this big rock again.*

The door to the main office swung open. A deputy she
didn't recognize stood there. "You've got a call." He
opened the cell door, shackled her and led her to a small
metal table on which sat a phone. It would be her mother,
she supposed. Rhyme was going to call the woman and
give her the news. Or maybe it was her best friend in
New York, Amy.

But when she picked up the receiver, the thick chains
clinking, she heard Lincoln Rhyme's voice. "How is it in
there, Sachs? Cool?"

"It's all right," she muttered.

"That lawyer'll be here tonight. He's good. He's been
doing criminal law for twenty years. He got off a suspect
in a burglary *I* made a case against. Anybody does that,
you *know* they have to be good."

"Rhyme, come on. Why even bother? I'm an outsider
who broke a murderer out of jail and killed one of the
local cops. It doesn't get any more hopeless than that."

"We'll talk about your case later. I've got to ask you
something else. You spent a couple of days with Garrett.
Did you talk about anything?"

"Sure we did."

"What?"

"I don't know. Insects. The woods, the swamp." Why was he asking her these things? "I don't remember."

"I *need* you to remember. I need you to tell me everything he said."

"Why bother, Rhyme?" she repeated.

"Come on, Sachs. Humor an old crip, will you?"

. . . chapter forty

Lincoln Rhyme was alone in the impromptu lab, gazing at the evidence charts.

FOUND AT PRIMARY CRIME SCENE—
BLACKWATER LANDING

Kleenex with Blood
Limestone Dust
Nitrates
Phosphate
Ammonia
Detergent
Camphene

FOUND AT SECONDARY CRIME SCENE—
GARRETT'S ROOM

Skunk Musk
Cut Pine Needles
Drawings of Insects

Pictures of Mary Beth and Family
Insect Books
Fishing Line
Money
Unknown Key
Kerosene
Ammonia
Nitrates
Camphene

FOUND AT SECONDARY CRIME SCENE—QUARRY

Old Burlap Bag—Unreadable Name on It
Corn—Feed and Grain?
Scorch Marks on Bag
Deer Park Water
Planters Cheese Crackers

FOUND AT THE SECONDARY CRIME SCENE— MILL

Brown Paint on Pants
Sundew Plant
Clay
Peat Moss
Fruit Juice
Paper Fibers
Stinkball Bait
Sugar
Camphene
Alcohol
Kerosene
Yeast

Then he studied the map, eyes tracing the course of the Paquenoke River as it made its way from the Great Dismal Swamp through Blackwater Landing and meandered west.

There was a peak in the stiff paper of the map—a wrinkle that made you itch to smooth it.

That's been my life for the past few years, Lincoln Rhyme thought: itches that can't be scratched.

Maybe, soon, I'll be able to do that. After Dr. Weaver cuts and stitches and fills me up with her magic potions and youthful shark . . . maybe then I'll be able to run my hand over maps like this, flatten out a little crinkle.

An unnecessary gesture, pointless, really. But what a victory it would be.

Footsteps sounded. Boots, Rhyme deduced from the sound. With hard leather heels. From the interval between the steps it had to be a tall man. He hoped it would be Jim Bell and it was.

Breathing carefully into the sip-and-puff controller, Rhyme turned away from the wall.

"Lincoln," the sheriff asked. "What's up? Nathan said it was urgent."

"Come on in. Close the door. But first—is anybody in the hall?"

Bell gave a faint smile at this intrigue and looked. "Empty."

Rhyme reflected that the man's cousin, Roland, would have tacked on a Southernism of some sort. "Quiet as a church on payday" was one that he'd heard the northern Bell use from time to time.

The sheriff swung the door shut then walked to the table, leaned against it, crossed his arms. Rhyme turned slightly and continued to study the map of the area. "Our map doesn't go far enough north and east to show the Dismal Swamp Canal, does it?"

"The canal? No, it doesn't."

Rhyme asked, "You know much about it?"

"Not really," Bell said deferentially. He'd known Rhyme for only a short while but must've sensed when to play straight man.

"I've been doing a little research," Rhyme said, nodding at the phone. "The Dismal Swamp Canal's part of the Intracoastal Waterway. You know you can take a boat all the way from Norfolk, Virginia, down to Miami and not have to sail on open sea?"

"Sure. Everybody in Carolina knows about the Intracoastal. I've never been on it. I'm not much of a boater. I got seasick watching *Titanic*."

"Took twelve years to dig the canal. It's twenty-two miles long. Dug completely by hand. Amazing, don't you think? . . . Relax, Jim. This's going someplace. I promise you. Look at that line up there, the one between Tanner's Corner and the Paquenoke River. G-11 to G-10 on the map."

"You mean, *our* canal. The Blackwater Canal?"

"Right. Now, a boat could sail up that to the Paquo then to the Great Dismal and—"

The approaching footsteps weren't half as loud as Bell's had been, with the door being shut, and there was little warning before it swung open. Rhyme stopped speaking.

Mason Germain stood in the doorway. He glanced at Rhyme then at his boss and said, "Wondered where you'd got to, Jim. We got to make a call to Elizabeth City. Captain Dexter has some questions 'bout what happened at the 'shiners' cabin."

"Just having a chat with Lincoln. We were talking about—"

But Rhyme interrupted him quickly. "Say, Mason, I wonder if you could give us a few minutes alone here."

Mason glanced from one to the other. He nodded slowly. "They're in a mind to talk to you pretty soon, Jim." He left before Bell could respond.

"Is he gone?" Rhyme asked.

Once again Bell glanced down the corridor then nodded. "What's this all about, Lincoln?"

"Could you check out the window? Make sure Mason's left? Oh, and I'd close that door again."

Bell did. Then he walked to the window and looked

out. "Yeah. He's headed up the street. Why all this . . . ?" He lifted his hands to complete the thought.

"How well do you know Mason?"

"As good as I know mosta my deputies. Why?"

"Because he murdered Garrett Hanlon's family."

■

"*What?*" Bell started to smile but the expression faded fast. "Mason?"

"Mason," Rhyme said.

"But why on earth?"

"Because Henry Davett paid him to."

"Hold up," Bell said. "You're a couple steps past me."

"I can't prove it yet. But I'm sure."

"Henry? What's his involvement?"

Rhyme said, "It all has to do with the Blackwater Canal." He fell into his lecturing mode, eyes on the map. "Now, the point of digging the canals in the eighteenth century was having dependable transport because the roads were so bad. But as the roads and railroads got better, shippers stopped using the waterways."

"Where'd you find all this out?"

"Historical Society in Raleigh. Talked to a charming lady, Julie DeVere. According to her, Blackwater Canal was closed just after the Civil War. Wasn't used for a hundred thirty years. Until Henry Davett started running barges on it again."

Bell nodded. "That was about five years ago."

Rhyme continued, "Let me ask—you ever wonder why Davett started using it?"

The sheriff shook his head. "I remember some of us were a little worried kids'd try to swim out to a barge and get hurt and drown but none of 'em ever did and we never thought any more about it. But now you mention it I don't know *why* he'd use the canal. He's got trucks coming and going all the time. Norfolk's nothing to get to by truck."

Rhyme nodded up at the evidence chart. "The answer's right up there. That one bit of trace I never did find a source for: camphene."

"The stuff in the lanterns?"

Rhyme shook his head, grimaced. "No. I made a mistake there. True, camphene *was* used in lanterns. But it's also used in something else. It can be processed to make toxaphene."

"What's that?"

"One of the most dangerous pesticides there is. It was used mostly in the South—until it was banned in the eighties by the EPA for most uses." Rhyme shook his head angrily. "I assumed that because toxaphene was illegal there was no point in considering pesticides as the source for the camphene and that it had to be from old lanterns. Except we never *found* any old lanterns. My mind got into a rut and it wouldn't get out. No old lamps? Then I should have gone down the list and started looking for insecticide. And when I did—this morning—I found the source of the camphene."

Bell nodded, fascinated. "Which was where?"

"Everywhere," Rhyme said. "I had Lucy take samples of dirt and water from around Tanner's Corner. There's toxaphene all over the place—the water, the land. I should've listened to what Sachs told me the other day when she was searching for Garrett. She saw huge patches of barren land. She thought it was acid rain but it wasn't. Toxaphene did that. The highest concentrations are for a couple of miles around Davett's factory—Blackwater Landing and the canal. He's been manufacturing asphalt and tar paper as a cover for making toxaphene."

"But it's banned, I thought you said."

"I called an FBI agent friend of mine and he called the EPA. It's not completely banned—farmers can use it in emergencies. But that's not how Davett's making his millions. This agent at the EPA explained something called the 'circle of poison.' "

"Don't like the sound of that."

"You shouldn't. Toxaphene *is* banned here but the ban in the U.S. is only on *use*. It can be made here and sold to foreign countries."

"And *they* can use it?"

"It's legal in most Third World and Latin American countries. That's the circle: Those countries spray food with pesticides and send it back into the U.S. The FDA only inspects a small percentage of imported fruits and vegetables so there are plenty of people in the U.S. still poisoned, even though it's banned."

Bell gave a cynical laugh. "And Davett can't ship it on the roads because of all the counties and towns that won't let any toxic shipments go through 'em. And the ICC logs on his trucks'd show what the cargo is. Not to mention the public relations problem if word got out what he was doing."

"Exactly," Rhyme said, nodding. "So he reopened the canal to send the toxaphene through the Intracoastal Waterway to Norfolk, where it's loaded onto foreign ships. Only there was a problem—when the canal closed in the eighteen hundreds the property around it was sold privately. People whose houses butted up against the canal had the right to control who used it."

Bell said, "So Davett paid them to lease their portion of the canal." He nodded with sudden understanding. "And he must've paid a lot of money—look at how big those houses are in Blackwater Landing. And think about those nice trucks and Mercedeses and Lexuses people're driving around here. But what's this about Mason and Garrett's family?"

"Garrett's father's land was on the canal. But he wouldn't sell his usage rights. So Davett or somebody in his company hired Mason to convince Garrett's father to sell and, when he wouldn't, Mason picked up some local trash to help him kill the family—Culbeau, Tomel and O'Sarian. Then I'd guess that Davett bribed the executor of the will to sell the property to him."

"But Garrett's folks died in an accident. A car accident. I saw the report myself."

"Was Mason the officer who handled the report?"

"I don't remember but he could've been," Bell admitted. He looked at Rhyme with an admiring smile. "How on earth d'you figure this out?"

"Oh, it was easy—because there's no frost in July. Not in North Carolina anyway."

"Frost?"

"I talked to Amelia. Garrett told her that the night his family was killed the car was frosty and his parents and sister were shivering. But the accident happened in July. I remembered seeing the article in the file—the picture of Garrett and his family. He was in a T-shirt and the picture was of them at a Fourth of July party. The story said the photo was taken a week before his parents were killed."

"Then what was the boy talking about? Frost, shivering?"

"Mason and Culbeau used some of Davett's toxaphene to kill the family. I talked to my doctor over at the medical center. She said that in extreme cases of neurotoxic poisoning the body spasms. That's the shivering Garrett saw. The frost was probably fumes or residue of the chemical in the car."

"If he saw it why didn't he tell anybody?"

"I described the boy to the doctor. And she said it sounds like he got poisoned too that night. Just enough to give him MCS—multiple chemical sensitivity. Memory loss, brain damage, severe reaction to other chemicals in the air and water. Remember the welts on his skin?"

"Sure."

"Garrett thinks it's poison oak but it isn't. The doctor told me that skin eruptions are a classic symptom of MCS. Breaking out when you're exposed to trace amounts of substances that wouldn't affect anybody else. Even soap or perfume'll make your skin erupt."

"It's making sense," Bell said. Then, frowning, he added, "But if you don't have any hard evidence then all we've got is speculation."

"Oh, I should mention"—Rhyme couldn't resist a faint smile; modesty was never a quality that he wore well— "I've *got* some hard evidence. I found the bodies of Garrett's family."

. . . chapter forty-one

At the Albemarle Manor Hotel, a block away from the Paquenoke County lockup, Mason Germain didn't wait for the elevator but climbed the stairs, covered with threadbare tan carpet.

He found Room 201 and knocked.

"S'open," came the voice.

Mason pushed the door open slowly, revealing a pink room bathed in orange, afternoon sunlight. It was painfully hot inside. He couldn't imagine that the occupant of the room liked it this way so he assumed that the man sitting at the table was either too lazy to turn on the air conditioner or too stupid to figure out how it worked. Which made Mason all the more suspicious of him.

The African American, lean and with particularly dark skin, wore a wrinkled black suit, which looked completely out of place in Tanner's Corner. Draw attention to yourself, why don't you? Mason thought contemptuously. Malcolm Goddamn X.

"You'd be Germain?" the man asked.

"Yeah."

The man's feet were on the chair across from him and when he withdrew his hand from under a copy of the *Charlotte Observer* his long fingers were holding a long automatic pistol.

"That answers one of my questions," Mason said. "Whether you got a gun or not."

"What's the other?" the man in the suit asked.

"Whether you know how to use it."

The man said nothing but carefully marked his place in a newspaper story with a stubby pencil. He looked like a third-grader struggling with the alphabet.

Mason studied him again, not saying a word, then felt an infuriating trickle of sweat running down his face. Without asking the man if it was all right Mason walked to the bathroom, snagged a towel and wiped his face with it, dropped it on the bathroom floor.

The man gave a laugh, as irritating as the bead of sweat had been, and said, "I'm gettin' the distinct impression you don't much like my kind."

"No, I guess I don't," Mason answered. "But if you know what you're doing, what I like and what I don't aren't important."

"That's completely right," the black man said coolly. "So, talk to me. I don't want to be here any longer than I have to."

Mason said, "Here's the way it's shaking out. Rhyme's talking to Jim Bell right now over in the County Building. And that Amelia Sachs, she's in the lockup up the street."

"Where should we go first?"

Without hesitating Mason said, "The woman."

"Then that's what we'll do," the man said as if it were *his* idea. He slipped the gun away, placed the newspaper on the dresser and, with a politeness that Mason believed was more mockery than anything else, said, "After yourself." And gestured toward the door.

■

"The bodies of the Hanlons?" Jim Bell asked Rhyme. "Where are they?"

"Over there," Rhyme said. Nodding to a pile of the bones that had been in Mary Beth's backpack. "*Those're* what Mary Beth found at Blackwater Landing," the criminalist said. "She thought they were the bones of the survivors of the Lost Colony. But I had to break the news to her that they're not that old. They looked decayed but that's just because they were partially burned. I've done a lot of work in forensic anthropology and I knew right away they've been in the ground only about five years—which is just how long ago Garrett's folks were killed. They're the bones of a man in his late thirties, a woman about the same age who'd borne children and a girl about ten. That describes Garrett's family perfectly."

Bell looked at them. "I don't get it."

"Garrett's family's property was right across Route 112 from the river in Blackwater Landing. Mason and Culbeau poisoned the family then burned and buried the bodies and pushed their car into the water. Davett bribed the coroner to fake the death report and paid off somebody at the funeral home to pretend to cremate the remains. The graves're empty, I guarantee. Mary Beth must've mentioned finding the bones to somebody and word got back to Mason. He paid Billy Stail to go to Blackwater Landing to kill her and steal the evidence—the bones."

"*What?* Billy?"

"Except that Garrett happened to be there, keeping an eye on Mary Beth. He was right, you know: Blackwater Landing *is* a dangerous place. People *did* die there—those other cases in the last few years. Only it wasn't Garrett who killed them. It was Mason and Culbeau. They were murdered because they'd gotten sick from the toxaphene and started asking questions about why. Everybody in town knew about the Insect Boy so Mason or Culbeau killed that one girl—Meg Blanchard—with the hornets' nest to make it look like he was the killer. The others they hit over the head and pitched into the canal to drown. People who didn't question getting sick—like Mary Beth's father and Lucy Kerr—they didn't bother with."

"But Garrett's fingerprints were on the shovel . . . the murder weapon."

"Ah, the shovel," Rhyme mused. "Something very interesting about that shovel. I stumbled again. . . . There were only *two* sets of fingerprints on it."

"Right, Billy's and Garrett's."

"But where were Mary Beth's?" Rhyme asked.

Bell's eyes narrowed. He nodded. "Right. There were none of hers."

"Because it wasn't *her* shovel. Mason gave it to Billy to take to Blackwater Landing—after wiping his own prints off it, of course. I asked Mary Beth about it. She said that Billy came out of the bushes carrying it. Mason figured it would be the perfect murder weapon—because as an archaeologist Mary Beth'd probably have a shovel with her. Well, Billy gets to Blackwater Landing and sees Garrett with her. He figures he'll kill the Insect Boy too. But Garrett got the shovel away and hit Billy. He thought he killed him. But he didn't."

"Garrett didn't kill Billy?"

"No, no, no. . . . He only hit Billy once or twice. Knocked him out but didn't hurt him that seriously. Then Garrett took Mary Beth away with him to the moonshiners' cabin. Mason was the first on the scene. He admitted that."

"That's right. He took the call."

"Kind of a coincidence that he was nearby, don't you think?" Rhyme asked.

"I guess. I didn't think about it at the time."

"Mason found Billy. He picked up the shovel—wearing latex evidence gloves—and beat the boy until he died."

"How do you know that?"

"Because of the position of the latex prints. I had Ben reexamine the handle of the shovel an hour ago with an alternative light source. Mason held the shovel like a baseball bat. That's not how somebody would pick up evidence at a crime scene. And he adjusted his grip a number of times to get better leverage. When Sachs was at the crime scene she said the blood pattern showed Billy'd been hit first in the head and knocked down. But he was still alive. Until Mason hit him in the neck with the shovel."

Bell looked out the window, his face hollow. "Why would Mason kill Billy?"

"He probably figured that Billy'd panic and tell the truth. Or maybe the boy was conscious when Mason got there and said he was fed up and wanted out of the deal."

"So that's why you wanted Mason to leave . . . a few minutes ago. I *wondered* what that was about. So how're we going to prove all of this, Lincoln?"

"I've got the latex prints on the shovel. I've got the bones, which test positive for toxaphene in high concentrations. I want to get a diver and look for the Hanlons' car in the Paquenoke. Some evidence will've survived— even after five years. Then we should search Billy's house and see if there's any cash there that can be traced to Mason. And we'll search Mason's house too. It'll be a tough case." Rhyme gave a faint smile. "But I'm good, Jim. I can do it." Then his smile faded. "But if Mason doesn't turn state's evidence against Henry Davett it's going to be tough to make the case against *him*. All I've got's that." Rhyme nodded to a plastic exemplar jar filled with about eight ounces of pale liquid.

"What's that?"

"Pure toxaphene. Lucy got a sample from Davett's warehouse a half hour ago. She said there must've been ten thousand gallons of the stuff there. If we can establish a compositional identity between the chemical that killed Garrett's family and what's in that jar we might convince the prosecutor to bring a case against Davett."

"But Davett helped us find Garrett."

"Of course he did. It was in his interest to find the boy—and Mary Beth—as fast as possible. *Davett* was the one who wanted her dead most of all."

"Mason," Bell muttered, shaking his head. "I've known him for years. . . . You think he suspects?"

"You're the only one I've told. I didn't even tell Lucy—I just had her do some legwork for me. I was afraid somebody'd overhear and word'd get back to Mason or Davett. This town, Jim, it's a nest of hornets. I don't know who to trust."

Bell sighed. "How can you be so sure it's Mason?"

"Because Culbeau and his friends showed up at the moonshiners' cabin just after we figured out where it was. And Mason was the only one who knew that . . . aside from me and you and Ben. He must've called Culbeau and told him where the cabin was. So . . . let's call the state police, have one of their divers come on down here and check out Blackwater Landing. We should get on those warrants to search Billy's and Mason's houses too."

Rhyme watched Bell nod. But instead of going to the phone he walked to the window and slid it shut. Then he stepped to the door again, opened it, looked out, closed it.

Locked the latch.

"Jim, what're you doing?"

Bell hesitated then took a step toward Rhyme.

The criminalist looked once into the sheriff's eyes and gripped the sip-and-puff controller quickly between his teeth. He blew into it and the wheelchair started forward. But Bell stepped behind him and yanked the battery cable free. The Storm Arrow eased forward a few inches and stopped.

"Jim," he whispered. "Not you too?"

"You got that right."

Rhyme's eyes closed. "No, no," he whispered. His head dipped. But only a few millimeters. As with most great men Lincoln Rhyme's gestures of defeat were very subtle.

V

The Town Without Children

chapter forty-two

Mason Germain and the sullen black man moved slowly through the alley next to the Tanner's County lockup.

The man was sweating and he slapped in irritation at a mosquito. He muttered something and wiped a long hand over his short kinky hair.

Mason felt an urge to needle him but resisted.

The man was tall and by stretching up on his toes he could look into the lockup window. Mason saw that he wore short black boots—shiny patent leather—which for some reason added to the deputy's contempt for the out-of-towner. He wondered how many men he'd shot.

"She's in there," the man said. "She's alone."

"We're keeping Garrett on the other side."

"You go in the front. Can somebody get out through the back?"

"I'm a deputy, remember? I got a key. I can unlock it." He said this in a snide tone, wondering again if this fellow was halfway bright.

He got snide in return. "I was only asking if there's a *door* in the back. Which I don't know, never having been in this swamp of a town before."

"Oh. Yeah, there's a door."

"Well, let's go then."

Mason noticed that the man's gun was in his hand and that he hadn't seen him draw it.

■

Sachs sat on the bench in her cell, hypnotized by the motion of a fly.

What kind was it? she wondered. Garrett would know in an instant. He was a warehouse of knowledge. A thought occurred to her: There'd be that moment when a child's knowledge of a subject surpasses his parents'. It must be a miraculous thing, exhilarating, to know that you'd produced this creation who'd outsoared you. Humbling too.

An experience that she now would never know.

She thought once again about her father. The man had *diffused* crime. Never fired his gun in all his years on duty. Proud as he was of his daughter, he'd worried about her fascination with firearms. "Shoot *last*," he'd often remind her.

Oh, Jesse. . . . What can I say to you?

Nothing, of course. I can't say a word. You're gone.

She thought she saw a shadow outside the lockup window. But she ignored it, and her thoughts slipped to Rhyme.

You and me, she was thinking. *You and me.*

Recalling the time a few months ago, lying together in his opulent Clinitron bed in his Manhattan town house, as they watched Baz Luhrmann's stylish *Romeo and Juliet,* an updated version set in Miami. With Rhyme, death always hovered close and, watching the final scenes of the movie, Amelia Sachs had realized that, like Shakespeare's characters, she and Rhyme were in a way starcrossed lovers too. And another thought had then flashed through her mind: that the two of them would also die together.

She hadn't dared share this thought with rationalist Lincoln Rhyme, who didn't have a sentimental cell in his brain. But once this notion had occurred to her it seated itself permanently in her psyche and for some reason gave her great comfort.

Yet now she couldn't even find solace in this odd thought. No, now—thanks to her—they'd live separately and die separately. They'd—

The door to the lockup swung open and a young deputy walked inside. She recognized him. It was Steve Farr, Jim Bell's brother-in-law.

"Hey there," he called.

Sachs nodded. Then she noticed two things about him. One was that he wore a Rolex watch, which must've cost half the annual salary of a typical cop in North Carolina.

The other was that he wore a sidearm and that the holster thong was unsnapped.

Despite the sign outside the door to the cells: PLACE ALL WEAPONS IN THE LOCKBOX BEFORE ENTERING THE CELL AREA.

"How you doing?" Farr asked.

She looked at him, gave no reaction.

"Being the silent type today, huh? Well, miss, I got good news for you. You're free to go." He flicked at one of his prominent ears.

"Free? To go?"

He fished for his keys.

"Yep. They've decided the shooting was accidental. You can just leave."

She studied his face closely. He wasn't looking her way.

"What about the disposition report?"

"What's that?" Farr asked.

"Nobody charged with a crime can be released from custody without a disposition report waiving charges, signed by the prosecutor."

Farr unlocked the cell door and stood back. Hand hovering near the pistol butt. "Oh, maybe that's how you do things in the big city. But down here we're a ton more casual. You know, they say we move slower in the South. But that ain't right. No, ma'am. We're really more efficient."

Sachs remained seated. "Can I ask why you're wearing your weapon in the lockup?"

"Oh, this?" He tapped the gun. "We don't have any hard-and-fast rules about that sort of thing. Now, come on. You're free to leave. Most people'd be jumping up and down at that news." He nodded toward the back of the lockup.

"Out the back door?" she asked.

"Sure."

"You can't shoot a fleeing prisoner in the back. That's murder."

He nodded slowly.

How was it set up? she wondered. Was there someone else outside the door to do the actual shooting? Probably. Farr bangs himself on the head and calls for help. Fires a shot into the ceiling. Outside, somebody—maybe a "concerned" citizen—claims he heard the gun and assumes Sachs is armed, shoots her.

She didn't move.

"Now stand up and git your ass outside." Farr pulled the pistol from his holster.

Slowly she stood.

You and me, Rhyme . . .

■

"You were pretty close, Lincoln," Jim Bell said.

After a moment he added, "Ninety percent right. My experience in law enforcement is that's a good percentage. Too bad for you *I'm* the ten percent you missed."

Bell shut off the air conditioner. With the window closed the room heated up immediately. Rhyme felt sweat on his forehead. His breathing grew labored.

The sheriff continued, "Two families along Blackwater Canal wouldn't grant Mr. Davett easements to run his barges."

A respectful *Mister* Davett, Rhyme noted.

"So his security chief hired a few of us to take care of the problem. We had a long talk with the Conklins and they decided to grant the easement. But Garrett's father never would agree. We were going to make it look like a car crash and we got a can of that shit"—he nodded to the jar on the table—"to knock them out. We knew the family went out to dinner every Wednesday. We poured the poison into the car's vent and hid in the woods. They got in and Garrett's father turned on the air conditioner. The stuff sprayed out all over them. But we used too much—"

He glanced again at the jar. "That there's enough to kill a man twice over." He continued, frowning at the memory. "The family started twitching and convulsing. . . . Was a hard thing to see. Garrett wasn't in the car but he ran up and saw what was going on. He tried to get inside but couldn't. He got a good whiff of the stuff, though, and it was like he became this zombie. He just stumbled off into the woods 'fore we could catch him. And by the time he surfaced—a week or two later—he didn't remember what'd happened. That MCS thing you were mentioning, I guess. So we just let him be for the time being—too suspicious if he was to die right after his family did.

"Then we did just what you figured. Set fire to the bodies and buried them at Blackwater Landing. Pushed the car into the inlet by Canal Road. Paid the coroner a hundred thousand for some ginned-up reports. Whenever we heard that somebody else'd got a funny kind of cancer and was asking questions why, Culbeau and the others took care of them."

"That funeral we saw on the way into town. You killed that boy, didn't you?"

"Todd Wilkes?" Bell said. "No. He did kill himself."

"But because he was sick from the toxaphene, right? What'd he have, cancer? Liver damage? Brain damage?"

"Maybe. I don't know." But the sheriff's face said that he knew only too well.

"But Garrett didn't have anything to do with it, did he?"

"No."

"What about those men at the moonshiners' cabin? The ones who assaulted Mary Beth?"

Bell nodded again, grimly. "Tom Boston and Lott Cooper. They were part of it too—they handled testing a lot of Davett's toxins out in the mountains where it's less populated. They knew we were looking for Mary Beth but when Lott found her I guess he decided they'd hold off letting me know until they'd had some fun with her. And, yeah, we hired Billy Stail to kill her but Garrett got her away 'fore he could."

"And you needed me to help you find her. Not to save her—but so you could kill her and destroy any other evidence she might've found."

"After you found Garrett and we brought him back from the mill, I left the door to the lockup open so Culbeau and his buddies could, let's say, *talk* Garrett into telling us where Mary Beth was. But your friend went and busted him out before they could snatch him."

Rhyme said, "And when I found the cabin you called Culbeau and the others. Sent them there to kill us all."

"I'm sorry . . . it's all become a nightmare. Didn't want it to but . . . there you have it."

"A hornets' nest . . ."

"Oh, yeah, this town's got itself a few hornets."

Rhyme shook his head. "Tell me, are the fancy cars and the big houses and all the money worth destroying the entire town? Look around you, Bell. It was a child's funeral the other day but there were no children at the cemetery. Amelia said there are hardly any kids in town anymore. You know why? People're sterile."

"It's risky when you bargain with the devil," Bell said shortly. "But, far as I'm concerned, life's just one big trade-off." He looked at Rhyme for a long moment, walked to the table. He pulled on latex gloves, picked up the toxaphene jar. He stepped toward Rhyme and slowly began to unscrew the lid.

■

Steve Farr roughly led Amelia Sachs to the back door of the lockup, the pistol firmly in the square of her back.

He was making the classic mistake of holding the muzzle of his weapon against the body of his victim. It gave her leverage—when she stepped outside she'd know exactly where the gun was and could sweep her elbow into it. With some luck Farr would drop the weapon and she'd sprint as fast as she could. If she could make it to Main Street there'd be witnesses and he might hesitate to shoot.

He opened the back door.

A stream of hot sunlight flooded into the dusty lockup. She blinked. A fly buzzed around her head.

As long as Farr stayed right up against her, pressing the gun into her skin, she'd have a chance. . . .

"What now?" she asked.

"Free to go," he said cheerfully, shrugging. She tensed, about to swing into him, planning every move. But then he stepped back fast, shoving her outside into the scruffy lot behind the jail. Farr remained inside, well out of reach.

From nearby, behind a tall bush in the field, she heard another sound. The cocking of a pistol, she thought.

"Go ahead," Farr said. "Git on outa here."

She thought of *Romeo and Juliet* again.

And of the beautiful cemetery on the hill overlooking Tanner's Corner they'd driven past what now seemed like a lifetime ago.

Oh, Rhyme . . .

The fly zipped past her face. Instinctively she brushed it away and began to walk forward into the low grass.

■

Rhyme said to Bell, "Don't you think somebody might wonder if I die this way? I can hardly open a jar by myself."

The sheriff responded, "You bumped the table. The lid wasn't on tight. It splashed on you. I went for help but we couldn't save you in time."

"Amelia's not going to let it go. Lucy won't either."

"Your girlfriend's not going to be a problem for very much longer. And Lucy? She might just get sick again . . . and this time there might not be anything to cut off to save her."

Bell hesitated only a moment then he stepped close and poured the liquid over Rhyme's mouth and nose. The rest he splashed onto the front of his shirt.

The sheriff dropped the jar onto Rhyme's lap, stepped back fast and covered his own mouth with a handkerchief.

Rhyme's head jerked back, his lips parted involuntarily and some of the liquid slipped into his mouth. He began to choke.

Bell pulled off the gloves and stuffed them into his slacks. He waited a moment, calmly studying Rhyme, then walked toward the door slowly, unlocked it, swung it open. He called, "There's been an accident! Somebody, I need help!" He stepped into the corridor. "I need—"

He walked right into Lucy Kerr's line of fire, her pistol aimed steadily at his chest.

"Jesus, Lucy!"

"That's enough, Jim. Just hold it right there."

The sheriff stepped back. Nathan, the sharpshooting deputy, walked into the room, behind Bell, and snagged the sheriff's pistol from its holster. Another man entered—a large man in a tan suit and white shirt.

Ben too ran inside, ignored everyone else and hurried to Rhyme, wiping the criminalist's face with a paper towel.

The sheriff stared at Lucy and the others. "No, you don't understand! There was an accident! That poison stuff spilled. You've got to—"

Rhyme spit on the floor and wheezed from the astringent liquid and the fumes. He said to Ben, "Could you wipe higher on my cheek? I'm afraid it'll get into my eyes. Thank you."

"Sure, Lincoln."

Bell said, "I was going for help! That stuff spilled! I—"

The man in the suit pulled handcuffs off his belt and ratcheted the loops around the sheriff's wrists. He said, "James Bell, I'm Detective Hugo Branch with the North Carolina State Police. You're under arrest here." Branch looked at Rhyme sourly. "I *told* you he'd pour it on your shirt. We should've put the unit someplace else."

"But you got enough on tape?"

"Oh, plenty. That's not the point. The point is those transmitters cost *money.*"

"Bill me," Rhyme said acerbically as Branch opened Rhyme's shirt and untaped the microphone and transmitter.

"It was a setup," Bell whispered.

You got that right.

"But the poison . . ."

"Oh, it's not toxaphene," Rhyme said. "Just a little moonshine. From that jar we tested. By the way, Ben, if there's any left, I could use a sip just now. And, Christ, could somebody get that AC going?"

■

Tense, cut to the left and run like hell. I'll get hit but if I'm lucky it won't stop me.

When you move they can't getcha . . .

Amelia Sachs took three steps into the grass.

Ready . . .

Set . . .

Then a man's voice from behind them, inside the lockup area, called, "Hold it, Steve! Put the weapon on the ground. Now! I'm not telling you again!"

Sachs spun around and saw Mason Germain, his gun pointed at the shocked young man's crew-cut head, his round ears crimson. Farr crouched and set the gun on the floor. Mason hurried forward and cuffed him.

Footsteps sounded from outside, leaves rustled. Dizzy from the heat and the adrenaline, Sachs turned back to the field and saw a lean black man climbing out of the bushes, holstering a big Browning automatic pistol.

"Fred!" she cried.

FBI agent Fred Dellray, sweating furiously in his black suit, walked up to her, brushing petulantly at his sleeve. "Hey, A-melia. My, it is too too too hot down here. I don't like this town one tiny bit. And look at this suit. It's all, I don't know, dusty or something. What is this shit, pollen? We don't have this stuff in Man-hattan. Look at this sleeve!"

"What're you doing here?" she asked, dumbfounded.

"Whatcha think? Lincoln wasn't sure who he could trust and who he couldn't so he had me fly down and hooked me up with Deputy Germain here to keep an eye on you. Figured he needed some help, seeing as how he couldn't trust Jim Bell or his kin."

"Bell?" she whispered.

"Lincoln thinks he put this whole thing together. He's finding out for sure right now. But looks like he was right, that being his brother-in-law." Dellray nodded at Steve Farr.

"He almost got me," Sachs said.

The lean agent chuckled. "You weren't in a single, solitary lick of danger, no way. I had a bead on that fellow right 'tween his big ears from the second the back door opened. He'd so much as squinted out a target at you he'da been way, way gone."

Dellray noticed Mason studying him suspiciously. The agent laughed, said to Sachs, "Our friend in the con-stab-ulary here don't like my kind much. He told me so."

"Wait," Mason protested. "I only meant—"

"You meant federal agents, I'm betting," Dellray said.

The deputy shook his head, said gruffly, "I meant Northerners."

"True, he doesn't," Sachs confirmed.

Sachs and Dellray laughed. But Mason remained solemn. But it wasn't cultural differences that made him somber. He said to Sachs, "Sorry, but I'll have to take you back to the cell. You're still under arrest."

Her smile faded, and Sachs looked once more at the sun dancing over the scruffy yellow grass. She inhaled the scorching air of the out-of-doors once, then again. Finally she turned and walked back into the dim lockup.

chapter forty-three

"*You* killed Billy, didn't you?" Rhyme asked Jim Bell.

But the sheriff said nothing.

The criminalist continued, "The crime scene was unprotected for an hour and a half. And, sure, Mason was the first officer. But *you* got there before he arrived. You never got a call from Billy saying that Mary Beth was dead and you started to worry so you drove over to Blackwater Landing and found her gone and Billy hurt. Billy told you about Garrett getting away with the girl. Then you put the latex gloves on, picked up the shovel and killed him."

Finally the sheriff's anger broke through his facade. "Why did you suspect *me*?"

"Originally I *did* think it was Mason—only the three of us and Ben knew about the moonshiners' cabin. I assumed he called Culbeau and sent him there. But I asked Lucy and it turned out that Mason called *her* and sent her to the cabin—just to make sure Amelia and Garrett didn't get away again. Then I got to thinking and I realized that at the mill Mason tried to shoot Garrett.

Anybody in on the conspiracy would want to keep him alive—like you did—so he could lead you to Mary Beth. I checked into Mason's finances and found out he's got a cheap house and is in serious hock to MasterCard and Visa. Nobody was paying *him* off. Unlike you and your brother-in-law, Bell. You've got a four-hundred-thou-sand-dollar house and plenty of cash in the bank. And Steve Farr's got a house worth three ninety and a boat that cost a hundred eighty thousand. We're getting court orders to take a peek in your safe-deposit boxes. Wonder how much we'll find there."

Rhyme continued. "I was a little curious why Mason was so eager to nail Garrett but he had a good reason for that. He told me he was pretty upset when you got the job of sheriff—couldn't quite figure out why since he had a better record and more seniority. He thought that if he could collar the Insect Boy the Board of Supervisors'd be sure to appoint him sheriff when your term expired."

"All your fucking playacting. . . ." Bell muttered. "I thought you only believed in evidence."

Rhyme rarely sparred verbally with his quarry. Banter was useless except as a balm for the soul and Lincoln Rhyme had yet to uncover any hard evidence on the whereabouts and nature of the soul. Still, he told Bell, "I would've *preferred* evidence. But sometimes you have to improvise. I'm really *not* the prima donna everybody thinks I am."

■

The Storm Arrow wheelchair wouldn't fit into Amelia Sachs's cell.

"Not crip accessible?" Rhyme groused. "That's an A.D.A. violation."

She thought his bluster was for her benefit, letting her see his familiar moods. But she said nothing.

Because of the wheelchair problem Mason Germain

suggested they try the interrogation room. Sachs shuffled in, wearing the hand and ankle shackles that the deputy insisted on (she had, after all, already managed one escape from the place).

The lawyer from New York had arrived. He was gray-haired Solomon Geberth. A member of the New York, Massachusetts and D.C. bars, he had been admitted to the jurisdiction of North Carolina *pro hac vice*—for the single case of *People v. Sachs.* Curiously, with his smooth, handsome face and mannerisms even smoother he seemed far more a genteel Southern lawyer out of a John Grisham novel than a bulldog of a Manhattan litigator. The man's trim hair glistened with spray and his Italian suit successfully resisted wrinkles even in Tanner's Corner's astonishing humidity.

Lincoln Rhyme sat between Sachs and her lawyer. She rested her hand on the armrest of his injured wheelchair.

"They brought in a special prosecutor from Raleigh," Geberth was explaining. "With the sheriff and the coroner on the take I don't think they quite trust McGuire. Anyway he's looked over the evidence and decided to dismiss the charges against Garrett."

Sachs stirred at this. "He did?"

Geberth said, "Garrett admitted hitting the boy, Billy, and *thought* he killed him. But Lincoln was right. It was Bell who killed the boy. And even if they brought him up on assault charges Garrett was clearly acting in self-defense. That other deputy, Ed Schaeffer? His death's been ruled accidental."

"What about kidnapping Lydia Johansson?" Rhyme asked.

"When she realized that Garrett had never intended to hurt her she decided to drop the charges. Mary Beth did the same. Her mother wanted to go ahead with the complaint but you should've heard that girl talk to the woman. Some fur flew during *that* conversation, I'll tell you."

"So he's free? Garrett?" Sachs asked, eyes on the floor.

"They're letting him out in a few minutes," Geberth told her. Then: "Okay, here's the laundry, Amelia: the prosecutor's position is that even if Garrett turned out not to be a felon, you aided in the escape of a prisoner who'd been arrested on the basis of probable cause and you killed an officer during the commission of that crime. The prosecutor's going for first-degree murder and throwing in the standard lesser-included offenses: both manslaughter counts—voluntary and involuntary—and reckless homicide and criminally negligent homicide."

"First degree?" Rhyme snapped. "It wasn't premeditated; it was an accident! For Christ's sake."

"Which is what I'm going to try to show at trial," Geberth said. "That the other deputy, the one who grabbed you, was a partial proximate cause of the shooting. But I guarantee they'll get the reckless homicide conviction. On the facts there's no doubt about that."

"What's the chance of acquittal?" Rhyme asked.

"Bad. Ten, fifteen percent at best. I'm sorry, but I have to recommend you take a plea."

She felt this like a blow to her chest. Her eyes closed and when she exhaled it was as if her soul had fled from her body.

"Jesus," Rhyme muttered.

Sachs was thinking about Nick, her former boyfriend. How, when he was arrested for hijacking and taking kickbacks, he refused a plea and took the risk of a jury trial. He said to her, "It's like what your old man said, Aimee—when you move they can't get you. It's all or nothing."

It took the jury eighteen minutes to convict him. He was still in a New York prison.

She looked at the smooth-cheeked Geberth. She asked, "What's the prosecutor offering for the plea?"

"Nothing yet. But he'll probably accept voluntary manslaughter—if you do hard time. I'd guess eight, ten years. I have to tell you, though, that in North Carolina it'll be *hard* time. No country clubs here."

Rhyme grumbled, "Versus a fifteen percent chance of acquittal."

Geberth said, "That's right." Then the lawyer added, "You have to understand that there aren't going to be any miracles here, Amelia. If we go to trial the prosecutor's going to prove that you're a professional law enforcer and a champion marksman and the jury's going to have trouble buying that the shooting was accidental."

Normal rules don't apply to anybody north of the Paquo. Us or them. You can see yourself shooting before you read anybody their rights and that'd be perfectly all right.

The lawyer said, "If that happens they could convict you of murder one and you'll get twenty-five years."

"Or the death penalty," she muttered.

"Yes, that's a possibility. I can't tell you it isn't."

For some reason the image that came into her mind at this moment was of the peregrine falcons that nested outside of Lincoln Rhyme's window in his Manhattan town house: the male and the female and the young hawk. She said, "If I plead to *in*voluntary how much time will I do?"

"Probably six, seven years. No parole."

You and me, Rhyme.

She inhaled deeply. "I'll plead."

"Sachs—" Rhyme began.

But she repeated to Geberth, "I'll plead."

The lawyer rose. He nodded. "I'll call the prosecutor right now, see if he'll accept it. I'll let you know as soon as I hear anything." With a nod at Rhyme the lawyer left the room.

Mason glanced at Sachs's face. He stood and walked to the door, his boots tapping loudly. "I'll leave you two for a few minutes. I don't have to search you, do I, Lincoln?"

Rhyme smiled wanly. "I'm weapon-free, Mason."

The door swung shut.

"What a mess, Lincoln," she said.

"Uh-uh, Sachs. No first names."

"Why not?" she asked cynically, nearly a whisper. "Bad luck?"

"Maybe."

"You're not superstitious. Or so you're always telling me."

"Not usually. But this is a spooky place."

Tanner's Corner. . . . The town with no children.

"I should've listened to you," he said. "You were right about Garrett. I was wrong. I looked at the evidence and got it dead wrong."

"But I didn't *know* I was right. I didn't *know* anything. I just had a hunch and I acted."

Rhyme said, "Whatever happens, Sachs, I'm not going anywhere." He nodded down at the Storm Arrow and laughed. "I couldn't get very far even if I wanted to. You do some time, I'll be there when you get out."

"Words, Rhyme," she said. "Only words. . . . My father said he wasn't going anywhere either. That was a week before the cancer shut him down."

"I'm too ornery to die."

But you're not too ornery to get *better,* she thought, to meet someone else. To move on and leave me behind.

The door to the interrogation room opened. Garrett stood in the doorway, Mason behind him. The boy's hands, no longer in shackles, were cupped in front of him.

"Hey," Garrett said in greeting. "Check out what I found. It was in my cell." He opened his fist and a small insect flew out. "It's a sphinx moth. They like to forage in valerian flowers. You don't see 'em much inside. Pretty cool."

She smiled faintly, taking pleasure in his enthusiastic eyes. "Garrett, there's one thing I want you to know."

He walked closer, looked down at her.

"You remember what you said in the trailer? When you were talking to your father in the empty chair?"

He nodded uncertainly.

"You were saying how bad you felt that he didn't want you in the car that night."

"I remember."

"But you know why he didn't want you. . . . He was trying to save your life. He knew there was poison in the car and that they were going to die. If you got in the car with them you'd die too. And he didn't want that to happen."

"I guess I know that," he said. His voice was uncertain and Amelia Sachs supposed that rewriting one's history was a daunting task.

"You keep remembering it."

"I will."

Sachs looked at the tiny, beige moth, flying around the interrogation room. "You leave anybody in the cell for me? For company?"

"Yeah, I did. There's a couple of ladybugs—their real name is ladybird beetles. And a leafhopper and syrphus fly. It's cool the way they fly. You can watch 'em for hours." He paused. "Like, I'm sorry I lied to you. The thing is, if I hadn't I never would've got out and I couldn't've saved Mary Beth."

"That's all right, Garrett."

He looked at Mason. "I can go now?"

"You can go."

He walked to the door, turned and said to Sachs, "I'll come and, like, hang out. If that's okay."

"I'd like that."

He stepped outside, and through the open door Sachs could see him walk up to a four-by-four. It was Lucy Kerr's. Sachs saw her get out and hold the door open for him—like a mom picking up her son after soccer practice. The jail door closed and shut off this domestic scene.

"Sachs," Rhyme began. But she shook her head and started shuffling back toward the lockup. She wanted to be away from the criminalist, away from the Insect Boy, away from the town without children. She wanted to be in the darkness of solitude.

And soon she was.

■

Outside of Tanner's Corner, on Route 112, where it's still two-lane, there's a bend in the road, near the Paquenoke River. Just off the shoulder is a thick growth of plume grass, sedge, indigo and tall columbines showing off their distinctive red flowers like flags.

The vegetation creates a nook that's a popular parking space for Paquenoke County deputies, who sip iced tea and listen to the radio as they wait for the display on their radar guns to register 54 mph or higher. Then they accelerate onto the highway in pursuit of the surprised speeder to add another hundred dollars or so to the county treasury.

Today, Sunday, as a black Lexus SUV passed this jog in the road the radar gun on Lucy Kerr's dashboard registered a legal 44. But she put the squad car in gear, flipped the switch starting the gumball machine atop the car and sped after the four-by-four.

She eased close to the Lexus and studied the vehicle carefully. She'd learned long ago to check the rearview mirror of cars she was stopping. You look at the drivers' eyes and you can pretty much get a feel for what other kinds of crimes they might be committing, if any, beyond speeding or a broken taillight. Drugs, stolen weapons, drinking. You get a feel for how dangerous the pullover will be. Now, she saw the man's eyes flick into the mirror and glance at her without a hint of guilt or concern.

Invulnerable eyes . . .

Which made the anger in her all the hotter and she breathed hard to control it.

The big car eased onto the dusty shoulder and Lucy pulled in behind it. Rules dictated that she call in for a tag, tax and warrants check but Lucy didn't bother with this. There was nothing that DMV could report that would be of any interest to her. With trembling hands she opened the door and climbed out.

The driver's eyes now shifted to the sideview mirror and continued to examine her clinically. They registered some surprise, noticing, she supposed, that she wasn't in her uniform—just jeans and a work shirt—though she was wearing her weapon on her hip. What would an off-duty cop be doing pulling over a driver who hadn't been speeding?

Henry Davett rolled down his window.

Lucy Kerr looked inside, past Davett. In the front passenger seat was a woman in her early fifties, with a dryness to her sprayed blond hair that suggested frequent beauty parlor shampoos. She wore diamonds on wrist, ears and chest. A teenage girl sat in the back, flipping through boxes of CDs, mentally enjoying the music that her father wouldn't let her listen to on the Sabbath.

"Officer Kerr," Davett said, "what's the problem?"

But she could see in his eyes, now no longer in reflection, that he knew exactly what the problem was.

And still they remained as guilt-free and in control as when he'd noticed the gyrations of the flashing lights on her Crown Victoria.

Her anger tugged at its restraints and she snapped, "Get out of the car, Davett."

"Honey, what did you do?"

"Officer, what's the point of this?" Davett asked, sighing.

"Out. Now." Lucy reached inside and popped the door locks.

"Can she do that, honey? Can she—"

"Shut up, Edna."

"All right. I'm sorry."

Lucy swung the door open. Davett unsnapped his seat belt and stepped out onto the dusty shoulder.

A semi sped past and wrapped its wake around them. Davett looked distastefully at the gray Carolina clay settling on his blue blazer. "My family and I are late for church and I don't think—"

She took him by the arm and pulled him off the shoulder, into the shade of wild rice and cattails; a small stream, a feeder to the Paquenoke, ran beside the road.

He repeated with exasperation, "What is the point?"

"I know everything."

"Do you, Officer Kerr? Do you know *everything*? Which would be?"

"The poison, the murders, the canal . . ."

Davett said smoothly, "I never had a bit of direct contact with Jim Bell or anybody else in Tanner's Corner. If there were some damn crazy fools on my payroll who hired some other damn crazy fools to do things that were illegal that's not my fault. And if that happened I'll be cooperating with the authorities one hundred percent."

Unfazed by his suave response she growled, "You're going down with Bell and his brother-in-law."

"Of course I'm not. Nothing links me to a single crime. There're no witnesses. No accounts, no money transfers, no evidence of any wrongdoing. I'm a manufacturer of petrochemical-based products—certain cleaners, asphalt and some pesticides."

"Illegal pesticides."

"Wrong," he snapped. "The EPA still allows toxaphene to be used in some cases in the U.S. And it's not illegal at all in most Third World countries. Do some reading, Deputy: without pesticides malaria and encephalitis and famine'd kill hundreds of thousands of people every year and—"

"—and give the people who're exposed to it cancer and birth defects and liver damage and—"

Davett shrugged. "Show me the studies, Deputy Kerr. Show me the research that proves that."

"If it's so fucking harmless then why did you stop shipping it by truck? Why did you start using barges?"

"I couldn't get it to port any other way—because some knee-jerk counties and towns've banned transportation of some substances they don't know the facts about. And I didn't have the time to hire lobbyists to change the laws."

"Well, I'll bet the EPA'd be interested in what you're doing here."

"Oh, please," he scoffed. "The EPA? Send them out. I'll give you their phone number. *If* they ever get around to visiting the factory they'll find permissible levels of toxaphene everywhere around Tanner's Corner."

"Maybe what's in the *water* alone is at a permissible level, maybe what's in the *air* alone, maybe the local *produce* alone. . . . But what about the combination of them? What about a child who drinks a glass of water from his parents' well then plays in the grass then eats an apple from a local orchard then—"

He shrugged. "The laws're clear, Deputy Kerr. If you don't like them write your congressman."

She grabbed him by the lapel. She raged, "You don't understand. You are going to prison."

He pulled away from her, whispered viciously, "No, *you* don't understand, Officer. You're way out of your depth here. I'm very, very good at what I do. I do not make mistakes." He glanced at his watch. "I have to go now."

Davett walked back to the SUV, patting his thinning hair. The sweat had darkened it and stuck the strands into place.

He climbed in and slammed the door.

Lucy walked up to the driver's side as he started the engine. "Wait," she said.

Davett glanced at her. But the deputy ignored him. She was looking at his passengers. "I'd like you to see what Henry did." Her strong hands ripped her own shirt open. The women in the car gaped at the pink scars where her breasts had been.

"Oh, for pity's sake," Davett muttered, looking away.

"Dad . . ." the girl whispered in shock. Her mother stared, speechless.

Lucy said, "You said that you don't make mistakes, Davett? . . . Wrong. You made this one."

The man put the car in gear, clicked on his turn signal, checked his blind spot and eased slowly onto the highway.

Lucy stood for a long moment, watching the Lexus disappear. She fished in her pocket and pinned her shirt closed with several safety pins. She leaned against her car for a long moment, fighting tears, then she happened to look down and notice a small, ruddy flower by the roadside. She squinted. It was a pink moccasin flower, a type of orchid. Its blossoms resemble tiny slip-on shoes. The plant was rare in Paquenoke County and she'd never seen one as lovely as this. In five minutes, using her windshield ice scraper, she'd uprooted the plant and had it packed safely in a tall 7-Eleven cup, the root beer sacrificed for the beauty of Lucy Kerr's garden.

. . . chapter forty-four

A plaque on the courthouse wall explained that the name of the state came from the Latin *Carolus,* for Charles. It was King Charles I who granted a land patent to settle the colony.

Carolina . . .

Amelia Sachs had assumed the state was named for Caroline, some queen or princess. Brooklyn born and raised, she had little interest in, or knowledge of, royalty.

She now sat, handcuffed still, between two guards on a bench in the courthouse. The redbrick building was an old place, filled with dark mahogany and marble floors. Stern men in black suits, judges or governors, she assumed, looked down on her from oil paintings as if they knew she was guilty. There didn't seem to be air-conditioning but breezes and the darkness cooled the place thanks to efficient eighteenth-century engineering.

Fred Dellray ambled up to her. "Hey there—you want some coffee or something?"

The left-field guard got as far as "No speaking to the—" before the Justice Department ID card crimped off the recitation.

"No, Fred. Where's Lincoln?"

It was nearly nine-thirty.

"Dunno. You know that man—sometimes he just *appears*. For a man who doesn't walk he gets around more'n anybody I know."

Lucy and Garrett weren't here either.

Sol Geberth, in a rich-looking gray suit, walked up to her. The guard on her right scooted over and let the lawyer sit down. "Hello, Fred," the lawyer said to the agent.

Dellray nodded, but coolly, and Sachs deduced that, as with Rhyme, the defense lawyer must've gotten acquittals for suspects that the agent had collared.

"It's a deal," Geberth said to Sachs. "The prosecutor's agreed to involuntary manslaughter—no other counts. Five years. No parole."

Five years . . .

The lawyer continued. "There's one aspect to this I didn't think about yesterday."

"What is it?" she asked, trying to gauge from the look on his face how deep this new trouble ran.

"The problem is you're a cop."

"What does that have to do with anything?"

Before he could say anything Dellray said, "You being a law en-*forcement* officer. Inside."

When she still didn't get it the agent explained, "Inside *prison*. You'll have to be segregated. Or you wouldn't last a week. That'll be tough, Amelia. That'll be nasty tough."

"But nobody knows I'm a cop."

Dellray laughed faintly. "They'll know ever-single-thing there is to know 'bout you by the time you get yourself issued your jumpsuit and linen."

"I haven't collared anybody down here. Why would they care that I'm a cop?"

"Don't make a splinter of difference where you're from," Dellray said, eyeing Geberth, who nodded in confirmation. "They ab-so-lutely won't keepya in general population."

"So it's basically five years in solitary."

"I'm afraid so," Geberth said.

She closed her eyes and felt nausea course through her.

Five years of not moving, of claustrophobia, of nightmares . . .

And, as an ex-convict, how could she possibly think about becoming a mother? She choked on the despair.

"So?" the lawyer asked. "What's it going to be?"

Sachs opened her eyes. "I'll take the plea."

■

The room was crowded. Sachs saw Mason Germain, a few of the other deputies. A grim couple, eyes red, probably Jesse Corn's parents, sat in the front row. She wanted badly to say something to them but their contemptuous gaze kept her silent. She saw only two faces that looked at her kindly: Mary Beth McConnell and a heavy woman who was presumably her mother. There was no sign of Lucy Kerr. Or of Lincoln Rhyme. She supposed that he didn't have the heart to watch her being led off in chains. Well, that was all right; she didn't want to see *him* under these circumstances either.

The bailiff led her to the defense table. He left the shackles on. Sol Geberth sat beside her.

They rose when the judge entered and the wiry man in a bulky black robe sat down at the tall bench. He spent some minutes looking over documents and talking with his clerk. Finally he nodded and the clerk said, "The people of the state of North Carolina versus Amelia Sachs."

The judge nodded to the prosecutor from Raleigh, a tall, silver-haired man, who rose. "Your Honor, the defendant and the state have entered into a plea arrangement, whereby the defendant has agreed to plead guilty to second-degree manslaughter in the death of Deputy Jesse Randolph Corn. The state waives all other charges and is recommending a sentence of five years, to be served without possibility of parole or reduction."

"Miss Sachs, you've discussed this arrangement with your attorney?"

"I have, Your Honor."

"And he's told you that you have the right to reject it and proceed to trial?"

"Yes."

"And you understand that by accepting this you will be pleading guilty to a felony homicide charge."

"Yes."

"You're making this decision willingly?"

She thought of her father, of Nick. And of Lincoln Rhyme. "I am, yes."

"Very well. How do you plead to the charge of second-degree manslaughter brought against you?"

"Guilty, Your Honor."

"In light of the state's recommendation the plea will be entered and I am hereby sentencing you—"

The red-leather doors leading to the corridor swung inward and with a high-pitched whine Lincoln Rhyme's wheelchair maneuvered inside. A bailiff had tried to open the doors for the Storm Arrow but Rhyme seemed to be in a hurry and just plowed through them. One slammed into the wall. Lucy Kerr was behind him.

The judge looked up, ready to reprimand the intruder. When he saw the chair he—like most people—deferred to the political correctness that Rhyme despised and said nothing. He turned back to Sachs. "I'm hereby sentencing you to five years—"

Rhyme said, "Forgive me, Your Honor. I need to speak with the defendant and her counsel for a minute."

"Well," the judge grumbled, "we're in the middle of a proceeding. You can speak to her at some future time."

"With all respect, Your Honor," Rhyme responded, "I need to speak to her *now*." His voice was a grumble too but it was much louder than the jurist's.

■

Just like the old days, being in a courtroom.

Most people think that a criminalist's only job is finding and analyzing evidence. But when Lincoln Rhyme was head of the NYPD's forensics operation—the Investigation and Resources Division—he had spent nearly as much time testifying in court as he did in the lab. He was a good expert witness. (Blaine, his ex-wife, often observed that he preferred to *perform* in front of people—herself included—rather than interact with them.)

Rhyme carefully steered up to the railing that separated the counsel tables from the gallery in the Paquenoke County Courthouse. He glanced at Amelia Sachs and the sight nearly broke his heart. In the three days she'd been in jail she'd lost a lot of weight and her face was sallow. Her red hair was dirty and pulled up in a taut bun—the way she wore it at crime scenes to keep the strands from brushing against evidence; this made her otherwise beautiful face severe and drawn.

Geberth walked over to Rhyme, crouched down. The criminalist spoke to him for a few minutes. Finally, Geberth nodded and rose. "Your Honor, I realize this is a hearing regarding a plea bargain. But I have an unusual proposal. There's some new evidence that's come to light—"

"Which you can introduce at trial," the judge snapped, "if your client chooses to reject the plea arrangement."

"I'm not proposing to introduce anything to the court; I'd like to make the *state* aware of this evidence and see if my worthy colleague will agree to consider it."

"For what purpose?"

"Possibly to alter the charges against my client." Geberth added coyly, "Which may just make Your Honor's docket somewhat less burdensome."

The judge rolled his eyes, to show that Yankee slickness counted for zip around these parts. Still, he glanced at the prosecutor and asked, "Well?"

The D.A. asked Geberth, "What sort of evidence? A new witness?"

Rhyme couldn't control himself any longer. "No," he said. "Physical evidence."

"You're this Lincoln Rhyme I've been hearing about?" the judge asked.

As if there were *two* crip criminalists plying their trade in the Tar Heel State.

"I am, yes."

The prosecutor asked, "Where is this evidence?"

"In my custody at the Paquenoke County Sheriff's Department," Lucy Kerr said.

The judge asked Rhyme, "You'll agree to be deposed, under oath?"

"Certainly."

"This's all right with you, Counselor?" the judge asked the prosecutor.

"It is, Your Honor, but if this is just tactical or if the evidence turns out to be meaningless, I'll pursue interference charges against Mr. Rhyme."

The judge thought for a moment then said, "For the record, this is not part of any proceeding. The court is merely lending itself to the parties for a deposition prior to arraignment. The examination will be conducted pursuant to North Carolina Rules of Criminal Procedure. Swear the deponent."

Rhyme parked in front of the bench. As the Bible-clutching clerk approached uncertainly, Rhyme said, "No, I can't raise my right hand." Then recited, "I swear that the testimony I am about to give is the truth, upon my solemn oath." He tried to catch Sachs's eye but she was staring at the faded mosaic tile on the courtroom floor.

Geberth strolled to the front of the courtroom. "Mr. Rhyme, could you state your name, address and occupation."

"Lincoln Rhyme, 345 Central Park West, New York City. I'm a criminalist."

"That's a forensic scientist, is that right?"

"Somewhat *more* than that but forensic science is the bulk of what I do."

"And how do you know the defendant, Amelia Sachs?"

"She's been my assistant and partner on a number of criminal investigations."

"And how did you happen to come to Tanner's Corner?"

"We were assisting Sheriff James Bell and the Paquenoke County Sheriff's Department. Looking into the murder of Billy Stail and the abductions of Lydia Johansson and Mary Beth McConnell."

Geberth asked, "Now, Mr. Rhyme, you say you have new evidence that bears on this case?"

"Yes, I do."

"What is that evidence?"

"After we learned that Billy Stail had gone to Blackwater Landing to kill Mary Beth McConnell I began speculating why he'd done that. And I concluded that he'd been paid to kill her. He—"

"Why did you think he was paid?"

"It's obvious why," Rhyme grumbled. He had little patience for irrelevant questions and Geberth was deviating from his script.

"Share that with us, if you would."

"Billy had no romantic relationship with Mary Beth of any kind. He wasn't involved in the murder of Garrett Hanlon's family. He didn't even know her. So he'd have no motivation to kill her other than financial profit."

"Go on."

Rhyme continued, "Whoever hired him wasn't going to pay by check, of course, but in cash. Deputy Kerr went to the house of Billy Stail's parents and was given permission to search his room. She discovered ten thousand dollars hidden beneath his mattress."

"What was there about this—"

"Why don't I just finish the story?" Rhyme asked the lawyer.

The judge said, "Good idea, Mr. Rhyme. I think counsel's laid enough groundwork."

"With Officer Kerr's assistance I did a friction ridge analysis—that's a *fingerprint* check—of the top and bottom bills in the stacks of cash. I found a total of sixty-one latent fingerprints. Aside from Billy's prints, two of these prints proved to be from a person involved in this case. Deputy Kerr got another warrant to enter that individual's house."

"Did you search it too?" the judge asked.

He replied with forced patience, "No, *I* didn't. It wasn't *accessible* to me. But I *directed* the search, which was conducted by Deputy Kerr. Inside the house she found a receipt for the purchase of a shovel identical to the murder weapon, eighty-three thousand dollars in cash, secured with wrappers identical to the ones around the two stacks of money in Billy Stail's house."

Dramatic as ever, Rhyme had saved the best till the last. "Deputy Kerr also found bone fragments in the barbecue behind that premises. These fragments match the bones of Garrett Hanlon's family."

"Whose house was this?"

"Deputy Jesse Corn's."

This drew some loud murmurs from the courtroom pews. The prosecutor remained unfazed but sat up slightly, his shoes scuffling on the tile floor, and whispered to his colleagues as they considered the implications of the revelation. In the gallery Jesse's parents turned to each other, shock in their eyes; his mother shook her head and started to cry.

"Where exactly are you going, Mr. Rhyme?" the judge asked.

Rhyme resisted telling the judge that the destination was obvious. He said, "Your Honor, Jesse Corn was one of the individuals who had conspired with Jim Bell and

Steve Farr to kill Garrett Hanlon's family five years ago and then to kill Mary Beth McConnell the other day."

Oh, yeah. This town's got itself a few hornets.

The judge leaned back in his chair. "This has nothing to do with me. You two duke it out." Nodding from Geberth to the prosecutor. "You got five minutes then she accepts the plea bargain or I'll set bail and schedule trial."

The prosecutor said to Geberth, "Doesn't mean she didn't kill Jesse. Even if Corn was a co-conspirator he was still the victim of a homicide."

Now the Northerner got to roll *his* eyes. "Oh, come on," Geberth snapped, as if the D.A. were a slow student. "What it means is that Corn was operating *outside* his jurisdiction as a law enforcer and that when he confronted Garrett he was a felon and armed and dangerous. Jim Bell admitted they were planning on torturing the boy to find Mary Beth's whereabouts. Once they found her, Corn would've been right there with Culbeau and the others to kill Lucy Kerr and the other deputies."

The judge's eyes swept from left to right slowly as he watched this unprecedented tennis match.

The prosecutor: "I can only focus on the crime at hand. Whether Jesse Corn was going to kill anybody or not doesn't matter."

Geberth shook his head slowly. The lawyer said to the court reporter, "We're suspending the deposition. This is off the record." Then, to the prosecutor: "What's the point of proceeding? Corn was a killer."

Rhyme joined in, speaking to the prosecutor. "You take this to trial and what do you think the jury's going to feel when we show the victim was a crooked cop planning to torture an innocent boy to find a young woman and then murder her?"

Geberth continued, "You don't want this notch on your grip. You've got Bell, you've got his brother-in-law, the coroner. . . ."

Before the prosecutor could protest again Rhyme looked up at him and said in a soft voice, "I'll help you."

"What?" the prosecutor asked.

"You know who's behind all this, don't you? You know who's killing half the residents of Tanner's Corner?"

"Henry Davett," the prosecutor said. "I've read the filings and depos."

Rhyme asked, "And how's the case against him?"

"Not good. There's no evidence. There's no link between him and Bell or anybody else in town. He used middlemen and they're all stonewalling or out of the jurisdiction."

"But," Rhyme said, "don't you want to nail him—before any more people die of cancer? Before more children get sick and kill themselves? Before more babies are born with birth defects?"

"Of course I want to."

"Then you need *me*. You won't find a criminalist anywhere in the state who can bring Davett down. I can." Rhyme glanced at Sachs. He could see tears in her eyes. He knew that the only thought in her mind now was that, whether they sent her to jail or not, she hadn't killed an innocent man.

The prosecutor sighed deeply. Then nodded. Quickly, as if he might change his mind, he said, "Deal." He looked at the bench. "Your Honor, in the case of the People versus Sachs, the state is withdrawing all charges."

"So ordered," said the bored judge. "Defendant is free to go. Next case." He didn't even bother to bang down his gavel.

. . . chapter forty-five

"I didn't know whether you'd show up," Lincoln Rhyme said.

He was, in fact, surprised.

"Wasn't sure I was going to either," Sachs replied.

They were in his hospital room at the medical center in Avery.

He said, "I just got back from visiting Thom on the fifth floor. That's pretty odd—*I'm* more mobile than he is."

"How is he?"

"He'll be fine. He should be out in a day or two. I told him he was about to see physical therapy from a whole new angle. He didn't laugh."

A pleasant Guatemalan woman—the temporary caregiver—sat in the corner, knitting a yellow-and-red shawl. She seemed to be weathering Rhyme's moods though he believed that this was because she didn't understand English well enough to appreciate his sarcasm and insults.

"You know, Sachs," Rhyme said, "when I heard you'd busted Garrett out of detention it half occurred to me you'd done it to give me a chance to rethink the operation."

A smile curved her Julia Roberts lips. "Maybe there was a bit of that."

"So you're here now to talk me out of it?"

She rose from the chair and walked to the window. "Pretty view."

"Peaceful, isn't it. Fountain and garden. Plants. Don't know what kind."

"Lucy could tell you. She knows plants the way Garrett knows bugs. Excuse me, *insects*. A bug is only one type of insect. . . . No, Rhyme, I'm not here to talk you out of it. I'm here to be with you now and to be in the recovery room when you wake up."

"Change of heart?"

She turned to him. "When Garrett and I were on the run he was telling me about something he read in that book of his. *The Miniature World*."

"I have a new respect for dung beetles after reading it," Rhyme said.

"There was something he showed me, a passage. It was a list of the characteristics of living creatures. One of them was that healthy creatures strive to grow and to adapt to the environment. I realized that's something *you* have to do, Rhyme—have this surgery. I can't interfere with it."

After a moment he said, "I know it's not going to cure me, Sachs. But what's the nature of our business? It's little victories. We find a fiber here, a partial latent friction ridge there, a few grains of sand that might lead to the killer's house. That's all I'm after here—a little improvement. I'm not climbing out of this chair, I know that. But I need a little victory."

Maybe the chance to hold your hand for real.

She bent down, kissed him hard, then sat on the bed.

"What's that look, Sachs? You seem a bit coy."

"That passage in Garrett's book?"

"Right."

"There was another characteristic of living creatures I wanted to mention."

"Which is?" he asked.

"All living creatures strive to continue the species."

Rhyme grumbled, "Do I sense another plea bargain here? A deal of some kind?"

She said, "Maybe we can talk about some things when we get back to New York."

A nurse appeared in the doorway. "I need to take you to pre-op, Mr. Rhyme. You ready for a ride?"

"Oh, you bet I am. . . ." He turned back to Sachs. "Sure, we'll talk."

She kissed him again and squeezed his left hand, where he could, just faintly, feel the pressure in his ring finger.

■

The two women sat side by side in a thick shaft of sunlight.

Two paper cups of very bad vending-machine coffee were in front of them, perched on an orange table covered with brown burn marks from in the days when smoking had been permitted in hospitals.

Amelia Sachs glanced at Lucy Kerr, who sat forward, hands together, subdued.

"What's up?" Sachs asked her. "You all right?"

The deputy hesitated then finally said, "Oncology's on the next wing over. I spent months there. Before and after the operation." She shook her head. "I never told anybody this but the Thanksgiving Day after Buddy left me I came here. Just hung out. Had coffee and tuna sandwiches with the nurses. Isn't that a kick? I could've gone to see my parents and cousins in Raleigh for turkey and dressing. Or my sister in Martinsville and her husband— Ben's parents. But I wanted to be where I felt at home. Which sure wasn't in my house."

Sachs said, "When my father was dying my mom and I spent three holidays in the hospital. Thanksgiving, Christmas and New Year's. Pop made a joke. He said we had to make our Easter reservations early. He didn't live that long, though."

"Your mom's still alive?"

"Oh, yeah. She gets around better than I do. I got Pop's arthritis. Only in spades." Sachs nearly made a joke about that being why she was such a good shot—so she wouldn't have to run down the perps. But then she thought of Jesse Corn, flashed back to the dot of the bullet on his forehead, and she remained silent.

Lucy said, "He'll be all right, you know. Lincoln."

"No, I don't know," Sachs responded.

"I've got a feeling. When you've been through as much as I have—in hospitals, I mean—you get a feeling."

"Appreciate that," Sachs said.

"How long do you think it'll be?" Lucy asked.

Forever . . .

"Four hours, Dr. Weaver was saying."

In the distance they could just hear the tinny, forced dialogue of a soap opera. A distant page for a doctor. A chime. A laugh.

Someone walked past then paused.

"Hey, ladies."

"Lydia," Lucy said, smiling. "How you doing?"

Lydia Johansson. Sachs hadn't recognized her at first because she was wearing a green robe and cap. She recalled that the woman was a nurse here.

"You heard?" Lucy asked. "About Jim and Steve getting arrested? Who would've thought?"

"Never in a million years," Lydia said. "The whole town's talking." Then the nurse asked Lucy, "You have an onco appointment?"

"No. Mr. Rhyme's having his operation today. On his spine. We're his cheerleaders."

"Well, I wish him all the best," Lydia said to Sachs.

"Thank you."

The big girl continued down the corridor, waved, then pushed through a doorway.

"Sweet girl," Sachs said.

"You imagine that job, being an oncology nurse? When I was having my surgery she was on the ward every day. Being just as cheerful as could be. More guts than I have."

But Lydia was far from Sachs's thoughts. She looked at the clock. It was eleven A.M. The operation would start any minute now.

■

He tried to be on good behavior.

The prep nurse was explaining things to him and Lincoln Rhyme was nodding but they'd already given him a Valium and he wasn't paying attention.

He wanted to tell the woman to be quiet and just get on with it yet he supposed that you should be extremely civil to the people who're about to slice your neck open.

"Really?" he said when she paused. "That's interesting." Not having a clue what she'd just told him.

Then an orderly arrived and wheeled him from pre-op into the operating room itself.

Two nurses made the transfer from the gurney to the operating table. One went to the far end of the room and began removing instruments from the autoclave.

The operating room was more informal than he'd thought. The clichéd green tile, stainless-steel equipment, instruments, tubes. But also lots of cardboard boxes. And a boom box. He was going to ask what kind of music they'd be listening to but then he remembered he'd be out cold and wouldn't care about the sound track.

"It's pretty funny," he muttered drunkenly to a nurse who was standing next to him. She turned. He could see only her eyes over the face mask.

"What's that?" she asked.

"They're operating on the one place where I need anesthetic. If I had my appendix out they could cut without gas."

"That's pretty funny, Mr. Rhyme."

He laughed briefly, thinking: So, she knows me.

He stared at the ceiling, in a hazy, reflective mood. Lincoln Rhyme divided people into two categories: traveling people and arrival people. Some enjoyed the journey more than the destination. He, by his nature, was an arrival person—finding the answers to forensic questions was his goal and he enjoyed getting the solutions more than the process of seeking them. Yet now, lying on his back, staring into the chromium hood of the surgical lamp, he felt just the opposite. He preferred to exist in this state of hope—enjoying the buoyant sensation of anticipation.

The anesthesiologist, an Indian woman, came in and ran a needle into his arm, prepared an injection, fitted it into the tube connected to the needle. She had very skillful hands.

"You ready to take a nap?" she asked with a faint, lilting accent.

"As I'll ever be," he mumbled.

"When I inject this I'm going to ask you to count down from one hundred. You'll be out before you know it."

"What's the record?" Rhyme joked.

"Counting down? One man, he was much bigger than you, got to seventy-nine before he went under."

"I'll go for seventy-five."

"You'll get this operating suite named after you if you do that," she replied, deadpan.

He watched her slip a tube of clear liquid into the IV. She turned away to look at a monitor. Rhyme began counting. "One hundred, ninety-nine, ninety-eight, ninety-seven . . ."

The other nurse, the one who'd mentioned him by name, crouched down. In a low voice she said, "Hi, there."

An odd tone in the voice.

He glanced at her.

She continued, "I'm Lydia Johansson. Remember me?" Before he could say of course he did, she added in a dark whisper, "Jim Bell asked me to say good-bye."

"No!" he muttered.

The anesthesiologist, eyes on a monitor, said, "It's okay. Just relax. Everything's fine."

Her mouth inches from his ear, Lydia whispered, "Didn't you wonder how Jim and Steve Farr found out about the cancer patients?"

"No! Stop!"

"I gave Jim their names so Culbeau could make sure they had accidents. Jim Bell's my boyfriend. We've been having an affair for years. He's the one sent me to Blackwater Landing after Mary Beth'd been kidnapped. That morning I went to put flowers down and just hang out in case Garrett showed up. I was going to talk to him and give Jesse and Ed Schaeffer a chance to get him—Ed was with us too. Then they were going to force him to tell us where Mary Beth was. But nobody thought he'd kidnap *me*."

Oh, yeah, this town's got itself a few hornets. . . .

"Stop!" Rhyme cried. But his voice came out as a mumble.

The anesthesiologist said, "Been fifteen seconds. Maybe you're going to break that record after all. Are you counting? I don't hear you counting."

"I'll be right here," Lydia said, stroking Rhyme's forehead. "A lot can go wrong during surgery, you know. Kinks in the oxygen tube, administering the wrong drugs. Who knows? Might kill you, might put you in a coma. But you sure aren't going to be doing any testifying."

"Wait," Rhyme gasped, "wait!"

"Ha," the anesthesiologist said, laughing, her eyes still on the monitor. "Twenty seconds. I think you're going to win, Mr. Rhyme."

"No, I don't think you are," Lydia whispered and slowly stood as Rhyme saw the operating room go gray and then black.

. . . chapter forty-six

This really *was* one of the prettiest places in the world, Amelia Sachs thought.

For a cemetery.

Tanner's Corner Memorial Gardens, on a crest of a rolling hill, overlooked the Paquenoke River, some miles away. It was even nicer here, in the graveyard itself, than viewed from the road where she'd first seen it on the drive from Avery.

Squinting against the sun, she noticed the glistening strip of Blackwater Canal joining the river. From here, even the dark, tainted water, which had brought so much sorrow to so many, looked benign and picturesque.

She was in a small cluster of people standing over an open grave. A crematory urn was being lowered by one of the men from the mortuary. Amelia Sachs was next to Lucy Kerr. Garrett Hanlon stood by them. On the other side of the grave were Mason Germain and Thom, with a cane, dressed in his immaculate slacks and shirt. He wore a bold tie with a wild red pattern, which seemed appropriate despite this somber moment.

Black-suited Fred Dellray was here too, standing by himself, off to the side, thoughtful—as if recalling a passage in one of the philosophy books he enjoyed reading. He would have resembled a Nation of Islam reverend if he'd been wearing a white shirt instead of the lime-green one with yellow polka dots on it.

There was no minister to officiate, even though this was Bible-waving country and there'd probably be a dozen clerics on call for funerals. The mortuary director now glanced at the people assembled and asked if anybody wanted to say something to the assembly. And as everyone looked around, wondering if there'd be any volunteers, Garrett dug into his baggy slacks and produced his battered book, *The Miniature World*.

In a halting voice the boy read, " 'There are those who suggest that a divine force doesn't exist, but one's cynicism is truly put to the test when we look at the world of insects, which have been graced with so many amazing characteristics: wings so thin they seem hardly to be made of any living material, bodies without a single milligram of excess weight, wind-speed detectors accurate to a fraction of a mile per hour, a stride so efficient that mechanical engineers model robots after it, and, most important, insects' astonishing ability to survive in the face of overwhelming opposition by man, predators and the elements. In moments of despair, we can look to the ingenuity and persistence of these miraculous creatures and find solace and a restoration of lost faith.' "

Garrett looked up, closed the book. Clicked his fingernails nervously. He looked at Sachs and asked, "Do you, like, want to say anything?"

But she merely shook her head.

No one else spoke and after a few minutes everyone around the grave turned away and meandered back up the hill along a winding path. Before they crested the ridge that led to a small picnic area the cemetery crews had already begun filling in the grave with a backhoe.

Sachs was breathing hard as they walked to the crest of the tree-covered hill near the parking lot.

She recalled Lincoln Rhyme's voice:

That's not a bad cemetery. Wouldn't mind being buried in a place like that. . . .

She paused to wipe the sweat from her face and catch her breath; the North Carolina heat was still relentless. Garrett, though, didn't seem to notice the temperature. He ran past her and began pulling grocery bags from the back of Lucy's Bronco.

This wasn't exactly the time or place for a picnic but, Sachs supposed, chicken salad and watermelon were as good a way as any to remember the dead.

Scotch too, of course. Sachs dug through several shopping bags and finally found the bottle of Macallan, eighteen years old. She pulled the cork stopper out with a faint pop.

"Ah, my favorite sound," Lincoln Rhyme said.

He was wheeling up beside her, driving carefully along the uneven grass. The hill down to the grave was too steep for the Storm Arrow and he'd had to wait up here in the lot. He'd watched from the hilltop as they buried the ashes of the bones that Mary Beth had found at Blackwater Landing—the remains of Garrett's family.

Sachs poured scotch into Rhyme's glass, equipped with a long straw, and some into hers. Everyone else was drinking beer.

He said, "Moonshine is truly vile, Sachs. Avoid it at all costs. This is much better."

Sachs looked around. "Where's the woman from the hospital? The caregiver?"

"Mrs. Ruiz?" Rhyme muttered. "Hopeless. She quit. Left me in the lurch."

"Quit?" Thom said. "You drove her nuts. You might as well have fired her."

"I was a saint," the criminalist snapped.

"How's your temperature?" Thom asked him.

"It's fine," he grumbled. "How's *yours*?"

"Probably a little high but *I* don't have a blood pressure problem."

"No, you've a bullet hole in you."

The aide persisted, "You should—"

"I said I'm fine."

"—move into the shade a little farther."

Rhyme groused and complained about the unsteady ground but he finally maneuvered himself into the shade a little farther.

Garrett was carefully setting out food and drink and napkins on a bench under the tree.

"How're you doing?" Sachs asked Rhyme in a whisper. "And before you grumble at me too—I'm not talking about the heat."

He shrugged—this, a *silent* grumble by which he meant: I'm fine.

But he wasn't fine. A phrenic-nerve stimulator pumped current into his body to help his lungs inhale and exhale. He hated the device—had weaned himself off it some years ago—but there was no question that he needed it now. Two days ago, on the operating table, Lydia Johansson had come very close to stopping his breathing forever.

In the waiting room at the hospital, after Lydia had said good-bye to Sachs and Lucy, Sachs had noticed that the nurse vanished through the doorway marked NEUROSURGERY. Sachs had asked, "Didn't you say that she works in oncology?"

"She does."

"Then what's she doing going in there?"

"Maybe saying hello to Lincoln," Lucy suggested.

But Sachs didn't think that nurses paid social calls to patients about to be operated on.

Then she thought: Lydia would know about new cancer diagnoses among residents from Tanner's Corner. She then recalled that somebody had given information to Bell about cancer patients—the three people in Blackwater

Landing that Culbeau and his friends had killed. Who better than a nurse on the onco ward? This was far-fetched but Sachs mentioned it to Lucy, who pulled out her cell phone and made an emergency call to the phone company, whose security department did a down-and-dirty pen-register search of Jim Bell's phone calls. There were hundreds to and from Lydia.

"She's going to kill him!" Sachs had cried. And the two women, one with a weapon drawn, had burst into the operating room—a scene right out of a melodramatic episode of *ER*—just as Dr. Weaver was about to make the opening incision.

Lydia had panicked and, trying to escape, or trying to do what Bell had sent her for, ripped the oxygen tube from Rhyme's throat before the two women subdued her. From that trauma and because of the anesthetic Rhyme's lungs had failed. Dr. Weaver had revived him but, afterward, his breathing hadn't been up to par and he'd had to go back on the stimulator.

Which was bad enough. But worse, to Rhyme's anger and disgust, Dr. Weaver refused to perform the operation for at least another six months—until his breathing functions were completely normalized. He'd tried to insist but the surgeon proved to be as mulely as he was.

Sachs sipped more scotch.

"You told Roland Bell about his cousin?" Rhyme asked.

She nodded. "He took it hard. Said Jim was the black sheep but never guessed he'd do anything like this. He's pretty shaken up by the news." She looked northeast. "Look," she said, "out there. Know what that is?"

Trying to follow her eyes, Rhyme asked, "What're you looking at? The horizon? A cloud? An airplane? Enlighten me, Sachs."

"The Great Dismal Swamp. That's where Lake Drummond is."

"Fascinating," he said sarcastically.

"It's full of ghosts," she added, like a tour guide.

Lucy came up and poured some scotch into a paper cup. Sipped it. Then made a face. "It's awful. Tastes like soap." She opened a Heineken.

Rhyme said, "It costs eighty dollars a bottle."

"Expensive soap, then."

Sachs watched Garrett as he shoveled corn chips into his mouth then ran into the grass. She asked Lucy, "Any word from the county?"

"On being his foster mom?" Lucy asked. Then shook her head. "Got rejected. The being single part isn't an issue. They have a problem with my job. Cop. Long hours."

"What do *they* know?" Rhyme scowled.

"Doesn't matter what they know," she said. "What they *do* is the thing that's important. Garrett's being set up with a family up in Hobeth. Good people. I checked them out pretty good."

Sachs didn't doubt that she had.

"But we're going on a hike next weekend."

Nearby Garrett eased through the grass, stalking a specimen.

When Sachs turned back she saw Rhyme had been watching her as she gazed at the boy.

"What?" she asked, frowning at his coy expression.

"If you were going to say something to an empty chair, Sachs, what would it be?"

She hesitated for a moment. "I think I'll keep that to myself for the time being, Rhyme."

Suddenly Garrett gave a loud laugh and started running through the grass. He was chasing an insect, which was oblivious to its pursuer, through the dusty air. The boy caught up with it and, with outstretched arms, made a grab for his prey then tumbled to the ground. A moment later he was up, staring into his cupped hands and walking slowly back to the picnic benches.

"Guess what I found," he called.

"Come show us," Amelia Sachs said. "I want to see."

AUTHOR'S NOTE

I trust North Carolinians will forgive me for rearranging the geography and educational system of the Tar Heel State a bit to suit my nefarious means. If it's any consolation, they can rest assured that I did this with the utmost respect for the state with the best basketball teams in the country.

ABOUT THE AUTHOR

Jeffery Deaver is the author of fifteen suspense novels, including the *New York Times* bestsellers *The Empty Chair, The Devil's Teardrop,* and *The Coffin Dancer,* as well as *The Bone Collector,* now a major motion picture from Universal starring Denzel Washington, and his newest hardcover, *The Blue Nowhere.* As William Jeffries, he is the author of *Shallow Graves, Bloody River Blues,* and *Hell's Kitchen.* His books have been translated into twenty-five languages and he is a four-time Edgar Award nominee. Deaver was born in Chicago, attended the University of Missouri, and received a law degree from Fordham University in New York. He has residences in California and Virginia. Readers can visit his Web site at www.jefferydeaver.com.

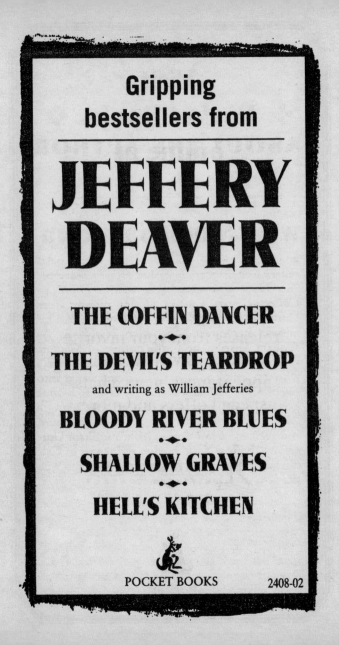

Gripping
bestsellers from

JEFFERY DEAVER

THE COFFIN DANCER

THE DEVIL'S TEARDROP

and writing as William Jefferies

BLOODY RIVER BLUES

SHALLOW GRAVES

HELL'S KITCHEN

POCKET BOOKS

2408-02

Visit
❖ **Pocket Books** ❖
online at

www.SimonSays.com

Keep up on the latest new
releases from your favorite
authors, as well as author
appearances, news, chats,
special offers and more.

SIMON & SCHUSTER
A VIACOM COMPANY
www.SimonSays.com

Pocket
Books

2381-01

SIMON & SCHUSTER HARDCOVER
PROUDLY PRESENTS

THE BLUE NOWHERE

Jeffery Deaver

Available May 2001
from
Simon & Schuster Hardcover

Turn the page for a preview of
The Blue Nowhere. . . .

I

The Wizard

It is possible . . . to commit nearly any crime by computer. You could even kill a person using a computer.

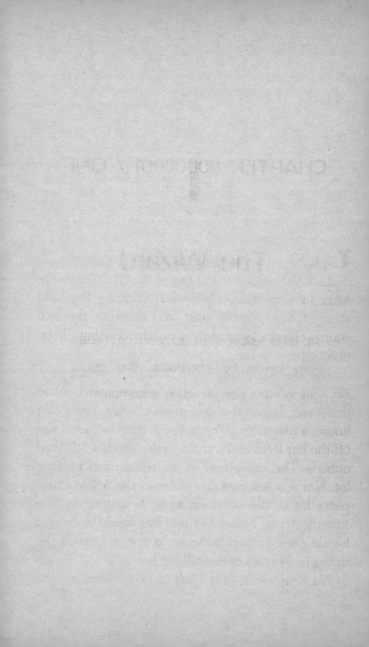

CHAPTER 00000001 / ONE

The battered white van had made her uneasy.

Lara Gibson sat at the bar of Vesta's Grill on De Anza in Cupertino, California, gripping the cold stem of her martini glass and ignoring the two young chip-jocks standing nearby, casting flirtatious glances at her.

She looked outside again, into the overcast drizzle, and saw no sign of the windowless Econoline that, she believed, had followed her from her house, a few miles away, to the restaurant. Lara slid off the bar stool and walked to the window, glanced outside. The van wasn't in the restaurant's parking lot. Nor was it across the street in the Apple Computer lot or the one next to it, belonging to Sun Microsystems. Either of those lots would've been a logical place to park to keep an eye on her—if the driver had in fact been stalking her.

No, the van was just a coincidence, she

decided—a coincidence aggravated by a splinter of paranoia.

She returned to the bar and glanced at the two young men who were alternately ignoring her and offering subtle smiles.

Like nearly all the young men here for happy hour they were in casual slacks and tie-less dress shirts and wore the ubiquitous insignia of Silicon Valley—corporate identification badges on thin canvas lanyards around their necks. These two sported the blue cards of Sun Microsystems. Other squadrons represented here were Compaq, Hewlett-Packard and Apple, not to mention a slew of new kids on the block, start-up Internet companies, which were held in some disdain by the venerable Valley regulars.

At thirty-two, Lara Gibson was probably five years older than her two admirers. And as a self-employed businesswoman who wasn't a geek—connected with a computer company—she was easily five times poorer. But that didn't matter to these two men, who were already captivated by her exotic, intense face surrounded by a tangle of raven hair, her ankle boots, a red-and-orange gypsy skirt and a black sleeveless top that showed off hard-earned biceps.

She figured that it would be two minutes before one of these boys approached her and she missed that estimate by only ten seconds.

The young man gave her a variation of a line

she'd heard a dozen times before: *Excuse me don't mean to interrupt but hey would you like me to break your boyfriend's leg for making a beautiful woman wait alone in a bar and by the way can I buy you a drink while you decide which leg?*

Another woman might have gotten mad, another woman might have stammered and blushed and looked uneasy or might have flirted back and let him buy her an unwanted drink because she didn't have the wherewithal to handle the situation. But those would be women weaker than she. Lara Gibson was "the queen of urban protection," as the *San Francisco Chronicle* had once dubbed her. She fixed her eyes on the man's, gave a formal smile and said, "I don't care for any company right now."

Simple as that. End of conversation.

He blinked at her frankness, avoided her staunch eyes and returned to his friend.

Power . . . it was all about power.

She sipped her drink.

In fact, that damn white van had brought to mind all the rules she'd developed as someone who taught women to protect themselves in today's society. Several times on the way to the restaurant she'd glanced into her rearview mirror and noticed the van thirty or forty feet behind. It had been driven by some kid. He was white but his hair was knotted into messy brown dreadlocks. He wore combat fatigues and, despite the overcast and misty rain, sunglasses. This was, of course, Silicon Valley, home of slackers and hackers, and it wasn't unusual to stop in Starbucks for a vente skim latte and be waited on by a polite teenager with a dozen body piercings, a shaved head and an outfit like an inner-city gangsta's. Still, the driver had seemed to stare at her with an eerie hostility.

Lara found herself absently fondling the can of pepper spray she kept in her purse.

Another glance out the window. She saw only fancy cars bought with dot-com money.

A look around the room. Only harmless geeks.

Relax, she told herself and sipped her potent martini.

She noted the wall clock. Quarter after seven. Sandy was fifteen minutes late. Not like her. Lara pulled out her cell phone but the display read NO SERVICE.

She was about to find the pay phone when she glanced up and saw a young man enter the bar and wave at her. She knew him from somewhere but couldn't quite place him. His trim but long blond hair and the goatee had stuck in her mind. He wore white jeans and a rumpled blue work shirt. His concession to the fact he was part of corporate America was a tie; as befit a Silicon Valley businessman, though, the design wasn't stripes or Jerry Garcia flowers but a cartoon Tweety Bird.

"Hey, Lara." He walked up and shook her hand,

leaned against the bar. "Remember me? I'm Will Randolph. Sandy's cousin? Cheryl and I met you on Nantucket—at Fred and Mary's wedding."

Right, *that's* where she recognized him from. He and his pregnant wife sat at the same table with Lara and her boyfriend, Hank. "Sure. How you doing?"

"Good. Busy. But who isn't around here?"

His plastic neckwear read *Xerox Corporation PARC*. She was impressed. Even nongeeks knew about Xerox's legendary Palo Alto Research Center five or six miles north of here.

Will flagged down the bartender and ordered a light beer. "How's Hank?" he asked. "Sandy said he was trying to get a job at Wells Fargo."

"Oh, yeah, that came through. He's at orientation down in L.A. right now."

The beer came and Will sipped. "Congratulations."

A flash of white in the parking lot.

Lara looked toward it quickly, alarmed. But the vehicle turned out to be a white Ford Explorer with a young couple inside.

Her eyes focused past the Ford and scanned the street and the parking lots again, recalling that, on the way here, she'd glanced at the side of the van as it passed her when she'd turned into the restaurant's parking lot. There'd been a smear of something dark and reddish on the side; probably mud but she'd thought it almost looked like blood.

"You okay?" Will asked.

"Sure. Sorry." She turned back to Will, glad she had an ally. Another of her urban protection rules: Two people are always better than one. Lara now modified that by adding, Even if one of them is a skinny geek who can't be more than five feet, ten inches tall and is wearing a cartoon tie.

Will continued, "Sandy called me on my way home and asked if I'd stop by and give you a message. She tried to call you but couldn't get through on your cell. She's running late and asked if you could meet her at that place next to her office where you went last month, Ciro's? In Mountain View. She made a reservation at eight."

"You didn't have to come by. She could've called the bartender."

"She wanted me to give you the pictures I took at the wedding. You two can look at 'em tonight and tell me if you want any copies."

Will noticed a friend across the bar and waved—Silicon Valley may extend hundreds of square miles but it's really just a small town. He said to Lara, "Cheryl and I *were* going to bring the pictures this weekend to Sandy's place in Santa Barbara. . . ."

"Yeah, we're going down on Friday."

Will paused and smiled as if he had a huge secret to share. He pulled his wallet out and flipped it open to a picture of himself, his wife and a very tiny, ruddy baby. "Last week," he said proudly. "Claire."

"Oh, adorable," Lara whispered.

"So we'll be staying pretty close to home for a while."

"How's Cheryl?"

"Fine. The baby's fine. There's nothing like it. . . . But, I'll tell you, being a father totally changes your life."

"I'm sure it does."

Lara glanced at the clock again. Seven-thirty. It was a half-hour drive to Ciro's this time of night. "I better get going."

Then, with a thud of alarm, she thought again about the van and the driver.

The dreadlocks.

The rusty smear on the battered door. . . .

Will gestured for the check and paid.

"You don't have to do that," she said. "I'll get it."

He laughed. "You already did."

"What?"

"That mutual fund you told me about at the wedding. The one you'd just bought?"

Lara remembered shamelessly bragging about a biotech fund that had zoomed up 60 percent last year.

"I got home from Nantucket and bought a shit-load of it. . . . So . . . thanks." He tipped the beer toward her. Then he stood. "You all set?"

"You bet." Lara stared uneasily at the door as they walked toward it.

It was just paranoia, she told herself. She thought momentarily, as she did from time to time, that she should get a real job, like all of these people in the bar. She shouldn't dwell so much on the world of violence.

Sure, just paranoia . . .

But, if so, then why had the dreadlocked kid sped off so fast when she'd pulled into the parking lot here and glanced at him?

Will stepped outside and opened his umbrella. He held it up for both of them to use.

Lara recalled another rule of urban protection: Never feel too embarrassed or proud to ask for help.

And yet as Lara was about to ask Will Randolph to walk her to her car after they got the snapshots she had a thought: If the kid in the van really *was* a threat, wasn't it selfish of her to ask him to endanger himself? Here he was, a husband and new father, with other people to depend on him. It seemed unfair to—

"Something wrong?" Will asked.

"Not really."

"You sure?" he persisted.

"Well, I think somebody followed me here to the restaurant. Some kid."

Will looked around. "You see him?"

"Not now."

He asked, "You have that Web site, right? About how women can protect themselves."

"That's right."

"You think he knows about it? Maybe he's harassing you."

"Could be. You'd be surprised at the hate mail I get."

He reached for his cell phone. "You want to call the police?"

She debated.

Never feel too embarrassed or proud to ask for help.

"No, no. Just . . . would you mind, after we get the pictures, walking me to my car?"

Will smiled. "Of course not. I don't exactly know karate but I can yell for help with the best of them."

She laughed. "Thanks."

They walked along the sidewalk in front of the restaurant and she checked out the cars. As in every parking lot in Silicon Valley there were dozens of Saabs, BMWs and Lexuses. No vans, though. No kids. No bloody smears.

Will nodded toward where he'd parked, in the back lot. He said, "You see him?"

"No."

They walked past a stand of juniper and toward his car, a spotless silver Jaguar.

Jesus, did *everybody* in Silicon Valley have money except her?

He dug the keys out of his pocket. They walked to the trunk. "I only took two rolls at the wedding. But some of them are pretty good." He opened the trunk and paused and then looked around the parking lot. She did too. It was completely deserted. His was the only car there.

Will glanced at her. "You were probably wondering about the dreads."

"Dreads?"

"Yeah," he said. "The dreadlocks." His voice was different, flatter, distracted. He was still smiling but his face was different now. It seemed hungry.

"What do you mean?" she asked calmly but fear was detonating inside her. She noticed a chain was blocking the entrance to the back parking lot. And she knew he'd hooked it after he'd pulled in—to make sure nobody else could park there.

"It was a wig."

Oh, Jesus, my Lord, thought Lara Gibson, who hadn't prayed in twenty years.

He looked into her eyes, recording her fear. "I parked the Jag here a while ago then stole the van and followed you from home. With the combat jacket and wig on. You know, just so you'd get edgy and paranoid and want me to stay close. . . . I know all your rules—that urban protection stuff. Never go into a deserted parking lot with a man. Married men with children are safer than single men. And my family portrait? In my wallet? I hacked it together from a picture in *Parents* magazine."

She whispered hopelessly, "You're not . . . ?"

"Sandy's cousin? Don't even know him. I picked Will Randolph because he's somebody you *sort of* know, who *sort of* looks like me. I mean, there's no way in the world I could've gotten you out here alone if you hadn't known me—or thought you did. Oh, you can take your hand out of your purse." He held up her canister of pepper spray. "I got it when we were walking outside."

"But . . ." Sobbing now, shoulders slumped in hopelessness. "Who *are* you? You don't even know me. . . ."

"Not true, Lara," he whispered, studying her anguish the way an imperious chess master examines his defeated opponent's face. "I know everything about you. Everything in the world."

Step by step, destiny has brought a sorcerer, a witch, a warrior, a scholar, a shape-shifter and a lost soul to the land of Geall—and to the Valley of Silence. It is here that their voices will ring out against those of evil.

The fate of every world hangs in the balance, as humanity rallies behind a newly crowned queen in a clash with a vampire who has reigned for centuries...

Valley of Silence

Third in a new trilogy from the #1 *New York Times* bestselling author

Number-one *New York Times* bestselling author Nora Roberts presents the electrifying conclusion to her powerful new trilogy. Worlds have collided and centuries have elapsed as six people have brought their unique powers, their courage and their hearts to a battle that could drown humanity in darkness . . .

Her face, so pale when she'd removed her cloak, had bloomed when her hand had taken the sword. Her eyes, so heavy, so somber, had gone as brilliant as the blade. And had simply sliced through him, keen as a sword, when they'd met his . . .

In the kingdom of Geall, the scholarly Moira has taken up the sword of her people. Now, as queen, she must prepare her subjects for the greatest battle they will ever fight—against an enemy more vicious than any they have seen. For Lilith, the most powerful vampire in the world, has followed the circle of six through time to Geall.

Moira also has a personal score to settle. Vampires killed her mother—and now, she is ready to exact her revenge. But there is one vampire to whom she would trust her soul . . .

Cian was changed by Lilith centuries ago. But now, he stands with the circle. Without hesitation, he will kill others of his kind—and has earned the respect of sorcerer, witch, warrior and shape-shifter. But he wants more than respect from Moira—even though his desire for her makes him vulnerable. For how can a man with an eternity to live love a woman whose life is sure to end—if not by Lilith's hand, then by the curse of time?

"[Roberts] is one of the best writers in the romance world."
—*The Best Reviews*

Turn the page for a complete list of titles by
Nora Roberts and J. D. Robb
from the Berkley Publishing Group . . .

Nora Roberts & J. D. Robb

REMEMBER WHEN

Nora Roberts

HOT ICE	SANCTUARY
SACRED SINS	HOMEPORT
BRAZEN VIRTUE	THE REEF
SWEET REVENGE	RIVER'S END
PUBLIC SECRETS	CAROLINA MOON
GENUINE LIES	THE VILLA
CARNAL INNOCENCE	MIDNIGHT BAYOU
DIVINE EVIL	THREE FATES
HONEST ILLUSIONS	BIRTHRIGHT
PRIVATE SCANDALS	NORTHERN LIGHTS
HIDDEN RICHES	BLUE SMOKE
TRUE BETRAYALS	ANGELS FALL
MONTANA SKY	

Series

Circle Trilogy

MORRIGAN'S CROSS
DANCE OF THE GODS
VALLEY OF SILENCE

In the Garden Trilogy

BLUE DAHLIA
BLACK ROSE
RED LILY

Key Trilogy

KEY OF LIGHT
KEY OF KNOWLEDGE
KEY OF VALOR

Three Sisters Island Trilogy

DANCE UPON THE AIR
HEAVEN AND EARTH
FACE THE FIRE

Gallaghers of Ardmore Trilogy

JEWELS OF THE SUN
TEARS OF THE MOON
HEART OF THE SEA

Born In Trilogy

BORN IN FIRE
BORN IN ICE
BORN IN SHAME

Chesapeake Bay Saga

SEA SWEPT
RISING TIDES
INNER HARBOR
CHESAPEAKE BLUE

Dream Trilogy

DARING TO DREAM
HOLDING THE DREAM
FINDING THE DREAM

Anthologies

FROM THE HEART
A LITTLE MAGIC
A LITTLE FATE

MOON SHADOWS
(with Jill Gregory, Ruth Ryan Langan, and Marianne Willman)

The Once Upon Series
(with Jill Gregory, Ruth Ryan Langan, and Marianne Willman)

ONCE UPON A CASTLE	ONCE UPON A ROSE
ONCE UPON A STAR	ONCE UPON A KISS
ONCE UPON A DREAM	ONCE UPON A MIDNIGHT

J. D. Robb

NAKED IN DEATH	BETRAYAL IN DEATH
GLORY IN DEATH	SEDUCTION IN DEATH
IMMORTAL IN DEATH	REUNION IN DEATH
RAPTURE IN DEATH	PURITY IN DEATH
CEREMONY IN DEATH	PORTRAIT IN DEATH
VENGEANCE IN DEATH	IMITATION IN DEATH
HOLIDAY IN DEATH	DIVIDED IN DEATH
CONSPIRACY IN DEATH	VISIONS IN DEATH
LOYALTY IN DEATH	SURVIVOR IN DEATH
WITNESS IN DEATH	ORIGIN IN DEATH
JUDGMENT IN DEATH	MEMORY IN DEATH

Anthologies

SILENT NIGHT
(with Susan Plunkett, Dee Holmes, and Claire Cross)

OUT OF THIS WORLD
(with Laurell K. Hamilton, Susan Krinard, and Maggie Shayne)

BUMP IN THE NIGHT
(with Mary Blayney, Ruth Ryan Langan, and Mary Kay McComas)

Also available . . .

THE OFFICIAL NORA ROBERTS COMPANION
(edited by Denise Little and Laura Hayden)

Valley
of Silence

Nora Roberts

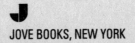

JOVE BOOKS, NEW YORK

THE BERKLEY PUBLISHING GROUP
Published by the Penguin Group
Penguin Group (USA) Inc.
375 Hudson Street, New York, New York 10014, USA
Penguin Group (Canada), 90 Eglinton Avenue East, Suite 700, Toronto, Ontario M4P 2Y3, Canada
(a division of Pearson Penguin Canada Inc.)
Penguin Books Ltd., 80 Strand, London WC2R 0RL, England
Penguin Group Ireland, 25 St. Stephen's Green, Dublin 2, Ireland (a division of Penguin Books Ltd.)
Penguin Group (Australia), 250 Camberwell Road, Camberwell, Victoria 3124, Australia
(a division of Pearson Australia Group Pty. Ltd.)
Penguin Books India Pvt. Ltd., 11 Community Centre, Panchsheel Park, New Delhi—110 017, India
Penguin Group (NZ), Cnr. Airborne and Rosedale Roads, Albany, Auckland 1310, New Zealand
(a division of Pearson New Zealand Ltd.)
Penguin Books (South Africa) (Pty.) Ltd., 24 Sturdee Avenue, Rosebank, Johannesburg 2196,
South Africa

Penguin Books Ltd., Registered Offices: 80 Strand, London WC2R 0RL, England

This is a work of fiction. Names, characters, places, and incidents either are the product of the author's imagination or are used fictitiously, and any resemblance to actual persons, living or dead, business establishments, events, or locales is entirely coincidental. The publisher does not have any control over and does not assume any responsibility for author or third-party websites or their content.

VALLEY OF SILENCE

A Jove Book / published by arrangement with the author

PRINTING HISTORY
Jove mass-market edition / November 2006

Copyright © 2006 by Nora Roberts.
Excerpt from *Angels Fall* copyright © 2006 by Nora Roberts.
Cover design by Richard Hasselberger.
Cover illustration by Pyrographx/David S. Reinhardt.
Stepback art: Mountain Range by Carl Lyttle/Getty Images; Lightning by Daniel Furon/Getty Images.
Text design by Kristin del Rosario.

ISBN: 0-515-14167-4

JOVE®
Jove Books are published by The Berkley Publishing Group,
a division of Penguin Group (USA) Inc.,
375 Hudson Street, New York, New York 10014.
JOVE is a registered trademark of Penguin Group (USA) Inc.
The "J" design is a trademark belonging to Penguin Group (USA) Inc.

PRINTED IN THE UNITED STATES OF AMERICA

10 9 8 7 6 5 4 3 2 1

To my own circle,
friends and family.

Good and evil, we know, in the field of this world
grow up together almost inseparably.
—JOHN MILTON

Presume not that I am the thing I was.
—SHAKESPEARE

Prologue

◈

There were pictures in the fire. Dragons and demons and warriors. The children would see them, as he did. The old man knew the very young and the very old often saw what others could not. Or would not.

He had told them much already. His tale had begun with the sorcerer who was called by the goddess Morrigan. Hoyt of the Mac Cionaoith was charged by the gods to travel to other worlds, to other times, and gather an army to stand strong against the vampire queen. The great battle between human and demon would take place on the sabbot of Samhain, in the Valley of Silence, in the land of Geall.

He had told them of Hoyt the sorcerer's brother, killed and changed by the wily Lilith, who had existed near a thousand years as a vampire before making Cian one of her kind. Nearly another thousand years would pass for Cian before he would join Hoyt and the witch Glenna to make those first links in the circle of six. The next links were forged by two Geallians—the shifter of shapes and the scholar who traveled between worlds to gather in those first days. And the last of the circle was joined by the warrior, a demon hunter of the Mac Cionaoith blood.

The tales he had told them were of battles and courage, of death and friendship. And of love. The love that had bloomed between sorcerer and witch, and between the shifter and the warrior, had strengthened the circle as true magic must.

But there was more to tell. Triumphs and loss, fear and valor, love and sacrifice—and all that came with the dark and the light.

As the children waited for more, he wondered how best to begin the end of the tale.

"There were six," he said, still watching the fire while the children's whispers silenced and their squirming stilled in anticipation. "And each had the choice to accept or refuse. For even when worlds are held in your hands, you must choose to face what would destroy them, or to turn away. And with this choice," he continued, "there are many other choices to be made."

"They were brave and true," one of the children called out. "They chose to fight!"

The old man smiled a little. "And so they did. But still, every day, every night of the time they were given, that choice remained, and had to be made anew. One among them, you remember, was no longer human, but vampire. Every day, every night of the time they were given, he was reminded he was no longer human. He was but a shadow in the worlds he had chosen to protect.

"And so," the old man said, "the vampire dreamed."

Chapter 1

✦

He dreamed. And dreaming, he was still a man. Young, perhaps foolish, undoubtedly rash. But then, what he believed was a woman had such beauty, such allure.

She wore a fine gown in a deep shade of red, more elegant than the country pub deserved, with its long, sweeping sleeves. Like a good claret it poured over her form to set her pure white skin glowing. Her hair was gold, the curls of it glinting against her headdress.

The gown, her bearing, the jewels that were sparkling at her throat, on her fingers, told him she was a lady of some means and fashion.

He thought, in the dim light of the public house, she was like a flame that burned at shadows.

Two servants had arranged for a private room for her to sup before she swept in, and simply by being had silenced the talk and the music. But her eyes, blue as a summer sky, had met his. Only his.

When one of the servants had come out again, walked to him and announced that the lady requested he dine with her, he hadn't hesitated.

Why would he?

He might have grinned at the good-natured comments of the men he was drinking with, but he left them without a thought.

She stood in firelight and candlelight, already pouring wine into cups.

"I'm so glad," she said, "you would agree to join me. I hate to dine alone, don't you?" She came toward him, her movements so graceful she almost seemed to float. "I'm called Lilith." And she handed him wine.

In her speech there was something exotic, some cadence of speech that hinted of hot sand and riotous blooming vines. So he was already half seduced, and completely enchanted.

They shared the simple meal, though he had no appetite for food. It was her words he devoured. She spoke of the lands to which she had traveled, those which he'd only read of. She had walked among the pyramids, she told him, in the moonlight, had ridden the hills of Rome and stood in the ruined temples of Greece.

He had never traveled beyond Ireland, and her words, the images they invoked, were nearly as exciting as she herself.

He thought she was young to have done so much, but when he said as much she only smiled over the rim of her cup.

"What good are worlds," she asked, "if you don't make use of them? I'll make use of much more. Wine to be drunk, food to be tasted, lands to be explored. You're young," she said with a slow and knowing smile, "to settle for so little. Have you no wish to see beyond what you've seen?"

"I thought perhaps to take a year when I'm able, to see more of the world."

"A year?" With a light laugh, she snapped her fingers. "That is a year. Nothing, a blink of time. What would you do if you had an eternity of time?" Her eyes seemed like depthless blue seas as she leaned toward him. "What would you do with it?"

Without waiting for his answer, she rose, leaving the trail of her scent behind as she walked to the small window. "Ah, the night, it's so soft. Like silk against the skin." She turned back with a gleam in those bold blue eyes. "I am a night creature. And so, I think, are you. We, such as we, are at our best in the dark."

He had risen when she did, and now as she came back to him, her scent and the wine swam through his senses. And something more, something thick and smoky that hazed over his mind like a drug.

She tipped her head up, and back, then laid her mouth over his. "And why, when we're best in the dark, would we spend the dark hours alone?"

And in the dream, it was like a dream, misty and muddled. He was in her carriage, with her full white breasts in his hands, her mouth hot and avid on his. She laughed when he fumbled with her kirtle, and spread her legs in seductive invitation.

"Strong hands," she murmured. "A pleasing face. It's what I need, and need, and take. Will you do my bidding?" With another light laugh, she nipped at his ear. "Will you? Will you, young, handsome Cian with the strong hands?"

"Aye, of course. Aye." He could think of nothing but burying himself in her. When he did, with the carriage swaying madly, her head fell back in abandon.

"Yes, yes, yes! So hard, so hot. Give me more, and more! And I'll take you beyond all that you know."

As he plunged, his breath coming short as he neared climax, her head reared up again.

Her eyes were no longer blue and bold but red and feral. The shock that rushed into him had him trying to pull back, but her arms suddenly wrapped around him, implacable as iron chains. Her legs hooked around his waist, keeping him inside her, trapped. While he struggled against her impossible strength, she smiled with fangs gleaming in the dark.

"What are you?" There were no prayers in his head; fear left no room for them. "What are you?"

Her hips continued to rise and fall, riding him, so he

was helplessly driven closer to peak. She fisted a hand in his hair, yanking back his head to expose his throat. "Magnificent," she said. "I am magnificent, and so will you be."

She struck, the fangs piercing his flesh. He heard his own scream, somewhere in the madness and pain he heard it. The burn was unspeakable, searing through skin, into blood, beyond the bone. And mixed with it, sliding through it was a terrible, terrible pleasure.

He came, in the whirling, singing dark, betrayed by his body even as it dipped toward death. He struggled still, some part of him clawing for the light, for survival. But the pain, the pleasure dragged him deeper into the abyss.

"You and I, my handsome boy. You and I." She dipped back, cradling him in her arms now. With her own fingernail, she sliced a shallow slice across her breast so that blood dripped from it as it did, horribly, from her lips. "Now drink. Drink me, and you are forever."

No. His lips wouldn't form the word, but it screamed through his mind. Feeling his life slipping away, he struggled weakly for that last hold on it. Even when she pulled his head to her breast he fought her with what was left of him.

Then he tasted it, the rich and heady flavor that flowed from her. The bulging life of it. And like a babe at its mother's breast, he drank his own death.

The vampire woke in absolute dark, in absolute silence. Such was the way for him since the change so long ago, that he roused each sunset with not even the sound of his own heartbeat to stir the air.

Though he had dreamed the dream countless times over countless years, it disturbed him to fall from that edge yet again. To see himself as he'd been, to see his own face—one he'd not seen while awake since that night—made him edgy and annoyed.

He didn't brood over his fate. That was a useless occupation. He accepted and used what he was, and had through his personal eternity accumulated wealth, women, comfort, freedom. What else could a man want?

Having no heartbeat was a small price to pay, in the larger scheme of things. A heart that beat aged and weakened, and eventually stopped like a broken clock in any case.

How many bodies had he seen decay and die over his nine hundred years? He couldn't count them. And while he couldn't see the reflection of his own face, he knew it was the same as the night Lilith had taken him. The bones were still strong, the skin over them firm, supple and unlined. His eyes were sharp of sight and unfaded. There was not, and would never be, any gray in his hair, any sagging in his jowls.

Perhaps there were times, in the dark, in private, when he used his fingers to see his own face. There the high, prominent cheekbones, the shallow cleft in the chin, the deep-set eyes he knew were a strong blue. The blade of his nose, the firm curve of his lips.

The same. Always the same. But still, a small indulgence to spend a moment reminding himself.

He rose in the dark, his leanly muscled body naked, shook back the black hair that framed his face. He'd been born Cian Mac Cionaoith, and had gone by many names since. He was back to Cian—his brother's doing. Hoyt would call him nothing else, and since this war he'd agreed to fight might end him, Cian decided it was only right he should wear the name of his birth.

He'd prefer not to be ended. In his opinion, only the mad or the very young considered dying an adventure. But if that was his fate, at this time and place, at least he'd go out with style. And if there were any justice in any world, he would take Lilith with him to dust.

His eyes were as keen as his other senses, so he moved easily in the dark, going to a chest for one of the packets of blood that had been transported from Ireland. Apparently, the gods had deemed to allow the blood, as well as the vampire who required it, to travel through worlds from their circle of stones.

Then again, it was pigs' blood. Cian hadn't fed on humans in centuries. A personal choice, he mused as he broke open the packet, poured its contents into a cup. A matter of will, he thought, and well, manners, come to that. He lived among them, did business with them, slept with them when he was in the mood. It seemed rude to feed off them.

In any case, he'd found it simpler to live as he liked, to stay off the radar, if he didn't kill some hapless soul on a nightly basis. Live feeding added both thrill and flavor nothing else matched, but it was, by nature, a messy business.

He'd grown accustomed to the more banal flavor of pigs' blood, and the simple convenience of having it at his fingertips rather than having to go out and hunt something up every time hunger stirred in him.

He drank the blood as a man might his morning coffee—out of habit and the need for a kick on waking. It cleared his mind, jump-started his system.

He troubled neither with candles nor fire as he washed. He couldn't say he was overly pleased with the accommodations of Geall. Castle or not, he imagined he was as out of place in this medieval atmosphere as both Glenna and Blair.

He'd lived through this sort of era once, and once was enough for anyone. He preferred—much preferred—the daily conveniences of indoor plumbing, electricity, Chinese bloody take-out, come to that.

He missed his car, his bed, the damn microwave. He missed the life and sounds of city life and all it offered. Fate would have given him a solid kick in the ass if it ended him here, in the era, if not the world, of his beginnings.

Dressed, he left his room to make his way to the stables, and his horse.

There were people about—servants, guards, courtiers—those who lived and worked within the Castle Geall. Most avoided him, averting their eyes, quickening their pace.

Some made the sign against evil behind their backs. It didn't trouble him.

They knew what he was—and had seen what creatures like him were capable of since Moira, the scholarly gladiator, had battled one in the playing field.

It had been good strategy, he thought now, for Moira to ask him along with Blair and Larkin to hunt down the two vampires who'd killed her mother, the queen. Moira had understood the importance, the value of having vampires brought back alive so the people could see them for what they were. And see Moira herself fight and end one, proving herself a warrior.

She would, in a matter of weeks, lead her people to war. When a land had been at peace as long as Geall was reputed to have been, it would take a strong leader, a forceful one, to whip farmers and merchants, ladies-in-waiting and creaky advisors into soldiers.

He wasn't sure she was up to the task. Brave enough, he mused as he slipped out of the castle, crossed a courtyard toward the stables. More than bright enough. And it was true she'd honed considerable fighting skills over the past two months. No doubt she'd been trained since birth in matters of state and protocol, and her mind was clever and open.

In peace, he imagined she'd rule her pretty little world quite well. But in wartime, a ruler was general as well as figurehead.

If it had been up to him, he would have left Riddock, her uncle, in charge. But little of this business was up to him.

He heard her before he saw her, and scented her before that. Cian very nearly turned around to go back the way he'd come. It was just another annoyance to come across the woman when he'd been thinking of her.

The problem was, he thought of her entirely too often.

Avoiding her wasn't an option as they were inexorably bound together in this war. Slipping away now unseen was easily done. And cowardly. Pride, as always, refused to let him take the easy way.

They'd housed his stallion at the far end of the stables, two stalls away from any of the other horses. He understood and tolerated the fact that the grooms and farriers were wary of tending to the horse of a demon. Just as he was aware either Larkin or Hoyt groomed and fed his temperamental Vlad in the mornings.

Now it seemed Moira had taken it upon herself to spoil the animal. She had carrots, Cian saw, and was balancing one on her shoulder, cajoling Vlad to nip it off.

"You know you want it," she murmured. "It's so tasty. All you have to do is take it."

He'd thought the same about the woman, Cian mused.

She was gowned, her dress draped over a plain linen kirtle, so he assumed whatever training she'd done that day was complete. Still, she dressed simply for a princess, in quiet blue with only a hint of lace at the bodice. She wore the silver cross, one of nine Hoyt and Glenna had conjured. Her hair was loose, all that glossy brown falling down her back to her waist, and crowned with the thin circlet of her office.

She wasn't beautiful. He reminded himself of that often, nearly as often as he thought of her. She was, at best, a pretty thing. Slender and small-framed, small of feature as well. But for the eyes. They were long and dominant in that face of hers. Dove gray when she was quiet, pensive, listening. Hell smoke when she was roused.

He'd had his choice of great beauties in his time—as a man with any sense and skill would given a few centuries. She wasn't beautiful, but he couldn't, for all the effort, lock her out of his mind.

He knew he could have her if he put any of that effort into a seduction. She was young and innocent and curious, and therefore, very susceptible. Which was why, above all else, he knew he'd be better off seducing one of her ladies if he wanted the entertainment, the companionship, the release.

He'd had his fill of innocence long ago, just as he'd had his fill of human blood.

His horse, however, appeared to have less willpower. It took only moments before Vlad dipped his head and nipped the carrot from Moira's shoulder.

She laughed, stroked the stallion's ears as he chomped. "There now, that wasn't so hard, was it? We're friends, you and I. And I know you get lonely from time to time. Don't we all?"

She was lifting another carrot when Cian stepped out of the shadows. "You'll make a puppy out of him, then what sort of war horse will he be come Samhain?"

Her body jerked, then stiffened. But when she turned toward Cian, her face was composed. "Sure you don't really mind, do you? He so enjoys a bit of a treat now and then."

"Don't we all," he murmured.

Only the faintest flush of heat along her cheekbones betrayed any embarrassment at being overheard. "The training went well today. People are coming in from all over Geall. So many willing to fight we've decided we'll be setting up a second training area on my uncle's land. We'll have Tynan and Niall working there."

"Lodging?"

"Aye, that's becoming a bit of a thing. We'll house as many here as we can manage, and at my uncle's as well. There's the inn, and many of the farmers and crofters nearby are sheltering family and friends already. No one will be turned off. We'll find a way."

She fiddled with her cross as she spoke. Not, Cian thought, out of fear of him, but out of nervous habit. "There's food as well to think of. So many had to leave their crops and cattle behind to come here. But we'll manage. Have you eaten?"

She flushed a little deeper as soon as the words were out. "What I meant is there'd be supper in the parlor if—"

"I know what you meant. No. I thought to see to the horse first, but he appears well groomed and fed." On the heels of the words, Vlad bumped his head against Moira's shoulder. "And spoiled," Cian added.

Her brows drew together as they did, he knew, when she

was annoyed or thoughtful. "It's only carrots, and they're good for him."

"Speaking of food, I'll need blood in another week. You might make certain the next pigs that are slaughtered, their blood isn't wasted."

"Of course."

"Aren't you the cool one."

Now the faintest sign of irritation crossed her face. "You take what you need from the pig. I'm not after turning my nose up at a slab of bacon, am I?" She shoved the last carrot into Cian's hand and started to sweep out.

She stopped herself, "I don't know why you fire me up so easily. If you mean to or not. And no." She held up a hand. "I don't think I want to know the answer to that. But I would like to speak to you for a moment or two about another matter."

No, avoiding her wasn't possible, he reminded himself. "I have a moment or two."

She glanced around the stables. It wasn't only horses that had ears in such places. "I wonder if you could take that moment or two to walk with me. I'd be private on this."

He shrugged, and giving Vlad the last carrot joined Moira to walk out of the stables. "State secrets, Your Highness?"

"Why must you mock me?"

"Actually, I wasn't. Irritable tonight, are you?"

"It might be I am." She shoved back the hair that spilled over her shoulder. "What with war and end of days, and the practical matters of washing linens and providing food for an army meanwhile, it might be I am a bit irritable."

"Delegate."

"I am. I do. But it still takes time and thought to push chores into other hands—finding the right ones, explaining how it must be done. And this isn't what I wanted to speak to you about."

"Sit."

"What?"

"Sit." He took her arm, ignoring the way the muscles tensed against his hand, and pulled her down onto a bench.

"Sit, give your feet a rest if you won't turn off that busy brain of yours for five minutes."

"I can't remember the last time I had an hour, all to myself and a book. Well, I can, actually. Back in Ireland, in your house. I miss it—the books, the quiet of them."

"You need to take it, that hour now and again. You'll burn out otherwise, and won't be any good to yourself or anyone else."

"My hands feel so full, they make my arms ache." She looked down at them where they lay in her lap, and sighed. "And there, I'm off again. What is it Blair says? Bitch, bitch, bitch."

She surprised a laugh out of him, and turned her head to smile into his face.

"I suspect Geall has never had a queen such as you."

And her smile faded away. "No, you've the right of that. And we'll soon see. We go tomorrow, at first light, to the stone."

"I see."

"If I lift the sword from it, as my mother did in her time, and her father in his, and back to the first, Geall will have a queen such as me." She looked off, over the shrubberies toward the gates. "Geall will have no choice in it. Nor will I."

"Do you wish it otherwise?"

"I don't know what I wish, so I don't wish at all— except that it was done and over. Then I could do, well, whatever needs to be done next. I wanted to tell you." She shifted her gaze from whatever she saw in her mind, and met his eyes again. "I'd hoped we'd find a way to do this thing at night."

Soft eyes, he thought, and so serious. "It's too dangerous to have any sort of ceremony outside after sunset beyond the castle walls."

"I know it. All who wish to witness this rite may attend. You can't, I know. I'm sorry for it. It feels wrong. I feel the six of us, our circle, should be together at such a time."

Her hand reached up for her cross again. "Geall isn't yours, I know that as well, but the moment of this, it's important for what comes after. More than I knew before. More than I could have known."

She took a shaky breath. "They killed my father."

"What are you saying?"

"I have to walk again. I can't sit." She got up quickly, rubbing her arms to warm them from the sudden chill in the air, and in her blood. She moved through the courtyard into one of the gardens.

"I haven't told anyone—I didn't mean to tell you. What purpose does it serve? And I've no proof, just a knowing."

"What do you know?"

Easier than she'd believed it would be to talk to him, to tell him, she realized, because he was also so to the point. "One of the two that killed my mother, that you brought here. The one I fought." She held a hand up, and he watched her draw in her composure again. "Before I killed it, he said something of my father, and how he died."

"Likely trying to get a rise out of you, break your concentration."

"It did that well enough, but was more, you see. I know it, inside me." Looking at him, she pressed a hand to her heart. "I knew it when I looked at the one I killed. Not just my mother, but my father as well. I think Lilith sent them here this time because she'd had success with it before. When I was a child."

She continued to walk, her head bowed with the weight of her thoughts, her circlet glinting in the light of the torches. "They thought it was a bear gone mad. He was in the mountains, hunting. He was killed, he and my mother's young brother. My uncle Riddock didn't go as my aunt was close to her time with child. I . . ."

She broke off again as footsteps echoed, keeping her silence until the sound of them drifted away. "They thought, those who found them and brought them home, they thought it was animals. And so it was," she continued with steel in her tone now. "But these walk like a man. She sent them to kill him, so there would be no child but me."

She turned to him then, the torchlight washing red over

her pale face. "Perhaps, at that time, she knew only the ruler of Geall would be one of the circle. Or perhaps it was easier to kill him than me at that time, as I was hardly more than a baby and kept close watch on. Plenty of time for her to send assassins back for me. But instead they killed my mother."

"Those that did are dead."

"Is that comfort?" she wondered, and thought—from him—it likely was an offer of it. "I don't know what to feel. But I know she took my parents from me. She took them to stop what can't be stopped. We'll meet her on the battlefield come Samhain, because it's meant. Whether I fight as queen or not, I fight. She killed them for nothing."

"And nothing you could have done would have stopped it."

Yes, comfort, she thought again. Oddly, his pithy statement gave her just that. "I pray that's true. But I know because of what was done, what was not done, what had to be, what comes tomorrow is more important than rite and ritual. Whoever holds that sword tomorrow leads this war, and wields it with the blood of my murdered parents. She couldn't stop it. She cannot stop it."

She stepped back, gestured up. "Do you see the flags? The dragon and the claddaugh. The symbols of Geall since its beginning. Before this is done, I will ask that one more be hoisted."

He thought of all she might choose—a sword, a stake, an arrow. Then he knew. Not a weapon, not an instrument of war and death, but a symbol of hope and endurance. "A sun. To shed its light on the world."

Surprise, with pleasure running just behind it, lit her face. "Aye. You understand my thinking, and the need. A gold sun on the white flag to stand for the light, the tomorrows we fight for. This sun, gold as glory, will be the third symbol of Geall, one I bring to it. And damned to her. Damned to her and what she brought here."

Flushed now, Moira drew a deep breath. "You listen well—and I talk too much. You must come inside. The others will be gathering for supper."

He touched a hand to her arm to stop her. "Earlier I thought you'd make a poor wartime queen. I believe it might have been one of the rare times I was wrong."

"If the sword is mine," she said, "you will be wrong."

It occurred to him as they started inside, that they'd just shared their longest conversation in the two months they had known each other.

"You need to tell the others. You need to tell them what you believe about your father. If this is a circle, there should be no secrets to weaken in."

"You're right. Aye, you've the right of it."

Her head was lifted now, her eyes clear as she led the way.

Chapter 2

❖

She didn't sleep. How could a woman sleep on what was, in Moira's mind, essentially the last night of her life? If in the morning it was her destiny to free the sword from its stone scabbard, she would be queen of Geall. As queen she would rule and govern and reign, and those were duties she'd been trained for since birth. But as queen on this coming dawn and the ones to follow, she would lead her people to war. If it wasn't her destiny to raise the sword, she would follow another, willingly, into battle.

Could weeks of training prepare anyone for such an action, such a weight of responsibility? So this night was the last she could be the woman she'd believed she would be, even the queen she'd hoped she might be.

Whatever dawn brought her, she knew nothing would ever be quite the same again.

Before her mother's death, she'd believed this coming dawn was years away. She'd assumed she would have years of her mother's company and comfort and counsel, years of peace and study so that when her time came she'd be not only ready for the crown, but worthy of it.

A part of her had assumed her mother would reign for decades longer, and she herself would marry. In the dim and distant future, one of the children she bore would take the crown in her stead.

All of that had changed on the night of her mother's death. No, Moira corrected, it had changed before, years before when her father had been murdered.

Perhaps it had not changed at all, but was simply unfolding as the pages of the book of fate were written.

Now she could only wish for her mother's wisdom, and look inside herself for the courage to bear both crown and sword.

She stood now on the high reaches of the castle under a thumbnail moon. When it waxed full again, she would be far from here, on the cold ground of a battlefield.

She'd come to the battlement because she could see the torches lighting the playing field. Here the sights and sounds of night training could reach her. Cian, she thought, used hours of his night to teach men and women how to fight something stronger and faster than humans. He would push them, she knew, until they were ready to drop. As he had pushed her, and the others of the circle, night after night during their weeks in Ireland.

Not all of them trusted him, she knew that as well. Some actively feared him, but that might be to the good. She understood he wasn't after making friends here, but warriors.

In truth, he'd had a strong part of making one of her.

She thought she understood why he fought with them— or at least had a glimmer of understanding why he would risk so much for humankind. Part of it was pride of which she knew he had abundance. He would not bow to Lilith. Part, whether he admitted it or not, was loyalty to his brother. And the rest, well, it dealt with courage and his own conflicted emotions.

For he had emotions, she knew. She couldn't imagine how they struggled and whirled inside him after a thousand years of existence. Her own were so conflicted and torn after only two months of blood and death she hardly recognized herself.

What must it be like for him, after all he'd seen and done, all he'd gained and lost? He knew more than any of them of the world, of its pleasures, its pains, its potentials. No, she couldn't imagine what it was like to know all he knew and still risk his own survival.

That he did risk it, that he was even now lending his time and skill to train troops, earned her respect. While the mystery of him, the hows and whys of him, continued to fascinate.

She couldn't be sure what he thought of her. Even when he'd kissed her—that single hot and desperate moment— she couldn't be sure. And getting to the inside of matters had always been irresistible to her.

She heard footsteps, and turning, saw Larkin coming toward her.

"You should be in your bed," he said.

"I'd only stare at the ceiling. The view's better here." She reached for his hand—her cousin, her friend—and was instantly comforted. "And why aren't you in yours?"

"I saw you. Blair and I went out to help Cian for a bit." Like hers, his gaze scanned the field below. "I saw you standing up here alone."

"I'm poor company, even for myself tonight. I only wish it were done, then there would be what happens next. So I came up here to brood over it." She tipped her head toward his shoulder. "It passes the time."

"We could go down to the family parlor. I'll let you beat me at chess."

"Let me? Oh, will you listen to him." She looked up at him. His eyes were golden brown, long-lidded like her own. The smile in them didn't quite mask his concern. "And I suppose you've *let* me win the hundreds of matches we've had over the years."

"I thought it good for your sense of confidence."

She laughed even as she poked him. "It's confident I am I can beat you at chess nine times out of every ten."

"We'll just put that to the test then."

"We will not." Now she kissed him, brushing his tawny hair away from his face. "You'll go to your bed and to your lady, and not spend these hours distracting me from my sorry mood. Come, we'll go in. It may be the limited view of my ceiling will bore me to sleep after all."

"You've only to tap on the door if you're wanting company."

"I know it."

Just as she knew she would keep her own counsel until the first light of dawn.

But she did not sleep.

In the way of tradition she would be dressed and tended to by her ladies in the last hour before dawn. Though it was urged on her, she refused the red gown. Moira knew well enough it wasn't a color that flattered her, however royal it might be. In its stead she wore the hues of the forest, a deep green over a paler green kirtle.

She agreed to jewels—they had been her mother's after all. So she allowed the heavy stones of citrine to be fastened around her neck. But she would not remove the silver cross.

She would wear her hair down and uncovered, and sat letting the female chatter chirp around her as Dervil brushed it tirelessly.

"Will you not eat just a little, Highness?"

Ceara, one of her women, once again urged a plate of honey cakes on her. "After," Moira told her. "I'll feel more settled after."

Moira got to her feet, her relief profound when Glenna stepped into the room. "How wonderful you look!" Moira held out her hands. She'd chosen the gowns herself for both Glenna and Blair, and saw now she'd chosen well. Then again, she thought, Glenna was so striking there was nothing that wouldn't flatter her.

Still, the choice of deep blue velvet highlighted her creamy skin and the fire of her hair.

"I feel a bit like a princess myself," Glenna told her. "Thank you so much. And you, Moira, look every inch the queen."

"Do I?" She turned to her glass, but saw only herself. But she smiled when she saw Blair come in. She'd chosen russet for Blair, with a kirtle of dull gold. "I've never seen you in a dress."

"Hell of a dress." Blair studied her friends, then herself. "We've got that whole fairy tale thing going." She threaded her fingers through her short, dark hair to settle it into place.

"You don't mind then? Tradition requires the more formal attire."

"I like being a girl. I don't mind dressing like one, even one who's not in my own fashion era." Blair spotted the honey cakes, and helped herself to one. "Nervous?"

"Well beyond it. I'd like a moment with the ladies Glenna and Blair," Moira told her women. When they scurried out, Moira dropped into the chair in front of the fire. "They've been fussing around me for an hour. It's tiring."

"You look beat." Blair sat on the arm of the chair. "You didn't sleep."

"My mind wouldn't rest."

"You didn't take the potion I gave you." Glenna let out a sigh. "You should be rested for this, Moira."

"I needed to think. It's not the usual way of it, but I want both of you, and Hoyt and Larkin to walk with me to the stone."

"Wasn't that the plan?" Blair asked with her mouth full.

"You would be part of the procession, yes. But in the usual way, I would walk ahead, alone. This must be, as it always has been. But behind me, would be only my family. My uncle, and my aunt, Larkin, my other cousins. After them, according to rank and position would walk others. I want you to walk with my family, as you are my family. I do this for myself, but also for the people of Geall. I want them to see what you are. Cian isn't able to be part of this, as I wish he could."

"It can't be done at night, Moira." Blair touched a hand to Moira's shoulder. "It's too much of a risk."

"I know. But while the circle won't be complete at the place of the stone, he'll be in my thoughts." She rose now to go to the window. "Dawn's coming," she murmured. "And the day follows."

She turned back as the last stars died. "I'm ready for what comes with it."

Her family and her women were already gathered below. She accepted the cloak from Dervil, and fastened the dragon brooch herself.

When she looked up from the task, she saw Cian. She assumed he might have stopped for a moment on his way to retire, until she saw he carried the cloak Glenna and Hoyt had charmed to block the killing rays of the sun.

She stepped away from her uncle's side, and up to Cian. "You would do this?" she said quietly.

"I rarely have the opportunity for a morning walk."

However light his words, she heard what was under them. "I'm grateful you've chosen this morning to take one."

"Dawn's broke," Riddock said. "The people wait."

She only nodded, then drew up her hood as was the custom before stepping out into the early light.

The air was cool and misty with barely a breeze to stir the fingers of vapor. Through the rising curtain of it, Moira crossed the courtyard to the gates alone, while her party fell in behind her. In the muffled quiet, she heard the morning birds singing, and the faint whisper of the damp air.

She thought of her mother, who had once walked this way on a cool, misty morning. And all the others who'd walked before her out of the castle gates, across the brown road, over the green grass so thick with dew it was like wading through a river. She knew others trailed behind her, merchants and craftsmen, harpers and bards. Mothers and daughters, soldiers and sons.

The sky was streaked with pink in the east, and the ground fog sparkled silver.

She smelled the river and the earth, and continued up, over the gentle rise with the dew dampening the hem of her gown.

The place of the stone stood on a faerie hill where a little glade of trees offered shelter. Gorse and moss grew, pale yellow, quiet green, over the rocks near the holy well.

In the spring there would be the cheery orange of lilies, dancing heads of columbine, and later the sweet spires of foxglove, all growing where they would.

But for now, the flowers slept and the leaves of the trees had taken on that first blush of color that portended their death.

The sword stone itself was wide and white, altarlike on an ancient dolmen of flat gray.

Through the leaves and the mists, beams of sun lanced, crossing that white stone and glinting on the silver hilt of the sword buried in it.

Her hands felt cold, so very cold.

All of her life she had known the story. How the gods had forged the sword from lightning, from the sea, and the earth and the wind. How Morrigan had brought it and the altar stone herself to this place. And there she had buried it to the hilt, carved the words on the stone with her fiery finger.

SHEATHED BY THE HAND OF GODS
FREED BY THE HAND OF A MORTAL
AND SO WITH THIS SWORD
SHALL THAT HAND RULE GEALL

Moira paused at the base of the stones to read the words again. If the gods deemed it, that hand would be hers.

With her cloak sweeping over the dew-drenched grass, she walked through sun and mist to the top of the faerie hill. And took her place behind the stone.

For the first time she looked, and she saw. Hundreds of people, her people, with their eyes on hers spread over the field, down toward that brown ribbon of road. Every one of them, if the sword came to her, would be her responsibility. Her cold hands wanted to shake.

She calmed herself as she scanned the faces and waited for the trio of holy men to take their places behind her.

Some were still coming over that last rise, hurrying lest they miss the moment. She wanted her breath steady when she spoke, so waited a little longer and let herself meet the eyes of those she loved best.

"My lady," one of the holy men murmured.

"Yes. A moment."

Slowly, she unpinned the brooch, passed her cloak behind her. The wide sweep of her sleeves flowed back as she lifted her arms, but she didn't feel the chill against her skin. She felt heat.

"I am a servant of Geall," she called out. "I am a child of the gods. I come here to this place to bow to the will of both. By my blood, by my heart, by my spirit."

She took the last step toward the stone.

There was no sound now. It seemed even the air held its breath. Moira reached out, curled her fingers around the silver hilt.

And oh, she thought as she felt the heat of it, as she heard somewhere in her mind the murmur of its music. Of course, aye, of course. It's mine, and always was.

With a whisper of steel against rock, she drew it free and raised its point to the sky.

She knew they cheered, and some of them wept. She knew that to a man they lowered to one knee. But her eyes were on that point and the flash of light that streaked from the sky to strike it.

She felt it inside her, that light, a burst of heat and color and strength. There was a sudden burn on her arm, and as if the gods etched it, the symbol of the claddaugh formed there to brand her queen of Geall. Rocked by it, thrilled and humbled, she looked down at her people. And her eyes met Cian's.

All else seemed to melt away in that moment, for a

moment. There was only him, his face shadowed by the hood of his cloak, and his eyes so brilliant and blue.

How could it be, she wondered, that she should hold her destiny in her hand, and see only him? How, meeting his eyes like this, could it be like looking deeper, deeper yet, into her own destiny?

"I am a servant of Geall," she said, unable to look away from him. "I am a child of the gods. This sword, and all it protects is mine. I am Moira, warrior queen of Geall. Rise, and know I love you."

She stood as she was, the sword still pointing skyward as the hands of the holy man placed the crown on her head.

He was no stranger to magic, the black or the white, but Cian thought he'd never seen anything more powerful. Her face, so pale when she'd removed her cloak, had bloomed when her hand had taken the sword. Her eyes, so heavy, so somber, had gone as brilliant as the blade.

And had simply sliced through him, keen as a sword, when they'd met his.

There she stood, he thought, slender and slight, and as magnificent as any Amazon. Suddenly regal, suddenly fierce, suddenly beautiful.

What moved inside him had no place there.

He stepped back, turned to go. Hoyt laid a hand on his arm.

"You must wait for her, for the queen."

Cian lifted a brow. "You forget, I have no queen. And I've been under this bloody cloak long enough."

He moved quickly. He wanted to get away from the light, from the smell of humanity. Away from the power of those gray eyes. He needed the cool and the dark, and the silence.

He was barely a league away when Larkin trotted up to him. "Moira asked me to see if you wanted a ride back."

"I'm fine, but thanks."

"It was amazing, wasn't it? And she was . . . well, brilliant as the sun. I always knew she'd be the one, but seeing it happen is a different matter. She was queen the moment she touched the sword. You could see it."

"If she wants to stay queen, have anyone to rule, she better make use of that sword."

"So she will. Come now, Cian, this isn't the day for gloom and doom. We're entitled to a few hours of joy and celebration. And feasting." With another grin, Larkin gave Cian an elbow poke. "She might be queen, but I can promise the rest of us will eat like kings this day."

"Well, an army travels on its belly."

"Do they?"

"So it was said by . . . someone or another. Have your feasting and celebration. Tomorrow queens, kings and peasants alike best be preparing for war."

"Feels like we've been doing nothing else. Not complaining, mind," he continued before Cian could speak. "I guess the matter is I'm tired of preparing for it, and want to get to it."

"Haven't had enough fighting the last little while?"

"I've payment to make for what was nearly done to Blair. She's still tender along the ribs, and wears down quicker than she'd admit." His face was hard and grim as he remembered it. "Healing fast, as she does, but I won't forget how they hurt her."

"It's dangerous to go into battle with a personal agenda."

"Ah, bollocks. We've all of us something personal to settle, or what's the point? And you won't tell me that a part of you won't be going into it with what that bitch did to King in your mind and in your heart."

Because Cian couldn't deny it, he left it alone. "Are you . . . escorting me back, Larkin?"

"As it happens. There was some mention of me throwing myself bodily over you to shield you from the sunlight should the magic in that cloak fade out."

"That would be fine. We'd both go up like torches." Cian said it casually, but he had to admit he felt easier when he stepped into the shadow cast by Castle Geall.

"I'm also asked to request you come to the family parlor if you're not too weary. We're to have a private breakfast there. Moira would be grateful if you could spare a few minutes at least."

She would have liked a few minutes herself, alone. But Moira was surrounded. The walk back to the castle was a blur of movement and voices wrapped in mists. She felt the weight of the sword in her hand, the crown on her head even as she was swept along by her family and friends. Cheers echoed over the hills and fields, a celebration of Geall's new queen.

"You'll need to show yourself," Riddock told her. "From the royal terrace. It's expected."

"Aye. But not alone. I know it's the way it's been done," she continued before her uncle could object. "But these are different times. My circle will stand with me." She looked at Glenna now, then Hoyt and Blair. "The people won't just see their queen, but those who have been chosen to lead this war."

"It's for you to say, you to do," Riddick said with a slight bow. "But on such a day, Geall should be free of the shadow of war."

"Until Samhain has passed, Geall remains always in the shadow of war. Every Geallian must know that until that day, I rule with a sword. And that I'm part of six the gods have chosen."

She laid a hand on his as they passed through the gates. "We will have feasting and celebration. I value your advice, as always, and I will show myself, and I will speak. But on this day, the gods have chosen both queen and warrior in me. And this is what I will be. This is what I'll give to Geall, to my last breath. I won't shame you."

He took her hand from his arm, brought it to his lips. "My sweet girl. You have and always will bring me nothing but pride. And from this day, to my last breath, I am the queen's man."

The servants were gathered, and knelt when the royal party entered the castle. She knew their names, their faces. Some of them had served her mother before Moira herself was born.

But it was no longer the same. She wasn't the daughter of the house now, but its mistress. And theirs.

"Rise," she said, "and know I am grateful for your loyalty and service. Know, too, that you and all of Geall have my loyalty and service as long as I am queen."

Later, she told herself as she started up the stairs, she would speak with each of them individually. It was important to do so. But for now, there were other duties.

In the family parlor the fire roared. Flowers cut fresh from garden and hothouse spilled from vases and bowls. The table was set with the finest silver and crystal, with wine waiting for Moira's inner circle to toast the new queen.

She took a breath, then two, trying to find the words she would say, her first, to those she loved best.

Then Glenna simply wrapped arms around her. "You were magnificent." She kissed both Moira's cheeks. "Luminous."

The tension she'd held tight in her shoulders eased. "I feel the same, but not. Do you know?"

"I can only imagine."

"Nice job." Blair stepped up, gave her a quick hug. "Can I see it?"

Warrior to warrior, Moira thought and offered Blair the sword.

"Excellent," Blair said softly. "Good weight for you. You expect it to be crusted with jewels or whatever. It's good that it's not. It's good and right that it's a fighting sword, not just a symbol."

"It felt as though the hilt was made for my hand. As soon as I touched it, it felt . . . mine."

"It is." Blair handed it back. "It's yours."

For the moment, Moira set the sword on the table to accept Hoyt's embrace. "The power in you is warm and steady," he said close to her ear. "Geall is fortunate in its queen."

"Thank you." Then she let out a laugh as Larkin swept her off her feet and in three dizzying circles.

"Look at you. Majesty."

"You mock my dignity."

"Always. But never you, *a stór.*"

When Larkin set her back on her feet, she turned to Cian. "Thank you for coming. It meant a great deal to me."

He neither embraced nor touched her, but only inclined his head. "It was a moment not to be missed."

"A moment more important to me that you would come. All of you," she continued and started to turn when her young cousin tugged on her skirts. "Aideen." She lifted the child, accepted the damp kiss. "And don't you look pretty today."

"Pretty," Aideen repeated, reaching up to touch Moira's jeweled crown. Then she turned her head with a smile both shy and sly for Cian. "Pretty," she said again.

"An astute female," Cian observed. He saw the little girl's gaze drop to the pendant he wore, and in an absent gesture lifted it so that she could touch.

Even as Aideen reached out, her mother all but flew across the room. "Aideen, don't!"

Sinann pulled the girl from Moira, gripped her tight against her belly, burgeoning with her third child.

In the shocked silence, Moira could do no more than breathe her cousin's name.

"I never had a taste for children," Cian said coolly. "You'll excuse me."

"Cian." With one damning look toward Sinann, Moira hurried after him. "Please, a moment."

"I've had enough moments for the morning. I want my bed."

"I would apologize." She took his arm, holding firm until he stopped and turned. His eyes were hard; blue stone. "My cousin Sinann, she's a simple woman. I'll speak with her."

"Don't trouble on my account."

"Sir." Pale as wax, Sinann walked toward them. "I beg your pardon, most sincerely. I have insulted you, and my queen, her honored guests. I ask your forgiveness for a mother's foolishness."

She regretted the insult, Cian thought, but not the act. The child was on the far side of the room now, in her father's arms. "Accepted." He dismissed her with barely a glance. "Now if you'll release my arm. Majesty."

"A favor," Moira began.

"You're racking them up."

"And I'm in your debt," she said evenly. "I need to go out, onto the terrace. The people need to see their queen, and, I feel, those who are her circle. If you'd give me a few minutes more of your time I'd be grateful."

"In the buggering sun."

She managed a smile, and relaxed as she recognized the frustration in his tone meant he'd do as she asked. "A few moments. Then you can go find some solitude with the satisfaction of knowing I'll be envying you for it."

"Then make it quick. I'd enjoy some solitude and satisfaction."

Moira arranged it deliberately, with Larkin on one side of her—a figure Geall loved and respected—and Cian on the other. The stranger some of them feared. Having them flank her would, she hoped, show her people she considered them equals, and that both had her trust.

The crowd cheered and called her name, with the cheers rising to a roar when she lifted the sword. It was also a deliberate gesture for her to pass that sword to Blair to hold for her while she spoke. The people should see that the woman Larkin was betrothed to was worthy to hold it.

"People of Geall!" She shouted it, but the cheering continued. It came in waves that didn't ebb until she stepped closer to the stone rail and raised her hands.

"People of Geall, I come to you as queen, as citizen, as protector. I stand before you as did my mother, as did her sire, and as did all those back to the first days. And I stand as part of a circle chosen by the gods. Not just a circle of Geallian rulers, but a circle of warriors."

Now she spread her arms to encompass the five who stood with her. "With these who stand with me, that circle is formed. These are my most trusted and beloved. As a citizen, I ask you give them your loyalty, your trust, your respect as you do me. As your queen, I command it."

She had to pause every few moments until the shouts and cheers abated again. "Today, the sun shines on Geall. But it will not always be so. What is coming seeks the dark, and we will meet it. We will defeat it. Today, we celebrate, we feast, we give thanks. Come the morrow, we continue our preparations for war. Every Geallian who can bear arms will do so. And we will march to *Ciunas*. We will march to the Valley of Silence. We will flood that ground with our strength and our will, and we will drown those who would destroy us in the light."

She held her hand out for the sword, then held it high again. "This sword will not, as it has since the first days, hang cool and quiet during my reign. It will flame and sing in my hand as I fight for you, for Geall, and for all humankind."

The roars of approval rose like a torrent.

Then there were screams as an arrow streaked the air.

Before she could react, Cian shoved her down. Under the shouting and chaos, she heard his low, steady cursing. And felt his blood warm on her hand.

"Oh God, my God, you're shot."

"Missed the heart." He spoke through gritted teeth. She saw the pain on his face as he pushed away from her to sit.

When he reached up to grip the arrow out of his side, Glenna dropped to a crouch, pushed his hand aside. "Let me see."

"Missed the heart," he repeated, and once again gripped the arrow. He yanked it out. "Bugger it. Bloody fucking hell."

"Inside," Glenna began briskly. "Get him inside."

"Wait." Though her hand trembled a little, Moira gripped Cian's shoulder. "Can you stand?"

"Of course I can bloody stand. What do you take me for?"

"Please, let them see you." Her free hand fluttered over his cheek for just an instant, like a brush of wings. "Let them see us. Please."

When she linked her fingers with his she thought she saw something stir in his eyes, and felt its twin shift inside her heart.

Then it was gone, and his voice was rough with impatience. "Give me some damn room then."

She got to her feet again. Below was chaos. The man she assumed was the assassin was being kicked and pummeled by every hand or foot that could reach him.

"Hold!" She shouted it with all her strength. "I command you, hold! Guards, bring that man to the great hall. People of Geall! You see that even on this day, even when the sun shines on us, this darkness seeks to destroy us. And it fails." She gripped Cian's hand, lifted it high with her own. "It fails because there are champions in this world who would risk their lives for another."

She laid a hand on Cian's side, felt his wince. Then held up her bloody hand. "He bleeds for us. And by this blood he shed for me, for all of you, I raise him to be Sir Cian, Lord of Oiche."

"Oh, for Christ's sake," Cian muttered.

"Be quiet." Moira said it softly, with steel, and her eyes on the crowd.

Chapter 3

◈

"Half-vamp," Blair announced as she strode back into the parlor. "Multiple bite scars. Crowd did a number on him," she added. "A regular human would be toast after the beating he took. And he's not feeling so well himself."

"He can be treated after I've spoken to him. Cian requires care first."

Blair looked over Moira's shoulder to where Glenna was bandaging Cian's side. "How's he doing?"

"He's angry and uncooperative, so I would say he's doing well enough."

"We can all be grateful for his reflexes. You handled it," Blair added, looking back at Moira. "Kept your cool, kept control. Tough first day on the job, nearly getting assassinated and all that, but you did good."

"Not good enough to have anticipated a daylight attack. To remember that not all Lilith's dogs require an invitation to come within these walls." She thought of how Cian's blood had run against her hand—warm and red. "I won't make that mistake again."

"None of us will. What we need is to get information out of this asshole Lilith sent. But there's a problem. He either can't or won't speak English. Or Gaelic."

"He's mute?"

"No, no. He talks, it's just none of us can understand him. Sounds Eastern European. Maybe Czech."

"I see." Moira glanced back at Cian. He was stripped to the waist, with only the bandage against his skin. Annoyance more than pain darkened his face as he sipped from a goblet she assumed held blood. Though he didn't look to be in the best of moods, she knew she was about to ask another favor.

"Give me a moment," she murmured to Blair. She approached Cian, ordering herself not to shrink under his hot blue stare. "Is there something more that can be done for you, to make you more comfortable?"

"Peace, quiet, privacy."

Though each of his words had the lash of a whip, she kept her own calm and pleasant. "I'm sorry, but those items are in short supply right at the moment. I'll order them up for you as soon as I can."

"Smart-ass," he mumbled.

"Indeed. The man whose arrow you intercepted speaks in a foreign tongue. Your brother told me once that you knew many languages."

He took a long, deep drink, with his eyes deliberately on hers. "It's not enough that I *intercepted* the arrow? Now you want me to interrogate your assassin?"

"I would be grateful if you would try, or at least interpret. If indeed, his tongue is one you know. There are likely a few things in the world you don't know, so you may be of no use to me at all."

Amusement flickered briefly in his eyes. "Now you're being nasty."

"Tit for tat."

"All right, all right. Glenna, my beauty, stop hovering."

"You lost considerable blood," she began, but he only lifted the goblet.

"Replacing, even as we speak." With a slight grimace, he got to his feet. "I need a goddamn shirt."

"Blair," Moira said in even tones, "would you fetch Cian a goddamn shirt?"

"On that."

"You've made a habit of saving my life," Moira said to Cian.

"Apparently. I'm thinking of giving that up."

"I could hardly blame you."

"Here you go, champ." Blair offered Cian a fresh white shirt. "I think the guy's Czech, or possibly Bulgarian. Can you handle either of those?"

"As it happens."

They went into the great hall where the assassin sat, bruised, bleeding and chained, under heavy guard. That guard included both Larkin and Hoyt. When Cian entered, Hoyt stepped away from his post.

"Well enough?" he asked Cian.

"I'll do. And it cheers me considerably that he looks a hell of a lot worse than I do. Pull your guards back," he said to Moira. "He won't be going anywhere."

"Stand down. Sir Cian will be in charge here."

"Sir Cian, my ass." But he only muttered it as he approached the prisoner.

Cian circled him, gauging ground. The man was slight of build and dressed in what would be the rough clothes of a farmer or shepherd. One eye was swollen shut, the other going black and blue. He'd lost a couple of teeth.

Cian snapped out a command in Czech. The man jolted, his single working eye rolling up in surprise.

But he didn't speak.

"You understood that," Cian continued in the same language. "I asked if there are others with you. I won't ask again."

When he was met with silence, Cian struck out with enough force to have the prisoner slamming back against the wall, along with the chair he was chained to.

"For every thirty seconds of silence, I'll give you pain."

"I'm not afraid of pain."

"Oh, you will be." Cian jerked the chair and the man upright, kept his face close. "Do you know what I am?"

"I know what you are." The man used his bloodied mouth to sneer. "Traitor."

"That's one viewpoint. But the important thing to remember is that I can give you pain beyond what even such as you can stand. I can keep you alive for days, weeks, come to that. And in constant agony." He lowered his voice to a hiss. "I'd enjoy it. So let's begin again."

He didn't bother to ask the question, as he'd warned he wouldn't repeat it.

"Could use a spoon," he said conversationally. "That left eye looks painful. If I had a spoon handy, I could scoop it right out of its socket for you. Of course, I could use my fingers," he continued when that eye wheeled wildly. "But then I'd have a mess on my hands, wouldn't I?"

"Do your worst," the man spat out—but he'd begun to tremble a little. "I'll never betray my queen."

"Bollocks." The shudders and sweat told him this one would be easily and quickly broken. "You'll not only betray her before I'm done with you, you'll do it dancing the hornpipe if I tell you to. But let's just be quick and direct as we've all better things to do."

The man's head jerked back as Cian moved. But instead of going for the face as his quarry anticipated, Cian reached down, gripped the man's cock. And squeezed until there was nothing but screams.

"There's no one else! I'm alone, I'm alone!"

"Be sure." Cian only increased the pressure. "If you lie, I'll find out. And then I'll begin to cut this piece of you off, one inch at a time."

"She sent only me." He was weeping now, tears and snot running down his face. "Only me."

Cian eased the pressure a few fractions. "Why?"

The only answer was raw, rough gasps, and Cian tightened the vise of his fingers again. "Why?"

"One could slip through easily, unnoticed. Un . . . unremarked."

"The logic of that has spared you, at least for the moment, from becoming a eunuch." Cian strolled over, got himself a chair. After placing it in front of the prisoner, he straddled it. And spoke in conversational tones even as the man whimpered. "Now, this is better, isn't it? Civilized. When we're done here, we'll see to those injuries."

"I want water."

"I'm sure you do. We'll get you some——after. So for now, let's talk a bit about Lilith."

It took thirty minutes——and two more sessions of pain——before he was satisfied he knew all the man could tell him. Cian got to his feet again.

The would-be assassin was weeping uncontrollably now. Perhaps from the pain, Cian thought. Perhaps from the belief it was ended.

"What were you before she took you?"

"A teacher."

"Did you have a wife, a family?"

"They were no use but food. I was poor and weak, but the queen saw more in me. She gave me strength and purpose. And when she slaughters you, and these . . . ants who crawl with you, I'll be rewarded. I'll have a fine house, and women of my choosing, wealth and power."

"Promised you all that, did she?"

"That and more. You said I could have water."

"Yes, I did. Let me explain something to you about Lilith." He moved behind the man, whose name he'd never asked, and spoke quietly in his ear. "She lies. And so do I."

He clamped his hands on the man's head and in one fast move, broke his neck.

"What have you done?" Shocked to the pit of her belly, Moira rushed forward. "What have you done?"

"What needed doing. She sent only one——this time. If it upsets your sensibilities, you might want to have your guards take that out of here before I brief you."

"You had no right. No right." Her belly wanted to revolt as it had constantly since he'd begun the torturous interrogation. "You murdered him. What makes you any different from him that you would kill him without trial, without sentence?"

"The difference?" Coolly, Cian lifted his brows. "He was still mostly human."

"Is it so little to you? Life? Is it so little?"

"On the contrary."

"Moira. He's right." Blair moved between them. "He did what had to be done."

"How can you say that?"

"Because I'd have done the same. He was Lilith's dog, and if he'd escaped, he'd have tried again. If he couldn't get to you, he'd kill whoever he could."

"A prisoner of war—" Moira began.

"There are no prisoners in this," Blair interrupted. "On either side. If you'd locked him up, you'd take men out of training, off patrol, to guard him. He was an assassin, a spy sent behind lines during wartime. And mostly human is generous," she added with a glance at Cian. "He'd never be human again. If it had been a vampire in that chair, you'd have staked him without thought or hesitation. This isn't any different."

A vampire didn't leave its body broken on the floor, Moira thought, still chained to a chair.

Moira turned to one of the guards. "Tynan, remove the prisoner's body. See that it's buried."

"Majesty."

She saw Tynan's quick glance at Cian—and recognized the steely approval in the look.

"We'll go back to the parlor," she continued. "No one has eaten. You can . . . brief us while we do."

"Lone gunman," Cian said, and wished almost wistfully for coffee.

"Makes sense." Blair helped herself to eggs and a thick slice of fried ham.

"Why?" Moira addressed the question to Blair.

"Okay, they've got some half-vamps trained for combat." She nodded at Larkin. "Like the ones Larkin and I dealt with that day at the caves, but it takes time and effort. And it takes a lot of work and will to keep one in thrall."

"And if the thrall is broken?"

"Insanity," Blair said briefly. "Total breakdown. I've heard stories of half-vamps gnawing off their own hand to get free and back to their maker."

"He was doomed before he came here," Moira murmured.

"From the minute Lilith got her hands on him, yeah. My take on this was it was supposed to be a quick hit, suicide mission. Why waste more than one? Things go right, you only need one."

"Yes, one man, one arrow." Moira considered it. "If he's skilled enough and fortunate enough, the circle is broken, Geall is without a ruler only moments, really, after it regains one. It would have been a good and efficient strike."

"There you go."

"But why did he wait until we were back? Why not try for me at the stone?"

"He didn't get there in time," Cian said simply. "He misjudged the distance he had to travel, and arrived after it was done. You were closed in by people on your way back, and he wasn't able to get a clear shot. So he joined the parade, so to speak, and bided his time."

"Eat something." Hoyt dished food onto Moira's plate himself. "So Lilith knew that Moira would go to the stone today."

"She has her ear to the ground," Cian confirmed. "Whether or not she'd planned to send someone to try to disrupt the ritual, and the result before Blair tangled with Lora is debatable. She was pissed," he said. "Wild, according to our late, unlamented archer. As I've said before, her relationship with Lora is strange and complicated, but very deep, very sincere. She ordered an archer chosen for this while she was still half-crazed. Sent him on horseback for speed—and they have only a limited number of horses."

"And how is the little French pastry?" Blair wondered.

"Scarred and screaming when the man left, and being tended to by Lilith personally."

"More important," Hoyt broke in, "where is Lora, and where are the rest of them?"

"Our informant, while handy with a bow, wasn't particularly observant or astute. The best I could get puts Lilith's main base a few miles from the battlefield. He described what seems to be a small settlement, overlooked by a good-sized farm with several cottages and a large stone manor house, where I'd say the gentry who owned the land lived. She's in the manor house."

"Ballycloon." Larkin looked at Moira, saw her face was very pale, her eyes very dark. "It must be Ballycloon, and the O Neills's land. The family we helped the day Blair and I were checking the traps, the day Lora ambushed her, they were coming from near Drombeg, and that's just a bit west of Ballycloon. We would have gone farther east, to check the last trap, but . . ."

"I was hurt," Blair finished. "We went as far as we could. And lucky for us. If she'd already made her base when we dropped in, we'd have been seriously outnumbered."

"And seriously dead," Cian added. "They moved in the night before your altercation with Lora."

"There would have been people there still, or on the road." It knotted Larkin's stomach to think of it. "And the O Neills themselves. I don't know if they've reached safety. How can we know how many . . ."

"We can't," Blair said flatly.

"You, you and Cian, you thought we should move everyone out, force them out if necessary, from all the villages and farms around the battleground. Burn the houses and cottages behind them so Lilith and her army would have no shelter. I thought it was cold and cruel of her. Heartless. And now . . .

"It can't be changed. And I couldn't, wouldn't," Moira corrected, "have ordered homes burned. Perhaps it would have been wiser, and stronger, to do just that. But those whose homes we destroyed would have lost the heart they need to fight. So it's done this way."

She had no appetite for the food on her plate, but she picked up her tea to warm her hands. "Blair and Cian know strategy, as Hoyt and Glenna know magic. But you and I, Larkin, we know Geall and its people. We would have broken their hearts and their spirits."

"They'll burn what they don't need or want," Cian told her.

"Aye, but it won't be our hands that light the torch. That will matter. So we believe we know where they are. Do we know how many?"

"He started out with multitudes, but he was lying. He didn't know," Cian said. "However much Lilith may use mortals, she wouldn't count them in her inner circle, or trust any with salient information. They're food, they're servants, they're entertainment."

"We can look." Glenna spoke for the first time. "Hoyt and I, now that we have a general area, can do a locator spell. We should be able to get harder data. Some idea of the numbers. We know from Larkin's trip to the caves and his look at their arsenal they were armed for a thousand or more."

"We'll look." Hoyt laid his hand over Glenna's. "But what I think Cian isn't saying is whatever the numbers they have, whatever we have, in the end they'll have more. Whatever weapons they have will be more. Lilith has had decades, perhaps centuries, to plan this moment. We've had months."

"And still we'll win."

Cian lifted a brow at Moira's statement. "Because you're good and they're evil?"

"No, and there's nothing so simple as that. You yourself are proof of that, for you're neither like her nor like us, but something else altogether. We'll win because we'll be smarter, and we'll be stronger. And because she has no one like the six of us standing with her."

She turned from him to his brother. "Hoyt, you are the first of us. You brought us together."

"Morrigan chose us."

"She, or fate, selected us," Moira agreed. "But it was you who began the work. It's you who believed, who had the power and the strength to forge this circle. So do I believe it. I rule Geall, but I don't rule this company."

"Nor do I."

"No, none of us do. We must be as one, for all our differences. So we look to each other for what we need. I'm far from the strongest warrior here, and my magic is but a shadow. I don't have Larkin's skills, nor the steeliness of mind to kill in cold blood. What I have is knowledge and authority, so I offer those."

"You have more," Glenna told her. "A great deal more."

"I will have more, before it's done. There are things I must do." She got to her feet. "I'll return to work on whatever is necessary as soon as I'm able."

"Pretty royal," Blair commented after Moira left the room.

"Carrying a lot of weight with it." Glenna turned to Hoyt. "Agenda?"

"Best to see what we can of the enemy. Then I'm thinking fire. It's still one of our most formidable weapons, so we should charm more swords."

"Risky enough to put swords in some of the hands we're training," Blair put in. "Much less flaming ones."

"You'd be right." Hoyt considered, nodded. "It will be up to us then, won't it, to decide who'll be—what is it?—issued that sort of weapon. Good men should be placed in positions as close to Lilith's base as we can manage. They'd need shelter that's safe after sunset."

"It's barracks you're meaning. There are cottages and cabins, of course." Larkin narrowed his eyes in thought. "Other shelters can be built in the daylight hours if need be. There's an inn as well, between her base and the next settlement."

"Why don't we go take a look?" Blair shoved her plate aside. "You and Glenna can look your way, and Larkin and I can do a fly-by. You up for the dragon?"

"I am." He smiled at her. "Especially when you're doing the riding."

"Sex, sex, sex. The guy's a machine."

"On that note," Cian said dryly, "I'm going to bed."

With a quick squeeze of Glenna's hand, Hoyt murmured, "A moment," then followed his brother.

"I need a word with you."

Cian flicked him a glance. "I've had my quota of words this morning."

"You'll have to swallow a few more. My rooms are closer, if you would. I'd prefer this private."

"Since you'd just dog me to my room and pester me until I want to rip your tongue out, your rooms will do."

Servants bustled on the route between the parlor and bedchambers. Preparations for the feasting, Cian thought, and wondered if it was Hoyt's talk of fire that put him in mind of Nero and his fiddle.

Hoyt stepped into a chamber, then immediately threw out an arm to block Cian from entering. "The sun," was all he said, then moved quickly to pull the coverings over the windows.

The room plunged into gloom. Without thinking, Hoyt gestured toward a brace of candles. They flared into light.

"Handy bit of business that," Cian commented. "I'm out of practice lighting tinderboxes."

"It's a basic skill, and one you'd have yourself if you'd ever put your mind and time into honing your power."

"Too tedious. Is that whiskey?" Cian moved straight to a decanter, and poured. "Oh, such sobriety and disapproval." He read his brother's expression clearly as he took the first warm sip. "I'll remind you that it's the end of my day—well past it, come to that."

He glanced around, began to wander. "Smells female. Women like Glenna always leave something of themselves behind to remind a man." Then he dropped down into a chair, slouching, stretching out his legs. "Now, what is it you're bound and determined to bore me with?"

"There was a time you enjoyed, even sought my company."

Cian's shoulders moved in something too lazy to be called a shrug. "I suppose that means nine hundred years of absence doesn't make the heart grow fonder."

Regret showed on Hoyt's face before he turned away to add turf to the fire. "Are you and I to be at odds again?"

"You tell me."

"I wanted to speak with you alone about what you did with the prisoner."

"More humanity heard from. Yes, yes, I should have patted his head so he could stand trial, or before the tribunal, whatever goes for the name of justice in this place. I should've invoked the sodding Geneva Convention. Well, bollocks."

"I don't know this convention, but there could be no trial, no tribunal on such a matter at such a time. That's what I'm saying, you great irritating idiot. You executed an assassin, as I would have done—but with more tact and, well, stealth."

"Ah, so you'd have slithered down to whatever cage they put him in and put a knife between his ribs." Cian raised his eyebrows. "That's all right then."

"It's not. None of it's all right. It's a bloody nightmare is what it is, and we're all having it. I'm saying you did the necessary. And that for his trying to kill Moira, whom I love as I did my own sisters, and for putting an arrow in you, I'd have done for him. I've never killed a man, for these things we've ended these past weeks haven't been men, but demon. But I'd have killed this one if you hadn't been there ahead of me."

Hoyt paused, caught his breath if not his composure. "I wanted to say as much to you so you'd know my feelings on it. But it seems I waste both our time as you couldn't give a damn in hell what my feelings are."

Cian didn't move. His only change was to shift his gaze from his brother's furious face down to the whiskey in his hand. "I do, as it happens, give several damns in hell what your feelings are. I wish I didn't. You've stirred things in me I'd calmed too long ago to remember. You've slapped family in my face, Hoyt, when I'd buried it."

Crossing over, Hoyt took the chair that faced his brother's. "You're mine."

Now when Cian lifted his eyes to his brother's they were empty. "I'm no one's."

"Maybe you weren't, from the time you died until the time I found you. But it's no longer true. So if you give those damns, I'm saying to you I'm proud of what you're doing. I'm saying I know it's harder for you to do this thing than any of us."

"Obviously, as demonstrated, killing vampires or humans isn't difficult for me."

"Do you think I don't see how some of the servants melt away when you're near? That I didn't see Sinann rush to take her child, as if you might have snapped its neck as you did the assassin's? These insults to you don't go unnoticed."

"Some aren't insulted to be feared. It doesn't matter. It doesn't," he insisted when Hoyt's face closed up. "This is a fingersnap of time for me. Less. When it's done, unless I get a lucky stake through the heart, I'll go my way."

"I hope your way will bring you, from time to time, to see me and Glenna."

"It may. I like to look at her." Cian's grin spread, slow and easy. "And who knows, she may eventually come to her senses and realize she chose the wrong brother. I've nothing but time."

"She's mad for me." His tone easy again, Hoyt reached over, took Cian's glass of whiskey and had a sip himself.

"Mad is what she'd have to be to put her lot in with you, but women are odd creatures. You're fortunate in her, Hoyt, if I've failed to mention it before."

"She's the magic now." He passed the glass back. "I'd

have none that mattered without her. My world turned when she came into it. I wish you had . . ."

"That isn't written in the book of fate for me. The poet's may say love's eternal, but I can tell you it's a different matter when you've got eternity, and the woman doesn't."

"Have you ever loved a woman?"

Cian studied his whiskey again, and thought of the centuries. "Not in the way you mean. Not in the way you have with Glenna. But I've cared enough to know it's not a choice I can make."

"Love is a choice?"

"Everything is." Cian tossed back the last of the whiskey, then set the empty glass aside. "Now, I choose to go to bed."

"You chose to take that arrow for Moira today," Hoyt said as Cian started for the door.

Cian stopped, and when he turned his eyes were wary. "I did."

"I find that a very human sort of choice."

"Do you?" And the words were a shrug. "I find it merely an impulsive—and painful—one."

He slipped out to make his way to his own room on the northern side of the castle. Impulse, he thought again, and, he could admit to himself, an instant of raw fear. If he'd seen the arrow fly a second later, or moved with a fraction less speed, she'd be dead.

And in that instant of impulse and fear, he'd seen her dead. The arrow still quivering as it pierced her flesh, the blood spilling the life out of her onto her dark green gown and the hard gray stones.

He feared that, feared the end of her, where she would be beyond him. Where she would go to a place he couldn't see or touch. Lilith would have taken one last thing from him with that arrow, one last thing he could never regain.

For he'd lied to his brother. He had loved a woman, despite his best—or worst—intentions, he loved the new-crowned queen of Geall.

Which was ridiculous, and impossible, and in time

something he'd get over. A decade or two and he'd no longer remember the exact shade of those long gray eyes. That quiet scent she carried would no longer tease his senses. He'd forget the sound of her voice, the look of that slow, serious smile.

Such things faded, he reminded himself. You had only to allow it.

He stepped into his own room, closed and bolted the door.

The windows were covered, and no light was lit. Moira, he knew, had given very specific orders on how his housekeeping should be done. Just as she'd specifically chosen that room, a distance from the others, as it faced north.

Less sunlight, he mused. A considerate hostess.

He undressed in the dark, thought fleetingly of the music he liked to play before sleep, or on wakening. Music, he thought, that filled the silence.

But this time and place didn't run to CD players, or cable radio or any damn thing of the sort.

Naked, he stretched out in bed. And in the absolute dark, the absolute silence, willed himself to sleep.

Chapter 4

✦

Moira stole the time. She escaped from her women, from her uncle, from her duties. She was already guilty, already worried she'd be a failure as a queen because she so craved her solitude.

She would have bartered two days' food, or two nights' sleep, for a single hour alone with her books. Selfish, she told herself as she hurried away from the noise, the people, the questions. Selfish to wish for her own comfort when so much was at stake.

But while she wouldn't indulge herself with books in some sunny corner, she would take the time to make this visit.

On this day she was made queen, she wanted, and she needed, her mother. So hiking up her skirts, she went as fast as she was able down the hill, then through the little gap in the stone wall that bordered the graveyard.

Almost instantly she felt quieter of heart.

She went first to the stone she'd ordered carved and set when she'd returned to Geall. She'd set one herself for King in Ireland, in the graveyard of Cian and Hoyt's ancestors. But she'd vowed to have one done here, in honor of a friend.

After laying a handful of flowers on the ground, she stood and read the words she'd ordered carved in the polished stone.

King
*This brave warrior lies not here
but in a faraway land.
He gave his life for Geall,
and all humankind.*

"I hope you would like it, the stone and the words. It seems so long ago since I saw you. It all seems so long, and still hardly more than a hand clap. I'm sorry to tell you Cian was hurt today, for my sake. But he's doing well enough. Last night we spoke almost as friends, Cian and I. And today, well, not altogether friendly. It's hard to know."

She laid a hand on the stone. "I'm queen now. That's hard to know as well. I hope you don't mind I put this monument here, where my family lies. For to me, that's what you were for the short time we had. You were family. I hope you're resting now."

She stepped away, then hurriedly back again. "Oh, I meant to say, I'm keeping my left up, as you taught me." By his grave she lifted her arms in a boxing stance. "So, for all the times I don't get a fist in my face, thank you."

With the rest of the flowers in the crook of her arm, she picked her way through the long grass, the stones, to the graves of her parents.

She laid flowers at the base of her father's stone. "Sir. I hardly remember you, and I think the memories—most of them—that I have are ones mother passed to me. She loved you so, and would speak of you often. I know you were a good man, for she wouldn't have loved you otherwise. And all who speak of you say you were strong and kind, and quick to laugh. I wish I could remember the sound of that, of your laugh."

She looked over the stones now, to the hills, the distant mountains. "I've learned you didn't die as we always thought, but were murdered. You and your young brother. Murdered by the demons who are even now in Geall, preparing for war. I'm all that's left of you, and I hope it's enough."

She knelt now, between the graves, to lay the rest of the flowers over her mother. "I miss you, every day. I had to go far away, as you know, to come back stronger. *Mathair.*"

She closed her eyes on the word, and on the image it brought to her, clear as life.

"I didn't stop what was done to you, and still I see that night as if behind a mist. Those that killed you have been punished, one by my own hand. It was all I could do for you. All I can do is fight, and lead my people to fight. Some of them to their death. I wear the sword and the crown of Geall. I will not diminish it."

She sat awhile, with just the sound of the breeze through the tall grass and the shifting lights of the sun.

When she rose, turned toward the castle, she saw the goddess Morrigan standing at the stone wall.

The god wore blue today, soft and pale and trimmed in deeper tones. The fire of her hair was unbound to lay flaming over her shoulders.

Her hands empty of flowers, her heart heavy, Moira walked through the grass to meet her.

"My lady."

"Majesty."

Puzzled by Morrigan's bow, Moira clasped her hands together to keep them still. "Do gods acknowledge queens?"

"Of course. We made this place and deemed those of your blood would rule and serve it. We're pleased with you. Daughter." Laying her hands lightly on Moira's shoulders, she kissed both her cheeks. "Our blessings on you."

"I would rather you bless my people, and keep them safe."

"That is for you. The sword is out of its scabbard. Even

when it was forged, it was known that one day it would sing in battle. That, too, is for you."

"She's already spilled Geallian blood."

Morrigan's eyes were as deep and calm as a lake. "My child, the blood Lilith has spilled would make an ocean."

"And my parents are only drops in that sea?"

"Every drop is precious, and every drop serves a purpose. Do you lift the sword only for your own blood?"

"No." Shifting, Moira gestured. "There's another stone here, standing for a friend. I lift the sword for him and his world, and for all the worlds. We're all a part of each other."

"Knowing this is important. Knowledge is a great gift, and the thirst to seek it even greater. Use what you know, and she will never defeat you. Head and heart, Moira. You are not made to give greater weight to one than the other. Your sword will flame, I promise you, and your crown will shine. But what you hold inside your head and your heart is the true power."

"It seems they're full of fear."

"There's no courage without fear. Trust and know. And keep your sword at your side. It's your death she wants most."

"Mine? Why?"

"She doesn't know. Knowledge is your power."

"My lady," Moira began, but the god was gone.

The feast required yet another gown and another hour of being fussed over. With so much on her hands, she'd left the matter of wardrobe to her aunt, and was pleased to find the gown beautiful and the watery blue color flattering. She enjoyed pretty gowns and taking a bit of time to look her best.

But it seemed she was being laced into a new one every time she turned around, and subjected to the chirping and buzzing of her women half the day.

She could admit she missed the freedom of the jeans

and roomy shirts she'd worn in Ireland. Beginning the next day, however it shocked the women, she would dress as best suited a warrior preparing for battle.

But for tonight, she'd wear the velvets and silks and jewels.

"Ceara, how are your children?"

"Well, my lady, and thank you." Standing behind Moira, Ceara continued to work Moira's thick hair into silky braids.

"Your duties and your training keep you from them more than I would wish."

Their eyes met in the mirror. Moira knew Ceara to be a sensible woman, the most centered, in her opinion, of the three that waited on her.

"My mother tends them, and is happy to do so. The time I take now is well spent. I'd rather lose these hours with them than see them harmed."

"Glenna tells me you're very fierce in hand-to-hand."

"I am." Ceara's face tightened with a grim smile. "I'm not skilled with a sword, but there's time yet. Glenna's a good teacher."

"Strict," Dervil piped in. "Not as strict as the lady Blair, but demanding all the same. We run, every day, and fight and tumble and carve stakes. And end each day with weary legs, bruises and splinters."

"Better to be weary and bruised than dead."

At Moira's flat comment, Dervil flushed. "I meant no disrespect, Majesty. I've learned a great deal."

"And are, I'm told, becoming a demon with a sword. I'm proud. And you, Isleen, are said to have a good hand with a bow."

"I do." Isleen, the youngest of the three flushed with the compliment. "I like it better than the fighting with fists and feet. Ceara always knocks me down."

"When you squeal like a mouse and flutter your hands, anyone could knock you down," Ceara pointed out.

"Ceara's taller, and her arms longer than yours, Isleen. So," Moira said, "you have to learn to be faster, and sneakier.

I'm proud of all of you, for every bruise. Tomorrow, and every day after, for no less than an hour each day, I'll be training with you."

"But, Majesty," Dervil began, "you can't—"

"I can," Moira interrupted. "And I will. I'll expect each of you, and the other women to do their best to knock *me* down. It won't be easy." She stood when Ceara stepped back. "I've learned a great deal as well." She lifted her crown, placed it on her head. "Believe me when I tell you I can knock the three of you, and any else who comes, on your arse."

She turned, resplendent in shimmering blue velvet.

"Any who puts me on mine, or bests me with bare hands or any weapon will be given one of the silver crosses Glenna and Hoyt has charmed. This is my best gift. Tell the others."

It was, Cian thought, like walking into a play. The great hall was the stage, and festooned with banners, enlivened with flowers, blazing with candles and firelight. Knights and lords and ladies were decked in their very best. Doublets and gowns, jewels and gold. He spotted several men and women sporting footwear with the long and pointed upturned toes that he recalled were fashionable when he'd been alive.

So, he thought, even regrettable styles spanned worlds.

Food and drink were so plentiful he imagined the long tables groaned under the platters and pitchers. There was music, bright and lively, from a harper. The talk he overheard ran the gamut. Fashion, politics, sexual gossip, flirtations and finance.

Not so different altogether, he mused, from his own nightclub back in New York. The women wore less there, of course, and the music was louder. But the core of it hadn't changed overmuch through the centuries. People still liked to gather together over food and drink and music.

He thought of his club again, and asked himself if he

missed it. The nightly surge, the sounds, the press of people. And realized he didn't, not in the least.

Very likely, he decided, he'd been growing bored and restless, and would have moved on shortly in any case. It had only taken his brother's sweep through time and space, having Hoyt land—more or less—on his doorstep to up the timetable.

But without Hoyt and his mission from the gods, moving out would have meant a change of name and location, a shifting of funds. Complicated, time-consuming—and interesting. Cian had had more than a hundred names and a hundred homes, and still found the forming of them interesting.

Where might he have gone? he wondered. Sydney perhaps, or Rio. It might have been Rome or Helsinki. It was only a matter, essentially, of sticking a pin in a map. There were few places he hadn't been already, and none he couldn't have made his base if he chose.

In his world, in any case. Geall was a different matter. He'd lived through this sort of fashion and culture once, and had no desire to repeat himself. His family had been gentry, and so he'd attended his share of high-flown feasts.

All in all he'd have preferred a snifter of brandy and a good book.

He didn't intend to stay long, and had come only because he knew someone would come looking for him. While he was confident he could have avoided whoever had come hunting him, he would never avoid the haranguing Hoyt would subject him to the next day.

Easier altogether to put in an appearance, toast the new queen, then slip away.

He had drawn the line at wearing the formal doublet and accessories that had been delivered to his room. He might have been stuck in a medieval timeline, but he'd be damned if he'd dress for it.

So he wore black, pants and sweater. He hadn't packed a suit and tie for this particular journey.

Still he smiled with some warmth at Glenna who drifted

up to him in emerald green, in what he thought had been termed a *robe deguisee* at one time. Very formal, very elegant, and showcasing her very lovely breasts with its low and rounded neckline.

"Now here's a vision I prefer to any goddess."

"I almost feel like one." She spread her arms so the full bell sleeves swayed. "Heavy though. It must be ten pounds of material. I see you went for a less weighty ensemble."

"I believe I'd stake myself before I squeezed into one of those getups again."

She had to laugh. "Can't blame you, but I'm getting a kick out of seeing Hoyt all done up. For me—maybe for you after all this time—it's like a costume ball. Moira chose regal black and gold for the house sorcerer. It suits him, as your more contemporary choice does you. Still, this whole day has been like a very strange dream."

"I was thinking a very strange play."

"Yeah, that works. Whatever, tonight's feasting is a short and colorful respite. We managed to do some scouting today, Hoyt and I magically, Larkin and Blair with the fly-over. We'll fill you in when—"

She broke off at the sound of trumpets.

Moira made her entrance, the train of her gown flowing behind her, her crown flaming in the light of a hundred candles.

She glowed, as queens should, as women could.

As his unbeating heart tightened in his chest, Cian thought: Bloody, buggering hell.

He had no choice but to join the others at the high table for the feast. Leaving beforehand would have been an overt insult—not that he minded that overmuch—but it would have drawn attention. So he was stuck again.

Moira sat at the center of the table, flanked by Larkin and her uncle. Cian, at least, had Blair beside him, who was both an informative and entertaining companion.

"Lilith hasn't burned anything yet, which was a surprise," she began. "Probably too busy nursing Fifi. Oh, question. The French bitch has been around about four hundred years, right? And you more than double that. How come both of you still have accents?"

"And why is it Americans believe everyone should speak as they do?"

"Good point. Is this venison? I think it's venison." She took a bite. "It's not too bad."

She wore siren red, which left a portion of her strong shoulders bared. Her short cap of hair was unadorned, but there were ornate gold medallions, nearly big as a baby's fist, dangling from her ears.

"How do you hold your head up with those earrings?"

"Suffering for fashion," she said easily. "So they've got horses," she continued. "A couple of dozen in various paddocks. Might be more stabled. I figure why not have Larkin put down, and we could run the horses off. Just make a nuisance of ourselves. Maybe—if I can talk him into it—light a few fires. Vamps stay inside, they burn. Come out, they burn."

"Good thinking. Unless, of course, she had guards posted inside, with bows."

"Well, yeah, like I didn't think of that. I figure I'll wing a few flaming arrows down, get their attention. I pick my target—cottage nearest the biggest paddock. Gotta be some troops in there, stands to reason. Imagine my surprise and chagrin when the arrows bump off the air, like it was a wall."

His eyes narrowed as he shifted to face her. "Are you talking force field? What is this, bloody *Star Trek*?"

"That's what I said." In tune with him, Blair punched his shoulder. "She's got that wizard of hers, that Midir, working overtime by my guess. And their base camp's in a protective bubble. Larkin flew down, to get a closer look, and we both got a jolt. Like an electric shock. Pisser."

"Yes, it would be."

"Then the man himself comes out—from the big house, the manor house? Creepy-looking guy, let me say. Flying black robes, lots of silver hair. He just stands there, so we're looking down at him, he's looking up at us. Finally, I get it.

Mexican standoff. We can't get anything through, but neither can they. When the shield's up, they're locked down, we're locked out. Good as a freaking fortress. Better."

"She knows how to make the best use of the people she brings in," Cian mused.

"Looks that way. So I was lowered to making rude gestures, just so it wasn't a waste of time. She'd lower the shield at night, wouldn't she?"

"Possibly. Even if they brought enough food with them, the nature of the beast is to hunt. She wouldn't want her troops to get stale, or too edgy."

"So, maybe we can make a night run at it. I don't know. Something to think about. That's haggis, isn't it?" She wrinkled her nose. "I'm skipping that." She leaned a little closer to him, lowered her voice. "Larkin says the word's gone out on how you dealt with the guy who tried to kill Moira. You've got the castle guards and the knights behind you on that one."

"It hardly matters."

"You know better than that. You get what's essentially going to be this army's first line not just accepting you, but respecting you, it matters. Sir Cian."

He winced, visibly. "Just don't."

"Kind of rings for me. This Jell-O sort of thing is a little gritty. Do you know what it is?"

Cian waited, deliberately, until she'd taken a second bite. "Jellied internal organs—likely pig."

When she choked, the laugh just rolled out of him.

It was such a strange sound, Moira thought. To hear him laugh. Strange, a little wicked, and very appealing. She'd made a misstep with the clothes she'd sent for him. He was too much a creature of his own time—or what had come to be his own time—to put on garb from hers.

But he'd come, and she hadn't been sure he would. Not that he'd spoken a word to her. Not a single word.

He'd killed for her, she thought, but didn't speak to her.

So she would put him out of her mind, as he'd so obviously put her out of his.

She only wished the evening would end. She wanted her bed, she wanted sleep. She wanted to peel off the heavy velvet and slide blissfully—for one night—into the dark.

But she had to make a show of eating, despite her lack of appetite. She had to make a pretense, at least, of paying attention to conversations even though her eyes wanted to close.

She'd had too much wine, felt too warm. And there were hours yet before she could lay down her head.

Of course, she had to stop, to smile, and to drink every time one of the knights was moved to toast her. At the rate they were moving, her head would likely spin right off the pillow.

It was with huge relief that she was finally able to announce the dancing could begin.

She had to stand for the first set, as it was expected of her. And found she felt better for moving, for the music.

He didn't dance, of course, but only sat. Like a dyspeptic king, she thought, foolishly irritated because she'd *wanted* to dance with him. His hands on her hands, his eyes on her eyes.

But there he sat, gazing down on the masses and sipping his wine. She spun with Larkin, bowed to her uncle, clasped hands with Hoyt.

And when she looked back again, Cian was gone.

He wanted air, and more, he wanted the night. The night was still his time. What lived inside the mask of a man would always crave it, and always seek it.

He went up, and out, where the dark was thick and the music from the hall only a silvery echo. Clouds had rolled over the moon, and the stars were smothered by them. Rain would come before morning; he could already smell it.

Below, there were torches to light the courtyards, and guards stood at post at the gates, on the walls.

He heard one of them cough and spit, and the quick flap of the flags overhead in a sudden kick of wind. He could hear, if he tuned himself to it, the rustle of mice in their nest tucked in a gap of the stones, or the papery swish of the wings of a bat that circled overhead.

He could hear what others didn't.

He scented human—that salt on the flesh, and the rich run of blood beneath it. There was a part of him—always— that burned a little with the need. To hunt, to kill, to feed.

That burst of blood in the mouth, in the throat. The sheer life of it that could never be tasted in what came in cool packs of plastic. Hot, he remembered, always hot, that first taste. It heated all the places that were cold and dead, and for that moment, life—or its shadow—stirred inside that cold and that dead.

It was good to remember, now and then, the unspeakable pleasure of it. Good to remember what he pit his will against. Vital to remember what it was those they fought craved.

The humans did not, could not. Not even Blair who understood more than most.

Still they would fight, and they would die. More would come behind them to fight, and to die. Some would run, of course—some always did. Some would break with fear and simply stand and be slaughtered, like rabbits caught in a jacklight.

But most wouldn't run, wouldn't hide, wouldn't freeze in terror. In all the years he'd watched humans live and die, he knew when their backs were pressed hardest to the wall, they fought like demons.

If they won, they would end up romanticizing the whole business, songs and stories. Old men would sit by fires years from now and speak of the glory days while they showed their scars.

And others of them would wake in cold sweats from reliving the horror of war in their dreams.

If he lived, what would it be for him? he wondered. Glory days or nightmares? Neither, he thought, for he wasn't human enough to spend his time on what was over and done.

If Lilith managed to end him, well, true death was an experience he'd yet to have. It might be interesting.

And because he heard what others didn't, he caught the footsteps on the stone stairs. Moira's footsteps, as he knew her gait as well as her scent.

He nearly melted back into the shadows, then cursed himself for being a coward. She was only a woman, only a human. She could and would be nothing more to him.

When she stepped out, he heard her sigh once, long and deep as if she'd just shed some enormous weight. She moved to the stone rail, tipped her head back, closed her eyes. And breathed.

Her face was flushed from the heat of the fire, the exertion of the dance, but there were shadows of fatigue haunting her eyes.

Someone had worked slender braids through her long hair, so the weaving of them with their thin ropes of gold rippled through the rain of glossy brown.

He saw the minute she sensed she wasn't alone. The sudden stiffening in her shoulders, and the slide of her hand into the folds of her gown.

"If you've a stake tucked in there," he said, "I'd as soon you didn't point it in my direction."

Though her shoulders didn't relax, her hand dropped to her side as she turned. "I didn't see you. I wanted some air. It's so warm inside, and I've drunk too much."

"More that you didn't eat enough. I'll leave you to your air."

"Oh, stay. I'm only taking a moment, then you can have the damned air to yourself again." She pushed at her hair, then cocked her head.

He got a good look at her face now, her eyes, and thought, yes, indeed, the little queen was on the way to being plowed.

"Do you come out here to think deep thoughts? I can't decide if deep thoughts require space like this, or are better turned over in confines. I imagine you have many thoughts, with all that you've seen."

She stumbled a little, laughed a little when he caught her arm. And immediately released it.

"You're so careful not to touch me," she commented. "Unless you're saving me from death or injury. Or bashing at me in training. I find that interesting. You're a man of interests, how do you find it?"

"I don't."

"Except for that one time," she continued as if he hadn't spoken, and moved a step closer. "That one time you touched me good and proper. You put your hands on me then, and your mouth. I've wondered about that."

He very nearly took a step in retreat, and the realization of it mortified him. "It was meant to teach you a lesson."

"I'm a scholar, and I do love my lessons. Give me another then."

"The wine's made you foolish." He was annoyed with the stiff and pompous sound of his own voice. "You should go in, have your ladies take you to your bed."

"It has made me foolish. I'll be sorry for it tomorrow, but well, that's tomorrow, isn't it? Oh, what a day this has been for me." She did a slow turn that had her skirts swaying over the stones. "Was it only this morning I walked to the stone? How could it be only this morning? I feel I've carried that sword and the stone with it through this day. Now I'm setting them down, until tomorrow, I'm setting them down. I'm the worse for drink, and what of it?"

She stepped closer yet, and pride wouldn't let him back away.

"I'd hoped you'd dance with me tonight. I hoped, and I wondered what it would be like to have you touch me when it wasn't in a fight or out of manners or mistake."

"I wasn't in the mood for dancing."

"Oh, and you're full of moods, you are." She watched his face carefully, studying him, he thought, as she might the pages of a book. "And sure, so am I. I was in an angry mood when you kissed me before. And a little frightened around it. I'm not angry or frightened now. But I think you are."

"Now you're adding ridiculous to foolish."

"Prove it then." She closed that last bit of distance, tipped up her face to his. "Teach me a lesson."

He could hardly be damned for it. He'd been damned long before. He wasn't gentle; he wasn't tender. But yanked her against him and nearly off her feet before his mouth swooped down to plunder hers.

He tasted the wine and the warmth—and a recklessness he hadn't anticipated. That, he knew, was his mistake.

She was ready for him this time. Her hands were in his hair, her mouth open and avid. She didn't melt against him in surrender, or shudder from the onslaught. She strained for more.

Need clawed at him, one more demon sent to torture him.

She wondered the air between them didn't smoke, wondered how it was both of them didn't simply erupt into flame. This was fire, in the blood, in the bone.

How had she lived all of her life without it?

Even when he released her, pushed her back, it stayed inside her like a fever.

"Did you feel that?" Her whisper was full of wonder. "Did you feel that?"

The taste of her was inside him now, and everything in him craved more of her. So he didn't answer, didn't speak at all. He slipped into the dark and was gone before she could take another breath.

Chapter 5

◈

She awoke early and energized. All through the day before she'd dragged such weight with her, as if it had been shackled to her leg. Now that chain was broken. It didn't matter that rain poured out of moody gray skies that smothered even a hint of sun. She had the light inside her again.

She dressed in what she thought of as her Irish clothes—jeans and a sweatshirt. The time for ceremony and decorum was past, and sensibilities be damned until she could spend time soothing them again.

She might be a queen, she thought as she twisted her hair into a long, single braid, but she would be a working one.

She would be a warrior.

She laced on her boots, strapped on her sword. This woman Moira saw in the looking glass, she recognized and approved of. She was a woman with purpose, and power, and knowledge.

Turning, she studied the room. The queen's chamber, she thought. Once her mother's sanctuary, and now hers. The bed was wide and beautifully draped in deep blue velvet and frothy snow-white lace, for her mother had loved the soft and the pretty. The posts were thick, polished Geallian oak, and deeply carved with Geall's symbols. Paintings that graced the walls were also of Geall, its fields and hills and forests.

On a table near the bed stood a small portrait in a silver frame. Moira's father had watched over her mother every night—now he would watch over his daughter.

She glanced over toward the doors that led to her mother's balcony. The drapes were still pulled tight there, and she would leave them that way. At least for now. She wasn't ready to open those doors, to step out on the stones where her mother had been slaughtered.

Instead, she would remember the happy hours she'd spent with her mother in this chamber.

She went out, making her way to the door of Hoyt and Glenna's chamber where she knocked. Because it took several moments, she remembered the hour. She'd nearly stepped away again, hoping they hadn't heard her knock when the door opened.

Hoyt was still pulling on his robes. His long dark hair was tousled, and his eyes heavy with sleep.

"Oh, I beg your pardon," she began. "I didn't think—"

"Has something happened? Is something wrong?"

"No, no, nothing. I didn't think how early it was. Please, go back to your bed."

"What is it?" Glenna moved into view behind him. "Moira? Is there a problem?"

"Only with my manners. I was up and about early, and wasn't considering others would still be abed, especially after last night's festivities."

"It's all right." Glenna laid a hand on Hoyt's arm, signaling him to step aside. "What did you need?"

"Only a private word with you. The truth of the matter is I was going to ask if you'd have breakfast with me in my mother's—in my sitting room, so I could speak with you about something."

"Give me ten minutes."

"Are you certain? I don't mind waiting until later in the day."

"Ten minutes," Glenna repeated.

"Thank you. I'll see food's prepared."

"She looks . . . ready for something," Hoyt commented when Glenna went to the bowl and basin to wash.

"Or other." Glenna dipped her fingers into the water, focused. She might not be able to take a shower, but she'd be damned if she'd wash in cold water.

She did the best she could with what she had as Hoyt beefed up the fire. Then, giving into vanity, she did a subtle glamour.

"It might be she just wants to talk about today's training schedule." Glenna fixed on earrings she'd have to remember to take off for training. "I told you she's offered a prize—one of our crosses—to any of the women who takes her down in a match today."

"It was clever of her to offer a prize, but I wonder if it would be the best use of the cross."

"There were nine of them," Glenna reminded him as she dressed. "Five for us, and King's, of course, making six. The two we agreed to give to Larkin's mother and pregnant sister. There's a purpose for the ninth. This may be it."

"We'll see what the day brings." He smiled as she pulled a gray sweater over her head. "How is it, *a ghrá*, that you look lovelier every morning?"

"You've got love in your eyes." She turned into his arms when he moved to her—and looked wistfully at the bed. "Rainy morning. It'd be nice to snuggle in for an hour and have my way with you." She tipped her head up for a kiss. "But it looks like I'm having breakfast with the queen."

Moira was, as was her habit, sitting by the fire with a book when Glenna entered. Moira looked up, smiled sheepishly.

"Shame on me, taking you from your husband and your warm bed at such an hour."

"Queen's privilege."

With a laugh, Moira gestured to a chair. "The food will

be along. One day, if the seeds I brought and potted thrive, I'll be able to have the orange juice in the mornings. I miss the taste of it."

"I'd kill for coffee," Glenna admitted. "Then again, in a way, I am. For coffee, apple pie, TiVo and all things human." She sat and studied Moira. "You look good," she decided. "Rested, and as Hoyt said, ready."

"I am. Yesterday, there was so much inside my head and my heart, so it was all so very heavy. The sword and the crown were my mother's, and only mine now because she's dead."

"And you've had no time to grieve, not really."

"I haven't, no. Still, I know she would want me to do as I have, for Geall, for all, and not close myself off somewhere to mourn for her. And I had fear as well. What manner of queen would I be, and at such a time."

With some satisfaction, Moira looked down at her rough pants and boots. "Well, I know what manner of queen I'll try to be. Strong, even fierce. There's no time to sit on a throne and debate matters. Politics and protocol, they'll have to wait, won't they? We've had our ceremony and our celebration, and they were needed. But now it's time for the dirt and the sweat of it."

She got to her feet when the food was brought in. She spoke to the young boy—still sleepy around the edges—and the serving girl who was with him.

Spoke easily, Glenna noted. Called them both by name as the food and dishes were laid out. And while they both looked puzzled by their queen's choice of dress, Moira ignored it, dismissing them with thanks—and orders she and her guest not be disturbed.

When they sat together, Glenna noticed that Moira, who'd picked at her food for days, ate with an appetite to rival Larkin's.

"It'll be muddy and miserable for training today," Moira began, "and that's good, I'm thinking. Good discipline. I wanted to say that while I'll be participating, and likely every day now, you and Blair are still in charge of the thing. I want everyone to see that I'm training, just like the rest. That I'll get dirty and bruised."

"Sounds like you're looking forward to it."

"By the gods, I am." Moira scooped up eggs she'd coached the cooks to prepare as Glenna often had. Scrambled up with chunks of ham and onion right in them. "Do you remember when Larkin and I first came through the Dance to Ireland? I could plant an arrow anywhere I liked, nine of ten, but any one of you could plant *me* on my arse without half trying."

"You always got up."

"Aye, I always got up. But I'm not so easy to plant these days. That's something I want everyone to see as well."

"You showed them a warrior when you fought and killed the vampire."

"I did. Now I'll show them a soldier who takes her lumps. And there's more I want of you."

"I thought there was." Glenna poured them both more tea. "Spill it."

"I've never explored the magic I have. It isn't much of a thing, as you've seen yourself. A bit of a healing gift, and a kind of power that can be opened and reached by others with more. As you and Hoyt have done. Dreams. I've studied dreams, read books on their meanings. And books on magic itself, of course. But it seemed to me there was no real purpose for what I had other than to offer some ease to someone in pain. Or a way of knowing which direction to take to find a buck when hunting. Little things. Small matters."

"And now?"

"And now," Moira said with a nod. "I think there's a purpose, and there's a need. I think I need all I have, all I am. The more I know what's in me, the better I use it. When I touched the sword, when I put my hand on its hilt, it poured into me. The knowing that it was mine, had always been mine. And a power with it, like a strong wind, just blowing into me. More through me, I think. Do you know?"

"Exactly."

Nodding again, Moira continued to eat. "I've neglected this because it wasn't a particular interest. I wanted to read and to study, to hunt with Larkin, to ride."

"To do the things a young woman enjoys," Glenna interrupted. "Why shouldn't you have done what you liked to do? You didn't know what was coming."

"I didn't, no. I wonder, if I'd looked deeper, if I might have."

"You couldn't have saved your mother, Moira," Glenna said gently.

Moira looked up, her eyes very clear. "You see my thoughts so easily."

"I think because in your place, I'd have the same ones. You couldn't have saved her. More—"

"Weren't meant to," Moira finished. "I'm coming around to that, inside my heart. But if I'd explored what I have, I might have seen something of what was coming. For whatever difference it would have made. Like Blair, I've seen the battleground in dreams. But unlike her, I didn't face it. I turned away. That's done, too. I'm not . . . wait." She searched for the phrase. "Beating myself up? Right?"

"Yeah, that's right."

"I'm not beating myself up over it. I'm after changing it. So I'm asking, if you can make the time to help me hone whatever I might have, the way I've honed my fighting skills."

"I can. I'd love to."

"I'm grateful."

"Don't be grateful yet. It'll be work. Magic's an art, and a craft. And a gift. But comparing it to your physical training isn't far off. It's also, well, like a muscle." Glenna tapped a hand on her biceps. "You have to exercise it, and build it. Like medicine it's said we practice magic, so it's never done."

"Every weapon I take into battle is another strike against the enemy." Brows lifted, Moira flexed her arm. "So I'll build that muscle as I have this one, strong as I can.

I want to crush her, Glenna. More than defeat her, to crush her. For so many reasons. My parents, King. Cian," she added after a pause. "He'd dislike that, wouldn't he, knowing I think of him as a victim?"

"He doesn't see himself that way."

"He doesn't, refuses to. It's why he thrives, in his way. He's made his . . . I can't say peace as he's not a peaceful sort, is he? But he's accepted his lot. I suppose, in some sort of way, he's embraced it."

"I'd say you have his number, as much as any could."

Moira hesitated now, making a business of rearranging the food left on her plate. "He kissed me again."

"Oh. Oh." And after a pause. "Oh."

"I made him."

"Not to belittle your charm or powers, I don't think anyone can make Cian do much of anything he doesn't want to do."

"Could be he wanted to, but he wasn't going to until I pushed him into it. I'd had a bit to drink."

"Hmm."

"I wasn't the worse for it," Moira said with a laugh that had some nerves at the edges. "Not really. Just a little looser in my manners, so to speak, and more determined in my mind. I wanted air and some quiet, so I went up, out on one of the battlements. There he was."

She pictured it again. "He might have gone anywhere, and sure I could have gone somewhere else. But neither of us did, so we both ended up in the same place, at the same time. In the night," she said quietly. "With the music and the lights barely reaching us."

"Romantic."

"I suppose it was. With the rain that would come before dawn just beginning to scent the air, and the thin slice of moon very white against the sky. There's a mystery to him I keep wanting to pick at until I find the pieces of it."

"You wouldn't be human if you didn't find him fascinating," Glenna said. They both knew what she hadn't said. He wasn't. He wasn't human.

"He was being all stiff, the way he can be with me, and it was irritating. And well, I'll admit, challenging. At the same time . . . It comes in me sometimes, when I'm with him. The way knowledge does, or magic. Something rising."

She pressed a hand to her belly, then drew it upward toward her heart. "Just . . . pulling up from the center of me. I never had strong feelings, in this way, for a man. Little flutters of them, you know? Comfortable and interesting, but not strong and hot. There's something about him that compels me. He's so . . ."

"Sexy," Glenna finished. "At the outrageous level."

"I wanted to know if it would be like it had been the other time, the only time, when we'd both been so angry and he'd taken hold of me. I told him to do it again, and wouldn't take no for an answer."

She cocked her head now, as if puzzling it out. "Do you know, I think I made him nervous. Seeing him flustered a bit, and trying not to be, that was as intoxicating to me as the wine had been."

"God yes." On a long breath, Glenna picked up her tea. "It would be."

"And when he kissed me it was like the other time, only more. Because I was waiting for it. For that moment, he was as much caught as I was. I knew it."

"What are you looking for from him, Moira?"

"I don't know. Perhaps just that heat, just that power. That pleasure. Is it wrong?"

"I can't say." But it worried her. "He'd never be able to give you more. You have to understand that. He wouldn't stay here, and even if he did, for a time, you could never have a life with him. You're stepping onto dangerous ground."

"Every day from now till Samhain is dangerous ground. I know what you're saying is good, solid sense, but still in my mind and heart I want. I need to let them both settle a bit before I know what should be done about it next. But I do know that I don't want to go into battle stepping back from this only because I'm afraid of what it could be, or what it couldn't."

After a moment's debate, Glenna sighed. "It may be good solid sense, but I very much doubt I'd take my own advice if I were in your place."

Reaching over, Moira took Glenna's hand. "It helps, being able to talk to another woman. Just to be able to say what's in my mind and heart to another woman."

In another part of Geall, in a house shrouded against even the weak and watery light, two other females sat and talked.

It was the end of their day, not the beginning, but they shared a quiet meal.

Quiet because the man they were draining was beyond protest or struggle.

"You were right." Lora leaned back, delicately dabbing blood from her lips with a linen cloth. The man had been chained to the table between them as Lilith wanted her injured companion to sit, to eat, rather than lie in bed and sip from cups. "Getting up, having a civilized kill was what I needed."

"There, you see." Pleased, Lilith smiled.

Lora's face was still badly burned. The holy water that bitch of a demon hunter had hurled at her had wreaked terrible damage. But Lora was healing, and the good fresh meal would help her get her strength back.

"I wish you'd eat a little more though."

"I will. You've been so good to me, Lilith. And I failed you."

"You didn't. It was a good plan, and nearly worked. It's you who paid such a high price for it. I can't stand to think of the pain you were in."

"I would have died without you."

They had been lovers and friends, competitors and adversaries. They had been everything to each other for four centuries. But Lora's injuries, the near end of her, had brought them closer than they'd ever been.

"Until you were hurt, I didn't know how much I loved

and needed you. Here now, sweetheart, just a little more."

Lora obeyed, taking the man's limp arm, sinking her fangs into the wrist.

Before the burns, she'd been pretty, a youthful blonde with a swaggering style. Now her face was raw and red, riddled with half-healed wounds. But the glassy glaze of pain had faded from her blue eyes, and her voice was coming back strong again.

"It was wonderful, Lilith." She sat back again. "But I just can't drink another drop."

"Then I'll have it taken away, and we'll sit by the fire for a bit before bed."

Lilith rang a little gold bell, signaling one of the servants to clear. The leftovers, she knew, would hardly go to waste.

She rose to help Lora across the room where she'd already had pillows and a throw placed on the sofa.

"More comfortable than the caves," Lilith commented. "But still I'll be glad to be out of this place, and into proper accommodations."

She settled Lora before she sat, regal in her red gown, her hair piled high and gold as she'd wanted to add a touch of glamour to the evening.

Her beauty hadn't diminished in the two thousand years since her death.

"Do you have pain?" she asked Lora.

"No. I feel almost myself. I'm sorry I behaved so childishly yesterday morning, when that bitch flew over on her ridiculous dragon-man. Seeing her again just brought it all flooding back, all the fear, the agony."

"We gave her a surprise though, didn't we?" Soothing, Lilith smoothed the throw, tucking it around Lora. "Imagine her shock when her arrows met Midir's shield. You were right to talk me out of killing him."

"The next time I see her, I won't weep and hide under the covers like a frightened child. The next time I see her, she dies, by my hand. I swear it."

"Do you still have a yearning to change her, for a playmate?"

"I'd never give that whore such a gift." Lora's mouth tightened on a snarl. "She'll get only death from me." Then with a sigh, Lora laid her head on Lilith's shoulder. "She would never have been what you are to me. I thought to have a bit of fun with her. And I thought she'd be entertaining for both of us in bed—all that energy and violence inside her was so appealing. But I could never have loved her as I love you."

She tilted her head up now so their lips met in a long, soft kiss. "I'm yours, Lilith. Eternally."

"My sweet girl." Lilith pressed another kiss to Lora's temple. "Do you know when I first saw you, sitting alone on the dark, damp streets of Paris, weeping, I knew you'd belong to me."

"I thought I loved a man," Lora murmured. "And he loved me. But he used me, spurned me, tossed me aside for another. I thought my heart was broken. Then you were there."

"Do you remember what I said to you?"

"I will never forget. You said, 'My sweet, sad girl, are you all alone?' I told you my life was over, that I would be dead of grief by morning."

Lilith laughed, stroked Lora's hair. "So dramatic. How could I resist you?"

"Or I you. You were so beautiful—like the queen you are. You wore red, as you do tonight, and your hair so bright, all curls. You took me to your house, and fed me bread and wine, and listened to my sad tale and dried my tears."

"So young and charming you were. So sure this man who had cast you aside was all you could ever want."

"I don't remember his name now. Or his face."

"You came so willingly into my arms," Lilith murmured. "I asked if you would wish to stay young and lovely forever, if you would wish to have power over men like the one who hurt you. You said yes, and yes again. Even when I tasted you, you held tight to me and said again, yes and yes."

Hints of red stained the whites of Lora's eyes as she remembered that magnificent moment. "I'd never known such a thrill."

"When you drank from me, I loved you as I had no other."

"And when I lived again, you brought him to me, so I could have the one who scorned me for my first kill. We shared him, as we've shared so much."

"When Samhain comes, we will share all there is."

While the vampires slept, Moira stood on the playing field. She was filthy and drenched. Her hip throbbed from a blow that had slipped past her guard, and her breath was still wheezing out of her lungs from the last bout.

She felt wonderful.

She held out a hand to help Dervil to her feet. "You did very well," Moira told her. "You nearly had me."

Wincing, Dervil rubbed her ample rump. "I think not."

Hands on hips, her head covered with a wide-brimmed and now sodden leather hat, Glenna surveyed both of them. "You stayed on your feet longer this time, and got back on them quicker." She nodded approval at Dervil. "Improvement. From what I'm told there are several men on the other side of this field that you could take."

"There are several men on the other side of the field she *has* taken," Isleen called out, and got a number of bawdy laughs.

"And I know what to do with them when I take them," Dervil retorted.

"Put some of that energy into your next match," Glenna suggested, "and you might win it instead of ending up in the mud. Let's finish up with some archery practice, and call this a day."

Even as the women responded with relief that the session was nearly done, Moira waved a hand. "I haven't yet met Ceara in hand-to-hand. I've been saving what I'm told is the best for last. So I can retire full champion from the field."

"Cocky. I like it." Blair spoke as she moved through the rain and the mud. "Weapon details moving along," she added. "We've kicked production up a notch." She tipped back her head. "Let me tell you, this rain feels great after a couple hours with an anvil and forge. So, what's the score here?"

"Moira's taken all comers with sword and hand-to-hand. She's challenged Ceara here to a bout before we finish up with bows."

"Good enough. I can take a group to the targets while you finish up here."

There was immediate and vocal protest from the women who were eager to watch the last match.

"Blood-thirsty." Blair nodded approval. "I like that, too. All right, ladies, give them room. Who's your money on?" she murmured to Glenna as the two women squared off.

"Moira's hot, and motivated. She's just plowed through the field today. I'd have to put my money on her."

"I'll take Ceara. She's tricky, and she's not afraid to take a hit. See," she added when Ceara went sprawling facedown in the mud, and sprang up again to charge.

She feinted, pivoting at the last minute, then swept up a foot to catch Moira mid-body. The queen shot back from the hit, managed to catch her balance and duck the next blow. She came up hard, flipped Ceara over her shoulder. But when she spun around, Ceara wasn't flat on her back, but had pumped off her own hands, and striking out with her feet, kicked Moira into the mud.

Moira was up quickly, and with a light in her eyes. "Well now, your reputation hasn't been exaggerated, I see."

"I'm after the prize." Ceara crouched, circled. "Be warned."

"Come get it then."

"Good fight," Blair commented as fists and feet and bodies flew. "Ceara, keep your elbows up!"

Glenna jabbed Blair with her own. "No coaching from

the peanut gallery." But she was smiling, not just because it was a good, strong fight, but because the rest of the women were shouting and calling out advice.

They'd made themselves a unit.

Moira fell back, scissored out her legs and swept Ceara's from under her. But when she rolled up again to pin her opponent, Ceara thrust up and flipped Moira over her head.

There were several sounds of sympathy as Moira landed with a bone-rattling thud. Before she could shove up again, Ceara was straddling her, an elbow to Moira's throat, and a fist to her heart.

"You're staked."

"Damn me, I am. Get off me, gods' pity, you're crushing my lungs."

She sucked in breath as she struggled to push her still vibrating body into a sitting position. Ceara simply dropped down to sit in the mud beside her, and the two of them panted and eyed each other.

"You're a great bitch in battle," Moira said at length.

"The same to you, with all respect, my lady. I've bruises on top of my bruises now, and knots on top of those."

Moira swiped some of the mud from her face with her forearm. "I wasn't fresh."

"That's true, but I could take you fresh as well."

"I think you're right. You won the prize, Ceara, and won it fair. I'm proud to have been bested by you."

She offered her hand, and after shaking it, raised it high. "Here's the champion of the hand-to-hand."

There were cheers, and in the way of women, hugs. But when Ceara offered a hand to help Moira to her feet, Moira waved her off. "I'm just going to sit here another minute, catch my breath. Go on, get your bow. And with that you nor any will best me."

"It couldn't be done if we had a thousand years. Your Majesty?"

"Aye? Oh God, I won't sit easy for a week," she added, rubbing her sore hip.

"I've never been prouder of my queen."

Moira smiled to herself, then simply sat quiet, taking stock of her aches and pains. Then her gaze was drawn up to the spot where she'd stood with Cian the night before.

And there he was, standing in the gloom and the rain, looking down at her. She could feel the force of him through the distance, the allure he exuded, she thought, as other men never could.

"So what are you looking at?" she said to herself. "Is it amusing to you to see me on my arse in the mud?"

Probably, she decided, and who could blame him? She imagined she made quite the picture.

"We'll have a match of our own, I'm thinking, sooner or later. Then we'll see who bests who."

She pushed herself to her feet, gritted her teeth against the need to limp. So she could walk away steady, and without a backward glance.

Chapter 6

After scraping off an acre of mud, Moira joined the others for a strategy session. She walked in at that tenuous point between discussion and argument.

"I'm not saying you can't handle yourself." Larkin's tone as he addressed Blair had taken on that last ragged edge of patience. "I'm saying Hoyt and I can manage this."

"And I'm saying three would get it done faster than two."

"What would that be?" Moira asked.

The answer came from several sources, with steadily rising voices.

"I can't make much of that out." She held up a hand for peace as she took her seat at the table. "Am I understanding that we're after sending a party out to set up a base near the battlefield, scouting as they go?"

"With the first troops moving out behind them, in the morning," Hoyt finished. "We have locations marked where shelter can be found. Here," he said, tapping the map spread out on the table. "A day's march east. Then another, a day's march from that."

"But the fact is, with Lilith dug in here." Blair laid her fist on the map. "She's taken the advantage of primo location and facilities. We can crisscross our bases, establish a kind of jagged front line. But we need to start moving troops, and we need to secure bases for them before we send them out. Not only along the route, but at the best points near the valley."

"True enough." Considering, Moira studied the map. She saw how it was meant to work, with daylight jumps from position to position. "Larkin can cover the distance faster than any—we'd agree on that?"

"The way things are. But if we recruited other dragons—"

"Blair, I've said that can't be."

"Dragons?" Moira held up a hand again to silence Larkin's interruption. "What do you mean?"

"When Larkin shape-shifts he can communicate, at least on a rudimentary level, with what he becomes," Blair began.

"Aye. And?"

"So if he calls other dragons when he's in that form, why couldn't he convince some of them to follow him—with riders?"

"They're peaceful, gentle creatures," Larkin interrupted. "They shouldn't be drawn into something like this where they could be harmed."

"Wait, wait." Rolling it over in her mind, Moira sat back. "Could it be done? I've seen some take a baby in as a kind of pet from time to time, but I've never heard of anyone riding a full-grown dragon except in stories. If it could be done, it would allow us to travel swiftly, and even by night. And in battle . . ."

She broke off when she saw Larkin's expression. "I'm sorry, truly. But we can't be sentimental about it. The dragon is a symbol of Geall, and Geall needs its symbols. We ask our people, our women, the young ones, the old ones, to fight and to sacrifice. If such a thing could be done, it should be done."

"I don't know if it can be."

Moira knew when Larkin was being mule-headed. "You'll need to try. We love our horses, too, Larkin," Moira reminded him. "But we'll ride them into this. Now, Hoyt, would you tell me plain, is it best for you and Larkin to go on your own, or for the three of you to do this?"

He looked pained. "Well, you've put me between the wolf and the tiger, haven't you? Larkin's concerned that Blair's not fully recovered from the attack."

"I'm good to go," she insisted, then punched Larkin—not so lightly—in the arm. "Want to go one-on-one with me, cowboy, and find out?"

"Her ribs still pain her by end of day, and the shoulder that was hurt is weak yet."

"I'll show you weak."

"Now, now, children." Glenna managed to sound light and sarcastic. "I'm going to stick my neck into this. Blair's fit for duty. Sorry, honey," she said to Larkin, "but we really can't keep her on the disabled list."

"It would be best if she went." Hoyt sent a look of sympathy toward Larkin. "With three, we shouldn't need to be gone more than a day. The first troops could be sent out at first light, and make their way to the first post."

"That leaves three of us here to continue to work and train and prepare." Moira nodded. "This would be best. Would you think Tynan should lead those first troops, Larkin?"

"Do you ask as a sop to my wounded pride, or because you want my opinion of it?"

"Both."

She charmed a reluctant laugh out of him. "Then, aye, he'd be the one for it."

"We should get started." Blair glanced around the table. "With the time Larkin can make in the air, we'd be able to set up the first base, maybe the first two, before nightfall."

"Take whatever you need," Moira told them. "I'll speak to Tynan, and have him lead the first troops out at dawn."

"She'll be expecting you." Cian spoke for the first time since Moira had entered. "If Lilith hasn't thought of this move, one of her advisors would have. She'll have troops posted to intercept and ambush."

Blair nodded. "Figured that. It's why we're better with three, and coming from the air. They won't take us by surprise, but we might just take them."

"Better chance of that if you come from this direction." He got up to come around to the map and illustrate. "Circle around, come at the first location from the east or the north. More time, of course, but they'd likely be watching for you from this direction."

"Good point," Blair acknowledged, then gave Larkin a considering frown. "Hoyt and I could put down, out of sight, and send our boy here to get the lay. Maybe as a bird, or some animal they wouldn't think twice about seeing in the area. Have to take extra provisions," she added, "the way he burns up the fuel with the changes, but better safe than otherwise."

"Keep it small," Cian warned Larkin. "If you go as a deer or any sort of game, they might shoot you for sport or an extra meal. They'll be bored by this time, I'd imagine. If the weather there's as it's been here today, they'll likely be inside or under shelter. We don't care to be drenched any more than humans do."

"Okay, we'll work it out." Blair got to her feet. "Any magic tricks up your sleeve," she said to Hoyt, "don't forget to pack them."

"Be careful." Glenna fussed with Hoyt's cloak as they stood at the gates.

"Don't worry."

"Goes with the territory." She held both hands on his cloak as she looked up into his eyes. "We've stuck pretty tight together since this started, you and I. I wish I were going with you."

"You're needed here." He touched her cross, then his own. "You'll know where I am, and how I am. Two days, at most. I'll come back to you."

"Make damn sure of it." She pulled him to her, kissed him hard and long while her heart trembled. "I love you. Be safe."

"I love you. Be strong. Now go inside, out of the rain."

But she waited while Larkin shimmered into the dragon, then Hoyt and Blair loaded on the packs and weapons. She waited while they vaulted on the dragon's back, and rose up, flying through the gray curtain of rain.

"It's hard," Moira said from behind her, "to be the one who waits."

"Horrible." She reached back, took a strong grip on Moira's hand. "So keep me busy. We'll go in, have our first lesson." They turned, walked away from the gates. "Do you remember when you first knew you had power?"

"No. It wasn't definite, as it was with Larkin. It was more that I sometimes knew things. Where to find something that was lost. Or where someone was hiding if we were playing a game. But it always seemed it could have been as much luck, or just good sense as anything else."

"Was your mother gifted?"

"She was. But softly, if you understand me. A kind of empathy, you could say. A gift for growing things." Idly she tossed her braid behind her shoulder. "You've seen the gardens here, and those were her doing. If she was able to attend a birth or help at a sick bed, she could bring comfort and ease. I thought of what she had, and what I have, as a kind of woman's magic. Empathy, intuition, healing."

They stepped through the archway, moved to the stairs. "But since I began to work with you and Hoyt, I felt more. Like a stirring. It seemed to me it was a kind of echo, or reflection of the stronger power both of you have. Then I took hold of the sword."

"A talisman, or conduit," Glenna speculated. "Or more simply a key that opened a door to what was already in you."

She led the way into the room where she and Hoyt worked. It wasn't so different from the tower room in Ireland. Bigger, Moira thought, and with an arched doorway that led to one of the castle's many balconies.

But the scents were the same, herbs and ash and something that was a mix of floral and metallic. A number of Glenna's crystals were set around on tables and chests. As much Moira supposed for aesthetics as for magical purposes.

There were bowls and vials and books.

And crosses—silver, wood, stone, copper—hung at every opening to the outside.

"Damp and chilly in here," Glenna commented. "Why don't you light the fire?"

"Oh, of course." But when Moira started across to the wide stone hearth, Glenna laughed and grabbed her hand.

"No, not like that. Fire. It's elemental, one of the basic skills. To practice magic, we utilize the elements, nature. We respect them. Light the fire from here, with me."

"I wouldn't know how to begin."

"With yourself. Mind, heart, belly, bone and blood. See the fire, its colors and shapes. Feel the heat of it, smell the smoke and burning turf. Take that from your mind, from inside you, and put it in the hearth."

Moira did as she was told, and though she felt something ripple along her skin, the turf remained quiet and cold.

"I'm sorry."

"No. It takes time, energy and focus. And it takes faith. You don't remember taking your first steps, pulling yourself up with your mother's skirts or on a table, or how many times you fell before you stood. Take your first step, Moira. Hold out your right hand. Imagine the fire lighting inside you, hot, bright. It flows out, up from your belly, through your heart, down your arm to your fingertips. See it, feel it. Send it where you will."

It was almost a trance, Glenna's quiet voice and that building of heat. A stronger ripple now, under her skin, over it. And a weak tongue of flame spurted along a brick of turf.

"Oh! It was a flash inside my head. But you did most of it."

"A little of it," Glenna corrected. "Just a little push."

Moira blew out a long breath. "I feel I've run up a mountain."

"It'll get easier."

Watching the fire catch hold, Moira nodded. "Teach me."

By the end of two hours, Moira felt as though she'd not only climbed a mountain, but had fallen off one—on her head. But she'd learned to call and somewhat control two of the four elements. Glenna had given her a list of simple spells and charms to practice on her own.

Homework, Glenna had called it, and the scholar in Moira was eager to apply herself to it.

But there were other matters to be seen to. She changed to more formal attire, fixed the mitre of her office on her head, and went to meet with her uncle regarding finance.

Wars cost coin.

"Many had to leave their crops unharvested," Riddock told her. "Their flocks and herds untended. Some will surely lose their homes."

"We'll help them rebuild. There will be no tax or levy imposed for two years."

"Moira—"

"The treasury will stand it, Uncle. I can't sit on gold and jewels, no matter what their history, while our people sacrifice. I would melt the royal crown of Geall first. When this is done, I will plant crops. Fifty acres. Another fifty for grazing. What comes from it will be given back to those who fought, the families of any who perished or were injured serving Geall."

He rubbed his own aching head. "And how will you know who has served and who has hidden themselves away?"

"We'll believe. You think I'm naive and softhearted. Perhaps I am. Some of that will be needed from a queen when this is done. I can't be naive and softhearted now, and I must push and prod and ask my people to give and give. I ask a great deal of you. You're here, while strangers turn your home into a barracks."

"It's nothing."

"It's very much, and won't be the last I ask of you. Oran marches tomorrow."

"He's spoken to me." There was pride in Riddock's voice, though his eyes were heavy with sorrow. "My younger son is a man, and must be a man."

"Being yours he could be no less. For now, even as troops begin to march, work has to continued here. Weapons must be forged, people must be fed and housed. Trained. Whatever is required you have leave to spend. But . . ." She smiled now, thinly. "If any merchant or craftsman seeks too heavy a profit, he will have an audience with the queen."

Riddock returned her smile. "Very well. Your mother would be proud of you."

"I hope she would. I think of her every day." She rose, and the gesture brought him to his feet. "I must go to my aunt. She's so good to stand as chantelain these weeks."

"She enjoys it."

"I wonder that she could. The kitchens, the laundry, the sewing, the cleaning. It's beyond my ken with so many to tend. I'd be lost without her."

"She'll be pleased to hear it. But she tells me you come, every day, to speak with her, and to tour those kitchen, the laundry. Just as I'm told you go speak to the smithies, the young ones you have carving stakes. And today you trained with the other women."

"I never thought my office would be an idle one."

"No, but you need rest, Moira. Your eyes are shadowed."

She told herself to ask Glenna to teach her to do a glamour. "There's time enough to rest when this is done."

She spent an hour with her aunt going over household accounts and duties, then another speaking with some of those who performed those duties.

When she started toward the parlor with the idea of a light meal and a vat of tea, she heard Cian's laugh.

It relieved her to know he was keeping Glenna company, but she wondered if she herself had the energy to deal with him after such a long day.

She caught herself turning away, felt a quick flare of anger. Did she need a headful of wine just to sit comfortably in the same room with him? What sort of coward was she?

Straightening her spine, she strode in to see Glenna and Cian sitting by the fire with fruit and tea.

They looked so easy with each other, Moira thought. Did Glenna find it comforting or strange that Cian looked so like his brother? Little differences, of course. That cleft in Cian's chin his brother lacked. And his face was leaner than Hoyt's, his hair shorter.

There was his posture, and his movements. Cian always seemed at his ease, and walked with a near animal fluidity.

She liked watching him move, Moira admitted. He always put her in mind of something exotic—beautiful in its way, and just as lethal.

He knew she was there, she was sure. She'd yet to see anything or anyone come up on him with him unaware. But he continued to slouch in the chair where most men would rise when a woman—much less a queen—entered the room.

It was like his shrug, she thought. A deliberate carelessness. She wished she didn't find that so appealing as well.

"Am I interrupting?" she asked as she crossed the room.

"No." Glenna shifted to smile at her. "I asked for enough for three, hoping you'd have time. Cian's just been entertaining me with stories of Hoyt's exploits as a child."

"I'll leave you ladies to your tea."

"Please don't go." Before he could rise, Glenna took his arm. "You've been working hard to keep me from worrying."

"If you knew it, I wasn't working hard enough."

"You gave me a breather, and it's appreciated. Now, if everything's gone as planned, they should be at the projected base. I need to look." Her hand was steady as she poured tea for Moira. "I think it would be better if we all looked."

"Can you help them if . . ." Moira let it trail off.

"Hoyt's not the only one with magic up his sleeve. But I'll be able to see more clearly, and help if necessary if the two of you work with me. I know you've had a long one, Moira."

"They're my family as well."

With a nod, Glenna rose. "I brought what I thought I'd need." She retrieved her crystal globe, some smaller crystals, some herbs. These she arranged on the table between them. Then she took off her cross, circled the ball with its chain.

"So." She kept her voice light, placed her hands over the ball. "Let's see what they're up to."

It had rained across Geall, making the trip a small misery. They'd circled wide, coming down nearly a quarter mile east of the farm they intended to use for a base. Its location was prime, nearly equidistant from the land Lilith now occupied and the field of battle.

Because it was, Cian's assumption that it would be laid for ambush rang true.

The two riders dismounted from the dragon's back, then off-loaded packs and supplies. There was some cover—the low stone wall separating the fields, and the scatter of trees that ran with it.

Nothing stirred in the rain.

Dragon turned to man, and Larkin scooped both hands through his dripping hair. "Filthy day all in all. You saw the goal right enough?"

"Two-story cottage," Blair answered. "Three outbuildings, two paddocks. Sheep. No smoke or sign of life, no horses. If they're there, they'd have guards posted, a couple in each building, most likely. Taking shifts while the others sleep. They'd need food, so they may have prisoners. Or if they're traveling light, they'd have what they need in canteens—water bags."

"I could risk a look," Hoyt said. "If she sent along any with power though, they could sense it, and us."

"Simpler if I take a run at it." Larkin paused to crunch into an apple. The long trip had hunger gnawing at his belly. "They wouldn't put up the shield, as they have around their main base. Not if they're hoping to snatch some of us if and when we come along."

"Go in small," Blair reminded him. "Cian had a good point about that."

"Aye, well." He stuffed some bread in his mouth. "A mouse is small enough and worked before. It'll take longer than it would as wolf or deer." He slipped off his cross. "You'll need to keep this for me."

"I hate this part." Blair took the cross. "I hate you going in without a weapon or shield."

"Have a little faith." He cupped her chin, kissed her. Then stepping back changed into a small field mouse.

"Can't believe I just kissed that," Blair muttered, then closed her hand tight over his cross as the mouse streaked across the grass. "Now we wait."

"Best if we take precautions. I'll cast a circle."

Larkin was nearly to the first outbuilding when he spotted the wolf. It was large and black, crouched in a thicket of berries. It paid no mind to him while its red eyes scanned the field and the road to the west. Still, he gave it a wide berth before squirming under the doorway.

It was a rough stable, and there were two horses in the stalls. And two vampires seated on the floor having a game of dice. The mouse cocked its head in some surprise. Larkin hadn't considered vampires would game. The wolf, he deduced, was their outlook. A signal from it, and they'd come to action. But for now, they were too involved in the dice to notice a small mouse.

There were swords, and two full quivers with bows. Inspired, he dashed over to where the bows rested against a stall. And busily gnawed at the strings.

One vampire was cursing his fellow's luck when Larkin scrambled out again.

He found similar setups in each building, with the main body of the troop in the cottage. Though he smelled blood, he saw no human. In the cottage, four vampires slept in the loft while five others kept watch.

He did what could be done by a mouse to sabotage, then hurried away again.

He found Hoyt and Blair where he'd left them, sitting now on a damp blanket in a circle that simmered low. "Fifteen by my count," he told them. "And a wolf. We'd need to get past that one for any chance at taking the others by surprise."

"Have to be quiet then." Blair picked up a bow. "And from downwind. Hoyt, if Larkin can give me the exact position, is there a way you can help me see it?"

"I can give you the exact position," Larkin said before Hoyt spoke, "because we'll be going together now. You won the round to come, but you won't go into that nest of demons alone."

"She won't, no. Of the three of us, you've the best hand with a bow, so you'll take the shot," Hoyt told Blair. "But we'll be covering your flank while you're at it. I'll do what I can to help you get a clear shot."

"No point in arguing that one moves faster and quieter than three? Didn't think so," Blair said when she met stony silence. "Let's move out then."

They had to circle widely to keep out of sight, and prevent their scent from carrying. But when they came up behind the wolf, Blair shook her head. "I don't think I can get the heart from here. Moira, maybe, but I'm not that good. Gonna take more than one shot."

She thought it over, saw how it could best be done.

"You take the first one," she whispered to Larkin. "Get as close as you can. If it rears or rolls, shifts around, I can take it. One, two," she added, using her fingers. "Has to be fast, has to be quiet."

He nodded, pulled an arrow from the quiver, notched it in his bow. It was a long shot for him, and the angle poor. But he took aim, breathed out, breathed in. And let the arrow fly.

It took the wolf between the shoulder blades, and its body jerked up. Blair's arrow struck home.

"Nice work," she said as black smoke and ash flew.

Hoyt started to speak, then Glenna's voice sounded in his head as clearly as if she'd been standing beside him.

Behind you!

He spun, pivoted. A second wolf leaped, its body slamming Hoyt aside, knocking him to the ground as it fell on Larkin. Man and wolf grappled, an instant only. Even as Blair drew her sword, and Hoyt his, the wolf was rolled beneath a bear.

The bear's claws swiped, slicing deep across the throat. There was a gush of blood. The bear collapsed on the black ash, and became a man again.

Blair dropped to her knees, running her hands frantically over Larkin. "Are you bit? Are you bit?"

"No. Scratched up here and there. No bites. Ah, the stench of that one." Out of breath, he pushed to his elbows, looked down in disgust at his bloody shirt. "Ruined a good hunting tunic." He looked over at Hoyt. "All right then?"

"I might not have been. Glenna. They must be watching. I heard her in my head." Hoyt held out a hand to help Larkin to his feet. "If you wear that, they'll smell us a half league away. You'll need to . . . wait, wait." And his smile came slow and grim. "I've an idea."

The black wolf crouched over the bloody figure, and from outside the rear of the stables, sent out a low howl. In moments, a vampire armed with a battle-ax opened the door.

"What do we have here?" He glanced over his shoulder. "One of the wolves brought us a present."

Facedown, Hoyt let out a quiet moan.

"It's still alive. Let's get it inside. No need to share it with the others, right? I could use something fresh for a change."

As they stepped out, the second spared the wolf a brief grin. "Yeah, good dog. Let's just have a—"

He exploded into ash as Blair rammed the stake through

his back and into his heart. The second didn't have time to lift his ax before Hoyt sprang off the ground and sliced his sword through its neck.

"Yeah, good dog." Blair mimicked the vampire, and added a quick ruffle of Larkin's fur. "I say we stick with a winner, use the same gambit on the next outbuilding."

They had nearly identical results with the second building, but on the third, only one came out. It was obvious by the way he glanced surreptitiously back at his post that he intended to keep the unexpected meal for himself. When he rolled Hoyt over, the unexpected meal put a stake through his heart.

Using hand signals now, Blair indicated she would go in first, with Hoyt covering her.

Quick and quiet, she thought as she slipped inside. She saw the other guard had made himself a cozy nest with blankets and was taking an afternoon nap in what she thought was a dovecote.

He was actually snoring.

She had to bite back the half a dozen smart remarks that trembled on her tongue, and simply staked him while he slept.

She blew out a long breath. "I don't mean to complain, but this is almost embarrassing, and a little bit boring."

"You're disappointed we're not fighting for our lives?" Hoyt asked.

"Well, yeah. Some."

"Take heart." Larkin stepped in, surveyed the area. "There are nine in the cottage, where we'll be severely outnumbered."

"Ah, thanks, honey. You always know just what to say to perk me up." She hefted the battle-ax she'd taken from the first kill. "Let's go kick some ass."

Bellied down behind a water trough, Blair and Hoyt studied the cottage. The wounded man/wolf gambit wasn't going to work here, and the alternate they'd agreed on was risky.

"He's already gone through a lot of changes," Blair murmured. "It starts taking a toll."

"He ate four honey cakes."

She nodded, hoping it was fuel enough as the dragon landed lightly on the thatched roof. Larkin shimmered free of it, then picked up the scabbard and the sheath for his stake. He signaled down to them before swinging down to peer in one of the second-story windows.

Apparently, Blair thought, he didn't have to change into a monkey to climb like one. Larkin held up four fingers.

"Four up, five down." She moved into a crouch. "Ready?"

Keeping low, they rushed to either side of the doorway. As agreed, she counted to ten. Then kicked in the door.

With the battle-ax, she decapitated the one on her right, then used the staff of it to block the hack of a sword. Out of the corner of her eye she saw a ball of fire flash into Hoyt's hand. Something screamed.

From overhead, Larkin and a vampire flew off the loft to land hard on the floor. She tried to hack her way to him, took a hard kick in her healing ribs. The pain and the force knocked her back into a table that broke beneath her weight.

She used the splintered leg to dust the one that leaped on her. Then she threw the makeshift stake, striking one that rushed Hoyt from behind. She missed the heart, swore and shoved herself breathlessly to her feet.

Hoyt thrust out with a back kick that made her warrior's heart sing. When the vampire fell, Larkin finished it with a sword clean through the throat.

"How many?" Blair shouted. "How many?"

"I took two," Hoyt said.

"Four, by the gods." Even as he grinned, he was grabbing Blair's arm. "How bad?"

"Off my game. Caught my ribs. I only got two. There's another left."

"Gone out the window above. Here, sit, sit. Your arm's bleeding as well."

"Shit." She looked down, saw the gash she hadn't felt. "Shit. Your nose is bleeding, mouth, too. Hoyt?"

"A few nicks." He limped toward them. "I don't think we'd need worry overmuch about the one that escaped. But I'll be doing a spell to revoke any invitation. Let me see what I can do for your arm."

"Spell first." Breathing through her teeth, she looked at Larkin. "Four, huh?"

"It seems two of them were mating, and distracted with it when I came through the window. So I had them both with one blow."

"Maybe we should only count that as one."

"Oh, no, we won't." He finished tying a field dressing on her wounded arm, swiped blood from under his own nose. "Jesus, I'm starving."

It made her laugh, and despite her aching ribs, she wrapped her arms around him to hug.

"They're fine." Glenna let out a shuddering breath. "A little battered, a little bloody, but fine. And safe. Sorry, sorry. But watching it like this, not being able to help . . . I'm just going to have a short breakdown."

As promised, she buried her face in her hands and wept.

Chapter 7

✦

Escaping, Cian left Glenna to Moira. In his experience, women dealt best with women's tears. His own
reaction to what they'd seen in the crystal hadn't been fear,
or relief, but sheer and simple frustration.

He'd been delegated to do no more than watch while
others fought. Cozied in the bloody parlor with women and
teacups, like someone's aged grandfather.

While the training sessions were some level of entertainment, he hadn't had a good fight since they'd left Ireland. Hadn't had a woman in longer than that. Two very
satisfying ways of releasing tension and energy had been
denied to him—or he was denying them to himself.

Hardly a wonder, he thought, he was tied up in nasty
knots over a pair of steady gray eyes.

He could seduce a serving girl, but that was fraught with
complications and probably not worth the time or effort.
He could hardly pick a fight with one of the very handy humans, which was too damn bad.

If he went out on a hunt he could likely scare up at least
one or two of Lilith's troops. But he couldn't rev himself

up to go out into the endless rain on the chance of a lucky kill.

At least back in his own time, his own world, he'd had work to occupy him. Women if he wanted one, of course, but work to pass the time. The endless time.

With none of those options available to him, he closed himself in his room. He fed, and he slept.

And he dreamed as he hadn't dreamed in decades and more of hunting human.

The strong and salty scent of them stung the air, rising as even their puny and smothered instincts warned them they were prey.

It was a seductive and primitive perfume to stir needs in the belly and in the blood.

She was only a whore, working the alleyways of London. Young though, and fair enough despite her trade, which told him it was unlikely she'd been at it very long. As the aroma of sex clung to her, he knew she'd made a few coppers that night.

He could hear tinny music and the raucous, drunken laughter from some gin parlor, and the clopping of a carriage horse moving away. All distant—too distant for her human ears to catch. And too distant for her human legs to run, if she tried.

She hurried through the thick yellow fog, quickening her pace with nervous glances over her shoulder as he deliberately allowed her to hear his footsteps behind her.

The smell of her fear was intoxicating—so fresh, so alive.

It was so easy to catch her, to cover the squeak of her mouth with his hand—to cover the rabbit-rapid jump of her heart with the other.

So amusing to see her eyes take in his face, young and handsome—the expensive clothing—and go sly, go coy, as he eased his hand from her mouth.

"Sir, you frighten a poor girl. I thought you be a brigand."

"Nothing of the sort." The cultured accent he used was

in direct opposition to squawking cockney. "Simply in need of a little comfort, and willing to pay your price."

With a flutter and a giggle, she named one he knew would be double her usual rate. "For that I think you should make me very comfortable."

"I'm sorry to ask for pay from such a fine and handsome gentleman, but I have to earn my keep, I do. I have a room nearby."

"We won't need it."

"Oh!" She laughed when he pulled up her skirts. "Here, is it?"

With his free hand he yanked down her bodice, covered her breast. He needed to feel her heart, beating, beating, beating. He drove into her, pumping hard so that her bare buttocks slapped against the damp stone wall of the alley. And he saw the shock and surprise in her eyes that he could give her pleasure.

That beat beneath his hand quickened, and her breath went short and expelled on gasps and moans.

He let her come—a small gesture—and let her dazed and sleepy eyes meet his before he showed his fangs.

She screamed—just a quick, high sound he cut off when he sank his fangs into her throat. Her body convulsed, bringing him to a very satisfactory orgasm as he fed. As he killed.

That beating under his hand slowed, stilled. Stopped.

Replete and sated, he left her in the alley with the rats, the price she'd named tossed carelessly beside her. And he strolled away to be swallowed by the thick yellow fog.

He woke in the here and now on an oath. The dream memory had awakened appetites and passions long suppressed. He almost, almost, tasted her blood in his throat, almost smelled the richness of it. In the dark, he trembled a little, an addict in withdrawal, so forced himself to get up and drink what he allowed himself as substitute for human.

It will never satisfy you. It will never fill you. Why do you struggle against what you are?

"Lilith." He said it softly. He recognized the voice in his

head, understood now who and what had put that dream into his mind.

Had it even been his memory? It seemed false now that he was steadier, like a stage play he'd stumbled into. But then he'd killed his share of whores in alleys. He'd killed so many, who could remember the details?

Lilith shimmered into the dark. Diamonds glittered at her throat, her ears, her wrists, even in her luxurious hair. She wore a gown of regal blue trimmed in sable, cut low to highlight the generous mounds of her breasts.

She'd gone to some trouble with her dress and appearance, Cian thought, for this illusionary visit.

"There's my handsome boy," she murmured. "But you look tense and tired. Hardly a wonder with what you've been up to." She wagged her finger playfully. "Naughty of you. But I blame myself. I wasn't able to spend those formative years with you, and as the twig is bent."

"You deserted me," he pointed out. Though he didn't need them, he lighted candles. Then poured himself a cup of whiskey. "Killed me, changed me, set me on my brother, then left me broken at the bottom of the cliffs."

"Where you let him toss you. But you were young, and rash. What could I do?" She tugged her bodice lower to show him the scar of the pentagram. "He burned me. Branded me. I was no good to you."

"And after? The days and months and years after." Odd, he thought, odd to realize he had this resentment, even this hurt buried inside him. Like a child tossed aside by its mother. "You made me, Lilith, birthed me, then left me with less sentiment than an alley cat leaves a deformed kitten."

"You're right, you're right. I can't argue." She wandered the room, lazy sweeps that had the skirts of her gown brushing through a table. "I was careless with you, darling boy. And what did I do but take out my temper for your brother on you. Shame on me!"

Those pretty blue eyes twinkled with merriment, and the curve of her lips was charmingly female. "But you did so well for yourself—initially. Imagine my shock when Lora told me the rumors I'd heard were true, and you'd stopped hunting. Oh, she sends her regards, by the way."

"Does she? I imagine she's a pretty sight at the moment."

Lilith's smile faded, and a hint of red showed in her eyes. "Careful there, or when the time comes it won't just be that fucking demon hunter I rip to pieces."

"Think you can?" He slouched into a chair with his whiskey. "I'd wager you on that, but you wouldn't be able to pay up, being a pile of ash at the end of it."

"I've seen the end of it, in the smoke." She came to him, leaning over the chair—so real he could almost smell her. "This world will burn. I'll have no need of it. Every human on this foolish island will be slaughtered, screaming and drowning in their own blood. Your brother and his circle will die most horribly. I have seen it."

"Your wizard would hardly show you otherwise," Cian said with a shrug. "Were you always so gullible?"

"He shows me *truth*!" She shoved away, her gown sweeping in a furious arch. "Why do you persist in this doomed adventure? Why do you oppose the one who gave you the greatest gift? I came here to offer you a truce—a private and personal agreement, just between you and me. Step away from this, my darling, and you have my pardon. Step away and come to me, and you have not only my pardon but a place at my side come the day. Everything you hunger for and have denied yourself I'll lay at your feet—in repentance for abandoning you when you needed me."

"So, I just go back to my time, my world, and all's forgiven?"

"I give you my word on it. But I'll give you much, much more if you come to me. To me." She purred it, molding her breasts with her hands. "Remember what we shared that night? The spark, the heat of it?"

He watched her run her hands over her body, white against red. "I remember, very well."

"We can have that again, and more. You'll be a prince in

my court. And a general, leading armies instead of slogging through the muck with humans. You'll have your pick of worlds and all their pleasures. An eternity of desires met."

"I remember you promising something along those lines before. Then I was alone, broken and lost, with the graveyard dirt barely washed off me."

"And so this is my penance. Come now, come. You have no place here, Cian. You belong with your own kind."

"Interesting." He tapped his fingers on the side of his cup. "So, all I need do is take your word that you'll reward me rather than torturing and ending me."

"Why would I destroy my own creation?" she replied in reasonable tones. "And one who's proven himself to be a strong warrior?"

"For spite, of course, and because your word is as much an illusion as your appearance here. But I'll give you mine on one vital matter, Lilith, and my word is as hard and as bright as those diamonds you're wearing. It will be I who comes for you. It will be I who does for you."

He picked up a knife and slashed it over his own palm. "I swear it to you, in blood. Mine will be the last face you see."

Fury tightened her face. "You've damned yourself."

"No," he murmured when her image vanished. "You damned me."

It was deep night, and he was done with sleep.

At least at such an hour he could wander where he liked without bumping into servants or courtiers or guards. He'd had enough of company—human and vampire. Still he needed distraction, movement, something to clear away the bitter dregs of the dream, and the visitation that followed it.

He admired the architecture of the castle—something a few steps up, and over into fantasy than what would have been usual when he was alive. It was storybook, inside and out, he mused, with the shifting lights of torches rising from their dragon sconces, the tapestries of faeries and festivals, the polished, jewel-toned marble.

Of course, it hadn't been built as a fortress, but more as a lavish home. Fit, most certainly, for a queen. Until Lilith, Geall had existed in peace and so could focus its energies and intellects on art and culture.

He could, in the quiet and dark, take time to study and admire the art—the paintings and tapestries, the murals and carvings. He could drift through the dark with the perfume of hothouse flowers sweetening the air or wander to the library to peruse the tall shelves.

Since its creation, Geall had been a land for art and books and music rather than warfare and weaponry. How apt, how cold, that both gods and demons should select such a place for bloody war.

The library, as Moira had indicated when falling in love with his own, was a quiet cathedral of books. He'd passed some of his time with a few of them already, and had been both interested and entertained that the stories he'd found there weren't so different from ones written in his own lifetime.

Would Geall, if it survived, produce its own Shakespeare, Yeats, Austen? Would its art go through revivals and renaissance and offer its version of Monet or Degas?

A fascinating thought.

For now, he was too restless, too edgy to settle himself down with a book, and instead moved on. There were rooms he'd yet to explore, and by night he could go wherever he wanted.

As he walked through shadows, the rain drummed steadily.

He moved through what he supposed had been a kind of formal drawing room and was now serving as an armory. He lifted a sword, testing its weight, its balance, its edge. Geall's craftsmen might have devoted their time, previously, to arts, but they knew how to forge a sword.

Time would tell if it would be enough.

Without aim, he turned and stepped into what he saw was a music room.

A gilded harp stood elegantly in one corner. A smaller

cousin, shaped just as a traditional Irish harp, graced a stand nearby. There was a monochord—an early forefather of the piano—enhanced with lovely carving on its soundbox.

He plucked its string idly, pleased its sound was true and clear.

There was a hurdy-gurdy, and when he turned its shaft, slid the bow over its strings, it sang with the mournful music of bagpipes.

There were lutes and pipes, all beautifully crafted. There was comfortable seating, and a pretty hearth from the local marble. A fine room, he mused, for musicians and those who appreciated the art.

Then he saw the vielle. He lifted it. It's body was longer than the violin that would come from it, and it held five strings. When the instruments had been popular, he'd had no interest in such matters. No, he'd been for killing whores in alleyways.

But when a man has eternity, he needs hobbies and pursuits, and years to study them.

He sat with the vielle over his lap, and began to play.

It came back to him, the notes, the sounds, and calmed him as it was said music could do. With the rain as his accompaniment, he let himself fall into the music, drifted away on the tears of it.

She would never have come upon him without him being aware otherwise.

She'd heard it, the quiet sobbing of music as she'd made her own wanderings. She'd followed it like a child follows a piper, then stood just inside the doorway, stunned and enchanted.

So, Moira thought, this is how he looks when he's peaceful, and not just pretending to be. This is how he might have looked before Lilith had taken him, a little dreamy, a little sad, a little lost.

All that had stirred and risen inside her for him seemed to come together inside her heart as she saw him unmasked. Sitting alone, she thought, seeking the comfort of music. She wished she had Glenna's skill with paints or chalk, for she would have drawn him like this. As few, she was sure, had ever seen him.

His eyes were closed, his expression, she would have said, caught somewhere in the misty place between melancholy and contentment. Whatever his thoughts, his fingers were skilled on the strings, long and lean, seducing the instrument into wistful music.

Then it stopped so abruptly she let out a little cry of protest as she stepped forward with her candle. "Oh please, continue, won't you? Sure it was lovely."

He had preferred she come at him with a knife than that innocent, eager smile. She wore only nightrobes, white and pure, with her hair unbound to fall like the rain over her shoulders. The candlelight shifted over her face, full of mystery and romance.

"The floors are cold for bare feet," was all he said, and rose to set the instrument down.

The dreamy look was gone from his eyes, so they were cool again. Frustrated, she set the candle down. "They're my feet, after all. You never said you played."

"There are a lot of things I never said."

"I have no skill at all, to the despair of my mother and every teacher she hired to school me in music. Any instrument I picked up would end by making a sound like a cat being trod on."

She reached over, ran her hand over the strings. "It seemed like magic in your hands."

"I've had more years to learn what interests me than you've been alive. Many times more years."

She looked up now, met his eyes. "True enough, but the time doesn't diminish the art, does it? You have a gift, so why not accept a compliment on it with some grace?"

"Your Majesty." He bowed deeply from the waist. "You honor my poor efforts."

"Oh bugger that," she snapped and surprised a choked laugh out of him. "I don't know why you look for ways to insult me."

"A man must have a hobby. I'll say good night."

"Why? This is your time, isn't it, and you won't seek your bed. I can't sleep. Something cold." She hugged her elbows, shivered once. "Something cold in the air woke me." Because she was watching him, she caught the slight change in his eyes. "What? What do you know? Has something happened. Larkin—"

"It's nothing to do with that. He and the others are well enough as far as I know."

"What then?"

He debated for a moment. His personal desire to be away from her couldn't outweigh what she should know. "It's too cold in here for nighttime confessions."

"Then I'll light the fire." She walked to the hearth, picked up the tinderbox that rested there. "There was always whiskey in that painted cabinet there. I'd have some."

She didn't have to see to know he'd lifted a brow, a gesture of sarcasm, before he crossed to the cabinet.

"Did your mother always fail to teach you that it would be considered improper for you to be sharing a fire and whiskey alone with a man, much less one who is not a man, in the middle of the night?"

"Propriety isn't an immediate concern of mine." She sat back on her haunches, watching for a moment to be sure the turf caught. Then she rose to go to a chair, and held out her hand for the whiskey. "Thanks for that." She took the first swallow. "Something happened tonight. If it concerns Geall, I need to know."

"It concerns me."

"It was something to do with Lilith. I thought it was just my own fears, creeping in while I slept, but it was more than that. I dreamed of her once, more than a dream. You woke me from it."

And had been kind to her after, she remembered. Reluctant, but kind.

"It was something like that," she continued, "but I didn't dream. I only felt . . ."

She broke off, her eyes widening. "No, not just felt. I heard you. I heard you speaking. I heard your voice in my head, and it was cold. *It will be I who does for you.* I heard you say that, so clearly. As I was waking, I thought I would freeze to death if you spoke so cold to me."

And had felt compelled to get out of bed, she thought. Had followed his music to him. "Who was it?"

Later, he decided, he might try to puzzle out how she could hear, or feel, him speak in her dreams. "Lilith."

"Aye." Her eyes on the fire, Moira rubbed a hand up and down her arms. "I knew. There was something dark with the cold. It wasn't you."

"You could be sure?"

"You have a different . . . hue," she decided. "Lilith is black. Thick as pitch. You, well, you're not bright. It's gray and blue. It's twilight in you."

"What is this, an aura thing?"

The chilly amusement in his tone had a flush creeping up her neck. "It's how I see sometimes. Glenna told me to pursue it. She's red and gold, like her hair—if you have an interest in it. Was it a dream? Lilith?"

"No. Though she sent me one that may have been a memory. A whore I fucked and killed in the filth of a London alley." The way he lifted his glass and drank was a callous punctuation to the words. "If it wasn't that particular one, I fucked and killed others, so it hardly matters."

Her gaze never wavered from his. "You think that shocks me. You say it, and in that way, to put something cruel between us."

"There's a great deal of cruelty between us."

"What you did before that night in the clearing in Ireland when you first saved my life isn't between us. It's behind you. Do you think I'm so green I don't know you've had all manner of women, and killed all manner of them as well? You only insult me, and your own choices since by pushing them into the now."

"I don't understand you." What he didn't understand he usually pursued. Understanding was another kind of survival.

"Sure it's not my fault, is it? I make myself plain in

most matters. If she sent you the dream, true or not, it was to disturb you."

"Disturb," he repeated and moved away toward the fire. "You are the strangest creature. It excited me. And it unnerved me, for lack of a better term. That was her purpose, and she succeeded very well."

"And having served her purpose, dug into some vulnerability in you, she came to you. The apparition of her. As Lora did with Blair."

He turned back, holding the whiskey loosely in one hand. "I got an apology, centuries overdue, for her abandonment of me when I was only days into the change, and near dead from Hoyt tossing me off a cliff."

"Perhaps tardiness is relative, given the length of your existence."

Now he did laugh, couldn't stop himself. It was quick and rich and full of appreciation. "Aye, the strangest creature, with a sharp wit buried in there. She offered me a deal. Are you interested to hear it?"

"I am, very interested."

"I have only to walk away from this. You and the others, and what comes on Samhain. I do that, and she'll call it quits between her and me. Better, if I walk away from you, and into her camp, I'll be rewarded handsomely. All and anything I can want, and a place at her side. Her bed as well. And any others I can to take to mine."

Moira pursed her lips, then sipped more whiskey. "If you believe that, you're greener than you think me."

"I was never so green as you."

"No? Well, which of the two of us was green enough to sport with a vampire and let her sink fangs into him?"

"Hah. You've got a point. But then you've never been a randy young man."

"And women, of course, have no interest in carnal matters. We much prefer to sit and do our needlework with prayers running through our heads."

His lips twitched before he shook his head. "Another point. In any case, no longer being a randy young man or with any sprig of green left in me, I'm fully aware Lilith would imprison and torture me. She could keep me alive, as it were, for . . . well, ever. And in unspeakable pain."

He considered it now, his thoughts sparked by the brief debate with Moira. "Or, more likely, she'd keep her word—on sex and other rewards—for as long as it suited her. She would know I'd be useful to her, at least until Samhain."

In agreement, Moira nodded. "She would bed you, lavish gifts on you. Give you position and rank. Then, when it was done, she'd imprison and torture you."

"Exactly. But I have no intention of being tortured for eternity, or being of use to her. She killed a good man I had affection for. If for nothing else, I owe her for King."

"She would have been displeased by your refusal."

He sent Moira a bland look. "You're the queen of understatement tonight."

"Then let me also be the mistress of intuition and say you told her you would make it your mission to destroy her."

"I swore it, in my own blood. Dramatic," he said, glancing at the nearly healed wound on his hand. "But I was feeling theatrical."

"You make light of it. I find it telling. You need her death by your own hands more than you'll say. She doesn't understand that, or you. You need it not just for retribution, but to close a door." When he said nothing, she cocked her head. "Do you think it odd I understand you better than she? Know you, better than she could."

"I think your mind is always working," he replied. "I can all but hear the wheels. It's hardly a surprise you're not sleeping well these past days with all the bloody noise that must go on inside that head of yours."

"I'm frightened." His eyes narrowed on her face, but she wouldn't meet them now. "Frightened to die before I've really lived. Frightened to fail my people, my family, you and the others. When I feel that cold and dark as I did tonight, I know what would become of Geall if she wins this.

Like a void, burned out, hulled, empty and black. And the thought of it frightens me beyond sleep."

"Then the answer must be she can't win."

"Aye. That must be the answer." She set the whiskey aside. "You'll need to tell Glenna what you told me. I think it would be harder to get the answer if there are secrets among us."

"If I don't tell her, you will."

"Of course. But it should come from you. You're welcome to play any of the instruments you like whenever you're moved to. Or if you'd rather be private, you could take any you like to your room."

"Thank you."

She smiled a little as she got to her feet. "I think I could sleep for a bit now. Good night."

He stayed as he was as she retrieved her candle and left him. And stayed hours longer in the fire-lit dark.

In the raw, rainy dawn Moira stood with Tynan as he and the handpicked troops prepared to set out.

"It'll be a wet march."

Tynan smiled at her. "Rain's good for the soul."

"Then our souls must be very healthy after these last days. They can move about in the rain, Tynan." She touched her fingers lightly to the cross painted on his breastplate. "I wonder if we should wait until this clears before you start this journey."

With a shake of his head, he looked beyond her to the others. "My lady, the men are ready. Ready to the point that delay would cut into morale and scrape at the nerves. They need action, even if it's only a long day's march in the rain. We've trained to fight," he continued before she could speak again. "If any come to meet us, we'll be ready."

"I trust you will." Had to trust. If not with Tynan, whom she'd known all of her life, where would she begin? "Larkin and the others will be waiting for you. I'll expect their return shortly after sunset, with word that you arrived safe and have taken up the post."

"You can depend on it, and on me. My lady." He took both her hands.

Because they were friends, because he was the first she would send out, she leaned up to kiss him. "I do depend." She squeezed his fingers. "Keep my cousins out of trouble."

"That, my lady, may be beyond my skills." His gaze shifted from her face. "My lord. Lady."

With her hands still caught in Tynan's, Moira turned to Cian and Glenna.

"A wet day for traveling," Cian commented. "They'll likely have a few troops posted along the way to give you some exercise."

"So the men hope." Tynan glanced over to where nearly a hundred men were saying goodbye to their families and sweethearts, then turned back so his eyes met Cian's. "Are we ready?"

"You're adequate."

Before Moira could snap at the insult, Tynan roared out a laugh. "High praise from you," he said and clasped hands with Cian. "Thank you for the hours, and the bruises."

"Make good use of them. *Slán leat.*"

"*Slán agat.*" He shot Glenna a cocky grin as he mounted. "I'll send your man back to you, my lady."

"See that you do. Blessed be, Tynan."

"In your name, Majesty," he said to Moira, then wheeled his mount. "Fall in!"

Moira watched as the scattered men formed lines. And watched in the rain as her cousin Oran and two other officers rode out, leading her foot soldiers to the first league toward war.

"It begins," she murmured. "May the gods watch over them."

"Better," Cian said, "if they watch over themselves."

Still he stood as she did until the first battalion of Geall's army was out of sight.

Chapter 8

Glenna frowned over her tea as, with Moira's prodding, Cian related his interlude with Lilith. The three of
them took the morning meal together, in private.

"Similar to what happened with Blair then, and with me
back in New York. I'd hoped Hoyt and I had blocked that
sort of thing."

"Possibly you have, on humans," he added. "Vampire to
vampire is likely a different matter. Particularly—"

"When the one intruding is the sire," Glenna finished.
"Yes, I see. Still, there should be a way to shut her out."

"It's hardly worth your time and energies. It's not a
problem for me."

"You say that now, but it upset you."

He glanced at Moira. "Upset is a strong word. In any
case, she left in what we'll call a huff."

"Something good came out of it," Glenna continued.
"For her to come to you, try to deal, she can't be as confident as she'd like to be."

"On the contrary, she believes, absolutely, that she'll
win. Her wizard's shown her."

"Midir? You said nothing of this last night."

"It didn't come up," Cian said easily. In truth, he'd thought long and hard before deciding it should be told. "She claims he's shown her victory, and in my opinion, she believes. Any losses we've dealt her thus far are of little importance to her. Momentary annoyances, slaps to the pride. Nothing more."

"We make destiny with every turn, every choice." Moira kept her eyes level with Cian's. "This war isn't won until it's won, by her, by us. Her wizard tells her, shows her, what she wants to hear, wants to see."

"I agree," Glenna said. "How else would he keep his skin intact?"

"I won't say you're wrong, either of you." With a careless shrug, Cian picked up a pear. "But that kind of absolute belief can be a dangerous weapon. Weapons can be turned against the one who holds them. The deeper we prick under her skin, the more reckless she might be."

"Just what do we use for the needle?" Moira demanded.

"I'm working on that."

"I've something that may work." Glenna narrowed her eyes as she stirred her tea. "If her Midir can open the door for her to come into your head, Cian, I can open it, too. I wonder how Lilith would like a visit."

Biting into the pear, Cian sat back. "Well now, aren't you the clever girl?"

"Yes, I am. I'll need you. Both of you. Why don't we finish off breakfast with a nice little spell?"

It wasn't little, and it wasn't nice. It took Glenna more than an hour to prepare her tools and ingredients.

She ground flourite, turquoise, set them aside. She gathered cornflower and holly, sprigs of thyme. She scribed candles of purple, of yellow. Then set the fire under her cauldron.

"These come from the earth, and now will mix in water." She began to sprinkle her ingredients into the cauldron.

"For dreaming words, for sight, for memory. Moira, would you set the candles in a circle, around the cauldron?"

She continued to work as Moira set the candles. "I've actually been thinking about trying this since what happened with Blair. I've been working it out in my head how it might be done."

"She's hit you hard every time you've used magic to look into her bases," Cian reminded her. "So be sure. I wouldn't enjoy having Hoyt try to toss me off a cliff again because I let something happen to you."

"It won't be me—at least not front line." She brushed her hair back as she looked over at him. "It'll be you."

"Well then, that's perfect."

"It's risky, so you're the one who has to be sure."

"Well, it's the guts and glory business, isn't it?" He moved forward to peer into the cauldron. "And what will I be doing?"

"Observing, initially. If you choose to make contact . . . it'll be up to you, and I'll need your word that you'll break it off if things get dicey. Otherwise, we'll yank you back—and that won't be pleasant. You'll probably have the mother of all headaches, and a raging case of nausea."

"What fun."

"Fun's just beginning." She walked over, unlocked a small box. Then held up a small figure carved in wax.

Cian's brows shot up. "A strong likeness. You are clever."

"Sculpting's not my strongest skill, but I can handle a poppet." Glenna turned the figure of Lilith around so Moira could see. "I don't generally make them—it's intrusive, and dangerous to the party you've captured. But the harm-none rule doesn't apply to undead. Present company excepted."

"Appreciated."

"There's just one little thing I need from you."

"Which is."

"Blood."

Cian did nothing more than look resigned. "Naturally."

"Just a few drops, after I bind the poppet. I have nothing of hers—hair, nail clippings. But you mixed blood, once upon a time. I think it'll do the job." She hesitated, twisting the chain of her pendant around her fingers. "And maybe this is a bad idea."

"It's not." Moira set the last candle. "It's time we push into her mind, as she's pushed into all of ours. It's a good, hot needle under the skin, if you're asking me. And Cian deserves to give her a taste of her own."

She straightened. "Will we be able to watch?"

"Thirsty for some vengeance yourself?" Cian questioned.

Moira's eyes were cold smoke. "Parched. Will we?"

"If all goes as it should." Glenna took a breath. "Ready for some astral projection?" she asked Cian.

"As I'll ever be."

"Step inside the circle of candles, both of you. You'll need to achieve a meditative state, Cian. Moira and I will be your watchers, and the observers. We'll hold your body to this plane while your mind and image travel."

"Is it true," Moira asked her, "that it helps hold a traveling spirit to the safety of its world if it carries something from someone of it?"

Glenna pushed at her hair again. "It's a theory."

"Then take this." She tugged off the band of beads and leather that bound her braid. "In case the theory's true."

After giving it a dubious frown, Cian shoved it in his pocket. "I'm armed with hair trinkets."

Glenna picked up a small bowl of balm. "Focus, open the chakras," she said as she rubbed the balm on his skin. "Relax your body, open your mind."

She looked at Moira. "We'll cast the circle. Imagine light, soft, blue light. This is protection."

While they cast, Cian focused on a white door. It was his habitual symbol when he chose to meditate. When he was ready, the door would open. And he would go through it.

"He has a strong mind," Glenna told Moira. "And a great deal of practice. He told me he studied in Tibet.

Never mind," she said with a wave of her hand. "I'm stalling. I'm a little nervous."

"Her wizard isn't any stronger than you. What he can do, you can do."

"Damn right. Gotta say though, I hope to hell Lilith is sleeping. Should be, really should be." Glenna glanced at the window at the thinning rain. "We're about to find out."

She'd left an opening in the poppet, and prepared to fill it with grains of graveyard dirt, rosemary and sage, ground amethyst and quartz.

"You have to control your emotions for the binding, Moira. Set aside your hatred, your fear. We desire justice and sight. Lilith can be harmed, and we can use magic to do so, but Cian will be a conduit. I wouldn't want any negativity to backwash on him."

"Justice then. It's enough."

Glenna closed the poppet with a plug of wax.

"We call on Maat, goddess of justice and balance to guide our hand. With this image we send magic across air, across land." She placed a white feather against the doll, wrapped it in black ribbon. "Give the creature whose image I hold, dream and memory ancient and old."

She handed the ritual knife to Moira, nodded.

"Sealed by blood she shed, bound now with these drops of red."

Cian showed no reaction when Moira lifted his hand to draw the knife over his palm.

"Mind and image of the life she took joins her now so he may look. And while we watch we hold him safe in hand and heart until he chooses to depart. Through us into her this magic streams. Take our messenger into her dream. Open doors so we may see. As we will, so mote it be."

Glenna held the poppet over the cauldron, and releasing it, left it suspended on will and air.

"Take his hand," she said to Moira. "And hold on."

When Moira's hand clasped his, Cian didn't go through the door. He exploded through it. Flying through a dark even his eyes couldn't conquer, he felt Moira's hand tighten strong on his. In his mind, he heard her voice, cool and calm.

"We're with you. We won't let go."

There was moonlight, sprinkling through the dark to bring blurry smears of shape and shadow. There were scents, flowers and earth, water and woman.

Humans.

There was heat. Temperature meant little to him, but he could feel the shift of it from the damp chill he'd left behind. A baking heat, eased only a little by a breeze off the water.

Sea, he corrected. It was an ocean with waves lapping at the sugar of sand. And there were hills rising up from the beach. Olive trees spread over the terraces of those hills. And on one of the rises—the highest—stood a temple, white as the moonlight with its marble columns overlooking that ocean, the trees, gardens and pools.

Overlooking, too, the man and woman who lay together on a white blanket edged in gold on the sparkling sand near the play of white foam.

He heard the woman's laugh—the husky sound of a roused woman. And knew it was Lilith, knew it was Lilith's memory, or her dream he'd fallen into. So he stood apart, and watched as the man slid the white robe from her shoulders, and bent his head to her breasts.

Sweet, so sweet, his mouth on her. Everything inside her ebbed and flowed, as the tide. How could it be forbidden, the beauty of this? Her body was meant for his. Her spirit, her mind, her soul had been created by the gods as the mate for his.

She arched, offering, with her fingers combing gently through his sun-kissed hair. He smelled of the olive trees, and the sunlight that ripened their fruit.

Her love, her only. She murmured it to him as their lips met again. And again, with a hunger that built beyond bearing.

Her eyes were full of him when at last his body joined with hers. The pleasure of it brought tears glimmering, turned her sighs to helpless gasps.

Love swarmed through her, pounded in her heart, a thousand silken fists. She held him closer, closer, crying out her joy with an abandon that dared even the gods to hear.

"Cirio, Cirio." She cradled his head on her breast. "My heart. My love."

He lifted his head, brushing at her gilded hair. "Even the moon pales against your beauty. Lilia, my queen of the night."

"The nights are ours, but I want the sun with you—the sun that gilds your hair and skin, that touches you when I cannot. I want to walk beside you, proud and free."

He only rolled onto his back. "Look at the stars. They're our torches tonight. We should swim under them. Bathe this heat away in the sea."

Instantly pique hardened the sleepy joy from her face. "Why won't you speak of it?"

"It's too hot a night for talk and trouble." He spoke carelessly as he sifted sand through his fingers. "Come. We'll be dolphins and play."

But when he took her hands to pull her up she drew them away with a sharp, sulky jerk. "But we *must* talk. We must plan."

"My sweet, we have so little time left tonight."

"We could have forever, every night. We have only to leave, to run away together. I could be your wife, give you children."

"Leave? Run away?" He threw back his head with a laugh. "What foolishness is this? Come now, come, I have only an hour left. Let's swim awhile, and I'll ride you on the waves."

"It's not foolishness." This time she slapped his hand away. "We could sail from here, to anywhere we wished. Be together openly, in the sunlight. I want more than a few hours in the dark with you, Cirio. You promised me more."

"Sail away, like thieves? My home is here, my family. My duty."

"Your coffers," she said viciously. "Or your father's."

"And what of it? Do you think I would smear my family name by running away with a temple priestess, living like paupers in some strange land?"

"You said you could live on my love alone."

"Words are easy in the heat. Be sensible." His tone cajoling, he skimmed a finger down her bare breast. "We give each other pleasure. Why does there need to be more?"

"I *want* more. I love you. I broke my vows for you."

"Willingly," he reminded her.

"For love."

"Love doesn't feed the belly, Lilia, or spend in the marketplace. Don't be sad now. I'll buy you a gift. Something gold like your hair."

"I want nothing you can buy. Only freedom. I would be your wife."

"You cannot. If we attempted such madness and were caught, we'd be put to death."

"I would rather die with you than live without you."

"I value my life more, it seems, than you value either of ours." He nearly yawned, so lazy was his voice. "I can give you pleasure, and the freedom of that. But as for a wife, you know one has already been chosen for me."

"You chose me. You said—"

"Enough, enough!" He threw up his hands, but seemed more bored by the conversation than angry. "I chose you for this, as you chose me. You were hungry to be touched. I saw it in your eyes. If you've spun a web of fantasy where we sail off, it's your own doing."

"You pledged yourself to me."

"My body. And you've had good use of it." He belted on his robes as he rose. "I would have kept you as mistress, happily. But I have no time or patience for ridiculous demands from a temple harlot."

"Harlot." The angry flush drained, leaving her face

white as the marble columns on the hillside. "You took my innocence."

"You gave it."

"You can't mean these things." She knelt, clasping her hands like a woman at prayer. "You're angry because I pushed you. We'll speak no more of it tonight. We'll swim, as you said and forget all these hard words."

"It's too late for that. Do you think I can't read what's in your mind now? You'll nag me to death over what can never be. Just as well. We've challenged the gods long enough."

"You can't mean to leave me. I love you. If you leave me, I'll go to your family. I'll tell—"

"Speak of this, and I'll swear you lie. You'll burn for it, Lilia." He bent down, ran a finger over the curve of her shoulder. "And your skin is too soft, too sweet for the fire."

"Don't, don't turn from me. It will all be as you say, as you like. I'll never speak of leaving again. Don't leave me."

"Begging only spoils your beauty."

She called out to him in shock, in terrible grief, but he strode away as if he couldn't hear her.

She threw herself down on the blanket, wildly weeping, pounding her fists. The pain of it was like the fire he'd spoken of, burning through her so that her bones seemed to turn to ash. How could she live with the pain?

Love had betrayed her, and used her and cast her aside. Love had made her a fool. And still her heart was full of it.

She would cast herself into the sea and drown. She would climb to the top of the temple and fling herself off. She would simply die here, from the shame and the pain.

"Kill him first," she choked out as she raged. "I'll kill him first, then myself. Blood, his and mine together. That is the price of love and betrayal."

She heard a movement, just a whisper on the sand, and flung herself up with the joy. He'd come back to her! "My love."

"Yes. I will be."

His hair was black, flowing past his shoulders. He wore long robes the color of the night. His eyes were the same, so black they seemed to shine.

She grabbed up her toga, held it to her breasts. "I am a priestess of this temple. You have no leave to walk here."

"I walk where I will. So young," he murmured as those black eyes traveled over her. "So fresh."

"You will leave here."

"In my time. I've watched you these past three nights, Lilia, you and the boy you waste yourself on."

"How dare you."

"You gave him love, he gave you lies. Both are precious. Tell me, how would you like to repay him for his gift to you?"

She felt something stir in her, the first juices of vengeance. "He deserves nothing from me, neither he nor any man."

"How true. So you'll give to me what no man deserves."

Fear rushed in, and she ran with it. But somehow he was standing in front of her, smiling that cold smile.

"What are you?"

"Ah, insight. I knew I'd chosen well. I am what was before your weak and rutting gods were belched out of the heavens."

She ran again, a scream locked in her throat. But he was there, blocking her way. Her fear had jumped to terror. "It's death to touch a temple priestess."

"And death is such a fascinating beginning. I seek a companion, a lover, a woman, a student. You are she. I have a gift for you, Lilia."

This time when she ran, he laughed. Laughed still when he plucked her off her feet, tossed her sobbing to the ground.

She fought, scratching, biting, begging, but he was too strong. Now it was his mouth on her breast, and she wept with the shame of it even as she raked her nails down his cheek.

"Yes. Yes. It's better when they fight. You'll learn. Their

fear is perfume; their screams music." He caught her face in his hand, forced her to look at him.

"Now, into my eyes. Into them."

He drove himself into her. Her body shuddered, quaked, bucked, from the shock. And the unspeakable thrill.

"Did he take you so high?"

"No. No." The tears began to dry on her cheeks. Instead of clawing, beating, her hands dug into the sand searching for purchase. Trapped in his eyes, her body began to move with his.

"Take more. You want more," he said. "Pain is so . . . arousing."

He plunged harder, so deep she feared she might rend in two. But still her body matched his pace, still her eyes were trapped by his.

When his went red, her heart leaped with fresh fear, and yet that fear was squeezed in a fist of terrible excitement. He was so beautiful. Her human lover pale beside this dark, damning beauty.

"I give you the instrument of your revenge. I give you your beginning. You have only to ask me for it. Ask me for my gift."

"Yes. Give me your gift. Give me revenge. Give me—"

Her body convulsed when his fangs struck. And every pleasure she had known or imagined diminished beside what rushed into her. Here, here was the glory she'd never found in the temple, the burgeoning black power she'd always known stretched just beyond her fingertips.

Here was the forbidden she'd longed for.

It was she, writhing in that pleasure and power, that brought him to climax. And she, without being told, reared up to drink the blood she'd scored from his cheek.

Smiling through bloody lips, she died.

And woke in her bed two thousand years after the dream.

Her body felt bruised, tender, her mind muddled. Where was the sea? Where was the temple?

"Cirio?"

"A romantic? Who would have guessed." Cian stepped out of the shadows. "To call out for the lover who spurned and betrayed you."

"Jarl?" It was the name she'd called her maker. But as dream separated from reality, she saw it was Cian. "So, you've come after all. My offer . . ." But it wasn't quite clear.

"What became of the boy?" As if settling in for a cozy chat, Cian sat on the side of the bed.

"What boy? Davey?"

"No, no, not the whelp you made. Your lover, the one you had in life."

Her lips trembled as she understood. "So you toy with my dreams? What does that matter to me?" But she was shaken, down to the pit of her. "He was called Cirio. What do you think became of him?"

"I think your master arranged for him to be your first kill."

She smiled with one of her sweetest memories. "He pissed himself as Jarl held him out to me, and he sniveled like a child as he begged for his life. I was new, and still had the control to keep him alive for hours—long after he begged for his death. I'll do better with you. I'll give you years of pain."

She swiped out, cursed when her raking nails passed through him.

"Entertaining, isn't it? And Jarl? How long before you did for him."

She sat back, sulking a little. Then shrugged. "Nearly three hundred years. I had a lot to learn from him. He began to fear me because my power grew and grew. I could smell his fear of me. He would have ended me, if I hadn't ended him first."

"You were called Lilia—Lily."

"The pitiful human I was, yes. He named me Lilith when I woke." She twirled a lock of her hair around her finger as she studied Cian. "Do you have some foolish hope that by learning my beginning you'll find my end?"

She tossed the covers aside, rose to walk naked to a silver pitcher.

When she poured the blood into a cup, her hands trembled again.

"Let's speak frankly here," Cian suggested. "It's only you and I—which is odd. You don't sleep with Lora or the boy, or some other choice today?"

"Even I, occasionally, seek solitude."

"All right. So, to be frank. It's strange, isn't it, disorienting, to go back even in dreams to human? To see your own end, own beginning as if it just happened. To feel human again, or as best we can remember it feels to be human."

Almost as an afterthought, she shrugged into a robe. "I would go back to being human."

His brows lifted. "You? Now you surprise me."

"To have that moment of death and rebirth. The wonderful, staggering thrill of it. I'd go back to being weak and blind, just to experience the gift again."

"Of course. You remain predictable." He got to his feet. "Know this. If you and your wizard steer my dreams again, I'll return the favor, threefold. You'll have no rest from me, or from yourself."

He faded away, but he didn't go back. Though he could feel the tugs from Moira's mind, from Glenna's will, he lingered.

He wanted to see what Lilith would do next.

She heaved the cup and what was left of the blood in it against the wall. She smashed a trinket box, pounded holes into the wall with her fists until they bled.

Then she screamed for a guard.

"Bring that worthless wizard to me. Bring him in chains. Bring him— No, wait. Wait." She turned away in an obvious fight for control. "I'll kill him if he crosses paths with me now, then what good will he be to me? Bring me someone to eat."

She whirled back. "A male. Young. Twenty or so. Blond if we have one. Go!"

Alone, she rubbed her temple. "I'll kill him again," she

murmured. "I'll feel better then. I'll call him Cirio, and kill him again."

She snatched her precious mirror from the bureau. And seeing her own face reminded her why she would keep Midir alive. He'd given her this gift.

"There I am," she said softly. "So beautiful. The moon pales, yes, yes, it does. I'm right here. I'll always be here. The rest is ghosts. And here I am."

Picking up a brush, she began to groom her hair, and to sing. With tears in her eyes.

"Drink this." Glenna pushed a cup to Cian's lips, and immediately had it pushed aside.

"I'm fine. I'm not after drinking whiskey, or swooning on you without it."

"You're pale."

His lips quirked. "Part of the whole undead package. Well. That was quite a ride."

Since he refused it, Glenna took a sip of the whiskey herself, then passed it off to Moira. "E-ticket. She didn't sense us," she said to Moira. "I'd like to think my blocks and binding were enough, but I think, in large part, she was just too caught up to feel us."

"She was so young." Moira sat now. "So young, and in love with that worthless prick of a man. I don't know what language they were speaking. I could understand her, strangely enough, but I didn't know the tongue."

"Greek. She started out a priestess for some goddess. Virginity's part of the job description." Cian wished for blood, settled for water. "And save your pity. She was ripe for what happened."

"As you were?" Moira shot back. "And don't pretend you felt nothing for her. We were linked. I felt your pity. Her heart was broken, and moments later, she's raped and taken by a demon. I can despise what Lilith is and feel pity for Lilia."

"Lilia was already half mad," he said flatly. "Maybe the change is what kept her relatively sane all this time."

"I agree. I'm sorry," Glenna said to Moira. "And I got no pleasure out of seeing what happened to her. But there was something in her eyes, in her tone—and God, in the way she ultimately responded to Jarl. She wasn't quite right, Moira, even then."

"Then she might have died by her own hand, or been executed for killing the man who used her. But she'd have died clean." She sighed. "And we might not be here, discussing the matter. It all gives you a headache if you think about it hard enough. I have a delicate question, which is more for my own curiosity than anything else."

She cleared her throat before asking Cian. "How she responded, as Glenna said. Is that not usual?"

"Most fight, or freeze with fear. She, on the other hand, participated after the . . . delicacy escapes me," Cian admitted. "After she began to feel pleasure from the rape. It was rape, no mistake, and no sane woman gains pleasure from being brutalized and forced."

"She was already his before the bite," Moira murmured. "He knew she would be, recognized that in her. She knew what to do to change—to drink from him. Everything I've read has claimed the victim must be forced or told. It must be offered. She took. She understood, and she wanted."

"We know more than we did, which is always useful," Cian commented. "And the episode unnerved her, an added benefit. I'll sleep better having accomplished that. Now it's past my bedtime. Ladies."

Moira watched him go. "He feels. Why do you think he goes to such lengths to pretend he doesn't?"

"Feelings cause pain, a great deal of the time. I think when you've seen and done so much, feelings could be like a constant ache." Glenna laid a hand on Moira's shoulder. "Denial is just another form of survival."

"Feelings loosed can be either balm or weapon."

What would his be, she wondered, if fully freed?

Chapter 9

The rain slid into a soggy twilight that curled a smoky fog low over the ground. As night crept in, no moon, no stars could break through the gloom.

Moira waded through the river of fog over the courtyard to stand beside Glenna.

"They're nearly home," Glenna murmured. "Later than we'd hoped, but nearly home."

"I've had the fires lit in your room and Larkin's, and baths are being prepared. They'll be cold and wet."

"Thanks. I didn't think of it."

"When we were in Ireland, you thought of all the comfort details. Now it's for me." Like Glenna, Moira watched the skies. "I've ordered food for the family parlor, unless you'd rather be private with Hoyt."

"No. No. They'll want to report everything at once. Then we'll be private." She lifted her hand to grip her cross and the amulet she wore with it. "I didn't know I'd be so worried. We've been in the middle of a fight, outnumbered, and I haven't obsessed like this."

"Because you were with him. To love and to wait is worse than a wound."

"One of the lessons I've learned. There have been so many of them. You'd be worried about Larkin, I know. And about Tynan now. He has feelings for you."

Moira understood Glenna didn't mean Larkin. "I know. Our mothers hoped we might make a match of it."

"But?"

"Whatever needs to be there isn't there for me. And he's too much a friend. Maybe having no lover to wait for, no lover to lose, makes it easier for me to bear all of this."

Glenna waited a beat. "But."

"But," Moira said with a half laugh. "I envy you the torture of waiting for yours."

From where she stood Moira saw Cian, the shape of him coming through the gloom. From the stables, she noted. Rather than the cloak the men of Geall would wear against the chill and rain, he wore a coat similar to Blair's. Long and black and leather.

It billowed in the mists as he crossed to them with barely a sound of his boots against the wet stones.

"They won't come any sooner for you standing in the damp," he commented.

"They're nearly home." Glenna stared up at the sky as if she could will it to open and send Hoyt down to her. "He'll know I'm waiting."

"If you were waiting for me, Red, I wouldn't have left in the first place."

With a smile, she tipped her head so it leaned against his shoulder. When he put his arm around Glenna, Moira saw in the gesture the same affection she herself had with Larkin, the kind that came from the heart, through family.

"There," Cian said softly. "Dead east."

"You see them?" Glenna strained forward. "You can see them?"

"Give it a minute, and so will you."

The moment she did, her hand squeezed Moira's. "Thank God. Oh, thank God."

The dragon soared through the thick air, a glimmer of gold with riders on its back. Even as it touched down, Glenna was sprinting over the stones. When he dismounted, Hoyt's arms opened to catch her.

"That's lovely to see." Moira spoke quietly as Hoyt and Glenna embraced. "So many said goodbye today, and will tomorrow. It's lovely to see someone come home to waiting arms."

"Before her, he'd most often prefer coming back to solitude. Women change things."

She glanced up at him. "Only women?"

"People then. But women? They alter universes just by being women."

"For better or worse?"

"Depends on the woman, doesn't it?"

"And the prize, or the man, she's set her sights on." With this, she left his side to rush toward Larkin.

Despite the fact that he was dripping, she hugged him hard. "I have food, drink, hot water, all you could wish. I'm so glad to see you. All of you." But when she would have turned from Larkin to welcome the others, he gripped her hard.

Moira felt her relief spin on its head to fear.

"What? What happened?"

"We should go in." Hoyt's voice was quiet, and tight. "We should go in out of the wet."

"Tell me what happened." Moira drew away from Larkin.

"Tynan's troop was set upon, at the near halfway point."

She felt everything inside her freeze. "Oran. Tynan."

"Alive. Tynan was injured, but not seriously. Six others . . ."

She took Larkin's arm, digging her fingers in. "Dead or captured?"

"Five dead, one taken. Several others wounded, two badly. We did what we could for them."

The cold remained, like ice over her heart. "You have the names? The dead, the wounded, and the other?"

"We have them, yes. Moira, it was young Sean taken. The smithy's son."

Her belly twisted with the knowledge that what the boy faced would be worse than death. "I'll speak to their families. Say nothing to anyone until I've spoken to their families."

"I'll go with you."

"No. No, this is for me. You need to get dry and warm, and fed. It's for me to do, Larkin. It's my place."

"We wrote down the names." Blair took a scrap of paper out of her pocket. "I'm sorry, Moira."

"We knew this would come." She slipped the paper inside her cloak, out of the wet. "I'll come to the parlor as soon as I'm able, so you can tell me the details of it. For now, the families need to hear this from me."

"Lot of weight," Blair declared when Moira walked away.

"She'll bear it." Cian looked after her. "It's what queens do."

She thought it would crush her, but she did bear it. While mothers and wives wept in her arms, she took the weight. She knew nothing of the attack, but told each and every one their son or husband or brother had died bravely, died a hero.

It was what needed to be said.

It was worse with Sean's parents, worse to see the hope in the blacksmith's eyes, the tears of that hope blurring his wife's. She couldn't bring herself to snuff it out, so left them with it, with the prayers that their son would somehow escape and return home.

When it was done, she went to her rooms to put the names into a painted box she would keep now beside her bed. There would be other lists, she knew. This was only the first. And every name of every one who gave his or her life would be written down, and kept in that box.

With it, she put a sprig of rosemary for remembrance, and a coin for tribute.

After closing the box, she buried her need for solitude, for grieving, and went to the parlor to hear how it had been done.

Conversation stopped when she entered, and Larkin rose quickly.

"My father has just left us. I'll go bring him back if you like."

"No, no. Let him be with your mother, your sister." Moira knew her pregnant cousin's husband was to lead tomorrow's troop.

"I'll warm you some food. No, you will eat," Glenna said even as Moira opened her mouth. "Consider it medicine, but you'll eat."

While Glenna put food on a plate, Cian poured a stiff dose of apple brandy into a cup. He took it to her. "Drink this first. You're white as wax."

"With this I'll have color, and a swimming head." But she shrugged, tossed it back like water.

"Have to admire a woman who can take a slug like that." Impressed, he took the empty glass, then went back to sit.

"It was horrible. At least I can admit that here, to all of you. It was horrible." Moira sat down at the table, then pressed her hands to her temples. "To look into their faces and see the change, and know they'll forever be changed because of what you've brought to them. To what's been taken from them."

"You didn't bring it." Anger lashed in Glenna's voice as she slapped a plate down in front of Moira. "You didn't take it."

"I didn't mean the war, or the death. But the news of it. The hardest was the one who was taken prisoner. The smithy's boy, Sean. His parents still have hope. How could I tell them he's worse than dead? I couldn't cut that last thread of hope, and wonder if it would be kinder if I had."

She let out a breath, then straightened. Glenna was right, she would eat. "Tell me what you know."

"They were in the ground," Hoyt began, "as they were when they set upon Blair. Tynan said no more than fifty, but the men were taken by surprise. He told us it seemed they didn't care if they were cut down, but charged and fought like mad animals. Two of our men fell in the first instant, and they gained three horses from us in the confusion of the battle."

"Nearly a third of the horses that went with them."

"Four, maybe five of them took the smithy's son, alive from what those who tried to save him said. They took him off, heading east, while the rest held their line and battled back. They killed more than twenty, and the others scattered and ran as the tide turned."

"It was a victory. You have to look at it that way," Blair insisted. "You have to. Your men took out over twenty vamps on their first engagement. Your casualties were light in comparison. Don't say every death is one too many," she added quickly. "I know that. But this is the reality of it. Their training held up."

"I know you're right, and I've already told myself the same. But it was their victory, too. They wanted a prisoner. No reason else to take one. Their mission must have been to take one alive, whatever the cost of it."

"You're right, no argument. But I don't see that as a victory in their column. It was stupid, and it was a waste. Say five for the prisoner. Those vamps had stayed and fought, they'd have taken more of ours—alive or dead. My take is that Lilith ordered this because she was feeling pissy, or it was impulse. But it was also bad strategy."

Moira ate food she couldn't taste while she considered it. "The way she sent King back to us. It was petty, and vicious. But playful in her way. She thinks these things will undermine us, crush our spirits. How can she know us so little? You've lived half her time," she said to Cian. "You know better."

"I find humans interesting. She finds them . . . tasty at best. You don't have to know the mind of a cow to herd them up for steaks."

"Especially if you've got a whole gang to handle the roping and riding," Blair put in. "Just following your metaphor," she said to Cian. "I hurt her girl, so she needs some payback for that. We took three of her bases—should add we cleared out the second two locations this morning."

"They were empty," Larkin stated. "She hadn't bothered to set traps there, or base any of her troops. Added to that, Glenna told us how you played with her while we were gone."

"Sum of it is, this was tit for tat. But she loses more than we do. Doesn't make it any easier on the families of the dead," Blair added.

"And tomorrow, I send more out. Phelan." Moira reached out for Larkin. "I can't hold him back. I'll speak to Sinann, but—"

"No, that's for me. I expect our father has already talked to her, but I'll see her myself."

She nodded. "And Tynan? His wounds?"

"A gash along the hip. Hoyt treated the wounded. He was doing well when we left them. They're secured for the night."

"Well then. We'll pray for sun in the morning."

She had another duty to see to.

Her women had a sitting room near her own chambers where they could sit and read, or do needlework, or gossip. Moira's mother had made it a cheerful, intensely female space with soft fabrics, many cushions, pots filled with flowering plants.

The fire here was habitually of apple wood for the scent, and there were wall sconces of pretty winged faeries.

When she was crowned, Moira had given her own women leave to make any changes they liked. But the room remained as it had in all her memory.

Her women were there now, waiting for her to retire for the night, or simply dismiss them.

They rose when she entered, and curtseyed.

"We're all women here now. For now, in this place, we're all only women." She opened her arms to Ceara.

"Oh, my lady." Ceara's eyes, already red and swollen from weeping overflowed as she rushed into Moira's embrace. "Dwyn is dead. My brother is dead."

"I'm sorry. I'm so sorry. Here now, here." She led Ceara to a seat, holding her close. And she wept with her as she'd wept with Ceara's mother, and all the others.

"They buried him there, in a field by the road. They couldn't even bring him home. He had no wake."

"We'll have a holy man consecrate the ground. And we'll build a monument to those who fell today."

"He was eager to go, to fight. He turned and waved at me before he marched off."

"You'll have some tea now." Her own eyes red from weeping, Isleen set the pot down. "You'll have some tea, Ceara, and you, my lady."

"Thank you." Ceara mopped at her damp face. "I don't know what I'd have done these past hours without Isleen and Dervil."

"It's good that you have your friends. But you'll have your tea, then you'll go to your family. You'll need your family now. You have my leave for as long as you want it."

"There's something more I want, Your Majesty. Something I ask you to give me, in my brother's name."

Moira waited, but Ceara said nothing more. "Would you ask me to give you my word on something without knowing what I promise?"

"My husband marches tomorrow."

Moira felt her stomach sink. "Ceara." She reached over, smoothed a hand on Ceara's hair. "Sinann's husband marches with the sunrise as well. She carries her third child, and still I can't spare her from his leaving."

"I don't ask you to spare me. I ask you allow me to march with him."

"To—" Stunned, Moira sat back. "Ceara, your children."

"Will be with my mother, and as safe and well as they can be, here, with her. But my man goes to war, and I've trained as he has. Why am I to sit and wait?" Ceara held out her hands. "Peck at needlework, walk in the garden when he goes to fight. You said we would all need to be ready to defend Geall, and worlds beyond it. I've made my-self ready. Your Majesty, my lady, I beg your leave to go with my husband on the morrow."

Saying nothing, Moira got to her feet. She moved to the window to look out at the dark. The rain, at last, had stopped, but the mists from it swarmed like clouds.

"Have you spoken with him on this?" Moira asked at length.

"I have, and his first thought was for my safety. But he understands my mind is set, and why."

"Why is it?"

"He's my heart." Ceara stood, laid a hand on her breast. "I wouldn't leave my children unprotected, but trust my mother to do all she can for them. My lady, have we, we women, trained and slogged in the mud all this time only to sit by the fire?"

"No. No, you haven't."

"I'm not the only woman who wants this."

Moira turned now. "You've spoken to others." She looked at Dervil and Isleen. "Both of you want this as well?" She nodded. "I see I was wrong to hold you back. Arrangements will be made then. I'm proud to be a woman of Geall."

For love, Moira thought as she sat to make another list of names. For love as much as duty. The women would go, and fight for Geall. But it was the husbands and lovers, the families inside of Geall that made them reach for the sword.

Who did she fight for? Who was there for her to turn to the night before a battle, to reach for that warmth, for that reason to fight?

The days ticked away, and Samhain loomed like a bloodied ax over her head. And here she sat, alone as she sat alone every night. Would she reach for a book again, or another map, another list? Or would she wander the room again, the gardens and courtyards, wishing for . . .

Him, she thought. Wishing he would put his hands on her again and make her feel so full, so alive, so bright. Wishing he'd share with her what she'd seen in him the night he'd played music and had stirred her heart as truly as he'd stirred her blood.

She'd fought and she'd bled, would fight and bleed again. She would ride into battle as queen, with the sword of gods in her hand. But here she sat in her quiet room, wishing like a blushing maid for the touch and the heat of the only one who'd ever made her pulse quicken.

Surely that was foolish and wasteful. And, it was an insult to women everywhere.

She rose to pace as she considered it. Aye, it was insulting, and small-minded. She sat and wished for the same reasons she'd held back sending the women on the march. Because it was traditional for the man to come to the woman. It was traditional for the man to protect and defend.

Things had changed, hadn't they?

Hadn't she spent weeks in a world and time where women, like Glenna and Blair, held their own—and more—at every turn?

So, if she wanted Cian's hands on her, she'd see that he put them there, and that would be that.

She started to sweep out of the room, remembered her appearance. She could do better. If she was about to embark on seducing a vampire, she'd have to go well armed.

She stripped off her dress. She might have wished for a bath—or oh, the wonderfully hot shower of Ireland—but she made do washing from the basin of scented water.

She creamed her skin, imagined Cian's long fingers skimming over it. Heat was already balling in her belly and throbbing along nerves as she chose her best nightrobe.

Brushing her hair she had a moment to wish she'd asked Glenna to teach her how to do a simple glamour. Though it seemed to her that her cheeks were becomingly flushed, her eyes held a glint. She bit her lips until they hurt, but thought they'd pinked and plumped nicely.

She stood back from the long glass, studied herself carefully from every angle. She hoped she looked desirable.

Taking a candle she left the room with the sheer determination she wouldn't return to it a virgin.

In his room, Cian pored over maps. He was the only one of the circle who'd been denied a look at the battlefield, either in reality or dreams. He was going to correct that.

Time was a problem. Five days' march, well, he could ride it in two, perhaps less. But that meant he'd need a safe place to camp during the daylight.

One of the bases the others had secured would do. Once he'd taken his survey, he could simply relocate in one of those bases until Samhain.

Get out of the bloody castle, and away from its all-too-tempting queen.

There'd be objections—that was annoying. But they could hardly lock him in a dungeon and make him stay put. They'd be leaving themselves in another week or so. He'd just ride point.

He could ride out with the troops in the morning, if the sun stayed back. Or simply wait for sundown.

Sitting back he sipped blood he'd laced with whiskey— his own version of a sleep-inducing cocktail. He could just go now, couldn't he? No arguments from his brother or the others if he just rode off.

He'd have to leave a note, he supposed. Odd to have people who'd actually be concerned for his welfare, and somewhat pleasant though it added certain responsibilities.

He'd just pack and go, he decided, pushing the drink aside. No muss, no fuss. And he wouldn't have to see her again until they caught up to him.

He picked up the band of beaded leather he'd failed to give back, toyed with it. If he left tonight, he wouldn't have to see her, or smell her, or imagine what it would be like to have her under him in the dark.

He had a bloody good imagination.

He got to his feet to decide what gear would be most useful for the journey, and frowned at the knock on his door.

Likely Hoyt, he decided. Well, he just wouldn't mention his plans, and thereby avoid a long, irritating debate on the matter. He considered not answering at all, but silence and a locked door wouldn't stop his brother the sorcerer.

He knew it was Moira the moment his hand touched the latch. And he cursed. He opened the door, intending to send her on her way quickly so he could be on his.

She wore white, thin, flowing white, with something filmy over it that was nearly the same gray as her eyes. She smelled like spring—young and full of promise.

Need coiled inside him like snakes.

"Do you never sleep?" he demanded.

"Do you?" She swept by him, the move surprising him enough that he didn't block it.

"Well, come right in, make yourself at home."

"Thank you." She said it politely, as if his words hadn't dripped with sarcasm. Then she set down her candle and turned to the the fire he hadn't bothered to light.

"Let's see if I can do this. I practiced until my ears all but bled. Don't speak. You'll distract me."

She held out a hand toward the fire. Focused, imagined. Pushed. A single weak flame flickered, so she narrowed her eyes and pushed harder.

"There!" There was absolute delight in her voice when the turf caught.

"Now I'm surrounded by bloody magicians."

Both her hair and her robes fanned out as she turned. "It's a good skill, and I intend to learn more."

"You won't find a tutor in sorcery here."

"No." She brushed back her hair. "But I think in other

things." Walking back to the door, she locked it, then turned to him. "I want you to take me to bed."

He blinked as otherwise he might have goggled. "What?"

"There's not a thing wrong with your hearing, so you heard me well enough. I want to lie with you. I thought I might try being coy or seductive, but then it seemed to me you'd have more respect for plain speaking."

The snakes coiled inside him began to writhe. And bite. "Here's plain speaking. Get out."

"I see I've surprised you." She wandered, running a finger over a stack of books. "That's not easy to do, so as Blair would say, points for me." She turned again, smiled again. "I'm green at this, so tell me, why would a man be angry to have a woman want to lie with him?"

"I'm not a man."

"Ah." She lifted a finger to acknowledge his point. "But still, you have needs, desires. You've desired me."

"A man will put his hand on nearly any female."

"You're not a man," she shot back, then grinned. "More points for me. You're not keeping up."

"If you've been drinking again—"

"I haven't. You know I haven't. But I've been thinking. I'm going to war, into battle. I may not live through it. None of us may. Good men died today, in mud and blood, and left broken hearts behind them."

"And sex reaffirms life. I know the psychology of it."

"That, aye that, true enough. And on a more personal level, I'm damned—I swear it—if I'll die a virgin. I want to *know* what it is. I want to feel it."

"Then order up a subject for stud, Majesty. I'm not interested."

"I don't want anyone else. I never wanted anyone before you, and haven't wanted any but you since I first saw you. It shocked me, that I could have any such feelings for you, knowing what you are. But they're inside me, and they won't leave. I have needs, like anyone. And wiles enough, I think, to overcome your resistance if need be—though you may no longer be a randy young man."

"Found your feet, haven't you?" he muttered.

"Oh, I've always had them. I'm just careful where I step." Watching him, measuring him, she trailed a hand down one of the bedposts. "Tell me, what difference would it make to you? An hour or two. You haven't had a woman in some time, I'm thinking."

He felt like an idiot. Stiff and foolish and needy. "That wouldn't be your concern."

"It might be. I've read that when a man's been denied, we'll say, for a while, it can affect his performance. But you shouldn't worry about that, as I've nothing to compare it to."

"Isn't that lucky for me? Or would be if I wanted you."

Her head cocked, and all he could see on her face was curiosity and confidence.

"You think you can insult me away. I wager—any price you name—that you're hard as stone right now." She moved toward him. "I want so much, Cian, for you to touch me. I'm tired of dreaming of it, and want to feel it."

The ground was crumbling under his feet. Had been, he knew, since the moment she'd walked in. "You don't know what you're asking, what you're risking. The consequences are beyond you."

"A vampire can lie with a human. You won't hurt me." She reached up, drew the cross over her head, set it aside on the table.

"Trusting soul." He tried for sarcasm, but the gesture had moved him.

"Confident. I don't need or want a shield against you. Why do you never say my name?"

"What? Of course, I do."

"No, you don't. You refer to me, but you never look at me and say my name." Her eyes were smoke now, and full of knowledge. "Names have power, taken or given. Are you afraid of what I might take from you?"

"There's nothing for you to take."

"Then say my name."

"Moira."

"Again, please." She took his hand, laid it on her heart. "Don't do this."

"Cian. There's your name from me. Cian. I think if you don't touch me, if you don't take me, a part of me will die before I ever go to battle. Please." She framed his face in her hands, and saw—at last—what she needed to see in his eyes. "Say my name."

"Moira." Lost, he took her wrist, turned his lips into her palm. "Moira. If I wasn't damned already, this would send me to hell."

"I'll try to take you to heaven first, if you teach me."

She rose to her toes, drawing him down. Her sigh trembled out when his lips met hers.

Chapter 10

He'd believed his will would prevent this. A thousand years, he thought, and sank into her, and the male still deluded itself it could control the female.

She was leading him, and had in her way been leading him to this from the first instant. Now he would take what she offered him, what she demanded from him, however selfish the act. But he would use the skill of a dozen lifetimes to give her what she wanted in return.

"You're foolish, reckless to give up your innocence to such as me." He skimmed a fingertip across her collarbone. "But you won't leave now until you have."

"Virginity and innocence aren't always the same. I lost my innocence before I met you." The night her mother had been murdered, she thought. But memories of that weren't for tonight.

Tonight was for knowing him.

"Should I disrobe for you, or is that for you to do?"

He gave a short, almost pained laugh before resting his brow to hers in a gesture she found surprisingly tender. "In such a hurry," he murmured. "Some things, especially the first time they're tasted, are better savored than gulped."

"There, you see. I've learned something already. When you kiss me, things wake up inside my body. Things I didn't know were sleeping there until you. I don't know what you feel."

"More than I'd like." He combed his fingers through her hair as he'd longed to for weeks. "More than could be good for either of us. This . . ." He kissed her, softly. "Is a mistake." And again, deeper.

Like her scent, her taste was of springtime, of sunlight and youth. He craved the flavor of it, filled himself on it and the quick catch of her breath as he skimmed his teeth lightly, very light, over her bottom lip.

He let his hands plunge into her hair, the long, sleek fall of it, then under it to tease and waken the nerves along her spine.

When she trembled, he brought his hands to her shoulders to slide the robes down and bare that soft flesh for his lips. He could feel the yielding in her as well as the tremors, and when his mouth brushed along her throat, that seductive pulsing of blood under the skin.

She didn't jolt when his teeth grazed there, but stiffened when he brushed his hand over her breast.

No one had ever touched her so intimately. The flash of heat his hands brought her was a shock, as was the knowledge only a thin layer of material was between his hand and her flesh.

Then even that was gone, and her nightrobes pooled around her feet. Her hand came up instinctively to cover herself, but he only took it, nipped his teeth lightly at her wrist while his eyes watched hers.

"Are you afraid?"

"A little."

"I won't bite you."

"No, no, not of that." She turned the hand he held so her palm cupped his cheek. "There's so much happening inside of me. So much new. No one's ever touched me like this." Gathering her courage, she took his other hand, brought it to her breast. "Show me more."

He brushed his thumb over her nipple, watched the shock of pleasure flicker over her face. "Turn that busy mind off, Moira."

It was already as if mists clouded it. How could she think when her body was swimming in sensation?

He lifted her off her feet so that her face was suddenly on level with his. Then his mouth took hers into the heat again.

The bed was beneath her? Had he crossed the room? How had . . . but her mind misted over again as his hands, his mouth, slid like flaming velvet over her body.

She was a feast, and he'd fasted far too long. But still he sampled slowly, lingering over tastes and textures. And with each shiver, each sigh or gasp, she fed his own arousal.

When her curious hands came too close to breaking his control, he caught them in his own, trapping them as he slowly, mercilessly ravished her breasts.

She was building beneath him; he could feel the power filling her, harder, fuller. And when he pushed her to peak, she bowed up, riding it with a strangled cry.

She melted down, her hands going limp under his.

"Oh." The word was a long expulsion of breath. "Oh, I see."

"You think you do." His tongue traced over the thick beat of the pulse in her throat. As she sighed, he glided his hand between her legs, and sliding into the wet heat, showed her more.

Everything went bright. It blinded her, the brilliance of it all but seared her eyes, her skin, her heart. She was nothing but feelings now, a mass of pleasures beyond any possibility. She was the arrow from the bow, and he'd shot her high, on an endless flight.

His hands simply ruled her until she was a hostage to this never-ending need. Half-mad she struggled with his shirt.

"I need—I want—"

"I know." He pulled off his shirt so she could touch and taste him in turn. And let himself glide on the pleasure of her eager explorations. Her breath against his skin, warm and quick, her fingers tracing, then digging. When her hands gripped his hips, he let her help him strip the rest of his clothes away.

And wasn't sure whether to be amused or flattered when her eyes went huge.

"I . . . I didn't realize. I've seen a cock before, but—"

Now he laughed. "Oh, have you now?"

"Of course. Men bathe in the river, and well, and being curious . . ."

"You've spied on them. A man's pride isn't at its, ah, fullest after a bath in a cold river. I won't hurt you."

He'd have to, wouldn't he? she thought. She'd read of such things, and certainly she'd heard the women speak of it. But she wasn't afraid of the pain. She feared nothing now.

So she laid back again, braced for him. But he only began to touch her again, rouse her again, undo her again as if she were a knot of string.

He wanted her drenched, drowning, beyond thought and nerves. That tight and slender body she'd stiffened in anticipation went loose again. Warm and soft again, with that erotic flush of blood spreading under the skin.

"Look at me. Moira *mo chroi*. Look at me. Look into me."

This he could do, with will and control. He could ease that moment, that flash of pain and give her only the pleasure. When those heavy gray eyes blurred, he pierced her. He filled her.

Her lips trembled, and the moan they formed was low and deep. He kept her trapped in his eyes as he began to move, long, slow thrusts that had the thrill of it rippling over her face, over her body.

Even when he released her from the thrall, when she began to move with him, her eyes stayed locked on his. Her heart was raging, a wild drum against his chest, so vital it seemed—for a moment—as if it beat inside him.

She came with a cry of wonder and abandonment. At last, at last, he let his own need take him with her.

She curled up against him, a cat who'd lapped up every drop of cream. He would, he was sure, berate himself later for what he'd done. But for now he was content to wallow a bit.

"I didn't know it could be like that," she murmured. "So enormous."

"Being so well-endowed, I've likely ruined you for anyone else."

"I didn't mean the size of your pride, as you called it." Laughing, she looked up at him, and saw from his lazy smile he'd understood her meaning perfectly. "I've read of the act, of course. Medical books, storybooks. But the personal experience of it is much more satisfying."

"I'm happy to have assisted you in your research."

She rolled over so she could splay herself on him. "I'll need to do considerably more research, I'm thinking, before I know all there is to know. I'm greedy for knowledge."

"Damn you, Moira." he said it with a sigh as he played with her hair. "You're perfect."

"Am I?" Her already glowing cheeks went pinker with pleasure. "I won't argue because I feel so perfect right now. Thirsty though. Is there any water about?"

He nudged her aside, then rose to fetch the jug. She sat up as he poured, and her hair spilled over her shoulders and breasts. He thought if he had a heartbeat, the sight of her like this might stop it.

He handed her the cup, then sat across from her on the bed. "This is madness. You know it."

"The world's gone mad," she replied. "Why shouldn't we have a piece of it? I'm not being foolish, or careless," she said quickly, laying a hand over his. "I have to do so many things, Cian, so many things where there's no choice for me. This was my choice. My own."

She drank, handed him the cup so he could share. "Will

you regret something that gave us pleasure and harmed no one?"

"You haven't thought about what others will think of you for sharing a bed with me."

"Listen to you, worrying about my reputation of all things. I'm my own woman, and I don't need to explain to anyone whose bed I share."

"Being queen—"

"Doesn't make me less a woman," she interrupted. "A Geallian woman, and we're known for making up our own minds. I was reminded of that earlier tonight." Now she rose, picking up her outer robe to wrap it around her.

He thought it was like she wrapped herself in mist.

"One of my ladies, Ceara—do you know who I mean?"

"Ah, tall, dark blond hair. She took you down in hand-to-hand."

"That she did. Her brother was killed today, on the march. He was young, not yet eighteen." It pierced her heart, again. "I went to the sitting room where my ladies gather and found her there when I would have given her leave to be with her family."

"She's loyal, and thinks of her duty to you."

"Not just to me. She asked if I would give her one thing, in her brother's name. One thing." Emotion quivered in her voice before she conquered it. "And that was to march in the morning with her husband. To go from here, from her children, from safety and face whatever might be on the road. She's not the only woman who asks to go. We're not weak. We don't sit and wait, or no longer will. I was reminded of that tonight."

"You'll let her go."

"Her, and any who wish it. In the end, some who may not wish it will be sent. I didn't come to you because I'm weak, because I needed comfort or protection. I came because I wanted you. I wanted this."

She cocked her head, and with a little smile, let the robe fall. "Now it seems I'm wanting you again. Do I need to seduce you?"

"Too late for that."

Her smile widened as she moved toward the bed. "I've heard—and I've read—that a man needs a bit of time between rounds."

"You force me to repeat myself. I'm not a man."

He grabbed her hand, flipped her onto the bed—and under him.

She laughed, tugged playfully at his hair. "Isn't that handy, under the circumstances."

Later, for the first time in too long to remember, Cian didn't slip into sleep in silence, but to the quiet rhythm of Moira's heart.

It was that heart that woke him. He heard the sudden and rapid beat of it even before she thrashed in sleep.

He cursed, remembering only then she wasn't wearing her cross, nor had he taken any of Glenna's precautions against Lilith's intrusion.

"Moira." He took her shoulders, lifting her. "Wake up."

He was on the point of shaking her out of it when her eyes flew open. Instead of the fear he'd expected, he saw grief.

"It was a dream," he said carefully. "Only a dream. Lilith can't touch you in dreams."

"It wasn't Lilith. I'm sorry I woke you."

"You're shaking. Here." He pulled up a blanket, tossed it over her shoulders. "I'll get the fire going again."

"No need. Don't trouble," she said even as he got up. "I should go. It must be nearing dawn."

He simply crouched down, placed the turf in the hearth. "You won't trust me with this."

"It's not that. It's not." She should have gotten up quickly, she realized. Left straight on waking. For now she couldn't seem to move. "It wasn't Lilith, it was just a bad dream. Just . . ."

But her breath began to hitch and heave.

Rather than go to her, he lit the turf, then moved around the room to light candles.

"I can't speak of it. I can't."

"Of course you can. Maybe not to me, but to Glenna. I'll go wake her."

"No. No. No." She covered her face with her hands.

"So." Since he was up, and unlikely to sleep again for now, he poured himself a cup of blood. "Geallian women aren't weak."

She dropped her hands, and the eyes she'd hidden with them went hot with insult. "You bloody bastard."

"Exactly so. Run back to your room if you can't handle it. But if you stay, you'll pull out whatever's knotted up your guts. Your choice." He took a chair. "You're big on choices, so make one."

"You want to hear my pain, my grief? Why not to you then, who it would mean so little to? I dreamed, as I do over and over, of my mother's murder. Every time, it's clearer than it was before. At first, it was so muddled and pale—like I saw it through a smear of mud. It was easier then."

"And now?"

"I could see it."

"What did you see?"

"I was sleeping." Her eyes were huge on his face, and full of pain. "We'd had supper, and my uncle, Larkin, the family had come. A little family party. My mother enjoyed having them every few months. We had music after, and dancing. She loved to dance, my mother. It was late when we went to bed, and I fell asleep so quickly. I heard her scream."

"No one else heard?"

Moira shook her head. "No. She didn't scream, you see. Not out loud. I don't think she screamed out loud. In her head, she did, and I heard it in mine. Just once. Only once. I thought I imagined it, must have imagined it. But I got up, and went down to her room. Just to ease my mind."

She could see it even now. She hadn't bothered with a candle because her heart was beating so fast and hard. She'd simply run from her room and down to her mother's door.

"I didn't knock. I was saying to myself, no, you'll wake her. Just ease inside and see for yourself that she's sleeping.

"But when I opened the door, she wasn't in her bed, she wasn't sleeping. I heard such sounds, such horrible sounds. Like animals, like wolves, but worse. Oh, worse."

She paused, tried to swallow through her dry throat. "The doors to her balcony were open, and the curtains moving with the breeze. I called out for her. I wanted to run to the doors, but I couldn't. My legs felt as if they'd turned to lead. I could barely make one step in front of the other. I can't say it."

"You can. You walked to the door, to the balcony door."

"I saw . . . Oh God, oh God, oh God. I saw her, on the stones. And the blood, so much blood. Those things were . . . I'll be sick."

"You won't." He got up now, crossed to her. "You won't be sick."

"They were ripping at her." And the words tore out of her now. "Ripping at her body. Demons, things of nightmares, tearing at my mother. I wanted to scream, but I couldn't scream. I wanted to run out and beat them off. One, one looked at me. His eyes red, my mother's blood all over his face. My mother's blood. He charged at the door, and I stumbled back. Back, away from her when I should have gone to her."

"She was dead, Moira, you knew it. You'd be dead if you'd stepped out that door."

"I should have gone to her. It leaped at me, and then I screamed, and screamed and screamed. Even when it fell back as if it had struck a wall, I screamed. Then it all went to black. I did nothing but scream while my mother lay bleeding."

"You're not stupid," he said flatly. "You know you were in shock. You know that what you saw was the same as being struck a stunning physical blow. Nothing you could have done would have saved your mother."

"How could I leave her there, Cian? Just leave her

there." Tears spilled from her eyes to slide down her cheeks. "I loved her more than anything in this world."

"Because your mind couldn't cope with what you saw, with what was—to you—impossible. She was already dead, before you came into the room. She was dead, Moira, the moment you heard her scream."

"How can you be sure? If—"

"They were assassins. They would have killed her instantly. What came after was indulgence, but death was the goal."

Now he took her cold hands in his to warm them. "She would have had only a moment to feel afraid, to feel the pain. The rest, she was beyond the rest of it."

She went very still, stared hard into his eyes. "Will you swear to me you believe that?"

"It's not a matter of believing, but knowing. I can swear that to you. If they'd wanted to torture her, they'd have taken her somewhere where they could have taken their time. What you saw was a cover-up. Wild animals, it would have been said. The way it was with your father."

She let out a long breath, then another as she saw the horrible logic of it. "I've been sick at the thought that she might have been alive when I got there. Still alive while they tore at her. It's somehow easier to know she wasn't."

She knuckled a tear away. "I'm sorry I called you a bastard."

"I pissed you off."

"With cool deliberation. I haven't spoken of that night to anyone before this. I couldn't pull it out of me and look at it, speak of it."

"Now you have."

"Maybe now that I have I won't see her the way she was that night. Maybe I'll see her as she was when she was alive, and happy. All those paintings I have inside my head of her, instead of that last one. Would you hold on to me for a bit?"

He sat, put his arm around her, stroked her hair when she rested her head on his shoulder. "I feel better that I've told you. It was kind of you to piss me off so I would."

"Anytime."

"I wish I could stay, just stay here in the dark and quiet. Stay with you. But I need to go and dress. I need to see the troops off at first light."

She tipped her head up. "Will you kiss me good morning?"

He met her lips with his, drew the kiss out until it brought a pang to his belly.

She opened sleepy eyes. "I could feel that one right down to the soles of my feet. I hope that means I'll walk lighter today."

Rising, she reached for her robes. "You could miss me a little these next hours," she told him. "Or just lie when I see you again and say you did."

"If I tell you I missed you, it won't be a lie."

Dressed, she caught his face in her hands for one more kiss. "Then I'll settle for whatever happens to be the truth."

She picked up her candle, went to the door. After shooting him a last quick grin over her shoulder, she unlatched it.

And opened it an instant before Larkin could knock.

"Moira?" His smile was quick and baffled. It faded instantly when he saw the rumpled bed and Cian lazily wrapping a blanket around his waist.

It was wild rage now that had him shoving Moira aside and charging.

Cian didn't bother to block the blow, but took it full on the face. The second fist he caught in his hand an inch before it struck. "You're entitled to one. But that's enough."

"He's entitled to nothing of the sort." Moira had the presence of mind to shut and latch the door. "Strike out again, Larkin, I'll kick your arse myself."

"You fucking bastard. You'll answer for this."

"Undoubtedly. But not to you."

"It will be me, I promise you."

"Stop it. I mean it!"

When Larkin's fists bunched again, Moira had to fight the urge to bean him with a candlestick. "Lord Larkin, as your queen I command you to step back."

"Oh, don't start bringing rank into it," Cian said easily. "Let the boy try to defend his cousin's honor."

"I'll beat you bloody unconscious."

Out of patience, Moira shoved between them. "Look at me. Damn your thick skull, Larkin, look at me. What room are we in here?"

"The bloody buggering bastard's."

"And do you think he dragged me in here by the hair, forced himself on me? You're a numbskull is what you are. I walked here, and I knocked on Cian's door. I pushed myself into this room, into this bed, because it's what I wanted."

"You don't know what—"

"If you dare, if you *dare* to say to me that I don't know what I want I'll beat *you* bloody unconscious." She drilled a finger into his chest to emphasize the point. "I've a right to this private matter, and you've no say in it at all."

"But he—you. It's not proper."

"Bollocks to that."

"It's hardly a surprise your cousin objects to you sleeping with a vampire." Cian moved away from them, picked up his cup. Deliberately he dipped a finger in, licked the blood from it. "Nasty habit."

"I won't have you—"

"Wait." Larkin interrupted Moira's furious spate. "A moment. I'd like to speak with Cian in private. Talk only," he said before Moira could object. "My word on it."

She pushed a hand through her hair. "I don't have time for either of you, and this foolishness. Be men then, and discuss what is none of your business or concern as if I'm addle-brained. I have to dress and speak to the troops who march today."

She strode to the door. "I'll trust you not to kill each other over my private relationships."

She went out, slammed the door.

"Make it quick," Cian snapped. "I'm suddenly weary of humans."

The worst of the temper had faded out of Larkin's face.

"You think I hit you, that I'm angry because of what you are. I would have had the same reaction, done the same to any man I'd found her with like this. She's my girl, after all. It wasn't part of what I was thinking, as I wasn't thinking in any case."

He shifted his feet, blew out a hard breath. "And now that I do, well, it adds a complicated layer to it all. But I don't want you thinking I planted one on you because you're a vampire. The fact is, I don't think of you that way unless, well, unless I think about it. You're a friend to me. You're one of the six of us."

Even as he spoke, the flush of temper came back. "And I'm saying clear, me demanding, here and now, what the sodding hell you were thinking of taking advantage of my cousin has nothing to do with whether or not you have a fucking heartbeat."

Cian waited a moment. "Are you done with that part of the speech?"

"I am, until I have an answer."

With a nod, Cian sat, picked up his cup again. "You put me in a position, don't you? Calling me a friend, and one of you. I may be the first, but I'll never be the second."

"Bollocks. That's a kind of way out of things. I trust you as I trust few others. And now you've seduced my cousin."

Cian let out a snorting laugh. "You're not giving her enough credit. Neither did I." Idly, Cian traced a finger over the beaded leather. "She unraveled me like a ball of yarn. It doesn't excuse not making her leave, but she's persuasive and stubborn. I couldn't— I didn't resist her."

He glanced over at the maps he'd neglected since she'd knocked on the door. "It won't be a problem as I'm leaving tonight. Earlier if the weather cooperates. I want a firsthand look at the battlefield. So she's safe from me, and me from her, until this is over."

"You can't. You can't," Larkin repeated when Cian merely lifted a brow. "If you go like this, she'll think it's because of her. It'll hurt her. If I'm responsible for you planning to leave—"

"I'd decided it before she came here last night. Partially because I'd hoped to keep my hands off her."

Obviously frustrated, Larkin dragged his hands through his hair. "As you didn't make it away quick enough for that, it'll just have to wait. I'll take you there myself, by air, in a few days or whenever it can be done. But we six need to be together."

Calmer, Larkin studied Cian's face. "We need to be one circle. This is bigger than lying with or not lying with each other. And that, now that my blood's cooler, I can say is between the two of you. It's not my place to interfere. But damn it," he continued, "I'm going to ask you one thing. I'm going to ask you as a friend, and as her blood kin standing for her father. Have you feelings for her? True feelings?"

"You play the friendship card handily, don't you?"

"You are my friend, I care for you as I would a brother. That's the truth from me."

"Damn it." Cian slammed down the cup, then scowled at the blood that splattered on the maps. "You humans crowd me with these feelings. You push them at me, and into me without a single thought for how I can survive them."

"How can you survive without them?" Larkin wondered.

"Comfortably. What difference does it make to you what I feel? She needed someone."

"Not someone. You."

"Her mistake," Cian said quietly. "My damnation. I love her, or I would have taken her before this for the sport of it. I love her, or I'd have sent her away from me last night. How, I'm not sure, but I love her otherwise I wouldn't feel so goddamn desperate. And you repeat that to anyone, I'll snap your head from your shoulders, friend or not."

"All right." With a nod, Larkin got to his feet, offered his hand. "I hope you'll make each other as happy as you're able, for as long as you're able."

"Hell." Cian accepted the hand. "What the hell are you doing here at this hour anyway?"

"Oh, I forgot completely. I thought you'd not yet be in bed. I wanted to ask if you'd be willing to let us—my family—mate your stallion with one of our mares. She's in season, and your Vlad would be a fine sire."

"You want to use my horse as stud?"

"I would, yes, if it's no problem for you. I'd have her brought to him this morning."

"Go ahead. I'm sure he'll enjoy it."

"Thanks for that. We'll pay you the standard fee."

"No. No fee. We'll consider this a gesture between friends."

"Between friends then. Thanks. I'll just go and find Moira, and let her break her temper over my head as I deserve." Larkin paused at the door. "Oh, the mare I've in mind for your stallion. She's fetching."

The quick grin, the quick wink as Larkin went out had Cian laughing despite the mess of the morning.

Chapter 11

At Moira's orders, the flags flew at half-staff, and pipers played a requiem in the dawn light. She would do more, if the gods were willing, for those who gave their lives in this war. But for now, this was all that could be done to acknowledge the dead.

Standing in the courtyard, she was torn between grief and pride as she watched the men and women—the warriors—prepare for the long march east. She'd already bid her farewells to her women, and to Phelan, her cousin's husband.

"Majesty." Niall, the big guard who was now one of her trusted captains, stepped before her. "Should I order the gates opened?"

"In a moment. You wish you were going today."

"I serve at your pleasure, my lady."

"Your wishes are your own, Niall, and I understand them. But I need you here a bit longer. You'll have your time soon enough." They would all have their time, she thought. "Your brother and his family? How are they?"

"Safe, thanks to Lord Larkin and the lady Blair. Though my brother's leg is healing, he won't be able to fight on his feet."

"There will be more to this than swinging a sword on the battlefield."

"Aye." His hand closed over the hilt of the blade at his side. "But in truth I'm ready to swing mine."

She nodded. "You will." She drew a breath. "Open the gates."

For the second time she watched her people march away from the safety of the castle. It would be a scene repeated, she knew, until she herself rode through the gates, leaving behind the very old, the very young, the ill and infirm.

"It's a clear day," Larkin said from beside her. "They should reach the first base safely."

Saying nothing, Moira looked over to where Sinann stood, a child in her arms, another in her belly, one more at her skirts. "She never wept."

"She wouldn't send Phelan off with tears."

"They must be like a flood inside her, yet even now she won't let her children see them. If courage of heart is a weapon, Larkin, we'll sweep the enemy out of existence."

When she turned to go he fell into step with her. "There wasn't time," he began, "to speak with you before. Or after."

"Before the ceremony." Her voice was cool as the morning now. "After you invaded my private life."

"I didn't invade it. I was just there, at what was an awkward time for everyone involved. Cian and I resolved matters between us."

"Oh, did you?" Her eyebrows winged up as she spared him a glance. "Hardly surprising, as men will resolve matters between them one way or another."

"Don't take that royal tone with me." He took her arm, drew her toward one of the gardens, and more privacy. "How, I'm asking you, would you expect me to react when I've seen you've been with him?"

"I suppose expecting you to be well-mannered enough to excuse yourself is too much to ask."

"That's damn right. When I think a man of damn near eternal experiences seduces you—"

"It was the other way around. Entirely."

He flushed, scratched his head, turned a frustrated circle. "I don't want to know the details of it, if you don't mind. I've apologized to him."

"And to me?"

"What do you want from me, Moira? I love you."

"I expect you to understand I'm a woman grown, and one capable of making her own decisions about taking a lover. Don't wince at the term," she snapped impatiently. "I can rule, I can fight, I can die if need be, but your sensibilities are bruised at the thought I can have a lover?"

He thought it over. "Aye. But they'll get over it. I only want, more than anything, never to see you hurt. Not in battle, not in the heart. Is that enough?"

Her feathers smoothed out, and her heart softened as it always did with him. "It must be, as I want the same for you. Larkin, would you say that I have a good, strong mind?"

"Almost too much of both at times."

"In my mind, I know that I can't have a life with Cian. In my head I understand that what I've done will one day cause me grief and pain and sorrow. But in my heart I need what I can have with him now."

She brushed her fingers over the leaves of a flowering shrub. The leaves would fall, she thought, with the first frost. Many things would fall.

"When I put my head and heart together, I know, in both, that he and I are better for what we gave to each other. How can you love and turn away?"

"I don' t know."

She looked back toward the courtyard where people were once again going about their business, their routines. Life went on, she mused, whatever fell. They would see that life went on.

"Your sister watched her man ride away from her, and

knows she might never see him alive again. But she didn't weep in front of him, or in front of their children. When she weeps, she'll weep alone. They're her tears to shed. So will mine be, when this ends."

"Will you do something for me?"

"If I can."

He touched her cheek. "When you have tears, will you remember I have a shoulder for you?"

She smiled now. "I will."

When they parted, she went to the parlor where she found Blair and Glenna already discussing the day's schedule.

"Hoyt?" Moira asked as she poured herself tea.

"Hard at work. We had a slew of new weapons finished yesterday." Glenna rubbed tired eyes. "We'll be charming them twenty-four/seven. I'm going to work with some of those who'll be staying here when the rest of us leave. Basic precautions, defensive, offensive tutorials."

"I'll help you with that. And you, Blair?"

"As soon as Larkin's finished playing pimp, we're—"

"I'm sorry, what?"

"He's got a horny mare, and cleared it with Cian to have Vlad give her a bang. She doesn't even get dinner and drinks first. I thought he told you."

"No, we had other matters, and it must have slipped his mind. So he's having Cian's stallion stand as stud." Her smile came slowly. Yes, life went on. "That's a fine thing. Strong and hopeful—and damn clever, too, as he may be starting a brilliant line there. So, that's what he was about, knocking on Cian's door before sunrise."

"He figured if Cian gave the go-ahead, he could— Wait." Blair held up a hand. "Replay. How do you know he knocked on Cian's door before sunrise?"

"Because I was just leaving the room when Larkin arrived." Moira sipped her tea calmly while Blair slanted a look at Glenna, then puffed out her cheeks.

"Okay."

"Aren't you going to berate and damn Cian for seducing an innocent?"

Blair ran her tongue over her teeth. "You were in his room. I don't think luring you in there to look at his etchings is his style."

Moira slapped a hand to the table with satisfaction. "There! I knew a woman would have more sense—and a bit more respect for my own wiles. And you?" She lifted her eyebrows at Glenna. "Have you nothing to say about it?"

"You're both going to be hurt, and you both know it already. So I'll say I hope you're both able to give and take whatever happiness you can, while you can."

"Thanks."

"Are you all right?" Glenna asked. "The first time is often difficult or a little disappointing."

Now Moira smiled fully. "It was beautiful, and thrilling, and more than I imagined. Nothing I'd played through my mind was near the truth of it."

"A guy isn't good at it after a few hundred years' practice," Blair speculated. "He'd be hopeless. And Larkin walked in when . . . he must've flipped."

"He punched Cian in the face, but they've made it up now. As men do when they pound each other. We've agreed that my choice of bedmate is mine, and moved on."

There was a moment of unified silence as all three women rolled their eyes.

"There's little time left before we leave the safety of this place. And, we can hope, plenty of time after Samhain to debate my choices."

"Then I'll move on, too," Blair told her. "Larkin and I— after considerable browbeating by yours truly—are heading out in a couple of hours to see if we can wrangle ourselves some dragons. He's still not sold on the idea, but he's agreed we'll give it a shot."

"If it's possible, it would be a great advantage for us." Propping her chin on her fist, Moira turned it over in her mind. "I think we could cull out those we feel may not be as strong on the field. If they could ride . . . archers in the air."

"Flaming arrows," Blair said with a nod. "Their aim doesn't have to be on the money."

"As long as they don't shoot the home team," Glenna finished. "There isn't much time left to train, but it's worth the try."

"Fire, aye," Moira agreed. "It's a strong weapon—stronger yet coming from the air. A pity you can't charm the sun onto the tip of an arrow, Glenna, then this would be done."

"I'm going to see if I can move Larkin along." Blair got to her feet, hesitated. "You know, my first time, I was seventeen. The guy, he was in a hurry, and left me thinking at the end: So this is it? BFD. Something to be said for being initiated by someone who knows what he's doing, and has a sense of style."

"There is." Moira's smile was slow and satisfied. "There certainly is." She sensed Blair and Glenna exchange another look over her head, so continued to drink her tea as Blair left the room.

"Do you love him, Moira?"

"I think there's a part of me, inside me, that's waited all my life to feel what I feel for him. What my mother felt for my father in the short time they had. What I know you feel for Hoyt. Do you think I only imagine it's love because of what he is?"

"No, no, I don't. I have strong, genuine feelings for him myself. They have everything to do with who he is. But, Moira, you know you won't be able to have a life with him. That is because of what he is. What neither of you can change any more than the sun can fly on an arrow."

"I listened to everything he and Blair have told us about . . . we'll say his species." And read, Moira thought, countless volumes of fact and lore. "I know he'll never age. He'll be forever as he was in that moment before he was changed. Young and strong and vital. I will change. Grow old, frailer, gray and lined. I'll have sickness, and he never will."

She rose now to walk to a window and the slant of sunlight. "Even if he loved as I love, it's no life for either of us. He can't stand here as I am now and feel the sun warm on my face. All we'd have is the dark. He can't have children. So I won't be able to take away from this even that much of him. I might think, just a year together, or five, or ten. Just that much. I might think and wish for that," she murmured. "But however selfish my own needs might be, I have a duty."

She turned back. "He could never stay here, and I can never go."

"When I fell in love with Hoyt, and believed that we'd never be able to be together, it broke my heart every day."

"But still, you loved him."

"But still I loved him."

Moira stood with the sun slanting at her back, glinting on her crown. "Morrigan said this is the time of knowing. I know my life would be less if I didn't love him. The more life, the longer and harder we'll fight to keep it. So, I have another weapon inside me. And I'll use it."

Moira discovered a long day of teaching children and the old how to defend themselves and each other from monsters was more tiring than hours of sweaty physical training. She hadn't known how hard it would be to tell a child that monsters were real after all.

Her head ached from the questions, and her heart was bruised from the fear she'd seen.

She stepped out into the garden for some air, and to check the sky, again, for Larkin and Blair's return.

"They'll be back before sunset."

She whirled at the sound of Cian's voice. "What are you doing? It's still day."

"Shade's deep here this time of day." Still, he leaned back against the stones, well out of direct light. "It's a pretty spot, a quiet one. And sooner or later, you end up here for a few minutes."

"So, you've studied my habits."

"It passes the time."

"Glenna and I have been with the children and the old

ones, teaching them how to defend themselves if there's an attack here after we leave. We can't spare many of the able-bodied to hold the castle."

"The gates stay locked. Hoyt and Glenna will add a layer of protection. They'll be safe enough."

"And if we lose?"

"There'll be nothing they can do."

"I think there's always something, if you put choice and a weapon in someone's hands." She walked toward him. "Did you come here to wait for me?"

"Yes."

"Now that I'm here, what do you choose to do?"

He stayed where he was, but she could see the war inside him. Though the air suddenly seemed to lash and swirl with that battle, she stood calmly, her eyes grave and patient.

He took her with both hands, a quick and violent jerk that slammed her body to his. His mouth was ravenous.

"A fine choice," she managed when she could speak again.

Then his lips were assaulting hers again, stealing both breath and will.

"Do you know what you've let loose here?" he demanded. Before she could speak, he turned, gripped her hands to drag her up onto his back.

"Cian, what—"

"You'd better hold on," he ordered, interrupting her baffled laugh.

He leaped up. Her arms tightened around his neck as she gasped. He'd simply soared up, more than ten feet in the air from a stand, and was scaling the walls.

"What are you doing?" She risked a look down, felt her stomach shudder at the drop. "You could have warned me you'd lost your bloody mind."

"I lost it when you walked into my room last night." Now he swung through the window, flicked the drapes shut behind him and plunged them into the dark. "This is the price you pay for it."

"If you'd wanted to come back inside, there are doors—"

She let out a quick cry of alarm when he swooped her up. It felt as though she was flying through the air, blind in the dark. Her next cry was of stunned excitement as she found herself under him on the bed, and his hands tugged aside clothes to take flesh.

"Wait. Wait. I can't think. I can't see."

"Too late for both." His mouth silenced her, and his hands drove her to a hard, violent crest.

Her body strained beneath his, and he knew she was reaching, reaching for the burning tip of that crest. Her breath sobbed against his lips as she reached it, and her body went limp.

He gripped her wrists in his hand, pulling her arms over her head. She was one long line of surrender now, and he sheathed himself in her.

She would have cried out again, but she had no voice. No sight, and with her hands captured, no hold. She could do nothing but feel as he plunged himself into her, battering her body with dark, desperate pleasure until she was writhing, then rising, then recklessly matching him beat for violent beat.

This time the hot tip of the crest shattered her.

She lay, scorched skin over melted bones, unable to move even when he left her to light the fire and candles.

"Choice isn't always an issue," he said, and she thought she heard liquid being poured into a cup. "Nor is it a weapon."

She felt the cup bump against her hand, and managed to open her heavy eyes. She made some sound, took the cup, but wasn't at all sure she could swallow any water.

Then she saw the raw red burn on his hand. She pushed up quickly, nearly sloshing water over the rim. "You've burned yourself. Let me see. I—" And she did see, that the mark was the shape of a cross.

"I would have taken it off." Hurriedly, she pushed the cross and chain under her bodice.

"Small price to pay." He lifted her wrist, noted the faint bruising. "I have less control with you than I'd like."

"I like that you have less. Give me your hand. I have a little skill with healing."

"It's nothing."

"Then give me your hand. It's good practice for me." She held hers out expectantly. After a moment he sat beside her, laid his hand in hers.

"I like that you have less," she said again, drawing his eyes to hers. "I like knowing I can be wanted that much, that there's something in me that pulls something in you enough that something strains, nearly snaps."

"Dangerous enough when you're dealing with a human. When a vampire's control snaps, things die."

"You'd never hurt me. You love me."

His face went carefully blank. "Sex rarely has anything to do with—"

"Being inexperienced doesn't make me stupid, or gullible. Is it better?"

"What?"

She smiled at him. "Your hand. The redness has eased."

"It's fine." He drew it away. In fact there was no longer any burning. "You learn quickly."

"I do. Learning is a passion for me. I'll tell you what I've learned of you, when it comes to me. You love me." Her lips were softly curved as she brushed at his hair. "You might have taken me last night—in fact you would have, with less resistance—if it had been just for sex. If it had been only need, only sex, you wouldn't have taken me with such care, or trusted me enough to sleep awhile with me."

She held up a finger before he could speak. "There's more."

"With you, there tends to be."

She rose, straightening her clothes. "When Larkin came in, you did nothing to stop him from striking you. You love me, so you were guilty about taking what you saw as my innocence. You love me, so you've watched me enough to know one of my favorite places. You waited for me there, then you brought me here because you needed me. I pull at you, Cian, as you pull at me."

She watched him as she sipped water. "You love me, as I love you."

"To your peril."

"And yours," she said with a nod. "We live in perilous times."

"Moira, this can never—"

"Don't tell me never." Passion vibrated in her voice and turned her eyes to hellsmoke. "I know. I know all about never. Tell me today. Between you and me let it be today. I have to fight for tomorrow, and the day after and into always. But with this, with you, it's just today. Every today we can have."

"Don't cry. I'd rather have the burn than the tears."

"I won't." She shut her eyes for a moment, and willed herself to keep her word. "I want you to tell me what you've shown me. I want you to tell me what I see when you look at me."

"I love you." He came to her, gently touched her face with his fingertips. "This face, those eyes, all that's inside them. I love you. In a thousand years I've never loved another."

She took his hand, pressed her lips to it. "Oh! Look. There's no burn now. Love healed you. The strongest magic."

"Moira." He kept her hand in his, then laid hers against his chest. "If it beat, it would beat for you."

Tears stung her eyes again. "Your heart may be still, but it isn't empty. It isn't silent because it speaks to me."

"And that's enough?"

"Nothing will ever be enough, but it will do. Come, we'll—"

She broke off when she heard shouting from outside. Turning, she rushed to the window, drew back one of the drapes. Her hand went to her throat. "Cian, come look. The sun's low enough. Come look."

The sky was full of dragons. Emerald and ruby and

gold, their sleek bodies soared above the castle like flashing jewels in the softening light. And their trumpeting calls were like a song.

"Have you ever seen anything so beautiful?"

When his hand laid on her shoulder, Moira reached up, clasped it. "Listen how the people cheer them. Look at the children running and laughing. It's the sound of hope, Cian. The sound, the sight."

"Getting them here, and getting them to be ridden, and to respond in battle like warhorses, two different matters, Moira. But yes, it's a beautiful sight, and a hopeful sound."

She watched as they began to land. "In all your years, I imagine there's little you haven't done."

"Little," he agreed, then had to smile. "But no, I've never ridden a dragon. And yeah, damn right I want to. Let's go down."

There was still enough sunlight that he needed the bloody cloak in open spaces. But despite it, Cian discovered he could still be enchanted and surprised—when he looked into a young dragon's golden eye.

Their sinuous bodies were covered in large, jewel-toned scales that were smooth as glass to the touch. Their wings were like gossamer, and kept close into the body when they grazed along the ground. But it was the eyes that captivated him. They seemed to be alive with interest and intelligence, even humor.

"Figured the younger ones would be easier to train," Blair said to him as they stood, watching. "Larkin's best at communicating with them, even in his regular form. They trust him."

"Which is making it harder on him to use them in battle."

"Yeah, my guy's a softie, and we went around and around about it. He was hoping to convince everyone we could use them for transportation only. But they could make a hell of a difference on the field. Or above it. Still, I have to admit, I get a little twinge at the idea myself."

"They're beautiful—and unspoiled."

"We're going to change the second part." Blair let out a sigh. "Everything's a weapon," she murmured. "Anyway, want to go up?"

"Bet your ass."

"First flight's with me. Yeah, yeah," she said when she saw the objection on his face. "You pilot your own plane, ride horses, leap tall buildings in a single bound. But you've never ridden a dragon, so you're not going solo yet."

She walked slowly toward one of ruby and silver. She'd ridden it back, and still held out her hand so it would test her scent. "Go ahead, let her get acquainted."

"Her?"

"Yeah, I checked out the plumbing." Blair grinned. "Couldn't help it."

Cian laid his hand on the dragon's side, worked his way slowly to the head. "Well now, aren't you a gorgeous one." He began to murmur to her in Irish. She responded with what could only be termed a flirtatious swish of her tail.

"Hoyt's got the same way with them you do." Blair nodded toward where Hoyt was stroking sapphire scales. "Must be a family trait."

"Hmm. Now why is it that Her Majesty there is mounting one by herself?"

"She's ridden a dragon before. That is, she's ridden Larkin in dragon form, so she knows the ropes. Not all she's riding lately."

"Beg your pardon?"

"Just saying. You two look a lot more relaxed than either of you did yesterday." She gave him a wide, toothy grin, then swung onto the dragon. "Alley-oop."

He mounted the same way he'd scaled the walls. With an easy and fluid leap. "Sturdy," Cian commented. "More comfortable than they look. Not so very different from horseback all in all."

"Yeah, if you're talking Pegasus. Anyway, you don't give them a little kick like a horse or cluck. You just—"

Blair demonstrated by leaning down on the dragon's

neck, gliding a hand over its throat. With a sound like silk billowing, it spread its wings. And it rose up into the sky.

"Live long enough," Cian said behind Blair, "you do every damn thing."

"This has got to be one of the best. There are still logistics. The care and feeding, dragon poop."

"I bet it'll make the roses bloom."

She threw back her head and laughed. "Could be. We've got to train them, and their riders. But these beauties catch on fast. Watch." She leaned to the right, and the dragon swerved gently to follow her direction.

"A bit like riding a motorcycle."

"Some of that principle. Lean into the turns. Look at Larkin. That showoff."

He was riding a huge gold, and doing fancy loops and turns.

"Sun's nearly set," Cian commented. "Give it a few minutes, so I won't fry, and we'll give him a run for his money."

Blair shot a look over her shoulder. "You got it. Going to say something."

"When did you not?"

"She's carrying the weight of the fricking world. If what you two have going lightens that a little, I'm for it. Being with Larkin shifted some of mine, so I hope it's working for the two of you."

"You surprise me, demon hunter."

"I surprise myself, vampire, but there it is. Sun's down. You ready to rock?"

With enormous relief, he shoved back the hood of the cloak. "Let's show your cowboy some real moves."

Chapter 12

✦

Davey had been Lilith's for nearly five years. She'd slaughtered his parents and younger sister one balmy summer night in Jamaica. The off-season vacation package—airfare, hotel and continental breakfast included—had been a surprise thirtieth birthday gift from Davey's father to his wife. Their first night there, giddy with holiday spirit and the complimentary glasses of rum punch, they had conceived a third child.

They were, of course, unaware of this, and had things gone differently the prospect of a new baby would have put the skids on tropical vacations for some time to come.

As it was, it was their last family holiday.

It had been during one of Lilith's brief and passionate estrangements from Lora. She'd chosen Jamaica on a whim, and entertained herself picking off locals and the occasional tourist. But she'd grown tired of the taste of the men who trolled the bars.

She wanted some variety—something a little fresher and sweeter. She found just what she was looking for with the young family.

She'd ended the mother's and little girl's giggling moonlight walk along the beach swiftly and viciously. Still she'd been impressed with the woman's panicked and ineffectual struggle, and her instinctive move to protect the child. As they'd satisfied her hunger, she might have left the man and boy splashing unaware in the surf down the beach. But she'd wanted to see if the father would fight for the son. Or beg, as the mother had begged.

He had—and had screamed at the boy to run. Run, Davey, run! he'd shouted. And his terror for his son enriched his blood to make the kill all the sweeter.

But the boy hadn't run. He'd fought, too, and that had impressed her more. He'd kicked and he'd bitten, and had even tried to leap on her back to save his father. It was the wildness of his attack combined with his angelic face that had decided her on changing him rather than draining him and moving on.

When she had pressed his mouth to her bleeding breast, she had felt something stirring inside her that had never stirred for another. The almost maternal sensation had fascinated and delighted her.

So Davey became her pet, her toy, her son, her lover.

It pleased her how quickly, how naturally he'd taken to the change. When she and Lora had reconciled, as they always did, Lilith had told her Davey was their vampiric Peter Pan. The little boy, eternally six.

Still like any boy of six, he needed to be tended to, entertained, taught. Only more so, in Lilith's opinion, as her Davey was a prince. As such, he had both great privilege, and great duty.

She considered this specific hunt to be both.

He quivered with excitement as she dressed him in the rough clothes of a peasant boy. It made her laugh to see his eyes so bright as she added to the game by smearing some dirt and blood on his face.

"Can I see? Can I look in your magic mirror and see myself? Please, please!"

"Of course." Lilith sent a quick and amused look toward

Lora—adult to adult. Picking up the game, Lora shuddered as she picked up the treasured mirror.

"You look terrifying," Lora told Davey. "So small and weak. And . . . *human!*"

Carefully taking the mirror, Davey stared at his reflection. And bared his fangs. "It's like a costume," he said, and giggled. "I get to kill one all by myself, right, Mama? All by myself."

"We'll see." Lilith took the mirror, and bent down to kiss his filthy cheek. "You have a very important part to play, my darling. The most important part of all."

"I know just what to do." He bounced up and down on his toes. "I practiced and practiced."

"I know. You've worked very hard. You're going to make me so proud."

She put the mirror aside, facedown, forcing herself not to take a peek at herself. Lora's burns were still raw and pink, and her reflection so distressing that Lilith only looked into the charmed mirror when Lora was out of the room.

At the knock at the door, she turned. "That will be Midir. Let him in, Davey, then go out and wait with Lucian."

"We're going soon?"

"Yes. In just a few minutes."

He raced to the door, then stood, shoulders straight while the sorcerer bowed to him. Davey marched out, her little soldier, leaving Midir to shut the door behind him.

"Your Majesty. My lady."

"Rise." Lilith gave a careless wave of the hand. "As you see, the prince is prepared. Are you?"

He stood, his habitual black robes whispering with the movement. His face was hard and handsome, framed by his flowing mane of silver hair. Eyes, rich and black, met Lilith's cool blue.

"He will be protected." Midir glanced toward the large chest at the foot of the bed, and the silver pot that stood opened on it. "You used the potion, as I instructed."

"I did, and it's your life, Midir, if it fails."

"It will not fail. It, and the chant I will use, will shield him from wood and steel for three hours. He will be as safe as he would be in your arms, Majesty."

"If not, I'll kill you myself, as unpleasantly as possible. And to make certain of it, you'll go with us on this hunt."

She saw, for just a moment, both surprise and annoyance on his face. Then he bowed his head, and spoke meekly. "At your command."

"Yes. Report to Lucius. He'll see you mounted." She turned away in dismissal.

"You shouldn't worry." Lora crossed to Lilith, slipped her arms around her. "Midir knows it's his life if any harm comes to our sweet boy. Davey needs this, Lilith. He needs the exercise, the entertainment. And he needs to show off a bit."

"I know, I know. He's restless and bored. I can't blame him. It'll be fine, just fine," she said as much to assure herself. "I'll be right there with him."

"Let me go. Change your mind and let me go with you."

Lilith shook her head, brushed a kiss over Lora's abused cheek. "You're not ready for a hunt. You're still weak, sweetheart, and I won't risk you." She took Lora's arms, gripped tight. "I need you on Samhain—fighting, killing, gorging. On that night, when we've flooded that valley with blood, taken what's ours by right, I want you and Davey at my side."

"I hate the wait almost as much as Davey."

Lilith smiled. "I'll bring you back a present from tonight's little game."

Davey rode pinion with Lilith through the moonstruck night. He'd wanted to ride his own pony, but his mama had explained that it wasn't fast enough. He liked going fast, feeling the wind, flying toward the hunt and the kill. It was the most exciting night he could remember.

It was even better than the present she'd given him on

his third birthday when she'd taken him through the summer night to a Boy Scout camping ground. And that had been such *fun*! The screaming and the running and the crying. The *chomp, chomp, chomp*ing.

It was better than hunting the humans in the caves, or burning a vampire who'd been bad. It was better than anything he could remember.

His memories of his human family were vague. There were times he woke from a dream and for a moment was in a bedroom with pictures of race cars on the walls and blue curtains at the windows. There were monsters in the closet of the bedroom, and he cried until she came.

She had brown hair and brown eyes.

Sometimes he would come in, too, the tall man with the scratchy face. He'd chase the monsters away, and she would sit and stroke his hair until he fell asleep again.

If he tried very hard, he could remember splashing in the water, and the feel of the wet sand going gooshy under his feet and the man laughing as the waves splashed them.

Then he wasn't laughing, he was screaming. And he was shouting: Run! Run, Davey, run!

But he didn't try very hard, very often.

It was more fun to think about hunting and playing. His mother let him have one of the humans for a toy, if he was very, very good. He liked best the way they smelled when they were afraid, and the sounds they made when he started to feed.

He was a prince, and could do anything he wanted. Almost.

He would show his mother tonight that he was a big boy now. Then there would be no more almost.

When they stopped the horses, he was almost sick with the thrill of what was to come. They would go on foot from here—and then it would be his turn. His mother held tight to his hand, and he *wished* she wouldn't. He wanted to march like Lucius and the other soldiers. He wanted to carry a sword instead of the little dagger hidden under his tunic.

Still, it was fun to go so fast, faster than any human, across the fields toward the farm.

They stopped again, and his mother crouched down to him to take his face in her hands. "Do just the way we practiced, my sweet boy. You'll be wonderful. I'll be very close, every minute."

He puffed out his chest. "I'm not afraid of them. They're just food."

Behind him Lucius chuckled. "He may be small, Your Majesty, but he's a warrior to the bone."

She rose, and her hand stayed on Davey's shoulder as she turned to Midir. "Your life," she said quietly. "Begin."

Spreading his arms in the black robes, Midir began his chant.

Lilith gestured so that the men spread out. Then she, Lucius and Davey moved closer to the farm.

One of the windows showed the flickering glow of a fire banked for the night. There was the smell of horses closed inside the stable, and the first hints of human. It stirred hunger and excitement in Davey's belly.

"Be ready," she told Lucius.

"My lady, I would give my life for the prince."

"Yes, I know." She laid a hand briefly on Lucius's arm. "That's why you're here. All right, Davey. Make me proud."

Inside the farmhouse, Tynan and two others stood guard. It was nearly time to wake their relief, and he was more than ready for a few hours' sleep. His hip ached from the wound he'd suffered during the attack on their first day's march. He hoped when he was able to close his gritty eyes he wouldn't see the attack again.

Good men lost, he thought. Slaughtered.

The time was coming when he would avenge those men on the battlefield. He only hoped that if he died there, he fought strong and brave first and destroyed a like number of the enemy.

He shifted his stance, preparing to order the relief watch when a sound brought his hand to the hilt of his sword.

His eyes sharpened; his ears pricked. It might have been a night bird, but it had sounded so human.

"Tynan."

"Yes, I hear it," he said to one of the others on guard.

"It sounds like weeping."

"Stay alert. No one is to . . ." He trailed off as he spotted a movement. "There, near the northmost paddock. Do you see? Ah, in the name of all the gods, it's a child."

A boy, he thought, though he couldn't be sure. The clothes covering him were torn and bloody, and he staggered, weeping, with his thumb plugged into his mouth.

"He must have escaped some raid near here. Wake the relief, and stay alert with them. I'll go get the child."

"We were warned not to step outside after sundown."

"We can't leave a child out there, and hurt by the look of him. Wake the relief," Tynan repeated. "I want an archer by this window. If anything out there moves but me and that child, aim for its heart."

He waited until the men were set, and watched the child fall to the ground. A boy, he was nearly sure now, and the poor thing wailed and whimpered pitifully as it curled into a ball.

"We could keep an eye on him until morning," one of the others on duty suggested.

"Are Geallian men so frightened of the dark they'd huddle inside while a child bleeds and cries?"

He shoved the door open. He wanted to move quickly, get the child inside to safety. But he forced himself to stop his forward rush when the boy's head came up and the round little face froze in fear.

"I won't hurt you. I'm one of the queen's men. I'll take you inside," he said gently. "It's warm, and there's food."

The boy scrambled to his feet and screamed as if Tynan had hacked him with a sword. "Monsters! Monsters!"

He began to run, limping heavily on his left leg. Tynan dashed after him. Better to scare the boy than to let him get away and very likely be a snack for some demon. Tynan caught him just before the boy managed to scramble over the stone wall bordering the near field.

"Easy, easy, you're safe." The boy kicked and slapped and screamed, shooting fresh pain into Tynan's hip. "You need to be inside. No one's going to hurt you now. No one . . ."

He thought he heard something—chanting—and tightened his grip on the child. He turned, ready to sprint back for the house when he heard something else, something that came from what he held in his arms. It was a low, feral growl.

The boy grinned, horribly, and went for his throat.

There was something beyond agony, and it took Tynan to his knees. Not a child, not a child at all, he thought as he fought to free himself. But the thing ripped at him like a wolf.

Dimly he heard shouts, screams, the thud of arrows, the clash of swords. And the last he heard was the hideous sound of his own blood being greedily drunk.

They used fire, tipping arrows with flame, and still, nearly a quarter of their number were killed or wounded before the demons fell back.

"Take that one alive." Lilith delicately wiped blood from her lips. "I promised Lora a gift." She smiled down at Davey who stood over the body of the soldier he'd killed. It swelled pride in her that her boy had continued to feed even when troops had dragged the body, with the prince clinging to it, away from the battle.

Davey's eyes were red and gleaming, and his freckles stood out like gold against the rosy flush the blood had given his cheeks.

She picked him up, held him high over her head. "Behold your prince!"

The troops who hadn't been destroyed in the brief battle knelt.

She lowered him to kiss him long and deep on his mouth.

"I want more," he said.

"Yes, my love, and you'll have more. Very soon. Toss that thing on a horse," she ordered with a careless gesture toward Tynan's body. "I have a use for it."

She mounted, then held out her arms so that Davey could leap into them. With her cheek rubbing against his hair, she looked down at Midir.

"You did well," she said to him. "You can have your choice of the humans, for whatever purposes you like."

The moonlight shone on his silver hair as he bowed. "Thank you."

Ooira stood in the brisk wind and watched dragons and riders circle overhead. It was a stunning sight, she thought, and would have sent her heart soaring under any other circumstances. But these were military maneuvers, not spectacle.

Still, she could hear children calling out and clapping, and more than a few of them pretending they were dragon or rider.

She smiled a greeting when her uncle strode over to watch beside her. "You're not tempted to fly?" she asked him.

"I leave it for the young—and the agile. It's a brilliant sight, Moira. And a hopeful one."

"The dragons have lifted the spirits. And in battle, they'll give us an advantage. Do you see Blair? She rides as if she was born on the back of one."

"She's hard to miss," Riddock murmured as Blair drove her mount toward the ground at a dizzying speed, then swept up again.

"Are you pleased she and Larkin will marry?"

"He loves her, and I can think of no other who suits him so well. So aye, his mother and I are pleased. And will miss him every day. He must go with her," Riddock said before Moira could speak. "It's his choice, and I feel—in my heart—it's the right choice for him. But we'll miss him."

Moira leaned her head against her uncle's arm. "Aye, we will."

She would be the only one to remain, she thought as she went inside again. The only one of the first circle who would remain in Geall after Samhain. She wondered how she would be able to bear it.

Already the castle felt empty. So many had already gone ahead, and others were busy with duties she'd assigned. Soon, very soon, she would leave herself. So it was time, she determined, to write down her wishes in the event she didn't return.

She closed herself in her sitting room and sat to sharpen her quill. Then changed her mind and took out one of the treasures she'd brought back with her from Ireland.

She would write this document, Moira determined, with the instrument of another world.

She'd use a pen.

What did she have of value, she wondered, that wouldn't by rights belong to the next who ruled Geall?

Some of her mother's jewelry, certainly. And this she began to disburse in her mind between Blair and Glenna, her aunt and cousin, and lastly, her ladies.

Her father's sword should be Larkin's, she decided, and the dagger he'd once carried would go to Hoyt. The miniature of her father would be her uncle's if she died before him, as her father and uncle had been fast friends.

There were trinkets, of course. Bits of this and that which she gave thought to bequesting.

To Cian she left her bow and quiver, and the arrows she'd made with her own hand. She hoped he'd understand that these were more than weapons to her. They were her pride, and a kind of love.

She wrote it all carefully, sealed it. She would give the document to her aunt for safekeeping.

She felt better having done it. Lighter and clearer in her mind somehow. Setting the paper aside, she rose to face the next task. Moving back into the bedroom, she crossed to the balcony doors. The drapes still hung there, blocking the light, the view. And now she drew them back, let the soft light spill through.

In her mind's eye she saw it again, the dark, the blood, the torn body of her mother and the things that mutilated her. But now she opened the door and made herself walk through them.

The air was cool and moist, and overhead the sky was full of dragons. Streaks and whirls of color riding the pale blue. How her mother would have loved the sight of them, loved the sound of the wings, the laughter of the children in the courtyard below.

Moira walked to the rail, laid her hands on it and felt the sturdy stone. And standing as her mother had often done, she looked out over Geall, and swore to do her best.

She might have been surprised to know that Cian spent a large portion of his restless day doing what she had done. His lists of bequests and instructions were considerably longer than hers and minutely more detailed. But then he'd lived considerably longer and had accumulated a great deal.

He saw no reason for any of it to go to waste.

A dozen times during the writing of it he cursed the quill and wished violently for the ease and convenience of a computer. But he kept at it until he believed he'd spread his holdings out satisfactorily.

He wasn't certain it could all be done as some of it would be up to Hoyt. They'd speak about it, Cian thought. If he could count on anything, he could count on Hoyt doing everything in his considerable power to fulfill the obligation Cian meant to give him.

All in all, he hoped it wouldn't be necessary. A thousand years of existence didn't mean he was ready to give it up. And he damn well didn't intend to go to hell until he'd sent Lilith there before him.

"You were always one for business."

He pushed to his feet, drawing his dagger in one fluid motion as he turned toward the sound of the voice. Then the dagger simply fell out of his limp fingers.

Even after a millennium, there can be shocks beyond imagining.

"Nola." His voice sounded rusty on the name.

She was a child, his sister, just as she'd been when he'd last seen her. Her long dark hair falling straight, her eyes deep and blue. And smiling.

"Nola," he said again. "My God."

"I thought you would say you have no god."

"None that would claim me. How can you be here? Are you here?"

"You can see for yourself." She spread her arms, then did a little turn.

"You lived, and you died. An old woman."

"You didn't know the woman, so I'm as you remember me. I missed you, Cian. I looked for you, even knowing better. For years I looked and I hoped for you and for Hoyt. You never came."

"How could I? You know what I was. Am. You understand that now."

"Would you have hurt me? Or any of us?"

"I don't know. I hope not, but I didn't see any reason to risk it. Why are you here?"

He reached out, but she held up her hand and she shook her head. "I'm not flesh. Only an apparition. Here to remind you that you may not be what you were when you were mine, but you're not what she would have made you."

Because he needed a moment, he bent to pick up the dagger he'd dropped, then sheathed it again. "What does it matter?"

"It does. It will." And apparition or not, her eyes swam as they locked on his. "I had children, Cian."

"I know."

"Strong, skilled, gifted. Your blood, too."

"Were you happy?"

"Oh, aye. I loved a man, and he loved me. We had those children, and lived a good life. And still my brothers left a place in my heart I could never fill. A little ache inside.

I would see you, and Hoyt, sometimes. In the water, or the mist, or the fire."

"There are things I've done I wouldn't have you see."

"I saw you kill, and feed. I saw you hunt humans as you'd once hunted deer. And I saw you stand by my grave in the moonlight and lay flowers on it. I saw you fight beside the brother we both love. I saw my Cian. Do you remember how you'd pull me up on your horse and ride and ride?"

"Nola." He rubbed his fingers over his brow. He hurt too much to think of it. "We're both dead."

"And we both lived. She came to my window one night."

"She? Who?" Inside him, he went cold as winter. "Lilith."

"We're both dead," Nola reminded him. "But your hands go to fists and your eyes go sharp as your dagger. Would you still protect me?"

He walked to the fire, kicked idly at the simmering turf. "What happened?"

"It was more than two years after Hoyt left us. Father had died and mother was ill. I knew she would never be strong again, that she would die. I was so sad, so afraid. I woke from sleep in the dark, and there was a face at my window. So beautiful. Golden hair and a sweet smile. She whispered to me, called me by name. 'Ask me in,' she said, and promised me a treat."

Nola tossed back her hair, and her face was full of disdain. "She thought since I was only a girl, the youngest of us, I'd be foolish, I'd be easy to trick. I went to the window, and I looked in her eyes. There's power in her eyes."

"Hoyt must have told you not to take such risks. He must have—"

"He wasn't there, and neither were you. There was power in me as well. Have you forgotten?"

"No. But you were a child."

"I was a seer, and the blood of demon hunters was in my veins. I looked in her eyes and I told her it was my blood who would end her. My blood who would rid the worlds of her. And for her there would be no eternity in hell, or any-where. Her damnation would be an end of all. She would be dust, and no spirit would survive."

"She wouldn't have been pleased."

"Her beauty remains even when she shows her true self. That's another power. I held up Morrigan's cross, that I wore always around my neck. The light flashed from it, like a sunbeam. She was screaming when she ran."

"You were always fearless," he murmured.

"She never came back while I lived, and never came again until you and Hoyt went home together. You're stronger than you were without him, and he with you. She fears that, hates that. Envies that."

"Will he live through this?"

"I can't know. But if he falls, it will be as he lived. With honor."

"Honor's cold comfort when you're in the ground."

"Then why do you hold your own?" she demanded with a whip of impatience in her voice. "It's honor that brings you here. Honor that you'll carry into battle along with your sword. She couldn't drain it out of you, and just the lit-tle she left was enough for you to draw on again. You made this choice. You've still more to make. Remember me."

"Don't. Don't leave."

"Remember me," she repeated. "Until we see each other again."

Alone, he sat, lowering his head into his hands. And re-membered far too much.

Chapter 13

For the most part, Cian avoided the tower room where Hoyt and Glenna worked their magicks. Such things often involved considerable light, flashes, fire and other elements unfavorable to vampires.

But in a way he hadn't—or hadn't admitted to in centuries—he needed his brother.

He noted before he knocked that one or both of his magically inclined relations had taken the precaution of drawing protection symbols on the tower door to keep the curious out. He'd have preferred to stay out himself, but he knocked.

When Glenna answered, there was a dew of sweat on her skin. Her hair was bundled up, and she'd stripped down to a tank and cotton pants. Cian lifted a brow.

"Am I interrupting?"

"Nothing physical, unfortunately. It's just viciously hot in here. We're working on a lot of heat and fire magicks. Sorry."

"I'm not bothered much by temperature extremes."

"Oh. Right." She closed the door behind him. "We've

got the windows blocked off—keeping everything contained—so you won't have to worry about the light."

"It's nearly sundown."

He looked over to where Hoyt stood over an enormous copper trough. Hoyt had his hands spread above it, and there was a sensation, even across the room, of more heat, of power and energy.

"He's fire-charging weapons," Glenna explained. "And I've been working on, well, it's a kind of bomb, really. Something we may be able to drop from the air."

"The NSO would love to have you on staff."

"I could be their version of Q." She swiped at her damp brow with the back of her hand. "You want a tour?"

"Actually . . . I wanted to . . . I'll just speak with Hoyt when he's not so involved."

"Wait." It was the first time Glenna could remember seeing Cian flustered. No, not flustered, she thought. Upset. "He needs a break. So do I. If you can stand the heat, just hang out a few more minutes. He's nearly done. I'm going to go get some air."

Cian caught her hand before she turned to go. "Thank you. For not asking."

"No problem. And if it is a problem, I'll be around."

When she went out, Cian leaned against the door. Hoyt remained just as he'd been, hands spread over the silver smoke that rose from the trough. His eyes were darkened as they were when he held his power strong and steady.

It had always been so, Cian thought, since they were children.

Like Glenna, Hoyt had stripped down for work, and wore a white T-shirt and faded jeans. It was odd, even after the past months, to see his brother in twenty-first-century clothing.

Hoyt had never been one for fashion, Cian recalled. But for dignity and purpose. However much they looked alike, they'd approached life from different poles. Hoyt for solitude and study, and he himself for society and business—and the pleasure both brought him.

Still, they'd been close, had understood each other on a level few others could. Had loved each other, Cian thought now, in a way that was as strong and as steady as Hoyt's power.

Then the world, and everything in it, had changed.

So what was he doing here? Looking for answers, for comfort, when he knew there could be neither? None of it could be taken back, not a single act, a single thought, a single moment. It was a foolish waste of time and energy on all counts.

The man who stood like a statue in the smoke wasn't the man he'd known, any more than he was the same man he'd been. Or a man at all for that matter.

Too much time spent with these people, these feelings, these needs made him forget what could never be altered. He pushed away from the door.

"Wait. A moment more."

Hoyt's voice stopped him—and it irritated him to understand Hoyt had known he wasn't simply shifting position but leaving.

Hoyt lowered his hands, and the smoke whisked away.

"Sure we'll go into this well-armed." Hoyt reached into the trough and lifted a sword by the hilt. Spinning, he pointed it toward the hearth. And shot a beam of fire.

"Will you be using one of these?" Hoyt turned the sword in his hand, eying its edge. "You've skill enough not to burn yourself."

"I'll use whatever comes best to hand—and do my best to stay away from those you arm who are considerably less skilled."

"It's not worry over poor swordsmanship that brings you here."

"No."

Since he was here, he'd do what he'd come to do. But he wandered the room first while Hoyt removed the other weapons from the trough. The room smelled of herbs and smoke, of sweat and effort.

"I've chased your woman away."

"I'll find her again."

"Since she's not here, I'll ask you. Are you afraid you'll lose her in this?"

Hoyt laid the last sword on the worktable. "It's my last thought before sleep, my first on waking. The rest of the time I try not to think of it—or let out the part of myself that wants to lock her away safe until this is over."

"She isn't a woman you could lock away, even with your skill."

"No, but knowing that doesn't stop the fear. Are you afraid for Moira?"

"What?"

"Do you think I don't know you're with her? That your heart is with her?"

"A temporary madness. It'll pass." At his brother's quiet, steady look, Cian shook his head. "I've no choice in it, and neither does she. What I am doesn't run to white picket fences and golden retrievers." He waved it away when Hoyt's look turned puzzled. "To home and hearth, brother. I can't give her a life—if I wanted to—and what passes for mine will go on long after hers is ended. And that's not what I've come to tell you."

"Tell me this first. Do you love her?"

It came into him, the truth of it, swirling through his heart and into his eyes. "She is . . . She is like a light for me when I've lived eternally in the dark. But the dark is mine, Hoyt. I know how to survive there, to be content and productive and entertained there."

"You don't say happy."

Frustration snapped into his voice. "I was happy enough before you came. Before you changed everything again, as surely as Lilith had done to me. What would you have me do? Wish for what you have, and will have with Glenna if you live? What good will it do me? Will it start my heart again? Can your magic do that?"

"No. I've found nothing that can take you back. But—"

"Let it be. I am what I am, and I've done more than well enough. I'm not whining about it. She's an experience.

Love is an experience, and I've always sought them out."
He dragged his hands through his hair. "Christ. Is there
anything to drink in this place?"

"There's whiskey." Hoyt lifted his chin toward a cabinet. "I'll have one as well."

Cian poured whiskey generously into cups, then crossed
to where Hoyt drew two three-legged stools together. So
Cian sat, and they drank for a few moments in silence.

"I've written out a document, a kind of will, should my
luck run out on Samhain."

Hoyt lifted his eyes from his whiskey and met Cian's. "I
see."

"I've accumulated considerable property and holdings,
assets, personal items. I expect you'll see to them, as I've
instructed."

"I will, of course."

"It'll be no small task as they're spread out over the
world. I don't keep a great many eggs in one basket. There
are passports and other identification papers in the New
York apartment, and in safety deposit boxes here and there.
If any are useful to you, you're welcome to them."

"Thanks for that."

Cian swirled the whiskey in his glass, kept his eyes on
it. "There are some things I'd like Moira to have, if you can
get them here."

"I'll get them here."

"I thought to leave the club and the apartment in New
York to Blair—and to Larkin. I think they'd suit them better than you."

"They would. They'll be grateful, I'm sure."

Annoyance rose up at his brother's easy and practical
tone. "Well, don't let sentiment choke you, as it's more
likely I'll be holding a wake for you than you for me."

Hoyt angled his head. "Do you think so?"

"I damn well do. You haven't had three decades and I've
had near a hundred. And you never were as good in a fight
as me when we were both alive, however many tricks you
have up your sleeve."

"But then again, as you said, we aren't what we were, are we?" Hoyt smiled pleasantly. "I'm determined we'll both come through this, but if you fall, well . . . I'll lift a glass to you."

Cian let out a half laugh as Hoyt did just that.

"And would you be wanting pipes and drums as well?"

"Oh, bugger it." Now a wicked gleam came into Cian's eyes. "I'll toss in some fifes for yours, then console your grieving widow."

"At least I won't have to dig a hole for you, seeing as you'll just be dust, but I'll show you the honor of having a stone carved. 'Here doesn't lie Cian, for he's blown off with the wind. He lived and he died, then stayed on like the last annoying guest to leave the ball.' Does that suit you?"

"I'm thinking I'll go back and change some of those bequests, for principle only, seeing as I'll be singing 'Danny Boy' over your grave."

"What's 'Danny Boy'?"

"A cliche." Cian picked up the bottle he'd set on the floor and poured more whiskey into the cups. "I saw Nola."

"What?" Hoyt lowered the cup he'd just lifted. "What did you say?"

"In my room. I saw Nola, spoke with her."

"You dreamed of Nola?"

"Is that what I said?" Cian snapped. "I said I saw her, spoke with her. As awake then as I am now, looking and speaking to you. She was still a child. Jesus, there isn't enough whiskey in the world for this."

"She came to you," Hoyt murmured. "Our Nola. What did she say?"

"She loved me, and you. She missed us. She'd waited for us to come home. Damn it. Goddamn it." He pushed up to pace. "She was a child, exactly as she'd been the last I saw her. It was a lie, of course. She'd grown up, grown old. She'd died and gone to dust."

"And why would she come to you as a grown woman, or an old one?" Hoyt demanded. "She came to you as you remembered her, as you think of her. She gave you a gift. Why are you angry?"

It was fury in him now, fury to wrap tight around the pain. "How can you know what it is to feel this, to have it ripping inside you? She looked the same, and I'm not. She talked of how I'd swing her up on my horse and take her riding. And it was like it was yesterday. I can't have those yesterdays in my head and stay sane."

He turned back. "At the end of this, you'll know you did what you could, what was asked of you—for her, for all of them. If you live, whatever pang you feel at leaving them behind will be balanced out by that knowing, and by the life you make with Glenna. I have to go back where I was. I have to. I can't take this with me and survive it."

Hoyt was quiet a moment. "Was she in pain, afraid, grieving?"

"No."

"And you can't take that with you and survive it?"

"I don't know, that's the plain truth. But I know that one feeling leads to another until you drown in them. I'm half drowned now with what's in me for Moira."

He calmed himself, sat again. "She wore the cross you gave her, Nola did. She said she wore it always, just as you told her. I thought you should know. And I thought you should know she told me Lilith had come back, and tried to lure her into an invitation."

As Cian's had done, Hoyt's hand fisted. "That hell-bitch went for our Nola?"

"She did, and got a boot up the ass for the trouble—metaphorically." He told Hoyt what Nola had said, watched Hoyt's grim face soften a little with pride and satisfaction. "Then she flashed that cross of yours and sent her packing. According to Nola she never came back again, until we did."

"Well now, well. Isn't that interesting. The cross didn't just shield the wearer, it frightened Lilith enough to send her haring off. That, and the prediction we'd end her."

"Which may be why she's so determined to end us."

"Aye. Nola's threat could have added weight to that. Imagine how it must have been for Lilith, being frightened off by a child."

"She wants her own back, no doubt of it. She wants to win this, of course. To set herself up as a kind of god, but under that, it's us. The six of us and the connection between us. She wants us destroyed."

"Hasn't had much luck with that, has she?"

"And what do you think of that? The gods depose, don't they? We've all of us had our close calls, and bled for it. But we're all of us, Lilith included, being driven toward one time and place. The fact of the matter is, I don't care for being led by the nose by gods any more than demons."

Hoyt lifted his brows. "What choice is there?"

"They all talk of choice, but which of us would turn away from this now? It's not just humans who have pride, after all. So, the time clicks away." He rose. "And we'll see what we see on that reckoning day. The sun's well down. I'm going out for air."

He walked to the door, paused to glance back. "She couldn't tell me if you survived it."

Hoyt lifted a shoulder, finished off his whiskey. Then he smiled. " 'Danny Boy,' is it?"

Cian went to see to his horse. Then, though he knew it was risky, saddled Vlad and rode out through the gates. He needed the speed, and the night. Maybe he needed the risk as well.

The moon was past half full now. When that circle was complete, blood—human and demon—would soak the ground.

He hadn't fought in other wars, hadn't seen the point of them. Wars for land, for riches and resources. Wars waged in the name of faith. But this one had come to be his.

No, it wasn't only humans who had pride, or even honor. Or love. So for all of that, this was his. If his luck was in, he'd ride one day again in Ireland—or wherever he chose. And he'd think of Geall with its lovely hills and thick forests. He'd think of the green and the tumbling water, the standing stones, and the fanciful castle on the rise near the river.

He'd think of its queen. Moira, with the long gray eyes and the quiet smile that masked a clever, flexible brain and a deep, rich heart. Who would have believed that after all these lifetimes he would be seduced, bewitched, drowned in such a woman?

He took Vlad leaping over stone walls, galloping over fields where the air was sweet and cool with the night. The moonlight rained down on the stones of her castle, and the windows glowed with candles and lamps. She'd kept her word, he thought, and had hoisted that third flag, so there was claddaugh, dragon, and now the bright gold sun.

He wished, with all that was in him, that she would give Geall, and all the worlds, the sun after the blood spilled.

Maybe he couldn't take all these feelings, these needs and wants with him and survive. But he wanted to take this. When he went back to the dark, he wanted to take this much of her, and have that single glimmer of light through all his nights.

He rode back, and found her waiting, with her bow in her hands and the sword of Geall strapped to her side.

"I saw you ride out."

He dismounted. "Covering my back, were you?"

"We'd agreed none of us would go out alone, particularly after dark."

"I needed it," was all he said, and led the stallion to the stables.

"So it seemed, from the way you were riding. I didn't see any hounds of hell, but it appeared you did. Would you trust one of the stable boys to cool him and settle him for the night? It helps them to have the work, as much as it might help you to have a wild ride."

"There's a scolding under that accommodating tone, Majesty. You do it very well."

"Learned at my mother's knee." She took the reins herself, then passed them with instructions to the boy who came hurrying out from the stables.

When she'd finished, she looked up at Cian. "Are you in a mood?"

"Always."

"I should have said a difficult mood, but the answer might be always to that as well. If you're not, more than usual, I'd hoped you'd have a meal with me. In private. I'd hoped you'd stay with me tonight."

"And if I am in a difficult mood?"

"Then a meal and some wine might sweeten it enough for you to lie with me, and stay with me. Or, we can argue over the food, then go to bed."

"I'd have to have taken a spill from the horse and damaged my brain to turn down that offer."

"Good. I'm hungry."

And furious, he thought with some amusement. "Why don't you get the lecture out of your system. It's liable to give you indigestion."

"I don't have a lecture, and if I did, it's not what would suit me." She walked—regally, he thought—across the courtyard. "What I'd like is to give you a good, strong kick in the ass for taking a chance like that. But . . ."

She drew a long breath, then a second as they entered the castle. "I know what it is to need to get away, to just go for a bit. How it feels you'll rip apart from the pressure inside if you don't. I can go into a book and be quiet in my mind again. You needed the ride, the speed of it. And, I think, there are times you just need the dark."

He said nothing until they'd come to the door of her room. "I don't know how you can understand me that way."

"I've made a study of you." Now she smiled a little, looking up and into his eyes. "I'm a good study. And added to it, you're inside my heart now. You're inside me, so I know."

"I haven't earned you," he said quietly. "That occurs to me now. I haven't earned you."

"I'm not a wage or a prize. I wouldn't care to be earned." She opened the door to her sitting room.

She'd had the fire lit, and the candles. The cold supper and the good wine were already laid out, with flowers from one of the hothouses.

"You've gone to some trouble." He shut the door behind them. "Thank you."

"It was for me, but I'm glad you like it. I wanted a night, just one, where it would be only the two of us. As if none of this was happening. Where we could sit and talk and eat. And where I might drink just a little too much wine."

She laid down her bow and quiver, unhooked her sword. "One night when we don't talk of battles and weapons and strategy. You'd tell me you love me. You wouldn't even have to say it, because I'd see it when you looked at me."

"I do love you. I looked back at the castle, and saw the glow in the windows from these candles. That's how I think of you. A steady glow."

She stepped toward him, took his face in her hands. "And if I think of you as the night, it's the mystery of it, and the thrill. I'll never be afraid of the dark again, because I've seen into it."

He kissed her brow, her temples, then her lips. "Let me pour you the first glass of too much wine."

She sat at the little table and watched him. This was her lover, she thought. This strange and compelling man who carried wars inside him. And she'd have this night with him, the whole of it, and a few hours of peace for them both.

She chose food for his plate, knowing it was a wifely gesture. She'd have that as well, this one night. When he sat across from her, she lifted her glass to his. "*Sláinte.*"

"*Sláinte.*"

"Will you tell me the places you've seen? Where you've traveled? I want to go there in my mind. I studied the maps in your library in Ireland. Your world is so big. Tell me the wonderful things you've seen."

He took her to Italy during the Renaissance, and Japan in the time of samurai, to Alaska during the gold rush, to Amazon jungles and to African plains.

He tried to paint quick snapshots with words, so she could see the variety, the contrasts, the changes. He could all but see her mind opening to take it in. She asked dozens of questions, particularly when something he related expanded or contradicted what she'd read when in his library.

"I've wondered what lies beyond the sea." She propped her chin on her fist as he poured more wine. "Other lands, other cultures. It seems that if we were once a part of Ireland, that there may be parts of Italy and America, Russia, all those wondrous places here, in this world, too. One day . . . I'd like to see an elephant."

"An elephant."

She laughed. "Aye, an elephant. And a zebra and a kangaroo. I'd like to see the paintings from the artists you've seen, and the ones I found in your books. Michelangelo and DaVinci, Van Gogh, Monet, Beethoven."

"Beethoven was a composer. I don't believe he could paint."

"That's right, sure, that's right. The *Moonlight Sonata*, and all those symphonies with numbers. It's the wine muddling it up a bit. I'd like to see a violin, and a piano. And an electric guitar. Do you play any of those?"

"Actually, it's a little known fact that there were six original Beatles. Never mind."

"I know. John, Paul, George and Ringo."

"You've got a memory like that elephant you'd like to see."

"As long as you remember it, it belongs to you. I'll likely never see an elephant, but I'll have orange trees one day. The seeds in the hothouse pots are sprouting." She held her thumb and forefinger up, close together. "That bit of green coming out of the dirt. Glenna tells me the blossoms will be very fragrant."

"Yes, they will be."

"And I took other things."

It amused him to hear the confessional tone in her voice. "So, you've sticky fingers, have you?"

"I thought, if I'm not meant to take them to Geall, they won't go. I took a cutting of your roses. All right, well, three cuttings. I was greedy. And a photograph Glenna took of Larkin and me. And a book. I confess it, I took a book right out of your library. It's a thief I am."

"Which book?"

"It was poems by Yeats. I wanted it particularly because he was Irish it said, and it seemed important I bring something that was written down by an Irishman."

Because you were Irish, she thought. Because the book was yours.

"And the poems were so beautiful and strong," she continued. "I told myself I was going to give it back to you once I'd copied more down, but that's a lie. I'm keeping it."

He laughed, shook his head. "Consider it a gift."

"Thank you, but I'll happily pay you for it." She rose, stepped over to where he sat. "And you may name the price." She sat on his lap, linked her arms around his neck. "He wrote something, your Yeats, that made me think of you, and especially what we have between us tonight. He wrote: 'I spread my dreams at your feet. Tread softly because you tread on my dreams.' "

She combed her fingers through his hair. "You can give me your dreams, Cian. I'll tread softly."

Impossibly moved, he rested his cheek against hers. "You're unlike any other."

"With you, I'm more than I ever was. Will you come out, stand for a while on the balcony with me? I'd like to look at the moon and the stars."

He rose with her, but when he turned, she drew him back. "No, the bedroom balcony."

He thought of her mother, of what she'd seen. "Are you sure?"

"I am. I stood out there today, alone. I want to stand there with you, in the night. I want you to kiss me there so I'll remember it all of my life."

"You'll want a cloak. It's cold."

"Geallian woman are made of sterner stuff."

And when she led the way, when her hand gripped his tight as she opened the balcony doors, he thought, yes, yes, she was.

Chapter 14

He kissed her on the balcony, and she would re-member it, all of it. She wouldn't forget the quiet mu-sic of the night, the chill in the air, the easy skill of his mouth.

Tonight she wouldn't think of sunrise and the obliga-tions that came with it. The night was his time, and while she was with him, it would be hers.

"You've kissed many women."

He smiled a little, brushed his lips over hers again. "I have."

"Hundreds."

"At least."

Her eyes narrowed. "Thousands."

"Very likely."

"Hmm." She wandered away from him, then turned, leaning back on the stone rail. "I think I'll make a decree, that every man must come and kiss their queen. So I can catch up. At the same time it would be a kind of study, a comparison. I could see how you rate in this particular skill."

"Interesting. I'm afraid you'd find your countrymen sadly lacking."

"Oh? How can you be sure? Have you ever kissed a man of Geall?"

He laughed. "Clever, aren't you?"

"So I'm told." She stayed as she was when he moved to her, when he caged her in by laying his hands on the rail on either side of her. "Does your taste run to clever women?"

"Currently, when their eyes are like night fog, and their hair the color of polished oak."

"Gray and brown. I always thought they were such dull colors, but nothing about me feels dull when I'm with you." She laid a hand on his heart. Though it didn't beat, she saw the pulse of it in his eyes. "I don't feel shy with you, or nervous. I did, until you kissed me."

She pressed her lips to where her hand had laid. "Then I thought, well of course. I should have known. A curtain lifted inside me. I don't think it will ever close again."

"You bring the light inside me, Moira." He didn't say, not to her, not to himself, that when he left her it would go out again.

"The moon's clear tonight, and the stars shine." She laid her hands on his. "We'll leave the drapes open until it's time for sleep."

She went inside with him, into a room shimmering with moonlight and candlelight. She knew what it would be now, the warmth that went to heat, and the heat that went to fire. And all the thrills and sensations that came between.

From somewhere outside an owl called. For its mate, she thought. She knew what it was now to pine for her mate.

She lifted off her circlet, set it aside, then reached up to take off her earrings. When she saw him watching her she realized these small acts, this prelude to disrobing, could arouse.

So she took them off slowly, watching him as he watched her. She took the cross she'd tucked under her bodice, drawing it over her head. This, she knew, was an act of trust.

"I have no ladies. Would you see to my laces?"

She turned her back, lifted her hair.

"I think I'll try to make a zipper. It's a simple thing, really, and makes dressing easier."

"A lot of charm is lost to convenience."

She sent him a smile over her shoulder. "Easy for you to say." But then again, feeling him loosen those laces brought a flutter to her belly. "What invention pleased you the most over your time?"

"Indoor plumbing."

The quickness of his answer made her laugh. "Larkin and I were spoiled, and miss it sorely. I studied the pipes and the tanks. I think I could fashion something like your shower."

"A queen and a plumber." He laid his lips on her shoulder as he eased the material away. "There's no end to your talents."

"I wonder how I'll be as a gentleman's valet." She turned to him. "I like buttons," she said as she began to undo his shirt. "They're sensible, and pretty."

So was she, he thought as she worked her way down efficiently. Then she shoved at her hair.

"I think I should cut this off. Like Blair's. That's sensible, too."

"No. Don't." His belly quivered as her fingers paused on the button of his jeans. His combed down through the length of her hair, from crown to waist. "It's beautiful. The way it falls over your shoulders, spills down your back. It all but glows against your skin."

Charmed, she glanced over toward the long looking glass. And was jolted to see herself standing half dressed. And alone.

She looked away quickly, sent him an easy smile. "Still, it's a great deal of trouble, and—"

"Does it frighten you?"

There was no point pretending she didn't understand

him. "No. It's a bit of a shock is all. Is it hard for you? Not being able to see your reflection?"

"It just is. You adjust. Just another irony. Here, you've got eternal youth, but you won't be able to admire yourself. Still . . ."

He turned her around so they both faced the mirror. Then he lifted her hair, let it fall. When she let out a laugh at watching her hair seem to fly around on its own, he laid his hands on her shoulders.

"There are always ways to amuse yourself," he told her. He lifted her hair again, and this time brushed his lips— and just a hint of teeth—along the nape of her neck.

He heard the quick intake of her breath, saw her eyes widen.

"No, no," he murmured when she started to turn. "Just watch." And trailed his fingers along her skin—bare shoulders, and down to where her loosened bodice clung tenuously to her breasts. "Just feel."

"Cian."

"Did you ever dream of a lover coming to you in the night, in the dark?" He nudged the dress down to her waist then glided his fingertips over her breasts. "Overtaking you. Hands and lips heating your skin."

She lifted her hands to his, needing to feel them. Then flushed and dropped them again as the reflection showed her cupping her own breasts.

Behind her, invisible, he smiled. "You said I didn't take your innocence. You might have been right, but I think I will now. It's . . . succulent, and what I am craves it."

"I'm not innocent," she said, but trembled.

"More than you know." He circled her breasts with his thumbs, moving in slowly until they rubbed stiffened peaks. "Are you afraid?"

"No." And shuddered. "Yes."

"A little fear can add to excitement." He pushed the dress to the floor, leaned close to her ear. "Step out," he whispered. "Now watch. Watch your body."

Fear twisted with arousal so it was impossible for her to

tell them apart. Her body was helpless, her mind transfixed. Hands and lips she couldn't see roamed over her, erotically intimate, lazily possessive. She could see herself quivering, and the startled pleasure on her own face.

The clouds of surrender in her own eyes.

Her phantom lover ran his hands down her, fingers toying, tracing, leaving a trail of shivering flesh. This time when they took her breasts, she covered his hands with hers, shameless.

She moaned for him, and still her eyes stayed on the glass. His scholar would never shut her eyes to new experience, to new knowledge. He could feel her trembles, and the instinctive movement of her hips as pleasure took her over. Candlelight played over her skin and sensation warmed it so it bloomed like a rose.

She moaned again as he trailed his fingers over her belly, and melting into him, hooked her arm back around his neck.

He only teased, skimming his fingers along her thighs, over the most sensitive flesh, hinting, only hinting at what was to come until her breath was sobbing out.

"Take," he murmured. "Take what you want." He gripped her hand, pressed it to his between her thighs. Trapped it there.

She felt her body buck against him, against herself as he stroked her toward a new, towering pleasure. His body was solid behind hers, and his voice murmured words she no longer understood, but in the glass there was only her own form, lost now to its own rising needs.

Release left her breathless, limp and amazed.

He spun her around so quickly she couldn't find her balance, and knew she'd have lost it again in any case when his mouth took hers with a wild urgency. She could only cling, could only give while her heart slammed an anvil beat against his chest.

Of all he'd had and taken and tasted, he'd never known such hunger. A kind of madness of need that could only be met with her. For all his skill, all his experience, he was helpless when she held him against her. As ready and wrecked as she, he pulled her to the floor, and plunged inside her to forge that first desperate link.

He turned her face to the mirror once again as he ravished her, as her body went wild under his strong, thrusting hips. And when she came, quaking, he chained need with will until her heavy eyes opened, met his. Until she saw who had her.

He took her again, building and building until her need paced his own. Then burying his face in her hair, emptied himself into her.

She might have lain there, spent, for the rest of her life, but he lifted her. Simply scooped her up, she realized, and stood with her in his arms all in one effortless motion.

And her heart did a little jig in her chest.

"It's foolish," she said as she nuzzled his neck, "and I'm thinking it's female. But I love it that you're so strong, and that for a moment when we love each other, I make you weak."

"There's a part of me, *mo chroi*, that's always weak when it comes to you."

My heart, he'd called her, and it made her own dance again. "Oh, don't," she said after he'd laid her on the bed and turned to close the drapes. "Not yet. There's so much night left." She rolled off the bed again and grabbed her night robe. "I'm going to get the wine. And the cheese," she decided. "I'm half starving again."

As she ran out he went to the fire, tossed on another brick of turf. He closed his mind to the part of him that asked what he was doing. Every time he was with her, there was another scar to his heart, for the day that would come when he'd never be with her again.

She'd survive it, he reminded himself. And so would he. Survival was something humans and demons had in common. Nothing really died of a broken heart.

She came back, carrying a tray. "We can eat and drink in bed, full of decadence." She set the tray on the bed, and climbed up after it.

"I've certainly given you enough of that."

"Oh?" She brushed back her hair and gave him a slow smile. "And here I was hoping there'd be more to come. But if you've shown me all you know, I suppose we can just begin repeating ourselves."

"I've done things you can't imagine. Things I wouldn't have you imagine."

"Now you're bragging." She made herself say it lightly.

"Moira—"

"Don't be sorry for what's between us, or for what you believe can't be, or shouldn't." Her gaze was clear, direct. "Don't be sorry when you look at me for whatever you might have done in the past. Whatever it was, each time, it was a step to bringing you here. You're needed here. I need you here."

He crossed to the bed. "Do you understand I can't stay?"

"Yes, yes. Yes. I don't want to speak of it, not tonight. Can't we have an illusion for just one night?"

He touched her hair. "I can't be sorry for what's between us."

"That's enough then." Had to be enough, she reminded herself, though with every minute that passed there was something inside her going wild, and wilder still with grief.

She lifted one of the goblets, offered it with a steady hand. When he saw it was blood, he lifted a brow at her.

"I thought you might need it. For energy."

He shook his head and sat on the bed with her. "So, should we talk about plumbing?"

She hadn't been sure what he'd say, but that was the last on any list she might have made. "Plumbing."

"You're not the only one who's made studies. Added to the fact that I was around when that kind of thing was being incorporated into daily life. I have some ideas how you could install some basics."

She smiled and sipped her wine. "Educate me."

They spent considerable time at it, with Moira going off

for paper and ink so they could draw basic diagrams. The fact that he took such an interest in something she imagined people of his time took for granted opened another facet of him for her.

But she realized she shouldn't have been surprised by it, not when she considered the extent of his library in Ireland. And in a house, she remembered, he didn't visit more than once or twice a year.

She understood, too, that he could have been anything he'd wanted. He had a quick, curious mind, clever hands, and from the way he'd played music, the soul of a poet. And a way with business as well, she reminded herself.

In Geall, in her time, he would have been prosperous, she was certain. Respected, even renowned. Other men would have come to him for advice and counsel. Women would have flirted with him at every opportunity.

But she and he would have met, and courted, and loved, she was sure of it. And he would have ruled by her side over a rich and peaceful land.

There would be children, with his beautiful blue eyes. And a boy—at least one boy—with that little cleft in the chin like his father.

And on nights like this, late and quiet, they'd talk of other plans for their family, for their people, for their land.

She blinked herself back when his fingers brushed her cheek.

"You need sleep."

"No." She shook her head, tried to refocus on the diagrams again—to hold off those minutes that drained away her time with him. "My mind was wandering off."

"You'd've been snoring in a minute."

"Well, what a lie. I don't snore." But she didn't argue when he gathered up the papers. She could barely keep her eyes open. "Perhaps we'll rest a little while."

She rose to snuff candles as he moved to close the drapes. But when she moved back toward the bed, he was opening the doors and stepping out.

"For heaven's sake, Cian, you're next to naked." Plucking

up his shirt, she hurried out after him. "At least put this on. You may not mind the cold, but I mind having one of the guards see you standing here in your altogether. It's not proper."

"There's a rider coming."

"What? Where?"

"Due east."

She looked east, but saw nothing. Still, she didn't doubt him. "A single rider?"

"Two, but the second's being led by the first. They're coming at a gallop."

With a nod, she strode back into the bedchamber and began to dress. "The guards are instructed not to pass anyone in. I'll have a look. It may be stragglers. If so, we can't leave them outside the gates and unprotected."

"Invite no one," Cian ordered as he yanked on his jeans. "Even if they're known to you."

"I won't, and neither will any of the guards." With a small pang of regret, she put on her circlet and became queen again. And as queen, she lifted her sword.

"It'll be stragglers," she said. "In need of food and shelter."

"And if not?"

"Then they've ridden a long way to die."

When she stood at the post on top of the wall she could see the riders, or the shape of them. Two as Cian had said, with the first leading the second horse. They wore no cloaks though there was a chill in the air, and a hint of the first frost.

She glanced at Niall who'd been awakened when the guards had spotted the riders. "I'll want a bow."

Niall gestured to one of the men, took a bow and quiver from him. "Seems fruitless for the enemy to ride straight at us. Two of them against us? And unable to pass through the gates unless we welcome them."

"Likely they aren't the enemy. But the gates aren't to be

raised until we know. Two men," she murmured as they rode close enough for her to be sure. "The one being led looks to be injured."

"No," Cian said after a moment. "Dead."

"How can you—" Niall cut himself off.

"You're certain?" Moira murmured.

"He's tied to the horse, and he's dead. So's the lead rider, but he's been changed."

"All right then." Moira let out a sigh. "Niall, tell the men to keep a sharp eye for others. They're to do nothing without a command. We'll see what this one wants. A deserter?" she said to Cian, then dismissed the idea before he answered. "No, a deserter would have gone as far east or north as possible, and kept hidden."

"Could be he thinks he has something to trade," Niall suggested. "Make us think the one he's bringing is still alive, so we'd let them in. Or he's got information he feels we'd value."

"No harm in listening," Moira began, then gripped Cian's hand. "The rider. It's Sean. It's Sean, the smithy's son. Oh God. Are you sure he's—"

"I know my own kind." And with eyes keener than Moira's he recognized the dead. "Lilith sent him—she can afford to lose one so newly changed. She sent him because you'd know him, and feel for him. Don't."

"He was little more than a boy."

"Now he's a demon. The other was spared that. Look at me, Moira." He took her shoulders, turned her to face him. "I'm sorry. It's Tynan."

"No. No. Tynan's at the base. We had word he reached it safely. Injured, but alive, and safe. It can't be Tynan."

She pushed away from Cian, leaning on the wall, straining her eyes. She could hear the murmurs now, then the shouts as the men began to recognize Sean. There was hope in the shouts, and welcome.

"It's no longer Sean." She lifted her voice, cut through the calls of the men. "They killed the one you knew and sent a demon with his face. The gates stay locked, and not a man here will pass what rides here through them. I command it."

She turned back. Every bone in her body went brittle as she saw Cian had been right. It was Tynan, or Tynan's mauled body, tied to the second horse.

She wanted to weep, wanted to burrow herself into Cian and scream and sob. She wanted to sink to the stones and cry out her grief and her rage.

She stood straight, no longer feeling the wind that blew at her cloak, at her hair. She notched the arrow, and she waited for the vampire to bring its vile gift.

"No one is to speak to it," she said coldly.

What had been Sean lifted its face, raised a hand to wave to those gathered on the wall.

"Open the gates!" it shouted. "Open the gates! It's Sean, the blacksmith's son. They may be after me still. I've Tynan here. He's badly hurt."

"You will not pass," Moira called out. "She killed you only to send you here to die again."

"Majesty." It managed an awkward bow as it pulled the horses to a halt. "You know me."

"Aye, I do. How did Tynan die?"

"He's hurt. He's lost blood. I escaped the demons and made my way to the farm, to the base. But I was weak and hurt myself, and Tynan, bless him, came out to help me. They set upon us. We barely escaped with our lives."

"You lie. Did you kill him? Did what she made you turn you so you'd kill a friend?"

"My lady." It broke off when she lifted the bow and aimed the arrow at its heart. "I didn't kill him." It held up its hands to show them empty of weapons. "It was the prince. The boy." It giggled, then pressed a hand to its mouth to muffle it in a gesture so like Sean's it ripped her heart. "The prince lured him outside and had the kill. I've only brought him back to you, as the true queen commanded. She sends a message."

"And what would it be?"

"If you surrender, and accept her as ruler of this world

and all others, if you place the sword of Geall in her hand, and set the crown on her head, you'll be spared. You may live out your lives here as you like, for Geall is a small world and of little interest to her."

"And if we don't?"

He took out a dagger, and leaning over, cut the ropes securing Tynan to the horse. A careless kick sent the body tumbling to the ground. "Then your fate is as his, as will be the fate of every man, every woman, every child who stands against her. You'll be tortured."

It ripped off its tunic, and the moonlight fell on the burns and gashes yet to heal on its torso. "Any who survive Samhain will be hunted down. We'll rape your women, we'll mutilate your children. When it's done, not a single human heart will beat on Geall. We are forever. You'll never stop the flood of us. Give your answer, and I'll take it to the queen."

"This is the answer of the true queen of Geall. When the sun rises after Samhain, you and all like you will be dust that blows out to sea on the wind. Nothing will be left of you in Geall."

She passed her bow back to Niall. "You have your answer."

"She'll come for you!" it shouted. "And for the traitor to his kind who stands beside you."

It wheeled the horse, kicked it to a gallop.

On the wall, Moira lifted her sword, and flinging it out, shot a stream of fire. The vampire screamed once as the flames struck, then the ball of fire that was left of it fell to the ground, and went to ash.

"He was of Geall," Moira murmured, "and deserved to end with its sword. Tynan—" Her throat simply locked.

"I'll bring him in." Cian touched her shoulder, and looked over her head into Niall's eyes. "He was a good man, and a friend to me."

Without waiting, Cian vaulted over the wall. He seemed almost to float to the ground.

Niall slapped the back of his hand on the arm of the

guard beside him when he saw the man made the sign against evil. "No man stands with me who insults Sir Cian."

Below, Cian picked Tynan up in his arms and, bearing his weight, looked up and met Moira's eyes.

"Open the gates," she ordered. "So Sir Cian can bring Tynan home again."

She tended the body herself, removing the torn and filthy clothes.

"Let me do this, Moira."

She shook her head, and began to wash Tynan's face. "This is for me. We were friends since childhood. I need to do this for him. I don't want Larkin to see him until he's clean."

Her hands trembled as she brushed the cloth gently over the tears and bites, but she never faltered.

"They were playmates, you see. Larkin and Tynan. Was it the truth, do you think, that the child did this to him?"

When Cian said nothing, she looked over.

"He's her child," Cian said at length. "He would be vicious. Let me wake Glenna, at least."

"She was fond of Tynan. Everyone was. No, there's no need for her to come now, so late. They tore my mother like this. Worse, even worse. And I turned away from that. I can't turn away from this."

"Do you want me to go?"

"You think because I see these wounds, these bites and tears, as if an animal had been at him, I could think you're the same as what did this? Do you think me so weak of mind and heart, Cian?"

"No. I think the woman I saw tonight, the woman I heard, has the strongest mind and heart I've ever known. I never ripped at a human that way."

He steadied himself as she turned those ravaged eyes on his again. "I need you to know that, at least. Of all the things I've done, and some were unimaginably cruel, I never did what was done to him."

"You killed more cleanly. More efficiently."

He felt the words slice into him. "Yes."

Moira nodded. "Lilith didn't train you, but abandoned you, so you have little of her in you. Not like this boy must. And, I think, some manner of your upbringing remained. Just as I heard Sean's tone, saw his mannerisms in that thing tonight, so some of yours stayed as they were. I know you're not human, Cian, just as I know you're not a monster. And I know there's some of both in you that has you constantly struggling to keep them balanced."

She washed Tynan's body as gently as she would have washed a child. When she was done she began to dress him in the clothes she'd had sent over from his quarters.

"Let me do that, Moira, for God's sake."

"I know you mean well. I know you're thinking of me. But I need to do this one thing for him. He was the first to kiss me." Her voice wavered a bit before she clamped down and finished. "When I was fourteen, and he two years older. It was very sweet, very gentle. Shy for both of us, as a first kiss in the springtime should be. I loved him. I think in a way like you loved King. She's taken that from us, Cian. Taken them from us, but not the love."

"I swear before any gods you wish, I'll end her for you."

"One of us will." She bent, brushed her lips over Tynan's cold cheek.

Then she stepped back from him.

Now she sank to the floor on a keening wail. When Cian knelt beside her, she curled into him and wept out her shattered heart.

Chapter 15

◈

They buried Tynan on a brilliant morning with cloud shadows dancing over the hills and a lark singing joyfully in a rowan tree. The holy man blessed the ground before they lowered him into it, with a fife and drum sounding the dirge.

All who knew him, and many who didn't, were there so that mourners stretched across the sun-drenched graveyard and up the rise toward the castle. The three flags of Geall flew at half staff.

Moira stood beside Larkin, dry-eyed. Though she heard Tynan's mother weeping, she knew her time for tears had passed. The others of her circle stood behind her, and she could feel them, took some comfort from that.

Now two stones would stand for friends here, along with the markers for her parents. All of them victims of a war that had raged long before she'd known of it. And would end with her, one way or another.

At last, she moved away to give the last moments to the family and their privacy. When Larkin took her hand, she gripped it firmly. She looked at Cian, could just see his eyes under the shadow of his hood. Then she looked at the others.

"We have work to do. Larkin and I need to speak with Tynan's family again, then we'll meet in the parlor."

"We'll head in now." Blair stepped forward, laid her cheek against Larkin's. Moira couldn't hear the words Blair murmured to him, but Larkin released her hand and pulled Blair into a hard embrace.

"We'll be in shortly." Larkin eased back, then took Moira's hand again. She would have sworn she could feel his grief coming through his skin.

Before Moira could move back toward the family, Tynan's mother broke away from her husband and pushed her way to Cian. Her eyes were still spilling tears.

"It's your kind did this. Your kind killed my boy."

Hoyt made a move forward, but Cian shifted to block his path. "Yes."

"You should be in hell instead of my boy being in the ground."

"Yes," Cian repeated.

Moira stepped up to put an arm around her, but the woman shook it off. "You, all of you." She whirled, jabbing out an accusing finger. "You care more about this *thing* than my boy. Now he's dead. He's dead. And you have no right to stand here by his grave." She spat at Cian's feet.

As she wept into her hands, her husband and daughters carried her off.

"I'm sorry," Moira murmured. "I'll speak with her."

"Leave her be. She wasn't wrong." Saying nothing more, Cian walked away from the fresh grave, and the lines of stones that marked the dead.

Niall caught up with him as he reached the gates. "Sir Cian, a word with you."

"You can have as many words as you want once I'm out of this shagging sun."

He didn't know why he'd gone to the graveyard. He'd seen more than enough dead in his time, heard more than enough weeping for them. Tynan's mother wasn't the only one who looked at him with fear and hate, and here he was out in the daylight with the only things between him and the killing sun some rough cloth and a charm.

His blood cooled the moment he was inside, out of the light.

"Say what you need to say." Cian shoved back the detested hood of the cloak.

"So I will." A big man with his usually cheerful face tight and grim, Niall nodded sharply. His wide hand rested on the hilt of his sword as he looked hard into Cian's eyes. "Tynan was a friend, and one of the best men I've known."

"You're saying nothing I haven't heard before."

"Well, you haven't heard me say it, have you? I saw what had become of Sean, what had been a harmless and often foolish lad. I saw him kick Tynan's body from the horse as if it were no more than offal to be tossed in a ditch."

"To him it wasn't any more than that."

Again, Niall nodded, and his fingers tightened on the sword's hilt. "Aye, that's what was made of him. And of you. But I watched you lift Tynan's body off the ground. I watched you carry it in, as a man would carry a fallen friend. I saw none of what was Sean in you. Tynan's mother's grieving. He was her first-born, and she's mad with grief. And she was wrong in what she said to you by his grave. He'd not have wanted you insulted by his blood. So as his friend, I'm telling you that. And I'm telling you any man who fights with me fights with you. That's my word on it."

He lifted his hand from the hilt of his sword and held it out to Cian.

Humans never failed to surprise him. Irritate, annoy, amuse, occasionally educate. But most of all they continued to surprise him with the twists and turns of their minds and hearts.

He supposed that was one reason he'd been able to live among them so long and still be interested.

"I'll thank you for it. But before you take my hand, you need to know that what was in Sean is in me. There's a thin difference."

"Not thin by my measure. And I'm thinking you'll use what's in you to fight. I'll put my back to yours, Sir Cian. And my hand's still out."

Cian shook it. "I'm grateful," he said. But when he went up the stairs, he went alone.

Heartsick, Moira walked back to the castle. There was little time for grieving, she knew, little time for comfort. What Lilith had done to Sean, to Tynan, she'd done to cut at their hearts. And she'd aimed well.

So they would heal them now with action, with movement.

"Can the dragons be used? Are they trained enough to carry men?"

"They're smart, and accommodating," Larkin told her. "Easily ridden by any who have a good seat, and aren't afraid of the height. But so far, it's been like a game for them. I can't say how they'll do in battle."

"For now, it's more a matter of transportation. You'd know the best of them, you and Blair. We'll need—" She broke off as her aunt crossed the courtyard to her. "Deirdre." She kissed her aunt's cheek, held an extra moment. She knew Larkin's and Tynan's mothers were close. "How is she?"

"She's prostrate. Inconsolable." Deirdre's eyes, swollen from her own tears, locked on Larkin's face. "As any mother would be."

He embraced her. "Don't fret for me, or for Oran."

"Now you ask the impossible." Still she smiled a little. But the smile faded as she turned to Moira again. "I know this is a difficult time, and you've much on your mind, on your heart. But I would speak with you. Privately."

"Of course. I'll join you shortly," she said to the others, then laid her arm around Deirdre's shoulders. "We'll go to my sitting room. You'll have tea."

"You needn't trouble."

"It'll do us both good." She caught the eye of a servant as they passed into the hall, and asked that tea be brought up.

"And Sinann?" Moira continued as they climbed the stairs.

"Fatigued, and full of grief for Tynan, of worry for her husband, her brothers. I couldn't allow her to go to the grave today, and made her rest. I worry for her, and the babe she carries, her other children."

"She's strong, and has you to tend her."

"Will it be enough if Phelan falls as Tynan has? If Oran has already . . ."

"It must be. We have no choice in this. None of us."

"No choice, but for war." Deirdre entered the sitting room, took a chair. Her face, framed by her wimple, was older than it had been weeks before.

"If we don't fight they'll slaughter us, as they did Tynan. Or do what they did to poor Sean." Moira went to the hearth to add bricks to the fire. Despite the bright autumn sun, she was cold to the bone.

"And fighting them, how many will die? How many will be slaughtered?"

Moira straightened, and turned. Her aunt wasn't the only one who would question, who would look to their queen for the impossible answer.

"How can I say? What would you have me do? You who were confidant to my mother before she was queen, and all during her reign. What would you have had her do?"

"The gods have charged you. Who am I to say?"

"My blood."

Deirdre sighed, looked down at her hands lying empty in her lap. "I'm weary, to the bottom of my soul. My daughter fears for her husband, as I do for mine. And for my sons. My friend buried her child today. And I know there is no choice in this, Moira. This blight has come to us, and must be cut out."

A servant hurried in with the tea.

"Leave it please," Moira said. "I'll pour. Is food being sent to the parlor?"

The young girl curtseyed. "Aye, Your Majesty. The cook was seeing to it when I left with the tea."

"Thank you. That's all then."

Moira sat, poured out the tea. "There's biscuits as well. It's good to have small pleasures in hard times."

"It's pleasures in hard times I need to speak with you about."

Moira passed the cup. "Is there something I can do to ease your heart? Sinann's and the children's?"

"There is." Deirdre took a small sip of the tea before setting the cup aside. "Moira, your mother was my dearest friend in this world, and so I sit here in her stead, and I speak to you as I would my own daughter."

"I'd have it no other way."

"When you spoke of this war that's upon us, you spoke of no choice. But there are other choices you've made. A woman's choices."

Understanding, Moira sat back. "I have."

"As queen, one who's claimed herself a warrior, one who's proven herself as one, you have the right, even the duty, to use any and all weapons that come to your hand to protect your people."

"I do, and I will."

"This Cian who comes here from another time and place. You believe the gods sent him."

"I know it. He fought by your own son. He saved my life. Would you sit here and look at me, and damn him as Tynan's mother damned him?"

"No." Deirdre took a careful breath. "In this matter of war, he is a weapon. By using him you may save yourself, my sons, all of us."

"You're mistaken," Moira said evenly. "He's not to be used like a sword. What he's done, and what he will do to cut out this blight, he does of his own will."

"A demon's will."

Moira's eyes chilled. "As you like."

"And you've taken this demon to your bed."

"I've taken Cian to my bed."

"How can you do this thing? Moira, Moira." She reached out her hands. "He's not human, yet you gave yourself to him. What good can come of it?"

"Much has already, for me."

Deirdre sat back a moment, pressed her fingers to her eyes. "Do you think the gods sent him to you for this?"

"I can't say. Did you ask yourself that question when you took my uncle?"

"How can you compare?" Deirdre snapped. "Have you no shame, no pride?"

"No shame, and considerable pride. I love him, and he loves me."

"How can a demon love?"

"How can a demon risk his life, time and again, to save humanity?"

"It's not his bravery I question, but your judgment. Do you think I've forgotten what it is to be young, to be stirred, to be foolish? But you're queen, and you have responsibility to your crown, your people."

"I live and breathe that responsibility, every moment, every day."

"And at night you bed a vampire."

Unable to sit any longer, Moira rose, moved to the window. The sun still shone, she thought, bright and gold. It sparkled on the grass, on the river, on the gossamer wings of dragons who flew lazy loops around Castle Geall.

"I don't ask you to understand. I demand your respect."

"Do you speak to me as my niece, or as the queen?"

She turned back, framed by the window and the sunlight. "The gods have deemed me both. You come to me out of concern, and that I accept. But you also come with condemnation, and that I don't. I trust Cian with my life. It's my right, my choice, to trust him with my body."

"And what of your people? What of those who question how their queen could take one of these creatures of darkness as lover?"

"Are all men good, Aunt? Are they all kind and good and strong? Are we as we're made, or how we choose to make ourselves thereafter? I'll say this about my people, about those I'll give my life fighting to defend. They have more important things to worry about, to think about, to talk about than what their queen does in the privacy of her bedchamber."

Deirdre got to her feet. "And when this war is over, will you continue this? Will you put this thing you love on the throne at your side?"

The sun still shone, Moira thought again, even when the heart goes bleak. "When this is over, if we live, he'll go back to his time and his place. I'll never see him again. If we lose, I'll give my life. If we win, I'll forfeit my heart. Don't speak to me of choices, of responsibilities."

"You'll forget him. When this is done, you'll forget him and this momentary madness."

"Look at me," Moira said quietly. "You know I won't."

"No." Deirdre's eyes swam with tears. "You won't. I'd spare you from this."

"I wouldn't. Not a moment of it. I've been more alive with him than I ever was before, or will be again. So no, not a moment of it."

They were all gathered in the parlor around the table and food when Moira came in. Glenna reached over to remove a cover from the plate at the head of the table.

"It should still be warm," she told Moira. "Don't waste it."

"I won't. We need to eat, to stay strong." But she stared at the food on her plate as if it were bitter medicine.

"So." Blair gave her a bright smile. "How's your day been so far?"

The laugh, however quick and humorless, eased some of the knots in Moira's stomach. "Crappy. That would be the word, wouldn't it?"

"Right down to the ground."

"Well." She made herself eat. "She's struck at us, as is her habit, to incite fear and carve away at morale and confidence. Some will believe what she had Sean tell us. That if we surrender, she'll leave us in peace."

"Lies are often more attractive than the truth," Glenna commented. "Time's running out either way."

"Aye. We, we six, will have to make preparation to leave the castle, head toward the battleground."

"Agreed." Hoyt nodded. "Before we do, we'll need to be certain the bases we've set up are still in our hands. If Tynan was killed, they may have taken that stronghold. We've only the word of a demon it was the child who killed him, and him alone."

"It was the child." Cian drank tea that was nearly half whiskey. "The wounds on the body," he explained. "They weren't made by a full-grown vampire. Still, it doesn't answer if the strongholds are still secured."

"Hoyt and I can look," Glenna said.

"I'll want you to, but looking isn't enough." Moira continued to eat. "We need to gather reports from those who survived."

"If they did."

She looked at Larkin and felt what he felt. The constant thrum of fear for Oran.

"If they did," she repeated.

"If she'd wiped out the base," Cian put in, "the messenger she sent would have bragged about it, and likely she'd have sent more bodies."

"Aye, I can see that. But to keep what she accomplished from happening again, we'll want to add reinforcements."

"You want us to go by dragon." Larkin nodded. "That's why you asked if they were ready to be ridden."

"As many as can be used for this. Those who must go on foot or horseback from here will, from today on, be watched over by riders in the air. If you, Larkin, and Blair could go this morning, take a small number with you. On dragon-back, you can travel to all the bases, transport more weapons, more men, see to the reports and what you think must be done when you see for yourself where we stand. You could be back before nightfall, or failing that, stay at one of the bases until the morning."

"You're cutting too many of us out by sending two," Cian interrupted. "And I should be the one to go."

"Hey." Blair wagged a piece of soda bread. "How come you get to have all the fun?"

"Practicalities. First, all but Glenna and I have seen some of the ground of or near the battlefield firsthand. It's time I got the lay of it. Second, with that bloody cloak, I can start the journey during the day, but I can travel more quickly and more safely than any of you at night. And being a vampire myself, I'll recognize signs of them quicker than even our resident demon hunter."

"He makes a good argument for it," Larkin pointed out.

"I've been planning to go, nose around a bit in any case. So this will kill all the birds with one stone. And the last of it, I think we can all agree, the mood here would settle if I wasn't around."

"She was out of line," Blair muttered.

Cian shrugged, knowing she spoke of Tynan's mother. "All a matter of perspective—and where you draw that line. Time's getting short, and one of us should be on the battleground, particularly at night when Lilith might be scouting around herself."

"You don't mean to come back," Moira said slowly.

"There's no point in it." Their eyes met, held, and said a great deal more than words. "One of the men can come back with your reports and so on. And I'd fill in the rest of it when all of you arrive."

"You've already decided this." Moira watched his face carefully. "I see. We're a circle here, equal links. For such a decision, I think we should all have a say. Hoyt?"

"I don't like any of us going off without the others, truth be told. But it needs to be done, and Cian makes the most sense of it. We can watch as we watched when Larkin went to the caves back in Ireland. If need be we can intervene." He looked at his wife. "Glenna?"

"Yes. Agreed. Larkin?"

"The same. With one change in it. I think you're wrong, Cian, to say we'd be cutting it too thin to send two out. I think no one goes on their own. I can get you there in dragon form. And," he continued before there were objections, "I'm more experienced with the dragons than you, should there be any trouble with them, or the enemy. So I'm saying we go together, you and I. Blair?"

"Damn it. Dragon-boy's right. You may move faster alone, Cian, but you're going to need a dragon wrangler to get there, especially if you're leading men."

"Yes, it's smarter." Glenna considered. "All around smarter. It gets my vote."

"And mine as well," Hoyt said. "Moira?"

"Then that's what we'll do." She got to her feet knowing she was sending the two men she loved most away from her. "The rest of us will finish the weapons, secure the castle and follow in two days."

"Big push." Blair considered, nodded. "We can do it."

"Then we will. Larkin, I'll leave it to you to pick the dragons for this, and to you and Cian to pick the men." Moira laid it out in her mind, the overview, the details. "I'll want Niall left back, if you will, to go at the end of it with the rest of us. I'll go now, see to the supplies you'll need."

When she'd done all she could, and hoping she was calm, Moira went to Cian's bedchamber. She knocked, then opened the door without waiting for his response. With the curtains drawn there was barely enough light to see, so she flicked her hand, her power toward a candle. The way the flame spurted warned her she wasn't as calm as she'd hoped.

He continued to pack what he wanted to take in a duffle.

"You said nothing of these plans to me."

"No."

"Were you going to leave in the night, with no word?"

"I don't know." He stopped, looked at her. There were a great many things he couldn't give her, or ask of her, he reflected. At least honesty was a quality they could share.

"Yes, at least initially. Then you came to my door one night, and my plans changed. Or, they were postponed."

"Postponed." She nodded slowly. "And when Samhain's come and gone, will you leave without a word?"

"Words would be useless, wouldn't they?"

"Not to me." There was panic rising up in her at the knowledge they were moving toward the end. How could she not have known that was waiting in her to push its way out and choke her? "Words would be precious to me. You want to leave. I can see it. You want to go."

"I should have gone before. If I'd been quicker, I'd have been out the door and gone before you came to me. You'd be better off for it. This . . . with me. It's no good for you."

"How dare you? How *dare* you speak to me like a child who wants too many sweets? I'm sick to death of being lectured on what I should think, feel, have, do. If you want to go, you'll go, but don't insult me."

"My going has nothing to do with what's between us. It's just something that has to be done. You agreed, and so did the rest."

"If I hadn't, they hadn't, you'd have gone anyway."

He watched her as he strapped on his sword. Pain was already slicing thin wounds in both of them, as he'd known it would from the moment he'd touched her. "Yes, but it's less complicated this way."

"Are you done with me then?"

"And if I am?"

"You'll be fighting on two fronts, you right bastard."

He laughed, couldn't help himself. It wasn't only pain between them, he realized. He'd do well to remember that. "Then it's lucky for me I'm not done with you. Moira, last night you knew you had to be the one to end what had once been a boy you'd known, you'd been fond of. I knew it, so I stopped myself from doing it, from sparing you from that. I know I have to go, and go without you for now. You know that, too."

"It doesn't make it easier. We may never be alone again, never be able to be with each other as we were again. I want more time—there hasn't been enough time, and I need more."

She moved to him, held him hard and tight. "We didn't have our night. It didn't last till morning."

"But the hours mattered, every minute of them."

"I'm greedy. And already fretting that you'll go while I stay."

Not just today, he thought. Both of them knew she didn't speak only of today. "Do women of Geall follow the tradition of sending their men off with a favor?"

"What would you have from me?"

"A lock of your hair." The sentiment of it surprised him, and embarrassed a little. But when she drew back, he could see his request had pleased her.

"You'll keep it with you? That part of me?"

"I would, if you'll spare it."

She touched her hair, then held up a hand. "Wait, wait. I have something. I'll have to get it." She heard the trumpet call of dragons. "Oh, they're ready for you. I'll bring it to you, outside. Don't leave. Promise me you'll wait until I come to say goodbye."

"I'll be there." This time, he thought as she rushed out.

Outside, in the shelter of shade, Cian studied the dragons Larkin had chosen, and the men they'd decided on together.

Then he frowned down at the ball of hardened mud Glenna held out to him. "Thanks, but I had quite enough at breakfast."

"Very funny. It's a bomb."

"Red, it's a ball of mud."

"Yes, a ball of earth—charmed earth, holding a ball of fire inside. If you drop it from the air." She used her hands waving them down as she made a whistling noise—then a puff of breath to simulate an explosion. "In theory," she added.

"In theory."

"I've tested it, but not from a dragon perch. At some point you could try it out for me."

Frowning, he turned it over in his hands. "Just drop it?"

"Right. Somewhere safe."

"And it's not likely to explode in my hands and turn me into a fireball?"

"It needs velocity and force. But it wouldn't hurt to be sure you had good altitude when it's bombs away." She rose on her toes, kissed him on both cheeks. "Be safe. We'll see you in a couple of days."

Still frowning, he secured the ball into one of the pockets of the weapon harness Blair had fashioned for Larkin.

"We'll be watching." Hoyt laid a hand on Cian's shoulder. "Try to stay out of trouble until I'm with you again. And you as well," he said to Larkin.

"I've already told him I'll kick his ass if he gets himself killed." Blair gripped Larkin's hair, pulled his head down for a hard kiss. She turned to Cian.

"We're not doing a group hug."

She grinned. "I'm with you on that. Stay away from pointy wooden objects."

"That's the plan." He looked over her head as Moira ran toward the stables.

"I'd hoped to be quicker," she said breathlessly. "You're ready then. Larkin. Be safe." She hugged him.

"And you." He gave her a last squeeze. "Mount your dragons!" he called out, and with a last flashing grin for Blair, changed.

"I have what you asked me for." Moira held out a silver locket while Blair harnessed Larkin. "My father gave it to my mother when I was born, so she could keep a lock of my hair in it. I left that one, and put in another."

And had added what magic she could.

Rising on her toes, she put the chain over his head. To make a point, to him, to any who watched, she took his face in her hands, and kissed him long and warm and tender.

"I'll have another of those waiting for you," she told him. "So don't do anything foolish."

He put on the cloak, lifting the hood and securing it. He mounted Larkin, looked into Moira's eyes.

"In two days," he said.

He rose up into the sky on the golden dragon. Others soared behind him, trumpeting.

As she watched, as those glints of color grew smaller with distance, Moira was struck with a sudden knowledge, a certainty that the six of them would not come back from the valley to Castle Geall as a circle.

Behind her, Glenna gestured to Hoyt, sending him away. She hooked an arm around Blair's waist, around Moira's. "All right, ladies, let's get busy packing and stacking so we can get you back together with your men."

Chapter 16

He wished for rain. Or at the very least a thick layer of cooling clouds to smother the sun. The damn cloak was hot as the hell he was eventually bound for. He just wasn't used to feeling extremes in temperatures.

Being undead, Cian mused, tended to spoil a man.

Soaring on a dragon was a thrilling experience, no question. For the first thirty minutes or so. And another thirty could be spent admiring the green and pastoral countryside below.

But after an hour in a fucking wool sauna, it was just misery.

If he had Hoyt's patience and dignity, he supposed he would ride steely-eyed and straight-backed until doomsday. Even with the intolerable heat melting the flesh from his bones. But then he and his twin had had some basic differences even before he'd become a vampire.

He could meditate, he supposed, but it seemed unwise to risk a self-induced trance. He had the sun beating overhead just waiting to fry him like bacon, and a magic bomb strapped on Larkin that for all he knew could burst into flame just for the fun of it.

Why exactly had he thought he had to do this idiotic thing?

Ah yes. Duty, honor, love, pride—all those emotional weights that dragged a man down into the drowning pool, however hard he struggled to keep his head above the surface. Well, there was no going back now. Not on the flight, not on the feelings crowding inside him.

My God, he loved her. Moira the studious, Moira the queen. The shy and the valiant, the canny and the quiet. It was stupid, destructive, hopeless to love her. And it was more real than anything he'd known in a thousand years.

He could feel the locket she'd put around his neck— another weight. She'd called him a bastard one minute, then had given him one of what he was certain was her most valued treasures the next.

Then again, she'd once aimed an arrow at his heart, then apologized with a simple sincerity and flushed mortification. It was probably at that moment when he'd fallen for her. Or at least tripped.

He continued to study the land as his mind wandered. Good farmland, he mused, with rich, loamy soil and gentle rises. Streams and rivers thick with fish running through forests that teemed with game. The mountains in the distance rich with minerals and marbles. Deep bogs for cutting turf for fuel.

She'd brought orange seeds through the Dance. Who would think of such a thing?

She'd need to plant them in the south. Did she know that? Foolish thought, the woman knew everything, or had a way of finding out.

Orange seeds and Yeats. And, because he'd seen it on the writing table in her sitting room, a roller ball pen.

So she'd grow her orange saplings in the hothouse, then plant them in the south of Geall. If they pollinated—and how could they refuse her?—she'd have an orange grove one day.

He'd like to see it, he realized. He'd like to see her orange blossoms bloom from the seeds she'd taken from his kitchen in Ireland.

He'd like to see her lovely eyes light with humor and appreciation as she poured a glass of the orange juice she'd become addicted to.

If Lilith had her day, there'd be no grove, no blossoms, no life here at all.

Already he could see some of the death, some of the destruction. What had been tidy cottages and little cabins were rubble of scorched rock and wood. Cattle and sheep continued to graze in the fields, but there were carcasses rotting in the sun under a black cloud of flies.

Cattle killed by deserters, he decided. Scavenging where and when they could.

They'd have to be hunted down and destroyed, every last one. If even one survived, it would feed and it would breed. The people of Geall and their queen would have to be cautious and vigilant long after Samhain.

He began to put his mind to that particular problem until, at last, Larkin began to circle.

"Thank all your gods," Cian murmured on the descent.

It was a neat and pretty farm, as farms went. Soldiers were spread out, training, posted at points for guards. Women were among them, working alongside the men. And the smoke that rose from the chimney carried a scent that told him there was stew in a pot, likely simmering throughout the day.

On the ground, hands were shading eyes as faces looked up, or were being raised in waves and salutes of welcome.

They were surrounded the minute Larkin landed. Cian dismounted, began to unload the supplies. He'd leave it to Larkin and the other men to answer questions, and ask them. Now, he needed shadow and shade.

"We haven't had any trouble at all." Isleen spooned up stew Cian didn't want. But he thought it best to wait to dip into his supply of blood until he had privacy.

Larkin dove into his bowl the instant they were set down. "Thanks," he said with his mouth full. "It's fine stew."

"You're very welcome. I'm doing the cooking by and large, so I'm thinking our troop here is eating better than the others." She dimpled into a smile. "We've been keeping up with our training, every day, and locking up tight before sunset. We haven't seen hide nor hair of anyone since we arrived and sent the other troop on its way."

"It's good to know that." Larkin picked up the tankard she'd set beside his bowl. "Could you do me a favor then, Isleen darling? Would you fetch Eogan—Ceara's Eogan. We've some talking to do."

"Sure I'll do that right away. Oh, and you can bed down here, or upstairs if you'd rather."

"We'll be moving on to the next base after a bit, and leaving three of the men we brought behind here with you."

"Oh. I noticed you brought red-haired Malvin along." She said it casually, with just the hint of a laugh. "I wonder if he'd be one you'd leave behind with us."

Larkin grinned and spooned up more stew. "That wouldn't be a problem, not at all. Fetch Eogan now, won't you, sweetheart?"

"You've had a bit of that, have you?" Cian murmured.

"Had— No." Then his tawny eyes glinted with humor. "Well, a bit, but nothing substantial you could say."

"How do you want to handle this business?"

"Eogan's a sensible man, a solid one. He'd have heard of Tynan by now from those we brought with us. So, I'll answer the questions he'll have on that. I'd like it best if you'd go over the precautions and orders again with him. Then if he's nothing more to report than we've just heard from Isleen, we'll leave Malvin and two others here, and go on to the next. Aren't you hungry then?"

"As a matter of fact, but I'll wait."

"Ah." Larkin nodded his understanding. "You have what you need in that area?"

"I do. The horses and cows are safe."

"I saw the carcasses along the way. Not like an army had fed, but a few scavengers. Deserters, would you say?"

"It's exactly what I'd say."

"An advantage now," Larkin murmured, "with her losing troops here and there. A problem for later."

"It will be, yes."

"We'll think of something." Larkin looked over as the door opened. "Eogan. We've much to talk about, and little time."

There was little more at the next stronghold, but at the third, Lilith had left her mark.

Two of the outbuildings had been burned to rubble, and in the fields the crops had been torched. The men talked of a night of fire and smoke, and the screams of the cattle as they were slaughtered.

With Larkin, Cian stood and studied the scorched earth.

"It's as you said, you and Blair. She would lay waste to the farms and the homes."

"Stone and wood."

Larkin shook his head. "Livestock and crops. Sweat and blood. Hearth and home."

"All of which can be bred and grown, shed and built again. Your men withstood the siege, with no casualties. They fought, and held the ground—and took some of Lilith's forces to hell. Your glass is miraculously half full, Larkin."

"You'd be right, I know it. And I hope if she tries to drink what's left in it, it burns her guts black. We'll move on then."

There were fresh graves at the next base, burned earth and wounded men.

The sick dread in Larkin's belly eased, finally, when he saw his younger brother, Oran, limp out of the farmhouse. He strode to Oran quickly, and in the way of men gave him a hard punch in the arm, then a bear hug.

"Our mother will be pleased you're among the living. How bad are your wounds?"

"Scratches. How is it at home?"

"Busy. I've seen Phelan at one of the other camps, and he's safe and well."

"It's good to hear. Good to hear. But I have hard news, Larkin."

"We know of it." He laid a hand on Oran's shoulder. His brother had been little more than a boy when he'd marched away from home, Larkin thought. Now he was a man, with all the weight that went with it. "How many besides Tynan?"

"Three more. And another I fear won't make the night. Two others taken, dead or alive, I can't say. It was a child, Larkin. A demon child who killed Tynan."

"We'll go inside, and talk of it."

They used the kitchen with Cian sitting back from the window. He understood why Larkin listened to the whole account, though they knew or could imagine most of it. Oran had to speak it all, see it all again.

"I'd had the watch before his, and was still sleeping when I heard the alarm. It was already too late for Tynan, Larkin, already too late. He'd gone out, alone, thinking there was a child hurt and lost and afraid. It lured him, you see, some distance from the house. And though there were men posted, bows ready, when it turned and ripped at him, it was too late."

He wet his throat with ale. "Men rushed out. I think back, I think, I was second in command, and should have ordered them to hold. It was too late to save him, but how could we not try? And because we did, more were lost."

"He would have done the same for you, for anyone."

"They took his body." Oran's young face was alive with grief, and his eyes very old. "We searched. The next morning we searched, for him and the two others, but found only blood. We fear they've been changed."

"Not Tynan." Cian spoke now, waited for Oran's weary gaze to meet his. "We can't say about the other two, but

Tynan wasn't changed. His body was brought back to Castle Geal. He was given a full burial early this morning."

"I'll thank the gods for that, at least. But who brought the body?"

As Larkin gave the account, Oran's face hardened again.

"Young Sean. We couldn't save him in the ambush along the road. They came out of the ground like hellhounds. We lost good men that day, and Sean was lost as well. Is he at peace now?" He looked to Cian. "Now that what took him over is gone, is he at peace?"

"I don't have the answer."

"Well, I'll believe he is, just as Tynan is, and the others we've buried. He can't be held accountable by men or gods for what was done to him."

They double posted guards for the night, and at Cian's instructions small bladders were filled with blessed water. These would be hooked to arrows. With this, even a miss of the heart would cause considerable damage, and possible death.

In addition, more traps had been set. Men who couldn't sleep whiled away the time carving stakes.

"Do you think she'll send out a raiding party tonight?" Larkin asked Cian.

They sat in what had been a small parlor, and was now in use for weapon storage.

"To one of the other points, she may. Here? Little point in it, unless she's bored—or wants to exercise some of her troops. She's done what she had in mind to do at this base." Since they were alone, Cian drank blood from a pottery cup.

"And if you were her?"

"I'd send out small parties to distract and harass. Chipping away at enemy troops and morale at every base. The trouble with that is your men tend to stand firm, while we know some of hers desert. But your individual losses echo with you, where hers mean less than nothing."

He drank again. "But then I'm not her. Being me, I'd find satisfaction in seeking out a raiding party, taking it by surprise before it reached its objective. And killing the hell out of it."

"Isn't that peculiar," Larkin said with a grin. "Not being her, and not being you, the exact same thought had planted itself in my mind."

"Well then. What are we waiting for?"

They left Oran in charge of the base. Though there was considerable argument, discussion, debate, Larkin and Cian set out alone. One dragon and one vampire, Cian had reasoned, could travel swiftly, and undetected.

If they found a party and opted to land for hand-to-hand, Larkin's weapon harness was well-loaded. Cian swung a quiver over his back, loaded extra stakes in his sword belt.

"It'll be interesting to see how the idea of aerial warfare flies—as it were."

"Ready then?" Larkin changed, stood gold and sinuous as Cian strapped on the harness.

They'd agreed to keep it short and simple. They would fly in widening circles, looking for any sign of a party or a camp. If they spotted one, they'd strike—quick and clean.

The flight up toward a moon approaching its third quarter was exhilarating. The freedom of the night swept over Cian. He flew without cloak or coat, reveling in the cool and the dark.

Beneath him, Larkin soared, his dragon's wings barely a whisper on the air, and so thin Cian could see the glimmer of stars through them when they swept the air.

Clouds drifted, thin wisps that slid like gauze over stars, sailed like ghost ships over the waxing moon.

Far below, the first fingers of fog began their crawl over the ground.

If nothing else, the pleasure of the flight balanced out the smothering discomfort of the day's journey. As if he sensed it, Larkin aimed higher, rising in lazy loops. For one indulgent moment, Cian closed his eyes and just enjoyed.

Then he felt it, a stroke along the skin. Cold, seeking fingers that seemed to slide into him and swirl through his blood. And a whisper inside his head, a quiet siren's song that called to what he was beneath the form of a man.

And when he looked down, the savage ground of the battlefield spread below.

Its utter silence was a scream of violence. It burned into him like molten steel, brilliant and dark, deep and primal. The grass was wild sharp blades, the rocks rough death. Then even they would give way to black pits of chasms and caves where nothing dared to crawl.

Guarded by the mountains the damned ground waited for blood.

He had only to lean forward—such a short distance—and sink his teeth in the neck of the dragon to find the blood of a man. Human and rich, that gush of life, and a taste no other living thing could match. A flavor he'd denied himself for centuries. And why? To live among them, to survive wearing the mask of one of them?

They were beneath him, so much less—fleas on a dog. They were nothing but flesh and blood, created for him to hunt. The hunger gnawed in him, and the desire, the feral thrill of it pumped through him like a heartbeat.

The memory of the kill, of that first hot spurt of life gushing into his mouth, riding down his throat, was glorious.

Shaking like an addict in the throes of withdrawal, he fought it. He would not end it this way. He would *not* go back to being a prisoner of his own blood.

He was stronger than that. Had made himself more than that.

His belly cramped with need and nausea as he leaned toward Larkin. "Put down here. Stay in this form. Be ready to fly again, to leave me if you need. You'll know."

It dragged at him, that cursed ground, as they lowered toward it. It murmured and sang and promised. It lied.

The heat was in him like a fever as he leaped down. He would not, he swore, he would not turn himself and kill a friend as he'd once tried to kill his brother.

"It's this place. It's evil."

"I told you not to change forms. Don't touch me!"

"I feel it inside me." Larkin's voice was calm and even. "It must burn in you."

Cian turned, his eyes red, his skin slicked with sweat from his inner war. "Are you stupid?"

"No." But Larkin hadn't, and didn't now draw a weapon. "You're fighting it, and you'll beat it back. Whatever it is this place calls to in you, there's more. There's what Moira loves."

"You don't know the hunger of it." Deep in his throat a groan waited. It hummed in Cian's ears, and with it, he could hear the beat of Larkin's pulse. "I can smell you, the human."

"Do you smell fear?"

Shudders ran through him, hard enough he thought his bones might crack to pieces. His head was screaming, screaming, and still he couldn't block out the sound, the vicious temptation of that beating heart.

"No. But there could be. I could bring it into you. Fear sweetens it. God, God, what sick hand forged this place?"

His legs wouldn't hold him, so he lowered to the ground and struggled to tighten his slippery grip on his will. As he did, he closed his fingers around the locket she'd put around his neck.

The sickness ebbed, just a little, as if a cool hand had stroked a fevered brow. "She brings me light, that's what she brings to me. And I take it, and feel like a man. But I'm not. This is a hard reminder that I'm not."

"I see a man when I look at you."

"Well, you're wrong. But I won't drink tonight, not from you. Not from a human. It won't swallow me tonight. And it won't take me like this again, now that I know."

The red was fading from his eyes as he looked up at Larkin. "You were a fool not to draw a weapon."

In answer, Larkin lifted the cross from its chain.

"It might have been enough," Cian considered. He scrubbed his sweaty palms dry on the knees of his jeans. "Fortunately for us both, we don't have to test it."

"I'll take you back."

Cian looked at the hand Larkin offered. Humans, he thought, trusting and optimistic. He took it, pulled himself to his feet. "No, we'll go on. I need to hunt something."

He'd won the battle, Cian thought as they rose into the air again. But he wouldn't deny he was relieved to be heading away from that ground.

And he was darkly thrilled when he spotted the movements below.

A dozen troops, he noted, on foot and moving with that fluid swiftness of his kind. For all the speed, there was a precision to it, an order in the ranks that told him they were trained and seasoned soldiers.

He felt the shift of the dragon's body when Larkin saw them, and once again Cian leaned down.

"Why don't we try out Glenna's newest weapon? When they cross the next field, fly directly over the center of the squad. They've got archers, so once the shit hits, you'll have to go into evasive maneuvers."

As Larkin flew into position, Cian reached into the harness pocket and took out the ball.

How is a dragon like a plane? he considered, and put his centuries of experience as a pilot to use gauging airspeed, distance, velocity.

"Bomb's away," he murmured, and let the ball drop.

It smashed into the ground, causing the baffled squad to stop, draw weapons. Cian was about to chalk Glenna's experiment up to a loss when there was a towering burst of flame. Those closest to it were simply obliterated, while a few others caught fire.

Watching the panic, hearing the screams, Cian notched an arrow. Ducks in a barrel, he mused, and picked off what was left.

Once again Larkin touched down, and changed. "Well." He kicked carelessly at a pile of ash. "That was quick."

"I feel better for having killed something, but it was detached, impersonal. Human style. Doesn't have the same kick as a true hunt. Same reason we don't use guns or modern weaponry," Cian added. "There's just no thrill in it."

"I'm sorry for that, but the results of it suit me well enough. And Glenna's fireball worked a treat, didn't it now?"

Larkin began to gather the weapons scattered over the ground. As he bent down, an arrow whizzed over his back, and planted itself in Cian's hip.

"Oh well, bugger it! I must have missed one."

"Take the harness." Larkin tossed it at Cian. "And get on."

He flashed to dragon, and since he considered the arrow might slow him down a little on foot, Cian vaulted up. He caught the next arrow in the air before it could strike. Then Larkin was rising and diving and swerving.

"There, I see them. Second party entirely. Likely a hunting party looking for stray humans or whatever comes to hand."

He used the bow again, taking out a few as they scattered and took cover.

"It's just no fun this way," he decided. Drawing his sword, he leaped off Larkin and dropped thirty feet to the ground.

If dragon's could curse, Larkin would have turned the air blue.

They came at Cian like the points of a triangle, two male, three female. He sliced the arrow coming at him in two with his sword, then spun the blade back to block the oncoming attack.

The dregs of what he'd felt on the battleground were in him, and he used them. That need for blood, if not to drink, then to shed it. He fought at first to wound, so he could smell it—the rich copper of it, and ride on it as he hacked and sliced.

The dragon's tail whipped down, slapped one of the females back as she lifted her bow again. Then its claws raked at the throat.

To amuse himself, Cian flipped back, shot a vicious kick into the face of an opponent. When it stumbled he took its head even as he yanked the arrow from its hip and plunged it into the heart of the one coming from his left.

He spun around, saw that Larkin had changed and was ramming a spent arrow in the heart of the last one.

"Is that it then?" Larkin said breathlessly. "Is that the last of them?"

"By my count."

"And you counted so well the last time." He rose, brushed himself off. "Bloody dust. Are you feeling more yourself now?"

"Top of the world, Ma." Cian rubbed absently at his wounded hip. Since it was pouring blood, he ripped off the sleeve of his shirt. "Give me a hand, will you? Quick field dressing."

"You want me to bandage your arse?"

"It not my ass, you git."

"Close enough." But Larkin walked over to see to it. "Drop your drawers then, sweetheart."

Cian spared him a single dark look, but obliged.

"And what do you think Lilith's mood will be when not a one of her raiding or hunting parties comes back?"

"She'll be pissed." Cian craned his head to watch Larkin's work. "Royally."

"Makes a body feel good, doesn't it? You'll have a fine hole in your bum for a bit."

"Hip."

"Looks like your ass to me. And I'm hungry enough to eat a donkey, hide and all. Time we went back, had ourselves a meal and a tankard. There, you'll do. It was a good night's work," he added when Cian pulled his pants up again.

"Turned out that way. It could have gone otherwise back there at the valley, Larkin."

Philosophically, Larkin pulled up some clumps of grass to wipe most of Cian's blood from his hands. "I don't think that's the truth of it. I don't think it could have gone any way but what it did. Now if your ass isn't too sore, you'll help me gather up all these nice weapons to add to our supply."

"Leave my ass out of it."

Together they began to gather swords, bows, arrows. "I'm sure that portion of you will be fine again shortly. If not, Moira'll kiss it well for you when they arrive."

Cian looked over as Larkin whistled a tune and loaded swords in the harness. "You're a funny guy, Larkin. A damn funny guy."

In Geall, Moira walked away from the crystal to stand at the window with her arms folded. "Am I mistaken in it, or were they not told to go check the bases, take no risks?"

"They disobeyed," Blair agreed. "But you've got to admit it was a good fight. And that fire ball was excellent."

"The delay's a little concern." Glenna continued to watch as they flew back toward base. "I'll work on that. I'm a little more worried about the effect the battlefield had on Cian."

"He fought it off," Hoyt replied. "Whatever tried to take hold of him, he fought it off."

"He did, to his credit," Glenna agreed. "But it was hard won, Hoyt. It's something we have to think about. Maybe we can work a charm or spell that will help him block it."

"No." Moira spoke without turning. "He'll do it himself. He'll need to. Isn't it his will that makes him what he is?"

"I suppose you're right." Glenna studied Moira's rigid back. "Just as I suppose the two of them had to go out tonight, and do what they did."

"That may be. Are they back safe yet?"

"Coming in for touchdown," Blair told her. "And all's quiet on the western front. Well, eastern front, but that doesn't have the same literary ring."

"Quiet for the moment." Moira turned back. "I think it's safe to say they'll be tucked up for the night now, and it's unlikely there'll be another raid on the base. We should all get some sleep."

"Good idea." Glenna gathered up the crystal.

They said good night, went their separate ways. But none of them went to bed. Hoyt and Glenna went to the tower to work. Blair headed to the empty ballroom to train.

Moira went to the library and pulled out every book she could find on the lore and legend and history of the Valley of Silence.

She read and studied until the first light of dawn.

When she slept, curled in the window seat as she'd often done as a child, she dreamed of a great war between gods and demons. A battle that had raged for a century, and more. A war that had spilled the blood of both until it ran like an ocean.

And the ocean became a valley, and the valley became Silence.

Chapter 17

"Sinann, you should be in bed still."

With her hand resting on her belly, Sinann shook her head at Moira. "I couldn't let my father leave without seeing him off. Or you." Sinann looked around the courtyard where horses and dragons and men were preparing for the journey. "It will seem so empty now, with so few of us left inside the walls." She managed a smile as she watched her father hoist her son high in the air.

"We'll come back, and the noise will be deafening."

"Bring them back to me, Moira." The strain began to leak through now, through her eyes, her voice. "My husband, my father, my brothers, bring them back to me."

She took Sinann's arms. "I'll do everything in my power."

Sinann pressed Moira's hand to her belly. "There's life. Feel it? Tell Phelan you felt his child move."

"I will."

"I'll tend your seedlings, and keep a candle lit until you all come home again. Moira, how will we know? How will we know if you . . ."

"You'll know," Moira promised. "If the gods don't send a sign of our victory, then we will. I promise. Now go kiss your father, and I'll kiss all your other men for you when I see them."

Moira moved to her aunt, touched a hand to Deirdre's arm. "I've spoken with the men I can leave with you. My orders are clear, simple and to be followed exactly. The gate stays locked, and no one leaves the castle—day or night—until word comes that the battle is done. I count on you as the head of my family who remains here, to see these orders are followed. You are my regent until my return. Or in the event of my death—"

"Oh, Moira."

"In the event of my death, you will serve until the next rightful ruler is chosen." She pulled off a ring that had been her mother's, and pushed it into Deirdre's hand. "This is a sign of your authority, in my name."

"I'll honor your wishes, your orders and that name. I swear it to you. Moira." She gripped her niece's hands. "I'm sorry we quarreled."

"So am I."

Though her eyes were wet, Deirdre managed a tremulous smile. "Though we both part here believing we had the right of it."

"We do. I don't love you less because of it."

"My child." Deirdre held her close. "My sweet girl. Every prayer I know goes with you. Come back to us. Tell my sons they have my heart and my pride."

"Sorry." Blair touched Moira's shoulder. "Everything's ready."

"I'll say goodbye to you." Deirdre stepped forward to kiss Blair's cheeks. "And trust you'll keep my eldest out of trouble."

"Do my best."

"You'll need to. He's a handful." She opened her mouth to speak again, then took a steadying breath. "I was going to say be safe, but that's not what warriors want to hear. So I'm saying fight well."

"You can count on it."

Without pomp or pageantry, they mounted horses and dragons. Groups of children were gathered, clucked over by the women who remained behind. The old leaned on walking sticks, or the arms of the younger.

There were tears glimmering. While they might look through the mist of them to loved ones leaving them behind, Moira knew they looked to her as well.

Bring them back to me. How many had that single desperate wish in their hearts and minds? Not all would have that wish granted, but she would—as she'd sworn to Sinann—do her best.

And she wouldn't leave them or lead them with tears.

Moira signalled to Niall who would lead the ground force. When he called for the gates to be raised, she lifted the sword of Geall high. And leading the last of the troops from Castle Geall, she shot an arc of fire into the pale morning sky.

The dragon riders arrived first to mobilize the troops. They would abandon the first base to begin the next leg of the march to the battlefield. Supplies and weapons were packed, and men were taken up on dragons, or onto horses when they arrived. Those who went on foot were flanked by riders—air and ground.

So they traveled across the land and the skies of Geall.

At the next stop they rested and watered their mounts.

"You'll have tea, my lady." Ceara joined Moira near a stream where dragons drank.

"What? Oh, thanks." Moira took the cup.

"I've never seen such a sight."

"No." Moira continued to watch the dragons, and wondered if any of them would see such a sight again. "You'll ride with your husband, Ceara."

"I will, my lady. We're near ready."

"Where is the cross you won, Ceara? The one you're wearing is copper."

"I . . ." Ceara lifted her hand to the copper cross. "I left it with my mother. Majesty, I wanted my children protected if . . ."

"Of course you did." She wrapped her fingers around Ceara's wrist and squeezed. "Of course." She turned as Blair strode toward them.

"Time to round them up. Mounts are rested and watered. Supplies and weapons are packed, except for what we're leaving behind with the squad that'll hold this base until tomorrow."

"The troops behind us should arrive well before sunset." Moira looked to the skies. "Do they have enough protection if there's a change in the weather. Natural or otherwise?"

"Lilith may have some snipers and scouts scattered this far west, but nothing the troops can't handle. We have to move on, Moira. Leap-frogging this way keeps soldiers from being exposed and vulnerable at night, but it takes time."

"And we've a schedule to keep," Moira agreed. "Give the order then, and we'll move on."

It was well past midday when the first of them arrived at their final destination. Below where she flew, men stopped and cheered. She saw Larkin come out of the house, lift his face. Then change into a dragon to fly up and join them.

And she saw the dark earth of fresh graves.

Larkin circled her with a quick, showy flourish, then paced himself to Blair's mount. Moira lost her breath when Blair stood on her dragon's back, then sprang off into the air. The cheers from below rose up like thunder as Blair landed on Larkin, and rode him down.

Like a festival, Moira thought, as other riders executed showy turns and dives. Perhaps they needed the show and the foolishness for these last few hours of daylight. Night would come soon enough.

She would have seen to her own mount as she had along the way, but Larkin plucked her off her feet, gave her a whirl and a kiss.

"That doesn't sweeten me up," she told him. "I've a bone to pick with you. You were to travel, gather reports and secure. Not go out looking for trouble."

"We do what we must when we must." He kissed her again. "And all's well, isn't it?"

"Is it?"

"It is. He is. Go inside. There are plenty here to see to the mounts. You've had a long journey. No trouble along the way, Blair says."

"No, none." She let him lead her inside.

There was a pot of stew simmering over the fire, and the scent of it, of men and mud filled the air. Maps were spread over a table where she imagined a family had once gathered. Hangings over the windows were homespun and cheerful, and the walls were clean and whitewashed.

Weapons stood at every door and window.

"You've a chamber upstairs if you want a bit of a rest."

"No, I'm fine. But in fact I could use a whiskey if there's any to be had."

"There is."

She could see by his face that Blair had come behind them.

"Mounts are being tended," Blair began. "Supplies and weapons unloaded. Hoyt's on it. What's the setup here?"

"We've troops bunking in the stables, the barn, the dovecote and the smokehouse as well as in here. There's a loft that's roomy enough, and we're using it as a kind of barracks."

He poured a whiskey as he spoke, cocked his head at Blair, but she shook hers.

"Sitting room here is serving as the main arsenal," he continued. "And we've weapons stockpiled in all the buildings. The men take shifts, day and night. Training continues daily. There were raids, as you know, but none since Cian and I arrived."

"Saw to that, didn't you?" Moira asked before she drank.

"We did, and gave Lilith a good boot in the arse. We lost

another man yesterday, one who was wounded in the raid that killed Tynan. He didn't die easy."

Moira looked down into her whiskey. "Are there more wounded?"

"Aye, but walking. There's a kind of parlor open to the kitchen, and we've been using that for tending those who need it."

"Glenna will have a look at that, and arrange it as she sees best. Well." She downed the rest of the whiskey. "We all know there's not enough room inside shelters for all the troops. Nearly a thousand here tonight, and half again that many who'll be here within the next two days."

"Then we'd better get busy making camp," Blair said.

There was some pride in it, Moira discovered, at seeing so many of her people—men and women, old and young—working together. Tents began to spread over the field while wood and turf was gathered for cook fires. Wagons of supplies were unloaded and stacked.

"You have your army," Glenna said from beside her.

"One day I hope crops will be planted here again instead of tents. There are so many. There never seemed so many before. Can you hold so many within a protective circle?"

Glenna's face tightened with sheer determination. "Lilith's pet dog managed to shield their entire base. I hope you're not suggesting Hoyt and I can't measure up."

"Wouldn't think of it."

"Damn big circle to cast," Glenna admitted. "And the sun's getting low, we'll have to get started. We could use you."

"I was hoping you could."

With them, Moira walked the field from end to end and, as Glenna had instructed, gathered blades of grass, small stones, bits of earth as she went. They met again in the center.

As word had passed that magic would be done, the troops fell silent. In the hush, Moira heard the first whispers of power.

They called on the guardians, east and west, north and

south. On Morrigan, their patron. She took up the chant with them as she'd been given it.

"In this place and in this hour, we call upon the ancient powers to hear our needs and grant our plea to shelter all in this company. Upon this grass, this earth, this stone, protection from harm bestow. Only life at its fullest may cross this ring, and none may enter with harm to bring. Within this circle that was cast no enemy nor his weapon may pass. Night or day, day or night shield earth and air within its light. Now our blood will seal this shield and circle it round this field."

As Hoyt and Glenna did, Moira cut her palm with an athame, then fisted it around the dirt, the grass, the stones she'd gathered.

It pumped and plunged through her, the heat—hers and theirs—and the wind they raised blew in widening circles, slapping at the tents, singing through the grass until it whipped around and around the edges of the field in a cyclone of light.

With Hoyt and Glenna, she threw down the blood-soaked earth, felt the shudder under her feet as three small flames bloomed and died. When they clasped hands, her body bowed back from the force of what joined them.

"Rise and circle," she shouted with them, "circle and close and bar this place from all our foes. Blood and fire here mix free, as we will, so mote it be."

Around the field red flames speared up. When the earth was scorched white in a perfect ring, the flames vanished in a thunderclap.

Moira's vision wavered, and the voices that spoke to her seemed to blur as well, as if the world were suddenly underwater.

When she came back to herself she was on her knees. Glenna was gripping her shoulders and saying her name.

"I'm all right. I'm all right. It was just . . . it was so much. Just need my breath back."

"Take your time. It was a powerful spell, only more so because we used blood."

Moira looked down at the slice on her hand. "Everything's a weapon," she stated. "As Blair says. Whatever it takes, as long as it works."

"I'd say it has," Hoyt said quietly.

Following his direction, Moira saw Cian standing outside the circle. Though the cloak protected him from the last rays of the sun, she could see his eyes, and the fury in them.

"Well then. We'll leave the men to finish setting up camp."

"Lean on me," Glenna told her. "You're white as a sheet."

"No, it won't do." Though her knees were still like pudding. "The men can't see me drooping now. I'm just a bit off in the stomach is all."

As she crossed the field, Cian turned on his heel and strode back to the house.

He was waiting inside, and something of his mood must have translated as he was alone.

"Are you trying to lay her out before Lilith gets the chance?" he demanded. "What are you thinking, dragging her into magicks like that, strong enough to brew up your own personal hurricane."

"We needed her," Hoyt said simply. "It isn't an easy matter to throw a net over an area so large that holds so many. And as it stopped you on the edge, the spell holds."

It hadn't just stopped him, but had shot jolts of electricity through him. He was surprised his hair wasn't standing on end. "She's not strong enough to—"

"Don't tell me what I'm not strong enough to do. I've done what was needed. And isn't that the same you'd say to me if I dared question your reckless journey to the valley? Both are done now, and we're able to stand here and argue about it, so I'd say both are well done. I'm told I have a chamber upstairs. Does anyone know where it might be?"

"First door, left," Cian snapped.

When she walked, haughtily, he thought, up the stairs, he cursed. Then followed her.

She sat in the chair by the fire that had yet to be lit, with her head between her knees.

"My head's light, and it doesn't need you bringing a scold down on it. I'll be myself again in a moment."

"You seem yourself to me." He poured water into a cup, held it down so she could see it. "Drink this. You're white as a corpse. I've made corpses with more color than you."

"A lovely thing to say."

"Truth is rarely pretty."

She sat back in the chair, studying him as she drank the water. "You're angry, and that's just fine and good, as I'm angry right with you. You knew I was here, but you didn't come down."

"No, I didn't come down."

"You're a great fool, is what you are. Thinking you'd ease back from me, that I'd let you. We've only days left before we end this thing, so you go ahead and take steps back from me. I'll just take them toward you until your back's in the corner. I've not only learned to fight, I've learned not to fight clean."

She gave a little shiver. "It's cold. I've nothing left after that spell to get the fire lit."

He moved toward the hearth, and before he bent down for the tinderbox, she took his hand. And she pressed it against her cheek.

It broke him, a snap like glass. He lifted her out of the chair, holding her off the floor while his mouth plundered hers. She simply wrapped herself around him, wantonly, arms and legs.

"Aye, that's better," she said breathlessly. "Much warmer now. The hours seemed endless since I watched you go. So little time, so little, for eternity."

"Look at me. Yes, there's that face." He held her close again so her head rested on his shoulder.

"Did you miss it, my face?"

"I did. You don't have to fight dirty when you've already carved yourself inside me."

"Easier to be angry with each other. It hurts less." She squeezed her eyes tight for a moment, then eased back when he set her on her feet. "I brought the vielle. I thought you might like to have it, to play it. We should have music, like we should have light and laughter, and all the things that remind us what we're ready to die for."

She walked to the window. "The sun's setting. Will you go back to the battlefield tonight?" She glanced around when he didn't speak. "We saw you go with Larkin two nights ago, and saw you go alone last night."

"Each time I go, I'm a little stronger. I won't be any good to you or myself if what's soaked into that ground turns me."

"You're right on that, and tonight I'll be going with you. You can waste time arguing, Cian," she said as he began to. "But I'll be going. Geall is mine, after all, and every inch of its ground, whatever is under it. I haven't been on the edges of that place since my childhood, except in my dreams of it. I need to see it, and at night, as it will be on Samhain. So I'll be going with you, or I'll be going alone."

"But I want to go! I want to. Please, please, please!" Lilith wondered if her head could actually explode from the boy's incessant whining and wheedling. "Davey, I said no. It's too close to Samhain, and much too dangerous for you to leave the house."

"I'm a soldier." His little face went sharp and vicious. "Lucius said so. I have a sword."

He unsheathed the small blade she'd had made for him—to her current regret—after his field kill. "It's just a hunting party," she began.

"I want to hunt. I want to fight!" Davey slashed at the air with his sword. "I want to *kill*."

"Yes, yes, yes." Lilith waved him away. "And you will, to your heart's content. *After* Samhain. Not another word!"

She snapped the order out while a tinge of red smeared the whites of her eyes. "I've had enough from you for one day. You're too young and too small. And that's the end of it. Now go to your room and play with that damned cat you wanted so much."

His eyes gleamed red, and his lips peeled back in a snarl that stripped away even the mask of human innocence. "I'm not too small. I hate the cat. And I hate you." He stormed off, his little legs pumping in his tantrum. He swung his sword wildly as he went, slicing through the torso of a human servant who wasn't quick enough to leap aside.

"Damnation! Look at that mess." Lilith threw up her hands at the blood spatter on the walls. "That boy's driving me mad."

"Needs a good swat, if you ask me."

Face livid now, Lilith rounded on Lora. "Shut your mouth! Don't tell me what he needs. I'm his mother."

"*Bien sur.* Don't bite at me because he's being a brat." Sulking, Lora slumped into a chair. Her face was nearly healed now, but the scars that remained burned into her like poison. "Simple to see where he gets his bitchy attitude."

One of Lilith's hands curled, the red-tipped nails like talons. "Maybe you're the one who needs a good swat."

Knowing Lilith could do worse than a swat in her current mood, Lora shrugged. "I wasn't the one who hammered at you the last hour, was I? I backed you up with Davey, and now you're taking it out on me. Maybe we're all on edge, but you and I should stick together."

"You're right, you're right." Lilith dragged her hands through her hair. "He actually gave me a headache. Imagine."

"He's just, how do they say it? Acting out. He's so proud of himself for that kill in the field."

"I can't let him go out."

"No, no." Lora waved a hand. "You did absolutely right. We've lost a hunting party and a raiding party, and it's no place for Davey out there. I still say you should've given him a good slap for talking back to you."

"He may get one yet. Have someone clean that up." She gestured vaguely toward the body of the servant. "Then make sure the hunting party gets on its way. Maybe they'll be luckier tonight and track down the odd human. The troops are tired of sheep's blood.

"Oh, one more thing," she said as Lora started out. "I want a little something to eat—to calm myself down. Do we have any children left?"

"I'll check."

"Something small in any case. I don't have much of an appetite tonight. Have it sent up to my room. I need some quiet."

Alone, she paced the room as if it were a cage. Her nerves were stretched, she could admit that. So much on her mind, so many details, so many responsibilities with it all coming to the end of the circle at last.

The loss of troops was infuriating and worrisome. Deserters had been a problem, but she sent out scavengers nightly to hunt them down and destroy them. It simply wasn't possible two full squads had deserted.

More human traps? she wondered. They were costing her dearly—and would cost the humans a great deal more when she was done.

No one understood the pressure she was under, the weight of her responsibility. She had worlds to decimate. Her destiny was pressing down on her and she was surrounded by fools and incompetents.

Now her own sweet Davey, her own darling boy, was behaving like a snarling, spitting brat. He'd actually sassed her, something she took from no one. She wasn't certain if she should be proud or furious.

Still, she thought, he'd looked so cute and fierce waving that miniature sword. And hadn't he nearly cut that stupid servant in two, then stomped right out, almost swaggered, without a backward glance?

It was annoying, of course, but how could she not be a little proud?

She walked to the door, stepped out so she could feel the night slide over her, into her. He felt trapped in this house, poor Davey. So did she. But soon . . .

Of course, of course, what a terrible mother she was! She'd arrange a hunt right here, on the shielded grounds. Just the two of them. It would perk up her appetite, her spirits. And Davey would be thrilled.

Pleased with the idea, she went back in, and stepping over the bleeding body, went upstairs.

"Davey. Where's my bad little boy? I have a surprise for you."

She opened the door of his room. The smell came first. There was a considerable amount of blood, on the floor, on the walls, on the bed covers she'd had made for him of royal blue silk.

Pieces of the cat were strewn everywhere. It had been, she recalled, a very large cat.

She sighed, then felt a laugh bubbling up. What a temper her little darling had.

"Davey, you naughty boy. Come out from wherever you're hiding, or I might change my mind about the surprise." She rolled her eyes. Being a mother was such work. "I'm not angry, my sweetheart. I've just had so much on my mind, and I forgot you and I need to have some fun."

She searched the room as she spoke, then frowned when she didn't find him. There were little pricks of concern as she stepped again. Lora dragged a woman behind her by a neck shackle.

"We're out of children, but this one's small."

"No, no, not now. I can't find Davey."

"Not in his room." Lora peeked in. "Ah, creative. He's hiding somewhere because you're angry with him."

"I have something . . ." Lilith pressed a hand to her belly. "Something tight inside me. I want him found. Quickly."

They called out a search, scoured the manor house, the

outbuilding, the fields within the protected area. The tightness in Lilith's belly became strangling knots when they discovered his pony missing.

"He's run away. He's run off. Oh, why didn't I make certain he was in his room? I have to find him."

"Wait. Wait," Lora insisted and grabbed Lilith hard. "You can't risk going outside the safety area."

"He's mine. I have to find him."

"We will. We will. We'll send our best trackers. We'll use Midir. I'll go myself."

"No." Struggling for calm, Lilith closed her eyes. "I can't risk you. Lucius. Find Lucius, and have him come to me in Midir's lair. Hurry."

She cooled her blood and her mind. To rule took heat, she knew, but it also took ice. It was ice she needed to hold strong until the prince was safe again.

"I depend on you, Lucius."

"My lady, I'll find him. I give you my word, and my word that I would give my life to see him safely home."

"I know it." She laid her hand on his shoulder. "There's no one I trust more. Bring him back to me, and anything you ask of me is yours."

She whirled on Midir. "Find him! Find the prince in the glass."

"I am searching."

On the wall was a large oval of glass. It reflected the wizard in his dark robes, the room where he worked his dark magicks, and none of the three vampires who watched him.

Smoke slithered over the glass, swirled, and clawed its way to the edges. Through the haze of it, night began to bloom. And in the night came the shadow of a boy on a pony.

"Oh there, there he is." Crying out, Lilith gripped Lora's hand. "Look how well he rides, how straight in the saddle. Where is he? Where in this cursed land is the prince?"

"He's behind the hunting party," Lucian told her as he studied the vision in the glass. "And moving toward the battleground. I know that land, my lady."

"Hurry then, hurry. Willful brat," she muttered. "I'll take your advice this time, Lora. When he's back he'll have a good hiding. Keep him in that glass, Midir. Can you send me to him, the illusion of me?"

"You ask for many magicks at once, Majesty." Robes swirling, he moved to his cauldron and, letting his hands flow through the air over it, brought up a pale green smoke.

"I'll need more blood," he told her.

"Human, I suppose."

His eyes glittered. "It would be best, but I can make do with the blood of a lamb or young goat."

"This is the prince," she said coldly. "We don't make do. Lora, have the one I was going to have brought in. Midir can have it."

In the dark, Davey rode quickly. He felt strong and fierce and fine. He would show them, show them all that he was the greatest warrior ever made. The Prince of Blood, he thought with a glinting smile. He'd make everyone call him that. Even his mother.

She'd said he was small, but he *wasn't*.

He'd thought to trail behind the hunting party, then move in among them and order them to let him take the lead. None would dare question the Prince of Blood. And he would have the first kill.

But something was pulling him away from them, from the scent of his own kind. Something strong and tempting. He didn't need to stay with a hunting party, trail along after them like a baby. They were all less than he was.

He wanted to follow the music that was humming in his blood, and the smell of ancient death.

He rode slowly now, and with excitement bubbling inside him. There was something wonderful out in the dark. Something wonderful and his.

In the moonlight he saw the battlefield, and the beauty of it made him shake as he did when his mother let him put himself into her and ride as if she were a pony.

While it burned through him he saw figures on the high ground. Two humans, he thought, and a dragon.

He would have them all, slaughter them, drain them, and take their heads to drop at his mother's feet.

No one would ever call him small again.

Chapter 18

There was a hard place in the middle of Moira's chest, like a fist poised to strike. Breathing around it was an effort, but she stood as Cian did, at the edge of Silence.

"What do you feel?" she asked him.

"Pulled. You're not to touch me."

"Pulled how?"

"Chains on my feet, around my throat, pulled in opposite directions."

"Pain."

"Yes, but it's mixed with fascination. And thirst. I can smell the blood in the ground. It's thick and it's rich. I can hear your heartbeat, taste your scent."

Yet his eyes were Cian's eyes, she thought. They didn't burn red as they had the night he'd come here with Larkin. "They'll be stronger here than on other ground."

He looked at her then, realizing he should have known she would understand that. "They'll be stronger here. There'll be more of them than there are of you. Driven by what's bred in this place, by Lilith's power over them, death won't mean to them what it does to you. They'll come and they'll come without thought of their own survival."

"You think we'll lose. We'll die here, every one of us."

Truth, he thought, would shield her better than platitudes. "I think the chances of beating this diminish."

"You may be right. I'll tell you what I know of this place. What I've read, and what I think is the truth of it."

She looked out again, across the pitted land called *Ciunas*. "Long, long ago, before the worlds had separated, and were one instead of many, there were only gods and demons. Man had yet to come between to fight either, to tempt either. Both were strong and fierce and greedy, both wanted dominion. But still, the gods, however cruel, didn't hunt and kill their own kind, didn't hunt and kill demons for sport or food."

"So had the margin of good against evil?"

"There has to be a line, even if it's only that. There was war. Eons of it, all leading to this place. This was their last battle. The bloodiest, the most vicious, and most fruitless, I think. There was no victory. Only an ocean of blood that rose here, formed this harsh valley, and in time ebbed away, so that blood soaked into the earth, deep and deep."

"Why here? Why in Geall?"

"I think when the gods made Geall, deemed it would live centuries in peace, in prosperity, this valley was the price. The balance."

"Now payment's due?"

"It's always been coming to this, Cian. Now the gods charge the humans to fight the battle with this demon that began as human. Vampire against what is its source and its prey. It balances here, or it all falls. But Lilith doesn't understand what may happen if she wins this."

"We'll burn out. My kind." He nodded, having come to the same conclusion himself. "In chaos nothing thrives."

Moira said nothing for a moment. "You're calmer now, because you're thinking."

He let out a half laugh. "You're right. Still, it's the last place in this world or any I'd want to spread out for a picnic."

"We'll have a moonlight one, after Samhain. There's a place that's a favorite of mine and Larkin's. It's—"

Though he'd told her not to touch him, he gripped her wrist now. "Ssh. Something . . ."

Saying nothing, Moira reached into the quiver on her back for an arrow.

In the shadows, Davey grinned and drew his treasured sword. Now, he would fight the way a prince was supposed to fight. He'd slice and thrust and bite.

And drink, and drink, and drink.

He leaned low over the saddle, preparing to loose a war cry. And Lilith appeared before him.

"Davey! You turn that pony around this minute and come home."

The fierceness on his face turned into a childish pout. "I'm hunting!"

"You'll hunt when and where I tell you. I don't have time for this nonsense, this worry. I have a war to wage."

Now his face tightened into stubborn lines, and his eyes gleamed against the dark. "I'm going to fight. I'm going to kill the humans, then you won't treat me like a baby."

"I made you, and I can *un*make you. You'll do exactly what I . . . what humans?"

He gestured with his sword. As she turned, and she saw, true fear bloomed in Lilith's belly. Uselessly she grabbed for the bridle, but her hand passed through the pony's neck.

"Listen to me, Davey. Only one of them is human. The male is Cian. He's very powerful, very strong, very old. You have to run. Make this pony run as fast as it can. You're not meant to be here. We're not meant to be here now."

"I'm hungry." His eyes were turning, and his tongue flicked out over fang and lip. "I want to kill the old one. I want to drink the female. They're mine, they're mine. I'm the Prince of Blood!"

"Davey, no!"

But with a violent kick of his heels, he sent the pony racing forward.

It was all so quick, Moira thought. Flashing moments. The silver snick of Cian's sword leaving its scabbard, the shift of his body in front of hers like a shield. The rider flew out of the dark, and her arrow was notched and ready.

Then she saw it was a child, a little boy on a sturdy roan pony. Her heart stumbled; her body jerked. And her arrow went wide of the mark.

The child was screaming, howling, snarling. A wolf cub on the hunt.

Lilith flew behind the pony, an emerald and gold she-demon, streaking through the air, hands curled into claws, fangs gleaming.

Moira's second arrow spiked through her heart and soared into the air.

"She's not real!" Cian shouted. "But he is. Take the dragon and go."

Even as she reached for a third arrow, Cian shoved her aside, leaping over the charging pony.

A little boy, Moira thought. A little boy with eyes burning red and fangs spearing. It waved a shortened sword, as it dragged on the reins. Lilith's screams were like lances of ice through Moira's brain as the boy tumbled off the pony and fell hard on the rocky ground.

It bled, Moira saw, where the rocks struck and scraped. It cried, as a boy would when he had a fall.

Her breath caught in denial as Cian advanced with the illusion of Lilith clawing at him with intangible hands. Sick in heart and mind, Moira lowered her bow.

The second rider came out of the moon-struck dark like fury. Not a boy now, but a man armed for battle, his broadsword already cleaving the air.

Cian pivoted, and met the charge.

Swords clashed and crashed, the deadly music of them ringing over the valley. Cian leaped, dismounting the rider with a vicious kick to the throat.

With no clear shot, Moira tossed down her bow and

drew her sword. Before she could rush to fight with Cian, the boy gained his hands and knees. He lifted his head, stared at her with those gleaming eyes.

It growled.

"Don't." Moira backed up a step as Davey crouched to spring. "I don't want to hurt you."

"I'll rip out your throat." His lips peeled back as he circled her. "And drink and drink. You should run. I like it best when they try to run."

"I won't run. But you should."

"Davey, run! Run now!"

He whipped his head toward Lilith and snarled like a rabid dog. "I want to play! Hide-and-seek. Tag, you're it!"

"I won't play." Moira circled with him, trying to work him back with thrusts of the sword.

He'd lost his sword in the fall, but Moira told herself she would use hers if he sprang at her. He wasn't unarmed; no vampire ever was. And those fangs glinted, sharp and keen.

She spun, kicking out, aiming low to hit him in the belly and drive him back.

Lilith's form crouched over him, hissing. "I'll kill you for that. I'll peel the skin from your bones before I do. Lucius!"

Lucius hacked out at Cian. There was blood on them both, blood in their eyes. They leaped at each other, meeting violently in midair.

"Run, Davey!" Lucius shouted. "Run!"

Davey hesitated, and something came over his face. Moira thought, for an instant, she could see the child the demon had swallowed. The fear, the innocence, the confusion.

He ran as a child runs, limping on his scraped knees. And gaining speed, gaining that eerie grace as he rushed toward the slashing swords.

Dropping her own sword, Moira grabbed up her bow. A moment too late, as Davey leaped onto Cian's back, struck with fang and fist. If she shot now, the arrow could go through the boy, and into Cian.

A fingersnap. More flashes of time. The boy tumbled

through the air, propelled by a savage blow. He knuckled his hands over his burning eyes and cried for his mother.

Again, Lilith called out. "Lucius, the prince! Help the prince."

His loyalty, his years of service cost him. As Lucius turned his head a fraction toward Lilith, Cian took it with one singing strike of his sword.

Davey scrambled to his feet, wild panic on his face now.

"Take him," Cian called out as Davey began to run. "Take the shot."

Now those flashes of time slowed down. Wild screams, wild weeping, echoing through the dragging air. The figure of a child running on bleeding, tired legs. Lilith, her face alive with fear and horror, standing between the child and Moira, her arms spread in defense or plea.

Moira looked into Lilith's eyes as her own blurred. Then with a tear in her heart, she blinked them clear, and sent the arrow flying.

The shriek was horribly human as the arrow passed through Lilith. That shriek went on and on and on as the arrow continued, straight and true into the heart of what had once been a little boy who'd played in the warm surf with his father.

Then Moira was standing alone with Cian on the edge of a valley that hummed with the hunger for more blood.

Cian bent, picked up the swords. "We need to go, now. She'll have already sent others."

"She loved him." Moira's voice sounded strange and thin to her own ears. "She loved the child."

"Love isn't exclusive to humans. We need to go."

Her mind dull, she tried to focus on Cian. "You're hurt."

"And I don't relish leaving any more blood here. Get mounted."

She nodded, taking her own weapons before pulling herself onto the dragon. "She'd killed him," Moira murmured as Cian vaulted on behind her. "But she loved him."

She said nothing more as they flew away from the battlefield.

* * *

Glenna took over the moment they got back, herding them both into the parlor for first aid.

"I'm not hurt," Moira insisted, but sat heavily. "I wasn't touched."

"Just sit." Glenna got to work on Cian's buttons. "Off with your shirt, handsome, so I can see the damage."

"Some cuts, a few punctures." He bit back a wince as he shrugged out of the shirt. "He was good with a sword, quick on his feet."

"I'd say you were better and quicker." Blair handed him a cup of whiskey. "That's a nasty bite on the back of your shoulder, pal. What? This guy fought like a girl?"

"It was the boy," Moira said before Cian could answer. She shook her head at the whiskey Blair offered. "Lilith's boy, the one she called Davey. He came at us, riding a little pony, waving a sword no bigger than a toy."

"He wasn't a boy," Cian said flatly.

"I know what he was." Moira simply closed her eyes.

"A kiddie vamp did all this?" Blair demanded.

"No." With some annoyance, Cian scowled at her. "What do you take me for? The soldier—trained and seasoned—Lilith must have sent after the whelp did this, except for the shagging bite."

"How do I treat it?" Glenna asked him. "A vampire bite on a vampire?"

"Like any other wound. You can sure as hell hold the holy water. It'll heal quick enough, like the others."

"It was a foolish risk going out there," Hoyt said.

"It was necessary," Cian shot back. "For me. And our happy news is whatever holds that place doesn't stop me from dusting another vampire. Moira." Cian waited until she opened her eyes and met his. "It had to be done. There might have been others coming behind the one she called Lucius. If I'd gone after the young one, it would have taken time and left you alone. He was no less your enemy because of his size."

"I know what he was," she said again. "He was what killed Tynan, what tried to kill Larkin. What would have killed us both tonight if it had gone another way. Still, I saw his face—under what it was, I saw his face. It was young and sweet. I saw Lilith's face, and it was the face of a mother, terrified for her child. I put the arrow into it as it ran away, crying for its mother. I know, whatever comes now, nothing I ever do will be worse than that. And I know I can live with it."

She let out a shuddering breath. "I think I'll be having that whiskey now after all. I'll take it up with me if you don't mind. I'm tired."

Cian waited until Moira left the room. "Lilith will try for her. She may not be able to get physically into the house, but in dreams, or illusions."

Hoyt rose. "I'll see to it, make certain the protection we have is strong enough."

"She won't want me now," Larkin murmured. "Or any of us," he added with a quiet look for Cian. "She'll need to curl up with it for a while. And she will live with it, just as she said."

He sat now, across from Cian. "You said the one you fought was called Lucius?"

"That's right."

"That's the one I tangled with, along with the boy, in the caves. I'd say you've just taken out one of Lilith's top men. A kind of general. This would be a very hard night for Lilith, thanks to you and Moira."

"She'll come harder now because of it. We've destroyed or damaged those closest to her, and she'll come at us like bloody vengeance."

"Let her come," Blair said.

She would have come, then and there, so mad was her fury, her rage, her grief. It took six guards, and Midir's magic to hold her down while Lora dosed her with drugged blood.

"I'll kill you all! Every one of you for this. Take your hands off me before I cut them off and feed them to the wolves."

"Hold her!" Lora ordered and forced more blood down Lilith's throat. "You can't go to their base tonight. You can't go with the army and attack. Everything you've worked and planned for would be lost."

"Everything is lost. She put an arrow in him." She whipped her head, flashed fangs and sank them into one of the restraining hands. Her own screams mixed with the howls of the wounded.

"Release her, and I'll take more than your hand," Lora warned. "There's nothing to be done for him, my love, my darling."

"It's a dream. Just a dream." Bloody tears ran down Lilith's face. "He can't be gone."

"There now, there." Signalling the others back, Lora gathered Lilith into her arms. "Leave us. All of you. Get out!"

She sat on the floor, rocking Lilith, cooing to her while their tears mixed together.

"He was my precious," Lilith wept.

"I know. I know, and mine."

"I want that pony found. I want it slaughtered."

"It will be. There now."

"He only wanted to play." Seeking comfort, she nuzzled at Lora's shoulder. "In a few days, I could have given him everything. And now . . . I'll peel the skin from her bones, pour her blood into a silver tub. I'll bathe in it, Lora. I swear it."

"We'll bathe together, while we drink from that turncoat who took Lucius."

"Lucius, Lucius." Tears ran faster. "He gave his eternity trying to save our Davey. We'll build a statue of him, of both of them. We'll grind the bones of humans and build it from their dust."

"They'd be so pleased. Come with me now. You need to rest."

"I feel so weak, so tired." With Lora's help she gained her feet. "Have whatever humans we have left in stock executed and drained. No, no, tortured and drained. Slowly. I want to hear their screams in my sleep."

Moira didn't dream. She simply dropped into a void and floated there. She had Hoyt to thank for the hours of peace, she thought as she began to wake. Hours of peace where she hadn't seen a child's face blurred together with that of a monster.

Now there was work to be done. The months of preparation had whittled down to days that could be counted in hours. While the vampire queen mourned, the queen of Geall would do whatever needed to be done next.

She stirred, sat up. And saw Cian sitting in the chair near the simmering fire.

"It's still shy of dawn," he said. "You could use more sleep."

"I've had enough. How long have you watched over me?"

"I don't count the time." She'd slept like the dead, he thought now. He hadn't counted the time, but he had counted her heartbeats.

"Your wounds?"

"Healing."

"You'd have had fewer of them, but I was weak. I won't be again."

"I told you to go. Didn't you trust me to deal with two of them, especially when one was half my size? Less."

She leaned back. "Clever of you to try to turn this into a matter of my trust in your fighting skills instead of my lack of spine."

"If you'd had less spine and more sense, you'd have gone when I told you to."

"Bollocks. The time for running is well done, and I would never have left you. I love you. I should have taken him with the sword, quickly. Instead, I wavered, and tried to find a way to drive him off so I wouldn't be the one to end him. That moment of weakness could have cost us both. Believe me when I tell you it's burned out of me."

"And the misplaced guilt that goes with it?"

"May take a bit longer, but it won't get in the way. We have only two days left. Two days." She looked toward the window. "It's quiet. This time just before dawn is quiet. She killed a young boy, and came to love what she'd made of it."

"Yes. It doesn't make either of them less of a monster."

"Two days," she said again, almost in a whisper. Something inside her was already dying. "You'll go when this is done, if we win, if we don't, you'll go back through the Dance. I'll never see you again, or touch you, or wake to find you've watched over me in the dark."

"I'll go," was all he said.

"Will you come, hold me now, before the sun comes?"

He rose, went to her. Sitting beside her, he drew her against him so her head lay on his shoulder.

"Tell me you love me."

"As I've loved nothing else." He met her lips when she turned them to his.

"Touch me. Taste me." She shifted so she lay over him, trembling body, seeking lips. "Take from me."

What choice did he have? She was surrounding him, saturating his senses, stoking his needs till they burned. Offering as much as demanding as she pressed his lips to her breast.

"Take more. More and more."

Her mouth was hot and desperate as she pulled away clothes, her teeth nipping at his jaw in sharp, quick bites while her breath shuddered.

She was alive now, burning and alive, with everything inside her rising, aching. How could she step back from this? The love, the heat, the *life*.

If she was destined to die in battle, then she'd accept it. But how could she live—day after day, night after night— without her heart?

She straddled him, taking him in, hips whipping as she fought to feel more, to take more. To know more.

Her eyes gleamed, almost a madness, and stayed locked on his. Then she leaned to him, and her hair fell, curtaining them both, trapping him in its texture and fragrance.

"Love me."

"I do."

His fingers dug into her hips as she drove him toward the jagged edge of peak.

"Touch me, taste me, take me." On a cry, she lowered her throat to his lips, pressed that soft flesh with its pounding blood against him. "Change me."

It was beyond him to stop the flood, it gushed through him, hot, strong, turbulent—and through her, he knew, as her body bucked and quaked. And shuddering, she rubbed that throbbing pulse against his mouth.

"Make me what you are. Give me forever with you."

"Stop." As his body shook, he shoved her away with a force strong enough to nearly send her to the floor. "You'd use what I am against me?"

"Yes." Her chest burned with the tears that streamed through her voice. "Anything, anyone. Why should we find this only to lose it? Two days, only two days left. I want more."

"There's no more to have."

"There could be. Lilith loved what she'd made, I saw it. You love me now, and I love you. We wouldn't stop with the change."

"You know nothing of it."

"I do." She grabbed his hand as he rolled out of bed. "There's nothing I haven't read. How can we just turn away from each other, and go on? Why should I choose death on the field rather than by your hand? It's not true death if you change me."

He pulled his hand free, then seemed to sigh. With a gentleness she couldn't see in his eyes, he framed her face. "Not for all the worlds."

"If you loved me—"

"A poor female trick, that phrase. Not worthy of you. If

I loved you less, I might do exactly what you ask. I have before."

He moved to the window. Dawn was upon them, but there was no need to draw the drapes. Dawn had come with rain.

"I cared for a woman once, long ago. And she loved me, or loved what she believed I was. I changed her because I wanted to keep her." He turned back to where Moira knelt on the bed, silently weeping. "She was beautiful and amusing and bright. We'd make interesting companions, I thought. And we were, for almost a decade until she ran afoul of a well-aimed torch."

"It wouldn't be that way."

"She was twice the killer I was. She liked children best. She was beautiful and amusing and bright—and no less so for the change. Only once she was like me, she put those qualities to use luring toddlers."

"I could never—"

"You could," he said flatly. "And most certainly would. I won't turn the brightest light of my life into a monster. No, I'd never see you like me."

"I don't see a monster when I look at you."

"I would be, again, if I did this. It wouldn't just be you who changed, Moira. Would you damn me all over again?"

She pressed her hands to her eyes. "No. No. Stay then." She dropped her hands. "Stay with me, as we are. Or take me with you. Once Geall is safe, I can leave it in my uncle's hands, or—"

"And what? Live in the shadows with me? I can't give you children. I can't give you any kind of true life. How will you feel in ten years, in twenty, when you age and I don't? When you look in the mirror and see in your nature what you'll never see in mine? We've already stolen these weeks. They'll have to be enough for you."

"Can they be for you?"

"They're more than I ever had, or thought to. I can't be a man, Moira, not even for you. But I can feel hurt, and you're hurting me now."

"I'm sorry, I'm sorry. I feel as if everything in me is being squeezed. My heart, my lungs. I had no right to ask you, I know it. I knew it even when I did. Knew it was selfish and wrong. And weak," she added, "when I'd sworn not to be weak again. I know it can't be. I know it can't. What I don't know is if you can forgive me."

He came to her again, sat beside her. "The woman I changed didn't know what I was until that moment. If she had, she'd have run screaming. You know what I am. You asked because you're human. If I don't need to ask you to forgive me for being what I am, you don't need to ask me to forgive you for being what you are."

Chapter 19

◈

For most of the day, Moira worked with Glenna forming, forging and charming the fireballs. Every hour or so two or three people would come into the tower and haul away what was done to store them in their stockpile outside.

"I never thought I'd say it," Moira began after the fourth straight hour, "but magic can be tedious."

"Hoyt would say what we're doing here is nearly as much science as magic." Glenna swiped at her damp face with her arm. "And yes, both can be boring as ever-living hell. Still, you're doing this with me cuts back on the time and increases the payload. Hoyt's bound to be closeted with Cian over maps and strategy all day."

"Which is probably just as tedious."

"Betcha more."

Once again Glenna walked the line of the hardened balls they'd made, hands stretched out, eyes focused as she chanted. From where she stood at the worktable Moira could see the constant use of power was taking its toll.

The shadows under Glenna's green eyes seemed to deepen every hour. And each time the flush the miserable heat brought to her cheeks faded, her skin looked more pale, more drawn.

"You should stop for a bit," Moira told her when Glenna completed the line. "Get some air, have a bite."

"I want to finish this batch, but I will take a minute first. It reeks of sulphur in here." She walked to the window, leaned out to draw in cool, fresh air. "Oh. This is a sight, Moira, come look. Dragons circling over tent city."

Moira wandered over to watch dragons, most of them mounted by riders training them to dive or turn on command. They were quick studies, she mused, and made a bold, bright show against a hazy sky.

"You're wishing you could take a picture of it, or sketch it at least."

"I'll spend the next ten years doing sketches and artwork of what I've seen these past months."

"I'll miss you so much when this is done and you're not here anymore."

Understanding, Glenna draped an arm over Moira's shoulders, then pressed a kiss to her hair. "You know if there's a way to come, we will. We'll visit you. We have the key, we have the portal, and if what we've done here doesn't earn the gods' blessing, nothing could."

"I know. As horrible as these past months have been in so many ways, they've given me so much. You and Hoyt and Blair. And . . ."

"Cian."

Moira kept her eyes on the dragons. "He won't come back to visit, with or without the blessing of the gods."

"I don't know."

"He won't, even if it were possible for him, he won't come back to me." Little deaths, Moira thought, every hour, every day. "I knew it all along. Wanting it different doesn't change what is, or can't be. It's one of the things Morrigan was telling me, about the time of knowing. Using my head and my heart together. Both my head and my heart know we can't be together. If we tried it would tear at us until neither of us could survive it. I tried to deny that, disgracing myself, hurting him."

"How?"

Before Moira could answer, Blair strode in. "What's up? A little girl time? What's the topic? Fashion, food or men? Oh-oh," she added when they turned and she saw their faces, "must be men, and me with no chocolate to pass around. Listen, I'll get out of your way, I just wanted to let you know the last incoming troops have been sighted. They'll be here within the hour."

"That's good news. No, stay a moment, would you?" Moira asked. "You should know what I was about to confess. Both of you have put your heart and blood into all of this. You've been the best friends to me I've ever had, or will have."

"You've got a serious voice on there, Moira. What did you do? Decide to turn to the dark side and hang out with Lilith?"

"It's not so far from that. I asked Cian to change me."

Blair nodded as she walked closer. "I don't see any bites on your neck."

"Why aren't you angry, or even surprised? Either one of you."

"I think," Glenna said slowly, "I might have done the same in your place. I know I'd have wanted to. If we walk away from this, Blair and I walk away with our men. You can't. Do you want us to judge you for trying to find some way to change that?"

"I don't know. It might be easier if you did. I used his feelings for me as weapons. I asked—all but begged him to make me like him when we were at our most intimate."

"Below the belt," Blair stated. "If I were going to do it, that's the method I'd have picked. He turned you down, which tells me there can't be any doubt what you are to him. Back to me again, I'd feel better knowing he was going to be just as miserable and alone as I was when he had to take a walk."

Moira let out a surprised and muffled laugh. "You don't mean that."

"I said it to lighten things up, but down in the gut? I don't know. I might. I'm sorry you're getting the shaft in this. Sincerely."

"Ah well, maybe I'll have a bit of luck and die in battle tomorrow night. That way I won't be miserable and alone after all."

"Positive thinking. That's the ticket." In lieu of chocolate, Blair gave her a hug. And met Glenna's eyes over Moira's shoulder.

It was important, Moira knew, for the last of the troops to be welcomed by their queen, and to show herself to as many as she could in the final hours before the last march. She walked among the tents as twilight came, as did the other members of the royal family. She spoke to all she could. She dressed as a warrior, with her cloak pinned with a simple claddaugh brooch and the sword of Geall at her side.

It was well after dark when she returned to the house, and to what she knew would be the final strategy meeting with her circle.

They were already gathered around the long table with only Larkin standing apart, scowling down at the fire. Something new, she thought with a little quiver in her belly. Something more.

She unpinned her cloak as she studied the faces of those she'd come to know so well.

"What plans are you making that has Larkin so worried?"

"Sit down," Glenna told her. "Hoyt and I have something. If it works," she continued as Moira walked to the table, "it would win this."

As Moira listened, the little quiver became a frozen knot. So many risks, she thought, so many contingencies, and so many ways to fail. For Cian most of all.

But when she looked into his eyes, she understood he'd already made his decision.

"It lays most on you," she said to him. "The timing . . . if it's off by a moment—"

"It lays on all of us. We all knew what we were taking on when we started this."

"No one of us should be risked more than the others," Larkin interrupted. "We may sacrifice one of us without need, without—"

"Do you think I bring this lightly?" Hoyt spoke quietly. "I lost my brother once, then found him again. Found more, I think, than either of us had before. Now doing this, doing what I was charged to do, I may lose him again."

"I'm not getting a sense of confidence in my abilities." There was a tankard on the table, and Cian lifted it to pour ale. "Apparently surviving over nine hundred years isn't considered a strong point on my résumé."

"I'd hire you," Blair said, and held out her cup. "Yeah, it's risky, a lot of steps, a lot of variables, but if it works, it'd be one hell of a thing. I'm figuring you'll make it through." She tapped her cup to Cian's. "So this has my vote."

"I'm not a strategist," Moira began. "And my magic is limited. You can do this?" she asked Hoyt.

"I believe it can be done." He reached for Glenna's hand.

"We got the idea, actually, from something you said back at Castle Geall," Glenna told her. "And we're using Geall's symbols. All of them. It would be strong magic, and—I think—though it takes blood to bind it, pure."

"I believe separately we have more true power than Midir." Hoyt scanned the faces around him. "Together, we'll crush him, and the rest."

Moira turned to Cian. "If you stayed back? A signal to you, to all of us once all the steps have been taken—"

"Lilith's blood on the battleground is essential. She has to be wounded, at least, by one of the six of us. And Lilith's mine," Cian said flatly. "If I get through or don't, she's mine. For King."

For King, Moira thought, and for himself as well. Once he'd been innocent, too. Once he'd been a victim and his life taken from him. She'd shed his blood, fed him hers. Now, what they'd shared might be vital to the survival of mankind.

She rose, carrying the weight of it, and walked to Larkin. "You've already decided." She looked back at the four who sat at the table. "Four of the six, so it would be done as you've planned however Larkin and I vote on this. But it's best if we're together. If the circle agrees, with no breaks, no doubts." She took Larkin's hand now. "It's best."

"All right. All right." Larkin nodded. "We're together then."

"If we could go over it oncemore." Moira came back to the table. "The details and the movements of it, then we'll pass this on to the squadron leaders."

It would be like a brutal and bloody dance, Moira thought. Sword, sacrifice and magic playing the tune. And the blood, of course. There must always be blood.

"The first preparations in the morning then." She'd risen to pour and pass short cups of whiskey for each. "Then we'll each do our part, and the gods willing, we'll end this. And end it, fittingly I think, with the symbols of Geall. Well, to us then and the hell with them."

When they'd drunk, she walked over to the vielle. "Would you play?" she asked Cian. "There should be music. We'll have music, and send it out to the night. I hope she hears it, and trembles."

"You don't play," Hoyt began.

"I didn't speak Cantonese once upon a time. Things change." Still Cian felt a little odd, sitting down with the vielle, testing the strings for tune.

"What is that thing?" Blair wondered. "Like a violin with gout?"

"Well, it would be a predecessor." He began to play, slowly, feeling his way back from war to music. The oddness faded away with the quiet, haunting notes.

"It's lovely," Glenna said. "A little heartbreaking." Because she couldn't resist, she went for paper and charcoal to sketch him as he played.

From outside, pipes and harps began to play, blending in with Cian's music.

Each note, Moira thought, like a tear.

"You've a hand with that," Larkin told Cian when the notes faded away. "And a heart for music, that's the truth. But would you be after playing something a bit livelier? You know, with a little jump to it?"

Larkin lifted his pipe and blew out quick, cheerful notes, so those echoes of melancholy were swept away in joy. More music poured in from outside, drums and fifes, as Cian matched melody and rhythm. With a quick hoot of approval, Larkin stomped his feet, his knees like loose hinges while Moira clapped the time.

"Come on then." Tossing his pipe to Blair, Larkin grabbed Moira's hands. "Let's show this lot how Geallians dance."

Laughing, Moira swung into step with him in what Cian saw was cousin to an Irish step-dance. Quick feet, still shoulders, all energy. He bent over the vielle, smiling a little at the persistence of the human heart as shadows and firelight played over his face.

"We won't let them get the better of us." Hoyt yanked Glenna to her feet.

"I can't do that."

"Sure you can. It's in the blood."

The floorboards rang with booted feet, and it flowed out into the night, the dance, the tune, the laughter. It was, Cian thought, so human of them, to take the joy, to not only use it, but to squeeze every drop of it.

There, his brother, the sorcerer who prized his dignity as much as his power, whirling around with his sexy red-headed witch who giggled like a girl as she tried to do the steps.

The kick-your-face-and-your-ass demon hunter mixing a little twenty-first-century hip-hop into the folk dance to make her shape-shifting cowboy grin.

And the queen of Geall, loyal, devoted and carrying the

weight of her world, flushed and glowing with the simple pleasure of music.

They might die tomorrow, every one, but by the gods, they danced tonight. Lilith, for all her eons, all her power and ambition would never understand them. And the magic of them, the light of them, might just carry the day.

For the first time, he believed—whether he survived or not—humankind would triumph. It couldn't be snuffed out, not even by itself. Though he'd seen, too often, it try.

There were too many others like these five, who would fight and sweat and bleed. And dance.

He continued to play when Hoyt paused long enough to drink some ale. "Send it to her," Cian murmured.

"Look at my Glenna, dancing as if she'd been born to it." Hoyt blinked, frowned. "What's that you said?"

Cian glanced up, no longer smiling though the music he played was as cheerful as a red balloon. "Send Lilith the music, send it out, just as Moira said. You can do that. Let's rub her fucking face in it."

"Then we will." Hoyt laid a hand on Cian's shoulder. "Damn right we will."

Power rippled, warming Cian's shoulder as he played, and played.

In the dark, Lilith stood watching her troops fight yet another training battle. As far as she could see—and her eyes were keen—vampires, half-vampires, human servants were spread in an army she'd spent hundreds of years building.

Tomorrow, she thought, they would swarm over the humans like a plague until the valley was a lake of blood.

And in it, she would drown that whore who called herself queen for what had been done to Davey.

When Lora joined her, they slid arms around each other's waists. "The scouts are back," Lora told her. "We outnumber the enemy by three to one. Midir is on his way, as you commanded."

"It's a good view from here. Davey would have enjoyed standing here, seeing this."

"By this time tomorrow, or soon after, he'll be avenged."

"Oh, yes. But it won't end there." She felt Midir as he climbed to the rooftop where she and Lora stood. "It begins soon," she said without turning to him. "If you fail me, I'll slit your throat myself."

"I will not fail."

"Tomorrow, when it begins, you'll be in place. I want you standing on the high ridge to the west, where all can see."

"Majesty—"

She turned now, her eyes cold and blue. "Did you think I'd let you stay here, locked and closeted within this shield? You'll do and be where I say, Midir. And you'll stand on that ridge so our troops, and theirs, can see your power. An incentive for them, and for you," she added. "Make your magic strong, or you'll pay the price of it during the battle, or after."

"I've served you for centuries, and still there is no trust."

"No trust between us, Midir. Only ambition. I prefer that you live, of course." She smiled now, thinly. "I have uses for you even after my victory. There are children inside Castle Geall, protected. I want them, all of them, when I've taken the night. From among them I'll choose the next prince. The others will make a fine feast. You'll stand on the ridge," she said as she turned back again. "And you'll cast your dark shadow. There's no cause for concern. After all, you've seen the outcome of this in your smoke. And so you've told me countless times."

"I would be more use to you here, with my—"

"Silence!" She snapped it out, tossed up a hand. "What's that sound? Do you hear it?"

"It sounds like . . ." Lora frowned out into the dark. "Music?"

"Their sorcerer sends it." Midir lifted face and hands

into the air. "I feel him reaching out, pale and petty power in the night."

"Make it stop! I won't be mocked on the eve of this. I won't have it. Music." She spat it out. "Human trash."

Midir lowered his arms, folded his hands. "I can do what you will, my queen, but they make a small and foolish attempt to anger you. See your own troops, training, wielding weapons, preparing for battle. And what does your enemy do with these final hours?" He dismissed them with a flick of his fingers that sizzled out fire. "They play like careless children. Wasting the short time they have left before the slaughter on music and dance. But if you will it—"

"Wait." She held up a hand again. "Let them have their music. Let them dance their way to death. Go back to your cauldron and smoke. And be prepared to take your place tomorrow, and hold it. Or I'll toast my victory with your blood."

"As you wish, Majesty."

"I wonder if he spoke the truth," Lora said when they were alone again. "Of if he hesitated to strike his power against theirs."

"It doesn't matter." Lilith couldn't let it matter, not this close to the fulfillment of all she coveted. "When everything is as I want it, when I crush these humans, drink their children, he'll have outlived his uses."

"*Certainement*. And his power could be turned against you once *he* has what he wants. What do you propose to do about him?"

"I'm going to make a meal of him."

"Share?"

"Only with you."

She continued to stand, watching the training. But the music, the damned music soured her mood.

It was late when Cian lay beside Moira. In these last hours, their circle was in three parts. He'd seen the fire flare and the candle flames flash, and knew Hoyt and Glenna were wrapped in each other.

As he'd been with Moira. As he imagined Larkin was with Blair.

"It was always meant to be this way," Moira said quietly. "The six of us making the circle, with each of us forming a stronger link with another. To gather together, to learn of and from one another. To know love. And this house is bright with love tonight. It's another kind of magic, and as powerful as any other. We have that, whatever comes."

She lifted her head to look down at him. "What I asked you to do was a betrayal."

"There's no need for that."

"No, I want to tell you what I know, as much as I know anything. It was a betrayal of you, of myself, of the others and all we've done. You were stronger, and now so am I. I love you with everything I am. That's a gift for both of us. Nothing can take it or change it."

She lifted the locket he wore. It held more than a lock of her hair, she thought. It held her love. "Don't leave this behind when you go. I want to know you have it, always."

"It goes where I go. My word on that. I love you with everything I am, and all I can't be."

She laid the locket back over his heart, then a hand over the stillness. Tears filled her, but she fought to hold them. "No regrets?"

"None."

"For either of us. Love me again," she murmured. "Love me again, one last time before dawn."

It was tender and slow, a savoring of every touch, every taste. Long, soft kisses were a kind of drug against any pain, silky caresses a balm over wounds that must be endured. She told herself her heart beat hard and strong enough for both of them now, this last time.

Her eyes stayed open and on his, drinking in his face so that at the peak of pleasure she saw him slide away with her.

"Tell me again," she murmured. "Once more."

"I love you. Eternally."

Then they lay together in the quiet. All the words had been said.

In the last hour before dawn they rose, the six, to prepare for the final march to battle.

They went on horse, on dragon, on foot, in wagons and carts. Above, clouds shifted over the sky, but didn't block out the sun. It beamed through them in shimmering fingers and sudden flashes to light the way to Silence.

The first arrived to lay traps in the shadows and in the caves while guards flew or rode over and around the valley with their eyes trained for any attack.

And there found traps laid for them. Under a man's feet, a pool of blood would spread, sucking him down. Ooze, black as pitch, bubbled up to burn through boots and into flesh.

"Midir's work," Hoyt spat as others ran to save who they could.

"Block it," Cian ordered. "We'll have a panic on our hands before we start."

"Half-vamps." Blair shouted the warning from dragon-back. "About fifty. First line, let's go." She dived down to lead the charge.

Arrows flew, and swords slashed. In the first hour, the Geallian forces were down fifteen men. But they held ground.

"They just wanted us to have a taste of it." With her face splattered with blood, Blair dismounted. "We gave them a bigger one."

"The dead and wounded have to be tended to." Steeling herself, Moira looked at the fallen, then away. "Hoyt's pushing back Midir's spell. How much is it costing him?"

"He'll have whatever he needs to have. I'm going up again, do a couple of circles. See if she's got any more surprises for us." Blair vaulted back on her dragon. "Hold the line."

"We weren't as prepared as we might have been for the traps, for a daylight attack." Sheathing his stained sword,

Larkin stepped to Moira. "But we did well. We'll do better yet."

He laid a hand on her arm, drawing her away so only she would hear. "Glenna says some are already here, under the ground. Hoyt can't work with her now, but she thinks between herself and Cian they can find at least some, and deal with it."

"Good. Even a handful will be a victory. I need to steady the archers."

The sun moved to midday, then beyond it. Twice she saw the ground open up where Glenna held a willow rod. Then the flash of fire as the thing burrowed in the earth caught the sun and flamed in it.

How many more, she wondered. A hundred? Five hundred?

"He's broken off." Hoyt swiped a hand over his sweaty face when he joined her. "Midir's traps are closed."

"You beat him back."

"I can't say. He may have gone to other work. But for now, he's blocked. This ground, it shakes the soul of a man. It pours up this evil it holds, all but chokes the breath. I'll help Cian and Glenna."

"No, you need to rest a few moments, save your energies. I'll help them."

Knowing he needed to gather himself, Hoyt nodded. But his eyes were grim as he scanned the valley, passed over where Glenna and Cian worked. "They won't be able to find them all. Not in this ground."

"No. But every one is one less."

Still when she reached Glenna, Moira could see the work was taking its toll. Glenna was pale, her skin clammy as Hoyt's had been. "It's time to rest," Moira told her. "Restore yourself. I'll work it awhile."

"It's beyond your power. It's on the edge of mine." Grateful, Glenna took the water bag Moira offered. "We've only unearthed a dozen. A couple more hours—"

"She needs to stop. You need to stop." Cian took Glenna's arm. "You're nearly tapped out, you know it. If you don't have anything left come sundown, what good will you be?"

"I know there are more. A lot more."

"Then we'll be ready when this ground spits them out. Go. Hoyt needs you. He's worn himself thin."

"Good strategy," Cian told Moira when Glenna walked away. "Using Hoyt."

"It is, but it's also true enough. We're draining them both. And you," she added. "I can hear in your voice how tired you are. So I'll say what you said to her. What good are you if you're worn out by sundown?"

"The bloody cloak smothers me. Then again, the alternative's not pleasant. I need to feed," he admitted.

"Then go, up to the high ground and see to it. We've done nearly all we can, all we set out to do by this time."

She saw Blair and Larkin with Hoyt and Glenna now. The six of them, together as the sun sank lower might push their strengths up again. They went across the broken ground, climbed over an island of pocked rock, and began up the hard slope.

Everything in her wanted to shudder when they reached the ridge. Even without Midir's spell, the ground seemed to pull at her feet.

Cian took out a water bag she knew held blood.

"Waiting on you," Blair began. "A lot of your troops have the jitters."

"If you're meaning they won't stand and fight—"

"Don't get all Geallian pride on me." Blair held up a hand for peace. "What they need is to hear from you, to get revved. They need their St. Crispin's Day speech."

"What's this?"

Blair arched her brows at Cian. "Guess you missed *Henry V* when you mowed through Cian's library."

"There were a lot of books, after all."

"It's about stirring them up," Glenna explained. "About getting them ready to fight, even die. Reminding them why they're here, inspiring them."

"I'm to do all of that?"

"No one else would have the same impact." Cian closed the water bag. "You're the queen, and while the rest of us might be generals, in a manner of speaking, you're the one they look to."

"I wouldn't know what to say."

"You'll think of something. While you are, Larkin and I will get your troops together. Add a little *Braveheart* to *Henry*," he said to Blair. "Get her on horseback."

"Excellent." Blair headed off to get Cian's horse.

"What did this Henry say?" Moira wondered.

"What they needed to hear." Glenna gave Moira's hand a squeeze. "So will you."

Chapter 20

"I don't have a thing in my head."

"It's not going to come from there. Or not only from there." Glenna handed Moira her circlet. "Head and heart, remember? Listen to both and whatever you say, it'll be the right thing."

"Then I wish you'd say it instead. Foolish to be afraid of speaking to them," Moira said with a weak smile. "And not as afraid to die with them."

"Put this on." Blair held out Moira's cloak. "Good visual, the cloak billowing in the wind. And speak up, kiddo. You have to project to the ones in the peanut gallery."

"I'll ask you what that means later." Moira took one huffing breath, then mounted the stallion. "Here we go then."

She walked the horse forward, then her heart gave a hard thud. There were her people, more than a thousand strong, standing with the valley at their backs. Even as the sun dipped lower in the sky, it glinted off sword and shield and lance. It washed over their faces, those who had come here, ready to give their lives.

And her head understood the words in her heart.

"People of Geall!"

They cheered as she trotted her horse in front of their lines. Even those already wounded called out her name.

"People of Geall, I am Moira, warrior queen. I am your sister; I am your servant. We have come to this time and this place by order of the gods, and so, to serve the gods. I know not all of your faces, all of your names, but you are mine, every man and woman here."

The wind caught at her cloak as she looked into those faces. "Tonight, when the sun sets, I ask you to fight, to stand this bitter ground that has already tasted our blood this day. I ask this of you, but you don't fight for me. You don't fight for the queen of Geall."

"We fight for Moira, the queen!" someone shouted. And again, her name rose up above the wind in cheers and chants.

"No, you don't fight for me! You don't fight for the gods. You don't fight for Geall, not this night. You don't fight for yourselves, or even your children. Not for your husbands, your wives. Your mothers and fathers."

They quieted as she continued to ride the lines, looking into those faces, meeting those eyes, "It's not for them you come here to this bitter valley, knowing your blood may spill on its ground. It's for all humankind you come here. For all humankind you stand here. You are the chosen. You are the blessed. All the worlds and every heart that beats in them is your heart now, your world now. We, the chosen, are one world, one heart, one purpose."

Her cloak snapped in the wind as the stallion pranced, and the dying sun glinted on the gold of her crown, the steel of her sword. "We will not fail this night. We cannot fail this night. For when one of us falls, there will be another to lift the sword, the lance, to fight with stake and fist the pestilence that threatens humanity and all it is. And if that next of us should fall, there will come another and another, and still more for we are the *world* here, and the enemy has never known the like of us."

Her eyes were like hell-smoke in a face illuminated with passion. Her voice soared over the air so the words rang out, strong and clear.

"Here, on this ground, we will drive them down even past hell." She continued to shout over the cheers that rippled and rose from the men and women like a wave. "We will not yield this night, we will not fail this night, but will stand and triumph this night. You are the heart they can never have. You are the breath and the light they will never know again. This night, they will sing of this Samhain, sing of The Battle of Silence, in every generation that comes after. They will sit by their fires and speak of the glory of what we do here. This night. The sun sets."

She drew her sword, pointed west where the sun had begun to bleed red. "Come the dark, we'll raise sword and heart and mind against them. And as the gods witness this, I swear it, we will raise the sun."

She sent fire rippling down the blade of her sword, and shooting into the sky.

"Not too shabby," Blair managed as the troops erupted with shouts and cheers. "Your girl's got a way with words."

"She's . . . brilliant." Cian kept his eyes on her. "How can they stand against that much light?"

"She spoke the truth," Hoyt stated. "They've never seen the likes of us."

The squadron leaders split the troops so they began to move into position. Moira rode back, dismounted.

"It's time," she said and held out her hands.

The six formed a circle to forge that final bond. Then released each other.

"See you on the flip side." Blair flashed a gleaming smile. "Go get 'em, cowboy." She leaped on her dragon, then shot skyward.

Larkin swung onto his own. "Last one to the pub when this is done buys the round." He flew up, and away from Blair.

"Blessed be. And let's kick ass." With Hoyt, Glenna started toward their posts, but she'd seen the look that had passed between the brothers. "What's going on with Cian? Don't lie this close to what might be bloody death."

"He asked for my word. If we're able to bring the spell into play, he asked for my word we not wait for him."

"But we can't—"

"It was the last he asked of me. Pray we won't have to make the choice."

Behind them, Moira stood with Cian. "Fight well," she said to him, "and live another thousand years."

"My fondest hope." He covered the lie by taking her hands a last time, pressing them to his lips. "Fight well, *mo croi*, and live."

Before she could speak again, he'd leaped onto his horse and galloped away.

From the air, Blair called out commands, directing her mount with her legs and scanning the ground for what would come with the dark. The sun fell, plunging the valley into night, and in that night, the ground erupted. They poured out of the ground, from earth, from rock, from crevice, in numbers too great to count.

"Show time," she whispered to herself, swinging south as arrows from Moira and her archers rained down. "Hold them, hold them." A quick glance to where Niall's foot soldiers' voices rose like chants told her Niall was waiting for the signal.

A little longer, a little more, she thought as vampires swarmed up the valley, as arrows pierced some, missed others.

She flashed the firesword and dove. As men charged, she yanked the rope on her harness, dropping the first bomb.

Fire and flaming shrapnel flew, and there were screams as vampires were engulfed. And still they spewed from the ground pushing their lines toward the Geallians.

Freed of his cloak, Cian sat his horse, his sword raised to hold the men at his back. Bombs exploded fire, scorching the enemy and the ground. But they came, slinking and slithering, clawing and leaping. On a cry of battle, Cian slashed his sword and led his troops into the firestorm.

With flashing hooves and hacking steel, he cleaved a hole in the advancing army's line. It closed again, surrounding him and his forces.

Screams came in a torrent.

On her sloping plateau, Moira gripped her battle-ax. Her heart knocked in her throat as she saw the vampires break through the line to the east. She led the charge even as Hoyt led his so that they took their warriors in a stream of steel and stake to flank the enemy's lines.

Over the screams, the crashes, the fire, came the trumpeting call of dragons. The next wave of Lilith's army was advancing.

"Arrows!" Moira shouted as her quiver emptied, and another, filled, was tossed at her feet.

She notched and loosed, notched and loosed until the air was so full of smoke the bow was useless.

She raised the fiery sword and rushed with her line into the thick of it.

Of all she'd feared, all she'd known, all she'd seen in the visions the gods had given her, what came through the smoke and stink was worse. Men and women already slaughtered, ash of vanquished enemy coating the bitter ground like fetid snow. Blood spurted like a fall of water, painting the yellowed grass red.

Shrieks, human and vampire, echoed in the dark under the pale, three-quarter moon.

She blocked a sword strike, and her body moved with the instinct of hard training to spin, to pivot, to block the next. When she leaped over a low slash, she felt the wind of the sword under her boots, and with a scream of her own slashed for the throat.

Through the haze she saw the dragon that held Blair spiraling to the ground with its side pierced with arrows. The ground was littered with stakes. Grabbing one in her free hand, she rushed forward, then flung it through the back and into the heart of one who charged at Blair.

"Thanks. Duck." Blair shoved Moira aside, and severed the sword arm of another. "Larkin."

"I don't know. They keep coming."

"Remember your own hype." Blair leaped up, striking with her feet, then rammed a stake through the one she'd kicked.

Then she was lost in the waves of smoke, and Moira was once again battling for her life.

As Blair hacked through the line, they closed in around her. She struck, sword, stake, fought to gain ground. And was suddenly soaked. As her attackers screamed from the flood of blessed water that rained down from above, Larkin flew out of the smoke, grabbing her lifted arm to haul her up behind him.

"Nice job," she told him. "Drop me off. There, big, flat rock."

"You drop me. It's my time to have a go down here. You're out of water, but there are two fireballs. She's pushing in hard from the south now."

"I'll give her some heat."

He leaped off, and she soared.

Through the melee, Hoyt searched with his eyes, with his power. He felt the brush of Midir's dark, but there was so much black, so much cold, he wasn't sure of its direction.

Then he saw Glenna, fighting her way back up a ridge. And standing on it like a black crow, was Midir. In horror, he watched a hand snake out of a fold of earth and rock and grab Glenna's leg. In his mind he heard her scream as she kicked, as she clawed to keep from being dragged into the crevice. Even knowing he was too far away, he rushed through swords. Continued to run even when the fire she shot from fingertips coated what dragged at her.

Sensing power, Midir hurled lightning, black as pitch, and had her flying back.

Mad with fear, Hoyt fought like a wild man, ignoring blows and gashes as he worked his way toward her. He could see the blood on her face as she answered Midir's lightning with white fire.

* * *

The stake missed Cian's heart by a hairsbreadth, and the pain buckled his knees. As he went down, he thrust his sword up, all but cleaving his attacker in two before he managed to roll. A lance dug into the stony ground beside him. He gripped it, heaved it up to strike at another heart. Then planting it, he vaulted up, kicking out to send another flying to the wooden stakes the Geallians had hammered into the ground.

He saw Blair through the smoke that billowed from the fireballs and flaming arrows. With a pump of his legs, he leaped up, grabbing her dragon's harness to swing behind her an instant before she released another bomb.

"Didn't see you," she called out.

"Got that. Moira?"

"Don't know. Take over here. I'm going down."

She jumped down to the table of a rock. Cian saw her flip off, shooting stakes from both hands before the haze buried her. He swung his mount, aiming his sword, sending out fire. The ground continued to pull at him; its intoxicating scents of blood and fear driving hunger into him as keenly as a sharpened stake.

Then he saw Glenna, struggling her way up a sheer slope, and outnumbered three-to-one. Her battle-ax flamed, and each time she took an enemy, more crawled their way up toward her.

And when he saw the black figure on the high ridge, he understood why so many would go against a single woman.

The power of the circle battled back the hunger as he swept through the air toward his brother's wife.

He sent three tumbling down against rock, into traps of stakes and pools of holy water with a wild strike from the dragon's tale. His sword took two more even as Glenna's fiery ax turned enemies into flaming dust.

"Give you a lift?" He swooped down, circled her waist with his arm and hauled her up.

"Midir. The bastard."

Understanding, Cian soared up again. But when he struck out with the dragon's tail, it bounced off as if it hit rock.

"He's shielded. The coward." Breath short and choppy, Glenna searched the ground for Hoyt. And felt the lock on her lungs release when she saw him fighting his way up the slope.

"Set me down on the ridge, and go."

"The hell I will."

"This is what's needed, Cian. It's magic against magic for this. This is why I'm here. Find the others, get ready. Because by all the gods and goddesses, we're going to do this."

"Okay, Red. My money's on you."

He flew over the ridge, pausing while she slid down. And left her to face the black sorcerer.

"So, the red witch has come here to die."

"I didn't come for the ambiance."

She raised a hand, and charged with a swing of her ax. The widening of his eyes told her the move had surprised him. The flaming edge of the ax cut through the shield, but the blade missed its mark. She was propelled back, lifted into the air, slammed hard into the ground.

Though she threw out her own power, the scorching heat of his black lightning seared the palms of her hands. She held them out, held her power in them as she pushed painfully to her feet.

"You can't win this," he told her as dark shimmered around him. "I've seen the end, and your death."

"You've seen what whatever devil you sold yourself to wants you to see." She hurled fire, and though he deflected it with a snap of his wrist, she knew he felt her burn even as she'd felt his. "The end's what we make it."

With icy fury on his face, he brought a cutting wind that slashed at her skin like knives.

They were holding, Blair thought. She believed they were holding, but for every foot of ground the Geallians held, more vampires swarmed through the night and over it.

She'd lost track of her kills. A dozen at least with sword

and stake, at least that many with air attacks. And still it wasn't enough. Bodies littered the ugly ground, and even her strength was pushed to its limit.

They needed to pull the rabbit out of the hat, she thought, and screamed in vengeance as she slayed a vampire who'd stopped to feed on one of the fallen.

Whirling, slashing at others, she saw Glenna and Midir on the high ridge, and the firestorm of black against white as they battled.

She grabbed a lance from a dead hand, shot it out like a javelin. The spear tip went through two vampires fighting back to back, and the wood pole pierced hearts.

Something leaped down from above. Her senses caught just the edge of it, and her instincts had her pumping up into a high, wide flip. She slashed her sword as she touched ground, and clashed it against Lora's.

"There you are." Lora slid her blade down until it met Blair's to form a V. "I've been looking for you."

"Been around. You got something on your face there. Oh! Gee, is that a scar? Did I do that? My bad."

"I'll be eating your face shortly."

"You know that's wishful thinking, right? In addition to being disgusting. Enough small talk for you?"

"More than."

The swords sang as they slid apart. Then the music crescendoed as blade struck blade.

In moments, Blair understood she was facing the most formidable enemy of her career. Lora might look like a B movie dominatrix wrapped in snug black leather, but the French bitch could fight.

And take a punch, she thought when she finally got past Lora's guard long enough to slam a fist in the vampire's face. Blair felt the burn shoot a line across her knuckles as fangs sliced her flesh.

Blair flipped up to the jagged teeth of a rock, hacked down. And met air as Lora rose off the ground as if she had wings. Lora's sword whistled past Blair's face, and the tip of it sliced her cheek.

"Oh, will that leave a scar?" Lora landed on the rock with her. "My bad."

"It'll heal. Nothing about you is going to last much longer."

She answered first blood with a lightning parry of her own, gashing Lora's arm, then followed it through with a ripple of fire.

But Lora's sword struck the blade aside, going black against the red flame. The fire spurted and died.

"You think we weren't ready for that?" Lora bared her teeth as they hacked and thrust and swung. "Midir's magic is more than your magicians can ever hope for."

"Then why don't all of your troops have swords like yours? He couldn't pull it off." Blair flew up again, flipping over and striking Lora with her feet. The vampire used the momentum to soar up, driving down with the sword on her descent.

Raising hers to block, Blair didn't see the dagger that flew out of Lora's other hand. She stumbled from the shock, the pain, when it pierced her side.

"Look at all that blood. It's just pouring out of you. Yum." Lora laughed, a tinkling sound of delight, when Blair fell to her knees. And her eyes gleamed red as she raised the sword high for the killing blow.

With a mad, undulating howl, the gold wolf pounced from above. Claws and fangs raked as he leaped over the swinging sword, as he lunged and snapped. When he bunched to spring for the throat, Blair cursed.

"No! She's mine. You gave your word." Her breath whistled as she stayed on her knees, the dagger still lodged in her side. "Back off, wolf-boy. Back the hell off."

The wolf shimmered into a man as Larkin stepped back. "Get it done then," he snapped, his eyes grim. "And stop messing about."

"Pussy-whipped, is he?" Lora circled so that she could keep them both in her line of sight—the bleeding woman, the unarmed man. "But he's right, we really should stop messing about. I've a busy schedule."

She swung the sword down, and Blair thrust hers up to meet it, to block it, to hold it. The muscles in her arms screamed with the strain and her side wept blood and agony.

"I'm no pussy," she panted. "He's not whipped. And you're done."

She yanked the dagger from her side, stabbed it to its bloodied hilt into Lora's belly.

"That hurts, but it's steel."

"So's this." With all her remaining strength, Blair shoved Lora's sword aside, and plunged her own into the vampire's chest.

"Now you're just annoying me." Lora hefted her sword, point down. "Now who's done?"

"You," Blair replied as the blade still in Lora's chest erupted with flame.

Burning, screaming, Lora started to tumble from the rock. Blair yanked the sword free, swung it, hard and true, and cut off the flaming head.

"Fucking well done." Blair stumbled, swayed, would have fallen if Larkin hadn't sprung forward to catch her.

"How bad? How bad?" He pressed his hand to her bleeding side.

"Through and through, I think. No organs hit. Quick patch to stop the bleeding and I'm back in the game."

"We'll see about that. Get on."

When he shimmered into a dragon, Blair crawled onto his back. As they soared she saw Glenna on the ridge clashing with Midir. And she saw her friend fall.

"Oh God, she's hit. She's done. How fast can you get there?"

Inside the dragon Larkin thought: Not fast enough.

G lenna tasted blood in her mouth. There was more seeping out of a dozen shallow slices in her skin. She knew she'd hurt him, knew she'd chipped at his shield, his body, even his power.

But she could feel her own power ebbing out of her along with her blood.

She'd done all she could, and it hadn't been enough.

"Your fire's cooling. Barely an ember left to glow." Midir stepped closer now to where she lay on the scorched and bloody ground. "Still it might be enough to trouble myself to take, along with what's left of your life."

"It'll choke you." She gasped out the words. He'd bled, she thought. She'd made him bleed onto the ground. "I swear it will."

"I'll swallow it whole. It's so small, after all. Can you see below, can you? Where what I helped wrought runs over you like locusts. It's as I foretold. And as you fall, one by one, my power grows. Nothing will hold it now. Nothing will stop it."

"I will." Hoyt swung, bloody and battered, over the lip of the ridge.

"There's my guy," Glenna managed, gritting her teeth against the pain. "I softened him up for you."

"Now here is something more to chew on." Whirling, Midir shot black lighting.

It crashed, sizzled, spewed bloody flames when it struck against Hoyt's blinding white. The force blew them both back, searing the air between them. On the ground, Glenna rolled away from a streaking line of flame, then clawed to her hands and knees.

Whatever she had left, she gathered to send to Hoyt. Closing a trembling hand around the cross at her neck she focused her power into it, and to its twin Hoyt wore.

While she chanted, the sorcerers—black and white—battled on the smoke-hazed ridge, and in the filthy air above it.

The fire that sliced at Hoyt carried the burn of ice. It sought his blood—what was shed, what it aimed to shed, to draw away his power.

It clawed and slashed at him while the air flashed and boomed with magicks, sending smoke billowing high to drown the swimming moon. The ground beneath his feet cracked, splitting fissures under the enormity of pressure.

While his lungs labored and his heart pounded, he ignored those earthy demands on his body, ignored the pains from his wounds and the sweat that ran salt into them.

He was power now. Beyond that moment at the beginning of this journey when he'd wavered for an instant over the black. Now, on this ridge over blood and death, over the courage of man, the sacrifice and the fury, he was the white-hot flame of power.

The cross he wore flashed silver and brilliant as Glenna joined her magic to his. With one hand he reached for hers, gripping it firmly when she linked fingers with him and pulled herself to her feet. With the other he raised a sword, and the fire on it went pure white.

"It is we who take you," Hoyt began and slashed away a thunderbolt with his sword. "We who stand for the purity of magic, for the heart of mankind. It is we who defeat you, who destroy you, who send you forever into the flames."

"Be damned to you!" Midir shouted, and lifting both arms hurled twin thunderbolts. Fear rushed over his face when Glenna waved a hand over the air and turned them to ash.

"No. Be damned to you." Hoyt swung down the sword. The white fire leaped from the blade to strike Midir's heart like steel.

Where he dropped and died, the ground turned black.

High ground, Moira thought. She had to get back to higher ground, regroup the archers. She'd heard the shouts warning that their line had broken again to the north. Flaming arrows would drive that invading force back, give the troops in its path time to forge their lines again. She searched through the melee for a horse or dragon that would take her where she knew she was most needed.

And looking up saw Hoyt and Glenna bathed in brilliant white, facing Midir. A spurt of fresh hope had her racing forward. Even as the ground seemed to catch at her feet, she swung her sword at an advancing enemy. The gash she served it slowed it down, and as she poised to strike again, Riddock took it from behind.

With a fierce grin, he charged with a handful of men toward the broken line. He lived, she thought. Her uncle lived. As she raced to join him, the ground bucked under her feet, sent her sprawling.

As she pushed up she looked down into Isleen's dead and staring eyes.

"No. No. No."

Isleen's throat was torn open, the leather strap where Moira knew she'd worn a wooden cross was snapped and soaked with blood. Grief struck so strong, so deep, she gathered the body up against her.

Still warm, she thought as she rocked. Still warm. If she'd been faster, she might have saved Isleen.

"Isleen. Isleen."

"Isleen. Isleen." The words were a mocking mimic as Lilith flowed out of the smoke.

She'd dressed for battle in red and silver, a mitre like Moira's banding her head. Her sword was bloody to its jeweled hilt. Seeing her crashed waves of fear and fury through Moira that had her surging to her feet.

"Look at you." The grace and deftness with which Lilith spun the sword as she circled warned Moira this vampire queen knew the art of the blade. "Small and insignificant, covered with mud and tears. I'm amazed I wasted so much time planning your death when it's all so simple."

"You won't win here." Queen to queen, Moira thought, and blocked Lilith's first testing thrust. Life against death. "We're beating you back. We'll never stop."

"Oh please." Lilith waved the words away. "Your lines are crumbling like clay, and I've two hundred yet in reserve. But that's neither here nor there. This is you and me."

With barely a blink, Lilith shot out a hand, grabbing the soldier who charged her by the throat. And snapping his neck. She tossed him carelessly to the ground, while slicing down at Moira's swinging fire sword.

"Midir has his uses," Lilith said when the fire died.

"I want to take my time with you, you human bitch. You killed my Davey."

"No, you did. And with what you made of him destroyed, I hope what he was, the innocent he was, is cursing you."

Lilith's hand streaked out, flashing like the fangs of a snake. She raked her nails down Moira's cheek.

"A thousand cuts." She licked the blood from her fingers. "That's what I'll give you. A thousand cuts while my army feeds its belly full on yours."

"You won't touch her again." On his stallion's back, Cian rode slowly forward, as if time had stopped. "You'll never touch her again."

"Come to save your whore?" From her belt, Lilith drew a gold stake. "Gilded oak. I had this made for you, for when I end you as I made you. Tell me, doesn't all this blood stir you? Warm pools of it, bodies not yet cooled waiting to be drained. I know what's in you wants that taste. I put it in you, and I know it as I know myself."

"You never knew me. Go," he said to Moira.

"Yes, run along. I'll find you later."

She flew at Cian, then sprang up a sword's length away to spin over his head. As she sliced down, her sword met air while he threw his body up and back, with the heels of his boots barely missing her face.

They moved so fast, that eerie speed, that Moira saw little more than a blur, heard the clash of swords like silver thunder. This would be his battle, she knew, the one only he could fight. But she wouldn't leave him.

Leaping onto the horse, she drove Vlad up blood-slicked rock until she was positioned over their heads. There she shot fire from her sword to hold off Lilith's men who tried to reach their queen. She vowed that she and the sword of Geall would stand for her lover to the last.

Lilith was skilled, Cian knew. After all, she had centuries to learn the arts of war just as he had. Her strength and speed were as great as his. Perhaps greater. She blocked him, drove him back, slithered away from the force of his attack.

This ground was still hers, he knew. This pocket of black. She fed off it, as he didn't dare. She fed off the screams that echoed through the air and the blood that seemed to spew through it like rain.

He fought her, and the war inside him, the thing that struggled to claw free and revel in what it was. What she'd made him. Taking her advantage, she beat his sword aside, and in that flash of an instant he was open, plunged the stake at his heart.

It struck with a force that sent him staggering back. But as her cry of triumph echoed away, he continued to stand whole and unharmed.

"How?" was all she said as she stared at him.

He felt the imprint of Moira's locket against his heart, and the pain was sweet. "A magic you'll never know." He sliced out, scoring across the scar of the pentagram. The blood that welled from the wound was black and thick as tar.

Pain and fury brought the demon to her eyes, the killing red. Now her screams rang as she came at him with a new and wild strength. He slashed back, spilled more blood, drove as he was driven as the locket seemed to pulse like a heart on his chest.

Her sword ripped down his arm, sending his clattering against the rocks. "Now you! Then your whore!"

When she charged, he gripped the wrist of her sword arm in his bloody hand. She smiled at him. "This way then. It's more poetic."

She bared her fangs to strike at his throat. And he plunged the stake she had made for him into her heart.

"I'd say go to hell, but even hell won't have you."

Her eyes went wide, faded to blue. He felt the wrist he held dissolve in his hand, and still those eyes stared into his another moment.

Then there was nothing but the ash at his feet.

"I've ended you," he declared, "as you ended me so long ago. That's poetic."

The ground under his feet began to quake. So, he thought, it comes.

The black stallion leaped from the rocks, scattering ash. "You've done it." Moira vaulted from the saddle into his arms. "You've beaten her. You've won."

"This saved me." He dragged her locket out, showed her the deep dent in the silver from the force of the stake. "You saved me."

"Cian." As the rock behind her split like an egg, she jumped down, and her face went pale again. "Hurry. Go, hurry. It's begun. Her blood, her end, was the last of it. They've started the spell."

"It's you who beat her, you who won. Remember that." He pulled her into his arms, crushed his mouth to hers. Then he was flying onto the horse, and was gone.

Everything around her was chaos. Screams and shouts through the haze, the moans of wounded, the rush of the enemy in mad retreat.

A gold dragon speared through it, Blair on its back. With the ground rippling in waves under her, Moira lifted her arms so Larkin could cradle her in his claws. She flew over the quivering land toward the high ridge.

On it, Hoyt gripped Moira's hand. "It must be now."

"Cian. We can't be sure—"

"I gave my word to him. It must be now." He raised their joined hands, and together they lifted their faces, their voices to the black sky.

"In this place once damned we hold the power, and we wield it in this final hour. On this ground blood was shed in blackest night, theirs for dark and ours for light. Black magic and demon here are felled by our hand, and now we claim this bloody land. Now call forth all we have done. Now through dark we raise the sun. Its light will strike our enemy. As we will, so mote it be."

The ground trembled, and the wind blew like a fury.

"We call the sun!" Hoyt shouted. "We call the light!"

"We call the dawn!" Glenna's voice rose with his, and the power grew as Moira clasped her free hand. "Burn off the night."

"Rise in the east," Moira chanted, staring through the

smoke that swirled up around them while Larkin and Blair completed the circle. "Spread to the west."

"It's coming," Blair cried. "Look. Look east."

Over the shadow of mountains the sky lightened, and the light spread and speared and grew until it was bright as noon.

Below, fleeing vampires burned to nothing.

On the rocky, broken ground, flowers began to bloom.

"Do you see that?" Larkin's hand tightened on Moira's, and his voice was thick, reverent. "The grass, it's greening."

She saw it, and the sweet charm of the white and yellow flowers that spread over its carpet. She saw the bodies of the fallen on the meadow of a lush and sun-lit valley.

But nowhere did she see Cian.

Chapter 21

✦

Though the battle was won, there was still work. Moira labored with Glenna in what Glenna called triage for the wounded. Blair and Larkin had taken a party out to hunt down any vampires that might have found shelter from the sun while Hoyt helped transport those whose wounds were less severe back to one of the bases.

After rinsing blood from her hands again, Moira stretched her back. And spotting Ceara wandering as if in a daze, rushed to her.

"Here, here, you're hurt." Moira pressed a hand to the wound on Ceara's shoulder. "Come, let me dress this."

"My husband." Her gaze roamed from pallet to pallet even as she leaned heavily against Moira. "Eogan. I can't find my husband. He's—"

"Here. He's here. I'll take you. He's been asking for you."

"Wounded?" Ceara swayed. "He's—"

"Not mortally, I promise you. And seeing you, he'll heal all the quicker. There, over there, you see? He's—"

Moira got no further as Ceara cried out and in a stumbling run rushed to fall to her knees beside where her husband lay.

"It's good to see, good for the heart to see."

She turned, smiled at her uncle. Riddock, his arm and leg bandaged, sat on a supply crate.

"I wish all lovers would be reunited as they are. But . . . we lost so many. More than three hundred dead, and the count still coming."

"And how many live, Moira?" He could see the wounds she bore on her body, and in her eyes the wounds she bore on her heart. "Honor the dead, but rejoice in the living."

"I will. I will." Still she scanned the wounded, those who tended them, and feared for only one. "Are you strong enough to travel home?"

"I'll go with the last. I'll bring our dead home, Moira. Leave that for me."

She nodded, and after embracing him went back to her duties. She was helping a soldier sip water when Ceara found her again.

"His leg, Eogan's leg . . . Glenna said he won't lose it, but—"

"Then he won't. She wouldn't lie to you, or to him."

On a steadying breath, Ceara nodded. "I can help. I want to help." Ceara touched her bandaged shoulder. "Glenna looked after me, and said I'm well enough. I've seen Dervil. She came through very well. Cuts and bruises for the most of it."

"I know."

"I saw your cousin Oran, and he said Sinann's Phelan's already on his way back to Castle Geall. But I haven't found Isleen as yet. Have you seen her?"

Moira lowered the soldier's head, then rose. "She did not come through."

"No, my lady, she must have. You just haven't seen her." Again, Ceara searched the pallets that stretched over the wide field. "There are so many."

"I did see her. She fell in the battle."

"No. Oh no." Ceara covered her face with her hands. "I'll tell Dervil." Tears flowed down her cheeks when she lowered her hands. "She's trying to find Isleen now. I'll tell her, and we'll . . . I can't fathom it, my lady. I can't fathom it."

"Moira!" Glenna called from across the field. "I need you here."

"I'll tell Dervil," Ceara repeated and hurried away.

Moira worked until the sun began to dim again, then exhausted and sick with worry, flew on Larkin to the farm where she would spend one last night.

He would be here, she told herself. Here is where he would be. Safe out of the sunlight, and helping organize the supplies, the wounded, the transportation. Of course, he would be here.

"Near dark," Larkin said when he stood beside her. "And there'll be nothing in Geall that will hunt in it tonight but that which nature has made."

"You found none at all, no enemy survivors."

"Ash, only ash. Even in caves and deep shade there was ash. As if the sun we brought burned through it all, and there was none of them could survive it no matter where they hid."

Her already pale face went gray, and he gripped her arm.

"It's different for him, you know it. He'd have had the cloak. He'd have gotten it in time. You can't believe any magic we'd bring would harm one of our own."

"No, of course. Of course, you're right. I'm just tired, that's all."

"You'll put something in your belly, then lay your head down." He led her into the house.

Hoyt stood with Blair and Glenna. Something on their faces turned Moira's knees to water.

"He's dead."

"No." Hoyt hurried forward to take her hands. "No, he survived it."

Tears she'd held for hours spilled out of her eyes and flooded her cheeks. "You swear it? He's not dead. You've seen him, spoken to him?"

"I swear it."

"Sit, Moira, you're exhausted."

But she shook her head at Glenna's words and kept her eyes on Hoyt's face. "Upstairs? Is he upstairs?" A shudder passed through her as she understood what she read in Hoyt's eyes. "No," she said slowly. "He's not upstairs. Or in the house, or in Geall at all. He's gone. He's gone back."

"He felt . . . Damnation, I'm sorry for this, Moira. He was determined to go, straight away. I gave him my key, and he was going by dragon-back to the Dance. He said . . ."

Hoyt took a sealed paper from a table. "He asked if I'd give you this."

She stared at it, and finally nodded. "Thank you."

They said nothing as she took the paper and went upstairs alone.

She closed herself in the room she'd shared with him, lit the candles. Then sitting, simply held the letter to her heart until she had the strength to break the seal.

And read.

Moira,

This is best. The sensible part of you understands that. Staying longer would only prolong pain, and there's been enough of it for a dozen lifetimes. Leaving you is an act of love. I hope you understand that, too.

I have so many pictures of you in my head. Of you sitting on the floor in my library surrounded by books, poring through them. Of you laughing with King or Larkin as you so rarely laughed with me in those first weeks. Courageous in battle or lost in thought. You never knew how often I watched you, and wanted you.

I'll see you in the morning mists, drawing a shining sword from a stone, and flying a dragon with arrows singing from your bow.

I'll see you in candlelight, holding out your arms

*to me, taking me into a light I've never known before
or will know again.*

*You've saved your world and mine, and however
many others there might be. I think you were right
that we were meant to find each other, to be together
to forge the strength, the power needed to save those
worlds.*

Now it's time to step away.

*I'm asking you to be happy, to rebuild your world,
your life, and to embrace both. To do less would be a
dishonor to what we had. To what you gave me.*

With you, somehow with you, I was a man again.

*That man loved you beyond measure. What I am
that is not a man loved you, despite everything. In all
the centuries I've loved you. If you loved me, you'll
do what I ask.*

*Live for me, Moira. Even a world apart, I'll know
that you do and be content.*

                                                    Cian

She would weep. A human heart needed to shed such a
deep well of tears. Lying on the bed where they'd loved
each other for the last time, she pressed the letter to her
heart, and let it empty.

*New York City
Eight weeks later*

He spent a great deal of time in the dark, and a
great deal of time with whiskey. When a man had eternity, Cian figured he could take a decade or two to brood.
Maybe a century since he'd given up the love of his endless
bloody life.

He'd come around, of course. Of course he would. He'd
get back to business. Travel for a while. Drink a bit longer
first. A year or two of a sodding drunk never hurt the undead.

He knew she was well, helping her people recover, planning the monument she would build in the valley come the next spring. They'd buried their dead, and she herself had read every name—nearly five hundred of them—at the memorial.

He knew because the others were back now as well, and had insisted on giving him details he hadn't asked for.

At least Blair and Larkin were in Chicago now and wouldn't be hammering at him to talk or get together with them. You'd think humans, after spending such an intense amount of time with him, would know he wasn't feeling sociable.

He was going to wallow, goddamn it. The lot of them would be long dead, by his estimation, before he was finished wallowing.

He poured more whiskey. He told himself at least he had enough standards left not to drink it straight from the bottle.

And here were Hoyt and Glenna nagging at him to spend Christmas with them. Christmas, for bleeding Judas's sake. What did he care for Christmas? He wished they would go the hell back to Ireland and the house he'd given them and leave him be.

Did they have Christmas in Geall? he wondered, running his fingers over the dented silver locket he wore night and day. He'd never asked about that particular custom—but why should he have. It would likely be Yule there, with burning logs and music. Whatever, it was nothing to him now.

But she should celebrate, Moira should. Light a thousand candles and set Castle Geall glowing. Hang the holly bushes and strike up the bloody band.

When the hell was this pain going to ebb? How many oceans of whiskey would it take to dull it?

He heard the hum of the elevator and scowled over at it. He'd told the shagging doorman no one was to be let up, hadn't he? He ought to snap the idiot's neck like a used chopstick.

But no matter, he mused, he'd locked the mechanism from inside as second line of defense.

They could come up, but they couldn't get in.

He could barely drum up a curse when the doors slid open, and he saw Glenna step into the dark.

"Oh for pity's sake." Her voice was impatient, and an instant later, the lights flashed on.

They seared his eyes so that this time his curses were loud and heartfelt.

"Look at you." She set aside the large and elegantly wrapped box she'd carried in. "Sitting in the dark like a—"

"Vampire. Go away."

"It reeks of whiskey in here." As if she owned the place, she walked into his kitchen and began making coffee. While it was brewing she came out to find him exactly as he'd been.

"Merry Christmas to you, too." She angled her head. "You need a shave, a haircut—and one day when you're not sulking I'm going to ask how you accomplish that sort of thing. A shave," she repeated, "a haircut, and since whiskey's not the only reek in here, a bath."

His eyes remained hooded, and his lips curved without a whiff of humor. "Going to give me one, Red?"

"If that's what it takes. Why don't you clean yourself up, Cian, come back to the apartment with me? We have plenty of leftover Christmas dinner. It's Christmas Day," she said to his blank look. "Nearly nine o'clock Christmas night, actually, and I've left my husband home alone because he's as stubborn as you and won't come back here without an invitation."

"That's something anyway. I don't want leftovers. Or that coffee you're making in there." He lifted his glass. "I've got what I want."

"Fine. Stay drunk and smelly and miserable. But maybe you'll want this, too."

She marched over to the box, hefted it, then brought it over to drop it in his lap. "Open it."

He studied it without interest "But I didn't get anything for you."

She crouched at his feet now. "We'll consider your opening it my gift. Please. It's important to me."

"Will you go away if I open it?"

"Soon."

To placate her, he lifted the lid with its silver paper and elaborate bow, brushed aside the top layer of sparkling tissue.

And Moira looked out at him.

"Ah, damn you, damn you, Glenna." Neither whiskey nor will could hold against the image of her. Emotion shook in his voice as he lifted the framed portrait. "It's beautiful. She's beautiful."

Glenna had painted her in that moment Moira had drawn the sword free from the stone. The dreaminess and power of it, with green shadows, silver mists, and the new queen standing with the shining sword pointed toward the heavens.

"I thought, hoped, that having it would remind you what you helped give her. She wouldn't have stood there without you. There'd be no Geall without you. I wouldn't be here without you. None of us would have survived this without each one of us." She laid a hand on his. "We're still a circle, Cian. We always will be."

"I did the right thing for her, leaving. I did the right thing."

"Yes." She squeezed his hand now. "You did the right thing, an enormous and pure act of love. But knowing you did the right thing for all the right reasons doesn't stop the pain."

"Nothing does. Nothing."

"I'd say time will, but I don't know if it's true." Sympathy swam in her voice, in her eyes. "I will say you have friends and family who love you, and will be there for you. You have people who love you, Cian, who hurt for you."

"I don't know how to take what you want to give me, not yet. But this." He traced his finger around the frame. "Thank you for this."

"You're welcome. There are photographs, too. Ones I took in Ireland. I thought you might like to have them."

He started to lift the next layers of tissue, then stopped. "I need a moment."

"Sure. I'll go finish the coffee."

Alone, he uncovered the large manila envelope, and opened it.

There were dozens of them. One of Moira and his books, and with Larkin outside. One of King reigning over the stove in the kitchen, of Blair, eyes intense, sweat sheening her skin as she held a sword in warrior position.

There was one of himself and Hoyt he hadn't known she'd taken.

As he studied each one his feelings swirled and mixed, pleasure and sorrow.

When he looked up at last he saw Glenna leaning against the doorjamb with a mug of coffee in her hand. "I owe you more than a gift."

"No, you don't. Cian, we're going back to Geall for New Year's. All of us."

"I can't."

"No," she said after a moment, and the understanding in her eyes nearly broke him. "I know you can't. But if there's any message—"

"There can't be. There's too much to say, Glenna, and nothing to say. You're sure you can go back?"

"Yes, we have Moira's key, and an assurance of Morrigan herself. You didn't wait around long enough for the thanks of the gods."

She walked over, set the coffee on the table beside him. "If you change your mind, we're not leaving until midday, New Year's Eve. If you don't, after that Hoyt and I will be in Ireland. We hope you'll come see us. Blair and Larkin are taking my apartment here."

"Vampires of New York, beware."

"Damn right." She leaned over, kissed him. "Happy Christmas."

He didn't drink the coffee, but he didn't drink any more whiskey either. Surely that was a step somewhere. Instead he sat and studied Moira's portrait, and the hours passed that way toward midnight.

A swirl of light brought him out of the chair. Since it

was the closest weapon, he grabbed the whiskey bottle by the neck. As he wasn't nearly drunk enough for hallucinations, he decided the goddess standing in his apartment was real.

"Well, this is a red-letter day. I wonder if such as you has ever paid a call on such as me before."

"You are of the six," Morrigan said.

"I was."

"Are. Yet you hold yourself apart from them again. Tell me, vampire, why did you fight? Not for me or mine."

"No, not for the gods. Why?" He shrugged, and now did drink from the bottle in a kind of defiance, of disrespect. "It was something to do."

"It's foolish for such as you to pretend with such as me. You believed it was right, that it was worth fighting for, even ending your own existence for. I've known your kind since they first crawled through the blood. None would have done what you did."

"You sent my brother here to see I fell into line."

The god lifted her brow at his tone, then inclined her head. "I sent your brother to find you. Your will was your own. You have love for this woman." She gestured toward Moira's portrait. "For this human."

"You think we can't love?" Cian's voice shook with rage, with grief. "You think we aren't capable of love?"

"I know that you are, and while that love may run deep in your kind, its selfishness runs as strong. But not yours." Robes flowing, she walked to the portrait. "She asked you to make her one of you, but you refused. You could have kept her had you done as she asked."

"Like a goddamn pet? Kept her? Damned her is what it would have done, killed her, crushed out that light in her."

"Given her eternity."

"Of dark, of a craving for the blood of what she'd been. Condemned her to a life that is no life. She didn't know what she asked me."

"She knew. Such a strong heart and mind she has, and courage, yet she asked and she knew, and would have given

you her life. You've done well, haven't you? You have culture and wealth, skills. Fine homes."

"That's right. Made something of my dead self. Why
shouldn't I?"

"And enjoy it—when you're not sitting in the dark
brooding over what can't be. What you can't have. You enjoy your eternity, your youth, your strength and knowledge."

He sneered now, damning the gods. "Would you rather I
beat my breast over my fate? Endlessly mourn my own
death? Is that what the gods demand?"

"We demand nothing. We asked, and you gave. Gave
more than we believed you would. If it were otherwise, I
wouldn't be here."

"Fine. Now you can go away again."

"Nor," she continued in the same easy tone, "would I
give you this choice. Continue to live, grow wealthier yet.
Century upon century, with no age, no sickness, and the
blessings of the gods."

"Got that already, without your blessing."

Her eyes sparkled a little, but he couldn't tell—didn't
care—if it was amusement or temper. "But now it's given
to you, the only of your kind who has it. You and I know
more of death than any human can. And fear it more. There
need be no end to you. Or you can have an end."

"What? Staked by the gods?" He snorted out a laugh,
took another long pull from the bottle. "Burned in god-
fire? A purification of my condemned soul?"

"You can be what you were, and have a life that comes
to an end as all do. You can be alive, and so age and sicken
and one day know the death as a man knows it."

The bottle slipped out of his fingers, thudded on the
floor. "What?"

"This is your choice," Morrigan said, holding out both
hands, palms up. "Eternity, with our blessing to enjoy it. Or
a handful of human years. What will you, vampire?"

* * *

In Geall, a quiet snow had fallen, a thin blanket over the ground. The morning sunlight glinted off it, and sparkled on the ice that coated the trees.

Moira passed her cousin's infant back to Sinann. "She's prettier every day, and I could spend hours just looking at her. But our company's coming after midday. I haven't finished preparing."

"You brought them home to me." Sinann nuzzled her daughter. "All I love. I wish you could have all you love, Moira."

"I had a lifetime in a few weeks." She gave the baby a last kiss, then glanced around in surprise as Ceara rushed in.

"Majesty. There's someone . . . downstairs, there's someone who wishes to see you."

"Who?"

"I . . . I was only told there's a visitor who's traveled far to speak with you."

Moira's eyebrows shot up when Ceara dashed away again. "Well, whoever it is has her fluttered up. I'll see you again later."

She went out, brushing at her trousers. They'd been cleaning for days in preparation of the new year and her most anticipated guests. To see them again, she thought, to speak with them. To watch Larkin grin over his new niece.

Would they bring any word, any at all, of Cian?

She pressed her lips together, reminded herself not to let her inner grieving show. It was a time of celebration, of holiday. She would not put a pall over Geall after all they'd fought to preserve.

Something trembled along her skin as she started down the stairs. Shivered up her spine and to the base of her neck where her lover had liked to press his lips.

Then it trembled in her heart, and she began to run. That trembling heart began to race. And then to soar.

What she believed never could be was, and he was there, standing there, looking up at her.

"Cian." The joy that had been shut away burst out of her, like music. "You came back." She would have launched herself into his arms, but he was staring at her so intently, so strangely she wasn't sure she'd be welcomed. "You came back."

"I wondered what I'd see on your face. I wondered. Can we speak in private?"

"Of course. Aye, we'll . . ." Flustered, she looked around. "It seems we are. Everyone's gone." What could she do with her hands to stop them from touching him? "How did you come? How—"

"It's New Year's Eve," he said, watching her. "The end of the old, the start of the new. I wanted to see you, on the edge of that change."

"I wanted to see you, no matter when or where. The others come in a few hours. You'll stay. Please say you'll stay for the feasting."

"It depends."

Her throat burned as if she'd swallowed flame. "Cian. I know what you said in your letter was true, but it was hard, so hard, not to see you again. To have our last moment together standing in blood. I wanted . . ." Tears flooded her eyes, and she nearly lost the war to will them back. "I wanted just a moment more. Now I have it."

"Would you take more than a moment, if I could give it?"

"I don't understand." Then she smiled and choked back a sob when he drew the locket she'd given him from under his shirt. "You still wear it."

"Yes, I still wear it. It's one of my most treasured possessions. I left nothing of me behind for you. Now I'm asking, would you take more than that moment, Moira? Would you take this?" He lifted her hand, pressed it to his heart.

"Oh, I was afraid you didn't want to touch me." Her breath shuddered out with relief. "Cian, you know, you must know, that I . . ."

The hand beneath his trembled, and her eyes went wide. "Your heart. Your heart beats."

"Once I told you if it could beat, it would beat for you. It does."

"It beats under my hand," she whispered. "How?"

"A gift from the gods in the last moments of Yule. They gave me back what was taken from me." Now he drew out the silver cross that hung around his neck with her locket. "It's a man who stands before you, Moira."

"Human," she whispered. "You live."

"It's a man who loves you." He pulled her toward the doors, flung them open so the sun poured over them. And because it was still so miraculous, he lifted his face, closed his eyes and let the stream of it bathe his face.

She couldn't stop the tears now, or the sobs that came with them. "You're alive. You came back to me and you're alive."

"It's a man who stands before you," he said again. "It's a man who loves you. It's a man who asks if you'll share the life he's been given, if you'll live it with him. If you'll take me as I am, and make a life with me. Geall will be my world, as you're my world. It will be my heart, as you're my heart. If you'll have me."

"I've been yours from the first moment, and I'll be yours until the last. You came back to me." She laid a hand on his heart, and the other on her own. "And my heart beats again."

She threw her arms around him, and those who'd gathered in the courtyàrd, and on the stairs cheered as the queen of Geall kissed her beloved in the winter sunlight.

"So they lived," the old man said, "and they loved. So the circle grew stronger, and formed circles out from it as ripples spread in a pool. The valley that had once been silent sang with music of summer breezes through green grass, the lowing of cattle. Of pipes and harps and the laughter of children."

The old man stroked the hair of a little one who'd climbed into his lap. "Geall flourished under the rule of Moira, the warrior queen and her knight. For them, even in the dark of night, a light shone.

"And that brings the tale of the sorcerer, the witch, the

warrior, the scholar, the shifter of shapes and the vampire to its own circle."

He patted the rump of the child on his lap. "Off with you now, all of you, while there's still sunlight to enjoy."

There were shouts and whoops, and he smiled as he heard the arguments already starting for who would be the sorcerer, who would be the queen.

Because his senses were still keen in some areas, Cian lifted his hand to the back of the chair, and covered Moira's.

"You tell it well."

"Easy to tell what you've lived."

"Easy to *enhance* what was," she corrected, coming around the chair. "But you stayed very close to the truth."

"Wasn't the truth strange and magical enough?"

Her hair was pure white, and her face as she smiled at him, lined with the years. And more beautiful than any he'd known.

"Walk with me before twilight comes." She helped him to stand, hooked her arm through his. "And are you ready for the invasion?" she asked, tipping her head toward his shoulder.

"When it comes, at least you'll be finished fussing over it."

"I'm so anxious to see them all. Our first circle, and the circles they've made. Once a year for the whole of them is so long to wait, even with the little visits between. And listening to little pieces of the tale brings it all back so clear, doesn't it?"

"It does. No regrets?"

"I've never had a one when it comes to you. What a fine life we've had, Cian. I know we're in the winter of it, but I don't feel the cold."

"Well, I do, when you put your feet on my arse in the night."

She laughed, turned to kiss him with all the warmth, all the love of sixty years of marriage.

"There's our eternity, Moira," he said, gesturing toward

their grandchildren, and great-grandchildren. "There's our forever."

Hands linked, they walked in the softening sunlight. Though their steps were slow and measured from age, they continued through the courtyards and the gardens, and out through the gates while the sound of children playing rang behind them.

High above on the castle peaks, the three symbols of Geall, the claddaugh, the dragon and the sun, flew—gold against the white.

Glossary of Irish Words, Characters and Places

a chroi (ah-REE), Gaelic term of endearment meaning "my heart," "my heart's beloved," "my darling"

a ghrá (ah-GHRA), Gaelic term of endearment meaning "my love," "dear"

a stór (ah-STOR), Gaelic term of endearment meaning "my darling"

Aideen (Ae-DEEN), Moira's young cousin

Alice McKenna, descendant of Cian and Hoyt Mac Cionaoith

An Clar (Ahn-CLAR), modern-day County Clare

Ballycloon (ba-LU-klun)

Blair Nola Bridgitt Murphy, one of the circle of six, the "warrior"; a demon hunter, a descendant of Nola Mac Cionaoith (Cian and Hoyt's younger sister)

Bridget's Well, cemetery in County Clare, named after St. Bridget

Burren, the, a karst limestone region in County Clare, which features caves and underground streams

cara (karu), Gaelic for "friend, relative"

Ceara, one of the village women

Cian (KEY-an) *Mac Cionaoith/McKenna,* Hoyt's twin brother, a vampire, Lord of Oiche, one of the circle of six, "the one who is lost"

Cirio, Lilith's human lover

ciunas (CYOON-as), Gaelic for "silence"; the battle takes place in the Valley of Ciunas—the Valley of Silence

claddaugh, the Celtic symbol of love, friendship, loyalty

Cliffs of Mohr (also Moher), the name given to the ruin of forts in the south of Ireland, on a cliff near Hag's Head, "Moher O'Ruan"

Conn, Larkin's childhood puppy

Dance of the Gods, the Dance, the place in which the circle of six passes through from the real world to the fantasy world of Geall

Davey, Lilith, the Vampire Queen's, "son," a child vampire

Deirdre (DAIR-dhra) *Riddock,* Larkin's mother

Dervil (DAR-vel), one of the village women

Eire (AIR-reh), Gaelic for Ireland

Eogan (O-en), Ceara's husband

Eoin (OAN), Hoyt's brother-in-law

Eternity, the name of Cian's nightclub, located in New York City

Faerie Falls, imaginary place in Geall

fàilte à Geall (FALL-che ah GY-al), Gaelic for "Welcome to Geall"

Fearghus (FARE-gus), Hoyt's brother-in-law

Gaillimh (GALL-yuv), modern-day Galway, the capital of the west of Ireland

Geall (GY-al), in Gaelic means "promise"; the city from which Moira and Larkin come; the city which Moira will someday rule

Glenna Ward, one of the circle of six, the "witch"; lives in modern-day New York City

Hoyt Mac Cionaoith/McKenna (mac KHEE-nee), one of the circle of six, the "sorcerer"

Isleen (Is-LEEN), a servant at Castle Geall

Jarl (Yarl), Lilith's sire, the vampire who turned her into a vampire

Jeremy Hilton, Blair Murphy's ex-fiancé

King, the name of Cian's best friend, whom Cian befriended when King was a child; the manager of Eternity

Larkin Riddock, one of the circle of six, the "shifter of shapes," a cousin of Moira, Queen of Geall

Lilith, the Vampire Queen, aka Queen of the Demons; leader of the war against humankind; Cian's sire, the vampire who turned Cian from human to vampire

Lora, a vampire; Lilith's lover

Lucius, Lora's male vampire lover

Malvin, villager, soldier in Geallian army

Manhattan, city in New York; where both Cian McKenna and Glenna Ward live

mathair (maahir), Gaelic word for mother

Michael Thomas McKenna, descendant of Cian and Hoyt Mac Cionaoith

Mick Murphy, Blair Murphy's younger brother

Midir (mee-DEER), vampire wizard to Lilith, Queen of the Vampires *miurnin* (also sp. miurneach [mornukh]), Gaelic for "sweetheart," term of endearment

Moira (MWA-ra), one of the circle of six, the "scholar"; a princess, future queen of Geall

Morrigan (Mo-ree-ghan), Goddess of the Battle

Niall (Nile), a warrior in the Geallian army

Nola Mac Cionaoith, Hoyt and Cian's youngest sister

ogham (ä-gem) (also spelled ogam), fifth/sixth century Irish alphabet

oiche (EE-heh), Gaelic for "night"

Oran (O-ren), Riddock's youngest son, Larkin's younger brother

Phelan (FA-len), Larkin's brother-in-law

Prince Riddock, Larkin's father, acting king of Geall, Moira's maternal uncle

Region of Chiarrai (kee-U-ree), modern-day Kerry, situated in the extreme southwest of Ireland, sometimes referred to as "the Kingdom"

Samhain (SAM-en), summer's end (Celtic festival); the battle takes place on the Feast of Samhain, the feast celebrating the end of summer

Sean Murphy (Shawn), Blair Murphy's father, a vampire hunter

Shop Street, cultural center of Galway

Sinann (shih-NAWN), Larkin's sister

sláinte (slawn-che), Gaelic term for "cheers!"

slán agat (shlahn u-gut), Gaelic for "good-bye," which is said to the person staying *slán leat* (shlahn ly-aht), Gaelic for "good-bye," which is said to the person leaving

Tuatha de Danaan (TOO-aha dai DON-nan), Welsh gods

Tynan (Ti-nin), guard at Castle Geall

Vlad, Cian's stallion

Turn the page for a look at

Angels Fall

by

Nora Roberts

Available in hardcover from G. P. Putnam's Sons.

Chapter 1

Reece Gilmore smoked through the tough knuckles of Angel's Fist in an overheating Chevy Cavalier. She had two hundred forty-three dollars and change in her pocket, which might be enough to cure the Chevy, fuel it and herself. If luck was on her side, and the car wasn't seriously ill, she'd have enough to pay for a room for the night.

Then, even by the most optimistic calculations, she'd be broke.

She took the plumes of steam puffing out of the hood as a sign it was time to stop traveling for a while and find a job.

No worries, no problem, she told herself. The little Wyoming town huddled around the cold blue waters of a lake was as good as anywhere else. Maybe better. It had the openness she needed—all that sky with the snow-dipped peaks of the Tetons rising into it, sober and somehow aloof gods.

She'd been meandering her way toward them, through the Ansel Adams' photograph of peaks and plains for hours. She hadn't had a clue where she'd end up when she'd started out that day before dawn, but she'd bypassed Cody, zipped through Dubois, and though she'd toyed with veering into Jackson, she'd dipped south instead.

So something must have been pulling her to this spot.

Over the past eight months, she'd developed a strong belief in following signs, and impulses. Dangerous Curves, Slippery When Wet. It was nice that someone took the time and effort to post those kinds of warnings. Other signs might be a peculiar slant of sunlight aimed down a back road, or a weather vane pointing south.

If she liked the look of the light or the weather vane, she'd follow, until she found what seemed like the right place at the right time. She might settle in for a few weeks— or as she had in South Dakota, a few months. Pick up some work, scout the area, then move on when those signs, those impulses, pointed in a new direction.

There was a freedom in the system she'd developed, and often—more often now—a lessening of the constant hum of anxiety in the back of her mind. These past months of living with herself, essentially *by* herself, had done more to smooth her out than the full year of therapy.

To be fair, she supposed the therapy had given her the base to face herself every single day. Every night. And all the hours in between.

And here was another fresh start, another blank slate in the bunched fingers of Angel's Fist.

If nothing else, she'd take a few days to enjoy the lake and the mountains, and pick up enough money to get back on the road again. A place like this—the signpost had said the population was 623—probably ran to tourism, exploiting the scenery and the proximity to the national park.

There'd be at least one hotel, likely a couple of B and Bs, maybe a dude ranch within a few miles. It might be fun to work at a dude ranch. All of those places would need someone to fetch and carry and clean, especially now that the spring thaw was dulling the sharpest edge of winter.

But since her car was now sending out thicker, more desperate smoke signals, the first priority was a mechanic.

She eased her way along the road that ribboned around the long, wide lake. Patches of snow made dull white pools in the shade. The trees were still there, wintering brown, but there were a few boats on the water. She could see a couple of guys in windbreakers and caps in a white canoe, rowing right through the reflection of the mountains. It was so clear she glanced up, almost expecting to see the canoe mirrored on the rough hills.

Across from the lake was what she decided was the business district. Gift shop, a little gallery. Bank, post office, she noted. Sheriff's office.

She angled away from the lake to pull the laboring car up to what looked like a big barn of a general store. There were a couple of men in flannel shirts sitting out front in stout chairs that gave them a good view of the lake.

They nodded to her as she cut the engine and stepped out, then the one on the right tapped the brim of his blue cap that bore the name of the store—Mac's Mercantile and Grocery—across the crown.

"Looks like you got some trouble there, young lady."

"Sure does. Do you know anyone who can give me a hand with it?"

He laid his hands on his thighs and pushed out of the chair. He was burly in build, ruddy in face, with lines fanning out from the corners of friendly brown eyes. When he spoke, his voice was a slow, meandering drawl.

"Why don't we just pop the hood and take a look-see?"

"Appreciate it." When she released the latch, he tossed the hood up and stepped back from the clouds of smoke. For reasons she couldn't name, the plumes and the fuss caused Reece more embarrassment than anxiety. "It started up on me about ten miles east, I guess. I wasn't paying enough attention. Got caught up in the scenery."

"Easy to do. You heading into the park?"

"I was. More or less." Not sure, never sure, she thought and tried to concentrate on the moment rather than the before or after. "I think the car had other ideas."

His companion came over to join them, and both men

looked under the hood the way Reece knew men did. With sober eyes and knowing frowns. She looked with them, though she accepted that she was as much of a cliché. The female to whom what lurked under the hood of a car was a foreign as the terrain of Pluto.

"Got yourself a split radiator hose," he told her. "Gonna need to replace that."

Didn't sound so bad, not too bad. Not too expensive. "Anywhere in town I can make that happen?"

"Lynt's Garage'll fix you up. Why don't I give him a call for you?"

"Lifesaver." She offered a smile and her hand, a gesture that had come to be much easier for her with strangers. "I'm Reece, Reece Gilmore."

"Mac Drubber. This here's Carl Sampson."

"Back East, aren't you?" Carl asked. He looked a fit fifty-something to Reece, and with some Native American blood mixed in once upon a time.

"Yeah. Way back. Boston area. I really appreciate the help."

"Nothing but a phone call," Mac said. "You can come on in out of the breeze if you want, or take a walk around. Might take Lynt a few to get here."

"I wouldn't mind a walk, if that's okay. Maybe you could tell me a good place to stay in town. Nothing fancy."

"Got the Lakeview Hotel just down aways. The Teton House, other side of the lake's some homier. More a B and B. Some cabins along the lake, and others outside of town rent by the week or the month."

She didn't think in months any longer. A day was enough of a challenge. And homier sounded too intimate. "Maybe I'll walk down and take a look at the hotel."

"It's a long walk. Could give you a ride on down."

"I've been driving all day. I could use the stretch. But thanks, Mr. Drubber."

"No problem." He stood another moment as she wandered down the wooden sidewalk. "Pretty thing," he commented.

"No meat on her." Carl shook his head. "Women today starve off all the curves."

She hadn't starved them off, and was, in fact, making a concerted effort to gain back the weight that had fallen off in the past couple of years. She'd gone from health club fit to scrawny and had worked her way back to what she thought of as gawky. Too many angles and points, too many bones. Every time she undressed, her body was like that of a stranger's to her.

She wouldn't have agreed with Mac's *pretty thing*. Not anymore. Once she'd thought of herself that way, as a pretty woman—stylish, sexy when she wanted to be. But her face seemed too hard now, the cheekbones too prominent, the hollows too deep. The restless nights were fewer, but when they came they left her dark eyes heavily shadowed and cast a pallor, pasty and gray, over her skin.

She wanted to recognize herself again.

She let herself stroll, her worn-out Keds nearly soundless on the sidewalk. She'd learned not to hurry—had taught herself not to push, not to rush, but to take things as they came. And in a very real way to embrace every single moment.

The cool breeze blew across her face, wound through the long brown hair she'd tied back in a tail. She liked the feel of it, the smell of it, clean and fresh, and the hard light that poured over the Tetons and sparked on the water.

She could see some of the cabins Mac had spoken of, through the bare branches of the willows and the cottonwoods. They squatted behind the trees, log and glass, wide porches and—she assumed—stunning views.

It might be nice to sit on one of those porches and study the lake or the mountains, to watch whatever visited the marsh where cattails speared up out of the bog. To have that room around, and the quiet.

One day maybe, she thought. But not today.

She spotted green spears of daffodils in a half whiskey barrel next to the entrance of a restaurant. They might have trembled a bit in the chilly breeze, but they made her think: spring. Everything was new in spring. Maybe this spring, she'd be new, too.

She stopped to admire the tender spouts. It was comforting to see spring making its way back after the long winter. There would be other signs of it soon. Her guidebook had boasted of miles of wildflowers on the sage flats, and more along the area's lakes and ponds.

She was ready for flowering, Reece thought. Ready for blooming.

Then she shifted her eyes up to the wide front window of the restaurant. More diner than restaurant, she corrected. Counter service, two- and four-tops, booths, all in faded red and white. Pies and cakes on display, and the kitchen open to the counter. A couple of waitresses bustled around with trays and coffee pots.

Lunch crowd, she realized. She'd forgotten lunch. As soon as she'd taken a look at the hotel, she'd . . .

Then she saw it in the window: the sign, hand-lettered.

COOK WANTED
INQUIRE WITHIN

Signs, she thought again, though she'd taken a step back before she caught herself. She stood where she was, taking a careful study of the set-up from outside the glass. Open kitchen, she reminded herself, that was key. Diner food— she could handle that in her sleep. Or would have been able to, once.

Maybe it was time to find out, time to take another step forward. If she couldn't handle it, she'd know, and wouldn't be any worse off than she was now.

The hotel was probably hiring, in anticipation of the summer season. Or Mr. Drubber might need another clerk at his store.

But the sign was right there, and her car had aimed

toward this town, and her steps had brought her to this spot, where daffodil shoots pushed out of the dirt into the first hesitant breaths of spring.

She backtracked to the door, took a long, long breath in, then opened it.

Fried onions, grilling meat—on the gamey side— strong coffee, a jukebox on country, and a buzz of table chatter.

Clean red floors, she noted, scrubbed white counter. The few empty tables had their lunch setups. There were photographs on the walls—good ones to her eye. Black and whites of the lake, of white water, of the mountains in every season.

She was still getting her bearings, gathering her courage, when one of the waitresses swung by her. "Afternoon. You're looking for lunch you've got your choice of a table or the counter."

"Actually, I'm looking for the manager. Or owner. Ah, about the sign in the window. The position of cook."

The waitress stopped, still balancing a tray. "You're a cook?"

There'd been a time Reece would have sniffed at the term—good-naturedly, but she'd have sniffed nonetheless. "Yes."

"That's handy, 'cause Joanie fired one a couple of days ago." The waitress curled her free hand, brought it up to her lips in the mime for drinking.

"Oh."

"Gave him the job in February when he came through town looking for work. Said he'd found Jesus and was spreading his word across the land."

She cocked her head and her hip, and gave Reece a sunny smile out of a pretty face. "He preached the Word, all right, like a disciple on crack, so you wanted to stuff a rag in his mouth. Then I guess he found the bottle, and that was that. So. Why don't you go right on and sit up at the counter. I'll see if Joanie can get out of the kitchen for a minute. How about some coffee?"

"Tea, if you don't mind."

"Coming up."

Didn't have to take the job, Reece reminded herself as she slid onto a chrome and leather stool and rubbed her damp palms dry on the thighs of her jeans. Even if it was offered, she didn't have to take it. She could stick with cleaning hotel rooms, or head out and find that dude ranch.

The juke switched numbers, and Shania Twain announced joyfully she felt like a woman.

The waitress tapped a short sturdy woman at the grill on the shoulder, leaned in. After a moment, the woman shot a glance over her shoulder, met Reece's eyes, then nodded. The waitress came back to the counter with a white cup of hot water, with a Lipton tea bag on the saucer.

"Joanie'll be right along. You want to order some lunch? Meatloaf 's house special today. Comes with mashed potatoes and green beans and a biscuit."

"No thanks, no, tea's fine." She'd never be able to hold anything more down, not with the nerves bouncing around in her belly. The panic wanted to come with it, that smothering wet weight in the chest.

She should just go, Reece thought. Go right now, and walk back to her car. Get the hose fixed and head out. Signs be damned.

Joanie had a fluff of blond hair on her head, a white butcher's apron splattered with grease stains tied around her middle, and high-topped red Converse sneakers on her feet. She walked out from the kitchen wiping her hands on a dishcloth.

And she measured Reece out of steely eyes that were more gray than blue.

"You cook?" A smoker's rasp made the brisk question oddly sensual.

"Yes."

"For a living, or just to put something in your mouth?"

"It's what I did back in Boston—for a living." Fighting nerves, Reece ripped open the cover on the tea bag.

Joanie had a soft mouth, almost a Cupid's bow, in contrast with those hard eyes. And an old, faded scar, Reece noted, that ran along her jawline from her left ear nearly to her chin.

"Boston." In an absent move, Joanie tucked the dishrag in the belt of her apron. "Long ways."

"Yes."

"I don't know as I want some East Coast cook can't keep her mouth shut for five minutes."

Reece's opened in surprise, then closed again on the barest curve of a smile. "I'm an awful chatterbox when I'm nervous."

"What're you doing around here?"

"Traveling. My car broke down. I need a job."

"Got references?"

Her heart tightened, a sweaty fist of silent pain. "I can get them."

Joanie sniffed, frowned back toward the kitchen. "Go on back, put on an apron. Next order up's a steak sandwich, med-well, onion roll, fried onions and mushrooms, fries and slaw. Dick don't drop dead after eating what you cook, you probably got the job."

"All right." Reece pushed off the stool and, keeping her breath slow and even, went through the swinging door at the far end of the counter.

She didn't notice, but Joanie did, that she'd torn the tea bag cover into tiny pieces.

It was a simple setup, she decided, and efficient enough. Large grill, restaurant-style stove, refrigerator, freezer. Holding bins, sinks, work counters, double fryer, heat suppression system. As she tied on an apron, Joanie set out the ingredients she'd need.

"Thanks." Reece scrubbed her hands, then got to work.

Don't think, she told herself. Just let it come. She set the steak sizzling on the grill while she chopped onions and mushrooms. She put the pre-cut potatoes in the fry basket, set the timer.

Her hands didn't shake, and though her chest stayed

tight, she didn't allow herself to dart glances over her shoulder to make sure a wall hadn't appeared to close her in.

She listened to the music, from the juke, from the grill, from the fryer.

Joanie tugged the next order from the clip on the round, and slapped it down. "Bowl of three-bean soup—that kettle there—goes with crackers."

Reece simply nodded, tossed the mushrooms and onions on the grill, then filled the second order while they fried.

"Order up!" Joanie called out, and yanked another ticket. "Reuben, club san, two side salads."

Reece moved from order to order, and just let it happen. The atmosphere, the orders might be different, but the rhythm was the same. Keep working, keep moving.

She plated the original order, turned to hand it to Joanie for inspection.

"Put it in line," she was told. "Start the next ticket. We don't call the doctor in the next thirty minutes, you're hired. We'll talk money and hours later."

"I need to—"

"Get that next ticket," Joanie finished. "I'm going to go have a smoke."

She worked another ninety minutes before it slowed enough for Reece to step back from the heat and guzzle down a bottle of water. When she turned, Joanie was sitting at the counter, drinking coffee.

"Nobody died," she said.

"Whew. Is it always that busy?"

"Saturday lunch crowd. We do okay. You get eight dollars an hour to start. You still look good in two weeks, I bump in another buck an hour. That's you and me and a part-timer on the grill, seven days a week. You get two days, or the best part of two off during that week. I do the schedule a week in advance. We open at six-thirty, so that means first shift is here at six. You can order breakfast all day, lunch menu from eleven to closing, dinner five to ten. You want forty hours a week, I can work you that. I don't pay any overtime, so you get stuck behind the grill and go over, we'll take it off your next week's hours. Any problem with that?"

"No."

"You drink on the job, you're fired on the spot."

"Understood."

"You get all the coffee, water, or tea you want. You hit the soft drinks, you pay for them. Same with the food. Around here, there ain't no free lunch. Not that it looks like you'll be packing it away while my back's turned. You're skinny as a stick."

"I guess I am."

"Last shift cook cleans the grill, the stove, does the lockdown."

"I can't do that," Reece interrupted. "I can't close for you. I can open, I can work any shift you want me to work. I'll work doubles when you need it, split shifts. I can flex time when you need me over forty. But I can't close for you. I'm sorry."

Joanie raised her eyebrows, sipped down the last of her coffee. "Afraid of the dark, little girl?"

"Yes, I am. If closing's part of the job description, I'll have to find another job."

"We'll work that out. We've got forms to fill out for the government. It can wait. Your car's fixed, sitting up at Mac's." Joanie smiled. "Word travels, and I've got my ear to the ground. You're looking for a place, there's a room over the diner I can rent you. Not much, but it's got a good view and it's clean."

"Thanks, but I think I'm going to try the hotel for now. We'll both give it a couple of weeks, see how it goes."

"Itchy feet."

"Itchy something."

"Your choice." With a shrug, Joanie got up, headed to the swinging door with her coffee cup. "You go on, get your car, get settled. Be back at four."

A little dazed, Reece walked out. She was back in a kitchen, and it had been all right. She'd been okay. Now that she'd gotten through it, she felt a little light-headed, but that was normal, wasn't it? A normal reaction to snagging a job, straight off the mark, doing what she was trained to do again. Doing what she hadn't been able to do for nearly two years.

She took her time walking back to her car, letting it all sink in.

When she walked into the mercantile, Mac was ringing up a sale at a short counter opposite the door. The place was what she'd expected. A little bit of everything: coolers for produce and meat, shelves of dry goods, a section for hardware, for housewares, fishing gear, ammo.

Need a gallon of milk and a box of bullets? This was the spot.

When Mac finished the transaction, she approached the counter.

"Car should run for you now," Mac told her.

"So I hear, and thanks. How do I pay?"

"Lynt left a bill here for you. You can run on by the garage if you're going to charge it. Paying cash, you can just leave it here. I'll be seeing him later."

"Cash is good." She took the bill, noted with relief it was less than she'd estimated. She could hear someone chatting in the rear of the store, and the beep of another cash register. "I got a job."

He cocked his head as she pulled out her wallet. "That so? Quick work."

"At the diner. I don't even know the name of it," she realized.

"That'd be Angel Food. Locals just call it Joanie's."

"Joanie's then. I hope you come in sometime. I'm a good cook."

"I bet you are. Here's your change."

"Thanks. Thanks for everything. I guess I'll go get myself a room, then go back to work."

"If you're still looking at the hotel, you tell Brenda on the desk you want the monthly rate. You tell her you're working at Joanie's."

"I will. I'll tell her." She wanted to take out an ad announcing it in the local paper. "Thanks, Mr. Drubber."

The hotel was five stories of pale yellow stucco that boasted views of the lake. It harbored a minute sundry shop, a tiny stand selling coffee and muffins, and an intimate linen-tablecloth dining room.

There was, she was told, high-speed Internet connection for a small daily fee, room service from seven A.M. to eleven P.M. and a self-service laundry in the basement.

Reece negotiated a weekly rate on a single—a week was long enough—on the third floor. Anything below the third was too accessible for her peace of mind, and anything above the third made her feel trapped.

With her wallet now effectively empty, she carted her duffle and laptop up three flights rather than use the elevator.

The view lived up to its billing, and she immediately opened the windows, then just stood looking at the sparkle of the water, the glide of the boats, and the rise of the mountains that cupped this little section of valley.

This was her place today, she thought. She'd find out if it was her place tomorrow. Turning back to the room, she noted the door that adjoined the neighboring guest room. She checked the locks, then pushed, shoved, dragged the single dresser in front of it.

That was better.

She wouldn't unpack, not exactly, but take the essentials and set them out. The travel candle, some toiletries, the cell phone charger. Since the bathroom was hardly bigger than the closet, she left the door open while she took a quick shower. While the water ran, she did the multiplication tables out loud to keep herself steady. She changed into fresh clothes, moving quickly.

New job, she reminded herself, and took the time and effort to dry her hair, to put on a little makeup. Not so pale today, she decided, not so hollow-eyed.

After checking her watch, she set up her laptop, opened her daily journal, and wrote a quick entry.

Angel's Fist, Wyoming
April 15

I cooked today. I took a job as a cook in a little diner-style restaurant in this pretty valley town with its big, blue lake. I'm popping champagne in my mind, and there are streamers and balloons.

I feel like I've climbed a mountain, like I've been scaling the tough peaks that ring this place. I'm not at the top yet, I'm still on a ledge. But it's sturdy and wide, and I can rest here a little while before I start to climb again.

I'm working for a woman named Joanie. She's short, sturdy, and oddly pretty. She's tough, too, and that's good. I don't want to be coddled. I think I'd smother to death that way, just run out of air the way I feel when I wake up from one of the dreams. I can breathe here, and I can be here until it's time to move again.

I've got less than ten dollars left, but whose fault is that? It's okay. I've got a room for a week with a view of the lake and the Tetons, a job, and a new radiator hose.

I missed lunch, and that's a step back there. That's okay, too. I was too busy cooking to eat, and I'll make up for it.

It's a good day, April fifteenth. I'm going to work.

She shut down, then tucked her phone, keys, driver's license, and three dollars of what she had left in her pockets. Grabbing a jacket, she headed for the door.

Before she opened it, Reece checked the peep, scanned the empty hall. She checked her locks twice, cursed herself, and checked a third time before she went back to her kit to tear a piece of Scotch tape off her roll. She pressed it over the door, well below eye level, before she walked to the door for the stairs.

She jogged down, counting as she went. After a quick debate, she left her car parked. Walking would save her gas money, even though it would be dark when she finished her shift.

Couple of blocks, that was all. Still, she fingered her key chain, and the panic button on it.

Maybe she should go back and get the car, just in case. Stupid, she told herself. She was nearly there. Think about now, not about later. When nerves began to bubble, she pictured herself at the grill. Good strong kitchen light, music from the jukebox, voices from the tables. Familiar sounds, smells, motion.

Maybe her palm was clammy when she reached for the door of Joanie's, but she opened it. And she went inside.

The same waitress she'd spoken to during the lunch shift spotted her, wiggled her fingers in a come-over motion. Reece stopped by the booth where the woman was refilling the condiment caddie.

"Joanie's back in the storeroom. She said I should give you a quick orientation when you came in. We got a lull, then the early-birds will start coming in soon. I'm Lindagail."

"Reece."

"First warning: Joanie doesn't tolerate idle hands. She catches you loitering, she'll jump straight down your back and bite your ass." She grinned when she said it in a way that made her bright blue eyes twinkle, deepened dimples in her cheeks. She had doll-baby blond hair to go with it, worn in smooth French braids.

She had on jeans, a red shirt with white piping. Silver and turquoise earrings dangled from her ears. She looked, Reece thought, like a western milkmaid.

"I like to work."

"You will, believe me. This being Saturday night, we'll be busy. You'll have two other waitstaff working—Bebe and Juanita. Matt'll bus, and Pete's the dishwasher. You and Joanie'll be manning the kitchen, and she'll have a hawk eye on you. You need a break, you tell her, and you take it. There's a place in the back for your coat, your purse. No purse?"

"No, I didn't bring it."

"God, I can't step a foot outside the house without mine. Come on then, I'll show you around. She's got the forms you need to fill out in the back. I guess you've done this kind of work before, the way you jumped in with both feet today."

"Yeah, I have."

"Restrooms. We clean the bathrooms on rotation. You've got a couple of weeks before you have that pleasure."

"Can't wait."

Linda-gail grinned. "You got family around here?"

"No. I'm from back east." Didn't want to talk about that, didn't want to think about that. "Who handles the fountain drinks?"

"Wait staff. We get crunched, you can fill drink orders. We serve wine and beer, too. But mostly people want to drink, they do it over at Clancy's. That's about it. Anything else you want to know, just give me a holler. I've got to finish the setups or Joanie'll squawk. Welcome aboard."

"Thanks."

Reece moved into the kitchen, took an apron.

A good, wide, solid ledge, she told herself. A good place to stand until it was time to move again.